FLICKER

Other Books by Theodore Roszak

The Dissenting Academy, editor and contributor
The Making of a Counter Culture: Reflections on the Technocratic Society and Its Youthful Opposition
Where the Wasteland Ends: Politics and Transcendence in Postindustrial Society
Masculine/Feminine, editor and contributor with Betty Roszak
Sources, editor and contributor
Unfinished Animal
Person/Planet: The Creative Disintegration of Industrial Society
The Cult of Information: A Neo-Luddite Treatise on High Tech, Artificial Intelligence, and the True Art of Thinking
The Voice of the Earth: An Exploration of Ecopsychology
Ecopsychology: Restoring the Earth, Healing the Mind, editor and contributor
America the Wise: The Longevity Revolution and the True Wealth of Nations
The Gendered Atom: Reflections on the Sexual Psychology of Science
Longevity Revolution: As Boomers Become Elders
World, Beware! American Triumphalism in an Age of Terror

Fiction
Pontifex
Bugs
Dreamwatcher
Flicker
The Memoirs of Elizabeth Frankenstein
The Devil and Daniel Silverman

FLICKER

A NOVEL BY
THEODORE ROSZAK

CHICAGO
REVIEW
PRESS

Library of Congress Cataloging-in-Publication Data
Roszak, Theodore.
    Flicker / Theodore Rozsak.
    p. cm.
    "The filmography of Max Castle": p. 589
    I. Title.
    PS3586.O8495F5 1991
    813'.54—dc20   90-24890
    CIP
    ISBN 1-55652-577-X

Grateful acknowledgment is given to the following for permission to reprint "The Second Coming" by W. B. Yeats (page 347). Reprinted with permission of Macmillan Publishing Company from *The Poems of W. B. Yeats*, edited by Richard J. Finneran. Copyright © 1924 by Macmillan Publishing Company, renewed 1952 by Bertha Georgia Yeats.

Cover design: Rachel McClain
Front cover image: Christian Michaels/Getty Images

This edition published in 2005 by
Chicago Review Press Incorporated
814 North Franklin Street
Chicago, Illinois 60610
ISBN 978-1-55652-577-3
Printed in the United States of America

The stronger the evil, the stronger the film.

ALFRED HITCHCOCK

CONTENTS

FLICKER

1 THE CATACOMBS

I saw my first Max Castle movie in a grubby basement in west Los Angeles. Nobody these days would think of using a hole in the wall like that for a theater. But in its time—the middle fifties—it was the humble home of the best repertory film house west of Paris.

Older film buffs still remember The Classic, a legendary little temple of the arts wedged unobtrusively between Moishe's Strictly Kosher Deli and Best Buy Discount Yard Goods. Now, looking back more than twenty years, I can see how appropriate it was that my first encounter with the great Castle should take place in what might have passed for a crypt. It was a little like discovering Christ in the catacombs long before the cross and the gospel became the light of the world. I came like the bewildered neophyte wandering into the dark womb of an unformed faith, and found . . . what? Not a sign of the kingdom and glory to come. Only a muffled rumor of miracles, an alien rite, an inscrutable emblem scratched on the crumbling wall. Still, in the deep core of his being, the seeker feels conviction stir. He senses the great hungering mystery that lurks before him amid the rubble and rat droppings. He stays and tastes of the sacrament. Transformed, he returns to the world outside bearing an apocalyptic word.

That was how I discovered Castle years before he acquired the cult following my life's work as scholar, critic, and enthusiast would one day bring him. In my case, the sacramental supper was a single flawed film, a dancing phantom of light and shadow only dimly perceived, less than half understood. Having begun its career as a censored obscenity, the poor, luckless thing had languished for decades in the deep vaults of defunct studios and uncaring collectors. That it had managed to survive at all—at one point as one of the lesser spoils of war, at another as an article of stolen goods—was a miracle in its own right. The words of Jesus, so we are told, once existed as nothing more than chalk scrawled on the pavement of bustling cities, trodden underfoot by busy merchants, scuffed by the feet of children at play, pissed upon by every passing dog. Castle's message to the world might just as well have been committed to the dust of the streets. A movie, a thin broth of illusion smeared across perishing plastic, is no less fragile. At a dozen points along the way, it might have vanished beneath the waves of neglect like so many film treasures before and since, an item of unsalvaged cultural flotsam that never found the eye to see it for what it was. That was what Castle's work needed: a beginner's eye—*my* eye, before it became too schooled and guarded, while it was still in touch with the vulgar foundations of the art, still vulnerably naive enough to receive that faint and flickering revelation of the dark god whose scriptures are the secret history of the movies.

Like most Americans of my generation, my love affair with the movies reaches back farther than I can remember. For all I can say, it began with prenatal spasms of excitement and delight. My mother was a great and gluttonous moviegoer, a twice-a-week, triple-feature and selected-short-subjects fiend. She used the movies the way millions of Americans did at the tail end of the dismal thirties: twenty-five cents' worth of shelter from the heat of summer and the cold of winter, a million dollars' worth of escape from the long, bitter heartbreak of the Depression. It was also the best way to avoid the landlord lurking on the doorstep at home to collect the back rent. It may be that more than a little of the archetypal detritus that fills the unswept corners of my mind—Tarzan's primordial mating call, the cackle of the Wicked Witch of the West, the blood-howl of the Wolf Man—infiltrated my fetal sleep through the walls of the womb.

In any case, I've always regarded it as prophetic that I was born in the year that is fondly remembered as the high noon of Hollywood's Golden Age—1939—the *annus mirabilis* when the great baronial studios showered the nation with a largesse of hits, just before the storms of war submerged cinematic dreams beneath historical night-mares. I gestated through *The Wizard of Oz, Snow White, Stage-coach, Wuthering Heights.* Mother's labor pains began, in fact, halfway through her third entranced viewing of *Gone With the Wind*—in sympathy, so she claimed, with Olivia de Havilland giving birth during the burning of Atlanta. (With the ambulance waiting at the curb, she refused to leave for the maternity ward until the management refunded her dollar-and-a-quarter admission—a hefty price in those days.)

Once born and breathing on my own, I was nursed through Joan Crawford matinees, I teethed on the Three Stooges. In early adolescence, I suffered my first confused sexual tremors when, at the action-packed conclusion of episode nine, we left Nylana, the blouse-bursting Jungle Girl, supine across a heathen altar, about to be ravished by a crazed witch doctor.

All this, the dross and froth of the movies, settled by natural gravitation into the riverbed of my youthful consciousness and there became a compacted sludge of crude humor and cheap thrills. But my devotion to film—to *Film*, the movies revered as the animated icons of high art—this began with The Classic during my first years at college. It was that period many now regard as the Heroic Age of the art-film house in America. Outside New York, there were at the time perhaps a few dozen of these cultural beacons in the major cities and university towns, many of them beginning to earn reasonably well from the newfound audience for foreign movies, some even taking on a few amenities: Picasso brush-stroke reproductions in the lobby, Swiss chocolates at the candy counter.

And then there were the struggling repertory and revival houses like The Classic, few in number, poor but pure. These weren't so much a business as a brave crusade dedicated to showing the films people *ought* to see, like them or not. Invariably, they were shoestring operations, store fronts with the windows paneled over and the walls painted black. You sat on folding chairs and could hear the projectionist fighting with his recalcitrant equipment behind a partition at the rear.

The Classic had taken up residence in a building that originally housed one of the city's first and finest picture palaces. On its opening night some time in the late twenties, a fire broke out and the place was gutted. Over the next twenty years, the surviving auditorium served as everything from a soup kitchen to a Chautauqua lecture hall. One-night-stand evangelists and passing medicine shows had frequently rented the space. Finally, before it closed down soon after the war, it had gone over to Jewish vaudeville. Faded posters for Mickey Katz as "Berny the Bull Fighter," "Meier the Millionaire," or "The Yiddisher Cowboy" could still be found hanging askew in the lobby when I started visiting. The Classic had been salvaged out of the building's capacious basement, which was as darkly sequestered as any Gothic dungeon. You entered along a dim alley next to Moishe's Deli off Fairfax Avenue. Several shadowed yards along, a discreet sign lit by a frame of low-wattage bulbs pointed around the back of the building and down a short flight of stairs. Even with people illegally huddled in the aisles, The Classic couldn't have held more than an audience of two hundred. There was only one touch of refinement: the price of the ticket included a small paper cup filled with a bitter brew that was to be my first bracing taste of espresso. Often the little cups got spilled, which left the theater's unscrubbed floors perpetually sticky underfoot.

The crowd I ran with in those early college days included an elite corps of theater-arts and film-studies majors who were advanced movie addicts. With religious scrupulosity, they took in everything that played at The Classic, which was run by one of their own kind from the previous generation, an early postwar dropout named Don Sharkey, who had discovered the art of cinema during a bohemian sojourn in Paris after being mustered out of the army. Sharkey and his woman friend Clare kept The Classic running on sweat capital and pure love. They sold the tickets, ran the projectors, mimeographed the film notes, and swept out—if any sweeping was ever done—at the end of the evening. Silent classics and vintage Hollywood movies rented cheap in those days, if you could get them at all. Even so, except for what they took in from the occasional second-run foreign film, Sharkey and Clare picked up little more than spare change from the business and had to earn from other jobs. The Classic was their way of getting others to chip in on the rentals so they could see the movies they wanted to see.

At the time, I was treading water at UCLA. My parents back in Modesto had me programmed for law school—my father's profession. I went along with the idea; anything that kept me out of the post–Korean War draft would do, and the easier the better. But it would never have occurred to me that the movies—this leftover childhood amusement—might be the subject of deep study and learned discourse. What was there to say about these cowboys and gangsters and glamour girls I had been watching since infancy in a state of semihypnotic fixation? I was bemused by the aesthetic furies that agitated my film-buff friends, the heady talk, the rarefied critical theory they exchanged among themselves as we sat drinking coffee at Moishe's after an evening at The Classic. I envied their expertise and sophistication, but I couldn't share in it. A great deal that fired them with ecstasy left me stone cold, especially the heavy-duty silent films in which The Classic specialized. Oh, I could handle Mack Sennett, Chaplin, Keaton. I had no trouble enjoying a kick in the pants, a pie in the face. But Eisenstein, Dreyer, Griffith struck me as lugubrious bores. Movies without sound (and at The Classic, too penurious to hire a pianist, the silents were shown *silent*, unrelieved by a hint of musical distraction, only the harsh liturgical rasp of the projector filling the hushed and lightless shrine) were my idea of a retarded art form.

What a young savage I was among the gourmets at The Classic's banquet table. I came with a voracious appetite for movies, but no taste. No, that's not true. I had taste: *bad* taste. Appalling taste. Well, what would you expect of someone raised on a steady diet of Monogram westerns, the Bowery Boys, Looney Tunes? For such items (I blush to say), I was blessed, or burdened, with total recall; no doubt it is all still buzzing around in my deep memory, a zany chaos of fistfights and pratfalls. At the age of ten, I could rattle off verbatim a half-dozen Abbott and Costello routines. At play in the streets, I could reconstruct in precise detail the shoot-em-up Saturday matinee exploits of Roy Rogers and Lash La Rue. My Curly the Stooge imitations were a constant household irritant.

Kid stuff. Later, in my high school years, the movies became kid stuff of another order. They were mirrors of the adolescent narcissism that blighted America of the fifties. It was that period when middle-class elders were finding all the illusions they needed on television, the family hearth of the new suburbia. By default their offspring became the nation's moviegoing public. Suddenly Hollywood found itself held to ransom by randy teenagers on wheels. Given the primary use the kids were making of drive-in theaters as do-it-yourself sex-education clinics, it was needlessly generous of the moviemakers to provide their work with any content at all. Make-out movies didn't exist to be watched; a blank screen would have done just as well. But those who came up for air long enough to take notice were apt to find that screen flooded with corrupting flattery, tales of moody youth grievously oppressed by insufficiently permissive parents who failed to take their least whim with the utmost and immediate seriousness. Like millions of others my age, I grasped at what I took to be a lifelong license *not* to grow up and rushed to pass myself off as the reincarnation of martyred James Dean—the surly slouch, the roguish clothes, the finely greased ducktail. A leather-clad, motorcycle-mounted Marlon Brando was constantly before my mind's eye, a wishful image of the perpetual untamed adolescent I wanted to be.

All this had nothing to do with the art of film; it was simply the stalled identity crisis of my generation. What was it, then, that drew a born-and-bred vulgarian like me to The Classic and its elite clientele? If I said it was a fascination with foreign films—especially with the French and Italian imports which the art houses of the time relied on to pay their bills—that might suggest some sudden refinement of taste. But no. Not immediately. Not consciously. Let me be honest. To begin with, the attraction was totally glandular. For me, as for thousands of moviegoers of the forties and fifties, foreign films meant sex—sex of a frankness American movies of the time weren't even trying to rival. For at least a few young, romantic years, European eroticism became my standard of grown-up sophistication.

Where else did I have to turn? I harbored every young man's curiosity about the mysteries of maturity. But the American movies that dominated my fantasy life were no help. On the contrary, they populated my head with treacherous delusions of womanhood. During that era of canting Eisenhower piety, the screen was peculiarly cluttered with a succession of vestal virgins—Audrey Hepburn, Grace Kelly, Deborah Kerr—who seemed to have been welded into their clothes at birth, and whose lovemaking reached its absolute libidinal limit with a dry-lipped kiss. Between the clavicle and the kneecap they had been anatomically expurgated by the Legion of Decency. Is this what I was to believe of women? Every bone in my pubescent body told me nothing human could draw a living breath and remain so antiseptic.

Yet, when Hollywood tried to smuggle a stronger dose of sex appeal through the tight cordon of censorship that surrounded it, things got even more bewilderingly unreal. The result was no improvement upon Nylana the Jungle Girl who had, for lack of anything better, been functioning as my make-believe love-slave since the age of ten. Jane Russell, Linda Darnell, Jayne Mansfield . . . their intimidating torsos, cantilevered and cross-braced, with cleavage calibrated to the last permissible millimeter—so much and no more—might have been fabricated by a team of structural engineers. Even Marilyn Monroe, the movies' closest approximation to sluttish abandon, always looked to me like a windup fiberglass doll designed to titillate by the numbers. Off camera, I imagined she was packed away in the special-effects storeroom along with King Kong and the Munchkins.

The Great Change came one Saturday during my senior year at Modesto High, when, in the company of two buddies, I drove to San Francisco on secret sexual maneuvers. Our object was to infiltrate the old Peerless Theater on Mission Street, then terminally tacky but still advertising "The Hottest Burlesque West of New York." Unable to pass ourselves off at the door as grown men, we grudgingly settled for second best: a selection of Tempest Storm strip flicks at an equally seedy showplace down the street. This was also "Adults Only," but the gates weren't so closely guarded. Slipping by the near-comatose ticket-taker, we eagerly seated ourselves in the oppressively grungy auditorium amid an audience of scattered single males slouched down to the ears in their seats. For the next hour, we were treated to a dimly photographed parade of bored and beefy ladies whose perfunctory bumping and grinding was more often off camera than on. When we finally got to Tempest Storm, she was as blurred an image as all the rest and no less concealed by tassles and bangles. This erotic delight was followed by a bonus: a silent reel of posture shots featuring a dozen or so rigidly positioned "artist's models" morosely shifting this way and that. Whenever the girls failed in their maladroit efforts to make sure that not more than the permissible half-nipple was revealed, chop! the film got edited with a meat-ax. Even seen from beginning to end a second time, these were meager rations, barely enough to give us the satisfaction of vindicated manhood.

Afterward, our lust unslaked and the night still young, we cruised the streets fruitlessly looking for more of the same. Finally, when we'd drifted out of the Tenderloin into more respectable parts of town, we were ready to give up and begin the long drive home. But then, in one of the city's better neighborhoods, we happened upon a demurely lit first-run movie house whose marquee advertised a film called *The Lovers*. This sounded promising, and indeed there were posters of a man and a woman and a bed. We decided to make a few exploratory passes.

The theater seemed suspiciously tasteful, much too swanky for a porn show. The glass doors were polished, the lobby inside carpeted, the man who took the tickets was dressed in jacket and tie. Moreover, the audience going in wasn't the scruffy crowd with whom we'd shared Tempest Storm's charms. The men buying tickets looked well-dressed, intelligent, reputable. They looked like our fathers, for God's sake! Moreover, they had *women* with them. How could a guy enjoy dirty movies with females present? We knew there had to be a catch. There was. This wasn't an American movie. It was *French*. That's why it cost so much. A whole dollar. More than Tempest Storm. Our doubts grew stronger when one of my companions perceptively noted, "It says subtitles." He made the observation as if he'd discovered a dubious clause in the small print of a contract. "That means they put all the talking in words at the bottom of the screen."

A foreign film. A film you had to *read*. Of course I'd heard about such movies. I'd even seen one the year before: Brigitte Bardot, though in a toned-down and domesticated version. With voice dubbed and bare posterior expurgated (how else could she have gained admittance to Modesto?) she'd come off seeming vastly overrated to me, a poor substitute for Mamie Van Doren, suffering from out-of-sync lips. Given our prurient mission that evening, the movie at hand seemed even less likely to be the merchandise we were shopping for. Still, it looked as if we might have no trouble getting into the place. There were young guys getting past the usher at the door, no questions asked. We could probably pass for college age—not that the management showed signs of caring. After a brief consultation, we decided to gamble the buck. It was a night for running risks.

As a mordant commentary on bourgeois marital habits, Louis Malle's *The Lovers*, that season's rage of the art houses, was lost on me. Nor did it matter in the least that to the critics' way of thinking, the story was feather-light and much too preciously played. But what did I know about critics? What did I know about thinking? For me, the movie was an excuse for the camera to loiter deliciously over the intimate details of an illicit love affair. A man and a woman share a bed, a bath. She yields to his touch with the easy grace of water stirred in a pool. Their lovemaking flows as lyrically as the gorgeous music that accompanies their brief romance. (A Brahms sextet, as I later learned. An unusual bit of film scoring.) I sat in the presence of this erotic dream dizzy with desire, convinced that, at last, I'd experienced the *real thing. This* was what it was all about—men and women together, the great guarded secret of what they did and how they did it when it didn't have to be done in the backseat of a car or in the uncertain privacy of somebody's parents' living room.

What did I see that was so arousing? It wasn't the few quick glimpses of nudity, nor the occasional caress that freely strayed across the woman's body. Rather it was the natural ease with which this man and this woman carried it off. So cool, so casual. When we see the lovers in the tub, we can tell they're really bare; there are no strategically positioned bubbles or reflections. But the camera, so cleverly handled, doesn't strain to reveal or conceal. When the woman rises from the water to reach for a towel, once again the camera is totally relaxed. It doesn't stare salaciously—the way I would've stared salaciously. Rather, like the true eye of an experienced lover, it scans the passage of her breasts, her navel, moving across this charged terrain with matter-of-fact nonchalance. Intimacies like these, the film seemed to say, are the unspectacular facts of adult life. One takes them in easy stride. For didn't we, the audience, know all about these things?

Like hell we did! Not me. Not my friends. Nevertheless, the film invited a blasé acceptance. And it was getting what it asked for. Because (my God!) in a theater filled to capacity, no horse laughs, no wolf whistles, never a giggle or gasp. This was some classy audience. Of course, all of us, adolescent and adult, were being artfully cued. Perhaps I even knew it. But I also enjoyed it, especially as the cueing was being done by this stunning actress who played the woman, Jeanne Moreau—or, as I remembered her name then, "Jeany Mor-e-oh." No great beauty by Hollywood standards. A plain face with bad skin. An unremarkable body. Rather limp and smallish breasts. But precisely for that reason, she took on a pungent reality. There could actually *be* such a woman. This is how she'd act in her bedroom, in her bathroom. And the way she moved, with such compliant carnality, I could imagine she was indeed naked under her clothes. Who could believe such a thing of Doris Day?

My buddies, I recall, were unimpressed. The film held no magic for them. They thought it compared poorly with Tempest Storm's more ritualized gyrations. (Also, they were outraged by the absence of popcorn.) But I left the theater intoxicated with Jeanne Moreau, by her suave, slightly bored permissiveness. I wanted more of these films. I wanted more of these women. Which was too much to expect of drowsy Modesto. But when, soon after, I moved to Los Angeles to start college, I was on the lookout for all the foreign movies I could find and so finally made my way to The Classic, where I quickly caught up on the whole postwar repertory of French and Italian films. I took in the heavy as well as the light—*Shoeshine* and *Open City*, along with *Beauties of the Night* and *House of Pleasure*—because you could never tell. In the middle of a grindingly morose neorealist drama, some deliciously unashamed sexual byplay (all I was really watching for) might suddenly light the screen.

By then, there were opportunists by the score cashing in on the belated American sexual revolution, filling slick magazines and slicker movies with topless vixens, buxom playmates. A few years farther down the line we would be treated to a surfeit of X-rated skin flicks that loaded the screen with genital gymnastics and full-frontal gynecology. But I'm recalling an illusion of another order, one that worked by understatement and elegant insouciance. Sometimes, in the Italian films of that period, the passions of men and women were lent a more bracing physicality by being blended into the rough grain of everyday life. Italian moviemakers admitted (almost reveled in) the existence of dirt in the streets, soiled clothing, cracked plaster. In super-hygienic, middle-class America, where I'd been raised, such grunginess was rarely on view. Yet, by some subtle magic that became my earliest appreciation of the art of film, these exotic images of a tawdriness I'd never experienced actually managed to make "real life" as I'd known it seem artificial, lacking the organic vitality they possessed. Silvana Mangano, laboring at the harvest in *Bitter Rice*, pauses to wipe her brow. Her hair is a magnificent straggly chaos. Her ample body streams with real sweat. There is damp hair beneath her upraised arm. Her shirt, loosely knotted at the midriff, gapes in the wind to bare the lush curve of her pendulous breasts. Nipples press assertively against the clinging cloth. Only a passing mirage on the screen. But to my captivated eye, the woman is palpably *there*. Almost discernibly, she smells of the earth, of forbidden female odors.

How diabolically ironic it was that I should have been summoned to the serious study of film by these French and Italian sirens. As I remember them now—Gina Lollobrigida, Simone Signoret, Martine Carol—they brim with the bright promise of love, the insurgent fertility of life. But the hunger of the flesh as I learned it from them was only the beginning of a darker adventure; though I could never have guessed it, beyond them lay the labyrinthine tunnel that led down and down into the world of Max Castle. There, among old heresies and forgotten deities, I would learn that both life and love can be bait in a deadly trap.

Still I must be grateful, knowing that the awkward desire these few fleeting moments of cinematic seduction quickened in me was the first early-morning glimmer of adulthood. Through them, I was learning the difference between the sexual and the sensual. Sex, after all, is a spontaneous appetite; it bubbles up from the adolescent juices of the body without shape or style. We are born to it like all the simple animals that mindlessly rut and mate. But sensuality—raw instinct reworked by art into a thing of the mind that can be played with endlessly—*that* is grown-up human. It idealizes the flesh into a fleshless emblem.

Plato (so some scholars believe) had something like the movies in mind when he wrote his famous Allegory of the Cave. He imagines an audience—it is the whole sad human race—imprisoned in the darkness, chained by its own deceiving fascinations as it watches a parade of shadows on the wall. But I think the great man got it wrong. Or let us say he couldn't, at that distance, know that the illusions of film, when shaped by a deft hand, may become true raptures of the mind, diamond-bright images of undying delight. At any rate, that's what these beauties of the screen became for me—enticing creatures of light, always there, unchanging, incorruptible. Again and again, for solace or inspiration, I reach back to recapture their charm, the recollection of something more real than my own experience.

One exquisite memory embodies that far-off period of youthful fantasy more vividly than all others. I see it as a softly focused square of light, and see myself dazzled and aroused, seated in the embracing darkness, savoring the enticement. It was, so I remembered, a moment from Renoir's *Une Partie de Campagne*. Then some years later I discovered that I was mistaken. I saw the movie again; it contains no such scene. I searched in other likely places; I never found it. I turned to friends and colleagues for help. "Do you remember the movie where . . . ?"

But they didn't.

Where does it come from? Is it some form of benign hallucination? Perhaps it is, after all, a composite creation pieced together from all the naively romantic images I bring away from those years, the memory of a love story I never saw, and yet of all the love stories I once wanted the movies to tell me. A voluptuous peasant girl waits at the edge of a wood for her lover. As naturally as she breathes, she removes her clothes and wades into the inviting river. The camera casually surveys her body, plump and rounded, not perfect but wholesome as fresh milk. The heat of an idyllic summer glows on her skin. She reaches up to tie back her unruly hair. The soft contour of her breast is revealed. Languidly, she stretches out over the bright water . . . she floats in the sunlight.

2 AN EROTIC EDUCATION

Which brings me to Clare, who turned my voyeuristic fantasies into flesh and blood and, in the process, taught me the art of film.

It was by way of my infatuation with foreign movies that I first took notice of Clare. That was surely the only way she could have caught my lusting adolescent eye, since she was nothing like the going standard of female beauty in late-fifties America, the era of the bouffant hairdo and the thrust brassiere. Plain and pockmarked at the cheeks, she nonetheless scorned the use of makeup and resolutely shielded her face behind heavy tortoiseshell glasses. Her hair, mousy-brown and coarse, was drawn back severely in a tight rubber-banded braid. She dressed on all occasions with an almost monastic austerity: a baggy black cardigan, long black skirt, black stockings, black flat-heeled shoes. Sometimes the cardigan was replaced by a baggy boatneck sweater that slid across her shoulders to left or right, revealing no trace of a bra strap in either direction. She was, in brief, everything I had grown up to regard as sexually disqualified. Moreover, she was old—certainly in her early thirties.

For months after I began attending The Classic, Clare was no more than a featureless fixture at the theater. She was simply the unsmiling, unwelcoming woman who sold tickets at the door, poured the espresso, and then stood morosely at the rear through every film, arms folded, smoking an illegal cigarette beneath The Classic's one, overworked air vent. At most, I registered her presence with distinct unease. Her manner was chill and dismissive, as if we, the patrons, were a necessary inconvenience in running the theater.

At the time I was keeping close company with one Geoff Reuben, a consummate film buff. Geoff had been born into the world of movies. His parents, along with countless uncles and aunts, worked for all the studios at various low-level jobs that nonetheless bespoke glamour to me. He'd become my constant companion at The Classic. There was in fact no way to avoid his companionship, since he came every night—usually bringing Irene, a film-studies graduate three years his senior and five years mine. At the time, Geoff and Irene were living together in an off-campus apartment. This made them my model of bohemian daring; it also further cemented the connection between cinema and sex in my fevered imagination. Irene may not have been much to look at; she was on the dumpy side and woefully bucktoothed, but how I wished I had a girl like her in my life, someone who had studied in Paris, spoke French, and had been to the Cinémathèque. Astutely picking up on my secret longing, Geoff had—quite generously—offered to share Irene with me.

I was astonished by the proposition. And more so still by the shameless, even coquettish, ease with which Irene accepted the prospect. At the time I didn't even know arrangements like this had a name. But I'd recently learned about something very like it. Where else but at the movies? Anna Magnani in *The Golden Coach* plays an adventuress who takes many lovers to her bed in no particular legal or emotional order, simply as whim and opportunity dictate. Now here across the table from me was a real live woman willing to do the same. The idea alone was enough to make me dizzy. But then, as I recall, I began to wonder if the idea alone might not be enough. What if it all went wrong somehow? What if Irene decided Geoff was more desirable? What if Irene couldn't satisfy two men? What if I couldn't satisfy one woman? What if there were big scheduling problems about the bedroom or the bathroom? How did something like this work anyway? Worst of all, what if it just proved to be . . . nothing much? That would be one great sexual fantasy blown to bits. Some things, I began to think, ought never to leave the realm of imagination.

Well, we went ahead and tried it . . . or were in the process of trying it. I would spend the occasional weekend in their apartment, and the occasional night in Irene's bed. As I'd suspected, on closer inspection Irene turned out to be built on the saggy-baggy side, rather too much the Earth Mother for my tastes. But then, couldn't the same be said about Anna Magnani herself? Yet, given the chance, she managed in role after role to come across with what the men in her life were after. I tried to think of Irene that way, and, at least with the lights out, it more or less worked—especially after I discovered how thrilling it was to hear the woman beside me in the dark whispering incomprehensible French endearments. And that wasn't Irene's only redeeming quality as a lover. She was quite the worldly young woman. She'd traveled, she'd moved in supremely brilliant intellectual circles, she had stories to tell. Once she'd sat behind Jean-Paul Sartre at the movies. A Jerry Lewis comedy.

"Jean-Paul Sartre went to see Jerry Lewis?"

"He goes to see every movie that plays in Paris. He's an absolute movie freak."

"I never realized."

"Oh yes. He has a whole philosophy about seeing things. He calls it 'violation by sight.' He says, 'What is seen is possessed; to see is to *deflower*.' It's all very phenomenological."

"Wow!"

" 'The unknown object is given as virgin. It has not delivered up its secret; man must snatch its secret away from it.' You see what he means?"

"Yes. Sort of. I guess . . ."

"Going to the movies. It's a kind of visual rape."

I'm sure what Jean-Paul Sartre had in mind as visual rape was very deep indeed. What I had in mind was Nylana the Jungle Girl hanging from the trees.

I can't say that the rest of my three-way relationship with Geoff and Irene was all that satisfying—except for the risqué air it allowed us to wear when we were out together in public. For, of course, we were doing nothing to keep our arrangement secret. Probably we just looked like three smug and giggly kids—but as it turned out, my daring little experiment with Geoff and Irene contributed just enough self-assurance to my otherwise unformed character to usher me into the great erotic adventure that lay at hand.

One night, after seeing *Hiroshima Mon Amour* at The Classic (as usual the movie was too deep for me; but, again as usual, I found the love scenes mesmerizing), Geoff, Irene, and I stopped off at Moishe's for strong coffee and film talk. This had become our almost nightly ritual. Irene, who always did most of the talking, was doing her best to explain how brilliantly Alain Resnais had used "hermeneutic reconfiguration" to achieve "cathartic excitation" . . . or something like that. Though I had learned to squint and nod knowingly in all the right places, the analysis, as she could tell, was wasted on me. "Don't you see," Irene insisted, "in the opening sequence we can't tell if that's sweat or atomic fallout covering the writhing naked bodies." Maybe we couldn't, but a lot I cared. Plain old writhing naked bodies on the screen were enough to give me my money's worth. Poor Irene had just about given up trying to enlighten the barbarian when Don Sharkey and Clare came in accompanied by a man and woman.

The woman, I noticed at once, was a slightly older replica of Clare: the same dour clothes, the same unadorned face, the same skinned-back hair. Geoff, one of Sharkey's fans, at once invited the new arrivals to join us. They did. And for the next few hours, Clare sat at the far end of the table immersed in heavy French conversation with her friends, who, I learned, were visitors from Paris, the publishers of a highly regarded cinema journal. The two women guzzled black coffee and smoked nonstop, one pungent French cigarette after another (Disque Bleu was the name of the brand. Where could I buy them, I wondered). Though I didn't understand a word of what they said, I was spellbound by their flow of heady discourse. I can't say if that was the first night I looked closely at Clare, but I surely looked. My gaze wandered from her to her friend and back, carefully comparing their identically bored, impassive faces, noting the air of absolute, if casual, authority that colored all they said. From my friends at the table I learned that the two women were disputing the relative merits of montage as opposed to *mise-en-scène* in the work of the New Wave directors—an issue that meant precisely nothing to me.

Slowly, as I watched, a bold hypothesis formed in my mind. Here were two women who chose to look unwomanly in exactly the same way. Two obviously smart women. Smart? For all I knew, judging from the intensity of their talk, *brilliant*. Two brilliant women, speaking French, smoking French cigarettes, discussing French film. Conclusion: the way they looked was . . . a *look*. A deliberate, carefully devised look. It struck me that I'd seen this look not two weeks before. It was in a movie: Jean Cocteau's *Orphée*. It was the look of the oh-so-sophisticated female students the hero meets at the café. And didn't the dark woman who played the figure of Death in the film affect much the same austere appearance?

What a dope I was! What I'd ignorantly mistaken for a drab and sexless absence of style was—so I decided that evening on the basis of no greater evidence than what I could see at the far end of the table—the look of French female intellect. These were women of ideas for whom life (and doubtless love) were far too serious, too *existentially* serious (I had lately learned the word in Philosophy 101) to allow them to waste time on frivolities like lipstick, nylons, underwear.

I was improvising wildly, for I knew nothing about Frenchwomen, or French intellect, or existential seriousness. Still, I relished the conjecture. Big ideas were careening through my head, colliding with conventional values and tastes. I was expanding the inherited standards of sexiness that had always governed my life. Right or wrong, here was a thought all my own, the first exploratory step I'd dared to take beyond the worldview of Modesto, California. Moreover, I was allowing this thought, along with my lascivious fascination for French cinema, to rub off on a woman—on Clare, who sold me the tickets of admission that opened this erotic rite of passage to me.

And then there came a moment that might have been among the least memorable in my life, a vapor of the mind that might have been quickly blown into forgetfulness. But before that could happen, events to come would reveal its importance, and the memory would be rescued from extinction: my first encounter with the name "Castle."

It was the Frenchwoman who brought it up. Turning to Clare, she said something in French which, like all the rest that passed between them, sailed by me without meaning. I was, however, listening intently enough to know it was a question—which led Clare to question back with a single word, "Castle?" Then, after a quick puzzled look at Sharkey beside her, she asked, "*William* Castle?"

The woman said, "No, *Max* Castle."

Clare turned to Sharkey again, asking in English, "Have you ever heard of a director named Max Castle?"

Sharkey, shrugging, passed the name down the table to his student contingent. "How about it, movie fans? You know of a Max Castle?"

Following Sharkey's inquiry, Clare sent a glance down the table. Her eyes went from Geoff to Irene to . . . me. A long, blank look. A nothing look. Our first encounter beyond the lobby of The Classic.

How I wished I could be the one to tell her what she wanted to know, to look bright and quick and knowledgeable. But I had no idea who this Castle was. At that point in my life, I had no idea who

D. W. Griffith was. What could I do but smile and stare back? I think I offered a doltish shrug, as if to apologize. But why? If she didn't know who Castle was, why should I?

At my elbow, however, sat someone who did. It was Geoff, as I might have expected. Geoff knew everything about movies right down to the names of the stuntmen who fell off horses in Johnny Mack Brown westerns. If a guy appeared in a minor horror flick wearing an ape suit, Geoff was sure to know who the guy in the suit was and, thanks to his family's connections, had probably been to lunch with him at one of the studios. Geoff may have been the world's first movie trivia master. As I would learn later, Clare despised movie trivia masters. She regarded them as a disease of the art form. But that night her question was right up Geoff's alley: a casual query about cinematic trash. "Sure," Geoff piped up brightly. He knew who this Max Castle was. He could even rattle off a brief filmography: *Count Lazarus, Feast of the Undead, Revenge of the Ghoul.*

"Oh yeah," Sharkey said, now flashing on the name—for he too was an accomplished trivialist. "The vampire guy. *House of Blood,* stuff like that, right?"

"Also *Shadows over Sing Sing,*" Geoff hastened to add. "That's his best."

Having acquired the information she sought, Clare pulled a supercilious face. "Oh. *That* Castle," she said, lending her tone an arrogantly dismissive chill. But she dropped the remark as if she might be covering up, still not entirely certain of her ground. Turning back to her friend, she asked a question that brought a long answer in French.

"What's she saying?" Geoff asked Irene.

Irene cocked an ear and translated for the two of us. "She says people are talking about him—this Castle. In Paris. Very important, she says."

Very important—but not, I could see, to Clare, who was exhaling a dense screen of cigarette smoke to hide the baleful expression she had assumed. She was clearly doubting every word she heard. I liked the way she looked: haughty, blasé, sullen. I wanted to look like that too. So I tried it, and it felt right. Dumb as I was about movies at that stage of my life, I had no trouble understanding her response. Vampires. Even I knew that wasn't *art,* wasn't the least bit like the things we came to The Classic to see: movies about tortured relationships, despair, and the meaninglessness of life—like *La Strada,*

The Bicycle Thief, or *The Seventh Seal.* Really good movies, as I understood it, made you want to go out and drown yourself. Vampire movies didn't do that. They were just junk. True, I liked movies about vampires. Werewolves too. But I knew better than to say so. That much I had learned: when you enjoyed junk, keep your mouth shut about it.

If only by the most tenuous thread of pretense and make-believe, I fancied that I was allied with Clare in her disdain for someone who made movies called *Feast of the Undead, House of Blood.* Imitating her in that small, secret exercise of critical discrimination, I felt intoxicatingly connected with some higher realm of the mind where she stood guard.

That night I fell in love with Clare. I couldn't have said so at the time, for, at nineteen, I didn't know love could attach to an intellectual ideal, let alone an intellectual ideal that came dressed like a woman. But from that evening on, whenever I attended The Classic, I looked forward in high anticipation to taking my ticket from Clare's hand. I even dared from time to time to speak to her—no more than small talk, a fumbling inquiry about the evening's program. "Who directed?" "Is this the uncut version?" "When was it made?" Dumb questions, but the best I could come up with.

Her answer was always the same impatient gesture. She would hand me the notes that went with each program. Price: one cent.

"One cent?" I remarked the first time I bought a copy.

"I don't write for nothing," she answered belligerently.

I knew that friends of mine who were regulars at The Classic treasured these notes and carefully filed them away for later use, often cribbing from them in their film courses. I, on the other hand, had always found them so analytically dense that I rarely troubled to read them. There were never less than several single-spaced paragraphs of mercilessly congested prose on each film, imperfectly typed, mimeographed on both sides, the ink bleeding through from back to front. I'd never found anything in them worth the eyestrain. But now I discovered that these unsigned notes were Clare's work—her special contribution to The Classic and, in the opinion of its more discriminating patrons, the theater's most distinctive feature.

I found out more about The Classic. The theater, it turned out, was rather less than half Sharkey's property and achievement. For all his windy self-importance, he seemed to be in charge of the projectors and the espresso machine and not much else. The truth was,

Sharkey was burning too much hash to be entrusted with more than minimal technical responsibilities, and even these were getting beyond him. The capital in the business was mainly Clare's, and the programs were wholly her choice. She tracked down the films, placed the orders, bargained with the distributors. Finally, when each program was scheduled, she provided the research and criticism that went into the notes. On every film she produced a savagely opinionated discussion, every point supported with scholarly precision. Where old films were concerned, she entered into minute comparisons of the various prints available. As I was soon to learn, in Clare's world, there was no bliss to compare with the discovery of a lost Von Stroheim scene or a Pabst without torn sprockets.

Accordingly, as my secret infatuation with Clare grew more intense, I too began to pore over these notes like The Classic's more addicted patrons. Much of what I found there—the abstruse issues under fierce debate, the historical allusions, the subtle critical nuances—escaped my understanding. Nevertheless, I saved the notes, read and reread them, struggling to appropriate their sophistication, or at least their vocabulary, if for no other reason than to place myself on speaking terms with their intimidating author. For years afterward, these ink-stained pages of pink and blue and green remained in a box in my closet, a souvenir as much of my first great romance as of my intellectual initiation into film culture. The box collected dust; the mimeographed sheets inside grew brittle with age; but at last these penny handouts, so often pirated by other film houses but of which I owned the complete original series, became the valued collector's item they deserved to be. At which point I contributed them with no little pride to the University of California film archives. Why should the gift have been so proudly presented and so eagerly received? Because the Clare I speak of, who labored with such love to produce this anonymous treasure trove of scholarship and opinion, was Clarissa Swann, then an unsung talent but destined in less than ten years to become America's premier film critic. It was no less an authority that was to become my private tutor in film.

I suppose, to begin with, I was nothing more to Clare than an amorous interlude during one of her many fallings out with Sharkey. Like most regular patrons of The Classic, I knew that she and Sharkey were more or less lovers who more or less lived together. But their relationship was a stormy one, punctuated as much by financial disaster as by chronic infidelities on both sides. There was no way to tell if the infidelities were the cause or the result of their business contretemps. In any case, both managed to slot numerous liaisons into their quarrelsome episodes. An eager, good-looking young man who had already begun an amateurish flirtation, I quickly qualified as a possible diversion for Clare. She was hardly one to let the discrepancy in our ages make any difference. The word was that she had taken up with many of the students who frequented The Classic. In my eyes, such gossip only served to envelop her with an enticing mystique of suave, continental promiscuity. By now I was prepared to believe that just possibly, without her glasses on, with her hair a bit fluffed, Clare might, in a dim light and with the benefit of peripheral vision, look enough like the French film beauty Maria Casares to be considered—well, attractive . . . if you overlooked her rather pudgy build, which the baggy sweater helped you to do.

As for myself, I was then living through the intoxication of Autant-Lara's *Devil in the Flesh*. Fantasies of the boyish Gérard Philipe yielding to the seduction of an older woman dazzled my imagination. I rather fancied I might make do as his blond American counterpart, a tall and slender youth, with the same quick smile and wide-eyed exuberance. I even had it on Irene's authority that in the throes of passion, I took on Gérard's feverish intensity: the trembling brow, the clenching jaw. As for his adolescent gaucherie, which I gathered his older female fans found charming, of this I had a plentiful supply.

One late night, Clare, minus Sharkey, who was rumored to be living at the beach with a recent coed conquest, wandered into Moishe's and took a lonely seat in a booth. A group of us who had been to The Classic that night—this time for a heavyweight Roberto Rossellini double bill—spotted her, but judged by her vacant and morose look that she preferred to be alone. Clare wasn't much of a mixer. I, however, caught her eye and offered my most boyish smile. At once, without altering her semitragic expression, she moved to sit beside me at our table, strategically segregating me from the others. It was the first time she'd acknowledged my existence as something other than a customer at The Classic.

"You're Alan?" she asked, looking up darkly from under drooping lids.

Why Alan, I wondered. "No, Jonathan. Jonathan Gates."

"Oh yes," she said as if remembering, though we'd never been introduced. Then she said nothing but sat staring fixedly into her coffee cup. Gropingly, I made conversation about the Rossellini movies, staying cautiously close to her program notes. I had gone on for several stumbling minutes before I realized that there were tears on her cheeks. She was crying, silently but tremulously. I shut up and reverted to bashful, attempting my best, ultrasensitive imitation of Gérard. After a long, awkward interval, she looked up.

"Come home with me," she said.

Close-up of young hero's face. Expression of bewildered delight and eager anticipation. Dissolve and cut.

I never found out why Clare was crying that night. I soon learned it was something she frequently did without any identifiable cause. It was part of her style, a symptom of some deep underground stream of angst that ran through her life, occasionally welling up to the surface. In any case, my curiosity about her secret sorrow was forgotten soon after we returned to her apartment. What followed wasn't my first sexual adventure, but it might as well have been. The quantity, intensity, above all the stunning variety of Clare's lovemaking reduced me to virginal status. I was blithely swept along in the torrent, accepting all that was thrust upon me, yielding all that was demanded. It was a night I never expected to be repeated.

Toward morning, in a condition torn between physical exhaustion and undiminished emotional frenzy, I found myself oddly positioned across Clare's bed, my face sunk between her corpulent thighs, performing as required, when I felt a tug at my hair. Lifting me from my diligent efforts, Clare looked at me quizzically down the length of her naked torso. "*Mother?* Is that what you're thinking of?"

Her juices still warm upon my cheeks, the look I returned was surely more quizzical than her own. For mother was—I hope—the farthest thought from my mind at that moment.

"I mean," Clare explained, "are you sure you've ever seen a Pudovkin?"

Even this didn't help. Was "pudovkin" perhaps a sexual code word? I was about to answer, yes, I'd seen a pudovkin before, when I realized she was resuming a line of conversation that had broken off some time before. In one of our brief respites, I'd apologetically mentioned my dislike for silent films—for, of course, between bouts of lovemaking, we talked film. Or rather, Clare talked, I listened. "Surely, that doesn't include the Russians," she had protested. "Dovzhenko, Eisenstein, Pudovkin . . ."

"Pudovkin?" Distractedly, I simply picked up on the last name in the series. "Well, yes, he's all right, I guess. But his movies are so slow, so heavy. . . ." Which was what I said about all silent movies that weren't comedies.

Now, some two hours later, Clare was returning to the subject, holding my head unsteadily balanced on her pubic bone. "*Mother*," she informed me, "is the only Pudovkin you can still rent in this country. And we haven't shown that at The Classic in over four years. The Museum of Modern Art used to have a bad print of *Storm over Asia*, but, God, that hasn't been available since 1948. So where have you seen any Pudovkins?"

"Well," I said, struggling to dredge up any Russian movies I could remember, "there was that picture about the czar last month—*Ivan the Terrible*."

Her belly shook with laughter beneath my chin. "Silly! That was *Eisenstein!*" And she abruptly returned my head to its salacious assignment. "Lover, you've got lots to learn."

One week later, I vacated Geoff and Irene's apartment and moved in with Clare. My education had begun.

There are moments when a door opens in the mind's eye, and through it we see the path that lies before us in life. Our talent, our calling. Years later that first experience of vocation may still glow as vividly as the recollection of our sexual awakening. In my case, the two moments are intertwined, and at the center of both there is the memory of Clare, lover and teacher. We both knew our relationship was bound to be perishable. The years we spent together were an erotic holiday. Clare never made a secret of the fact that she was grooming me to satisfy her ego; she never asked me to pretend she was more to me than a young man's sexual fantasy come to life. Of course, she *was* more than that. But whatever more she may have been, I understood I mustn't speak of it as "love"—a word she had banished from her autobiographical vocabulary. There was a defensive cynicism about Clare that led her to prefer a tougher style—an emotional abrasiveness, an unsparing contention of minds. For her, honesty between a man and a woman was a sort of martial art, a dry-eyed giving and taking of wounds. I dutifully absorbed many such wounds—hard critical knocks, put-downs, temperamental jabs. They hurt. But nothing hurt more than her ban upon tenderness. I sometimes ached to confess my real affection. Nevertheless, though I wasn't permitted to speak of it (and if I had, it would have been with a clumsiness she despised) I wasn't too green to know there was something rare and supremely precious between us—a marriage of mind and body.

There are two things movie fans around the world would one day come to know about Clarissa Swann. First, that she was a brilliant critic and stylist. Second, that she could be a pitiless butcher in an argument. The agility of her mind, the slashing acerbity of her wit are on public display in every line she ever wrote. But there was one thing I alone would know about the Clare who was, when I met her, a bitter and bitchy Nobody still years away from becoming the bitter and bitchy Somebody whose reviews would one day grace the pages of *The New York Times*. She could be generous to a fault, at least to someone who came to her, as I did, in submissive awe. Clare always needed an admiring audience, if only an audience of one. Adulation brought out the best in her, which was her honest passion to teach. That virtue was, however, mixed with a pugnacious need to flatten disagreement, to assail and destroy those who questioned her views. In the presence of resistance, she gave no quarter. Ridicule, sarcasm, insult became permissible weapons. But this was only because she *cared* about movies fanatically. In her life, the defense of cinematic excellence was a cause of supreme importance. She'd created her critical standards against fierce opposition and had suffered because of them.

When, in the mid-forties, she entered Barnard as a freshman, Clare precociously sought to merge her youthful love of film with the literary studies she chose as her major. In that period, the universities were adamantly closed to the vulgarity of mere movies. After all, what could Milton have in common with Mickey Mouse? Accordingly, Clare found herself penalized by hidebound academics whenever she dared to bring film into her classwork. The opposition of the day was unbudging; no one would admit the academic legitimacy of her interest. Before her sophomore year was finished, she quit college in an act of intellectual rebellion. The sting of that early rejection never healed. Years later, when her cause had been more than vindicated in the universities, part of her continued to live in those scorning classrooms, fighting old battles with smug professors for whom the printed word was the last word in culture.

When the war ended, she spent the remainder of the forties in Paris soaking up the lively appreciation of film that has characterized the French intelligentsia since the days of Louis Lumière. She worked (unpaid) as usher, ticket seller, concierge in the *ciné* clubs that began to reappear after the war. After two or three years of drudgery, she managed to become a research assistant (again unpaid) at the Ciné-mathèque, the mecca of the Parisian film community. There she quickly attached herself to the circle of New Wave theorists then forming around the influential French critic André Bazin. Her own education in film unfolded amid the raucous debates she heard waged in the clubs by the likes of Godard, Truffaut, Resnais. Eventually, thanks to a boost from the admiring Bazin, she picked up still another unpaid position editing and then writing—in French—for the land-mark journal *Cahiers du Cinéma*. In this way, she acquired the dis-tinctive Gallic intensity that would lend her work its peculiar appeal—though fortunately without the Gallic pomposity that frequently comes with it.

Somewhere along the line she met Sharkey, who, as Clare told it, was little more than an expatriate bum haunting the cafés of the Left Bank, and their always uneasy lust and disgust partnership began. With money from her parents, Clare bankrolled Sharkey's first film house in Paris. It did modestly well, showing mainly popular Amer-ican movies—Walt Disney, the Marx Brothers, Laurel and Hardy. At one point, it ran *Horsefeathers* for nine months solid; Clare claimed she could recite the entire film word perfect, and one night, with the aid of enough booze, she did . . . in forty-three minutes flat. Had she been the least bit drunker, she assured me, she could have in-cluded Harpo's pantomime bits. By the early fifties, Sharkey, con-vinced that in Paris he would always be a small fish in a big pond, was anxious to return to the States. With what they'd earned and learned from the Paris venture, he and Clare relocated to Los Angeles, Sharkey's hometown. The Classic never became the success they expected; still, it had served to hold them together in love and strug-gle—though for the life of me, I couldn't see why. Sharkey seemed so hopelessly punched-out, so lacking in the sophistication I found in Clare . . . what did she see in him? I didn't have the nerve to ask outright, but once when I edged close enough to the subject, Clare volunteered a sad, wistful confession.

"You'd never guess it, but once upon a time—about a million years ago—Sharkey was a beautiful animal. That's really all there ever was between us. Brute sexuality. His taste has always been abysmal, you know. Stuck at that macho-obnoxious level that certain penis-anxious male types think will keep them youthful. But he was as close as I would get to going to bed with Dana Andrews. Haven't you ever noticed the resemblance? It might still be there, if you restored the hair at the top and pared away the flab at the bottom. To tell you the truth, I haven't looked lately."

Dana Andrews? *Laura*'s Lieutenant Mark MacPherson? By God, she was right. I'd never studied Sharkey closely enough to notice. Now I did, and underneath the pouches and creases he did show the remnants of movie-star good looks. The flab in question, however, was more than a matter of physique. Whatever he might have been when Clare met him, he'd long since turned into an incorrigible floater. With The Classic as his base of operations, he seemed content to spend the rest of his years playing senior cinema guru to his own small circle of young, mainly pushover female admirers, spinning tales of his years among the New Wave directors. He'd developed a line of intellectualoid banter, liberally sprinkled with gutter French, which he'd haul out at parties. With luck, his act might just manage to get him into bed with the prettiest face in the crowd before he was too soused to carry on coherently.

Such pretentious dissipation might have satisfied Sharkey, but it was hardly what Clare was prepared to settle for. She wanted much more: success, acclaim, vindication. The occasional editing stints she picked up with students and professors were never going to bring her that. Her writing still appeared in esoteric French film journals— printed for no pay. That and her film notes, so assiduously researched and written, were all she had to show for herself at the age of thirty-two. It wasn't enough. For her, The Classic had become a drowning pool where she was sinking into obscurity.

From time to time, Clare took up with young men like myself, looking for the acquiescence and admiration that her undernourished ego craved. How often she found it, I can't say. But from me she received what she needed in abundance. An instinctive teacher, she quickly recognized me for the bright but unformed boy I was, and set to work fashioning me into both paramour and apprentice. At the time, a dismal interlude in her life, it may have been resignation that prompted her generosity. Seeing no future for herself, she labored to transplant her intellectual resources into my otherwise unoccupied young mind. All that was required of me was an unstinting willingness to be molded in her hands—to take over her knowledge, her values, above all her loyalties and antagonisms. For this, I was the ideal choice. Deference and passivity have always been my strong suit. I confess that my intelligence is that of the attentive follower, the gifted mimic.

But there was one thing more that suited me to Clare's tutelage. I don't know what luck Clare had with other young men, but her methods of instruction meshed perfectly with my belated sexual development. How shall I put it? Very well—Clare was as kinky as she was brilliant. And she didn't keep these qualities in separate compartments. Rather, she mixed sex and intellect in ways that might have shocked others and driven them off in bewilderment. But for me, I almost blush to admit, the combination worked perfectly.

A major part of what Clare taught me about film I learned in bed—and I don't mean in relaxed, postcoital conversation, but in active process. At first, until I grasped that this was Clare's preferred style of instruction, I found myself dumbfounded. When, in the act of love, she began to murmur a stream-of-consciousness lecture on Russian Formalism in my ear, I felt certain I should pause and take respectful note. But no. With a pelvic shove and a slap to my buttocks, she bullied me on, almost angrily. I continued; I accelerated the rhythm of our intercourse; her words flowed more rapidly, her voice grew stronger. Spread luxuriantly beneath me, with eyes closed, sweat beaded across her upper lip, she became more articulate by the moment, even as her breath caught and raced. That was the first session in what would become a frenzied cerebral-genital curriculum. In the nights that followed, the theories of Arnheim, Munsterberg, Mitry lathered from her like prepared lectures. What was more surprising—I was taking it all in! The ideas were registering vividly. It was as if my body, totally preoccupied with pouring its libidinous energy into Clare, transformed my brain into a *tabula rasa* on which every word could be imprinted.

When we'd finished on that first occasion, we lay for a long while in silent exhaustion. Then, as she reached for the inevitable cigarette at the bedside, Clare turned to me with a slyly provocative look. "Of course, you have to take Balázs into account as the definitive statement of Formalism." And when would I learn about Balázs, whoever he was? I knew it would be once again at Clare's quaint idea of the proper time.

I was an apt pupil and quickly adjusted to Clare's unique form of erotic pedagogy. Perhaps I was the only one of her lovers who ever had. In any case, my ready response to her eccentric ways cemented our relationship beautifully. I was learning in exactly the way she wanted to teach. I absorbed Kracauer's Realist theory while Clare held me nuzzling to her breast, maneuvering a teasing nipple between my lips; I mastered Bazin's Myth of Total Cinema while she performed a playful striptease-lecture; I received a magisterial analysis of the contrast between iconic and indexical imagery while busied in prolonged cunnilingual service, the lush river of my mentor's thought rising and dipping with the tempo of her excitement. Only gradually did I come to see that Clare's teaching technique wasn't designed entirely for my benefit. A compulsively cerebral woman, she was able to use these intellectual distractions to build her orgasms to the point of maximum intensity.

As for me, this unique instructional method has indelibly stamped my study of film with a remarkable quality. No matter how seemingly abstruse the concept, if I learned it from Clare, it remains suffused with sexual heat. Perhaps I find myself lecturing on Astruc's theory of the *caméra-stylo;* to my students, it is simply a piece of academic furniture—but remembering the wickedly inventive stimulus with which Clare once punctuated the idea, I am beset by subtle genital tremors. No one could understand the sensation. No doubt there's some Pavlovian principle involved.

The comic side of all this didn't escape us; that was part of the enjoyment. One night, after a particularly vigorous romp, I lay across Clare's body, my spent member still in place. Taking a bite of my ear, she announced, "Well, I think you're finally ready to learn about the possibilities of the deep shot." For years afterward, I couldn't view a good piece of depth-of-field cinematography without reexperiencing that night, that moment, and thrilling with a secret shudder of delight.

I remember those early years with Clare as the earthly paradise of my youth. Ecstasies of the mind, pleasures of the flesh mingled in our days and nights. She turned my world upside down and inside out, beginning with my ideals of feminine beauty. I'd never have thought, until Clare took me to her bed, that I could find such stimulation in an unshaven female leg or armpit. In that era of sterilized Styrofoam femininity, Clare was all natural odors and organic textures, a Neorealist movie heroine come to life. Just as dramatically, she revolutionized my taste in manners, morals, art, politics, even cuisine. I adopted her as my model in all these. I tried especially to affect her elitist style of mind, though far too stiltedly—with the result that from time to time Clare had to take me down a peg or two. As on the night I asked if she knew that Jean-Paul Sartre believed looking at movies was a kind of "violation by sight"—which was about all I knew about Jean-Paul Sartre, and that at secondhand.

"Yes, my dear," Clare answered wearily. "That's probably because every film student I've met since the publication of *Being and Nothingness* has been telling me. But we must be charitable. The man did go on to say a few intelligent things."

Snobbishness, Clare would have me know, was among the cardinal intellectual sins, a vice which she was spared by natural immunity. Her standards, however lofty, came naturally and spontaneously to her. They weren't a costume worn for effect; they were her life's blood. When is a snob *not* a snob? When she cares to the point of hurting about the bad taste of her inferiors—and will pay the price to teach them better. In Clare's case, that meant again and again running The Classic into the red trying to force-feed her tiny audience on works of taxing quality. As for example—the time she proudly hosted the First American Dziga Vertov Festival.

"Who?" I asked.

"Dziga Vertov," she repeated, as if I should know. I didn't. "The creator of the *Kino-Pravda* movement. It's one of the great experiments in documentary-film making. The Museum of Modern Art has the work of his entire school on loan from the Moscow Institute. It's a must."

Kino-Pravda turned out to be an hours-long montage of choppy, bizarrely edited newsreels from Russia of the 1920s and 1930s. Street scenes, barnyard scenes, endless footage of workers working, farmers farming, wheat growing. Now and then an interesting, if primitive innovation—as of 1932. One promising quick shot of a near-naked lady. Then more workers, more farmers. "Clare," Sharkey lamented after the first preview, "nobody wants to see fossils like this."

But Clare was adamant. "It's an important example of cinematic failure," she insisted and set about preparing a packet of mimeographed notes to explain the historical importance of that failure.

The first night of the festival, every ambulatory Bolshevik in Los Angeles showed up. An audience of eight. There was weak applause. The second night, an audience of zero. Clare ordered Sharkey to run the films anyway, while she sat in the empty Classic, tears in her eyes, a curse on her lips. "Have they no culture?" she moaned, asking of the multitudes who had not come.

From Clare, I also learned the rough-and-tumble pleasures of serious argument. Often simply to exercise my wits, she would take unpredictable issue with my unschooled likes and dislikes. To begin with, playing cautious, I sought always to echo her opinions, but I'd sometimes misjudge. Once, knowing her deep admiration for Ingmar Bergman, I ventured to praise his *Wild Strawberries*. Immediately, Clare flashed out at me, claiming to loathe the film. "Whining, menopausal self-indulgence," she called it—and for that night I was banished to the living-room couch to sleep alone. This was Clare's version of an "F." Trimming my sails accordingly, the next time Bergman came up I confidently disparaged his *Virgin Spring*, only to discover that Clare adored the picture, regarding it as an authentic cinematic fairy tale. Exiled for another night to the lonely couch.

Clare could be just such a baffling mixture of bullying egotism and Socratic provocation. She wanted agreement, but not slavish imitation. In effect she wanted me to make up my own mind to see things her way. I was more than willing to play along, but at times the twists and turns of Clare's critical logic left me dazzled. Especially so when she found herself surrounded by the agreement of her inferiors—which included just about every other critic in the country. Far be it from Clare to follow the herd, or even appear to do so. In the presence of unwelcome consensus, she would insist on finding a better reason to like or dislike, the one reason everybody else had stupidly overlooked. Or, just possibly, she might simply decide to reverse her views on the grounds that it was now time to elevate the discussion to a higher level of analysis. She did this in a mode that suggested, for lack of anyone better suited to the task, she would have to serve as her own most challenging interlocutor. At first I mistook this for a kind of mere game-playing on her part. But no, she meant it seriously. It was her way of raising the cultural stakes—and of driving herself toward a more demanding analysis.

I remember when this happened with François Truffaut, one of Clare's Parisian confreres whose early movies she'd praised to high heaven. But then when his *Jules et Jim* came out to nearly universal acclaim, she made an abrupt about-face, contending that it was time to teach the man a thing or two. Yes, *Jules et Jim* was a great movie. That was precisely the problem. It was *too* good, *too* clever, *too* self-assured, a facile Cartesian exercise in human relations that lacked a convincing emotional messiness. "A film you can love so much, you want to hate it."

When I finished typing her program notes for The Classic's second-run showing of the film, I let her know how surprised I was. "I thought you'd really like it. It's so true to life."

"Oh? Whose life?"

"Well, ours. Yours and mine . . . and Sharkey's. We're a sort of *ménage à trois*, aren't we?"

I might as well have stepped on a land mine. The emotional explosion that followed was my first lesson in how personally Clare could take a movie. "*Jules et Jim* is an exquisitely contrived piece of self-congratulatory masculine bullshit about a cardboard cutout of a woman who drives herself off a bridge because the two men who've shared her body turn out to be total jerks. Apparently Mr. Truffaut can't think of anything else the dumb broad might do with the rest of her life. Is that the kind of loser you think *I* am?" But she made sure to add, the outrage flaming in her eyes, "And, Goddamit! It's as close to a perfect movie as I've ever seen. Which makes it all the worse."

That little miscalculation cost me a full week's sentence on my solitary couch, including two humiliating nights that Clare spent with another student.

By the end of my first year with Clare, my intellectual course was set. I'd scrapped prelaw and, with a certain sense of pompous self-importance, declared myself a film-studies major specializing in history and criticism. Clare encouraged the choice, or rather demanded it—not entirely because of my aptitude, which was yet to put in an appearance. In me, she saw her chance to relive the education that had been denied to her. I went along unresistingly. Naive I may have been, but not too obtuse to overlook a golden opportunity when it presented itself. Clare was offering me a ready-made academic career. I grasped it. She, as a student during the war years, had been ahead of her time. Now, a decade and a half later, the universities were opening up eagerly to the study of film; at UCLA the subject was booming. If Clare had been willing to return to school—but she'd never have considered it—she would have had all the intellectual leverage she needed against the literary fuddy-duddies. I returned in her place, equipped with all her tastes and insights. But where she had been a pushy young woman in the stuffy male world of the academy, I arrived as a tactful young man, a good (meaning docile) student who had a positive knack for charming his teachers. Clare never could help raising hackles; it was her nature. Nevertheless, she reveled in my progress as she watched me move among the scholars with a smooth and soothing ease. I was her hand-groomed agent infiltrating the hostile citadel of the university, armed with her once-despised critical views, many of which I wasn't ashamed to take over like lessons learned by rote. Convinced of my teacher's brilliance—and all too aware of my own strictly second-rate talents—I was prepared to be the perfect conduit.

Over a three-year period together, Clare and I screened nearly the entire repertoire of film classics or at least as much as could be rented on the market. We arranged pioneering festivals and retrospectives both heavy (Fritz Lang, Von Sternberg, Renoir) and light (Buster Keaton, Fred Astaire, Harold Lloyd). Sometimes, when The Classic was running a special series, movies arrived four and five at a time, small towers of battered metal canisters that filled our tiny projection booth to the limit. Then I'd cut classes to sit with Clare through film after film, a veritable cinematic orgy. We brought in our meals—great, sopping corned-beef sandwiches from Moishe's—and didn't emerge again until after the evening program ended and we'd locked the doors. I came to think of the dark grotto of The Classic as a salt mine tunneling down into the bowels of the earth. Working through films with Clare, as she compiled her notes, was true intellectual labor: stop the movie, talk, run it again, talk some more, then run it again. If she judged we needed a closer reading, she could be a sure hand on the inching knob, expertly clicking the film along, exposing each delicate celluloid square to its ordeal by fire in the perilous film gate . . . eight seconds, nine, ten, and then on its way in just that last split second before it showed signs of melting. Her touch was the gift of instinct. On one occasion, we saw *Intolerance* through four times with Clare dissecting Griffith shot by shot, cut by cut, for my benefit. On another, she spent sixteen analytical hours on *Triumph of the Will*, teaching me Leni Riefenstahl's diabolical skills as a film propagandist, every angle of the camera, every least nuance of lighting. "The single most gifted woman filmmaker," Clare commented sourly, "and she had to be a fink."

What a joy it was exploring this phantasmagoria of the mind called movies! And what a privilege to have Clarissa Swann for my personal guide. Eventually there would be those who regarded her as a highly conservative critic, a remnant of the old school no longer in touch with the hot new ideas. But when I was her star pupil, she was among the few in America who were fully conversant with the latest European theories. Within the next few years, she would catch the crest of New Wave enthusiasm in America and ride it to a success she'd all but stopped hoping for. For whatever Clare did to make my mind the mirror of her own during that entrancing interval of my life, I can only be grateful. Because, for all her quirky angles and bitter antagonisms, she was a staunchly humanistic spirit. Though she could talk cinematic technique with the best of them, she never allowed the medium to outweigh the meaning of the film. She insisted that movies were something more than a bag of optical illusions; they were literature for the eye, potentially as great as anything ever written for the page. From her I learned always to listen for the statement, watch for the vision. Or at least that's how I looked at movies until Max Castle ushered me into a darker science of the cinema. At which point I discovered that as vast and well-furnished as Clare's intellectual universe might be, there was a trapdoor within it that opened into the uncharted depths.

One day while The Classic was featuring a Howard Hawks series, I arrived at the theater in the early afternoon hoping to sit through another of Clare's illustrated lectures on one of her favorite directors. But when I entered the darkened auditorium, there was already a movie on the screen—and it wasn't Howard Hawks. It was a dim, yellowing print with a blurry sound track, so crudely spliced and so bereft of sprockets that it lurched spastically through the projector, garbling the dialogue and chopping the images into near incoherence. The scene was a morose Gothic interior: vast halls, shadowy stairways, mullioned windows glowing with spooky moonlight. Buxom ladies wearing Regency gowns and carrying guttering candles wandered along eerie corridors in the dead of night; ghoulish servants lurked in the corners. I could recognize none of the actors. What I managed to catch of the mangled script was a compendium of clichés. "I thought I heard a scream in the night," one of the lusty beauties remarks. "I'm sure it was only the wind, milady," the cadaverous butler answers with a furtive roll of his eyes.

Now this, I felt absolutely certain, was a very bad movie. Still, if Clare was watching it . . . and not just watching it—devouring it. When I entered the projection booth where she was stationed at the little window, she was deeply immersed in the film, too absorbed to register my arrival with more than a quick, cool glance. Slipping up behind her, I offered the greeting she most appreciated: a kiss in the hollow of her neck, my hands, searching out the flesh of her belly, gliding gently upward. It was the way Jean-Claude Brialy embraces Juliette Mayniel in *Les Cousins*. (Were Juliette's breasts, like Clare's, also bare beneath her sweater?) Clare usually melted a bit when I did that. But this time she gave an annoyed start and pulled away.

"What's this?" I asked as I settled in beside her at the window.

"A bit of a lark," she answered impatiently. "It's called *Feast of the Undead*."

I didn't immediately place the title. Wanting to be sure of my ground, I waited a few minutes more, then ventured to comment, "It looks pretty . . . bad."

"It's crap."

"Oh." After a pause, I asked, "Why are we watching it?"

"*We* aren't. *I* am. You don't have to."

"Well, why are *you* watching it?"

"It may be the only Max Castle movie in captivity. At least it's the only one I've been able to get hold of."

Ah yes. Castle. The vampire guy. The one the French couple had mentioned at Moishe's that night. Since then, Clare had brought him up two or three times more. I recalled hearing her on the phone making inquiries with distributors and film libraries. I had the impression he was haunting her, I guessed because she felt irked that she hadn't been able to recognize his name when it came her way.

"It isn't in very good condition," I remarked, observing the obvious.

"Scrap quality. Best I could find. Channel Five was going to show this on the late, late, late show. Decided it was unprojectable. They don't even want it back. Good thing—because I've already burned about ten feet out of it in the machine. We may not make it to the end."

And we didn't. Five minutes farther along and the film caught fire in the midst of its grand, gory climax: an impaling scene of extraordinary vividness, the camera spiraling down upon the doomed vampire lord as if it were the very stake on which his life would expire. It was a dizzying, nauseating effect; I welcomed seeing it vanish from the screen before the blood gushed. With a curse Clare shut the projector down. "Worst thing is: somebody amputated all the credits. They do that on television with garbage like this. Leaves more time for commercials. There's some striking camera work—like that last shot. I wonder who did it." She carried the reel to the rewind table. "Damn their eyes for mutilating this!"

"But it's crap, isn't it?"

"Oh? Is it? You saw less than ten minutes of it, and you're so sure."

"Well, you said so."

"And you just go along with whatever you hear, is that right?"

"But aren't vampire movies crap?"

"Carl Dreyer made a pretty good one, as I recall."

Dumb mistake. Clare had shown *Vampyr* only last month. "Well, yes, I guess . . . I mean . . ."

"Think for yourself, Jonny."

"Actually, I sort of like horror movies."

"Which are, by and large, crap. But this one . . . there are some interesting bits. Like that final sequence—I wish I could've seen the whole thing."

"The impaling? Pretty extreme."

"Yes, wasn't it? But unusually extreme. Something about the twist he gives the camera . . . makes it seem the shadows are coming up to swallow you. Never saw anything like that before. I don't know . . . maybe the man had something."

"Dialogue sounded really clunky."

"Awful. But that wouldn't have bothered you if you'd seen the bedroom scenes a little earlier. You know, vampire seductions. Very explicit. I could swear there was actual fornication. Odd about that. When I looked again, I couldn't find it. Even so, I'd like to know how they snuck that part past the censors back then. Must have been 1937, 1938. Olga Tell was in the film. Would-be Garbo of that period. I didn't know she appeared in trash like this."

"I'd like to see those bedroom scenes," I told her. "Just for scholarly purposes."

"Out of luck, lover. That's the part that got burned up." Clare inspected the film and wagged her head. "This'll never make it through the machine again. I'm not even going to bother rewinding." She dropped the reel in its canister and dusted her hands over it. "We've got better stuff to watch."

As Clare began to load another movie, I asked, "If this is such trash, why do the French think it's so good?"

"The *French!*" Clare laughed. "You mean my two visiting friends and maybe a couple of their friends back on the Left Bank? That's probably the size of Castle's following. Of course, in France that counts as a 'movement.' "

"Well, anyway, why did they say it was important?"

"Defensive pretension. The froggies are like that about American

44

movies. They can't just enjoy something because it's funny or exciting or clever—not if it was made by money-hungry philistine slobs. If *they* like it, it's got to be 'important.' So they wrap it up in miles of theory."

I wanted to ask more, but Clare was growing impatient. She had *Twentieth Century* ready to go on the projector and insisted we get down to some "real movie making." So we did. But I had the clear impression she was rushing us along to other things, trying hard to dismiss *Feast of the Undead*. Why, I wondered. And what to make of her strange indecisiveness about Max Castle? "*Maybe* the man had something. . . ." *Maybe* had no place in her critical vocabulary. Usually she made fanatically final judgments, trusting her first impression all the way.

One more thing I couldn't easily shake off. All the while we sat together laughing our way through Howard Hawks's hard-boiled little farce, I kept remembering how reluctant Clare had been to take her eyes off that vile vampire flick, how she'd shrugged me aside to return to it with such concentration. What had she seen in that sadly tattered sample of Castle's work that I had missed?

A day or so later, wondering how much more I might be able to see of *Feast of the Undead*, I approached Clare asking where she'd stashed the reel. She shot me a disapproving look. "I told you it was scrap. I disposed of it."

"You threw it out?" I'd never known her to do that. She'd once told me that no film, whatever its quality or condition, should be destroyed. Movies, in her view, were scarce and fragile cultural documents; they ought to be preserved down to the last withering frame. I started to ask, "Weren't there any parts that might be . . ." but she cut me off.

"Forget it. I don't serve slop like that in this house."

That shut me up. But it left me more curious than ever. The next time I heard the name "Castle," I'd be sure to pay attention.

3 THE MAGIC LANTERN

The education I received from Clare was generous in its proportions and passionately imparted, but it didn't come free of charge. As I soon discovered, I was expected to work it off. A modest tuition to begin with but it soon grew. When Clare asked the first time if I would mind sweeping out The Classic one Saturday morning, I assumed she was asking a special favor and eagerly complied. God knows, the theater needed it. I would have guessed it hadn't been swept for months. But from that time forward, sweeping up became my regular Saturday chore. A few weeks later and I found myself scrubbing down and repainting the theater's closet-sized unisex toilet; soon after that, I was running errands of all descriptions.

Before long, I was asking myself how a tiny, hole-in-the-wall operation like The Classic could possibly require so much work. What with repairing, replacing, purchasing, cleaning, polishing, picking up and delivering, my unpaid labor was soon snowballing into a full-time job, most of it menial drudgery. Each morning at breakfast, as strictly as a general marshaling her army of one, Clare would tick off the chores I was expected to discharge that day. Order more coffee for the espresso machine, buy more toilet paper, replace the burnt-out light bulbs, fix the broken seats, tack down the carpet in the lobby, chase to the printers, the distributors, the post office, the bank. There came a point when I began to wonder if our love affair was really a way for Clare to make up for years of neglect to her capital investment with the benefit of cheap labor. So I complained, if feebly, reminding her that I did after all have classes to attend and assignments to do.

She dismissed the protest, insisting that my real education was happening at The Classic and included the slave labor I was performing. She never apologized for what she asked of me, never so much as said please. It was all work she'd done herself in the past to keep The Classic going. She simply ordered it done, and done cheerfully.

"It all belongs to the movies," she told me. "The pictures need a theater, the theater's a human habitat. Sure, this place has always

46

looked pretty crummy. That's because there's only so much I can do, and there's nobody to help. If I could afford to make it a picture palace, I would. Believe me, the art of the cinema begins with scraping the chewing gum off the seats."

Apologizing abjectly, I surrendered and did as I was told.

There was only one task in all the lot that was remotely intellectual. When Clare learned I was ten fast fingers on a typewriter, she at once put me to work typing her program notes. This assignment, what with all the revisions Clare now took the liberty of producing, often kept me up into the small hours of the night; but it meant that I'd be the first to read each new installment of her work. With me to take over the dog labor of cutting stencils, mimeographing, collating, stapling, her writing began to grow in length. Soon she was adding a monthly essay to the notes, several dense paragraphs of film history, criticism, and comment on the passing cinema scene. While I was no more than the hands that typed the words, I now felt I was some significant part of The Classic's cultural role; I'd given Clare the chance to unfold thoughts she hadn't the time to gather before.

It wasn't until well into the second year of my semivoluntary apprenticeship that Clare began to introduce me to the higher mysteries of programming, as well as accounting and budgeting—the "business end" of things. These she discharged from a cubbyhole office just above the theater where she kept her files, her personal archives, her legal papers and ledgers. Clare regularly spent two or three hours each working day on the telephone tracing films and bargaining with distributors. "Listen and take notes," she instructed me. "It's the only way to learn." And I'd glue my ear to the extension phone while she went about the tedious, time-consuming toil of securing the movies that were The Classic's staff of life. In those prehistoric days, when repertory and revival theaters were rare phenomena, the task of tracking down old and unusual films, finding decent prints, negotiating for them with hard-nosed and mercenary distributors often required the combined talents of a detective and a diplomat.

About this time, an envious Sharkey put in his bid for more of my services. Convinced that he was cruelly overworked in the projection booth, he saw no reason why he shouldn't share the slave. But Clare said nothing doing, turning his request away with a snappish finality that Sharkey never challenged.

At first I had the impression this was a matter of snobbery on Clare's part. As captain of the good ship Classic, she regarded the mechanical side of the enterprise as below decks and Sharkey as the hairy ape who stoked the boilers. Not that Clare couldn't handle the apparatus herself if the need arose. She took charge of the projectors whenever the two of us had a viewing session. Even on those occasions, however, she insisted on keeping me away from the machines. I assumed that, out of some uncustomary sense of kindness, she was sparing me the dirty work I ought to view with principled repugnance. But I was getting things wrong. Clare's seeming disdain for the projectionist's trade was simply a reflection of her rancor against Sharkey. If she was determined to keep me out of his domain, it was only because she felt that Sharkey had unloaded too much work upon her as it was. Her orders were absolute. "I don't want you lifting a finger to help that bum."

One day, without warning, Sharkey failed to report in. I arrived at the theater that evening to find Clare setting up for the scheduled screening, hefting film canisters, testing the projectors, and cursing Sharkey an inspired streak. It was hot, heavy work, but, stripped down to a clammy tanktop (in which she cut quite a sexy figure), she was going about it with complete self-assurance. "May I help?" I asked.

She refused. "If that son of a bitch knows you can run these fucking machines, he'll never show up. Goddamit! It's *his* job." I was assigned to the ticket counter and espresso machine.

Though Clare chewed him out royally when he returned, Sharkey's erratic absences continued, culminating in a week-long disappearance. We later discovered he'd spent the time in a Tijuana jail, charged with drunk and disorderly conduct. Clare had no choice but to hire a replacement; that was costly. The price of a union-scale projectionist could wipe out a week's worth of the theater's earnings. After that, she decided it was time for me to learn the projectors, even though she knew that once Sharkey had trained me, he would feel even more license to goof off. As eagerly as I looked forward to assisting Sharkey, I was troubled by one unresolved issue that lay between us. I had, after all, taken his woman from him . . . or at least that was the self-congratulatory slant I privately placed upon things. A man like Sharkey was bound to be hurting over that. Should I apologize . . . make excuses to save his pride? I needn't have worried. Without being asked, Sharkey put the matter to rest on our first night in the booth.

"Listen, pal, I want to thank you for helping me out with Clare."

Theodore Roszak

He dropped the remark as he pulled on the frayed undershirt that served as his official projectionist's uniform. As far as I can recall, this miserable little rag, sweated yellow front and back, was never sent out to be washed. "I've been hoping somebody would take the old girl off my hands for a while."

"Oh?" I said, shaping the vowel to mean *is that what I'm doing, helping you out?* And "Oh?" again, meaning *for a while?* Sharkey, assiduously polishing the projectors, failed to hear the implied questions.

"Seems like what our Miss Swann needs is something more on the effete side, you know? Lots more sex in the head. You're just the man for the job. See, the woman just never did know how to be an animal. God knows I've tried to warm her up. But it's like trying to move a glacier with your bare hands. Myself, I'm strictly a steak and potatoes man. And you can hold the potatoes, serve the meat raw. Now, Clare . . . like you've probably noticed, she's happy just to read the menu."

I'd noticed nothing of the sort. If anything, I found Clare's sexual appetite voracious, and her erotic imagination nearly overwhelming. But if that was the way Sharkey preferred to see it . . .

I remember distinctly the impression I carried away from that first lesson on the machines. Now that I was to lay hands on them in earnest, I realized what strange instruments they were. The picture out front on the screen that evening was Cocteau's *Beauty and the Beast*, a gossamer-fine fairy tale that came as close as any film ever has to capturing true magic. But here inside the dark, tiny hotbox at the rear of the theater was a brace of wheezing, rasping, thirty-five-millimeter projectors with no more magic to them than a couple of broken coffee grinders. And there was Sharkey, sweating over his task like some frenzied demon toiling in the bowels of hell, muttering away, pleading with these rattletrap monsters to please be on their best behavior. How could the delicately wrought elegance of such a movie emerge from these infernal contraptions? In the sweltering booth the machines, which broke down regularly, snagging and singeing the film, seemed at war with the hapless movie that was forced to run the risky gauntlet of their pitiless gears and wheels. From their menacing look and sound, the projectors might almost be intent on devouring the fragile artistry entrusted to their care.

"I didn't realize how old the machines were," I later observed to Clare.

49

"Old!" she responded gloomily. "They're antediluvian. It makes me shudder to put film through them. Christ! If only we could get far enough ahead around here to buy some decent equipment. I pray for the day."

But she was talking about thousands of dollars, and by then I knew The Classic limped along from week to week on a bank account that never rose above three low figures. For months at a time, it was all Clare could do to cover the rent and the bills. "I don't know which I'm more ashamed of," she confessed, "Sharkey or his machines."

Sharkey, on the other hand, loved his machines, and he loved teaching about them. All the more so since he'd built them with his bare hands from shreds and patches of discarded gear. On its mechanical side as in everything else, The Classic was a seat-of-the-pants operation, making do with secondhand and cast-off equipment, some of it just inches above the level of junk. Even my untutored eye could tell as much. But Sharkey took specific pride in the age of his projectors and the pedigree of their every salvaged part. The big, battered lamp boxes, for example. They bore a boldly scripted logo on their side whose paint had long since worn away; but the raised metal letters could still be made out. "See that," Sharkey announced to his gawking apprentice. "*Peerless.* Best brand there ever was. These honeys have seen duty in all the finest movie houses in L.A. Opened the old Pantages downtown. Chaplin, Valentino, Clara Bow—they all traveled through that box first run. Nobody's improved on Peerless in the last thirty-five years. Look at the weight of that metal. That's industrial-strength steel. Battleship quality."

Clinging precariously to the front of each superannuated lamp box and emitting a slow, steady drip of oil that spattered on newspapers Sharkey had spread beneath was a piece of machinery called the picture head. Sharkey's version was a jerry-built package of recycled gears, shutters, reels, and rollers. This I learned was the projector's principal muscular organ; its function was to marry each frame of the advancing film for a risky split second to the hotly concentrated blaze of projected light that gave the passing pictures their moment of life. Both heads bore the brand name Simplex, and their vintage was also antique. "Early thirties," Sharkey told me. "These date back to the opening of Grauman's Chinese. Best quality of the day. I must've rebuilt these babies down to the last screw. But I've got them tuned to perfection. Sure, they need a lot of help; but there's history in those gears. That makes a difference. You know, like they say with a Stradivarius: the wood remembers. Well, metal has its memories, believe me. I wouldn't trade Simplex here for anybody's so-called top of the line. Tacky—that's what they're building these days. These machines got faith in themselves; they were built with conviction. Back when the U.S.A. was king of the movie mountain. Don't be fooled by appearances. The way Dotty and Lilly handle film is a love affair. They just caress it along its way."

Dotty and Lilly were the pet names Sharkey had given his machines—after the Gish sisters. "But," I observed, "they do seem to chew up the film quite a bit."

"Bah!" Sharkey answered, looking wounded. "That's not their fault. It's the state of the film stock we get sent. Lots of it is scrap condition, ready for the garbage can. Torn sprockets, bad splices . . . the head can't get a grip on material like that. Look here."

He took me to the rewind table, where he was transferring that night's movie from its packing reel. This, as I learned, had to be done with each reel of every movie before it could be shown and then done again before the film could be returned to the distributor. As he went about the chore, Sharkey's trained eye would spot the breaks and burns and tears that might catch in the machine. These he would conscientiously repair—as many as a few dozen in any one film— making expert cuts and splices, so that he usually sent the movie back looking better than when it arrived. He cranked through the reel he was working on that evening, showing me the numerous trouble spots he'd have to patch. "Try running tenth-rate stock like that through a new machine; it'd be eaten alive. Believe me, old Simplex here has got a surgeon's touch."

Working with such old, eccentric equipment presented all sorts of problems for the neophyte projectionist. Everything seemed to require special handling. "What you're learning on these machines," Sharkey told me as if it were a rare honor, "you won't be able to transfer to another projector in the whole world. See, these machines got personality. You have to run them with charm." And so Sharkey did. On the job, he kept a steady flow of affectionate chatter going, as if he were coaxing along a team of aged thoroughbreds who, despite their faltering pace, retained the dignity of better days.

As I came to know Dotty and Lilly better, I developed a reasonable respect for the old girls' mechanical agility. Even more, there was one thing about them that was authentically amazing—at least to my amateur eye, a secret they kept hidden from sight in their inner sanctum. It was their light source. I'd always thought projectors simply used a very bright bulb. That was in fact true of The Classic's sixteen-millimeter machine. It was also a relic of the distant past, used when nothing but sixteen-millimeter prints could be ordered. But the thirty-five-millimeter projectors were another story. It was only when we wheeled them into position, like the big guns of our arsenal, that Sharkey believed we were showing *real* movies; thirty-five-millimeter film needed far more brightness than any bulb could produce in order to drive its image-bearing beams across the length of even a small movie house like The Classic and illuminate the screen with the vividness filmmakers expected for their work. In these machines, the light came from a living flame so savagely bright that the naked eye must never be exposed to it. The carbon arc that burned inside the Peerless lamp box could only be viewed through a tiny panel of welder's glass. "There's an angry jinni in there," Sharkey warned me. "And he's burning like all hellfire. Give him the chance and he'll singe a hole in your eye."

It was the intense heat of the arc light that accounted for the two huge serpentine ducts that rose from the projectors and traveled up through the ceiling toward the nearest window somewhere on the floor above. But the ducts were so turned upon themselves, the fans within them so dust-laden and decrepit, that the venting they achieved was minimal at best. Whenever the thirty-five-millimeter machines were in use, the projection booth became a sweatbox filled with the odor of ozone. Before each reel of film could be shown on these machines, it was the projectionist's job to relight and adjust the thin stick of carbon that produced this small, fierce flame—then to replace each stick as it rapidly consumed itself in the act of sacrificial illumination. "Sticks cost twenty bucks a pop," Sharkey told me. "So we burn 'em down as short as we can get away with. It's a major expense for us."

The carbon arc, so deeply sequestered in its protective shelter, teased my imagination. It was like some sacred presence ensconced in its tabernacle, the innermost mystery of the darkened temple, never to be looked upon by mortal eyes. Unfortunately, The Classic's antiquated equipment couldn't offer that enchanted presence the respect it deserved. Instead, the carbon fire in one of the projectors (it was Dotty) had become the prisoner of a ludicrous Rube Goldberg hookup. Because of the low ceiling and descending slope of the basement that was The Classic's auditorium, the projectors had to be mounted high and then tilted sharply forward at the rear of the room. This tilt was too steep for the waning strength of the spring that was designed to steadily advance Dotty's carbon rod as it burned down. And if the rod didn't advance as it burned, it would cool, grow dimmer, flicker, and finally go out—a common problem at The Classic. For such an ancient machine, Sharkey had never been able to find a spring with the right tension. So with a sort of spaced-out inspiration, he'd rigged up an ingenious little device that combined a lever, a pulley, a rocker arm, and a counterweight that would (supposedly) tug the carbon rod forward at just the right pace. But Sharkey had never been able to get the counterweight, which was simply a hook carrying miscellaneous nuts and washers, quite right. That forced him to spend a good deal of each screening adding weighted objects to the hook (or removing them), hoping someday to hit upon exactly the proper combination.

I recall that when Clare took over in the booth, it was this crazy task that most frazzled her; she had to resort to constant manual adjustments. Sharkey, on the other hand, found the problem an endless amusement. He'd even invented a playful little superstition about it. "Someday, when I find just the right weight, that's gonna be my lucky charm. And it's gonna give me three wishes."

"And what will they be?" I asked.

"Well, the *first* one will be to get out of this cellblock of a basement."

Which raised a question. "Why *are* we in the basement, Sharkey?" I asked. There was, after all, an abandoned auditorium of generous dimensions just one floor above our heads. And here we were down below, struggling to make do with a diminutive theater and a booth the size of a storeroom, which indeed is what it had originally been.

"That wasn't the plan," Sharkey explained. "At least it wasn't the plan to *stay* in the basement. Plan was to start here, make a small fortune, take over the whole building, rebuild upstairs, become a glorious artistic-commercial success grounded in the sophisticated good taste of the great American public. Boy, talk about having one's head up one's ass, I don't know where we got that little fantasy from. Maybe we were blowing too much grass. Have you seen upstairs?"

I'd managed to get a glimpse or two while I worked with Clare in her tiny office, which was as much of the upper stories as she had access to. Mostly the place was locked off or boarded up; what could be seen was dimly lit at best and shrouded in cobwebs. A nice interior for a spooky movie.

"It was once a true cinematic emporium," Sharkey went on. "Dates back to 1929. Guess what it was called? The Cinema Ritz. A true beauty of the period, all gilt and curlicues. But, it should have been named the Titanic."

"Why?"

"It was meant to be one of the first all-sound houses. Best equipment money could buy. The night it opened, the maiden voyage—disaster."

"What happened?"

Sharkey laid his hand on a stack of film canisters in one corner of the booth. It was the movie we would be screening that night: *Nothing Sacred*, part of a William Wellman festival. "*That's* what happened. Ka-plooey!"

I didn't understand.

"Nitrate film. All the old movies are on nitrate. Like this one we're showing. Nitrate is a killer. You didn't know that?"

At the time, I didn't.

"Well then, let me tell you the projectionist's basic facts of life—and death. There's nitrate and there's safety film. Everything up to postwar is nitrate. And, oh! that nitrate is a son of a bitch. That's what we got here tonight in these cans. And it might as well be high-octane gasoline. If it even gets near an open flame, bam!"

"But there's an open flame in the projector."

"Right. But properly shielded and surrounded by safeguards—so we hope. That's why I wouldn't trust anything but the old Peerless. It was built for the danger. You didn't know you were taking your life in your hands every time you screened one of the old film classics, eh? Well, you are. That's why I'm always so nerved up when we're showing them. Probably you noticed."

I hadn't. If anything, Sharkey always seemed blissfully laid back and unflappable in the booth. I told him so.

"That's because I burn some weed ahead of time. Just the right amount to keep me steady. If you feel the need, let me know."

Suddenly I felt more menaced in the booth than ever before.

"Anyway," Sharkey continued, "that's why we're working in this concrete bunker down here. You see all the asbestos on the ceiling, and the steel door? The fire chief is very particular about people like us. He lays down lots of rules. We just barely meet them. Actually, not quite. The ventilation's lousy, as you've doubtless noticed. But that only affects the health of the projectionist, so what the hell, says Miss Swann, the management."

"How bad was the damage upstairs, back in twenty-nine?"

"Gutted the whole projection booth and most of the balcony. Killed three people including the projectionist. So the whole upper rear of the place was boarded over. Ceiling too. It's supposed to be an Art Deco marvel: murals, lights, bas-relief. It got smoke-damaged from end to end. Nobody ever did the repairs. The old Ritz was just too elegant for anyone to restore. Place was dirt cheap to get. That's how come the old lady and me (don't tell Clare I called her that, okay?) could afford the rent. Idea was: we start in this little dungeon down here, save up, then buy the whole place and renovate. Well, it's five thousand plus bucks' worth of fixing just to rebuild the booth to code. Balcony's another five, six grand. Ceiling's another three, four, five. Floor needs redoing. Cleaning and patching and painting. You get the picture. A major capital investment. As it is, we can hardly keep this sinkhole going with hungry peons on the job—meaning you and me."

And slave labor it was, of the most relentless kind. I'd always imagined that projectionists had a soft touch. They simply pushed a button, then spent the rest of the evening enjoying the movie or reading a book, maybe stepping out for coffee and conversation. I couldn't have been more wrong. There was always something needing to be done—reels to be changed, the carbon to be lit, the lens to be adjusted, film to be rewound, a part to be oiled—and it all had to be done to the imperious rhythm of the projectors, in the fifteen- to-twenty-minute interval allowed by the reel being shown. For the month or more I spent with Sharkey learning the trade, we found little time for idle conversation, except for the hour or so before the program started or after it ended. Then, while we packed or unpacked film, set up or finished off for the evening, we had the chance to kibitz. Not that I expected to have much to talk about with Sharkey. Clare had convinced me that he was a cross between a boob and a boor. Certainly whenever he showed up drunk or strung out, which was most of the time, he could be an insufferable dolt. But having promised Clare he would train me, he went about it as an act of conscience, remaining clearheaded and diligent, perhaps out of some stubborn pride in his craft. He turned out to be a first-rate mentor.

More surprising, I discovered that he could be, after his own madcap fashion, an entertaining raconteur. I actually began to look forward to my sessions with him, perhaps because they provided a sort of comic relief from Clare's relentless intellectuality. In the course of our brief working relationship, Sharkey ushered me into the wackiest film talk I could have imagined, beginning with an infinitely convoluted exposition of *The Shanghai Gesture*, which he regarded as "metaphysical pornography on the highest level." From there he launched into an endless encomium on the films of Maria Montez and Judy Canova. The thesis of this labyrinthine disquisition seemed to be that they were the best actresses there ever were because they were so very, very bad. Or that, at least, is as much sense as I could make of it. Much of this I assigned to the state of chemical relaxation Sharkey brought with him to the job. Sheer stoned silliness.

But there was another set of rambling exchanges of a different character. Baffling as it was at the time, I would in later years have reason to recall what Sharkey once told me in all the detail I could muster. It would be his unwitting contribution to my study of Max Castle.

It began like this.

One evening while he was escorting me through the basic anatomy of the projector, Sharkey dropped a remark about "fusion frequency." "You know what that is, don't you?" he asked.

Of course I did, as any film student would. It was the speed at which the still images on the frames of a running film "fused" in the eye, giving the appearance of motion. Twenty-four frames per second.

"Damn, but that's a remarkable thing!" Sharkey went on, "when you stop to think about it. Ever think about it? It's remarkable. Because none of the pictures on this film is really moving, right? The old Simplex here's playing tricks on the eye. Clickety-click. Openshut. Off-on. Now you see it, now you don't. And every time you see it, your eye tells your brain it's moving. But it ain't. In here, inside the eyeball, there's this weird little gimmick—persistence of vision, right? And out there somewhere in the universe is this fusion frequency, just waiting for some machine to come along that can run pictures at the right speed. And one day the two of them get together, and you got"—Sharkey did a nasally *ta*-ta-ta-*ta* version of the 20th Century–Fox fanfare—"you got the *movies!*" Then, giving me a soulfully quizzical look: "Why should it be like that? The world didn't have to be like that. Every time I think about it, it just spooks me. I mean, who writes the script for things like that?" And then with a sudden, sobering change of tone that caught me off guard: "Work of the devil. Ever hear that one?"

I grinned back, assuming he was making some typically bizarre joke.

"Seriously," he insisted. "It's a lie, see? A hoax. *Contra naturam.* That's what the authorities used to call it. *Un*-natural."

"*What* authorities?"

He gave me a sly wink. It was one of his characteristic gestures when he was seeking to appear deeply significant. A wink and a low, dry whistle. "Well, I don't mean the Hays Office, buddy-boy. Goes a lot deeper than that. We came *that* close—a hairbreadth—to seeing moving pictures banned right out of existence."

"When was this?"

Sharkey shrugged. "Can't say for certain. It was all done under wraps. We never hear about these things on the outside, you know. Somewhere back in the nineteenth century. Time of Napoleon. There were all these heavy discussions inside the Vatican. Went on for years."

"The Vatican!"

"Sure. There was a whole brigade of holy fathers wanted to kill moving pictures stone-cold dead—as an offense against the faith."

Now I was convinced he was putting me on, which he often did. "Sure, sure. Movies in the time of Napoleon."

"I didn't say 'movies.' I said 'moving pictures.' You know about the Zoetrope."

I did. The Zoetrope was part of basic film history, mentioned in all the textbooks. It was a little carousel-like device with a series of drawings inside the drum, usually of a running or jumping figure in different positions. Spun at the right speed, it would blend the drawings together at their fusion frequency and make them seem to move. It had been a popular novelty in the last century.

"Zoetrope goes back to the infidel peoples," Sharkey went on. "The ancient wheel of life. There was this zonked-out Arab—Al-Hazen . . . something or other. H. P. Lovecraft has the lowdown on him. He worked out all the principles way back, just before the crusades, I think. And he wasn't the first. He was just picking it up from the heretics."

"What heretics?"

"Zoetrope worshipers. The first movie fans. They were all over the biblical lands there."

"Where did you say all this took place?"

"The biblical lands. You know . . . Arabia like. India. Katmandu."

"That's not 'biblical,' " I protested.

"Not now, no. But then it was. All the way out. East. Way east. Far as a camel could walk. Bible used to cover more ground then."

"*When?*"

"Thousand, two thousand years ago. The whole thing goes way back. Egypt maybe."

Sharkey could see I wasn't taking him seriously. But that didn't stop him. He rambled on, keeping things playful as if for the benefit of my untutored understanding. "Oh sure, the Zoetrope's just a harmless toy, right? But it's based on an illusion. Same illusion this projector's built around. That's what makes this a magic lantern. But what kind of magic? Maybe *black* magic." He gave me the wink and the whistle, then waited to see how things were registering.

"Where did you pick all this up, Sharkey?" I asked, letting my incredulity show, but politely.

"Met this priest in Paris back in the forties. He knew the whole story. See, originally—meaning all the way back, Dark Ages, like that—the church was totally down on moving pictures. Said the Zoetrope, anything like it, was an infernal engine. You got caught eyeballing one, they might burn you at the stake. No kidding. But there was this faction in the Vatican—the good guys, our team, so to speak— finally got the holy fathers turned around. The pope and all the rest, they decided that persistence of vision was an innocent amusement and an okay thing. Because, after all, God made the eye that way, didn't he? That's the ten-cent version of what they came up with. I mean: they were talking heavy-duty theology, you understand. When the authorities hold a powwow like that, it sends out vibrations in all directions, way beyond the pope's private parlor. Well, like I said, it finally came out the right way. Lucky for us. You know what would have happened if old Mother Church had clamped down on the Zoetrope? Very likely no Charlie Chaplin, no Donald Duck, no Rhett and Scarlett. You think I'm kidding? I'm not kidding. There are powers you don't go up against. If you do, you get creamed."

"Who was this priest?" I asked.

"Funny old bird. Name was Rosenzweig. A Jesuit. Actually, he wasn't a Jesuit anymore when we met him, Clare and me. He got unfrocked for making too many waves on the inside of the inside of things. See, he wouldn't give up. He was still fighting to get the decision reversed—but it was nothing doing. He was out on his ear. Used to mouth off for hours on the evils of the movies. Not what was *in* the movies, you understand. Sex, violence, profanity—he didn't care bat's crap about that. Just *movies*. The illusion, that's what had him pissed off. *Black magic,* was what he called it. He used to hang around the Cinémathèque trying to make converts. For him, that was Satanic headquarters. You can imagine how much luck he had there. He got to be quite a local character, coming around with his little pamphlets, speechifying at the drop of a hat. Boy, could he work himself into a lather. Foamed at the mouth. After a while, they decided to lock him out. He was getting to be a real nuisance. That's when he took a potshot at Henri Langlois."

"He tried to shoot Henri Langlois?"

"Yep. Quite a sensation. An act of cultural assassination. Missed by a hair. He was convinced Langlois was trafficking with the dark powers."

Henri Langlois was the head, heart, and soul of the Paris Ciné-mathèque, its founder, father-figure, and mad genius. But for him, there might never have been a French film community. He was one of Clare's great heroes.

"Were you there when this happened?" I asked.

"Nope. That was a year or so after we left for the States. Clare nearly had heart failure when she heard about it. She once got into a shouting match with Rosenzweig. One of those big, dumb arguments that used to break out at the Cinémathèque. Who knows? He might have tried to gun her down too. He got nearly mad enough to attack her, I recall."

"She never mentioned that."

"She won't talk about it."

"Sounds wild. I had no idea . . ."

"Basically," Sharkey continued, "Rosenzweig was a nut. That's obvious. But he was the kind of nut that makes you think. Because it's a damn good story, you know. Makes a lot of sense."

"What does?"

"Cinema theology. The good and the evil. Reality and illusion."

"You take all this seriously?"

"Damn right. It's just a matter of getting into—*really* getting into the magic of it. I mean: we're mucking around with the fundamental ontology of things here." Another wink and a whistle, this time more haughty, as if to add: *You didn't think I knew words like that, did you?* "What's real? What's not? The old magic lantern here"—he slapped the projector affectionately—"is basically one hell of a mind-fucker. You think the authorities don't care about that? Believe me, they care."

I left that night inclined to dismiss everything Sharkey had said as one of his patented exercises in surrealistic humor. I'd often heard him holding forth at parties, rambling on about flying saucers, miracle cures, the secrets of the pyramids. Only this evening, he hadn't been burning any grass; and his manner hadn't been all that comic. In fact, Sharkey had been about as serious as he ever got.

Another evening, another wild conversation.

This one started off almost rationally. Sharkey let fall a name I didn't recognize, so I asked, "Who?"

"Louis Aimé Auguste LePrince. You never heard of him? Look him up in the *Guinness Book of Records*. First man to show movies. You did hear of Edison, I imagine. Thomas Alva Edison?"

I assured him I knew who Edison was.

"Well, Americans like to think Edison invented the movies, right? That's just patriotic bullshit. What Tom Edison invented was the Kinetoscope, which was a souped-up peep show, that's all. Big deal. If anybody invented real movies—I mean *projected moving pictures*—it was LePrince. He got the whole works together. Camera, projector, lenses, celluloid film stock."

"When was this?"

"Eighteen-eighties."

"That early?"

"Yep. Not only that, but he was a zealot. Traveled the world pushing movies. London, New York, Chicago. He really wanted to see this technology take off. That's what did him in."

"How do you mean?"

"Dropped off the face of the earth. That's why the textbooks say so little about him. Listen, he was a real genius. He invented per-forated film, not Edison. Edison stole the idea from LePrince, not that he knew what to do with it except to stick it in his peep show. Also"—Sharkey's voice dropped into a confidential whisper—"here's the clincher. Louis Aimé was the first to use the Maltese cross gear. But that's a whole 'nother story."

I decided to let that other story wait and stick to LePrince. "You say he vanished?"

"In a puff. Without a trace. One of the great mysteries—1890. He went to visit his brother in the south of France. Mind you, he'd just done a big number at the Paris Opera. Projected movies. On a screen. The real thing. Great triumph. All the honchos in the French theater were there. Well, on his way back from seeing his brother, he disappeared off the train. Never heard from again."

I could tell there was more to the story. I waited for Sharkey to add the punch line.

"The ODs got him."

"The *who?*"

"Remember Papa Rosenzweig I told you about? He was one of them. Oculus Dei. The Eye of God. Did I get the Latin right? I think so. You dig the name? Eye of God—it sees things *right,* not like in the movies. If they were all like Rosenzweig—these ODs—they were the worst enemies us film folk ever had. Worse than the Legion of Decency, House Un-American Activities Committee, all that. Because they were out to kill the art, zap!"

"Well, who were they?"

One of his sly winks. *"Were?* What gives you the idea they're not still around? Just ask Miss Swann some time. They haven't given up on her."

"She's still in touch with them?"

"They're in touch with *her.* Or they'd sure like to be. Couple times since we left Paris they've dropped by for a chat, not that Clare'd give 'em the time of day. Allies is what they're after. Respectable-type brainy people like Our Lady of The Classic."

"Well, who *are* they?"

"Search me, kid. Only OD I ever met was Rosenzweig. And he wasn't saying. All I know is they were out to sabotage the movies from the word go."

"And you think they . . . what? *Murdered* LePrince?"

"Could be." Then, with a laugh, he added, "Or maybe Father Rosenzweig was just shitting us. Maybe he was the only OD there was."

"But there *was* a LePrince. And he did vanish."

"Oh yeah. But maybe he was just running out on his wife. Who knows?"

There was one more conversation I recall, the weirdest of all. It started while Sharkey was showing me how to clean the film gate of the projector. It occurred to me to ask him about the mechanism that caught the film by its sprocket holes and shoved it forward frame by frame. It's called the Maltese cross gear.

"You said LePrince invented that," I remarked.

"No, no. He was the first one to take it out in public—as part of his projector. You know why it's called a Maltese cross gear, don't you? Because that's the shape of a Maltese cross. And that's no accident."

"What's no accident?"

"That the most important part of the machine is shaped like a Maltese cross. You know about Malta, don't you?"

Of course I didn't know about Malta. I had no idea what he was talking about. So, as usual, I let him ramble on casually while he swabbed away at the innards of the projector.

"That's where the Hospitalers set up shop. Ran the island for two or three centuries. You've heard of the Hospitalers?"

Again, I hadn't.

"Medieval knights. Crusaders. All like that." Then, as if it were the main point: "They're the ones who got the Templars' loot. Plus all the secrets."

I stared back at him blankly.

"You know what happened to the Templars? Knights Templar? Shafted but good. By the pope himself. For heresy. Wiped out. Totally. Torture, disemboweling, burning at the stake . . . somebody ought to make a movie. By the time the old pope got finished, you couldn't find one hangnail of a Templar left. Except for those who hid out with the Hospitalers. Let's see—they went to Cyprus, then to Rhodes . . . or Sicily, was it? Finally to Malta. That's where they came up with the Maltese cross. The story is: the pope wiped out the Templars, but not the secret teachings. The Hospitalers got those. They held out on Malta until Napoleon put them out of business." With another wink: "And where did the teachings go after that, eh? Nobody knows."

I asked the obvious question. "What's all this got to do with the projector?"

Sharkey gave me the royally elevated eyebrow of surprise. "Well, where do you think this machine comes from? The whole thing depends on that gear. And who invented the gear? See, you got to get the cause and effect right, or it all comes out ass-backward. The cross didn't come first. The *gear* came first. The cross was based on the gear. Like a kind of emblem among the *cognoscenti*, get it?"

I was close to exasperation. I expected my banter with Sharkey to be amusing. This wasn't amusing, just mindless. "Sharkey, what the hell are you talking about? The movies are a modern thing . . . since Edison. Okay, let's say since LePrince. That's 1880, 1890."

"So the books say."

"You think the books are wrong?"

"Wouldn't be the first time. Look what they say about Houdini's dog."

I let that item pass. "So you think the motion picture projector was invented by . . . medieval knights . . . on Malta?"

"Why not?"

"Oh, come on! It's an electrical machine. It needs electricity. It needs a carbon arc."

Sharkey shrugged. "Not if you're running off ESP. I'm telling you, Jonny, these Templars and Hospitalers—they were like Rosicrucians. They were in touch with powers. Man, wouldn't you love to see some of them medieval movies! Tra-da-da-da-de-da! *The Return of Genghis Khan.*"

"Is this more of Father Rosenzweig's stuff?"

"Some of it, some of it. I looked a lot up myself. I got a great book on the Templars you can borrow. Heavy-duty scholarship. Story is they were in league with the devil. At least that's how the authorities want us to remember it. Black mass, virgin's blood, all that jazz."

"And you're telling me they invented the movies."

"Well, let's just say something like. Say a combination magic lantern and Zoetrope. Ran it off psychic energy, who knows? Maybe the old Templars were making movies out of pure astral projections."

"Sharkey, do you really believe any of this?"

"I keep an open mind," he answered.

"What about Clare? Have you ever talked about these things with her?"

"Hell, she knows about it. She met Rosenzweig. They argued the whole business every which way. But beyond a certain point of weirdness, Clare puts on the blinders. She's a bright lady, but she has her limits. She calls them her 'standards.' "

"And you don't believe in standards."

"Standards are for sluggers. Clare's a slugger. She likes a good fight; it's meat and drink to her. Me—I just lay back and enjoy. Don't get me wrong. As far as I'm concerned, Clare's the greatest. Only difference between us is, I think there's more to movies than meets the eye." Then with a wink and whistle, "Like with the vampire guy, right?"

"What vampire guy?"

"Old Slapsy-Maxy von Castle. *Feast of the Undead.*"

"Oh, that. What about it?"

"You think Maxy didn't know a thing or two about it?"

"About what?"

"Medieval movies. That was a medieval movie if I ever saw one. Any guy who can latensify a film like that has got to be in touch with powers. You wouldn't think black could get that black."

"You saw the picture?"

"Sure. First thing it came in. There were some plenty hot shots in that flick. How about that bedroom scene? Wow, wow!"

"Yeah, Clare told me."

"She didn't run it for you?"

"Not really. I just got in on the last part. Can't really say I saw it."

"Movies like that, you don't have to see more than a part. Like an ocular bouillon cube, you know? Pow! Comes through full strength."

"Funny thing about that film. Clare destroyed it."

Sharkey took the report in stride. "Not surprised. Must've scared her shitless."

"Come on. It wasn't that scary. There was hardly any blood."

"I'm talking about aesthetic principles. Which for Clare is more important than blood. You saw that impaling scene at the end? What's all her in-tel-lek-chul chit-chat up against a brain-bender like that?" Then, noticing my interest, Sharkey issued a warning. "Take my advice, don't mention any of this to Clare. She'll throw you out of bed. I speak from experience."

But I did mention it to Clare; I couldn't keep from doing it. Seeking to broach the subject as obliquely as possible, I decided LePrince might be the safest place to begin. But the man's name was hardly out of my mouth than she did in fact give me a look that made me fear she very well might drive me from the bed.

"You mean the guy who fell out of the train and was never heard from again?"

"Well, I gather nobody knows if he fell out of . . ."

"Of course he didn't. The Jesuits got him, right? Or was it the

Spanish Inquisition? Or the Rosicrucians? How did Sharkey tell the story this time?"

"You mean he made it up?"

"What do you think?"

"But there was a LePrince. I looked him up."

"Sure there was. And he disappeared. So what? That doesn't mean the flying saucers got him. My uncle Osbert disappeared. Ran off with the butcher's wife."

"But you did meet this priest, didn't you—Rosenzweig?"

"In the first place, he wasn't a priest. He *said* he was a priest. He was a crackpot is what he was. And in the second place, why don't you just shut up before I get sick?"

"Sharkey says Rosenzweig belonged to some sect that's been tailing you ever since you left Paris."

"Oh, sure! That's because I've got the secret of the thirty-nine steps."

"Well, are they?"

"Once or twice somebody came around. . . ."

"Aren't you worried about it?"

"If I had to worry about every nut case that wanders into The Classic . . ."

"Didn't this guy Rosenzweig try to kill Henri Langlois?"

"Yes, well . . . let's say I like to live dangerously."

"Sharkey says you had a couple big arguments with him. So I just wondered . . ."

"Argument! I don't waste my time arguing with crazies. My job was to bounce him out of the Cinémathèque when he came around. The man used to throw things at the screen. And he stank to high heaven."

"So you don't think there's anything to what Sharkey says . . . not at all?"

"Ha! Did he tell you about the Maltese cross?"

"Yeah."

"You know what that is? That's his seduction line. He uses it to pick up girls. Like the old one about the submarine races. 'Come up to the projection booth, let me show you the Maltese cross gear . . . well, well, isn't it hot in here? Why don't you take a few things off.' It usually works with bashful virgins, if they're nuts about movies." Clare gave me a suspicious squint. "I don't know what he's up to with you, but if he asks you to start taking showers with him after the show, watch out."

"Sharkey says that vampire film you had here, *Feast of the Undead*, was sort of what Rosenzweig was concerned about."

"Oh, is that what Sharkey says? Well, we do have to pay close attention to what Sharkey says, don't we?" Her voice was beginning to smolder.

"Well, I just wondered . . ."

"Three more words and you will be doing your wondering on the couch in the living room for the next few weeks." With that she turned away, curled up armadillo fashion, and pulled the covers over her ears.

I never brought up any of Sharkey's conversations again, but I did borrow the "heavy duty" piece of scholarship he'd mentioned. It turned out to be a fat pulp paperback with a gaudy cover showing scowling medieval knights whipping and branding seminude victims. The letters of the title, *Terror of the Templars*, were shaped from daggers of dripping gore. "Now At Last It Can Be Told," the cover copy announced. "The Unexpurgated True Blood-Chilling Story." Well, what else did I expect *ex libris* Don Sharkey? The closest the book came to having an author was a microscopic acknowledgment on the back of the title page: "Abridged and adapted from the original work by J. Delaville Le Roulx." For all the sensationalism of the edition, the text that bled through the translation retained a reasonably factual, at times stuffy, quality. Reading on and off over the next few months, I managed to stick with it all the way through. And damned if it wasn't a good story.

Theodore Roszak

4 VENETIAN MAGENTA

The voice on the phone was so breathy-confidential that Clare thought it might be an obscene call.

"Who the hell is this?" she demanded suspiciously. "Marcel? Marcel *who?*"

"Marcel, Chipsey Goldenstone's private secretary."

"Oh," Clare answered with more disgust in her tone than if it had been a masher on the line.

"Chipsey would like you to be apprised as to the fact that he is having a few *intime* friends around this Saturday one P.M. He will be making a large selection of filmland memorabilia available for acquisition from his late father's extensive private collection. We do hope you can join us on the occasion."

"By available for acquisition, I suppose you mean for sale," Clare said. "No freebies from Chipsey."

"Yes, you might put it that way."

"So Chipsey is cashing in on his old man's loot. Let's see—how long has Father Goldstein been moldering in the ground? All of a week, isn't it?"

"Mr. Ira Goldstein has been deceased for nearly a month."

"That long? Look, Marcel, I'm afraid I'm not in the market for filmland memorabilia. Unless, of course, that includes *films.*"

"Oh, it does. A large selection of such."

In a split second, Clare's expression shifted from indifferent to eager. "Are you serious?" she asked.

"Perfectly. As you may know, Mr. Goldstein *père* was an avid film collector."

"I know, I know!"

"Now, this is strictly confidential. A sizable proportion of Mr. Goldstein's films will be offered for purchase on Saturday to Chipsey's most *intime* friends."

"Does that include me?"

"I expect that it does. You *are* on the list."

67

"I'll be there," Clare promised. Then, beaming with excitement, she turned to me across the room. "The Goldstein Collection," she announced. "It's up for sale."

When Ira Goldstein's obituary appeared in the papers, Clare had given it about as much attention as the weather report. Movie moguls like the elder Goldstein were part of a world she despised. But when Chipsey's secretary mentioned movies for sale, she sat up and took notice. Old Ira was rumored to have one of the world's great private film libraries stashed away in the family vault. Clare kept close track of such holdings; she claimed to know every major collection in the country and many abroad. If she caught word of sales or auctions in the area, she was sure to attend and mingle. Even if she couldn't afford to buy—and she never could—it was useful to know who owned what, just in case they might be willing to rent. Her special interest in Ira Goldstein's films wasn't hard to understand. Notoriously, he never rented, he never screened. He held his films for purely speculative purposes and discussed them only with other, always well-heeled, collectors. This made his holdings a complete mystery, only now to be revealed. Clare would have had to be hospitalized to miss a chance at sizing up the Goldstein Collection.

I never expected to see anything connected with Chipsey Goldenstone have such an uplifting effect on Clare, least of all an arrangement that required her to identify herself as one of his *intime* friends. Chipsey was among the more exotic fauna of the local art film community. In conversations between Clare and Sharkey, his name had wafted past me several times before I asked who he was.

"An experimental filmmaker," Sharkey answered. "One of the best."

"An art-buggering asshole," Clare countered. "One of the worst." She elaborated on that description. "The best single contribution I could make to the art of the film would be to kill him the next time I see him."

Now, no one so described by Clare should have played any part in bringing Max Castle and me together. Yet, but for Chipsey Goldenstone's invitation to a movie auction that day, I might never have had the occasion to write these memoirs. A few months earlier, I'd seen ten struggling minutes of a Castle film so close to disintegrating on the reel that it had been an eyesore to watch. Whatever Clare might have spotted in *Feast of the Undead* through that jungle of careless splices and sprocket-tremors, I hadn't witnessed much more than an antiquated creep show. I would have come away from that brief sampling satisfied to dismiss the film as crap, trash, junk. Thanks to Chipsey, I was soon to experience my first dose of quality Castle.

Despised and rejected as he was by Clare, Chipsey could only have entered her life by the back door, that is, by way of Sharkey's fantasy world of petty vice and decadent taste. As I understood it, Sharkey had no sooner returned home from Paris than he fell in with the cast of transient hundreds that made up Chipsey's artistic-erotic entourage. "You can trust Sharkey to smell depravity a mile off," Clare told me. "And he'll run all the way to dive in."

For the most part, Chipsey's personal empire of sycophants and hangers-on seemed to be nothing more than a movable orgy that was in constant crepuscular migration between various seedy beach towns south of Santa Monica and many a classy canyon hideaway behind the Palisades. On occasion, this round of nonstop carousing paused long enough to produce outbursts of art, most of it financed by Chipsey and all of it (or at least as much as I had seen) excruciatingly inane. There were gallery openings for art so advanced it couldn't be distinguished from the plumbing fixtures; there were daring little magazines that never got beyond earthshaking issue number one; there were pretentious theater pieces that might be mistaken for bad burlesque; above all there were Chipsey's own movies. Years before I met Clare, Chipsey and Sharkey had dreamed up the idea of staging a festival of West Coast underground films, featuring Chipsey's work. Clare wasn't taken by the idea. She warned they'd never find enough quality to fill an intermission break.

"We have Chipsey's stuff," Sharkey reminded her.

"That's what I mean."

But Sharkey insisted and got his way, promising it would be a one-shot venture. The result was as dismal a collection of amateur efforts as Clare had feared. The festival would surely have been an exercise in financial masochism if it hadn't been lavishly underwritten by Chipsey and supplemented at the box office by the throng of parasitic admirers that followed him through life looking for favors or fixes or a high old time. Chipsey's cash and his pull transformed the potential disaster into an annual event that became The Classic's principal money-maker.

Grousing and grumbling, Clare accepted the money, but with it The Classic gained a certain dubious celebrity that made the profits especially galling. This had nothing to do with art, even bad art; it resulted from the high jinx and general hell-raising that accompanied the screenings. Chipsey's soirees, staged at a rambling, rustic-chic Topanga Canyon retreat, were infamous local happenings. They took the form of one seamless drunken brawl from the beginning to the end of the festival. Anybody might turn up and anything might happen. The press quickly elevated the event to a yearly staple of the social calendar. Reporters turned out in force to sample the booze, use the pool, enjoy the grass, wolf down the refreshments, and incidentally file stories filled with sexy gossip. They could be relied upon to season the papers with rumors of alcoholic debauchery that were invariably more exciting than any of the films that were shown. To Clare's chagrin, The Classic had become associated in the public mind with stories that sported headlines like "Film Folk Throw Big Binge," "Avant Garde Bares All at Film Fest."

But Clare's problems with the festival went deeper than that. Every time the event rolled around, it forced her to rethink her long, troubled history with the underground film movement. All she found there were jagged memories and painful ambivalence. During the early postwar years, when the New American Cinema (as it grandly called itself) was in its talking stage, Clare had eagerly allied herself with its theorists and impresarios. She made several trips to New York (at her own expense) to take part in conferences and panels that met to issue savage indictments of formula films, the studio system, censorship, blacklisting. Finally, there was a long, hard summer's unpaid labor helping Jonas Mekas launch *Film Culture*, the underground's chief journal. As long as there was the barest hope that Mekas' Film-Makers Cooperative might one day mature into something like the French New Wave, Clare clung to the cause tenaciously, contributing more time and money than she could afford.

In opposition, the enemies of the Hollywood establishment talked a good revolution. But once their films began to reach the screen, Clare lost heart. "Delusions of grandeur," she fumed. "A ton of pretentious self-congratulations for every minute of film, and not one of those minutes better than W. C. Fields on an off-day." It was the erotic clichés that troubled Clare the most, the endless repetition of peeping Tom naughtiness. When she reached her limit, she fired off a wickedly critical article to *Film Culture* calling avant-garde cinema "a wasteland of voyeurist fantasies." To Clare's angered amazement, the journal refused to print it. The result was a minor furor among the experimentalists that quickly lapped over into other journals. In the course of the give-and-take, some of Clare's more intemperate rejoinders were construed to imply an antihomosexual bias. That reading wasn't wholly inaccurate. Clare did harbor a decided hostility toward gays in the experimental film world. She never told me why; I suspect it had to do with a traumatic love affair somewhere in her past, a man she'd lost to another man. She tried to be discreet about her feelings. That was hard enough for Clare in the best of circumstances; under pressure, she barred no holds. The implicit soon became explicit.

"If we're going to wash our dirty linen in public," Clare charged, in a lacerating letter that was run in *The Moviegoer*, "let's be honest about the source of the stains. Wet dreams that are trying to pass themselves off as high art."

It didn't take long for this contretemps to catch the amused attention of mainstream observers. Much to Clare's surprise, *The New York Times* offered to buy her rejected article for its Sunday magazine. Wounded and furious, she snatched at the opportunity. It became her first piece to reach a major publication. She saw this as a breakthrough; her opponents regarded it as an act of treason.

Each year Sharkey's festival recalled the hurt feelings and bitter recriminations of that episode. Worse, it entangled the unsavory memories with someone who was quite simply the quintessence of everything Clare detested in the underground film community: Chipsey Goldenstone.

To her credit, Clare never tried to conceal her loathing for Chipsey, or even to soft-pedal it. Deception wasn't one of her talents, nor was tact among her virtues. The only reason Clare showed up at any of Chipsey's parties was to get drunk enough to revile him openly. For some reason I never grasped (could it have been sheer obtuseness on the man's part?) Chipsey simply refused to be insulted by Clare. Instead, he remained determined to claim her friendship. I was present at a screening when she was asked, in Chipsey's presence, what she thought of his movie. She answered, "Maybe you've heard: there's a species of pernicious slime that attaches itself to motion-picture film stock. Nobody knows how to kill it or even slow it down once it gets started. It creeps in along with the fringes of the reel and makes everything it touches sticky, off-color, and totally vile. When it gets done devouring a movie, there's nothing left in the can but a puddle of noxious syrup where you can't tell D. W. Griffith from Daffy Duck. *That's* what we just saw. It wasn't a film, it was fungus."

To which Chipsey replied in great good humor, "Ah, but that's just it, Clarissa. You see how you're forced to resort to organic images to critique my work. The germinal, the fertile, the seminal . . . that's exactly what I'm after. The fungi, for example, have always struck me as a life-affirming force. So alive, so irrepressible . . ."

Whatever Clare's opinion of Chipsey's films might be, she'd resigned herself to the fact that the festival's main purpose was to showcase his work. Which was, even in my amateur judgment, nauseatingly awful. The few examples I'd seen were hours-long vistas of naked bodies tangled into various acrobatic perversions. Sometimes anemic jazz played in the distant background; sometimes French poetry was read poorly and inaudibly. Invariably there was a sequence featuring some portion of the director's anatomy, his navel, an armpit, a crotch-shot of Chipsey's minimally garbed organ in a sequined and feathered snood. Or perhaps a pore-probing close-up of his face registering boundless ecstasy. As far as I could see, Chipsey's movies were nothing better than skin flicks. Rumor did have it that they were in lucrative demand on the fraternity-house and men's-club circuit.

Even so, Chipsey's accustomed style of consumption soared well beyond anything he could earn from mere pornography. His more visible means of support came from his father, one of the original Hollywood moguls of the Golden Age. At one time or another, Ira Goldstein had bankrolled all the great studio nabobs: Goldwyn, the Warners, Selznick, Cohn. Unlike them, however, Ira never pretended to be a producer, never cared to have his name on a film. He was content to be a backer pure, simple, and silent. In that strictly mercenary capacity, he accumulated a mint. He'd also acquired a reputation. Close friends—of which there weren't many—referred to him as Ira the Terrible. By others throughout the industry he was known as The Gonif, as in the phrase, "That gonif! He wants a bigger cut yet."

As savage as he might be in money matters, Ira was also credited with an uncanny instinct about movies. Some of his words of wisdom had become legendary. When Columbia came around looking for cash to finance a minor comedy called *Night Bus*, Ira wouldn't come across until the title was changed. "Put a name like that out front, you'll have the public lining up to catch the Greyhound for Pomona." He didn't like the studio's revised title much better (*It Happened One Night*) but he agreed to ante up on one condition. "I hear Louie wants to rent out the guy with the teeth—Gable, that's it. Stick him in there. Sure he can do comedy. Look at those ears. But make sure he shows his chest."

Ira was also among the first to put big money behind Walt Disney. "He's got a great idea, this boy. Why should we pay actors when we can buy pencils?" When Disney brought him some preliminary sketches for *Snow White*, Ira had a suggestion. "Put bigger warts on the witch and smaller boobs on the girl. Remember, this is for kids. The parents don't care the kids should be scared outa their skin, but God forbid you should give one of them a hard-on."

Chipsey's great problem in life as the unlovable son of an unlovable father was to be torn between feeble longings for artistic independence and overpowering greed. His solution to the dilemma was to anglicize the family name, then keep all the family money he could lay hands on. The money came his way, though it didn't always gush. Father Goldstein had more than once been heard openly referring to son Goldenstone as a "fruit," a "queer," even a "degenerate." Still, Ira had no place else to leave his fortune, so, grudgingly, he let it trickle down to Chipsey.

Clare's policy was to have nothing more to do with Chipsey than she had to, even when the festival was in progress. She reconciled herself to taking the money it produced, but normally scheduled those two weeks as her vacation, leaving The Classic in Sharkey's care. It was a gesture of contempt and disassociation. "If he ever got too stoned to turn the camera on," she once said of Sharkey as she made ready to clear out of town, "this crowd wouldn't know the difference. They'd think they were watching an experimental film." Unfortunately, this hands-off policy eventually backfired, landing Clare in a moral crisis that was to have far-reaching consequences for her and for me. That was the year of *Venetian Magenta*, one of the landmark events in the history of The Classic.

Since early on, Chipsey had been using the festival to showcase a multichaptered film opus called the "Venetian series." "Venetian" as in Venetian blind, before which a single fixed sixteen-millimeter camera was positioned to shoot a number of improvised episodes that were distinguished by nothing so much as their sheer silliness. The blind would open and we might see one of Chipsey's lovers shaving a live and clucking chicken. Maybe a half hour of that. Then the blind would close. Several minutes of that. Then it would open and we might see a gang of Chipsey's pals filling a tub with colored goo, clowning around, making a mess. Many minutes of that. Then a naked woman might leap into the tub and splash around. Many, many minutes of that. And so forth.

Each year, as an indication of the director's artistic growth, Chipsey's Venetian blind changed color. Thus, we had *Venetian Turquoise* followed by *Venetian Amber* followed by *Venetian Gold*. Chipsey insisted that with each new installment, the boundaries of film art were being flung back still farther into the creative unknown. He could talk endlessly about the symbolic meaning of the blind, of the chicken, of the tub, of action that took place behind the blind in contrast to action that took place *through* the blind. Nobody could possibly have traced the so-called "development" Chipsey claimed for the series, except for the fact that each installment was longer than the last. By the time we reached *Venetian Mauve*, we had passed the four-hour mark; this included a final ninety minutes during which we saw the blind and nothing but the blind, accompanied by a sound track filled with orgiastic giggles and grunts. Chipsey had lots to say about that final hour and a half. "You see the air of mystery it creates. It's taken directly from Egypt, ancient Egypt. The temple veil, the cult of Isis, that sort of thing. I'm definitely into an Egyptian phase."

Chipsey's films were all sent East to be shown in New York on the burgeoning underground circuit, where they were highly regarded among midnight-movie devotees. *Film Culture* first coined the term "Baudelairean cinema" as a slot in which to place the Venetian series. But *Venetian Mauve* was destined to be upstaged that year by an even more daring advance into decadence: Jack Smith's *Flaming Creatures,* which was hailed as the first film to show total male frontal nudity. A "dick show," as the aficionados termed it. This erotic revelation actually passed in a flash, surrounded by the sort of impromptu goofing off that had lately been given critical dignity among New York intellectuals as something called "camp." *Flaming Creatures* weighed in on the scales of outrageous misconduct as *high* camp; it at once became a minor *succès de scandale* which the police collaborated in publicizing by staging a few well-reported busts at which the film was confiscated and the theater owners momentarily arrested. This happened in Los Angeles when *Flaming Creatures* made its premiere. The result was to embolden Chipsey, who was determined not to be outdone by Smith, one of his old rivals for attention and acclaim. He at once announced that he too was prepared to go "all the way" in his next opus. This was *Venetian Magenta.*

Theodore Roszak

Shortly before its debut at The Classic Festival, Clare and I attended a preview. About an hour into the film, the trusty Venetian blind opened on the key sequence. There stood a figure wrapped from head to foot in aluminum foil!. An urgent whisper traveled around the darkened room; this was *Chipsey,* the director himself. The figure was delivering a muffled monologue, a lament that had something to do with the fact that he'd never been allowed to learn the rumba, how could his mother have been so cruel? He had a right to do the rumba, didn't everybody? He knew he could do the rumba, he could do it better than Rita Hayworth, but by the time he learned the rumba, everybody else was doing the samba. When would he ever have the chance to rumba? Oh, where were you, Xavier Cugat? Oh, where were the rumbas of yesteryear? In the background, the music was—what else?—a snappy little rumba.

At last Chipsey did indeed begin to rumba. Many minutes of that, leading up to the daring climax at which he stripped away the foil covering his crotch, revealing all. Several graphic, close-up seconds of that and the blind closed. Gasps and applause on all sides.

Afterward—two more hours of *Venetian Magenta* afterward—Clare and I bumped into Chipsey expounding upon the film to a group of admiring minions. He was holding forth on the deeper, existential meaning of the rumba and the artistic debt he would always owe to the great Cugat. Clare interrupted to ask, "But tell me, in that marvelous rumba section, what was that thing that showed through the tin foil at the end?"

Chipsey, startled, replied, "Why that was *me,* Clarissa. *All me,* the real, real thing."

"Oh," Clare said. "It looked just like a penis. Only much smaller."

It was one of the few thrusts that got through to Chipsey. "Well, wait till you see *Flaming Creatures,* my dear, before you make any comparisons. *Mine* is on view four seconds longer."

This became the most advertised word-of-mouth fact about that year's festival. Chipsey Goldenstone was going to show *his,* right up there on the screen for a record-breaking full-frontal nine seconds. Even the police knew. Especially the police. And they dutifully responded by breaking up the screening, grabbing the film, and busting Chipsey, Sharkey, and the projectionist, who happened to be me. The entire rowdy scene got on the television news that night with film clips of Chipsey raising histrionic Cain in the streets in front of the theater, proclaiming the freedom of artistic expression, denouncing the fascist cops. The result, as the case went to trial, was off-and-on flashes of publicity for The Classic, now firmly identified with the cause of the underground. Try as she might to fade out of sight, there was no way Clare as owner of the theater could avoid being dragged in by the press and the courts.

Though it was an agonizing bind to find herself in, Clare was no fink. She had no choice but to defend the theater, the film, and even—bitterest pill of all—Chipsey. "Valid? Do I think Mr. Goldenstone's film is valid?" she read herself saying in reports of the trial. "Well, I'm not about to let the police commissioner decide whether the movies I see are valid or not. Of course I believe it's valid, in the sense that . . ."

But whatever the qualifying remark might be, Clare came out of the crisis as a nationally recognized champion of underground cinema, committed to showing *Venetian Magenta* again, even if the courts forbade it. And she would have. But the courts didn't forbid it. The film was cleared by one of southern California's more liberal judges, who commented in his ruling that he couldn't believe anybody was likely to stay awake long enough to be corrupted by the offending scene. Chipsey became a hero; Clare became a heroine. A week after the decision, *Venetian Magenta* returned in triumph to The Classic. Thanks to much self-serving advance work by Chipsey, the screening took place with vast hoopla before an audience of more local notables than the little movie house could hold.

Halfway through the picture, Clare, who was putting in her obligatory civil-libertarian appearance, muttered to me, "If I have to sit through that rumba bit again, I'll throw up." We snuck out together to get coffee at Moishe's. Clare was no sooner seated than she let loose a flood of enraged tears. "I just had my theater swiped from me," she growled. "This isn't what I want. This isn't the movies."

I think that was the moment when Clare first took seriously the prospect of cutting free of The Classic to begin a new career. Ironically, the incident helped her achieve just that. She moaned and groaned for weeks over her enforced alliance with Chipsey and the underground, but there was no question about it: the publicity of the *Venetian Magenta* affair hastened the recognition she was soon to receive. Major magazines and newspapers were after her for articles; the NYU Film School invited her to give a series of lectures. "I can see it coming," she complained to me one night while she was taking time out from an article *Harper's* had commissioned. "I finally get a break, I get some attention, one-tenth of what I damn well deserve. And for sure somebody's going to say, 'She owes it all to Chipsey Goldenstone's prick.' "

Chipsey's invitation was to his father's mansion, an ersatz Renaissance villa with sprawling grounds that covered a few hundred acres of the Pacific Palisades, one of the original estates in the area. Normally, it was safely ensconced behind a stone wall and iron gates of medieval proportions—and probably guarded by ravenous hounds. But today it stood open to the world. We—Clare, Sharkey, and myself—had intended to come early, but by the time we arrived on Saturday afternoon, the place was already roaring with people. Chipsey's "few *intime* friends" turned out to be the usual mob gathered for the usual binge. The party looked as if it had begun the day before, or the day before that. There were at least three musical combos at work in the house and on the grounds: take your choice, jazz, rock, or rumba. The front lawn was paved nearly solid with cars parked every which way. The walk to the front door rivaled attending the Rose Bowl game.

Once we got inside, it seemed as if most of what was movable in the house was for sale. Sellers wearing pastel-colored straw hats milled through the crowd gleefully bargaining away all the senior Goldstein's furnishings, keepsakes, and cherished mementos. The scene reeked as much of filial vengeance as it did of greed. Chipsey had stationed a contingent of bare-chested bodybuilders at all the doors to check receipts as the merchandise was carried off. Flexing and posturing for one another's benefit, they managed to look more campy than intimidating.

"Our luck's run out," Clare muttered before we'd shouldered our way more than a few steps into the living room. She nodded toward someone who was struggling toward us through the crowd, waving and hailing. It was Chipsey, who had spotted us and was on his way over surrounded by an entourage of favorites, mainly pretty young men and boys. Chipsey always liked to be seen chatting with Clare; it was his main claim to having a brain. Now, since the trial, his association with her was a mandatory part of his role as Leading West Coast Voice of the American Underground. He was his usual outrageously euphoric self, beaming and bouncy. What was left of his perpetually platinum hair was slicked down into a Prince Valiant bob with bangs. He wore a bulky gym robe that was belted open to reveal lots of hairy human chest. Chipsey might almost have been mistaken for a slightly seedy prizefighter just come from a sparring session. His beefy body, tanned to a glowing cinnamon, still showed youthful muscle surviving beneath the blubber; his nose was squashed flat; his brows deeply lacerated and beaten into lumps. It was Chipsey's affectation to display both the muscles and the scars: evidence of his adventures among the rough trade of the local harbors and beaches.

"Are you moving in or moving out?" Clare asked after Chipsey had forced a wet kiss upon her.

"Moving in *here?*" Chipsey winced. His voice was a nasal buzz saw that could be heard above any tumult. "God help me, *never!* I grew up in this chamber of horrors. Too many vile childhood associations. I'm turning it into a spa. The Spa of the Stars. Herbal steaming. Shiatsu. Deep tissue massage. The Home of the Totally Permissive Jacuzzi. Of course the whole morbid dump will have to be gutted."

"You sound as if you enjoy the thought," Clare said. "Gutting the Goldstein family seat."

"Oh don't I!"

"Will there be films for sale?" Clare called out as Chipsey began melting away into the throng.

"Of course! What do you think? Bargains galore. Giveaways. Catch me later, Clarissa. I'll make sure they set aside something special for you."

But that was the last we saw of Chipsey or heard about movies until the day had wheeled round through night into the next morning.

Meanwhile, as the party ascended to ever dizzier alcoholic altitudes, Goldstein trivia began changing hands at wild prices . . . autographed photos, old shooting scripts, famous director's chairs. A pair of Eleanor Powell's tap shoes went for four hundred dollars. A crumpled box of "partially unused" Ramses condoms said to have belonged to Rudolph Valentino fetched an exuberant seven hundred and fifty. A greasy piece of lace and elastic that was described as the "epoch-making" brassiere worn by Jane Russell in *The Outlaw* sold for a thousand. Clare, drinking straight Scotch deeply and steadily, sat sullenly through the proceedings balanced on the brink of nausea. "In medieval Europe," she grumbled to me, "they used to sell the virgin's milk by the gallon. And we think *that* was the Dark Ages. When they get to Pola Negri's menstrual blood, I'm leaving."

Midnight came and went with still no sign of the promised film sale. By then the Goldstein mansion was a minor riot of gate-crashers and transient vandals. Filmland memorabilia, as well as a good deal of furniture, could be seen disappearing out all the doors. The body-builders had their hands full running down filchers on the lawn. One small brigade of thieves was caught trying to finesse a Wurlitzer organ through the rose garden. Looking for breathing space, Clare and I found our way to a thinly populated tile courtyard. We'd last seen Sharkey somewhere toward twilight; he was caught up in a nude volleyball game that seemed to be making do without a ball. Clare was by now at a high simmer of exasperation, kept from boiling over by frequent applications of liquor. As we sat together, we became aware of a conversation that was transpiring in syrupy tones between two men huddled on a garden swing just across from us. All we could see of them under the awning were two glowing cigarette tips in the shadows.

"It cost me a thousand, but I've always, *always* wanted it," one was saying.

"Well, I envy you, I *really* do."

"Wait until Howard hears I bought it. He'll just flip."

"It's *definitely* a collector's item."

"Oh, *more* than that. It's *absolutely* her best work as far as I'm concerned. I mean before this you could see the potential. But this is where she truly *emerges*. I say 'she,' but of course I'm convinced she was a man."

"You *really* think so?"

"With those shoulders? *Come on!*"

"You could be right. I admit I always had my suspicions. I mean the way I responded to her . . ."

"And those *deltoids?* Those are male deltoids if I've ever seen male deltoids."

"*Definitely* a masculine physique."

"They say she could press one hundred and fifty pounds."

"Well, I agree that this is where she achieves her, you know, maturity. But do you think it's more *fun?*"

"More fun than what?"

"Oh, say *Dangerous When Wet.*"

"Oh, come along! There's no comparison. The big finish in *Neptune's Daughter* is classic."

"With all the fountains, yes."

"I *really* get off on those fountains. And then, there's where she comes swinging in on the trapeze from God knows where and does this scissors thing with her legs. I mean she's like an ethereal being descending from heaven."

"Oh God, *yes*."

"I could watch that over and over."

"Good music too."

"Classic."

"But, you know, I think my *very* favorite is her big number in *Till the Clouds Roll By*."

"Oh well, that's *really* classic. That water-ski pyramid with all the guys . . ."

"That's the one I want. Do you think Chipsey has that?"

"Of course he does. But just in thirty-five-millimeter. He'll never sell that."

"You're sure?"

"Are you kidding? It's classic."

"Well, he sold you *Neptune's Daughter* and that's classic."

"Only the sixteen-millimeter. He'd never let the thirty-five-millimeter go. Besides, he wants to do a remake of the water-ski bit."

"*Does* he?"

"Uh-hm. To bring out all the erotic connotations."

Clare could hold back no longer. She crossed to the swing and asked, "Excuse me, but did I hear you say you bought a film—from Chipsey?"

I could tell by the long, frigid silence that her intrusion wasn't welcomed. I joined Clare and, squinting into the darkness, could make out two middle-aged men, one wearing a flowing silk gown, the other a T-shirt.

"I'm a friend of Chipsey's," Clare went on. "I came to look at the films."

Smugly, one of the men said, "Chipsey's been selling all evening. But just to his really *close* friends."

"I'm a really close friend, believe me," Clare insisted. "He invited me just for the films. Where are they being sold?"

"If Chipsey wanted you to know, you'd know without me telling you," was the snotty reply.

"Look, you can tell me," Clare snapped. "I'm not really a woman. Look at those deltoids." She held out one of her arms, flexing muscles.

The silk-gowned man sniffed and turned away. "Typical," he said.

"Okay, forget it, Peter Pan," Clare growled and spun away sharply, motioning me to follow. Then, turning at the entrance to the house, she called back. "She wasn't a man. She was a salmon. And the only movie she made that wasn't a cringe-fest was *Take Me Out to the Ball Game.*"

Clare had just passed from irritated to incensed. With me at her heels, she went tearing through the villa, asking after Chipsey, who seemed to have abandoned his guests. Passing a dark pantry off the kitchen, she picked up a familiar laugh. She found a light switch and flipped it. Inside she found Sharkey. Positioned precariously on his lap with both legs on his shoulders was a pretty young thing wearing a filmy dress. They were in the middle of something, Clare didn't bother to ask what.

"Where the hell have you been?" she shouted.

"Clare . . ." Sharkey answered, as if he weren't sure it was Clare. His pupils were dilated to the size of dimes. "Hey, I've been looking all over for . . ."

"Where's Chipsey? Is he selling movies or what?"

"Oh yeah, about that . . ." Sharkey began. The pretty young thing was sliding liquidly down his legs into an inebriated puddle on the floor. "Listen, don't worry. I told Chipsey to set something aside for me."

"For *you?* What about *me?*"

"For *us,* I mean."

"*Us* isn't *me.* Where're the films?"

"Uh . . . uh . . . uh . . ." Sharkey was trying to focus. He pulled himself to a standing position wobbling and naked, rubbing his brows. "The vault . . . there's a vault. But don't worry, it's taken care of."

"So what do I do—go through the house asking the way to the vault?"

Before Sharkey could answer, Clare had torn off to do just that. Along the way, those sober enough to be asked had no idea where the vault was. Clare and I made our way generally back and downward to a lower floor and then into the basement of the house. At the foot of a flight of stairs, we encountered one of Chipsey's bodybuilders struggling along a corridor, wheeling a hand dolly toward a rear exit. On the dolly was a heavy load of thirty-five-millimeter film cartons.

"I'm looking for Chipsey . . . in the vault," Clare informed the muscular lad, then followed where his chin inarticulately pointed. We turned a corner and heard a voice. Chipsey's.

"No, no, I really can't let it go that cheap. It's a classic." When he caught sight of Clare, he gave a whoop of delight. "Clarissa! Where have you been? My God, I was about ready to close the store." There was an anxious little man in a riotous Hawaiian shirt at his side, apparently a customer.

Chipsey had changed out of his boxer's robe. He was wearing something fluorescent and flowing and vaguely Arabian. A long, crooked stogie was fixed between his teeth. He was standing near the doorway of a good-sized storeroom that was caged in by floor-to-ceiling steel mesh. The storeroom was lined with enough racks to hold scores of films. Trouble was: there weren't scores of films. There weren't more than a scattered dozen. The place was stripped.

"Jesus!" Clare gasped. "Where's the collection?"

"Oh, most of it was sold off last week," Chipsey answered. "The big-ticket items, you know. The major collectors took the bulk of it."

Quickly Clare said, "I want their names . . . and what they bought."

"I can give you some of their names," he answered. "Oh, you'd know most of them. Roddy McDowall took a lot. People like that. Joshua Sloan from Chicago wanted to buy the whole works—and for a *very* good price, I can tell you. He and my father were old rivals at collecting. But I said, no, I have friends who deserve to share the wealth. But I really can't remember who bought what, it all went so fast. And actually it was quite informal. I'm not a great one for keeping accounts, you know. Frankly, these were private transactions. We wouldn't want the IRS knowing about it."

The Hawaiian shirt with whom Chipsey had been bargaining piped up to ask, "How about five hundred and fifty?"

"Oh, come now!" Chipsey replied. "This is vintage Sonja Henie. The Glenn Miller sound track alone is worth that much."

"Wasn't there an inventory for the collection?" Clare asked.

"Oh, I'm sure my parent kept one somewhere. He was positively psychotic about things like that. Very anal-retentive. I have no idea where it might be. I've been throwing out barrels of papers. Out, out, out. A clean sweep."

"Chipsey, that's so irresponsible," Clare protested. "You're running this like a goddam garage sale."

"Right you are, Clarissa. Out with all the Oedipal residues. But never fear. I've put something aside for you."

"Yes? What?"

Chipsey's disgruntled customer interrupted again. "Is the sound track in good condition? I mean if I'm paying for Glenn Miller . . ."

Impatiently, Chipsey informed his pesky customer, "The way my compulsively acquisitive parent looked after his possessions, it's probably a virgin film. He didn't collect these things to enjoy them. They were bloody investments. Most of them never came out of the can."

"Okay," the customer said, "how about six hundred and fifty?"

"Not even close," Chipsey sniffed and left the man to stew while he escorted Clare and me to a small row of sixteen-millimeter cartons high up on a rear rack. "I let Sharkey put these aside. Mind you, I could have sold them off days ago, but I agreed to hold them until you had a chance to make your choice."

Clare eagerly swept her eyes over the film cartons. For a moment she froze in astonishment, then turned back to Chipsey with a savage glare. "*That's* what you saved for me? *Jerry Lewis?*"

"It's what Sharkey picked out."

"Sharkey's a pinhead. This isn't even quality junk."

"Now, Clarissa, I can let you have those at a very good price."

"Don't call me Clarissa. From now on you don't know me well enough to call me Clarissa."

"Do you realize, Miss Swann, how much I could get for these movies? Jerry Lewis is going to be a cult phenomenon. He already is in Paris, you know."

"They like hot dogs in Paris too. So what? It's called intellectual slumming. You're a louse, Chipsey. You know I can't afford to buy anything, least of all *dreck* like this."

"I *was* going to let you choose one of these films as a *gift*. Just for friendship's sake. Well, not *The Stooge* or *The Bellhop*. I mean, those are classic. But any of the others . . ."

Chipsey's would-be customer came wandering into view around the end of one of the racks, still trying to clinch the deal on Sonja Henie. He stood by testily while Chipsey spoke.

Defeated, Clare sank down on a stack of film cartons, her head in her hands. "Christ, Chipsey, I would have been content just to know where the films were going. If you could have done that much, just to help keep track of the heritage."

"Do forgive me, Clare dear," Chipsey soothed, "but to be honest that just doesn't speak to me as an issue. These are old movies. Old, *old* movies. Of course, a scholar like yourself has to care about the past. But art is *now*. Art is the future, the prophetic impulse. For the artist, true art is the destroyer of the past and its defunct values. It's . . ."

"How about seven hundred bucks?" the Hawaiian shirt asked.

"*Sold American!*" Chipsey yipped, and the man started to write out a check. "I'll want to see a driver's license with that," he warned.

While Chipsey and his buyer were busy with their transaction, the oversized blond Apollo Clare and I had met on our way to the vault lumbered in with his hand dolly. "And that bunch," Chipsey said, pointing him toward the stack of cartons Clare was sitting on, "which the lady is warming for us with her pretty tush."

"Same car?" Apollo asked.

"Same car."

Clare moved out of the boy's way as he started loading the cartons, then suddenly let out a wrenching gasp. She leapt forward to take hold of his ample biceps. "My God, I can't believe it," she said.

Chipsey gave a proud, possessive snicker. "Yes, he *is* something to look at, isn't he? Clare, I'd like you to meet Jerome. Jerome is simply going to steal my next production. I don't blame you for your response. But I warn you, he's already spoken for."

But Clare was paying no attention whatever to Jerome. Her eyes were riveted to the cartons he was loading on the dolly.

"*This!* I want *this*," she announced.

Chipsey glanced at the cartons. "No, no. That's sold, Clare. Sorry."

"I'll pay you . . . a thousand dollars," she declared.

I wondered as she made the offer where Clare would get a thousand dollars. But she was already fumbling to find her poor, starving checkbook.

"No, no, please!" Chipsey protested. "It's sold. And for a great deal more than a thousand dollars, I can tell you."

But Clare persisted. "I'll give you . . . fifteen hundred."

"Clare, dear, you don't have fifteen hundred. You've already told me you don't have enough to buy Jerry Lewis. Besides fifteen hundred wouldn't come close."

Improvising frantically, Clare made a desperate proposition. "All right, I'll offer you sex. Sex means a lot to you, Chipsey, I know it does."

"Now, Clare." Chipsey gave a deep, throaty chuckle. "That's very, very sweet. But I don't think we're quite compatible."

"Not with *me*, you creep!" Clare snapped. "Don't be disgusting."

"Oh?"

"With . . . Jonny. I'll fix you up with Jonny." She grabbed me and pulled me over, too much like an item of merchandise.

"That's very generous of you, Clare," Chipsey said, giving me what I believe he intended as a seductive assessment. "And I'm sure Jonny would be worth every penny. But I doubt he'd come across."

Jolted, I stared at Clare. Then at Chipsey. I gave a little laugh to pick up on the joke. It was a joke . . . wasn't it?

"Shut up!" Clare growled at me, digging her nails into my arm. "He'll come across if I tell him to. Won't you, Jonny?"

It wasn't a joke.

Embarrassed and wounded, I decided to find out what my virtue was being traded for. I turned one of the cartons to see the label. And I understood. *Les Enfants du Paradis*. Clare's favorite film. In thirty-five-millimeter yet. I'd once heard her say she would kill to have her own print of it.

Chipsey continued to wave her off. "I'm sorry, Clarissa, but *Les Enfants* has been promised. It's a special favor. I can't go back on it—even for twice what you're offering."

"Promised to whom?"

"Jürgen Von Schachter." He offered the name with a smart-ass grin.

"Am I supposed to know who that is?"

"You mean you *don't*? I'm frankly amazed. He's Germany's most talked-about experimental director. I'd love to introduce you. He's somewhere on the premises. Gorgeous boy. Real aristocracy. Right down to the dueling scars. Except that *his* scars don't all show in public. I'm sure he'd be a count or a baron, if it weren't for whatever it is that seems to have deprived us of counts and barons. We'll be showing some of his films at the next festival. Exquisite work. Very Nietzschean, if you know what I mean. Cinema of Anguish he calls it. Deep, very deep."

"I can't wait to see it," Clare muttered. Clearly her mind was racing to find some way to lay hands on the film. But Jerome had started loading the cartons on his dolly. "Stop that!" Clare howled, taking a swipe at him with her open checkbook. "Leave that alone, you muscle-bound cocksucker!" Jerome, taken by surprise, backed off in slack-jawed amazement. Clare sank down beside the stack of cartons and passed her hand over it protectively as if she were comforting a dying child. More to herself than anyone else she said, "My mother took me to see *Les Enfants du Paradis*. It was my first great film experience."

Chipsey tried to sympathize. "I do understand, Clarissa. We all have our first time."

"Let me guess what yours was. *King Kong?*"

"No, as a matter of fact, it was Kenneth Anger's *Fireworks.*"

"Oh God," Clare moaned.

"I think I could honestly say I learned my total personal destiny from that movie. You know the big scene where the sailor's penis turns into a firecracker. . . ."

"Please stop, Chipsey," Clare begged. "I'm going to be sick."

"*Chacun à son goût*, Clarissa. Of course, later on Kenneth went completely superficial."

"Why does your Nietzschean pal want *Les Enfants du Paradis?*" Clare wanted to know. "What does it mean to him?"

"Well, actually he hates the film. Like myself, he sees it as totally retrograde and defunctive." Clare winced. Chipsey noticed. "Sorry, Clarissa, but art marches on, you know. Actually, Jürgen doesn't want the movie for himself. It's for his father. You see, during the war, the elder Von Schachter was something like the military minister of art or culture in occupied France. Did you know France was occupied during the war? By the Germans? Isn't that amazing? I never heard of that until Jürgen told me. Well, anyway, that's when *Les Enfants du Paradis* was produced. And it seems the old man was mixed up with the film somehow—making sure of its political tone and so forth. Or maybe just turning a blind eye, I don't know. The father's living in Argentina or Paraguay or someplace like that. Jürgen wants to send him the movie for his birthday. The man's quite sick, I understand. So you see, it's a sentimental gesture. I gather a couple of the girls in the movie were the elder Von Schachter's mistresses. Well, you can understand."

They say animals can smell an earthquake coming hours before it hits—some sort of instinctual ESP. That's what I felt standing beside Clare just then. The earth getting ready to split. The shock wave seemed to be rushing at us a mile a minute. But all she did was stand staring at Chipsey. A long, long stare. Then she gave a quizzical little smile and said very quietly, "Jürgen's father was the Nazi minister of culture in France. That's what you're telling me? And you're selling Jürgen this movie so he can send it to his father who's hiding out in Paraguay?"

"It might be Argentina. I forget which. I suppose it's a secret."

"Chipsey, this is insane," Clare was nearly squealing in protest. "Don't you know anything about this movie? It was made by starving actors in an occupied country. The whole cast and crew was mixed up with the Resistance; they risked their lives to hide members of the underground. This film . . . it was made in the belly of the beast, a celebration of life and love and art . . ." But Clare could see she was wasting her breath. Chipsey was simply staring back at her, blank and bored. "For Christ's sake, Chipsey, your boyfriend's goose-stepping father is a war criminal."

"Well, if you ask me," Chipsey said with a weary sigh, "I think people have blown this Hitler thing out of all proportion. Anyway, Clare, what do I care about politics? Especially old, *old* politics from way long ago?"

"Don't you realize what the Nazis did to homosexuals, as well as Jews?"

Chipsey assumed a deeply confidential tone. "Clarissa, I don't have a prejudiced bone in my body, you know that. But believe me, I've met plenty of Jews and queers who would've deserved it."

I was still waiting for the promised tremor to hit. It never came. I could see the knuckles of Clare's fisted hands turn white at her side. But the voice was dead steady and cool, as if it were somebody else's voice, not Clare's. "Chipsey, I'd love to meet Jürgen. Would you introduce us?"

"Delighted! As soon as we've finished up here."

"I'll tell you what," Clare answered. "I'll let Sharkey work something out with you about the Jerry Lewis stuff. Whatever he decides. He really is a better judge of such things than I could ever be."

"All right, if you want it that way."

Then, turning to me, she said, "And why don't you help Jerome load that film?" My bewildered stare only brought an intimidating shove in Jerome's direction. "It's a *long* movie. He's going to need help."

I had no idea why I should want to help Jerome, and Jerome showed no signs of wanting help from me. But after another, more insistent push and a muttered "Go *on!*" I did as I was told, though I felt rather like a kid being packed out of the way by his mother. I gathered Clare simply wanted me off the scene for some reason. Picking up one of the cartons Jerome hadn't stacked yet on his dolly, I started to tag along behind him.

"And come find me upstairs when you're finished," Clare called after me.

5 THE CHILDREN OF PARADISE CAPER

When I found Clare again, she was part of a small still relatively sober group that had drawn off into one corner of a glassed-in porch. There was a sweeping vista of the moon-silvered Pacific from here, but nobody was giving it any attention. Instead, like Clare, everyone was drawn up around Chipsey and the elegantly dressed young man who lounged beside him on an oversized pillow. Jürgen, I gathered. He was fair and lean to the point of being cadaverous; atop his head he carried some three inches of pompadoured Nordic locks. And, as Chipsey said, there were indeed scars—or at least one scar that showed, positioned rather too cutely under his left cheekbone. Though his face was frozen in a blank, bored expression, he seemed to be following what Clare had to say with great care, now and then giving a small twitch of amusement.

Moving in quietly behind Clare, I took my place at the fringe of the group and quickly picked up on the subject under discussion. Early German cinema. It was a topic on which I'd heard Clare hold forth many times. But this time there was something decidedly odd about what I was hearing. It was her tone. So calm and measured. So . . . respectful. She was explaining everything she said with great patience. *And* she was listening. Listening and nodding politely. Clare never behaved like that.

Then I heard Jürgen say, "But this man Kracauer—he is just shit, you know."

And Clare said, "Oh? Do you think so?"

And Jürgen said, "Obviously he has been hired by the Jews."

Now at that point, I would have expected Clare to go for the jugular like a wolf that scented blood. Siegfried Kracauer was one of the few philosophers of film for whom Clare had any respect. I'd heard her defend his book *From Caligari to Hitler* several times with impassioned conviction, as if she might have written it herself. That was a rare compliment for Clare to pay anybody.

Kracauer's big idea was that the Germans of Hitler's time had been driven crazy by the movies. Following the First World War, the country, still dazed by defeat, had been flooded with films that acted upon its wounded psyche like so many viruses. To begin with, there was *The Cabinet of Doctor Caligari,* a movie about madness and murder in which all the borders of sanity were systematically erased. Universally praised as high art, this film, along with a host of others, had saturated the German unconscious with a psychotic repertoire of ghouls, black magicians, vampires. Above all, the movies of that period had been obsessed with hypnotism. Again and again, the screen presented stories of mad doctors and master criminals who could mesmerize their helpless victims and then force them to commit hideous acts. Clear anticipations of Nazism, so Professor Kracauer believed. Such movies had poisoned the soul of the nation with images of perverted power. At last, along came *Der Führer,* who, like the evil hypnotist Caligari, spellbound the public and turned it into an army of murderous zombies.

Clare liked this idea. She thought it did justice to the strange, psychological influence of film in the modern world, its uncanny ability to charm and delude. She believed Kracauer was fighting for a deeply ethical understanding of that influence. I'd seen her explode with impatience at someone who dared to say that his book was somewhat overstated. "How can you overstate the danger of arsenic?" she demanded. But here she was now, sitting by demurely while a snotty stranger spat on work she admired with her whole heart.

What was going on?

In answer to Jürgen's crack about the Jews, all Clare did was smile (a bit sourly) and say, "You'll really have to take that up with Chipsey. He'd be in a better position than I to know. How about it, Chipsey? Are *your* people financing Professor Kracauer?"

Chipsey, flushed with drink, burst out in a dismissive laugh. "Clarissa, I don't understand a word that man writes. Besides, all these things you're talking about—and you are talking about them beautifully, my dear—they're practically prehistoric. My life, you must understand, happens in the creative present. Don't you agree, Jürgen? Art really must transcend these merely political ephemera."

Chipsey was a great one for pumping helium into any conversation. With his help, things bounced and floated aimlessly for several minutes more before they struck another snag. Clare had come back to Kracauer's book, trying as tactfully as before to explain this and that about it, when Jürgen interrupted to ask, quite casually, "And Von Kastell, for example? How would he fit in?"

Clare stopped short. "Who?" she asked back.

"Castle, if you prefer. Max Castle. Would you say this absurd theory applies to him?"

It must have seemed to her a lethal opening on Jürgen's part, more than she could resist. "Surely you aren't suggesting we give trash like *Feast of the Undead* serious critical attention!"

Jürgen waved her objection aside. "I mean, of course, his early films. His *German* films."

"Do any of them still exist?"

"Not many. My father personally destroyed several of his movies."

"Oh?"

"During the Reich. Part of the cultural policy."

"Well, if your father destroyed them, I would have loved to see them."

"He was, of course, only following orders."

"Of course."

"He was actually a great movie fan. Your Jean Harlow—she was a great favorite of his. Also Porky Pig."

"How nice. But he burned the movies anyway."

"Actually, he managed to save a few of them. Which is perhaps fortunate. There is some interest now in Castle's work—his early work. You know Victor Saint-Cyr in Paris?"

"Oh yes. We haven't been in touch for years."

"He contacted my father about some of Castle's things. Of course, Victor's approach, it will be very abstract, very Cartesian." He gave a derisive little giggle. "Very French."

At this point, Clare caught sight of me seated behind her and excused herself. "Please don't go away," she told Jürgen. "I'll be right back. I do so much want to continue." She hustled me across the room, asking, "Where the hell have you been all this time?"

"I was listening to you and . . ."

"You might have made your presence known," she scolded. "You think I was enjoying myself?"

"Well, it sounded . . ."

She cut me off in mid-sentence. "You know where his car is?"

"Yeah, it's a big white Mercedes. It's parked over . . ."

"You can find it again?"

"Sure."

"And the movie is in the car?"

"Yeah. Jerome was loading it into the trunk when I left."

"Now listen carefully. Would you say you were reasonably sober?"

"Well, I guess, more or less. . . ." Actually, I'd been guzzling all night long, matching her drink for drink. I rather wondered why she was looking so much less sloshed than I felt. I gathered her sense of urgency was keeping her focused.

"Then take a couple more stiff drinks. Because you'll never do what I want you to do if you're sober. First of all, go get Sharkey. Somebody said he's out at the pool. I don't care if you find him stuck in some chick all of his full three sad inches' worth. Pull him out. Are you following me?"

"Yes . . ."

"Then take him to Jürgen's car. And steal the movie."

These words seemed to take a long time getting to me, echoing down a winding, dreamy corridor. "Steal the movie? How can I do that?"

"Break into the car. Take the movie out of the car. Put it in your car. Drive it home. That's how you steal it."

"But his car is locked. Jerome had to use a key to . . ."

"That's why you need Sharkey. He knows all about breaking into cars and things like that."

"He does?"

"Probably he doesn't. Probably he's a fat liar. But he's been telling me for years about how he used to be a thief. He went through some romantic hoodlum phase in his distant, fictitious youth. If he's forgotten, remind him what a rogue he's supposed to be. But just get him to help you. If he's drunk enough, he'll do anything for kicks."

"But, Clare . . . *stealing?*"

She snapped back at me savagely, "This isn't stealing! This is a political act, understand? That warmed-over Hitler Jugend in there is absolutely *not* going to make a gift of *Les Enfants du Paradis* to his Gestapo father. Not if I can help it. Don't put it that way to Sharkey. It sounds too decent. Just tell him it's a caper. If he gives you any trouble, tell him I promise to go to every female I can find at this party and deliver a detailed critical review of his last ten years of sexual nonperformance."

"But what if we can't get into the car? What if . . . ?"

"If you can't get the film . . . burn the car."

"What?"

"Burn it. Blow it up. Destroy it."

"I don't know how to do that."

"Jesus! Drop a match in the gas tank."

"Oh, Clare . . . I can't . . . I don't . . ."

Suddenly, there were tears flooding from her eyes. Embarrassed, she slapped me hard across the chops. That really hurt, but it punctuated her absolute seriousness. "Listen, I'm in there fighting the Second World War all over again. I'm letting that Nazi faggot shit all over my best principles—just to keep him pinned down. Do you know what I've had to sit and listen to from that . . . that . . . I ought to get the Congressional Medal of Honor. Now you do what I tell you, or just never, never, *never* come looking for me again!"

"What if I get caught?"

"Well, I don't know. Shoot your way out."

"Clare!"

"It's pitch dark. Nobody will see you. If they do, play dumb. Play drunk. People have been swiping from this place all night. Who's going to care? I'll keep Chipsey and the *Übermensch* busy. Just work fast, that's all."

I stood helpless and shaken and despairing before her. Relenting, she raised herself and gave me the warmest kiss I'd ever had from her. "This means everything to me," she said. God, it was like Lauren Bacall sending Bogie into the night on a mission of danger. *Take care of yourself, darling. You're all I've got.* How could I refuse?

As I set off in search of Sharkey, I tried to justify what Clare was asking of me. I had to see it from her point of view. *Les Enfants du Paradis* wasn't simply another movie for her; it belonged in a special category all its own. It was a thing of beauty that had been bravely raised up in an act of defiance by its creators against the barbarian intruder. How could she let even one print of that film fall into the hands of the despoiler? I knew what she feared. Jürgen von Schachter's father would do something far worse than destroy this movie. He would *enjoy* it, as if he had the right to do that. Of course that mustn't happen!

I found Sharkey stoned and still nude in the company of a half-dozen stoned, nude people at the swimming pool. To my surprise, he responded eagerly to "the caper" as he gleefully envisioned it. "Wild!" he yipped. But not quite grasping the importance of secrecy, he loudly invited his swim mates to join us. Some, but not all, troubled to put on a robe or towel as we took off across the lawn. They in turn invited others along the way. By the time we reached the car, we'd become a raucous collection of amateur bandits making enough racket to be heard from one end of the estate to the other. Fortunately, we were not the only noisemakers on the grounds. A jazz combo had staked out some space on the roof of the villa and was filling the night with hot licks.

If somebody had filmed what happened during the next hour, Sharkey, Gates, and Company might have rivaled the best of the Keystone Cops. Sharkey assured me he could crack the car in thirty seconds flat. "Just the trunk," I told him, lighting the lock with match after match. But after he'd picked away at it for several minutes, one of the dizzy young women in our group decided to speed things along by heaving a large paving stone through a rear window. Her friends, not wanting to be left out of the fun, proceeded to smash the other windows.

"Hey, this is wild!" Sharkey wailed as he struggled into the car through the back window. "I'll have this buggy hot-wired in thirty seconds flat."

"No, no," I said. "We're not stealing the car. We don't want the car."

"We don't? What're we stealin', amigo?" he asked.

"The movie."

"What movie?"

"There's a movie in the car. In the trunk."

"No it isn't," Sharkey said. "Here it is—in the backseat."

I peered into the dark interior of the car. Sure enough, Sharkey was sprawling across a number of film cartons. "I thought it was in the trunk," I said.

"Well, is this a movie or is this a movie?" Sharkey asked and started pitching the cartons to me through the window. It was only then, as I stacked them on the lawn, that I realized we were a very long way from my car.

"Sharkey," I said, as I grunted over the heavy cartons, "we've got to get these all the way to the other side of the house."

"No sweat," Sharkey assured me. "Everybody! Lend me a hand," he shouted.

There were now several people hard at work on Jürgen's Mercedes, demolishing the headlights, amputating the windshield wipers, flatting the tires. Others, attracted to the spectacle, stood looking on amused. At Sharkey's call, they stumbled forward to pick up the cartons.

"Lead on, bwana!" Sharkey sang out, a film carton balanced on his head. "Into the bush. Boom-ba-ba-boom."

I gathered I was bwana and struck out into the darkness, but with no clear idea which way to head. Finding my car in the moonless night became a nightmare, but I seemed the only one to care. Behind me was a raggle-taggle safari of prancing and singing inebriates carrying film cartons on their heads, having the time of their lives. All along the way, Sharkey urged our queer trek on with jungle hoots and tom-tom rhythms beaten out on the carton he carried. We zigzagged around the villa and grounds for what seemed like hours before I spotted the car.

When the cartons had been dumped into the backseat, I sent Sharkey to tell Clare, but with no confidence he would make it back to her. Driving away, I was still trembling with guilt and the dread of being caught. I needn't have feared. Nobody who took part in the heist was likely to remember a thing the next day. Maybe I wouldn't remember myself; I'd followed Clare's advice and downed a few more drinks before going after Sharkey. Still, one thing stuck vividly in my mind on the way home. I was certain my wayward bearers had lost two or three cartons along the way. Perhaps a few of them were still meandering about the Goldstein estate with stray reels on their heads. There weren't more than five in the backseat; there should have been nearly twice that number.

I'd rescued only half the children of paradise. How would I explain that to Clare?

"You didn't lose two or three reels. You lost the whole damn thing."
"What d'you mean?"
"The whole film. You lost it."
"But it's in the car. In the backseat."
"There's a film in the car. But it isn't *Les Enfants du Paradis*."
"It isn't?"
"It isn't."
"Well, where's *Les Enfants du Paradis*?"
"You tell me."

Clare was hovering above me where I sat drooped over the kitchen table, swilling strong coffee, trying to muffle the pounding in my head with a cushion of caffeine. Under her insistent questioning, I felt like a cornered boxer hanging on the ropes. We looked a sight, the two of us. Red-eyed, sallow, bedraggled, the last people on earth who were qualified to be talking about the children of paradise.

Clare, I discovered, had collapsed toward dawn and spent what remained of the night at Chipsey's, sharing the living-room carpet with a few dozen other dissipated casualties. In the late morning, she got a lift home and found me still asleep. I woke under her pummeling to find her glaring down at me, demanding to know "Where is it? Where?"

I told her the film was in my car outside, but added that I might have lost a few reels along the way. She rushed out to check and came storming back into the apartment to tell me how complete my failure was.

"It was so dark. . . ." I explained feebly. "No, I didn't check the labels on the carton. Why should I? I wanted to get away fast. Sharkey was making such a rumpus. Oh, Clare . . . I thought they'd catch us all."

"All? How many people were in on this?"

"Dozens and dozens. Sharkey brought them along. They were trashing the car, and singing, and . . ."

Clare slumped into a chair and grabbed my coffee away. "So you fucked up. That Nazi louse got the movie after all. Oh God! I wish I could drop a bomb on somebody. Maybe *you*."

"But I did steal a film. I remember that. What film did we get?"

"Something called *Judas Castle*," Clare groaned.

"*Judas Castle*? I never heard of it."

"Is that so? Well, neither have I. Christ, what if it's one of Jürgen's masterpieces! If it is, I'll burn it."

Neither of us had much incentive to bring the film in for inspection, but finally I did: five battered thirty-five-millimeter cartons. On a few of the boxes I could see the remnants of stamps, labels, stenciled words—all in German. And along the side of each box the words *Judas Kastell*. Or *Kastell Judas*, written in a rapid, crooked scrawl. I unbelted each carton and inspected the film canisters inside. They were in remarkably good shape, tightly shut and undented as if they hadn't been handled much.

While I busied myself, Clare sat at the kitchen table bemoaning her loss. "Every night of my life, I'm going to know that some slimy fascist fugitive is ogling my favorite film. There were actresses who had to sleep with him to get the picture made. I never knew that. Damn, damn, damn!"

She put this melancholy theme through several variations, but it was the same lament. And it was my fault. I tried to console her, but not very effectively.

"Well . . . we did get *something*," I observed with unconvincing cheerfulness. "I don't think this could be Jürgen's work. It's a feature film in thirty-five-millimeter. Look what I found."

I held out a messy bundle of papers that had been jammed into one of the cartons. There were a couple of personal letters in English scratched off in longhand, others typed in German, and what looked like a manuscript: a piece of writing much inked out and corrected. This last item was written in French and tightly typed on legal-sized paper now crisp and brown with age.

"I think this is a movie called *Judas*. It was made by Max Castle . . . or Kastell. That's what this letter says. It's very old. Wasn't Jürgen saying something about Max Castle last night?"

Clare spread the letters on the table and studied them. As she did so, I noticed her expression alter. The anger and hurt melted away, replaced by deep concentration.

The first letter was from the Chicago film collector Joshua Sloan. Clare had dealt with him several times over the years, never very pleasantly. "Pompous old fart," was how she described him. Addressed to Ira Goldstein and dated 1946, this letter was part of a series (the rest missing) whose subject was a film swap. Old Ira was trading his private reserve of *The Wizard of Oz*, of which he apparently held several prints. Ira had been the film's principal backer; his role in the production was connected with one of his legendary bits of advice. He agreed to invest in the picture on one condition. "Absolutely you *don't* cast Shoiley. The public is sick of her already. You need a good singer. Get that whatsername . . . Judy Rooney. She'll work cheap."

The letter read:

Theodore Roszak

2724 Wacker Drive, Suite 22
Chicago, Illinois
January 16, 1946

Dear Ira:

So the miserly old fox is finally trading his *Wizards*. About time. And of all things, for Dietrichs! Can this mean there is some truth to the rumors we have all heard about Ira the Terrible's one-time intimate relations with Marlene the Magnificent? I do hope so.

I will confess that I am sorely tempted by your proposition. But *four* Marlenes for just *one* Judy! Come now!

Let me make a counter-proposal. I will reluctantly part company with *Shanghai Express* and *Blonde Venus*—both 16 mm., pristine condition. Hate to lose them, but how much longer can I go without a *Wizard* of my own? *Scarlet Empress* is, however, strictly off-limits. Still, think what you are getting. The sheer delight of Marlene vamping the Hot Voodoo in a gorilla suit. Surely it is one of von Sternberg's moments of sheer genius. Beauty and the Beast united. Delicious!

Clare looked up from the letter, an expression of pained disgust across her face. "I always suspected Sloan was a fruitcake. And he owns millions in film treasures. Jesus!"

The letter went on:

Of course, I've heard tell that you never actually look at what you collect. Can that be true? Hopeless philistine! Even so, you must see this from the connoisseur's viewpoint. There *are* pictures on these strips of film, and for some of us, they are dear in ways that money cannot measure. For that reason, *Scarlet Empress*, never!

Yours faithfully,
Josh

This was followed by a letter from Sloan dated February 21, 1946:

Dear Ira:

No wonder they call you the Shylock of the celluloid marketplace. Very well, I'll throw in *Morocco*, though God knows I hate surrendering Marlene's exquisite lebby impersonation. Movies were never tastefully bolder. That really ought to satisfy you. But I suspect it will not. In which case, let me sweeten the offer. I can put you on to an alternate supplier of Dietrichs. I know for certain that Curt Mangold in Toronto has at least three of her films, one of which is *Scarlet*

Empress. And I know he's willing to trade—for the right item. Now here's a hot tip. Curt has lately become passionately involved (filmically speaking) with Louise Brooks. And along that line, I have something that just might serve as tempting bait: a film called *Judas Jedermann,* directed by Max Castle (*né* von Kastell). Ever heard of it? I daresay not. I've been unable to find a listing for it anywhere since it came my way early this year. A mystery movie indeed. But there is the possibility—*just* the possibility—that luscious Louise makes her German film debut here.

How do I come to have the film? Bear with me while I boast a little. For the past year, I have enjoyed a most convenient cultural liaison with the War Department. I have agreed to purchase any unclaimed film (sight unseen and regardless of condition) that U.S. forces collect as spoils of war in occupied German territory. For these exalted cultural purposes, I am known officially as the American Universities Film Archive, headquartered at the U. of Chicago, where, one day, my collection will reside. All very public-spirited and academic, what? (Tax-deductible contributions always welcome.) Thus far, I have for mere nickels and dimes acquired some sixty films or fragments thereof, courtesy of the U.S. Army, mainly from bombed-out movie houses or military field theaters. (Can you guess what most of these turn out to be? Disney cartoons!) I have also picked up about a half-dozen prints of a little propaganda horror called *Jud Süss.* Would be willing to trade.

The Castle film, I am informed, was recovered (oddly enough) from an abandoned Catholic orphanage outside Dessau where it had been placed in storage by one of the producers at UFA studios, who feared that it would otherwise be destroyed by the Nazis. (Apparently Castle's work was among those on the agenda for liquidation.) Frankly, the film is a pig in a poke. I haven't viewed it myself and probably won't. German silents are a taste I have not acquired. In any case, my policy is not to expose these prehistoric nitrate jobs to the light of day. I trade them off (as is) as quickly as I can.

I don't know much about Castle myself. You may have come across him during his later, more obscure, Hollywood years. I once owned a film of his from that period, something he did for Republic called *Bum Rap*—a true stinker and chopped to ribbons besides. But I hear his early work is of some artistic interest—if you can find it. You know about his notoriously ill-fated *Martyr,* of course. That provides the tie-in with Louise. I have tracked down some old publicity material; it reports that her appearance as Mary Magdalen in *Martyr* was the *second* time she worked for Castle. About five years earlier, while Castle was still at UFA, she was cast in another Biblical opus of his that seems never to have been released. Now that might very well be *this* film, which seems to date from circa 1925. Whatever the movie is, it appears to be a complete, five reel, 35 mm. feature. Present it that way to Curt, and he is likely to bite.

Let's face it, Ira old friend. If I were your standard scholarly collector, I would treasure an item like this. But hopeless sentimentalist that I am, I simply must have *Wizard*. So I'm willing to include the Castle film with *Morocco* as the bargaining chip that could get you *Empress*. Deal?

Ever in hope,

Josh

There followed a letter in German from June of 1935. It was written on the letterhead stationery of the Universum Film Aktien Gesellschaft—UFA, the once famous studio that had established the German film industry, and which was taken over by the Nazis shortly after this letter was written. It was signed by a Thea von Pölzig who was identified as a senior studio executive. There was a rough pencil translation at the bottom of the letter, now barely legible, which might have been done for either Sloan or Goldstein. Where it had blurred away, Clare's German was strong enough to fill in. It read:

Dear Sister Irena:

We have received word that UFA can expect a visit from our ever-vigilant Reichsminister of Culture within the next several days. The result will no doubt be a significant reduction in the holdings of our film library. As good Germans, we will, of course, welcome this economy measure and the unsolicited lesson in Aryan aesthetic theory with which it is certain to be applied.

In order to save the Reichministry's valuable time, I am sending you a selection of films that I believe would otherwise take up an unwarranted amount of its critical attention and cost it the price of a good-sized bonfire. They are some of the early works of our own Max. You will please follow the instructions in my previous letters for their storage and safekeeping until further notice.

Cordially,

Thea

The oldest document in the bunch had the look of an office memo, again on UFA letterhead. It was dated May 14, 1924, and signed by the same Thea von Pölzig, whose title at that time was something like "Production Assistant." Once more, there was a translation penciled in across the bottom of the badly crumpled page. It read:

To: J.M.B.
From: T.V.P.

No use. *Judas Jedermann* will not be licensed for exhibition. Three meetings with the Censor's Office since last fall and no progress. They persist in their opinion that the film is obscene, even though they cannot (or will not) identify portions for editing. Following *Simon the Magician*, Max's reputation seems to stain everything he does indelibly. I recommend we withdraw *Judas* for at least a year. Meanwhile, you should seek release in the United States, perhaps through our connections at Universal.

Poor Max! If he has not already made up his mind, this news is sure to send him on his way. A prophet without honor . . .

Clare placed the letters in a neat pile to one side of the table. We were finally down to the manuscript. And here we found ourselves running an obstacle course. Clare's French would have been more than adequate to giving the piece a read, but the more closely she studied this withered and congested sheaf of papers, the more illegible it became. Inked out and written over, filled with typos, annotated along the margins in a private shorthand, it practically defied comprehension.

"Well . . . it's an interview. An interview with Castle," Clare observed. That much she could pin down by flipping through the first few pages. "Lots of mangled German scattered all over. Quotes, I guess. But, God, this will take hours to work through."

Shuffling further into the creased and faded pages, she came upon a folded envelope, itself covered with notes. It bore Swiss postage and a postmark for August 1939. The return address, cramped into one corner and barely legible, read: "MK, *Sturmwaisen*, Zurich." Clare loitered over the words. "MK. Max Kastell, right? But what's *Sturmwaisen*?" she asked, as if I might know. "Storm something. *Waisen* . . . that's waifs, orphans, something like that." The translation told us nothing. She shrugged and went on. The envelope was addressed, in a sweeping Germanic hand, to a Geneviève Joubert at *CinéArt* magazine in Paris.

"Ha!" Clare burst out. The name struck a chord. "I knew her. Not well, but we met a couple of times. In Paris after the war. She hung out at the Cinémathèque. Wrote for a number of publications. I liked her. Strong tastes. Lots of savvy. I suppose this could be her work.

She did some interviews. Directors mainly. I have a marvelous piece she did with Franju—before he was a name."

The envelope was too small to have held the bulky manuscript. It seemed empty, but wasn't. Opened and given a shake, it yielded a yellowed snapshot about passport size. Clare looked it over, then held it out to me. A man, perhaps in his thirties. Stern-faced, dark, messy hair falling into his eyes. "Castle . . . ?" she asked. "Could be a photo to accompany the article. If that's when the photo was sent, and *if* that's when the article was written, then this obviously never reached print. *CinéArt* went out of business when the war started—along with the rest of western civilization." Then she sighed. "There's no telling what all this is. Or why it's in with the film. But I don't see that we have any choice but to decipher it."

Inside, I gave a small, private prayer of thanks. The manuscript, along with the letters, had apparently distracted Clare's attention from my bungled attempt to capture *Les Enfants du Paradis*. Mercifully, she never mentioned the episode again.

"What about the film?" I asked. "Why don't we take it over to the theater and run it?"

Clare shook her head, opting for caution. "You have to be careful with old film stock like this. If it *is* as old as these letters from UFA say, you just can't expose it to the air. There have been cases of old nitrate films exploding if they're not handled right. We'd better leave this to Sharkey."

Sharkey had a good deal of experience with delicate film—repairing it, projecting it, reshooting it. It was a special skill that earned him some decent money from time to time. Reluctantly, Clare phoned the number we had for him—a temporary beach residence in Venice West. The groggy female voice that finally answered promised to pass the message along to Sharkey when he came to, but hinted he might not be ambulatory until much later in the day. It took three or four more calls and a deal of wrangling before Clare persuaded Sharkey to meet us at The Classic that Wednesday afternoon. When he showed up for the screening, he looked much the worse for several days and nights of hard partying. A blond, busty young thing named Shannon came with him; she looked all of sixteen. Clare treated her, as she did all Sharkey's inamoratae, with practiced cruelty—not that it made much of a dent on Shannon. She seemed to move in a semi-stupor.

I still had no idea who had broken off with whom in this latest, prolonged state of war between Clare and Sharkey. Each was behaving like the aggrieved party. After sparring through a few preliminary rounds of nasty knocks and jabs, Clare, as if calling for a truce, finally got to the subject of the Castle film.

"I don't suppose you remember the big screwup of the other night."

Sharkey squinted back at her uncertainly, as if there might be any number of big screwups he should remember but didn't. He had so far shown no sign whatever of recalling our misadventure with Jürgen's car.

"Okay, okay, never mind," Clare went on, summoning Sharkey to follow her back to the projection booth where the film was waiting. "Look, we want to screen this," she explained. "It's old. Very old. Pre-1925 possibly."

"Hey, wow!" Sharkey said. "Where'd you get this?"

"Promise not to tell? Jonny and a friend of his swiped it the other night."

"No kidding!" Sharkey was impressed. He glanced over at me. "Where'd you get it, pal?"

Clare cut me off. "That's top secret for now. We just want you to run this for us, if it's in any shape for that. Wouldn't trust anyone else with the assignment." Which was as close as I ever heard Clare come to giving Sharkey a kind word.

At once, everything between the two of them changed. A film—an undiscovered film—had entered their relationship, something that rose above personal hostilities. Hovering over the stack of cartons that held Max Castle's mysterious movie, they became totally clinical, partners in a professional enterprise.

"If this does date back to the twenties," Sharkey remarked as he pulled a canister out of its carton, "we may never get it out of the can. We might not have anything but yellow dust in here by now."

"It's been kept in film vaults for years," Clare said. "As far as we can tell, it hasn't been shown since it went into storage."

"Well, that could help, but . . . hello! What's this?" Sharkey was trying, without success, to slip a knife blade under the rim of the canister. "I'll be damned if this thing isn't soldered shut! Never saw that before. Well now, that's hopeful. But how do we get it open?"

After several minutes of trying in vain to pry the canister open, Sharkey had an idea. He hustled us out of The Classic and into a rear door at Moishe's. There he requested use of the deli's electric can opener. "If the can's been sealed tight, maybe we're in business."

We watched with mounting anticipation as Sharkey punched the opener into the first canister. There was a faint hiss. He looked up, startled. "Did you hear that? The thing's vacuum-packed. Who the hell vacuum-packs movies?" He quickly ran the opener around the rim of all five canisters, but he wouldn't open them until we were back in The Classic out of the bright light. There, slowly, he uncovered the first can. Inside was a full thirty-five-millimeter reel. Sharkey sent up a cheer. "This, my friends, is like finding a live dinosaur in Griffith Park." He quickly and expertly checked the film through, then announced it was in nearly perfect condition. He saw no breaks and the film stock seemed supple. "Okay," he said. "Suppose we run her once around the track."

Sharkey checked through all the reels, but could find no indication of the correct sequence. Each was marked, as the canisters had been, *Judas Jedermann*, but none was numbered. He chose a reel at random and proceeded to mount it on the projector. Within fifteen minutes, the four of us—Clare, Sharkey, myself, and a bored and bewildered Shannon—were watching a film that, very likely, had been made before any of us were born, and which might have been entombed ever since.

6 THE GRAVE ROBBER'S PROGRESS

The theater lights dim, the projector chatters, a shaft of light shoots across the darkness. Like the miraculous finger of God, it touches the waiting screen, void as a desert, and the screen comes alive with images. After a sleep of possibly four decades, the film *Judas Jedermann* awakens and moves before my eyes.

The experience is as vivid now as it was when it first happened. Allow me to pause at this point to recapture that moment of discovery full strength, realizing, as I do, how difficult it must be to imagine a time when the name of Max Castle was all but unknown, a cast-off on the cultural scrap heap. Some six months earlier I'd caught a few blurred and choppy minutes of the kind of movie the world remembered Castle for—or rather the kind of movie that explained why nearly nobody remembered him. I really couldn't say I'd seen *Feast of the Undead*, not even a fair sample; but I wouldn't have argued with Clare or anyone else who dismissed the man's work as garbage. That was one Max Castle movie; I was about to see another, the film that would mark the beginning of the Castle cult. No, not even the beginning. We stand at the door of the tomb, watching the first barely discernible twitch of a forgotten filmmaker's resurrection, uncertain whether the movement we see is real or a trick of the eye.

By the time a shambling and bleary-eyed Sharkey showed up to project the film, Clare and I had put in several days piecing together the surviving remnants of Castle's biography. There wasn't much to go on, and what there was included more rumor than fact. Certainly our research gave us no reason to believe that we were dealing with anything more than another of Hollywood's many hard-luck stories, a second-rater who washed out early and never made a comeback. Here's what little we knew about the man as we sat down to watch his *Judas Jedermann*.

Standard film histories remembered Castle (or Kastell, or von Kastell) as one of the early German Expressionist directors, a wunderkind who rose rapidly to prominence in the years immediately following World War One. He made his first movie before he was twenty years old, a thriller produced at the UFA Studios called *Die Träumende Augen (The Dreaming Eyes)*. It was listed in the filmographies as still another tale of hypnotism, lust, and bloody murder—obviously an imitation of *The Cabinet of Dr. Caligari* on which the young Castle had worked as an apprentice technician. With some digging, we were able to find a fragmentary reference to Thea von Pölzig at UFA; she was mentioned as the script editor for *The Dreaming Eyes*.

Following that apparently successful film, Castle fell in with a group of UFA directors who specialized in Gothic fantasies. They picked up the name *Die Grabräuber*—the Grave Robbers. At the time, their work was generally regarded as, at best, morbid, commercial trash. At worst, it was called decadent and psychotic. Yet, at one time or another during its brief existence, the group included such stellar talents as Joseph von Päppen, Franz Olbricht, Abel Völker—directors who were destined to change the course of moviemaking in Germany and America. Collectively, the young Grave Robbers won their spurs by inventing the entire repertoire of movie horrors: vampires, ghouls, homicidal sleepwalkers, werewolves. Their films were immensely popular with a war-weary German audience looking for supernatural escape.

Were Castle's movies of that period anything better than hackwork? It was impossible to say, since most, if not all, of these films had long since dropped out of sight. Producers and exhibitors of the time treated such work as dispensable merchandise. One authority on German films of the period touched briefly and disapprovingly cn Castle, singling him out as the most sensationally lewd of the Grave Robbers. But the same study included a tantalizing quotation from Abel Völker. "Even in those early days," the great director remarked, "we could see that young Max was the best among us. He thought about the medium of film more deeply—always innovating, innovating. Of course, the pictures we made at UFA then—they were rubbish. Even so Max always saw possibilities. Look, in these spook movies he made, the lighting technique—'split-lighting' he called it. Nobody yet has reproduced that. A great cinematic talent. Of course, later, it was very sad. Hollywood—it ate him alive."

About 1923, Castle got his chance to venture beyond the Gothic ghetto. UFA assigned him a film called *Simon the Magician.* He was given big-name talent to work with: Emil Jannings, Hanna Ralph, the young Peter Lorre. Once again, Thea von Pölzig's name appeared buried among the lesser credits as one of the set designers. There was little more we could find about the movie beyond a few passing references in a study of the German director Georg Pabst. The remarks had to do with Louise Brooks. Pabst was the man who turned Brooks into a star, featuring her as the classic vamp in his *Pandora's Box.* But before Pabst discovered her sexual allure, Castle had already used her as a slave girl in *Simon the Magician.* It was only a brief appearance for the young actress, but it nevertheless attracted considerable and scandalized attention. Hypnotized by Simon the black magician, she is induced to perform a dance that, as one critic reported it, began as offensively indecent and finished as intolerably obscene. Reputedly, the film contained lots of sadism and perversion, all thinly disguised as an edifying saga of early Christianity. Upon its release, it was met by a wave of public protest. Universally condemned as no better than smut, the movie was withdrawn, never again to find its

105

way to the screen. Along with other Castle movies, it may have eventually been destroyed by the Nazis as part of the "garbage culture" they meant to liquidate.

Where did *Judas Jedermann*, or *Judas Everyman* in its English translation, fit into Castle's early filmography? There was no record to be found of the picture anywhere. Possibly it was his last German production, destined to receive even less public exposure than *Simon the Magician*, perhaps none at all. We had to settle for whatever we could deduce from Thea von Pölzig's terse memo. Attacked by the censors before the final cut was completed, it was never released but simply boxed and shelved at UFA. Clare, still arguing with Jürgen von Schachter at the back of her mind, made a smug observation. Castle and the Grave Robbers sounded like exactly what Professor Kracauer set out to study in his book: filmmakers who had driven the German public crazy with paranoid terrors and ghastly fantasies. If the professor was correct, then, ironically, the Nazis were trying to destroy the very disease of which they were the major symptom.

In the mid-twenties, along with a boatload of German movie talent, Castle came to Hollywood. There he received the usual publicity buildup the studios reserved for foreign directors and stars. His name was now officially changed from Kastell to Castle, and in 1926 he was contracted by the fledgling MGM Studios to handle a big-budget historical production: *The Martyr*. It was, like *Simon the Magician*, a Christians-and-lions extravaganza, possibly meant to capitalize on the air of scandal surrounding Castle's censored German film. Rod La Rocque was signed for the title role, fresh from success with DeMille, and Louise Brooks was selected to play the role of Mary Magdalen in a reportedly sensational interpretation. Castle at once spirited his cast and crew away to Rome and Jerusalem to begin filming. The movie was one of the earliest to involve extensive (and expensive) location work, something the studio used for all it was worth in its publicity. Supposedly, *The Martyr* enjoyed one of the fattest production budgets in film history. Even so, it soared over cost within the first month of shooting. For the next year, the trade papers carried occasional items on the film's progress, its difficulties, its triumphs, its unprecedented scope and expense. There were rumors that Brooks had experienced an epiphany while filming at Golgotha.

When it was completed, the movie simultaneously launched Castle in America and sank him. He came in with a film thirty-one reels

106

long. Eleven hours. Metro refused to release it at even half that length and demanded major surgery. Castle refused. After months of haggling, the film was cut by the studio to a still weighty four hours. Castle threatened legal action to reclaim the edited footage. He argued that the film belonged to its maker, not to the studio, but the cause was hopeless. The case became moot when Metro announced that it had preemptively destroyed the unused material. Decrying the act as vandalism, Castle disowned *The Martyr* in its studio-revised form. As released by MGM, the movie proved to be both an artistic and financial disaster. It was withdrawn one week after its premiere, never again to be seen: another in the long list of Castle's lost films.

Following this debacle, no studio in America would hire Castle without placing him on a tight rein. There were a few more abortive contracts, but within two years of his arrival in the States, Castle had become one of the industry's least employable directors. In one of the trade journals for 1927 there was a brief note that mentioned he was assisting in some unspecified capacity at Universal on the silent original of *The Cat and the Canary*. The director on that archetypal piece of Hollywood Gothic was his recently arrived colleague Paul Leni. Possibly this was an odd job meant to keep him solvent while he and MGM wrangled over the cut on *The Martyr*. After that Castle dropped out of sight for three or four years, except for the occasional report on how his ill-fated litigation with MGM was going.

Then, in the thirties, he began a second, less celebrated, career, migrating along the low-rent fringes of the American studios as a free-lance director. Nobody would trust him with anything better than B-movies. Of these he did several—hack thrillers and horror films. A return to his Grave Robber period. From his childhood Sharkey thought he could just dimly recall a few of Castle's latter-day cheap-sters. "Classic awful" was the way he described them, not altogether disapprovingly. Clare, on the other hand, was quick to state that she'd never seen a Castle movie—other than *Feast of the Undead*, which she had only recently screened at The Classic. Her parents, she explained, wouldn't allow her to go to movies like that. Not because they were scary, she hastened to add, but because they were *bad*. Still, these pictures had been financially successful enough to keep Castle steadily employed. A few of them still got shown on late-night television or as midnight movies on Halloween.

We were able to find extremely little critical commentary on Castle's work. What there was dated back to the early thirties, all of it dealing with *The Martyr*. For the most part these were attempts to guess what the film might have looked like before MGM applied the knife. Was it perhaps a lost masterpiece? Clare managed to dig up one article along these lines that lent Castle a bit more stature in her eyes. It was a piece written by Alexander Woollcott for *The Dial* in which the noted critic used the fate of *The Martyr* as an opportunity to castigate the barbarism of Hollywood. While the essay pushed some praise Castle's way, it gave no details about the movie. As far as we could discover, that was the last time Castle or his work had enjoyed a glimmer of artistic visibility in America.

That brought us to the *CinéArt* interview. On this, Clare and I spent an entire evening and most of a night, picking our way through the rough French and German of the unpolished draft. There were passages that defied comprehension, even legibility. But we could recognize that the piece dealt mainly with some filming Castle was doing in France during the late thirties. This was the cloudiest part of his career, but also the part that most teased the curiosity. Seeking the opportunity for more ambitious work than Hollywood would permit, Castle had returned to Europe several times. There he traveled, did some shooting, and tried to raise money for his own work— apparently without much success. Certainly nothing he started during these junkets ever got completed. Even Geneviève Joubert—if she was indeed the author of the manuscript—hadn't seen more than a few rough-cut scenes. But these she wrote about in glowing terms as daring experimental efforts. At one point, she referred to them as the *fusée à temps*, the time bomb of modern cinema, unrecognized now, but destined to have the greatest impact in the future.

It was pretty obvious that Castle was cueing the author along these lines, shamelessly celebrating himself in vague but pretentious terms. At one point, he characterized himself as "the most unknown of film-makers." But he bravely accepted this role without self-pity, or so he claimed. As the author recorded it, ". . . he muses on the theme of the unknown creator . . . the creator *behind* the creator, the god without a face, without a name. He explains that in the film industry one's name does not always appear on one's work." Then, quoting Castle: "What is the director in America? The shop foreman. Under orders. You do part of a film, half of a film. In America, they have an art form called the patchwork. A dozen ladies come together, each sews on a patch, finally a pattern emerges. We have this in Hollywood too. A patch job, we call it. Two, three, four directors overlapping on one film. But it is not art, simply cheap production. Quite mad."

Here it was noted that Castle laughed sardonically and then went on. "Still, as we have mentioned, even on this crass assembly line, it is sometimes possible to do work of significance, provided one knows how to conceal the result. It is like magic tricks. Now you see it, now you don't." His interviewer, who apparently knew what this remark meant, agreed and then led the discussion off into a turgid digression which outran Clare's German, no doubt because so much of it was abbreviated or highly elliptical. Toward the end of this baffling passage, she came upon what seemed to be some notes the author had jotted down to elucidate the discussion. ". . . as if Rembrandt had treated his paintings with a glaze that covered more than it revealed. One had to wait for this glaze to fade, to fall away—perhaps for centuries. What then would we know of Rembrandt? Suppose his finest work lay hidden under a trivial doodle."

The interviewer asked only briefly and timidly about Castle's Hollywood potboilers. He responded to the question with good humor, claiming that he had come to enjoy making "these little toys." When his interviewer expressed surprise, he explained, "But these are the *true* movies, are they not? Movies for the millions. With these I reach the world of the streets. But I tell you this: this shit I am busily depositing in the movie houses across America is more fertile than the world knows. The eyes that can appreciate this work . . ." Here Clare paused to pick through the German word by word, "Let's see. He says 'the eyes . . . have not yet seen the light.' I suppose that means 'have not yet been born.' " Castle was coming across as bombastic. I could tell that Clare disapproved.

At several points in the interview, the author seemed to be quoting from a piece of writing that Castle was asked to elucidate. It took several readings before Clare got it clear that the quotes were from something Castle himself had written—an essay on film theory. But where had it been published? There was no indication. Clare was exasperated, for the quoted fragments managed to be intriguing without being illuminating. But then, that was very much the character of the entire piece. It left the reader wholly uncertain where Castle's words had been edited, paraphrased, reworked. There were large sections that had been inked out, others where the French and the German, both given, seemed to mean very different things. Yet there was just enough to get a hook into the mind—Clare's mind, at least—and to give the blurred impression of Castle as a serious (if often

109

pompous) thinker. Finally, Clare gave up, pretending to dismiss the tattered little manuscript as hopelessly obscure and probably not to be trusted. She didn't like the way Castle came across, didn't like the gullibility of his interlocutor. But in the months that followed, more than once I found her perusing the interview, trying to construe it more clearly. Mangled as it was, the item proved to be an effective piece of bait for both of us.

On the back of the last page, there was a personal memo scrawled by the author and a date—August 29, 1939. Two days before the outbreak of war. Whatever film Castle had come to France to make, it, too, remained unfinished.

On my own, I was able to make one marginally important contribution to our hasty research. Chased off to the library by Clare, I brought home several scraps of information on Castle and one item of substance: an article from a 1925 issue of *McClure's*. The magazine had run a brief essay-interview on Castle that dated from soon after his arrival in the United States. At the time, he was being trumpeted by MGM as the boy-genius of filmdom. The *McClure's* piece dealt mainly with his much-publicized movie *The Martyr*, which was then in the planning stage. The magazine wanted to treat the film as a major artistic undertaking. But what came through plainly in the article was Castle's minimal enthusiasm for the project. There had been so many of these biblical epics, he complained; it would be a welcome relief when he could get on to better things.

He was asked what sort of movie he would prefer to make. A movie about the movies, was Castle's answer. He already had the film scripted; he'd brought it with him from Germany. Would it be something like *Merton of the Movies* or *Ella Cinders*? No, no. Nothing so trivial. Castle had something far more ambitious in mind. "How the movies shape our soul," was the way he put it. His interviewer found this "darkly Germanic." What did it mean? Castle answered with a question. "Have you never wondered why they have such magic for us—the movie actors? The stars? Because of their riches, their glamour, do you think? No, there is something else. They are children of light." That was the name Castle intended to use for his film. *Children of Light*. "Think how we go to meet them—in a dark place, a theater, an underworld." Castle wanted to capture the power of that moment "when these strange creatures enter our lives, when they become the light that shineth in the darkness."

Snidely, Clare commented, "Good thing he never had a shot at making it. Sounds like a dud for sure."

And, of course, the movie never did get made. What lay ahead for Castle was the debacle of *The Martyr* and fifteen years riding a downward spiral. The last trace we could find of him were a couple of low-budget programmers released in 1941. They carried the not very encouraging titles *Kiss of the Vampire* and *Axis Agent*. After that, the only reference we could find was a brief obituary in the November 15, 1941 edition of *Variety*. It read:

> Max Castle, German film director who immigrated to Hollywood in 1925, was reported to be among those lost at sea when the free French freighter *Le Colombe* was torpedoed by a Nazi U-boat off the coast of Spain last Thursday. Castle is best remembered for the horror films *Count Lazarus, House of Blood*, and *Feast of the Undead.* One of the youngest directors in film history, he began his career at the age of nineteen with the UFA studios in Berlin. In the United States he directed at Universal, Paramount, Republic, Prestige International, and Allied Eagle. His most recent film was *Axis Agent* for Monogram. Castle was on his way to Switzerland to discuss a new production when he met his untimely end at the age of forty-two.

The film ran for just under ninety minutes. When it was finished, Sharkey was the first to speak, cracking a brittle silence.

"I give up. Was that a *movie?*"

Neither Clare nor I answered. We had no name for what we'd seen. We couldn't be certain that we'd viewed the whole film or that we'd seen it in anything like its correct sequence. What we'd watched was obviously a rough cut with all the ragged edges still showing. Yet, we knew that none of this mattered, for, after several minutes of talk, it was clear that the film, just as we had seen it, had *worked*. It had left us all with exactly the same experience of absolute, numbing horror. Not the horror of fear, but of revulsion. We'd been touched by an obscenity deliberately pressed to the limits of tolerance—and then held there in a risky balance for almost too long to bear, but not quite. Less artfully handled, the raw morbidity of the film might have driven us to stop the projector or leave the theater. But the experience had been so cleverly shaped and controlled that we stayed, we watched. We were held in spite of ourselves.

But by what? Curiosity? Or by some deeper aesthetic pleasure we would shudder to admit?

Our fascination had been so ingeniously captured that, for a long while afterward, everything Clare and Sharkey and I said about the film was shot through with an undertone of resentment. None of us wanted to admit that our sensibilities could be manipulated with such calculated skill. It's never easy to surrender to artistic genius, to admire a power that can reach in and violate the privacy of our most guarded feelings. Clare and Sharkey were sparring with the film, talking around and about its central effect. Oddly enough, it was Shannon who put an end to that. Young, vague, and impenetrably spacey, she was the first to lower her defenses and give the sense of moral anguish that enveloped all of us the appreciation it deserved. Her eyes still fixed glassily on the now darkened screen, she spoke over something Clare was saying, half-whispering the remark more to herself than to us.

"I guess that's how it would feel to be Judas. . . ."

Clare went silent. We waited for more, but that was all Shannon had to say. She sat playfully tugging at her long amber hair. Clare asked sharply, and a bit grudgingly, "How would you know?"

Shannon shrugged. "It's just I remember from school." She was talking about the Catholic school she hadn't yet graduated from. "We talked about that once—Judas and Jesus, you know. . . ."

The comment was so lamely made, it was difficult to take what she said seriously. Shannon's manner was all but completely mindless: the unfocused stare, the slack jaw, the sleepy voice. Nevertheless, her remark was the breakthrough, the handle we needed to get our first tentative grip on Castle's art. After some fashion we couldn't yet understand, this film had captured the essence of *being* Judas. Hence the title, *Judas Everyman*, the Judas in all of us. Perhaps it took someone still naively close enough to her religious background, like Shannon, to seize upon that experience fully. Sharkey, Clare, and I were all fashionably skeptical types. I doubt that any of us had ever pondered the crime of Judas before this. For us, it was part of a defunct religious mythology. Yet the film we'd just watched had brought that ancient act of treachery, the betrayal of a living god, to life within us. It had passed into our consciousness like swallowed filth. It was only after we'd admitted the film's disturbing impact that we could go on to the question we all wanted to ask. Clare raised it. "All right, how was it done?"

There was a belligerent edge to her question. I understood why. Castle's film contradicted everything she was teaching me. Nothing provoked her critical ire more than a production that was dominated by visual gimmicks, technical tricks. Clare regarded this as the besetting vice of film—to be swamped by its own rich technology. Precisely because this was so powerful a medium, she insisted that it must be disciplined by artistic discrimination. That was nothing less than an ethical principle for Clare; at the time, she was feeling the need to defend it with special tenacity. That summer the movie that was making the most waves in the art houses was a quirky little novelty called *Last Year at Marienbad,* an example of what some called "pure cinema." Clare, for all her love of French film, hated it. Where others saw a bold, new liberating use of the medium, Clare saw an arbitrary hash of mesmerizing images. A movie, she argued, isn't a Rorschach inkblot.

What, then, could she say of Max Castle's *Judas?* Here was a film that had no recognizable narrative structure. We couldn't even agree among ourselves on the sequence of reels. There was no obvious beginning, middle, end—no clear location in time or place, no clear distinction between reality, hallucination, dream. The movie was all visual contradiction and paradox. Its gritty *cinéma vérité* texture (remarkably ahead of its time, right down to its use of hand-held-camera technique) suggested a hyperrealistic story, almost a pseudodocumentary reconstruction of the life of Judas. But the film was anything but realistic. Contradicting its own camera style, it was a deeply psychological study, a carefully architectured nightmare that placed us inside the mind of the guilt-maddened Judas at some point after his great act of betrayal.

This wasn't, however, the historical Judas. It was indeed Judas-Everyman presented in modern dress, moving through a modern Everytown—"modern," meaning the wide-open, sin-ridden Berlin of the early 1920s, the cabarets, the brothels, the rathskellers. As far as we could tell, this Judas was a political fanatic, part of some underground revolutionary clique, who had ratted on a comrade; but the ideological coloration of the crime was deliberately obscure. One could read any number of interpretations into the movie, from radical to reactionary. All that mattered was the emotional convulsion through which the traitor was passing, and this unfolded, not as a story, but as a prolonged horror exquisitely studied from many sides. Although the film moved on the screen with a jagged, surging en-

113

ergy—the editing at points included more cuts than the eye could register, achieving a dizzy pace—all its power was focused on that single experience. As Clare put it, paying the film as much of a compliment as she could squeeze out, we were watching a piece of "cinematic sculpture"—a monumental symbol of guilt fashioned out of moving images.

The more we talked, the less certain we became that the film was actually as much of a rough cut as we'd initially assumed. Everything we'd seen needed to be there; every detail made its indispensable contribution, even the material which on first viewing had looked like outtakes. Take, for example, the now famous and much-studied sequence in which Judas (in fact or in fantasy) cuts off the hand that received the thirty pieces of silver. In the film this appears in three consecutive versions with a rough splice between each. One assumes the director hasn't yet chosen which to use, which to cut. But the effect this run of images produces, the agonizing sense of remorse, requires all three versions, each filmed at a different speed, each from a different angle, building up to the final slow-motion repetition that becomes so terrifying in the viewer's anticipation that one wants to hide one's eyes. Even the jumpy splices between the sequences add to the shock of the event, almost as if one felt the ax striking, cutting.

Clare was obviously reluctant to admit that techniques like this could have the effect they did. She insisted through two more viewings of the film that day—each time with a different sequence of reels—that there had to be some underlying narrative element, some line of psychological development that gave the film's images their compelling power. Now, so many years later, when the qualities of Castle's "lost films" (the *Judas* was the first to be found) have become so celebrated and widely imitated, it's difficult to imagine anyone holding out against them the way Clare did. She was resisting the push-button precision with which the *Judas* produced its effects. Grudgingly, she appreciated the achievement, but she wanted it to have something to do with aesthetic taste, with recognizable literary values. Even before we saw *Judas Everyman*, I can recall her telling me that if film or any artistic medium had the power to trigger our deep involuntary psychic machinery, it would be wrong to do so. It should be regarded as impermissible and no critic should accede to it. Art, she contended, must enter our lives through the discriminating mind. Otherwise, it might as well be a narcotic.

For several days, through repeated viewing of *Judas Everyman*,

Clare kept searching for the aesthetic method of the film—some subtle way in which a story line or character structure had been smuggled into Castle's images. Eventually, she made a quiet surrender. *Judas* wasn't film as she knew and loved film; but its emotional power was undeniable. Sharkey, on the other hand, received the film with unstinting enthusiasm. Its secret, he was convinced, lay in its purely formal properties: the editing, the lighting, the pacing, the camera angles. For the first time, I realized that, flabby as he was becoming in body and mind, Sharkey—if he managed to stay sober long enough—could still toss off an impressive job of film analysis. He was the one who called our attention to the way Castle used staircases throughout the film, always at crazy, vertiginous angles, the camera following a racing figure from behind—and always downward. The entire movie was tied together by the visual motif of reckless winding descent into engulfing shadows. Shame, panic, damnation . . . it was the perfect image.

Our last screening of the *Judas* that day became a grueling session of sequence-by-sequence dissection in which Sharkey tried to persuade Clare of his position. Only gradually did I come to realize that through some gap between Clare's reluctance and Sharkey's enthusiasm, an understanding of Max Castle that was all my own was being born. I listened to both; I leaned this way and that in agreement. But deep inside I knew that neither was right, because neither had yet absorbed the full thrust of the film. They were analyzing too soon, before they had opened themselves fully, as I felt I'd opened myself and wanted to open still further with each successive viewing, accepting the fearful penetration of Castle's art like a surgeon's blade that cuts to the quick in order to heal.

The film had meaning, as Clare insisted every movie must. But that meaning lay deeper than the literary qualities she looked for, deeper, too, than the technical tricks that preoccupied Sharkey. Even Shannon, who had exposed herself so unguardedly to Castle's power, hadn't followed her naive intuition far enough. Yes, we'd been made to feel the guilt of Judas. But why? For what purpose? Instinctively, I knew there was an answer to this question somewhere in the film. If I'd dared put it into words at that point, I would have said (not fully knowing what I meant when I said it) that the answer lay buried in the medium itself. I'd never until that day seen anything that needed so much to be a movie in order to say what it had to say. It needed this dark dungeon called the theater, this square of dancing light called the screen that was so much like the doorway into another realm, this hypnotic witness of the eye feeding upon the rush of pulsing images it watched.

It was something like this: imagine confronting the first human being who spoke. Nothing the creature said, no matter how eloquent, would be as important as the blunt fact of its speaking. This, apart from anything it said, would itself be a statement. And that statement would be: *I am human.* That was how Castle had used the medium of film. To say something that only this cunning art of light and darkness could say. Which was . . . ?

There I went blank. Only a spinning confusion filled my thoughts, as if I were staring down into an abyss. At some point along the line, one word flashed into my mind and I clung to it. *Unclean.* Unclean, meaning unholy, meaning profane, meaning hopelessly fallen. Unclean meaning taboo. I couldn't recall ever using the word in this sense. It was part of a religious vocabulary I knew only from books or from courses in school. I realized the experience was one of the world's oldest teachings—that a thing, an act, a person may be unclean, therefore abominable, therefore cast out and damned. I knew this, but had never felt it. Now the crime of Judas had rubbed off on me, and I could feel in the deep fibers of my being what it meant to be so indelibly sullied that the flesh itself would have to be peeled away to remove the stain.

While Clare and Sharkey debated the intricacies of Castle's art, this one thought echoed through me, a nagging disturbance. *The flesh itself . . . the flesh itself.*

On the day we first screened the *Judas*, as we sat through more viewings and endless analysis, we heard nothing more from Shannon after her one naively perceptive comment. While the rest of us— mainly Clare and Sharkey—talked away, she reverted to her vacant and airy lassitude. But she had one more thought about *Judas Everyman.* She offered it with her characteristic abstraction as we left the theater after our final screening of the film.

"Gee," she said, "it's enough to put you off sex for the rest of your life."

We waited for her to say more.

She didn't.

7 ZIP

I never mentioned it to Clare, but on the night following that first screening of *Judas Everyman,* Max Castle entered my dream life, where he has remained, off and on, ever since. Again and again, the now classic Castlean images which have been so often and expertly analyzed by film scholars—the crystal cup, the broken mirror, the ghostly play of moonlight refracted in water or vapor—haunted my sleep, convincing me that they had "taken" at some deep, psychic level and would stay with me, work at me. This was troubling, but it was also special. It was the first time anything about the art of film had penetrated my life so effectively. In an odd, secret sense, this made the movie "mine." I owned it in a way I felt Clare didn't, determined as she was to resist Castle's work. I couldn't know it at the time, but this difference of perception would one day lead to our parting of the ways. For the first time since I had met Clare, I knew I'd discovered something of my own.

Meanwhile, I remained her obedient pupil, learning all she had to tell me about Castle, mimicking her views. We knew the *Judas* was a great find. Of course, it would be shown at The Classic—an exclusive run that would be one of Clare's great coups. In those days, in the art-film business, a big success meant receiving the acclaim of a few dozen fellow fanatics. But Clare insisted the movie mustn't be shown by itself. She wanted something more scholarly and ceremonial. Her idea was: we'd rent as many of Castle's films as we could find and present the *Judas* as part of a festival—the world's first Max Castle film festival. She knew his silent films would probably be unavailable; perhaps they'd all been destroyed during the Nazi years. But she was sure we could round up some of his later American work. Her confidence puzzled me.

"Where are we going to get these movies?" I asked, bewildered by the ambition of her plans. "All you've been able to turn up is one burned-out print of *Feast of the Undead*," I reminded her, "which you scrapped."

She gave me a sly wink. "I've made further inquiries. Turns out your friend Geoff may be of some help."

Now that caught me off guard. Usually when she mentioned Geoff Reuben at all, which was rarely, Clare referred to him as "Geoff the jerk," someone for whom she never had a good word. A film-lore pack rat, Geoff could be the life of the party with his inexhaustible store of in-jokes and anecdotes; but whenever he approached Clare, whom he vastly admired, she brushed him off like two-legged dandruff. "He cheapens the art," she answered when I asked her one day why she treated him so wretchedly. "I'm sure he knows the brassiere size of every starlet in the business, but when it comes to talent, he couldn't tell Garbo from Harlow." Frivolous Geoff and sober Clare were hardly a compatible pair. What kind of help would she expect from him?

"After my French friends came visiting," she explained, "I got to wondering how Geoff happened to know so much about Castle. So I asked. Guess what? Your pal is helping catalogue a couple of studio libraries. A good job for a mental pygmy. He tells me he's gotten together a small cache of Castle films, mainly from Universal and Monogram. Not in good shape, he says—but maybe projectable with repairs."

No doubt Geoff got hired through family connections, but Clare was right: he was the ideal choice for the job, especially since the assignment had nothing to do with taste. On the contrary, what the studios needed was someone whose natural habitat was the cinematic garbage dump. Their object at that point in the industry's history was to get as much of their decaying inventory as possible off their shelves. This had nothing to do with the needs of repertory houses like The Classic. The reason was television. Thanks to the one-eyed monster, there was a booming market for vintage films, particularly old B-movies. These were being printed off in sixteen-millimeter by the carload and sold in package deals to run as filler material between commercials on the late show or Saturday children's programs. The studios were delighted to recycle such moldering antiquities, which they'd long since written off as a dead loss not even worth the cost of storage. Hopalong Cassidys, Tailspin Tommys, Andy Hardys, Charlie Chans . . . films that had died unmourned and been buried in unmarked graves were suddenly given a second life. But what this merchandising campaign required was a mindless enthusiast well-endowed with low commercial instincts who would delight in sorting through the junk; someone who could wander through acres of old celluloid and sing out, "Oh boy, Boston Blackie!" They couldn't have found a better man than Geoff Reuben. That was how he'd happened upon Max Castle's stuff, all but lost amid the dregs of the vault.

As instructed, I got in touch with Geoff and discovered he had about a half-dozen of Castle's quickie thrillers bundled up with some Bulldog Drummonds and Lone Wolfs waiting to be sold off to television distributors at rock-bottom prices. Flattered to be of service to Clare, he eagerly sent us everything he had for previewing, though with the warning that we might not find it in the best condition. That was a gross understatement. One film, *Kiss of the Vampire*, showed up missing two reels; another, *Count Lazarus*, turned out to be a mislabeled canister containing Abbott and Costello. Others were so stretched and curled they couldn't be fed through the projector.

For Clare, making the selections for our festival turned out to be an ordeal by aesthetic misery. It hurt her almost physically to look at damaged film—*any* film, even those of Max Castle, about whom she had such marked reservations. Clare registered every least jiggle in a reasonably good print as if it were a needle jab in the eye; a popping sound track was sheer torture for her. I was with her in one of the city's better first-run theaters when the movie slipped out of sync for not much longer than thirty seconds. Clare rose from her seat to shout obscenities at the nodding projectionist, and then chastised the audience on all sides for being too timid to speak up.

Picking our way through the remnants of Castle's work was especially tormenting for her, since she knew, with old films like these, every cut meant that something had vanished from the world forever; a scene shortened, a shot lost could never be made good. The one battered print there on the screen before us might be the last of the Mohicans. "Poor guy!" I heard her mutter more than once, meaning Castle, whose films, long neglected in the vaults of crassly uncaring studios, chopped and butchered by callous projectionists, had been pushed as close to the edge of extinction as a work of art can get.

It wasn't just Castle she was mourning; it was the terrible fragility of film—good film, bad film, all film. She'd raised the point with me many times. Movies are the most delicate of all human works. Paper and parchment can be cheaply replaced; sculpture lasts for centuries, architecture for millennia. But the plastic to which a movie clings so precariously is vulnerable to a hundred lethal hazards; to restore or reshoot is too costly except for the few films that can still earn the price of their survival at the box office. Whole scenes had been sense-lessly amputated from Castle's work, often leaving what survived incoherent. Where repairs had been attempted, they were slapdash. "Nobody deserves to be manhandled like that," Clare insisted, some-times visibly wincing as if she really cared about what had been lost. And yet, in the next breath, she might blithely refer to what she'd just watched with such furious concentration as "such shit." Her ambivalence kept me off balance. Why was she giving such close attention to work she seemed to despise?

Finally, with Sharkey's expert help, we managed to patch together six of the B-movies Castle had made between 1931 and 1941. Geoff, ransacking the vault at Universal, was able to unearth a presentable print of *Count Lazarus* and restore the missing reels of *Kiss of the Vampire*. Lucky for us. No sampling of Castle's films could do without a bloodsucker or two. Then there was *Shadows over Sing Sing*, Geoff's favorite Castle film. On first viewing, this seemed to be a standard thirties prison saga distinguished only by traces of some startling camera work: blazing hot highlights played off against shadows thick as oil. Clare must have viewed its closing sequence a dozen times, looking for more than I could find there, and once again coming away with an uncharacteristic indecision. "I don't know," she remarked more to herself than me the last time we sat through the movie, "there's something going on there. I wish I knew what."

She had the same uneasy response to *The Ripper Strikes*, the oldest of our Castle discoveries, dating back to 1931. One of the earliest Paramount B-movies, Geoff had picked it up at a film swap. I would have set it down as nothing more than a formula chiller featuring a dozen or so stiffly elegant representatives of the old Hollywood Raj plodding through an uninspired script with a studied British for-bearance. But halfway along, Clare turned to me to say, "Look what you're doing."

What was I doing? I wasn't aware until she called my attention to it. I was distractedly rubbing my hands over my arms, down my neck. She'd caught herself doing the same thing. Why?

"It's the fog," she said enigmatically, leaving me to work it out.

After a few moments of reflection, I saw what she meant. As trashy as *The Ripper Strikes* might have been, it was a study in the cinematics of fog. Not real fog, of course, but the billowy cotton-candy exhaust that gets blown out of a dry-ice machine. The film was filled with this usually negligible effect, not just the streets of the back-lot London sets, but the interiors as well. Rooms, corridors, staircases were lit with a hazy, swirling chiaroscuro that brought the terror of Ripper-haunted Whitechapel indoors. The fog seemed to be leaking off the screen, permeating the air about us, leaving a clammy scum upon the skin. Worse than unpleasant, the fog was threatening, I'd even have said evil. An appetite for blood inhabited it. And this had its effect on the story. The Ripper, played by a game but somewhat depleted Clive Brook, emerged as a tormented soul driven to kill by the fog which was, at one point in the film, referred to as "the devil's own breath."

"You're right," I told Clare. "I can almost feel it. Isn't that remarkable!"

But Clare was trying hard not to be sucked in. "Movies are for seeing," she grumbled. "Not for feeling or getting felt by. I like them to stay up there on the screen where they belong."

The Ripper Strikes was in such dreadful condition she was tempted to leave it out of our festival. But it was the first of Castle's cheapies, so it went in simply to balance *Axis Agent*, a run-of-the-mill wartime spy chase that was the last film Castle made before his death. By that late stage of his faltering career, he wasn't above "stealing from his betters," as Clare put it, eager to score some critical points against the man.

"How do you mean?" I asked.

"You mean you didn't notice? God, you're hopeless. All that deep focus, the shots from the floor, the camera peek-a-booing through the transom: it was all lifted straight out of *Citizen Kane*. A cut-rate version, but still recognizable. Also the sequence where all the German war vets get older and nastier each time the camera pans around the dinner table. That's the famous ten-year-breakfast scene from *Kane*. How could you miss it?"

Now that she mentioned it, I saw she was right and apologized. Apology not accepted. "Don't tell me you're sorry. Just learn!"

Much to my surprise and Clare's, the most distinguished of our discoveries turned out to be a 1935 Universal film with the unpromising title *Man into Monster*. This wasn't a monster film at all, but as Clare recognized about a half hour into the story, a retelling of Georg Büchner's *Wozzeck*, the strange tale of victimization that Alban Berg had turned into a controversial opera some ten years before the movie was made. Castle, who scripted the picture, had transposed the story to New York's Lower East Side and given it a brutal, journalistic realism that was well ahead of its time.

There were clearly a number of crude cuts in the print we had; we were sure whole scenes were missing, including the finish, where the dialogue seemed to have been hacked off in the middle of a sentence. Even so, what survived of the picture displayed remarkable sophistication. It must have slipped through the old Universal monster mill on the basis of its title alone. In a daring stroke, Clare decided to nominate it as possibly the first *film noir*. In those days, tracing the origins of *film noir* was a favorite game among movie scholars and critics, the cinematic equivalent of finding the source of the Nile among Victorian explorers. For the purposes of the festival, we decided to push that identity for most of the rest of Castle's movies, suggesting that, as ratty as many of them might be, they deserved to be recognized as among the earliest examples of *noir,* a genre that was usually dated from several years later and credited to more famous directors. We hoped that serving Castle's work up on that platter would lend a little academic class to the festival and perhaps make up for the obvious shoddiness of what we had to show. For despite Sharkey's best efforts to repair and restore, most of the films displayed abundant signs of wear and neglect: torn sprockets, breaks and burns that had never been patched; sound tracks that were often a blur of static, whines, and rumbles. There would have been no excuse for screening most of what we had to show if the *Judas* weren't there to provide a centerpiece. As Clare observed, it was a pity Castle's career didn't build up from *Judas* rather than down . . . and down and down from it.

By the time the Max Castle Film Festival arrived, I had, without realizing it, reached a state of euphoric expectation. This was, it suddenly occurred to me, the biggest project I'd taken on in my life, and I'd pursued it to a successful conclusion under the eye of a demanding mentor. It wouldn't have been Clare's style to lavish praise on her pupil's efforts; still, I could tell she was pleased with the result. Now my months of hard work would finally be crowned by five evenings of films featuring my own program notes. For the first time I had some idea of the gratification Clare must have found in running The Classic. The notes were, of course, carefully crafted to reflect as many of her views as possible. She'd sat through all the preview screenings tossing off remarks I knew she expected me to take down verbatim. I did. But when I had finished shaping them for the mimeograph machine, she surprised me by insisting that I claim them for my own. That struck me as curious. Clare wasn't the one to give away her intellectual wares. Nor did she seem to be granting me title to her critical judgments in a spirit of generosity. Rather I had the sense that she wanted the event to appear as somebody else's idea—not hers. As much as anything, she was washing her hands of responsibility.

As the first night of the festival approached, I had no idea quite what to expect, but Clare accurately recognized that I was looking for more than a week's worth of old movies at a hole-in-the-wall art house was likely to yield. "Don't get your hopes up, Jonny," she warned. "If we're lucky, we'll sell a dozen tickets."

We did better than that with *Judas.* Billed as a significant discovery, it drew a capacity Sunday evening audience. After that, we went begging. A double bill of *The Ripper Strikes* and *Axis Agent,* Castle's earliest and latest Hollywood films of the sound era, drew all of nine customers, only three of whom stayed through the second feature after watching the jumpy, dimly lit, nearly inaudible first. The following night was worse, bad enough to make me feel ill. *Man into Monster* and *Shadows over Sing Sing* brought us an audience of six. The closest we came to an expression of appreciation was to have one of our Classic regulars stop by afterward to remark, "I wondered why you were showing this old crud."

"Did you really think it would be crud?" Clare asked defensively.

"Of course."

"And now what do you think?"

"It's crud all right. But I can see what you're getting at in the notes. The shadows. It's all in the shadows, isn't it? Weird. It's going to give me bad dreams."

"Oh? Why?"

"Because somehow I think I know what it would be like to be on death row. Creepy. Especially since, like it says in the notes, the movie never tells you what the prisoner is condemned for. It's the best part I ever saw Tom Neal do."

The fellow had seen exactly what we had wanted him to see. Or rather what Clare wanted him to see; I'd simply taken the notes from her by dictation. She compared the camera work in *Shadows over Sing Sing* with Caravaggio, whose canvases can get so dark they give you eyestrain. But you keep staring, thinking there's something there you don't want to miss. "Caravaggio painting a Dick Tracy comic strip," was how Clare put it.

The next night brought us a nearly full house for *Count Lazarus* and *Kiss of the Vampire*. They were old horror clunkers that had a certain nostalgic appeal. People remembered them from childhood matinees or "Creature Features" television. The turnout perked up my spirits, at least until the first movie got rolling. At that point, something happened that nearly turned the evening into a disaster, a jarring disruption which was destined to give our makeshift festival an importance we could never have foreseen.

It began with a big, blowsy woman rushing in five minutes after *Count Lazarus* had started. She wore a howling flower-pattern dress pulled skin tight at the bust and bustle. Her hair was whipped up into a towering bouffant, bleached so white it might have glowed in the dark. She came in asking for help. Asking, then demanding, in a high, whining voice that sounded like a bad imitation of Shirley Temple pleading with Captain January. The more demanding she got, the more thrusting her abundant bosom became. Finally, Clare and I followed where she led. Outside, waiting at the top of the little flight of stairs that led down from the alley, sat a cadaverous old man who looked like a pile of bones stacked up in a wheelchair. Pale and drawn, he couldn't have weighed more than a ten-year-old boy, but his size was not entirely due to wastage. After a moment, I recognized that he was a dwarf; his legs barely made it over the front edge of the chair. He was wheezing so hard between hard drags on his cigarette that I couldn't hear a word he said. When I did, it turned out to be a muffled stream of abuse and curses. "What the hell is this?" he was asking. "A goddam tomb? A movie house in a basement! What the bejesus is goin' on here?"

Standing behind the old guy's chair was an even older-looking Japanese wearing a rumpled chauffeur's uniform. Between the lines that marked his face an expression of infinite exhaustion showed through. It was a muggy summer night; even so, the man in the chair kept a blanket wrapped tightly around himself and was still shivering under it, probably more with palsy than cold. He was wearing a zany porkpie hat that rested hard on his ears, pushing them out like small pink wings. The face between the ears had the look of a starved bird; it was one nasty collection of scowls and wrinkles from brow to chin. The cigarette screwed into the corner of his mouth seemed to be a permanent fixture.

With the old man wheezing and muttering all the way, the four of us—Clare, the woman, the Japanese chauffeur, and myself doing most of the work—levered the chair down the steps and into what passed for the lobby of The Classic, receiving no thank-you for our efforts. Crouching and lifting beside the old guy, I noticed the needle-thin plastic tubes that ran along his cheeks and up into his nostrils; they stemmed from the oxygen packet strapped to the chair, which was measuring out the whiffs and sniffs of air that kept his lungs supplied. The packet made a tiny gasping sound each time it pumped.

When Clare told the woman that the movie had already started, the old guy croaked, "I won't pay full price, not for half a picture."

"You missed the first five minutes, that's all," Clare said.

"Beginning's the best part," the old man retorted. "Don't pay full price," he instructed the woman. Two trembling hands poked out of the blanket and began struggling to replace the burned-down cigarette with a new one. The Japanese chauffeur supplied it and gave it a light. "Knock off a quarter, fifty cents, you hear?"

"Oh Christ!" Clare muttered, knowing that his raspy voice was getting loud enough to carry into the theater. "I'll let both of you in on one ticket. Satisfied?"

"Him, too," the old guy insisted, pointing to the chauffeur. "My bodyguard. Never budge without him."

"Okay, okay," Clare agreed. "But no smoking."

"You ain't got a smoking section?" the old man asked with an astonished stare.

"The smoking section is in the alley—where you just were."

"Shit! What kinda movie theater is this?"

"A small, dumpy one with lousy ventilation. If you don't like it, please leave."

Muttering, he sucked in a lungful of smoke and swallowed it forever before the chauffeur removed and discarded the cigarette. The woman paid for the single ticket and then awkwardly maneuvered the wheelchair through the curtained entrance of the theater.

That was the last we heard from the latecomers until the film ended—except for the old guy's steady coughing and rasping. When the screen finally went dark, he let out a hoot of derision. "Pigs!" he growled in a sandpaper falsetto. "Blood-suckin' pigs! You call that showin' movies? That's garbage. Phooey!" The woman got him back into the lobby, where he riveted Clare with a stare of icy contempt. "That ain't Max Castle you're showin'. Whatja do, run the movie through a meat grinder? You got no respect, you hear? Goddam vandals! I'm slappin' an injunction on this flea pit first thing in the mornin'. I'm puttin' you outa business."

The old guy chewed off his accusation in a venomously stinging Brooklynese, spitting the words out the side of his face that wasn't clamped down on the unlit cigarette. He was now shaking with enough rage to fall out of his chair. The woman steadied him while the chauffeur put a match to the much-chewed butt. He quieted down long enough to take a life-saving drag, then broke down in a cascade of coughing.

Clare fished the cost of admission out of the till and was eagerly refunding it to the woman with a not-too-polite request that they leave.

"Nothin' doin', sister," the old guy insisted. "You ain't buyin' me off. I'm puttin' you outa business, I mean it. You can't make corned-beef hash outa my work an' get away with it."

"*Your* work?" Clare was stymied by the remark.

"Me and Max. Like that." He held out two bony intertwined fingers. "The man was a genius. You're tearin' the heart outta him in there. I ain't gonna let you do it."

Clare eyed him narrowly, suddenly cooling her anger. "Who are you?" she asked.

"Lipsky," the old man shot back. "A lot that's gonna mean to you."

"*Arnold* Lipsky?"

The old man went silent, staring back at her in amazement. "Yeah, that's it."

"*Zip* Lipsky?"

"Right."

"*Glory Road? Johnny Champion? Symphony of a Million?*"

The old guy's etched-in scowl began to melt. Not much, but enough to allow a hint of suspicious surprise show through. His lips went soft, letting the cigarette drop into the folds of his blanket. The chauffeur went searching for it, found it, and repositioned it in his mouth.

"You know me?" he asked.

"One of the three best cinematographers there ever were."

"Yeah?" His eyes gave an aggressively inquisitive squint. "Who's the other two, I'd like to know?"

Quick as a wink, Clare answered, "Tissé . . . and Freund."

"Right about Freund," the old man agreed. "The guy never made

126

a bad shot. He learned a lot from Max, I'll bet you didn't know that. But *wrong* about Tissé."

"He taught Eisenstein everything he knew," Clare came back, challenging him.

"An' that was too bad for Eisenstein. Tissé—he could be tricky, but he couldn't be real. Stagey. He was stagey. You gotta be tricky *and* real."

"All right," Clare went on, now showing clear signs of high enjoyment. "What about . . . Georges Périnal?"

The old guy stared at her incredulously.

"*Blood of a Poet*," Clare added as if he might not recognize the name.

"Yeah, yeah, I know. Jesus, is that your idea of good shootin', that kinda French artsy-fartsy?"

"Okay, then. Sven Nyquist."

"Whatsa matter? You afraid to name any Americans?"

"Billy Bitzer."

"That's better. But, come on, that's Stone Age stuff. In them days, every time a guy picked up a camera, he invented somethin'. Besides, you can't tell what's him and what's Griffith."

"What about Jim Howe, then?"

"You think Howe was better'n me?" A hurt whine came into his voice.

"Well, he was pretty damn good."

"Good, sure. But better?"

Clare thought it over. "No, not better."

"Damn right."

She tried again. "Elgin Lessley?"

"Now you're talkin'. Lessley—that's real moviemakin'. Keaton woulda been lost without him. Trouble was: Elgin was a big nothin' with lights. Comedy don't let you do nothin' with lights. You gotta show all the details, see. Keep it square and bright."

As if she were playing a trump card, Clare said, "You want lights too? Okay. Gregg Toland."

Nodding thoughtfully, the old guy pondered the name with obvious respect. Almost wistfully, he said, "Yeah, yeah. Jesus, he was really somethin'. That deep-focus stuff—really gorgeous. Specially in *Grapsa Wrath*. That was his best. Better'n *Citizen Kane*, if you wanna know. Okay, you got me there."

Clare offered a tactful compromise. "Let's say: if he'd lived another ten years, he would've been . . . nearly as good as you."

Almost suspiciously, the old man asked, "You think I was *that* good, huh?"

"Good enough to win an Academy Award."

His face collapsed in disappointment. "Phaw! They give those away every year. What's that mean? You know how many klutzes got little gold statues? Hell, they give Billy Daniels one of those. A goddam fashion photographer was all he ever was."

"But *Glory Road* deserved an award," Clare insisted. "That's the difference. And," she added teasingly, "it wasn't even your best."

Lipsky studied Clare warily. "Oh yeah? So what was better, tell me that."

"*Prince of the Streets*—1943. With King Vidor."

The old guy spread his mouth in a delighted toothless grin and pointed a quivering finger at her. "Right! By Christ, that's right." He craned around to tell the woman behind him, "She's right. You hear that, by Jesus!"

"You didn't even get a nomination for that one. But it was still your best. Practically invented the Neorealist style."

Lipsky gave a contemptuous snort. "Too good for 'em, it was. Ahead of its time. Sons a bitches loved all that greasy newsreel shtick when the wops did it after the war. Sure. Cuz that was Your-o-peen. Jesus! You know what Rossellini said to me? Nineteen fifty-three. He let me do some shootin' for him after I got the bum's rush in the U.S. Said, 'Zip—you invented my movies.'" Then, turning tough guy again, he gave Clare a wised-up grimace. "You got it *almost* right, sister. *Prince of the Streets* was the *second*-best I ever did. The first best was *House of Blood*."

Clare was honestly astonished. "*House of Blood?*"

"Right! With Max. Shot it in eight days. Practically no retakes. Cleanest damn job I ever done. Beautiful!"

Clare sent a questioning glance my way.

"I came across that film in one of the catalogues," I explained, "but I couldn't find a print anywhere."

"Course not!" Lipsky snarled. "Scrapped it. Like all the best stuff Max did. They tried to scrap it all. Bastards!"

"Listen, Mr. Lipsky," Clare said eagerly, "we've got to talk."

"Yeah? About what?"

"About you. About your work. I'm a great admirer of yours."

"Yeah? Then what about in there?" He jerked a thumb toward the theater. "You're crucifyin' me in there. Me an' Max both."

"Those are the best prints we could find," Clare assured him. "Besides, I honestly didn't know that was *your* work. I mean—there *is* a Lipsky listed in the credits. But I didn't think it could be you."

Clare had mentioned the point while we were previewing Castle's films. The credits for three of them included an A. C. Lipsky as key grip. She'd asked, "Could that be Arnold Lipsky?" I recognized the name when she pointed it out. In the forties and fifties, Zip Lipsky became one of the celebrated Hollywood cameramen. He received a number of Academy Award nominations and one Oscar. In his time he was a minor legend around the studios, where his camera work was as distinctive as his physical build. Clare had also remarked that he dropped out of sight during the Hollywood blacklisting period, one of its many talented victims. We agreed that would be worth mentioning in the notes, but we couldn't be sure it was the same man.

"You're not listed for the camera work," Clare explained.

"Listed!" Lipsky scoffed. "Who the hell kept track of that on these quick hitters? Warren Kettle—they listed him. He got the paycheck. Hell, he was drunk from the first day. I shot the whole thing. That's *my* work, sister. And it looks like ground cow shit up there on the screen. It's a goddam sacrilege."

That night, I was running the projector. Which meant the second feature was now more than a half hour late in getting started. Even so, Clare and I hadn't yet succeeded in mollifying Lipsky. We had, however, managed to gather a small circle of spectators around us in the lobby. Some of them, film students who were regulars at The Classic, were more interested in the talk between Clare and Lipsky than in the movie that was waiting to be shown. Clare, offering her audience one of the rare apologies she ever gave, explained with a distinct note of pride in her voice, "This is Mr. Arnold Lipsky. Zip Lipsky. One of the great cinematographers of American film."

"Phaw! Cinematographer," Lipsky grumbled. "I was a *shooter*, that's what."

"One of the great shooters," Clare corrected. "The film you're about to see is one of Mr. Lipsky's uncredited works." Glancing at Lipsky, she asked, "Is that right? Your name isn't on this one either."

"It's mine," Lipsky announced belligerently. "Christ, I shot 'em all for Max. If he could get me, Max never used nobody else."

FLICKER

Kiss of the Vampire finally got shown—with Lipsky groaning and cursing in the back of the theater at every cut he could recognize. Halfway through, with a yip of pain, he decided to leave. That gave Clare the chance to hustle him off to Moishe's for a private talk. By the time I got there after running the film and closing down the house, Clare had found out something spectacular.

"He's got them all!" she announced as I slid into the booth beside her, across from Lipsky and the woman. "Castle's films. Or at least the ones he shot. How many did you say? Sixteen movies?"

"Seventeen," Lipsky answered smugly, "plus which I got the camera originals, sonny. Not this hashed-up crap you're showin'. Just the way Max wanted it. The whole works. Best stuff I ever did."

They'd managed to get him out of his wheelchair and into the rearmost booth of Moishe's. The little man's chin and shoulders just barely cleared the top of the table. He was wedged awkwardly between the wall and the big woman who still hadn't been introduced to me. I gathered she was Lipsky's wife, or possibly his nurse. The old guy was still smoking away like a furnace. In front of him there was a cup of hot water with a lemon slice floating in it.

"You really think some of these Castle films are better than *Glory Road* or *Prince of the Streets*?" Clare asked.

"Damn right! Cuz you know why? Me and Max, we was workin' on a total zilch budget. Leftover sets, lousy lights, almost no retakes. You *had* to be good. Good the *first* time. That's where I learned shootin'. Shit! *Glory Road*—we had a couple million bucks for that. A baboon can make a good picture for a million bucks. But when you're workin' on a shoestring—that's when you gotta have what it takes. Max planned every shot so careful . . . God, he was good. You see how close in we worked? That was to cut out all the phoney sets. You see how we used the edges of the screen? Spooky, huh? Never know what's comin' at y'. Learned it all from Max. From the ground up. Every trick there was. 'Silk from pig's ears' was what he called it. Max an' me. What a team!"

"Can . . . can we see the films?" I asked.

Apparently Clare had already raised the question. "Mr. Lipsky is being difficult about that."

"Damn right!" Lipsky shot back, putting on his tough-guy face. "Those pictures're mine. Nobody else's. Nobody's takin' 'em away. They did Max so much dirt. Me too. Goddam bloodsuckin' bandits."

130

"This would be a private screening," Clare said. "Just the two of us."

"Oh yeah? Next thing, you'll wanna show 'em in that fleapit of yours. One raw deal after another, that's what they give Max. So let 'em do without. Nobody sees them pictures but me."

"But why save the films if nobody can ever see them?" I asked.

The old man's face went enigmatic. "There's reasons," he sniffed. "I got a reason. I can do just what I want with them pictures. They're mine."

"But what harm could it do?" I pursued. "Clare and I—we'd really appreciate seeing them."

"Nothin' doin'." Lipsky was adamant. "After how I got burned in this town, I don't owe nobody any favors, see?" This was clearly a matter of vengeful pride with him.

Responding to a rub and stroke of the ankle under the table, I turned to the big woman across from me. I thought it was accidental contact at first. It wasn't. She was running her stockinged foot along my instep. Bewildered, I decided to treat the occasion as a chance to appeal to her. "We'd be very respectful," I said. "We really care about Castle's work."

The woman began to smile back. The smile didn't quit; it kept widening into something like a leer. And the leer became so frankly lascivious, I felt myself blushing. By now, her foot was probing its way up my trouser leg, her wiggly toes spelling out little lecherous messages all over my calf. She gave a flirtatious wink and leaned a meaty shoulder into the little man beside her. "Don't be so poo-poo, Zippy," she piped in her Shirley Temple voice. "Let him see the dumb ol' movies." To me, she said, "We got our own screening room and everything, just like a real picture show. You come up to our place and see the movie. We never have anybody visit." She started to act out a heavy pout. "I get *sooo* lonely."

"Nothin' doin'," Lipsky protested, holding firm.

The woman crowded him still harder, so that his wizened little figure began to disappear into her voluptuous bulk. "You wanna be tickled tonight or not?" she asked. "Huh, baby? Huh?"

"What's 'at gotta do with it?" Lipsky whined, now almost suffocated under her pressure.

Nodding across at me, her gaze shifting from lascivious to predatory, she mock-whispered, "He's sure a cutey. I want him to come see the pictures."

Clare came up with another idea. "What about the *Judas*?" she asked. "Wouldn't you like to see Max Castle's greatest film?"

"What're you sayin'?" Lipsky asked, suddenly alert and eager. "What'd she say?"

"*Judas Jedermann*," Clare replied. "We've got it. Wouldn't you like to see it without coming back to this fleapit, as you call it? We could show it for you privately. It's Castle's best film."

"Pfaa!" Lipsky refused to believe her. "How would you know? *Judas Yeh-mer . . . , Yeh . . . ber . . .* I never heard of no film by Max like that. You're bluffin'."

"*Judas Everyman* in English. You wouldn't have heard of it under that name either. It's been lost since the early twenties. It's in perfect condition."

Lipsky sent her a skeptical one-eyed squint. "How d'you know Max made it? Does it say so?"

"This is a rough cut . . . we think. No titles or credits. But it comes from somebody who knows it was his film."

"Yeah? Who?"

"Someone named Joshua Sloan."

Lipsky wagged his head. "Never heard of him. Who's that?" Then, stiffening noticeably, he asked, "One of them goddam orphans?"

"Orphans? Why, no. He's a film collector in Chicago," Clare answered.

"So how's he know Max made it?"

"There were some papers in with the film. A couple of them were from a Thea Von Pölzig at the UFA studios. She says . . ."

Lipsky flashed on the name. "Pull-zik! Christ! She still around? That skinny old bat! Them damn orphans live forever. Like zombies."

"As a matter of fact," Clare went on, "the film *was* found in an orphanage. In Germany. That's where Sloan got it."

Lipsky looked amazed. "The orphanage give him the picture?"

"No, the orphanage was bombed out. The film was found in the ruins."

"Good! They bombed it? Good!"

"Well, anyway," Clare continued, "that's how we know it's Castle's film. From this woman Von Pölzig's letter."

"Okay, this guy Sloan in Chicago, he got it from the orphanage." Lipsky gave Clare a narrow squint. "So how'd *you* get it?"

Clare hesitated, then went ahead and lied. "It was a gift from a local collector."

"Yeah? Who?"

"Ever hear of Ira Goldstein?"

"Goldstein! That *gonif!* He give you a film? For free? Not likely. Anyways, I thought he was dead."

"He is. I know his son. He's been selling some of Goldstein's films."

"Well, Goddamit! Nobody told me they was sellin' Max's pictures."

"There was just this one," Clare said.

"And how come they sold it to you?"

"Because people know I care about movies—good movies. And this is a good movie. Strange, but good. Maybe great."

"What d'you mean 'maybe'?" Lipsky asked aggressively. "It's Max's movie, isn't it?"

"Wouldn't you like to judge for yourself? It's very, very original. Lots of spectacular camera work. We could bring it to you. How about it, Mr. Lipsky? Fair exchange. We'll show you *Judas.* You show us your Castles."

"That's seventeen pictures for one. You call that fair?"

"But *Judas* is special. A true collector's item."

"It isn't worth seventeen to one."

"All right. How about just two for one? The two best Castle films. You pick them."

Lipsky hesitated, muttering and grimacing. Maybe he would have held out still longer, but the big woman closed in on him again with another nudge of her intimidating bosom. "Come on, Zippy. Don't be a poo-poo head!" she said, and, grudgingly, he caved in.

Before they left, we had their phone number and address and an arrangement to visit the following week. They drove off in an overaged Cadillac badly in need of body work, the Japanese chauffeur at the wheel, Lipsky in the back seat smoking and wheezing.

"What a pathetic old codger," Clare grumbled as we watched them pull away from Moishe's. "But he was once the best shooter in the business."

8 THE SALLYRAND

When Zip Lipsky built the place in the late forties, the big pastel house in the Los Feliz hills must have been the sort of showcase that was fashionable among the film-rich he had then just lately joined. Now it looked like a piece of crumbling wedding cake left over from the party. The pink stucco frosting had long since flaked and faded; a hundred earth tremors had left their graffiti of cracks in the walls; the drainpipes drooped at every corner. It was one of the houses that had helped the neighborhood go to seed. Not that you noticed the decay until you'd picked your way well up the overgrown driveway; the grounds behind the rusted iron fencing had run wild, covering the dilapidation of the property with a merciful obscurity.

Even when you got inside, you couldn't be sure the house was inhabited. The gloom dripped like syrup from every dark corner. The windows, weightily curtained and Venetian-blinded, let in only hints and splinters of light. We were met at the door—Clare, Sharkey, and myself—by the big woman. She was dressed as if for a party that might have been given the year Eisenhower was elected. I'd learned from Clare that she was Mrs. Lipsky. Her eyes went for me right away.

"Come to see the picture show?" she piped in her kewpie doll voice. She was carrying a very large drink. From the slurred sound of her words, I judged it wasn't her first of the day.

Most of the house we passed through looked and smelled unlived in, musty, and cobwebby. There was a lot of heavily upholstered furniture, blatantly tasteless, just as blatantly expensive, and all of a style—as if it had been bought in one big ostentatious splurge. There was the sense that the place was a crypt waiting for its corpse. The one note of color dimly discernible through the gloom was the movie posters that decorated the walls. Most of them were for Lipsky's pictures, but there were a few others more garish than the rest that arrested my attention at once, eliciting a special twinge of delight. They displayed an image that still vibrated deep in my secret inven-

134

tory of adolescent erotica. There she was in all her titillating glory: Nylana the Jungle Girl, she of the endless weekly perils. I lingered to examine each treasured depiction. Nylana being carried off across the treetops by a slavering gorilla. Nylana lifted high in the air, swooning and supine, about to be thrown into a pit of writhing snakes by a leering Arab. Nylana half-clothed and suspended by the wrists, struggling above a pyre of red-hot coals while wild-eyed savages cavorted under the Satanic gaze of a witch doctor. Each picture, though crudely rendered by some art-school reject of twenty years ago, brought back the rapine episode that had once taught me the dark psychology of sexual appetite.

Why was Nylana there, in this dismal tomb of a house? Were these remnants of Lipsky's waning career? Had he ever sunk so low in the tar pits of the movie industry?

At the distant rear of the house, we came upon the few rooms that still seemed to be in use: a kitchen in indescribable disorder and a large, glassed-in cabana that looked out upon a cracked and empty swimming pool now filled with debris. This part of the Lipsky home was permeated with the faintly medicinal odors of a sickroom. Here Mrs. Lipsky offered us drinks from a well-stocked wet bar and then led us to a cabin-sized outbuilding across the overgrown patio. This turned out to be a small, but well-kept projection room with seating for about a dozen. Here we found Lipsky, smoking and wheezing away in a plush armchair several times too large for his already small and now much-diminished dimensions. "You bring it?" he snarled as we entered. "The picture? You bring it? You ain't seein' anything if you didn't bring it."

He couldn't fail to see me loaded down with the canisters. Clare gestured me forward, and I presented them like a peace offering to the chief of a hostile tribe.

The chief was not placated. "What kept y'?" he snapped. Once again, on a warm day, he was wrapped in his blanket.

"You said two o'clock," Clare answered with strained patience. "We're early."

"So who told ja you could come early?" the little guy shot back. "I coulda been sleepin'."

Clare returned the volley gently. "But you're not, are you?"

Spotting Sharkey, Lipsky asked, "Who's that?"

"This is Don Sharkey," Clare said. "My partner. He's also a great admirer of your work."

Sharkey stepped forward to shake hands. "I'm pleased to . . ."

Lipsky cut him short, his gaze still on Clare. "I didn't say you could bring your whole damn family. What is this—a picnic?"

"Don is the best projectionist in the city," Clare explained.

"Hell he is," Lipsky shot back. "He don't touch none of my pictures. Only Yoshi handles my stuff." He gave a thumb-poke over his shoulder toward the projection booth where I could see someone at work on the machines.

"Well, Don's here to show *our* film," Clare said. "It has to be handled with complete professional care."

"Let's set up," Sharkey muttered sullenly, and led me off with the canisters. Clare and I had warned him not to expect the usual courtesies from Lipsky, but he was nonetheless wounded by the old man's abrupt dismissal.

"Your picture *first!*" Lipsky wheezed.

"Oh no," Clare countered, suspecting that Lipsky might hold out on us once he'd seen the *Judas*. "Yours first."

"Nothin' doin,' " Lipsky insisted. It seemed to be his habit to make the maximum trouble about everything that came up. I had the distinct feeling that he relished having someone to needle and was out to make the most of the opportunity. Maybe he even enjoyed Clare's pugnaciousness, though she was doing an unprecedented job of keeping it under control.

Sharkey and I looked over the projection booth while Clare and Lipsky wrangled. We were impressed. It was a better setup than we had at The Classic. There were two magnificent Century thirty-five-millimeter machines with big blowers vented through the ceiling. All the equipment was in prime condition, well-oiled and gleaming. Busily fussing over it was Yoshi, the old Japanese chauffeur who had driven Lipsky to The Classic. His face, as he worked, was skewed into a frown of pain.

"You're the projectionist?" Sharkey asked.

The old man answered, ticking it off on his fingers. "Gardener. Cook. Chauffeur. Crean-up. Arso projectionist, yes." His tone and expression made it clear that he felt vastly overworked.

"I hope you're a better projectionist than you are a gardener," Sharkey said. "This place looks like darkest Africa."

Yoshi pulled a sincerely sad face. "Too ord, too ord," he moaned, wagging his head. "Fingers too stiff." He held out two arthritic claws. "Prease, you can do machine?"

When Sharkey agreed, Yoshi gave a grateful bow, then slumped wearily into a chair.

"But we better not let your boss out there know," Sharkey remarked. "He says you're the only person who can show his movies."

Yoshi nodded. "Mr. Ripsky very good man. Ord friend. But sometimes fur of shit, you know."

After a half hour of wrangling, Clare and Lipsky had finally worked out a compromise on the screening order of the films. One of his first, then the *Judas*, then his other movie after that. What followed must have been the purest distillation of Max Castle's film art ever projected at a single showing. Three movies in pristine condition, just as their creator would have wished them to be seen. It was very nearly more than the eye and the mind could absorb. The two films Lipsky had chosen were *Count Lazarus* and *House of Blood*, at that time known to the world, if known at all, as nothing more than tawdry B-movies, the work of a marginal and now long dead talent whose career when he produced the films was bordering on well-deserved obscurity. Anyone reading the screenplays through line by line would have found nothing about these films that distinguished them from the general run of the genre. Just two more of Universal Studio's spooky doings. Even the cast was made up of actors and actresses who were the stock company of that era's werewolf and bloodsucker repertory. Evelyn Ankers, George Zucco, Anne Nagel, Glenn Strange, Dwight Frye. Yet there wasn't a frame of these movies— shown as the mind of Max Castle had conceived them—that wasn't touched with an uncanny power. We—Clare, Sharkey, and I—had all seen flashes of that power in the films we'd shown at the festival. But here the impact was whole and unrestrained. As with the *Judas*, I sat before the storm of images as if I were staring into a hurricane, struggling to keep my presence of mind before a shattering force. And that force was pure cinema: the elemental visual stuff of the art itself. Pictures in motion, one hammering image after another darting along unexplored optical rivers to reach the deep interior of the brain's shadowy continent.

It would have been enough to say that, by anybody's standards, these films were well crafted, so far beyond the ordinary studio standard that only their limited budget placed them in the category of B-movies. But there was more here, something that went beyond craftsmanship. There was in Castle's films a genuine horror, one that froze through to the bone. At no point could I have said precisely where the film's power lay—except that I was sure it was nothing I'd consciously seen that produced the effect. Rather, it was as if somewhere behind my eyes, another part of me was observing a different world, one in which the vampire and his victim were real, the supernatural events were real, the blasphemy was real. Again, the word "unclean" edged its way into my mind. *Unclean*, as only a thing risen from the grave to prey upon innocent blood could be unclean. The ghoul's essential obscenity was there before my eyes; it had touched me. Not me alone. Clare too. I could tell when the lights came up. She was wearing the same stiff-faced gaze that I'd seen when the *Judas* ended, the face of someone who refused to admit the experience she'd confronted. She managed to stick it out through the first movie, watching as intently as I had. But she wouldn't watch the *Judas* through again, nor *House of Blood*, even though Lipsky had called it his best work. Instead, she excused herself to wait for Sharkey and me in the kitchen.

I expected the old man to take offense at her departure; she was walking out on the film he considered his finest. He was too eagerly awaiting the *Judas* to care what Clare did. But Mrs. Lipsky, noting Clare's exit, lost no time in making the most of the opportunity. She quickly eased in beside me with a wink and a giggle. Ten minutes into the film and her foot began working aggressively at mine. Another five, and her hand was on my arm. "Excuse me," I said, running for cover. "I have to check the projector." I watched the rest of the movie with Sharkey from the booth.

Lipsky sat through the *Judas* with his attention riveted to the screen, his chicken-bone frame erect and alert. Even from the rear of the theater, his gasps of appreciation were audible, punctuating every key shot in the film. At several points, I could hear him muttering to himself, "That's it, Maxy . . . that's the ticket . . . perfect . . . perfect!" By the end of the film, he was accompanying every movement with body English, living the story. When the lights came back, he crumpled like a racer at the finish line. Mrs. Lipsky went to him to adjust his oxygen pack. "Poor Zippy!" she baby-talked him. "Does he get too 'cited?" Lipsky looked up at her, his eyes shining with tears and too choked to speak. He opened his mouth and closed it like a dying fish, but all that came out was, ". . . Max . . ."

He didn't stay to see the last movie, but made his way out of the room. Later, Sharkey and I found him with Clare in the kitchen, huddling over the table, the two of them filling the room with a pall of cigarette smoke. It looked as if a respectful conversation had been passing between them. I judged that seeing the *Judas* had mellowed the old guy and made him willing to talk, at least to Clare. When Sharkey and I arrived, he clammed up and moved off into the cabana. He made no reply to my thanks as we left. At the door, Mrs. Lipsky managed to get hold of my hand and give it a hard squeeze. "You hurry right back, y'hear?" she said. "We got lots and lots of movies to show."

On the way home, I was bursting to discuss the films. But Clare carried on as if she didn't hear me talking. "Poor sick old geezer." She sounded as if she really cared.

"Obnoxious little fart," Sharkey added.

"Be kind," Clare said. "He's flying on one lung. He won't last long. Emphysema. Worse, he's dying of terminal bitterness. He got kicked around a lot, you know. After they hit him with the blacklist, he had to shoot under other names to get work, or go begging around Europe. He was already too sick then for that. He's got a right to his grudge."

"How'd he get on the list?" Sharkey asked.

"I gather he was a political lefty from way back. Ran in his family. Just about the time Joe McCarthy invaded Hollywood, Zip got involved making a documentary on Paul Robeson—with a lot of his own money. Purely a labor of love. Next thing he knew, he was up shit creek. He was called before the committee. Uncooperative witness. Only reason he wasn't jailed was his health. Maybe also his size. Even McCarthy wasn't vile enough to bully a midget around in public. Anyway, there wasn't much publicity mileage in a mere cameraman. So they just destroyed his career. He fell a long way from the top of his profession. That leaves a lot of bruises."

"When did he start working with Castle?" I asked.

"That goes back farther than I would've guessed. Zip worked on *The Martyr.* He was on the film crew Castle took to Italy. He was one of the grips. He says everybody treated him like a sort of mascot— something dwarves have to live with. But not Castle. Castle began to groom him as a shooter. Zip was just a kid at the time. Of course, Castle wasn't that much older himself, but Zip remembers him as this sort of fatherly figure. Castle saw the talent in Zip and cared enough to bring it out. If I'm not mistaken, Zip rather worships the man for that. Apparently, Castle was going to make Zip his own personal handcrafted cameraman. After *The Martyr* crashed, Zip stuck by him. Quite a friendship. From the mid-thirties on, Zip was getting plenty of work on his own. Major studio stuff. A lot of junk, but some high-level things too. No matter what, he always insisted on working with Castle, even without credit. Here's a scoop for you. When Orson Welles came to RKO, one of the first people he talked to was Castle. Asked him what film he ought to make, now that he had a blank check from the studio. Castle suggested *Heart of Darkness*—the Conrad novel. It was a pet project he'd been nursing for years. Welles went for it. And Zip was going to be his shooter. Of course, that fell through. Welles went on to make *Citizen Kane* with Gregg Toland. Big loss for little Zip. But he got lucky, picked up other good things."

"What did he think of *Judas*?" I asked eagerly.

"Said he could see everything there he ever learned from Castle—plus a couple things more. All the . . . 'tricks' he calls them. They're a little cruder in *Judas*, but all there."

"Like what?"

"We didn't go into it that far. *I* didn't go into it that far. Not my interest. Anyway, Zip's not the one to give away very much. But I set you up with him."

"How do you mean?"

"He wants to see the *Judas* again. I said okay, but only if he'll let you see the rest of Castle's stuff. He agreed. Not enthusiastically, but he'll go along. Be sure to give him lots of strokes."

"Just me?" I asked. "Don't you want to be in on it?"

She paused thoughtfully before answering. "Let's let this be your little project, all right? It was hard enough to get him to agree to that much."

"Should I try to get the other films for The Classic?"

"Fat chance of that! He won't let the films out of his own possession."

"I could try."

"So try. See how far you'll get." She added with a teasing smile, "Mrs. L. might be of some help to you."

Knowing just what she meant, I nonetheless asked, "What do you mean?"

"Oh come on, Jonny! You can see the old girl's got the hots for you."

I tried to play innocent-dumb, not very convincingly.

"Cut it out, Jonny," Sharkey joined in. "You're in like Flynn there. Just play your cards right."

"Do you really think I should try using her influence . . . in that way?"

"All for the sake of art," Sharkey said.

Later that night I tried again to draw Clare out about the films we'd seen. She sidestepped every time. It was only after we'd gone to bed that I got a clear response, and a troubling one.

I'd been prattling on about *House of Blood*, assuming Clare would want to hear all about it. "It really is a shocker," I reported. "I can see why Zip is so proud of it. It's as cheap a piece of work as anything that ever came out of Universal in the old days, but the way they used the camera and the lighting . . . I was frankly scared out of my wits. I can't say why, but I was. There are some scenes that I'd swear are absolutely pornographic. Not actual sex, in fact, sort of . . . the opposite, if you know what I mean. You should see it. There's this one shot from over the bed, where the camera seems to just float and float like . . . well, a bat. Makes you almost nauseated. And then . . ."

In the darkness, Clare reached across to cover my mouth with her hand. Then, after a long silence, she whispered, "He's here. Can you tell?"

The words produced a distinct shiver, though I had no idea what she meant. "Who . . . ?" I asked.

"Castle. He's here—in the bed with us."

I shivered again. This wasn't like Clare. I had no idea how to reply. Then she ran her hand down my body, across my stomach, into the groin, caressing. "Here, Jonny. How did the movies make you feel *here?*"

Taken off guard, I had no answer to give. I lay there stupidly while Clare toyed with my strangely unresponsive member. To my amazement, I didn't want her hand where it was, doing what it did. Her touch brought with it what I might have called a sense of defilement, if I'd had the nerve to put the sensation in words. Even though I didn't, Clare could tell.

"Want me to stop, Jonny?" she asked. "*Why?* Because *he's* here. Somehow Castle's found a way to get between us. How does he do that?" There was a small, urgent tremor in her voice, almost as if she believed I might be able to answer the question for her. Clare didn't often reveal her vulnerabilities, but she was coming close to it that night. Of course, I had no answers to give her. I could only ask, "What about you? Does it have the same effect?"

141

"Me too! Goddamit! I feel the same way. Cold. Frozen solid. Like a puddle of dirty ice. I feel . . . ashamed. Of *what?* I don't know. And I don't like it. Movies are supposed to be the perfect pornographic medium, right? The ideal erotic turn-on. But not these movies. This is worse than porn. This is . . . I don't know what this is. It's what makes porn possible. It's the concentrated shame." Then, after a long pause, while her hand still stroked me, "How does he do it? That's what to find out, Jonny. What's the secret? Find it. And after you find it, *bury it.*"

She raised herself and leaned over me, breathing hard against my cheek, still working at me, beginning at last to get the reaction she wanted. "Now this is all I'll tell you about Max Castle's movies. I don't know what they're all about. I don't *want* to know. Just you be careful, lover, that the man doesn't get to you. If he begins to, remember *this*. Remember us together like *this*. Like *this*." She was astride me now, her thighs spread generously across my hips. For a time, her words faded into the rhythm of her laboring breath as she took her pleasure aggressively. We'd never made love that way, like rebellious subjects rising up against oppressive authority. Clare's use of my body that night could only be called belligerent, an act of war. Yet neither of us could say what it was that had brought such desperation into our bed.

When she'd finished with me, falling damp and exhausted across my chest, the words came back, close at my ear. "It could be he's the greatest there ever was. Quote me on that and I'll call you a liar. Because if I had my way, I'd see every one of his movies burned to fumes. Remember, Jonny, anything that makes *this* wrong is evil. Do you hear that, Herr Kastell? You're *evil, evil, evil.*"

I didn't realize it at the time, but that night Clarissa Swann delivered the only review of Max Castle's films she'd ever produce. And it came down to one sentence, one word.

Max Castle might have been *persona non grata* in the well-defended domain of Clare's cinematic taste, but for all her hostility, she couldn't exile him wholly from her thoughts. She was too helplessly addicted to film to deny herself work of that caliber. As deeply as his movies troubled her, they also fascinated. So a pattern arose, one which I'd dimly perceived forming when Clare first set me to work organizing the Max Castle Festival. She would deal with Castle through me. I would be her emissary dispatched to an enemy with

142

Theodore Roszak

whom she refused to have diplomatic relations. In a sense, I'd been granted a position of trust. Clare would learn about Castle primarily by way of my reports and evaluations. But there were times when I felt uncomfortably like a pair of tongs she was using to handle contaminated material.

For the next four months, I was a regular guest at the Lipsky house, sometimes coming as often as three times a week to sit in Zip's projection room studying the lost films of Max Castle. Though she never asked to be told, I knew that Clare expected a full account of my every visit. While I gave it, she would affect distraction, even unconcern. But I could feel the insistent pressure of her curiosity. She was taking in every word greedily, at times revealing more of her distaste than she'd have cared to know I saw.

My relationship with Zip, who sat through every screening with me, began in a distinctly unpromising way. He was at first determined to treat me as a nuisance and an interloper, tolerated only because I brought the *Judas* with me, a film he wanted to see again and again. Sometimes, in our early sessions, he would communicate with me only by way of impatient grunts and wheezes. If I dared to ask a question, he'd gasp out a contemptuous little smirk—as if to say, "Shows how much you know." But I was determined to overcome his petulance and learn what he had to tell me about Castle. I played deferential to the core, a role that came naturally to me. I was careful to compliment every film I saw lavishly, trying to massage my appreciation through his tough hide. Even so, it wasn't until the middle of the second month that I began receiving what were for Zip reasonably friendly responses. If I hadn't believed the glowing tributes I heaped upon his work—and Castle's—I would have burned with shame. But I came to see that this bitter old man was parched to the bone for the well-deserved recognition I was offering him. My words were a small rainfall of belated praise in the wasteland of his last years.

The breakthrough came unexpectedly in our second month together. We were watching one of Castle's more obscure products of the early thirties, *Zombie Doctor*. It was one of several films on which his name didn't appear. As late as 1938, Castle wasn't reconciled to permanent residence in the B-movie ghetto; he still hoped to move on to better things. He took the work but frequently directed under other names, among them Maurice Roche.

"Roche. You get it?" Zip asked with a wry squint. I didn't. "That's

143

from chess." I still didn't get it, but Zip offered nothing more than a haughty little sniff. "Max was a damn good chess player too. Beat the pants off everybody on the set. Brainy, that's what he was."

Chess, I gathered, was a pretty classy item in Zip's eyes, but it was clear he knew nothing about the game himself, so I asked no further. Later I worked it out on my own. *Roche* was the German for rook, castle. Zip knew of four other films Castle had directed under that *nom de film* before he finally agreed to put his own name on such humiliatingly substandard work.

Before the movie started I remarked to Zip that I'd seen it just a few months back on late-night television; I had no idea at the time that it was one of Castle's films. Zip shook his head dismissively. "You *think* you saw it, sonny. What you saw was chopped liver. This is the real thing. This you didn't see." There was a mischievous twinkle in his eye. "You ready?" he asked. I nodded that I was. "Okay, hold tight." And he gave the signal to Yoshi. The lights melted away. The movie started—but not in my eyes. In my ears. A thunderous burst of jungle drumming, a good fifteen seconds of it blasting out at full volume. Poor sound from a crackly sound track, but certainly loud.

Then the first image. A face, wild with fear, fills the screen. A black face, staring straight into the camera. The face turns, the man begins to run, stumbling through the undergrowth, his half-clothed body gleaming with sweat. His panicky breathing comes up loud to counterpoint the incessant drumming. The camera, hand-held and jiggling, pursues him like a tiger after its prey. The fleeing man throws terrified glances over his shoulder, running for all he is worth, panting, whimpering. The drumming accelerates. Voices come up, a ragged chorus of deep-throated howls and hoots, chanting to the racing rhythm. Only now, at least a minute into the action, does the first title appear. *Zombie Doctor.* Jagged letters blurring in and out of focus, using that sort of shimmering, fluid script that was a popular device in thrillers of the thirties. The rest of the titles follow in rapid succession, washing across the screen while the chase continues. But the eye scarcely takes them in; it is concentrated on the running man, sharing his terror.

Now this wasn't the way *Zombie Doctor* began in the version I'd seen. There we have the titles alone against a poorly drawn jungle background, accompanied by a piece of hackneyed studio scoring, in this case Universal's off-the-shelf thrills-and-chills music: a mewling electric organ over jittery fiddles. When I first saw the picture, I

144

assumed this was one of the movie's forced economies, never realizing that Castle had shot a totally different beginning.

It was at least a couple of minutes into the opening before I clearly registered the fact that I was witnessing two striking innovations. This might be the earliest movie to begin the action before the titles; this was also the longest tracking shot I'd ever seen, the camera relentlessly following the running man without a break through the entire credit sequence. As of the mid-thirties, a shot like this should have been a complete impossibility on a standard studio lot. There just wouldn't have been the space. Yet here we were watching what seemed like miles of ground racing by.

The sequence ends with the frightened man falling exhausted, writhing on the ground belly up, reaching to fend off his pursuers. His mouth gapes, too dry with fear to cry out. He gasps a stifled shriek as the camera bears in close. In the last split second, the camera swings dizzily around to show what he sees. Two, three, four horrific faces, twisted, demonic. Before the screen goes black, we just barely recognize that they are masks—the masks of the voodoo priests we meet later in the film. As it does so, the voices reach a yammering crescendo and give a final piercing shout. Silence. The movie begins. The audience (at least the audience that was me) starts the picture with adrenaline overflowing—and finishes on the margins of nausea transfixed by an image of unparalleled brutality: the film's hero expiring on an antheap where a gang of victorious zombies has left him crucified. The shot, taken overhead in cruelly slow motion, then tracks up and back, up and back . . . until the camera must have been shooting from the rafters. (How did Zip do it?) By that time, the victim has shrunk to the size of an insect in the eye of an uncaring god. Needless to say, the end, like the beginning of the film had been cut from the release version.

Zip made me wait until the movie was over before he'd answer any questions. That gave me the chance to mark another change from the release version of the film. In the *Zombie Doctor* I knew, the generic studio scoring was used throughout. Castle's original used voodoo drumming and voices; they were there all the time, building steadily through the film from slow and quiet to fast and furious. I asked Zip at once about the music.

"Yeah, they threw out all the drummin', the sons of bitches. Nigger music, they called it. Not what the audience expects. Blah, blah, blah. And, hell, they got Max's score for practically free."

"Free?"

"Yeah. See, we took over some Jungle Jim set; that's where we got the scenery from. The natives, too, buncha blacked-up extras in grass skirts. Maxie and me, we got in fast and told 'em to stay in their makeup while we shot some mob scenes. That's how we had to work on these cheapies. Used whatever was left over or layin' around. Right off, Max spots these couple of black guys—real blacks, I mean. From Jamaica they was, extras from the other movie. They was jammin' away on tom-toms in the alley outside. Just horsin' around. Max give 'em fifty bucks outa his own pocket, rustled 'em off to a soundstage, and asked 'em to knock out some music for us. Everything you heard there was from maybe an hour of recordin'. That's all the time Max could wangle. 'Gimme some voices too,' Max told 'em. 'But no English, just mumbo jumbo.' So the black guys threw that in too. Really cut loose, yippin' and howlin'. Christ! Maybe they thought Max was auditionin' them for a Tarzan movie or somethin'. He saw right away that was the music we needed. Real savage stuff. Terrific, huh?"

"And that tracking shot at the beginning?"

Zip gave a hoot. "Oh, that was a sucker! Nobody ever figured out how to do a shot like that on a studio lot except Max. We had it all planned out, Max and me. Spent a whole night settin' it up. See, we ran it in a figure eight, with all the phoney trees and vines blockin' in on all sides. Just kept that black guy runnin' around in circles, me on the hand dolly aimin' down his throat. Got the whole thing on the second try. But it was half a day's shootin'. Wasn't perfect, but that's all we had time for. Hell, nobody wasted dough back then on a credit sequence. But Max said, best thing we could do was start by scarin' the shit outa the audience. Maybe they wouldn't notice what a crummy movie this was. You see that little touch at the end, where I swish the camera? Hundred-eighty degrees, right on the button. I was layin' flat underneath, in between the actors. First time anybody ever pulled that off without a cut. I had to come right down off the dolly and make the pan just like that, one clean move, bull's-eye! And back then, the cameras was lots heavier too."

He let his mind drift back, his eyes squinching up as he reflected. "That black guy, the actor there . . . he was damn good. Looked just as scared as Max wanted. Forget his name. Never heard of him again." Then, belligerently, "I suppose that wasn't 'arty' enough for you. But lemme tell you, it was a plenty good movie for what we had to work

146

with, which was next to nothin'. We got whatever cast the studio had standin' by on the payroll that week. And film stock—strictly rationed. So much and no more. You think your Ing-o-mar Bergman could work with the spare change they give us? Ha!"

No matter how often I tried to assure Zip that I admired the movies he was showing me, he couldn't get over his defensiveness. "Really, Mr. Lipsky, I enjoyed the film. It had lots of good touches in it. Castle could certainly get a lot out of his actors. That was the best thing I ever saw Kent Taylor do. I'm just sorry the film's been damaged, if this is the only copy of the original . . ."

"Damaged! What d'you mean damaged?"

"The sprocket breaks in those two scenes. They come at important points. Even so," I hastened to assure him, "those sections have a tremendous impact. Really blood-curdling. But I think you'll admit, they'd be even better if they were repaired. You might want to let our projectionist, Don Sharkey, take care of that for you. That's his specialty, fixing up damaged films."

Zip let out a sour hiss. "You think I'd let one of Max's movies get damaged? Listen, sonny, every picture I got here is perfect. Mint condition. You don't believe me? Call Yoshi out here. Go on!"

Zip's lungs were too weak to do the job, so I gave a shout and old Yoshi came trudging in looking as fatigued and grouchy as ever.

"The big-cheese fil-um expert here," Zip said nodding toward me, "thinks he saw some torn sprockets there in the picture."

"Sprockets okay," Yoshi insisted.

"You show that part again," Zip instructed him. "Go on. Let him look for any torn sprockets. Tell you what, kiddo, I'll give you a hundred bucks for every one you find."

Puzzled, I followed Yoshi back to the booth where, reluctantly and letting me know it, he set up to rerun the last reel. When we got to the scene where the film skidded, he stopped and opened the projector. "Sprockets okay," he repeated angrily.

I unlocked the gate and slid my finger down the edge of the film inside, then looked closely. There was no sign of a single tear. I shrugged my shoulders at Yoshi and gave an embarrassed smile. "Well, it certainly *looks* like a tear," I told Zip when I returned, "but I can't find it."

Zip was amused by my confusion. "Of course you can't find it. Cause it ain't there, is why. That's no tear. That's a *slide*. It's s'posed to look like that." He gave a dry laugh.

"A slide?"

"Yeah, a slide. Sure you never heard of that. That's Max up to his tricks."

"But why would he want the film to look damaged?"

"Throws you off guard, don't it?" Zip replied slyly. "You think there's a tear, but your eye keeps watchin', right?" He gestured me back to the booth, saying, "You tell Yoshi to back that film up to the slide and run it again." He paused, eyeing me thoughtfully, then added, "And tell him I want the sallyrand."

"The what?"

"Sallyrand. Just tell him."

I did as I was told. In the booth, Yoshi fetched a small cardboard box down from a high shelf and sent me back with it. From the box Zip removed an object about the size of a flashlight and handed it to me for inspection. "Okay, Professor Know-it-all," he said in his most abrasively wise-guy voice, "this time take a gander through that." What he'd given me was a sort of viewer, rather like a kaleidoscope. Peering into it, I could see nothing but blurred white light.

"What's this?" I asked.

"Just point it at the screen and take a squint," Zip snapped impatiently, giving Yoshi the signal to run the film again. When *Zombie Doctor* returned to the screen, I stared through the device as instructed. I never saw it coming, but what happened next was an important moment, like the scene in Cocteau's *Orphée* when the hero steps through the mirror and enters the underworld. For the first time I was about to see beyond the surface of a Max Castle movie.

What I discovered there was a second series of images lightly but distinctly blurred across the screen. The images jittered vertically as if they were stuttering through a run of torn sprockets, but they nonetheless had a definite coherence. And what I saw—or thought I saw—in this bit of ghostly visual scoring radically deepened the story. It was nothing I could have taken in consciously, but I realized that the inexplicable impact of *Zombie Doctor* arose from this second, invisible, movie I was now watching, or rather now realized that I had been watching all along.

As Zip eventually explained it to me, Castle had been offered *Zombie Doctor* as a patch job. Edgar Ulmer, one of Universal's dependable hacks and a pal of Castle's from the old country, had shot some half-dozen scenes before he was taken off the picture. He recommended Castle as his replacement. It was a demeaning assignment, but Castle needed the work and the studio knew it. He was paid next to nothing and put on a bare-bones budget. At the time, zombies were a hot new item in the horror inventory. The movie was meant to capitalize on the success of *White Zombie,* a particularly lecherous Bela Lugosi vehicle of the year before. Castle was supplied with Ulmer's leavings, a half-baked screenplay, and a hard deadline. Two weeks.

The story was supposed to have something to do with Caribbean jungles, voodoo spells, and rampaging natives. Castle rapidly reworked the script, as he often did, to give it a distinctly more serious twist. In the film, a young American doctor—the Kent Taylor role—and his nurse-wife are brought to an unnamed island by missionaries to help them stop the spread of voodoo rites. The missionaries believe that poverty and disease are turning the natives back to the superstition of their tribal ancestors. The doctor is supposed to restore confidence in civilization. He does his best, but soon finds himself baffled by a strange plague that is sweeping the islands, turning the natives into walking dead men. He discovers that the problem is not a disease but a diabolical plot. There is a local plantation owner who has messianic ambitions in the islands. Castle became fascinated with this role and decided to develop it. Zip recalled that Castle tried to enlist his comrade Erich Von Stroheim for the part, seeking to give the role an ominous Germanic slant, but the imperious Von Stroheim considered the film beneath his dignity. Castle settled for George Zucco with a German accent, who put in a highly creditable performance, possibly his best.

As the story unfolds, the plantation boss is assisted by a voodoo priest who has the power to turn the natives into zombies willing to obey their master's commands without question. As Castle skewed the story, the petty island dictator takes on the megalomaniacal dimensions of a Hitlerian *Führer*. Recall, this was the early thirties; Castle's trashy little thriller may have been one of the earliest comments on totalitarianism to reach the American screen.

The film culminates in the usual clichéd action ending. The zombies carry off the doctor's wife, who is placed at the mercy of the voodoo priest. He threatens her with snakes and poison darts, and finally hypnotizes her into becoming the plantation boss's willing slave. There are sequences here that outdo the sexy suggestiveness of *White Zombie* and that were crudely edited by the studio before release. Our hero shows up in the nick of time to confront the boss. He has concocted a drug that cures the zombiism and brings people back to their senses. But the boss scoffs, telling the doctor that his mission is helpless. He—the boss—has discovered a greater secret than the doctor's medicine. Men *want* to be zombies; they will never accept the freedom the doctor offers them.

At this point, while the doctor and the boss scuffle, we have the first "slide," as Zip called it: a lightning-quick montage of mob scenes—massed throngs cheering, saluting, marching. They weren't distinct enough to be identified even when the film was clicked through frame by frame, but I took them to be newsreel clips of recent events, mainly Nazi rallies. Later, when the zombies, released from their spell, rise up to attack the doctor who has liberated them, we get the second slide. This time Zip's strange instrument revealed a blur of images showing men at war, charging across a battlefield, being gunned down by the hundreds. This might have been actual World War I newsreel footage. Here, in the middle of a second-rate horror movie, Castle had introduced an astonishingly original inter- pretation of zombiism. He'd fixed upon it as a symbol of the human desire for enslavement that was sweeping the world of his day.

"That's Max all over," Zip observed triumphantly. "He used every- thing. Everything a camera or a projector can do—he used it. Even the mistakes, the screw-ups. You should see what he could do with a flare on the film, or a ragged splice, like in the *Judas* there. Movin' pictures—Max knew 'em inside out." He gave a laugh. "I told Max, hey, we're gonna drive them projectionists nuts lookin' for that tear and not findin' it. Nah, says Max, they won't waste their time, not on crapola like this. That's what he was counting on. They'd run the picture, tears and all. Hell, they didn't care if it burned up in the machine. Back in those days, they wasn't even takin' trouble to save big-budget pictures once they got shown. What happened mostly with *Zombie Doctor* here was they just cut out the slides, which really loused up the story, y'know. They cut all that out with the witch doctor and the girl. Too sexy. Probably the best scene Wanda McKay ever did, too. Cut that. Cut the endin'—where the zombies gang up on the doctor an' knock him off. Studio said we couldn't make no picture where the zombies win. So chop! Off goes the great finish where they lynch the doctor. That's how Max saw it. He told 'em. 'The zombies're takin' over. Just look around you. People *like* bein' zombies.' They chopped it anyway. Movie didn't make any sense with the last scene cut out, but what'd they care? Pigs! Garbage was all they wanted."

"How did you do that—the slide?" Zip must have expected the question, but I might have predicted his response.

"Ha! Wouldn't you like to know?" He gave a stubborn sniff. "Nobody's gonna find out from me."

"And this?" I asked, holding up the viewer. "What did you say this was?"

He didn't answer until he had reached over and snatched it from me. "A sallyrand," he said. "That's what Max called it. You don't get that, do you? Don't know who Sally Rand was."

"I've heard the name," I said. "She was a dancer."

"A stripper she was. Get it? That's what this is: a stripper. It strips the film, so you can see what's underneath."

"I've never seen anything like that," I told him.

"Course not," Zip answered smugly. "And you won't never. Max invented that, so's he could do the secret stuff. Only his eye was so good, he didn't even need it. Second sight he had, when it come to movies."

"Secret stuff? Like what?"

"Like what you just seen there with the stripper." He was already stashing the odd little instrument away in its box.

"How is it made?" I asked. "Do you know?"

"Sure I do. Any shooter could make one. Just a couple lenses and a diffuser is all it is. Plus this little refractin' gizmo Max invented. Course you gotta position everything just right, which is tricky. But if that's all you got, you got nothin'."

"What do you mean?"

"Cuz the whole point is what's up there on the screen. If you got no split lightin', you don't see anything with the sallyrand. It's like you got a key but no lock, see?"

"Oh yes," I said, as if I understood. "Would you let me borrow the sallyrand?"

"Over my dead body!" he flashed out at me, then repeated the phrase, lending it a somber tone that rather worried me. Zip was inhabiting what looked too much like a dead body already.

As tactfully as possible I raised a small protest. "Don't you intend to tell anybody how Castle did these things—not ever?"

As if he'd been waiting all his embittered life to answer that one,

Zip rifled his answer back. "You think that's what Max'd want after how they screwed him over? Not on your life. Made him go beggin' work off all these crumb-bum no-talents. Katzman, Halperin, hacks like that. They had him doin' Fu Manchu, for God's sake! Max!"

I could see his jaw clenching with anger. "But he did have friends, didn't he?" I asked. "People who admired him and wanted to work with him. You told me Karl Freund gave him some help when he was down on his luck, and Murnau."

"Oh sure. Them krauts, they stuck together—except for the Big Dictator Von Sternberg there, stuck-up son of a bitch. Hell, why shouldn't they push some work Max's way? On a bad day when he was hung over to beat the band, he could still grind out a better movie than any of 'em. Right from the first, when he worked with what's-his-name-there Leni . . . Paul Leni. It was Max did all the lightin' on *The Cat and the Canary*. And that scene on the milk wagon, with all the hellfire. Sure that was Max. At least Leni was good on his own, and a right guy. Paid Max what he was worth. But now like Edgar brainless Ulmer—that was a different story. Cheez! Max give him all the best shots in *Black Cat*, rewrote the thing, redesigned it. You know for how much? Chicken feed."

"That's interesting," I commented. "Because actually Edgar Ulmer is very highly regarded these days. A few of his films have been called masterpieces."

Zip stared back at me almost cross-eyed with amazement. It was as if I'd slugged him with a blackjack. "Ulmer? By *who* is Ulmer regarded?"

"French critics for the most part. Mainly because of *Black Cat*. And *Detour*."

"French? You mean like . . . from *France*?" His expression began to tilt toward true anguish. I wondered if I should offer apologies. "Jeez, if that don't beat all! You mean . . . you mean, Ulmer . . . *Ulmer*?"

He was turning grey with disgust. I rushed to take what advantage I could of the moment. "You realize you could do a great deal to salvage Castle's reputation. There are directors who'd give their eye-teeth to learn what you could tell them about these unusual techniques."

He spit out an exasperated breath. "Who wants to hear from *me*, huh? The little freak, the commie runt. Flung me out on my ass is what they did. So let'm do without." Then, after a short private sulk, he looked up with a wily smile. "You don't know the half of it, what Max and me was up to." He was clearly aching to tell me, so I waited until he'd sucked a few more strangled drags out of his cigarette. "Eddy Puss. You heard of him?"

"Who?"

"College boy! Eddy Puss. Ancient Greek guy."

"Do you mean Oedipus? The Greek tragedy?"

"That's the ticket. Max and me were gonna make a movie about him."

"Oh? That's interesting."

"You think that's interesting, do you? Well, get a load of this. Max was gonna have the camera be this guy's eyes."

"That's clever. A first-person narrative."

Zip made a sour face. "First person . . . Get off it, professor. The movie was gonna show the story like Eddy saw it. You get me?"

"Yes, I think so."

"Hell, you do!" Zip spat back cantankerously. "The guy was *blind*. Didn't you know that?"

"Well, yes, he puts out his own eyes. That comes at the end. Of course there's another play by Sophocles that begins after Oedipus is already blind. It's called . . ."

"Yeah, yeah, yeah. That's the one, where the guy's blind. That's the movie Max was gonna make. *Through his eyes.* Catch?"

I didn't catch. "You mean a dark screen? All dark? But what would there be to look at?"

Zip started to laugh, then broke down in a racking cough. He loved being one up on "the professor"; that had become one of the pleasures he took in my company. When he got enough air back in his lungs, he went on. "There was gonna be plenty on that screen, take it from me. Max had it all worked out. We even shot some stuff—just on the quick and cheap." Zip assumed a crafty air. "That's where the underhold comes in."

Underhold?

When he saw I didn't understand, he repeated the word, hitting every syllable as if he were spelling it out for a child. "The un-der-hold. That's German."

Zip might have thought it was German, but he'd certainly gotten the word wrong. "German for what?"

"You're the professor. I thought professors was supposed to know German."

I'd never claimed to. But I could see it was useless to ask for clarification. As usual, Zip didn't have it to give. Castle, I gathered, had frequently used German to buffalo Zip. This was probably another instance. I filed the word away, hoping to discover its meaning later.

That evening when I returned to The Classic, my big news was about the sallyrand. Sharkey, with his technical turn of mind, was immediately fascinated, though he couldn't follow what Zip had told me about the instrument's construction. "What kind of lenses did he say were in there?"

"He didn't."

"Plus a diffuser, is that what he said?"

"Yeah. And some kind of refracting filter."

Sharkey wagged his head. "Can't feature that. You're sure he won't let you borrow the thing?"

"Absolutely. In fact, I got the idea he wished he hadn't shown it to me at all."

"Me too," Clare chimed in. "I wish he'd kept it to himself. Hocus-pocus."

Sharkey was amazed. "You mean you're not curious about how it works?"

"Not me," Clare answered. "I wouldn't touch the thing."

"You wouldn't?"

"If she'd had any sense, Madame Curie wouldn't have touched radium. Get the point?"

As for what Zip had told me about a production of *Oedipus*, that brought a blank, uncomprehending stare from both Clare and Sharkey. "A movie without pictures—I've heard of that," was Sharkey's comment. "It's called radio."

Seeking as best I could to clarify, I asked Clare if she'd ever come across a German word that sounded like "underhold." She hadn't; even after she'd paged through all the *unters* in her German dictionary, she couldn't come up with a good guess at what Zip might have in mind. Her conclusion was predictably dismissive. "A blank screen is what you get for free before the movie starts and after it's finished. In between there's supposed to be a work of art. Probably Herr Castle thought he could dispense with that little item."

"I don't think so. Zip said there'd be 'plenty' on the screen."

"Plenty of what?"

"He wouldn't tell me that. Maybe it has to do with the sallyrand."

Though I asked Zip about the sallyrand a couple more times, he slapped me down hard, refusing to talk further. "Forget it, wouldja? If I was you, I'd just forget I ever seen that damn thing. If them orphans knew I had one . . ."

Zip had mentioned "them orphans" a few times before, but without explaining who they might be. The one time I asked, he clammed up for the rest of the day. I'd learned to handle the subject gingerly. I paused, then put my question as casually as possible. "What would they do, these orphans?"

"Just never you mind."

And that was the last I heard from Zip about the sallyrand. It would be a long while before I saw one again.

Another two weeks went by before Zip made an important admission—almost a confession. By that time, thanks to my constant deference, he'd softened toward me, offering more about his work with Castle as he came to trust my appreciative responses. "Some of these tricks here—I can spot 'em . . . but the fact is, I don't always know just exactly how they was done." I could see how embarrassed he was to tell me this. "I mean—see, I wasn't in on that part of things."

Not knowing what to ask, I simply waited for him to tell me more.

"See, I did just about all the shootin'. I was the only shooter Max really trusted with a camera. But some of these tricks—like the slide and all like that—that was done in the editin'. Max sort of kept that to himself. Not cause he didn't trust me. Me an' Max—we was like that. Like he usta say, 'Zip, you are the *pure* technician. That's why you are my most valued associate.' His very words. 'You are my eyes and my hands.' That's what I was all right, Max's eyes and hands, doin' the job just like he wanted. You know how they treated me in the studios before Max came along? And *after*, too? Like some kinda lousy little monkey or somethin'. Usta give 'em a laugh to see me bustin' my guts with the big loads. I never backed off a job, I can tell y'. But I knew I could be a shooter. I had the eye, that's what I had. The rest don't matter. Max knew that. He spotted what I had. He gimme the chance to ride the camera. You know what that feels like? Man! There's nothin' like it."

Whenever Zip spoke of Castle, there was a thrill of pride in his voice. His little body actually seemed to take on size with the memory. But in what he said, I heard a different message, one that struck a deep note of pathos. I'd begun to wonder how much Zip really understood about Castle and about the meaning of his work. While Zip was forever telling me what great friends he and Castle were, I now felt certain their relationship hadn't been one of true partners, let alone equals. Rather, it struck me that just possibly what Castle most valued in Zip was his stubborn loyalty and willing subservience. Zip was always ready to be the unquestioning tool in his master's hand, a first-rate cameraman who could complete an assignment even when he didn't grasp its meaning.

I reported all this to Clare. "I think Castle exploited Zip quite a lot. Zip doesn't remember it that way, but I think Castle used him because he was easy to boss around."

Clare nodded agreement. "The more I learn about your Max Castle, the less I like him."

My Max Castle. That was becoming a fixed phrase in her vocabulary. *My* Max Castle. Not hers. This stubborn standoffishness on her part made me reluctant to convey the full flavor of some of Castle's movies. I began to soft-pedal the aspects of his work that most unsettled her—like the crushing sense of decadence that permeated *Zombie Doctor*. The zombies of the story weren't simply obedient robots. They were also endowed with a peculiarly physical repulsiveness: unnatural creations without soul or mind, clinging to the life of the body. I knew that if Clare had viewed the films, she would have done all she could to block that repellent experience out. I decided to block it for her.

On the other hand, by way of my reports, Clare's respect for Zip Lipsky was mounting by the week, despite his incessant crustiness. She asked me to find out more about his blacklisting period, and I did. It turned out that he wasn't all that political himself; his parents were the lifelong Lefties, communists of some prominence in the New York radical scene. They'd been at the famous Paul Robeson concert in the Catskills that got broken up by vigilante patriots in 1946. Old Mr. Lipsky had suffered a severe concussion in the riot. Zip was convinced it brought on his death about a year later. He got involved in the Robeson documentary that finally cost him his career more out of family loyalty than ideology.

Before that, at the beginning of the war, Zip had employed a Japanese gardener who got caught in the government roundup after Pearl Harbor. Just before the troops closed in, the gardener appealed to Zip to help keep his two young sons out of the camps. Zip agreed. He took Yoshi's two boys in for the duration, telling those who asked that they were Chinese refugees. In the camps, Yoshi had become seriously ill. When the war ended, Zip took him in too as a sort of semicompetent household factotum. As a result, Yoshi and his boys had become fanatically loyal to Zip. I'd seen the two sons helping out around the house and grounds on a couple of occasions, once doing what looked like a major roof repair.

A man who takes risks and does favors like that can be forgiven a good-sized load of bad temper. Clare decided to arrange a Zip Lipsky festival at The Classic, though we both wondered if he'd last long enough to see it. Each time I visited, he seemed to have visibly deteriorated. He was basically a fragile, rabbity man; even at his strongest, he couldn't have given his disease more than bones to gnaw on. Now it was as if the cigarettes he couldn't do without were smoking *him*, burning his insides to ashes. It was bad enough to watch the feisty little guy wasting away before my eyes; but his declining health was posing an odd problem for me. The sicker he became, the longer into the day he had to rest. Which meant that more and more often, when I arrived at the house, the ailing Zip was still asleep. And that presented an opportunity which the predatory Mrs. L. wasn't about to pass up.

9 THE PERILS OF NYLANA

Through my first two months as a guest in Zip Lipsky's home, I'd done my best to fend off the lady's insistent lechery by playing dumb. But there is a boundary beyond which dumb becomes idiotic, and I was well past that point with Franny—as she insisted I call her. Footsies under the table had long since given way to handsies in the darkness of the projection room. And the handsies were getting tighter, sweatier, more exploratory all the time. When I came and left, there were mushy kisses hello and goodbye at the door, with ever more insistent invitations to spend the night. "You're *sure* you don't wanna stay overnight? You're *sure?* Ah, come on . . . stay overnight. I gotta nice, big, soft bed waiting for you upstairs."

If Zip noticed any of this—and how could he miss it?—he didn't let on. I had the impression he was used to his wife's aggressive flirtatiousness, but that gave me no hint how far he'd be willing to let things go. Probably I could have deflected the overeager Franny indefinitely one way or another if it weren't for the fact that Zip's naps were lasting longer and longer. That sometimes gave Franny as much as a couple of hours with me alone on the days or evenings I came to watch films. She used the time trying, not at all subtly, to move me on to the couch or into one of the empty bedrooms, and then pouting like a real-life Betty Boop when I proved reluctant. My only way of stalling her was to make conversation. But I soon discovered there wasn't much Franny could make conversation about. Could she tell me anything about Max Castle? No, that was before she met Zip, which was just after the war started. All she knew was that Zip just practically worshiped the man, because who else would have given someone like Zip such a big break? What did she think of Castle's movies? Oh, they were so morbid, they made her feel just so depressed, why did anyone want to watch depressing things like that?

"I like love stories," she was quick to tell me. "Why don't we get some love stories to watch? Wouldn't that be nice? Did you ever see *Autumn Leaves*, where Joan Crawford (she was over fifty when she made that picture, no matter what they say) has this young guy—it was Kirk Douglas, I think, or maybe Cliff Robertson . . . no, it was Rock Hudson—anyway, he's half her age, and he goes all ga-ga over her."

Her habit was to prattle away in a squeaky little-girl voice, wrinkling up her nose and making her dimples show. She seemed to think that made her irresistibly charming.

Finally, as a last resort, we got around to talking about the posters on the wall. "*The Perils of Nylana*," I remarked, "I saw that. Every episode, some twice."

Franny's eyes popped. "You *did*? But you must of been just a baby."

"It was still running after the war."

"I didn't know you cared about things like serials. I thought you were too brainy for that."

"I was only a kid. Nylana was my first big heartthrob."

"She *was*?"

"I was really crazy about her."

"You mean like with sexual fantasies and all?"

"It was all very childish of course. But it leaves a mark. I didn't realize Zip ever worked on serials."

"Silly! Of course he didn't. When *Nylana* was made, Zip was in the big time."

"Oh. So why does he have these posters . . ."

"Well, I live here too. These are *my* posters. That's *me*."

"Who is?"

"Nylana the Jungle Girl. That's me. I mean that *was* me."

I stared at her in amazement. "Kay Allison is *you?*"

"Can't you tell? Oh come on, I haven't changed *that* much."

My God, I said to myself. "My God," I said out loud to her. "You're *really* Nylana?" No matter how I reshaped her pudgy, makeup-caked face in my mind, I couldn't find the features of my first love there. Kay Allison had been a lithe brunette beauty, wide-eyed and snub-nosed. Franny Lipsky was nothing like that. She might have been no older than her late forties, but her bulk and her general slovenliness made her seem much older.

Stupidly, I said, "But your name is Franny. . . ."

"My *real* name is Franny. Frances Louise Dukas. In the movies I was Kay Allison. Did you see *Nylana and The Cobra Cult* too?"

"Sure I did. And *Nylana and the Valley of Doom.*"

I should have realized that my answers might be encouraging her. They were, but in my astonishment I failed to notice and blundered on. "That was the one I liked best, where she—you—wore that leopard skin. . . ."

Giggling with delight, she scooted her chair around the table and jammed her knees into mine. "You saw me in my moment of stardom," she squealed. "Did you ever write to me for an autographed picture?"

"Yes, I did." I didn't tell her that I still had that picture carefully hidden away in my parents' basement with my collection of comic books and cereal-box prizes. By now that picture, which I hadn't laid eyes upon for years, was doubtless turning brown and fading. Perhaps the all-devouring Modesto mold had gotten to it. But the woman whose likeness it had once been was before me now, summoning back to life all that the picture had once represented.

"I'll tell you a secret," Franny whispered, leaning close. "I didn't sign those pictures myself. The studio did. Even way after my contract ended. But I got to see the letters. Oh, there were lots of boys who wrote to me. You should see some of the mash notes I got. Woo! Did they send you the one of me in the leopard skin? I hope they sent you that one."

"Yes, they did."

"Say, wasn't I something to see? That leopard skin, the way it fit—so tight, I could hardly move." She let out a flutter of giggles. "I musta fell outa that thing a dozen times. We had guys from all over the studio just standing around the set, waiting for me to fall out. Because you know, I did all my own stunts. God! I musta been out of my mind. That's really why I got the part, I think. They didn't have to hire a stunt girl. Whatever they told me to do, I just did it. Like once when I was being chased by that ape (that was Beany Wybrowsky, the football player, in the suit, you know), I had to swing by this rope over the crocodiles. And halfway across, guess what?" Another run of giggles. "Boom, boom. Out they came. Both barrels. I got so shook up, I missed my landing. So there I was like Gypsy Rose Lee hanging in midair. They didn't have enough money to reshoot, so they just made a quick cut. But, if you watch real close just at the end of that chapter, you can see me starting to show. Just a little flash there. Boy, I bet I gave some little boys out there a big thrill."

Oh God, I remembered! I remembered! I had stayed through three shows that day to see if my eyes had betrayed me.

"You know," Franny went on, "somebody did a real mean thing. They cut a frame outa that episode with me hanging out, and sold it around town as a naughty picture. Bet you'd like to see that, wouldn't ja? Huh? Well, I got a copy of that upstairs. What'y say? You wanna come up and see?"

I'd spent the years of my boyhood hoping there was a picture like that somewhere in the world. But of course I wouldn't admit that to her, even though she was now mussing my hair and maneuvering as if to sit down in my lap. "Whatever became of you?" I asked. "I mean . . . in Hollywood?"

She gave a sad little wincing smile and shrugged. It was the most genuine look she'd given me so far. "That was it. My whole career. I made all those serials in about one year. God, I can't even remember one from the other anymore. Then, they just stopped making serials. But after that, wherever I went for a job, I was always the Jungle Girl. And nobody wanted Jungle Girls anymore. Do you know, when I was first discovered—that's what they called it, you know, when some sleaze-ball took you home from one of those parties and rolled you in the hay: being *discovered*—this bald old geezer who said he was a producer said, 'You're gonna be a second Betty Grable.' You know." She spun around, hiked her skirt to mid-thigh, pulled it tight across the ample contours of her bottom, and smiled winsomely over her shoulder. The classic pinup-girl image. "I still got the gams, haven't I? Huh? Well, not bad for an old gal anyway. Every time I got discovered, I was gonna be a second somebody. Rita Hayworth. Linda Darnell. Maria Montez. Imagine—the second Maria Montez. What was that to be? That's when I knew I was sinking fast. Good ol' Zippy. He was a great one for taking people in."

"You met him when you were making the serials?"

"No, before that. When I was just a starlet. Starlet. You know what that means. It means showing up at a lot of parties and . . . you know. We met at some studio shindig. There was this real creep of a guy trying to proposition me into doing some skin flicks. Zippy could see how green I was. He warned me off and promised to get me a bit part in the movie he was shooting. That's how I got started. Once I had a scene with Barbara Stanwyck. *Lady of Burlesque.* You can see me over her shoulder. Zip got me the test for Nylana too. He was just this runty little guy, but he had a heart of gold. Lucky for me he concerned himself, because after Nylana, I was really getting desperate. You see, I always had this weight problem, boy did I! I just wasn't gonna be a starlet too much longer. And anyway, Zippy was getting pretty sick and needed somebody to look after him. So . . . but listen, this is the same bust you saw in that leopard skin. Forty inches. I haven't put on one fraction more. It's just . . . all the rest of me sort of caught up with my boobies."

She was standing over me, waggling the bosom that had haunted my boyhood. And in spite of myself, I was responding. Not to the bizarre woman who was disporting herself in front of me. I was being seduced by my own childhood fantasies.

During the days I spent in the Lipsky household, I learned a great deal about the magic of Max Castle's films. But, in her own way, Franny also taught me something about the delusionary power of the movies. For I did finally follow her upstairs to examine her photo of Nylana Unbound. And even if I'd protested (which I didn't), Franny would have insisted upon me making a critical comparison with the picture's unclad original. Yes, I had to agree, forty naked inches were forty naked inches and every bit as arousing. Because, though Franny was overweight and overaged and overbearing, some intangible part of her, more a property of my vestigial pubescent imagination than of the woman before me, was still *my* Nylana. Wrestling awkwardly with her across the bed in one of the abandoned upstairs rooms, I realized I was tunneling through the dark landscape of my own psyche, reconnecting with subterranean fountains of juvenile lust that I thought had long since run dry. But no, they were there, as effervescent as ever, the obsessive and utterly unreal images of desire that the movies implant in the adolescent mind. The beauty that never fades, the kiss that never ends, the night of passion that swells to crescendo on a Max Steiner theme and ends the film balanced forever on a pinnacle of undying intensity.

At the age of eleven, every boy becomes a demon driven by insatiable hungers. The picture shows of childhood feed that demon a feast of sexual expectations that can't possibly survive the messy, graceless ordinariness of their fulfillment. In every grown man, that demon lives on, secretly turning sullen and ugly with its disappointment, fighting off the maturity that it knows is nothing more than resignation. We spend our youth hunting for the reality we think lies on the other side of our illusions. What we find at the end of our search is what lies on the other side of the movie screen: a dark and desolate space that only reveals the unreality of what we pursued. So we spend our adulthood trying to recapture the illusions. Few of us do. But I was privileged to relive what others lose forever. Franny made that possible. Would she have been hurt to know that the moments we spent in ungainly and overheated intercourse were a private fantasy trip for me, that I was using her too-too-solid flesh to resurrect the phantom of Nylana? I don't think so. Because I was giving her the chance to be Nylana all over again. Her moment of stardom regained.

I could never tell if Zip suspected what Franny and I had gotten up to—not that it amounted to more than two or three steamy sessions before the fantasy wore thin for me and I became as evasive with her as before. I think Zip was beyond caring. Even in the course of the few months I spent with him, his blood was running slower and colder each time we met. Sometimes, as I sat beside him in the dark, the intervals between his labored wheezing grew so long, I wondered if he'd stopped breathing and would bend to listen closely until his gruff respiration sounded again.

Or if he did know about my interludes with Franny, he might

actually have been grateful. As Franny once confided to me, "Zip and me, we aren't *really* married, I mean the way regular people are. See, he's mostly been so awful sick, poor little guy. I'm more his sort of nurse, you know?"

As I understood it, Zip had spent the last twenty years of his life struggling to squeeze the oxygen through his moribund tissues. Perhaps it would have relieved him to know that Franny hadn't been condemned to a life of total abstinence. Or so I preferred to think.

By the time we'd gone through his collection of Castle films three times, I'd arrived at a disheartening conclusion. Zip simply didn't have much to tell me about the man he admired so greatly. Castle had clearly enveloped Zip with his charismatic charm; but he'd created that charm by holding back a lot and so cloaking himself with an air of mystery. Zip, for example, knew very little about Castle's work at UFA. "Water under the bridge," Zip reported more than once when I asked about Castle's early career. "Never said a word about it." Even for the Hollywood years when they were close associates, there were blank spots all through Zip's recollection—especially for several extended periods in the thirties, months at a time that Castle had spent in Europe trying to raise money for his independent productions. Zip had accompanied him on only one of these jaunts. On that trip—Zip remembered it as the summer of 1938—some scattered filming had actually been done in France, in Denmark, in Switzerland. It was while he was sorting through his dim memory of the trip that "the orphans" came up again.

"I guess the orphans were a big problem for Castle." I dropped the remark as if we'd talked about all this before.

"You can say that again." Zip fairly spat out the words. "Especially that Von Pull-zig dame. She really screwed up the works for us, the old bloodsucker."

"She was one of the orphans, was she?"

"Christ, yeah. She was one of the big-cheese orphans. She even scared Max. He hated her guts. Me too. You know what she called me? A *monkey*."

"But she helped launch Castle's career, I thought."

"Oh sure. She was his whatyoucall sponsor when he was a kid. But once them orphans get their claws in you, they don't let go. See, she never liked Max makin' any movies on his own that the orphans couldn't have their big say-so about."

"But how could they expect to influence his work from Europe?"

"They weren't just in Europe," he answered, as if I had asked a dumb question. "They were all over the studios right here. Like them goddam twins."

"Twins?"

"The Reinkings, the Reinkings. They did all Max's editing. That's where they stuck in all the tricks. See, they knew all about the flicker."

"The flicker?"

"Sure. That's what makes Max's pictures so good. The flicker. He knew how to use it just right. Him and the Reinkings."

"The flicker . . ." I groped my way ahead awkwardly. "That was one of the tricks."

"Nah!" Zip snapped, as if I should know better. "The flicker was how you made the tricks happen just right. First you had to get hold of the flicker, see? Then you could stick in all the tricks you wanted."

"Oh yes," I said, understanding nothing. "So the flicker was . . ."

"Was what?"

"I'm sort of . . . asking. What was the flicker?"

Zip went silent all of a sudden, as if he'd decided to slam on the mental brakes. "Wouldn't you like to know?" he said, reverting to his tough-guy mode.

By now I'd come to suspect that "wouldn't-you-like-to-know" was what Zip said when he had no answer to give. And when he ran out of answers, he began to grow cantankerous. I quickly shifted the discussion to new ground.

"How did you get along with the Reinkings?"

"Phaw! They treated me like absolute dirt, they did. Son-of-a-bitch stuck-up krauts. They usta call me 'the mechanic.' The *mechanic!* Can you beat that? Editin'—that was 'art,' see? That's how they saw it. But runnin' the camera—that was just bein' a mechanic. Every chance they got, they froze me out. Max—he woulda let me in on the editin'. But not them Reinkings."

"They were twins, you say—the Reinkings. Twin men . . ."

"*One* was a man. Heinzy was a man. God only knows what the other one was. That was Franzy. But I usta call 'em Hans an' Fritz."

"You couldn't tell whether the other one was a man or woman?"

"Them orphans could be queer. Queer. Like Von Pull-zig there. I guess she was a woman. But real dykey. I had my suspicions about her. I bet she shaved every morning. Wouldn't surprise me."

"So the twins were film editors. I don't remember seeing their names on any movies."

"They didn't care about that. They didn't want their names on anythin'. What they liked to do was work with the new editors—the greenhorns. Or with real goof-offs. And then they'd just sort of take over the job. See, they was real good, real sharp, I have to admit. Fast and good. And they was always hangin' around, givin' advice. Well, Heinzy give advice. Franzy—I never heard him say a word. A real spook he was. So people let 'em do this an' that. Especially with the cheapies. Nobody cared who worked on the cheapies."

"The studio let them get away with that?"

"*Somebody* in the studio let 'em. *Somebody* was keepin' 'em on the payroll."

"Who?"

"Wouldn't you like to know?"

"Which studio did they work for?"

"*All* the studios. Them orphans worked all over town."

"You mean there were lots of orphans—in all the studios?"

"Not a lot. I didn't say a lot. Just enough. In just the right places to stick their noses in."

"Why did Castle have so much to do with these orphans?"

He answered as if it were stupid to ask. "Hell, Max was an orphan himself. But he never treated me like dirt, like the rest of 'em."

"Max was an orphan?"

"You didn't know?"

"But you said Max hated this Von Pölzig woman."

"Right. Because Max wanted to go his own way. He wanted to make his own picture. So old bloodsucker Von Pull-zig, she got all in a huff. Snotty bitch. And, boy, did Max tell her off but good."

"This was in that summer—1938?"

"What else're we talking about? Sure. That summer. I thought Max was gonna haul off an' pop her one."

"Where did they have this argument?"

"I told you. In Europe there."

"I mean, was it in Paris . . . ?"

"In Zurich. When we was in Zurich. That's where the head orphanage was. Christ, that was some blowup."

"Do you remember what they said?"

"Nah! It was all in German. I couldn't pick up a word. But it was a plenty hot argument. That's when she called me a monkey. Max told me."

"So what came of it?"

"She screwed us but good. Made sure Max couldn't raise a nickel." Smugly, he added, "We had Garbo all lined up."

"Greta Garbo?"

"Was there any other Garbo you ever heard of? Max had her signed on the dotted line. Then, kapoot! No dough, no Garbo."

"You're saying that Max Castle was going to use Greta Garbo in one of his films?"

"You got it. Just her eyes. That's all he wanted. Just her eyes. We tried to set it up with her two, three times. Always fell through because of the dough. She wanted plenty. Fifty thousand bucks for maybe two, three hours of shootin'. Big money in those days."

"So Castle never got to film her?"

"Not after Von Pull-zig put the whammy on him. Max couldn't raise that kinda money. We got the eyes. But they wasn't Garbo's eyes."

"Whose eyes did you get?"

He gave me a foxy stare. "Guess."

"I give up."

"Come on. Whose eyes were next best to Garbo's? I mean if you wanted sad eyes. That's what Max wanted. Sad."

"Really, I have no idea."

"Ah, you don't know nothin'." Zip was forever losing his temper with me and condemning my gross ignorance. "Sylvia Sidney. Right? I mean just the eyes up close."

"Oh yes, now that you mention it."

"Damn right I'm right. Shooters know eyes. That's where you get the light from inside. The eyes. Sylvia Sidney. Terrific eyes. Maybe better'n Garbo. She worked cheap too. A thousand bucks she did it for. Sweet kid. I coulda gone for her."

"You shot her eyes, that's all?"

"Max had this thing about eyes. He collected 'em. Whenever he saw eyes he liked—like Garbo's there or Sylvia's—he tried to get 'em in front of the camera. Sometimes Max'd use a real stinky actor just cuz the guy had great eyes. Then Max'd make sure we got 'em filmed. For later."

"Later?"

"Later in his own movies. Max was carryin' a dozen movies in his head all the time I knew him, tryin' to scratch together the cash. All he ever got done was a scene here, a scene there, couple shots of this and that. When I started earnin' good money, I gave him lots of dough—but, hell, I was no Louis B. Mayer."

"How was he going to use these eyes?"

"Eyes meant somethin' special to Max. Know what he said once? 'God is in the eyes. The devil too, every time you blink.' " Zip peered sharply at me rather as if he wished I might explain the remark. When I didn't, he gave a grumpy little grunt and went on. " 'The eyes're the doors of heaven and hell,' he usta say." Zip paused again, studying me, clearly hoping I'd be suitably impressed. I offered him a nod and a thoughtful "Hm." That seemed to satisfy him. "What Max did was he snuck the eyes in behind the movie. Like in *House of Blood*. That was all eyes, in the shadows, all these doped-up actors we shot at one of Max's parties, while they was watchin' Olga do her dance."

"Olga . . . that's Olga Tell?"

"None other. She was Max's lady friend. Beautiful girl."

"What kind of dance?"

Zip's face went stone-wall blank. "None of your business, nosey!"

I quickly changed the subject. "So that's where all the eyes went— into *House of Blood*?"

"Not *all* of 'em. Some of 'em. Max and me, we had lots more. Some day he wanted to make a movie that was all eyes, nothin' but eyes. And, of course, split lightin'."

"Oh yes . . . split lighting. That was one of the tricks, wasn't it?"

Zip gave an exasperated hiss. "Nah! Split lighting was just split lighting. You could lay the tricks on top of it, if you wanted. But it wasn't a trick—like the slide."

"It was more like the flicker."

Another testy hiss. "Jesus, no! The flicker was always there. You could split light *over* the flicker, but you didn't have to. The split lightin' was just to bring out the flicker. The flicker is basic. It's like you could say the heartbeat. *Structure*, understand? That's how Max put it. Let's see . . . there was structure. And there was . . ." He was struggling to remember things he had memorized but never really understood. "God, I can't get it. They always used the German, you know—between themselves. *Overlay*. That's it. Structure and overlay. Tricks was overlay. They came mostly in the editin'. See, you don't have to know all that to do the shootin'."

"So the split lighting was completely separate from the tricks?"

"Right."

"It was a kind of lighting?"

"Right."

"And all these things—the split lighting, the tricks—were part of the underhold?"

"Yeah . . . sort of."

"And the underhold was . . . ?"

"Wouldn't you like to know?"

I dutifully reported all this to Clare, hoping that she'd pick up on some of what Zip left so obscure. But she knew nothing about slides and flickers and split lighting. "It sounds like a totally different species of filmmaking," she commented, giving the remark a distinctly disapproving twist. "Makes me feel like an old bard who's being told about some newfangled kind of literature called 'wri-ting.' "

"The trouble is," I explained, "I don't think Zip can tell me much more than he already has. Castle hired him to shoot his films, but Zip was never in on the editing. That was always done by Castle and the Reinkings. Zip thinks it was the Reinkings who blocked him out. But I'm not sure. It might have been Castle himself. Zip can be very loyal; but I sense that Castle didn't return that trust. Incidentally, Zip shot off a lot of footage that never seemed to have much connection with the movie they were working on. Extra stuff. Often got shot at Castle's house when he gave parties. He never left any film stock over. Used it all. In fact, he'd even go around the studio begging spare stock off other directors."

"What became of all the outtakes and extra footage?" Clare asked.

"Some of it might have gotten back to Zip, but I don't think very much. That's one of his grievances with the Reinkings. They kept a lot of what they edited for Castle."

"What happened to them after Castle's death?"

"Zip thinks they went back to Europe after the war. By that time Zip was well installed in the studios doing major pictures. He lost touch with Castle's circle, not that he ever had much rapport with any of them."

"But he says there were more of these orphans around?"

"That's what he remembers from when he was still working. He says he used to go out of his way to make sure none of them laid hands on any of his films. He hasn't been working for more than ten years now, so all this might have changed."

Clare pondered my report. "Remember when we unpacked the *Judas*? There was an envelope postmarked Zurich. It said something

168

about orphans. *Sturmwaisen,* wasn't that it? Find out about that if you can."

I said I'd try, but warned her, "Zip can be so touchy, especially when you get close to things he doesn't know. He gets angry and stubborn. And I think there's a lot he doesn't know."

I brought Clare my thoughts and speculations about Castle like so many gifts, hoping, in my naive way, that my service as an intermediary would lend me intellectual stature in her eyes. If it did, she didn't let it show. In fact, it sometimes seemed that my association with Castle was driving a wedge between us—as if I were a messenger contaminated by the unwelcome intelligence I brought.

One night, before I fell asleep beside her, I heard Clare musing over her last cigarette, "Ever since I got serious about movies—the night my mother took me to see *Les Enfants du Paradis*—I knew there was something there, deeper in. Something more than the glamour, the enchantment. Behind that. A power. Anything that could reach inside and take hold of you that way . . . I went back to see that movie seven times. I was just a kid, but I knew the whole civilized world was going up in smoke. And here was this work of exquisite beauty, so pure, so delicate. Like a flower growing on a battlefield. It was an intellectual ecstasy. But even then, I knew there were ways that power could be twisted. . . ." Then, after a long pause: "Suppose you were there, Jonny, when they invented fire. Suppose some genius of the species brought you the first torch. Such a gift. But suppose you could see—right there—the ruined cities, the charred flesh, the burning battlefields. What would you do, Jonny? What would you do? Drown the fire. Kill the inventor."

10 THE CELLULOID PYRE

Wandering through Zip's distant and darkening memories of Max Castle was becoming more and more of a mystery tour with each visit. His recollections were forever turning into culs-de-sac, labyrinths, locked doors. His great benefactor had left him with a backlog of oracular pronouncements and baffling incidents which the little guy had been puzzling over for years. As much as anything Castle had ever put on film, it was this lingering aura of strangeness that made him special to Zip, a wizard in touch with higher powers. My problem as the intruding scholar was to decide if Castle was the sorcerer his loyal apprentice still took him to be. Or was he a carnival faker willing to exploit the easy gullibility of those who trusted him?

There was one talk I had with Zip that managed to distill the enigmatic essence of his relationship with Castle. It raised a multitude of questions which, as usual, I stored away to be taken up later when I judged that Zip might be more forthcoming. But this time the questions would go permanently unanswered. Zip and I would never talk again.

We were watching Castle's final movie, *Axis Agent*. Since Zip didn't assist on the film, he hadn't been able to get hold of a good print. That made him reluctant to screen the picture. He was as sensitive to bad film as Clare. Twice before we'd gotten about a half hour into a less than perfect print, only to have him petulantly order Yoshi to stop. "I shoulda scrapped this piece of *dreck* years ago," he muttered. And back into the can it went.

This time we got through to the end, but it wasn't worth the time. Even making allowances for the inferior quality of the print, it was clear that this was among Castle's least distinguished efforts, bearing none of his artistic trademarks. Zip was sure the movie had been batted out in less than ten days and that a few other hands had patched it over here and there. In passing, I tossed off the observation I remembered Clare making the first time she saw the film—that there was a great deal in *Axis Agent* Castle had borrowed from *Citizen*

Kane. "I guess he was so rushed he had to lift a few things." I meant no disrespect by the remark, but at once Zip began to fume.

"Lift?" He turned on me with such pique that he immediately crumpled up in a spasm of coughing. I waited for him to continue. "Max never lifted nothin', junior. You got it exactly vicey-versy. Orson, he lifted from Max."

I'd learned not to contradict him too sharply, so I assumed an objectively inquisitive air. "Oh? Do you think so? But I thought *Citizen Kane* was completed before this film."

"Course it was."

"Then how could Orson Welles have lifted anything from *Axis Agent*?"

"He didn't, dumb-dumb. Not from the movie. From the horse's own mouth." When I didn't register comprehension, Zip blew out an exasperated sigh. "Boy, talkin' to you is like talkin' to a bowl of chop suey. Orson lifted from Max *direct* is what I'm tellin' you. The two of them, they had their heads together all the time Orson was makin' the movie. That Orson, he was some good listener. Picked up on every word Max said. And he was gettin' it all free of charge, just for the cost of the booze. That's how hungry Max was to get in on a first-class production."

"You're telling me Castle assisted on *Citizen Kane*?"

"What d'you mean 'assisted'? You ever hear anybody say Thomas Edison 'assisted' on the light bulb? Sure, Orson was a bright kid. But he didn't know beans about makin' movies when he come to RKO. Of course he had the instinct, you know? But without Max—and without Gregg Toland on the camera there—he woulda never got outa the bush leagues, believe me."

"Well, I'm certainly impressed to hear all this."

"Oh you are, are you, smarty-pants? Prob'ly you think that's some big deal, huh? Well, lemme tell you: *Citizen Kane* was second-best."

"What do you mean?"

"*Citizen Kane* wasn't what Max and Orson had in mind, not first off. First choice was the real lalapoloosa. And you know who woulda shot that one? *Me,* that's who. And, boy, it woulda stood your ears on end."

"What movie are you talking about, Zip?"

He passed me a cagey little squint. "*Hearta Darkness.* You ever hear of that? High-class literature. Joseph Comrade."

"Conrad."

171

"Yeah, well, whichever, that was number one top of the list. Max wanted to make that picture so bad. For years he wanted to make it, long as I knew him. He had this script he was promotin' all over the place, ever since he come from Germany. Nobody'd give him a tumble. Then Orson shows up in town, the fair-haired boy. He could write his own ticket. Studio big shots were standin' in line to give him money. But who's the first person he wants to see? Max Castle, you bet. 'They want me to make a movie,' he says. And what does Max do? Hands him the script. 'Make *Hearta Darkness*,' he tells Orson. 'You're the only one who can.' So Orson says, 'Great idea.' Smart boy he was. Knew a good thing when it fell in his lap. Spent his whole first year at RKO workin' on it with Max. Then, blooey! Studio puts the kibosh on it. And after all the shootin' Max and me did."

"You shot material for *Heart of Darkness*?"

"Didn't I just say so? And it wasn't easy, believe me. We were chasin' all over Mexico, sweatin' our balls off. Jeez, they got mosquitoes down there big as airplanes."

"Mexico?"

"Sure. For the jungle stuff. *Hearta Darkness*, that means the jungle, see? The jungle, that's the star of the movie. That's how Max saw it. Savage, you know. Like every minute it was gonna jump off the screen and eat you alive. I guess we really didn't have to go on location, but Max didn't wanna shoot around the studio. Didn't want nobody breathin' down our neck. And Orson, he had money to burn, right? So off we go to . . . where the hell was it? Yucatán, yeah. Nearly a month we were down there."

"What were you filming?"

"Like I said: the jungle. What the hell else is there to film in Yucatán? The jungle and the natives there. The Indians. Mean-lookin' buggers they were. Never wanted to turn my back on 'em. But Max slipped 'em some firewater and got 'em to do these dances. Wow, some dances. I filmed 'em, but believe you me, I was scared shitless. It was bad enough shootin' all those eyes. But those dances, I tell you I was shakin' so hard, I just about couldn't keep the camera steady. And I had to do all this hand-held stuff right in close. Boy!"

"You filmed their eyes?"

"Yeah. Mostly that's what Max wanted. Like in *House of Blood*, but lots scarier. He was gonna fill the whole jungle with eyes. I musta shot two, three reels of these Indian faces. They had real dangerous-

172

type eyes, especially the hungry ones. They didn't like us bein' there, you could tell. You could feel it comin' at you like poison arrows. That's what Max was after."

"But you never got the chance to use any of this footage?"

"Nope. And that ain't all the shootin' we did, either. We did plenty back at the studio. The stuff with Olga."

"Olga Tell, Max's girlfriend?"

"Yeah. Olga was a damn good sport, I can tell you. She'd do anythin' Max wanted. Sure as hell nobody else would do those scenes except some . . . well, that's not what Olga was. She was a good girl. Maybe a little wild—like, you know, these European girls are."

"What scenes are you talking about?" I asked.

Zip's voice dropped into a near whisper. "Weird stuff. Weird." Then, as if I'd made some challenging response, he snapped, "Hey, don't get no fancy ideas, sonny. It wasn't porn. Max never shot anything dirty. No sir! This was artistic, understand. Like in paintings with naked ladies." By now I'd learned that Zip was always somewhere in the middle of a private argument, part of a script that had been playing inside his head for years and which had little to do with anything I said.

"Of course it was artistic," I hastened to agree. "But what was it, exactly?"

"It was gonna be a movie inside a movie inside a movie, you get me? Nobody but Max could pull off somethin' like that—if they ever let him, which they didn't, so he couldn't. 'They're never gonna get to the bottom of this one if they dig a hundred years'—that's what Max said. He was gonna use all his tricks. See, he thought maybe this was his last chance to do good work, by latchin' on to Orson there. Only he didn't get his chance. Damn orphans saw to that. They aced Max out but good. No *Hearta Darkness*, the front office says. But it was the orphans pullin' their strings. Max knew. He was on their shit list and they were gonna keep him there just grindin' out the crud—like this here *Axis Agent*. Max, he was at the end of his rope. That's how come he started shootin' off his mouth every which way. He just didn't give a damn anymore. Like with Huston there. That's what really cooked old Maxy's goose, that goddam *Maltese Falcon*."

"Castle and Huston were friends?"

"Like *that* they were. Big drinkin' buddies. See, after *Hearta Darkness* crashed, Max was just about at rock bottom. He was practically

173

beggin' for work. Orson woulda took him on as assistant somethin' or other for *Citizen Kane,* but the studio wouldn't go for that, not after all the dough Max burned up in Mexico. So Max starts feedin' Huston all this stuff for *The Maltese Falcon.* The *real* story, you know." This came with a knowing wink. I had no idea what I was supposed to know, but I winked back anyway. "He was hopin' Huston could get him in on the picture someways. Huston tried, but it was no go. Max was gettin' froze out all over town."

"The real story. Was there a real story? I mean Sam Spade was fictitious, wasn't he?"

Zip wagged his head in disgust with my utter and unforgivable stupidity. "Not Sam Spade, dummy! I'm talkin' about the bird. The black bird. That goes way back. To Malta. You know, these knight guys in the iron clothes."

Zip was doing his best to sound impressively knowledgeable, but I could tell he was balancing on the edge of total ignorance. "Do you mean the Templars?"

Amazement flashed across his face. "You know about them, huh?" I sensed that Zip, suspecting I might know the answers to questions that had been haunting him for years, would have liked to ask me who these Templars were. I hoped he wouldn't. He didn't. Restraining his curiosity, he continued. "Course, Huston never used any of that stuff. I guess it wouldn't've fit too good in the movie he was makin'. Or maybe when he woke up next morning he was too hung over to remember what Max told him. But it sure got the orphans plenty steamed when they heard how Max was blabberin' away all over the lot. That's when they started sweet-talkin' him about comin' back so they could talk over a deal. Fat chance they was goin' to give Max any money."

"Back? To Germany?"

"To Zurich. To the head orphanage there. Ain't you listenin' at all? I told Max not to go. I told him the whole thing sounded fishy. But he wouldn't listen, he was so sore. A showdown, that's what he said he was after. Either they pony up the dough, he says, *or else.* Toward the end there, Max wasn't thinkin' too straight. He was drinkin' a lot, makin' all kinda threats. You don't mess with those orphans like that. They're mean, mean as hell."

"What exactly was he threatening to do?"

"Spill the beans."

"What beans?"

"All the inside dope, the secret stuff."

"What secret stuff?"

There was another of those strained, embarrassed pauses. Then: "Wouldn't you like to know?"

I moved to another position. "I'd love to see some of this film you shot in Mexico."

"Oh yeah? Well, you're not gonna. So there." He drilled me with a defiant stare, then melted into a sad grumble. "What I got left ain't worth lookin' at. Didn't even get it composited."

Composited. I gathered the word was another item in Castle's private cinematic vocabulary. What did it mean? I asked Zip. As usual, he answered as if I was forcing him to repeat the point. "You know— composited." He made an odd little gesture with his hands, one on top of the other, fingers knitted together. "That's what the editors did. Otherwise all you got is like an assembly print, see? It's all there, but it ain't . . . composited. Besides, what I got left ain't even all there. Best stuff's gone for good, and there wasn't much of that."

"Gone where?"

"Fish food. Bottom of the sea. Like I told you, the orphans said they wanted to talk money. So Max brung the film along to show 'em. Got torpedoed with him." Zip's voice fell away into a hushed tone. "If you ask me, they wouldn't've let Max come back anyway, even if he ever got there."

"What do you mean?"

"I think they were out to finish him off once and for all."

"You think they were that displeased with him?"

"Hell yes. Max was breakin' his vows."

"Vows?"

"You never heard of vows? Like in church? Don't you go to some kinda church?"

"I meant what vows was Castle breaking?"

"That was between him and the orphans. None of my business. All I know is Max, he just wanted to make movies, real good movies. But that's not what the orphans cared about. What they wanted was for him to sneak all this propaganda of theirs into the camera."

"Propaganda?"

"Secret propaganda. The kind you can't see is even there. Like I showed you with the sallyrand."

"What good is propaganda you can't see?"

Zip goggled at me in amazement. "That's the best kind. Which is the *worst* kind. Cuz it sneaks up on you, see?"

"What was this propaganda trying to get across?"

Suddenly Zip flushed with anger. "Not like what you're thinkin', sonny," he snapped.

"I'm not thinking anything," I protested. "I'm just trying to understand you, Zip."

"Max was no Nazi, get me? He wasn't nothin' political—like them orphans."

"The orphans were Nazis?"

Zip glared at me. "Did I say so?"

"Well, no, but . . ."

"Well, just stop the hell jumpin' the gun. They weren't Nazis, but they were pullin' for the Nazis, see?"

"But why?"

"Because they wanted to prove their point, and they didn't care how."

"What point?"

"About the *evilness*, like I told you." He had, of course, told me no such thing. Seeing me draw a blank, he sought to elucidate, enunciating with a beat between every word. "They—wanted—to—prove—about—the—evilness." And beyond that cryptically ominous pronouncement Zip wouldn't budge. When I tried to draw him out, he waved me off grumpily. "Are we gonna watch this movie or not?" was all he would say. So we settled back to watch our second feature of the afternoon.

Phantom of Murderers' Row was a grade-Z job Castle had churned out for Republic studios, once again under his pseudonym Maurice Roche. This movie, like a few others he had done, was also passing under an alias. Its original title was *Bum Rap*, the film Joshua Sloan had called "a true stinker" in one of his letters to Ira Goldstein. I'd sat through the film three times with Zip, finally deciding that Sloan's harsh opinion of it was right. The movie had only one thing to offer and that came at the very end: an execution scene that managed to wring more sickly terror out of the electric chair than any prison flick I'd ever seen. Paunchy, sourpussed old Barton MacLane, walking the last mile, is lacerated by shadows every step of the way until the image of the chair itself falls across him—his chest, his brow, his cheek—like the devil's own brand burning his guilt into his hide. He

176

wilts under the condemnation, falling to his knees, shrinking to the size of an insect as the chair, in several whiplash-quick cuts, swells into a tortuous mass of angles, a veritable alphabet of despair. As in so many Castle films, that one sequence—perhaps two minutes long—imprints itself more deeply on the mind than a dozen other films costing twenty times the money. At the picture's end, I found myself holding my breath. As was Zip. Or so I thought.

I'd become so accustomed to hearing the broken rhythm of Zip's lungs as they hitched and faltered beside me in the dark, that the night he stopped breathing for good, I didn't notice at all. Not until the movie ended and Yoshi brought up the lights. When I turned to Zip, I found him slumped in his chair, his face as gray as the ash drooping from the cigarette that had gone dead in his lips. His eyes were still staring out at the screen, seeing nothing. The last glimmer of light they had witnessed in this world was an image from a Max Castle film. Perhaps Zip would have wanted it that way, but I could think of nothing in *Phantom of Murderers' Row* that would offer a cheering segue into the afterlife. I reached over to feel for his pulse and found his hand already cold. Stepping quietly as if I might wake him, I slipped away into the projection booth and told Yoshi he'd best call an ambulance. He quickly bustled off toward Zip's chair to check for himself. I heard him let out a long, slow moan.

Meanwhile, I went in search of Franny and found her in the cabana stretched out asleep, snoring heavily, a copy of *The National Enquirer* spread across her stomach, a bottle of whiskey and a half-filled glass on the floor beside her. I bent to whisper her name at her ear and, when she woke, led her quickly away upstairs to the bedroom we hadn't used in the last two weeks. I wasn't sure I wanted to do more than hold her close and tell her about Zip as unjarringly as possible. But Franny was easily aroused, and I let her feelings run their course for what I knew would be our last time together. By now, she was no longer the reincarnated ghost of Nylana, but poor Franny herself, one of Hollywood's lesser meteors, long since burned to cold cinders in the dark night of neglect that has devoured many a brighter star.

When we'd finished, I hugged her to me until I could hear the wail of the ambulance siren in the distance. Then I told her about Zip. She took it bravely like bad news long expected, simply wilting in my embrace and letting quiet tears come. "He had a heart of gold," was all I heard her say.

Once or twice in the course of our last relatively friendly month together, I'd gotten up the nerve to tell Zip that he ought to give some thought to contributing his film collection to an archive . . . someday. He was weakening so steadily that I hesitated to talk about the matter in terms of wills or bequests, but he knew what I had in mind. "Don't you worry," he answered. "I got that all taken care of."

"Good," I said. But what did he have planned? "There's a fine archive at UCLA," I suggested. "They'd love to have the films."

"Sure, sure. And you know who else would love to have 'em? Them goddam orphans."

"Would they?"

"Damn right they would. But I ain't lettin' them lay their hands on Max's pictures, you can be sure of that."

"Well, if you put your collection in an archive, then you could be sure . . ."

Zip cut me off sharply. "I told you—it's all taken care of."

That was as far as I'd gotten in the week before he died. Afterward, I wanted a decent interval to pass before I raised the matter with Franny. In the meantime, there was Zip's funeral to get through. Franny seemed to have that well under control. Zip's death had hardly taken her by surprise; she'd been watching its steady approach for some fifteen years.

The day after Zip's death, she called to say she was holding a small ceremony that weekend and would I please come with Clare and Sharkey. I expected we'd gather in a local funeral home, but the place she named was in the desert near Barstow. "Why there?" I asked. She told me that Zip owned a piece of land; it was where his mother had been laid to rest after living out her last few years with Zip. He wanted the same for himself.

The trip was a three-hour drive, the last fifty miles of it a hard trek over ungraded Mojave roads. The land Zip owned turned out to be an undeveloped stretch of scrub desert marked only by remnants of wire fence and a Private Property sign. Most of the surrounding country was posted as an air-force gunnery range. It was the sort of area where people abandoned old cars. A few hundred yards beyond the boundary of Zip's land, near a clump of creosote bushes, were some mobile homes and a few shacks. I couldn't see that the place had any use except as a grave site. Maybe that was all Zip ever had in mind.

When we arrived, there were a few cars on the lot, one of them a

178

gardener's van that must have served as a hearse. A strip of black crepe streamed from the radio aerial. A group of about a dozen people were gathered near a mound that held a cheap wooden casket surrounded with flowers. Franny was there, wearing a tight, shiny black dress. Most of the others were Japanese. I recognized Yoshi among them with his two sons, all wearing black suits in the desert heat.

We seemed to be the last guests expected to arrive. After Franny welcomed us, a man stepped forward to speak. Clare later found out he was a minor screenwriter who had been blacklisted into oblivion with Zip in the fifties. Zip had kept him financially afloat until he went broke himself. The man delivered an overly long eulogy in a growly voice. He made Zip out to be an unsung hero of the witch-hunting period, but he said nothing about his films. Most of his words were whipped away by the wind.

When he finished, Yoshi and his sons moved everybody well back from the mound. Then at a signal from their father, who seemed to be in charge, the boys took automobile flares from their pockets, lit them, and jammed them under the riser that held the casket. Their movements were very precise, as if they'd rehearsed for the event. The flares sputtered and seemed to go out. Then there was a puff of smoke from under the riser and suddenly a small bright explosion of flames that swept up around the casket, which took fire immediately as if it had been soaked in gasoline. So we'd come to witness a cremation. Franny, standing beside me, whispered, "It's what Zip wanted."

We were standing out of the wind, but even so Sharkey caught a whiff of the black smoke that blew by on a wayward breeze. "Nitrate," he said. That's when I realized. As the flowers fell away, I saw the film reels stacked around the coffin. There were more of them crammed under the riser, already wrapped in thick ropes of smoke. I let out a gasp, just as Franny took hold of my arm. "It's what Zip wanted."

My heart shrank to the size of a small cold marble. I remembered Zip's ominous words: "That's all taken care of." I bent to whisper at Franny's ear, "What films are those?" She shook her head slowly as if to tell me not to ask. "Are those Castle's films?" I asked again.

She looked up at me with sorrowful, hollow eyes. "It's what Zip wanted."

Helplessly, I watched the gray, acrid cloud that was rising above the desert and scattering on the wind. A life's work up in smoke.

Now we all knew. The Lipsky film collection wasn't destined for any archive. In a final act of contempt and defiance, Zip had elected to use Max Castle's movies as the tinder that would burn his tired bones to ash. I turned, stunned and speechless, toward Clare. I could tell she had grasped what was happening. Yet I couldn't detect a sign of distress. I didn't want to believe it, but I could have described her expression as one of relief. I remembered the words she'd entrusted to me like a guilty confession: "If I had my way, I'd see his films burned to fumes."

For weeks after Zip Lipsky's funeral, I was desolate, all the more so as I came to realize that Clare refused to share my desolation. She wouldn't outspokenly endorse Zip's act of posthumous vandalism; but she wouldn't condemn it either. Nor would she spare me a word of sympathy for a loss that she could see I was taking very personally. Instead, she carried on, perversely, as if there were simply no way I could expect her to know what Zip's celluloid pyre had cost the world. After all, *she* hadn't seen the films. *She* had nothing to go on but my amateurish reports. What did it count for that one Jonathan Gates believed works of immortal genius had been obliterated? What was his judgment worth?

As Clare reminded me, "In 1947, Universal destroyed every silent movie in its library—just to save the storage costs. If I wanted to grieve over all the movies that ever got lost in the shuffle, I could find lots worse disasters to weep for than losing a dozen Max Castles. Hollywood's been treating its heritage like old Kleenex for generations: if you can't sell it, chuck it. Believe me, Jonny, this is a drop in the ocean."

I agreed but protested, "Aren't we the ones who are supposed to care about that?"

"I care a lot more that old Zip burned up all his better work too. Mint-condition prints of *Glory Road, Prince of the Streets,* the stuff he shot with Paul Robeson. I know what that was worth. Makes it a lot harder to put together a Lipsky retrospective."

Clare's stubborn pretense of unconcern brought me as close to anger as I'd ever dared to come with her. She seemed to be abandoning me to a terrible isolation. I was alone not only with the loss of Max Castle's work, but also with my appreciation of that work. His films—or at least his lost later films—now survived in my memory only. True, there was Franny, and there was Yoshi. They'd also seen them; but not with the same critical eye, the same depth of response I knew I'd brought to their viewing. That experience lived on exclusively in me, and with it a burdening sense of responsibility. Shouldn't I do *something* to make good for that loss before the images melted away in my remembrance?

I was into my second month of moping and sulking when the phone call came. It was Franny.

I hadn't parted from her gracefully at the funeral. I didn't want to. Stunned as I was to see Castle's films turning to vapor before my eyes, I couldn't think of what to say to her. I held her responsible for the act of devastation that had taken place. She could have saved what was being destroyed by simply ignoring Zip's vindictive request. But what right did I have at that moment in her life to accuse her? With Clare and Sharkey, I offered her a quick goodbye and left before the pyre had finished smoldering. I hoped my abrupt departure would be the end of our relationship. She'd always seemed pathetic to me. But the image I took away with me from Zip's funeral was that of a ridiculous, destructive slattern. That image had rapidly eclipsed whatever sweet, lingering memories of Nylana I still preserved. When I heard Franny's baby-talk voice on the phone, a sick anger rose in my throat. She wanted me to come visiting again.

"No, Franny," I said, making my reply as frosty as I knew how. "I don't see any point in that." Was she seriously proposing that our bizarre little affair go on? The thought was grotesque; I didn't care if my tone let her know it. I think it was the first time in my life I'd been so dismissively rude to anyone.

At the other end of the line, her voice lost its little-girl singsong and grew more sober. "I just thought we could maybe say goodbye a little nicer, you know. I'm selling off the house here and going home."

"Oh? Where's that?"

"I got family in Iowa. I'm going back."

"Uh-huh."

"Des Moines. I'm the farmer's daughter, did I ever tell you?"

"No."

"My folks disowned me when I ran off to be a movie star. Well, my father mainly. They're very religious people. But when I settled down with Zippy, they sort of forgave me, even though he was a dwarf and all. My father didn't go for that. But at least it was some kind of marriage and, well . . ."

181

I hoped she could hear my boredom in the silence.

". . . you see, I thought it would be nice to say goodbye like friends before I took off."

"Well, Franny, I'm really busy at school just now . . ."

"Sure, I know. But just an hour or so? See, Zippy left this stuff I think you'd like to have."

"Oh? What?"

"Well . . . the cameras, for one thing."

"Do you mean the projectors?"

"Cameras, projectors, a whole lot of stuff. I don't know what to do with it."

"You want to sell them?"

"Oh, you could just have them."

"Franny, you don't mean that. That's very expensive equipment."

"Well, I don't wanna have to sell them. And there's other things too."

"Like what?"

A teasing, girlish note returned to her voice. "Why don't you come and see?"

"Are there any films?"

"Could be . . ." And she would say nothing more.

I couldn't tell if Franny was leading me on. But the prospect of getting a bargain on Zip's Century projectors and bringing them back to The Classic was too much to forgo. I was at her house within the hour.

The realtor's "For Sale" sign on the front lawn had a "Sold" sticker pasted across it. There was an ominous piece of oversized earth-moving machinery parked in the driveway that seemed to have the house under siege. Inside, the Lipsky home had lost a lot of furniture. Whole rooms stood vacant, except for miscellaneous packing boxes here and there.

"They're gonna plow the whole place under and build an apartment house," Franny told me. "Can't hardly wait for me to leave. I got to be out by next week. I'm almost dizzy selling and packing. I don't know where I am anymore." She looked frazzled, her hair collapsed around her shoulders, her face shiny with sweat. She was a simpler, more honest Franny, and she was easier to like that way.

She was serious about the projectors. She fully intended to give them to me—along with everything else in the projection booth. That included the contents of a small storeroom filled with some good-looking camera equipment, the last remnants of Zip's career. "You could get a good price for all this," I told her.

"Yeah, well . . . I wouldn't feel good about selling Zip's stuff like that, just to strangers. I'd like for you and your friends to have it. Zip never showed his feelings too much, but he liked you. And that woman, Clare, he liked her a lot. What she said to him about his movies, that was the first nice thing anybody said to him in years. Is she your girlfriend, sort of?"

"Well, sort of . . ."

"Yeah, I sort of guessed." She made to smother a giggle. "I hope we didn't make her jealous?" Then, quickly sobering up, "She's very smart, I can tell. The intelligent type. Zip was real impressed with her. He told me. I think he'd like her to have this stuff."

When I entered the projection booth, my eye had gone at once to the high shelf where Yoshi had kept the sallyrand. There was no box there. Surveying the booth, I asked Franny "Do you know where the sallyrand might be?"

"The who?" She gave a puzzled smile, recognizing the name but not the object.

"It's a little viewing device about this big."

"Oh yeah, that. Sort of like a telescope . . . ?"

"That's it," I answered eagerly.

"Zip used to look at movies through it sometimes. God, I don't know where it could be." She tittered. "I never heard him call it a Sally Rand. Why would he call it that?"

I sidestepped explaining while I searched the booth. I found nothing. Franny could see I was disappointed. I hastened to let her know I was overwhelmed by her generosity. She was offering me a gift worth several thousand dollars. "I don't know what to say, Franny," I mumbled. "This is very good of you."

"Oh, listen, I got a good price for the house. This old dump, I thought I wouldn't get a dime. And Zip had something put aside. I don't have to make money on his equipment." Then, becoming worrisomely coquettish, she said, "Now I've also got something for just you especially." Taking my hand, she led me out of the projection room and back through the house. We were headed, as I feared, toward the stairs. She detected my hesitation. "Come on, don't be shy. I'm not gonna seduce you or anything. Honest." But she punctuated the promise with a naughty wink that made me uncertain.

We entered an empty upstairs room where a small collection of boxes stood near the door. From one of them she withdrew a scroll of paper. "I bet you'd like to have one of these—just for old times' sake." It was a Nylana poster. She was right. I was supremely grateful to have it. I noticed it was autographed. "To my favorite fan. Kay Allison."

"Now these books and all," she explained, sorting through the boxes, "they were Zip's favorite things. Lots of technical books. Some keepsakes. Scrapbooks. Couple of magazine stories on him. Isn't that the sort of thing you're studying in college?"

"Well, yes . . . more or less. You're sure you don't want to keep it yourself?"

"If I lug it all off to Iowa, it'll just molder away in my folks' attic or something. I'm no reader. And I got my own memories of Zippy, all I need. Maybe you'll find something that interests you. Oh, but this I'm keeping."

She plunged her hand into one box and pulled out a golden figurine. Zip's Oscar. "I think he'd want me to look after that." She smiled wistfully. "Sometime I can pretend I won it."

Hesitatingly, I reminded her, "You said there might be some films. . . ."

She took on a serious air. "Now about that, I got to explain to you. Because I know how you must've felt at the funeral. You see, that was all Yoshi's doing. He just practically idolized Zip. Whatever Zippy wanted, Yoshi was gonna do. Well, Zip told him he wanted those pictures used like you saw. Zippy had that written in his will, even. There was no talking Yoshi out of it. He's such a bossy guy. Him and me, we didn't ever get on so good, you might've guessed. Yoshi had this feeling that he knew Zippy a lot longer than I did, even if I was his wife. Which was true. So when it came to Zip's last will and testament, Yoshi simply took charge as if I couldn't be trusted to do a thing. He made the arrangements with this Japanese undertaker friend of his and everything. I told him I didn't think it was legal just to take Zippy's body like that and burn it. But Yoshi, he had this big grudge against the government, you know why. 'Shit on your laws,' he told me and just went right ahead. All I could think to do was keep my mouth shut and let him have his way. Which I did. Well, now he's moved out, and he won't be any the wiser."

She stepped across the room and threw open the door of a walk-in closet. Inside, stacked from floor to ceiling, were film canisters, dozens of them. I rushed to examine them and my heart sank. All the labels I could see read *Nylana. Nylana the Jungle Girl. Nylana and the Cobra Cult.* "Oh," I said, my voice catching with clear disappointment. "*Your* movies."

"It's all a big mess, I should warn you," she explained as she cracked open one of the canisters. "See, I had to do it all so fast and without much light. Yoshi was prowling around the place. I didn't want him to catch me at it."

"At what?"

"What I did was I put all those movies you and Zip were watching in these cans. And I put all the movies that were in here in those cans . . . see what I mean?"

"You mean you switched the films?"

"Yeah, that's what I did."

"So *these* are Max Castle's movies?"

"Yeah. Because I knew you didn't wanna see them burned up. I guess they were some important movies, huh?"

"Oh, Franny, I can't even tell you!"

"So this way, Yoshi thought he was doing what Zip wanted. I hope Zippy wouldn't hold it against me."

I wanted to take her in my arms and kiss her. Then it struck me. "But, Franny . . . you let the Nylana films get burned. All your movies. They would be very hard to replace."

She shrugged. "Oh, come on! That old crap? Who'd want to save that? Listen, those movies are a lot better the way you remember them than they ever really were. God, they were just awful! I was glad to see 'em go."

Then I did give her a hug. "Franny, I'm so grateful! I can't tell you! You saved the films."

"I might've missed some. Because, see, it wasn't easy to do. I was working so fast, with the Max movies piled up downstairs, and all these up here, back and forth, up and down. God, I never worked so hard. I kept getting all mixed up. There were so many damned cans! And some of them I couldn't get open, so I left them. And then I had all these reels all over the floor. I couldn't tell one from the other. So I'll bet they're all out of order."

"But you must have saved *most* of them."

"I tried to. Of course, I ran out of Nylana reels before I got all the movies switched around, so I had to stick some of the other movies in."

"What other movies?"

185

"Oh, Zippy had lots of movies laying around here. Mostly old silent pictures from way back."

"Like what?"

"I don't know which from which. I just took what I could find so Yoshi wouldn't notice any empty cans. Whatever the labels say, those are the movies I switched over."

I felt my way into the stacks of canisters at the rear of the closet and rotated some of them here and there to find the names. I spotted a few marked "Chaplin," some marked "Barrymore." "What Barrymore was this?" I asked.

"It was called *Don Juan*. Zippy liked that one."

Then I found several canisters labeled *Greed*. "*Greed*?" I asked her. "Zip had a print of *Greed*?"

"By that German guy—with the neck . . . ?"

"Erich Von Stroheim."

"Yeah, him. Zip liked that one too. He got it from Max, who was a friend of Stroheim."

"You mean one of the films that got burned up was a print of *Greed*?"

"If that's what it says on the can."

"Oh, Franny . . . do you realize how valuable that may have been?"

"Was it? I didn't know you cared about that one. Zip made me watch it once. It wasn't too good, believe me."

I didn't argue the point. Instead, I got to work loading everything Franny had to contribute into Sharkey's van. It was a ton of loot. Projectors, cameras, boxes of books, scores of film canisters . . . they filled the entire interior and the top carrier. Franny was being far too generous. If I had had the money, if Clare had had the money, I would have forced it on her. Yet, as precious a haul as it was, I would have traded all the equipment in the van for the sallyrand. That was the key to the magical kingdom. Where was it now? Before leaving, I made a tour of the house, checking closets, cupboards, drawers, finding nothing. Finally, I left a request with Franny to let me know if it turned up—though I wasn't hopeful. If there was one thing Zip was likely to make sure got destroyed upon his death, it was Max Castle's all-seeing eye. Sliding into the van, I thanked Franny one last time.

"Don't mention it," she insisted. "You were very, very nice to me, I want you to know. You brought me back some good old memories. Made me feel like a starlet again, you know? I hope you liked it too."

"I did. Every minute."

"Nice of you to say so. You know, there's nothing a movie star likes better than a few good fans. Even a little, used-up star like me. How about it?" she asked, putting out her arms. I walked into her embrace and we had one last mushy big kiss. "Wow! That's better than I ever got in the movies," she said. "And here, I want you to have this too." She quickly slipped an envelope inside my sweaty shirt. "A surprise for when you get home, okay?"

But I fetched the gift out at the first stoplight I hit heading west on Los Feliz Boulevard. It was a cracked and yellowed photograph. Nylana caught lusciously unveiled in the studio treetops. And it was autographed.

It took weeks to sort out the films Franny had saved for me. When the job was finished, I was delighted to discover she'd made a better job of it than she had realized. She hadn't lost a single reel of a Max Castle movie, but had simply scrambled them around. Her main screwup was to include miscellaneous pieces of other movies, those whose canisters she'd borrowed. That actually amounted to a bonus, a sort of surprise package of film fragments major and minor. There was one long-lost reel of Von Stroheim's *Greed,* some pieces of Murnau's *Sunrise,* and portions of Dreyer's *Joan of Arc* that Clare was certain she'd never seen before. The world's only surviving print of Chaplin's *How Slippery Sam Went for the Eggs* owes its existence to Franny Lipsky's great midnight rescue operation. "I only wish she'd saved more of everything that wasn't Castle," was Clare's comment. "Sounds as if there were some real gems." After a few private viewings, Clare and I decided to donate everything besides the Castle films to the UCLA film archives. There was one item in the haul, however, that I decided to keep for myself: five nonconsecutive episodes of *Nylana and the Cobra Cult.* While this was the rarest of the items Franny had preserved from destruction, it was also the least valuable. Yet for me it was pure nostalgic bliss to sit alone in The Classic after hours and see Nylana come to life again. There she was, Kay Allison, as beautiful as ever in her imperiled pulchritude. All mine, though, sad to say, the erotic charge of that once overpowering physique had waned. Was it because I had outgrown the charms of its exaggerated anatomy? Or because I could now claim carnal knowledge of that body in the imperfection of its later years? Perhaps Nylana had simply become too real to be the infinitely malleable fantasy she once was for me.

There was one more prize Franny had managed inadvertently to salvage, though it took me some time to register its value: three partially filled thirty-five-millimeter reels of unidentified outtakes, for the most part so badly over- or underexposed that for minutes at a time as I watched, I couldn't discern more than fleeting ghostly shapes. Where the film brightened enough to reveal more, all I could see was trees: the camera panning trees up close, at a distance, from a high angle, a low angle, moving among them slowly, rapidly. So much for the first two reels and nearly half of the third.

Then, after a lumpy splice, another brighter scene cut in. Blurred and at a distance, it looked at first like a long line of dolls. The camera came closer, the film cleared, and I saw.

These weren't dolls. They were human heads mounted higgledy-piggledy on long poles. Heads, half heads, skulls picked clean, jaw-bones. Where there were faces left, they were black and grotesquely primitive. Surely these were dummies carved from wood or shaped from *papier mâché* . . . but in the camera's perhaps deliberately fuzzy focus, they looked nauseatingly real. Suddenly the panning camera veered and moved in on one head, taking it in close-up. A fresh kill, still wet at the throat. The lifeless eyes goggled in terrible astonish-ment, the mouth gaped as if it might be struggling to voice a final scream left behind forever in its sundered body. The camera, ad-vancing rapidly and precisely (it was a patented Zip Lipsky hand-held maneuver), homed in on that hideous mouth, approached it, *entered* it. Swallowed. Darkness. A long darkness that allowed me time to remember . . . that fence. I knew that fence. Joseph Conrad had described it. He called it "that symbolic row of stakes" topped by "heads, black, dried, sunken." It stood in the deep jungle surrounding the encampment where Mr. Kurtz, the embodiment of white, western civilization at its highest, reverts to savagery.

So I'd discovered the footage Castle shot for his aborted *Heart of Darkness*—or as much of it as survived. When Zip had mentioned the project, I immediately got hold of the book and reread it. The fence was an image no one could forget. Apparently Castle had begun filming at just that point in the novel. I could see why Zip, with his sense of craftsmanship, had been unwilling to show the reel; it was a crude, preliminary effort, an assembly print at best, still waiting for choices to be made, effects to be introduced. Yet it let me see something of the story as Castle had understood it: the brooding jungle, the ghastly fence, the severed head that eats the audience alive.

Meanwhile, the darkness on the screen had given way to a new sequence roughly spliced into place. Eyes. Shot after shot of eyes, hard and hostile, the eyes of sullen natives who didn't trust the camera or those who had intruded it into their lives. Zip had said Castle wanted to fill the jungle with eyes. Here they were, though I had no idea how they might be integrated ("composited," wasn't that the word Zip used?) into the film. The eyes went on for several minutes, one pair following another. Toward the end of the sequence, the images began to skip back and forth between film positive and film negative: white-black, black-white, at first slowly, then more rapidly until the effect took on a dizzy, hypnotic attraction.

And then the eyes were gone, giving way to a badly fogged stretch of film. Dimly, I could make out an image, a human form that seemed to be dancing in slow motion, bending, turning. There were several takes of this sequence. In the fifth, the image was just bright enough for me to identify the figure as a woman. No doubt about that: she was totally naked, striking a number of startlingly lascivious postures. Her hair, long and blond, was whipped back across her face so that I had no chance of telling who this might be. But I gathered it must be Olga Tell, Castle's lovely and ever-compliant lady friend. If so, her reputation as one of the great screen beauties was well deserved. Even with her face obscured, she was displaying the most magnificent body I'd ever seen, and disporting it more wantonly than any queen of burlesque.

In the sixth take, there was a change. This time Olga was holding something between her jostling breasts. It glinted in the light revealing itself as a sword held inverted, the blade pumping rhythmically up and down between her thighs. She was maneuvering the nasty-looking weapon across and around her torso in a way that managed to be both menacing and erotic.

The seventh take was badly washed-out. Olga was just barely visible doing her phallic sword dance. But now she had company. A large, dark figure loomed up in the shadows behind her. By the quality of its movement—forceful, muscular—I judged it was a man. He wore a mask, but its features were wholly indistinct. His costume had loose, flapping sleeves that might almost have been wings. Embracing Olga from behind, he wrapped her in his flowing garment, drew her down

189

upon some kind of platform or table, and appeared to mount her. From that point on, as blurred as the film might be, there was no mistaking what was going on between the two figures: something that would never have cleared the censors of that day or this. Though there was no soundtrack, I could almost hear the ecstatic panting as the action reached its increasingly violent culmination. In its last several seconds, this portion of the film also began to oscillate between positive and negative, the alternation rhythmically timed to the accelerating climax of the sex act. Black-white, white-black, an intoxicating flicker that made the rough, fitful intercourse of man and woman all the more throbbingly powerful.

And there the reel broke off.

Now I knew why Zip had been so defensively quick to deny that he and Castle had filmed any "porn" in their sessions with Olga. Because if this wasn't porn, it was the next thing to it. Nevertheless, I made sure to convey his denial to Clare when she viewed the reel. As I expected, she scoffed. "Naked ladies doing bumps and grinds are always porn," she insisted. "Especially when they wind up underneath some muscular stud. Not remarkable that Castle should use his girlfriend that way. Pretty young things are always getting exploited in Hollywood. What mystifies me is what he expected to do with this stuff, except show it at private parties. He shot this in 1939, 1940. Even skin flicks back then weren't full frontal. Your Mr. Castle was a very kinky customer, Jonny."

I hazarded a few words in defense of the footage. "But the other things are pretty impressive, don't you think? The eyes, the fence . . ."

Clare shrugged. "A big maybe. All we have here is raw material. Who knows how Max Castle or Orson Welles might have used it? I certainly can't get a fix on what I've seen. It's like trying to guess what Van Gogh's next painting might be by studying the colors in his paint chest. In this case, we've got porn and gore and lots of big, scary eyes. Myself, I don't even like what I see on the palette. Somebody should turn *Heart of Darkness* into a movie. I'm glad Max Castle didn't."

"It might have been his best picture," I protested.

"That's what worries me. *Heart of Darkness* made by a brilliant nut who's on the side of the darkness."

Theodore Roszak

11 THE END OF THE AFFAIR

Once there was a time—how many can still remember?—when a Coke bottle qualified nowhere in the world as an aesthetic object. When Superman lay locked away and forgotten in children's comic books. When, though you searched the city (any city) from end to end, you couldn't find a single movie poster to decorate your walls or a T-shirt bearing James Dean's picture. When nobody except the sort of movie nut I had become could have told you from where Woody Allen got the line "Play it again, Sam," much less that he got it wrong.

In the university, at least in its more cloistered quarters, where I was busy carving a comfortable niche for myself, all this was as it should be. In the view of my academic masters, there was, between the fine and vulgar arts, a great gulf fixed. That gulf defined their role in life—which was to dig the ditch deeper, the better to defend high standards and good taste. To use an image they would have deplored: Culture-with-a-capital-C was Fay Wray, the unsullied virgin forever endangered by the King Kong of commerce and the mass media. In my habitual desire to please and succeed, I went along with that purpose; it seemed like a noble cause. I never dreamed that I might one day be among those who would betray the maiden to the ape. But I would. My love of movies—more specifically my fascination with Max Castle—was soon to make me a traitor within the citadel of intellect.

I can still remember the day when Clare began recruiting me for the job. Quite casually, she broke the news: King Kong had leapt the gulf and would soon have the frail and fainting beauty in his hairy paws. Did I know? Did I care? Were we to weep or cheer? Clare was giving me no cues, but remaining provocatively ambivalent.

The scene is a familiar one. Clare and I at breakfast. Before us, the usual meager fare. Mercilessly potent French coffee and toasted bagels. The two of us immersed in the Sunday New York Times. Having finished the Arts and Leisure section (always her prerogative

191

to read it first), Clare passed it across the table to me with a self-satisfied grin.

"They're finally catching up with us," she announced, leaving me to work out her meaning.

I took the paper from her and began to thumb through it. It was, of course, the *previous* Sunday's *Times*. In those days—the early sixties—it took four days for the Sunday edition to reach the provinces. Clare would buy it at the Farmers Market newsstand every Thursday, but never so much as glance at the headlines until Sunday morning. Then, ritualistically, that great, sagging, many-segmented carcass of a journal would be laid across the table and dissected layer by layer until breakfast had been prolonged into a reasonable facsimile of brunch. It didn't matter to Clare that the paper was a week out of date; when it came to film, her main reading matter, she operated from the assumption that the nation at large lagged behind the tastes she championed by a good five years.

After I'd searched several pages of the paper trying to guess which film review she might have had in mind, Clare reached across to stop me. "I mean this," she said with condescending patience, laying her finger on the lead article. Dutifully, I read the item through. No wonder I'd missed it. It had nothing to do with movies. It dealt with painting. The subject was a young artist, the latest find. A washed-out and vacuous youth, he didn't look like an artist or (judging from the interviewed quotes) talk like an artist. And the picture he had painted didn't look anything like the pictures artists painted. It was a picture of a soup can, an ordinary soup can—Campbell's tomato—but painted with all the loving care that Vermeer might have lavished on a still-life.

When I'd finished reading, I glanced at Clare, put on my most practiced knowing look, and nodded in thoughtful agreement. But she could tell I was faking. "Think about it, Jonny," she said. "This could solve an important problem for you."

And that, teasingly, was all she said, until a few days later. During a late-night intermission in our lovemaking, Clare fished a magazine from under the bed and dropped it with a slap across my bare loins. It was a heavy, slick job called *Artforum*, opened to the pages she wanted me to see. "For Chrissake," she muttered as I began to read, "do we have to wait for a money-grabbing jerk like this to teach us our cultural ABCs?"

The jerk in question was the same blank-faced young man I'd read about in the *Times* a few days before. He was the magazine's featured subject for the month. There spread before me was another of his works. A faded, muddy-colored portrait of Marilyn Monroe so exactly rendered that it might have been a photograph, but wasn't. It was a silkscreened picture, done not once, not twice, but over and over, like a face on a strip of film.

"You *do* get the point, don't you, lover?" she asked when I had finished reading.

Clare had been offering hints; I'd been pondering them. "You mean . . . study *Castle?*" I asked.

"Bright boy. If Pop can be art, it can sure as hell be scholarship."

That was the "problem" Clare had in mind. My graduate dissertation. The time had come for me to choose a topic. I'd been casting about none too brilliantly for some six months, trying to come up with one. My thoughts had been running in the standard academic grooves: something suitably filmological, dealing with respectable cinema. Great directors, masterworks of the screen. Or possibly a bit of high-toned theory. The sort of thing everybody did in film studies in those days. Every time I mentioned one of these possibilities to Clare, whose judgment mattered to me more than that of my professors, she'd respond with a pained expression. "Oh God! You'll die of boredom," she warned. "Worse, *I'll* die of boredom."

Now she was suggesting something that brought a glimmer of enthusiasm into her eyes. "Thanks to Nylana the Jungle Girl," Clare explained, "you practically own Max Castle's Hollywood career. Look what you have to draw on. Your own private collection of his uncut works."

"But they're only B-movies," I reminded her with great uncertainty. "I mean . . . they're junk."

"So what's Campbell's soup?" she fired back. "What's a smudgy picture of Marilyn Monroe? Don't you see? The Andy Assholes of the world are blurring the lines and winning prizes for doing it. Which means, at best, they're opening up possibilities. Castle is *good* junk, isn't he? Isn't that what *you* believe?" She emphasized the "you," as if maybe not *her*.

By this time, Clare had viewed all the Castle films I'd brought back from the Lipsky collection. She'd decided to screen them regularly at The Classic, though she insisted that I write the program notes for them. For her own part, she wouldn't offer Castle's films one friendly word of comment. Now she did—grudgingly.

"Take my word for it, Jonny, it's a significant discovery."

"You think so?"

"Even those tight-assed professors of yours should be able to see that. The barriers are coming down. In another ten years, we're going to have scholarly monographs on the films of Elisha Cook, Jr. What we've got to start doing is sorting out the good junk from the bad. Because the good junk—that's what we've got to make clear—is just the art that the mandarins wouldn't pay attention to. Like Shakespeare, once upon a time. Remember? He worked the wrong side of the river where the pimps and the whores and the groundlings hung out. He was good junk. So was Chaplin. And Keaton. And Groucho and Garbo."

Looking back now, it seems so obvious. But bear in mind how very new all this was at the time—and how very daring. The word Pop had only lately been coined by critics who were scrambling, as they had at least a score of times in the last century, to stretch the meaning of "art" still more hazardously thin, this time to cover pictures of soup cans and movie stars. The project had only just reached the popular press and was still knocking at the doors of the universities. But in the small, superheated world of film addicts where I was living at the time, we knew all about Pop before anybody got around to giving it a name. After all, we were the custodians of some very special pictures ourselves. Pictures that moved and spoke and glowed in the dark. Pictures that had been with us since our childhood, mingling with our dreams and fantasies. We knew how these pictures could bind the eye, steal the heart. They ruled our lives. They ruled everybody's life. We knew it and had long since faced up to it. To tell the truth, we relished it.

Finally, one of our kind made a movie about the power of movies. He was, of course, French. His movie came to America under the title *Breathless;* it was one of the major hits on the art-house circuit about the time I settled in at The Classic. In it, an American girl just out of college (it was Jean Seberg, exactly the right combination of blank innocence and spoiled-rotten moodiness) walks the streets of the Right Bank selling the *New York Herald Tribune,* getting casually involved in risky adventures with unsavory types. I remember that for months after I saw the movie, I wanted to be that footloose student wandering among the cafés, the bistros, the lowlife of Paris. It was an image of freedom, as well as dangerous fun.

But there was something more to the film than this precocious image of youthful American alienation. The male lead (Jean-Paul Belmondo, playing a lovable young hood) goes through the picture imitating his idol, Humphrey Bogart. So here was I, watching a movie, wanting to be a character in that movie. And there was Belmondo, himself a French movie idol, playing the part of someone who has modeled his life on the movies. And *what* movies? *American* movies. Old Warner Brothers cops-and-robbers junkers that nobody ever regarded as culture, let alone art. Yet, watching Belmondo, I could remember how I, in my boyhood, had come home from Saturday matinees mouthing the words of Bogie or John Wayne, aping the antics of Buster Crabbe locked in deadly comic-strip combat with Ming of Mongo. Had Homer or Dante or Rembrandt ever reached deeper into the shadowed bottoms of the mind than these celluloid heroes?

Here was a movie that *understood*. And when Belmondo the hoodlum-martyr is finally gunned down in the gutter, he goes out playing Bogart to the end, clinging to a precious remnant of film imagery that has become his life and death.

Not many months after *Breathless* opened, I bought my first movie poster and pinned it to the bedroom door as a gift for Clare. A larger-than-life blowup of Bogart and Bergman in a still from *Casablanca*. I bought it because it was there to be bought, in the bookshops and drugstores, soon to be joined by Laurel and Hardy, Astaire and Rogers, and top-shot bouquets of Busby Berkeley's near-nudie cuties. Novelty items, mass produced, mainly for college kids. Another year and I was meeting undergraduates at parties wearing T-shirts that told the world "I'm Doing All I Can for Regis Toomey."

Clare had lots of reservations about *Breathless*. They seemed to stem mainly from insults she'd once traded with Jean-Luc Godard when they crossed paths at the Cinémathèque. His impish decision to dedicate his film to Monogram Studios, that epitome of gutter culture, was one of those gestures of reverse snobbery that Clare deplored in the French. Still, the film brought back fond memories. "Believe it or not," she told me in a rare wistful moment, "I actually did the Jean Seberg bit in Paris. For about six months when things got tight and I didn't want to take money from home. Finally had to throw in the towel. The only way you could even earn lunch money as a newsy was by chiseling the tourists into paying a buck for a seventy-five-cent paper. On the other hand, if I'd looked as good as Seberg does in a T-shirt, I might've done lots better."

But Clare hadn't gone to Paris to hawk papers along the Champs-Elysées. She'd come on an intellectual pilgrimage in search of French cineasts who could discuss the films of Renoir, Cocteau, Buñuel. Much to her surprise, when she found the mentors she was seeking, they were as often as not more eager to talk about John Ford and Joseph Lewis and Raoul Walsh. Oh yes, the Americans were hopeless philistines, little better than savages actually. That went without saying. *But* when it came to film, that was a different matter. Hollywood, which was run by a collection of capitalist bandits, had nevertheless invented the western, the musical, Donald Duck. It had turned the rarefied art of cinema into the people's art of movies. And such good movies! To be sure, the Americans themselves had no idea what they were doing. Like true savages, they hadn't the ability to appropriate their own culture. That required the services of European, ideally French, intellect. It was all very dialectical—how something of such charm and fascination could issue from such a debased source.

Clare spent three years being patronized as a visiting barbarian by condescending French film connoisseurs. "Most of what they had to say about America was pretty screwy," she recalled. "That was back when Sartre was writing works of canonical ignorance like *The Respectful Prostitute*. Any stick to beat a dog with. They could never, never, never be simple, meaning honest. They could never just say they *liked* some good song and dance, or lots of brute action on the screen, the same way any proletarian meathead does."

By the time Clare's sojourn was over, European sophistication had taught her the virtues of American vulgarity. She brought that lesson home with her and invested it in The Classic. From the outset, she decided she'd never run the place simply as an art house. Alongside the foreign films that were The Classic's bread and butter, she'd show the good old American stuff her audience and their parents had grown up on. Slapstick comedy, cops and robbers, cowboys and Indians. Through her programming and her notes, she freely gave her audience the benefit of her European film studies, showing it how a Preston Sturges comedy or an MGM musical deserved the same critical appraisal as the great classics of the screen—and needed it more. Because, so Clare insisted, entertainment rules more lives than art, and rules them more despotically. People don't put up their guard when they're being entertained. The images and the messages slip through and take hold deeper.

"This country is a living picture show and doesn't know it," I remember her telling me the night we ran *Dr. Strangelove* at The Classic. "The kids grow up on John Wayne and Marilyn Monroe, but the professors go on teaching Chaucer, the intellectuals go on lint-picking their way through Wittgenstein. Christ! Bugs Bunny has more cultural clout in America than the hundred great books. Just look out the window, see how right Kubrick is. We've got gunslingers acting out *High Noon* in the White House. You don't find that kind of politics in Aristotle; you find it at the movies. Next time some president casts himself in a shootout like the Cuban missile crisis, we may all be dead. I wouldn't be surprised if we reach the point where America stops having elections and just holds auditions for high office. Then we can just send over to central casting for any two-bit actor who *looks* presidential."

She was exaggerating, but I took her point.

As Clare saw things, she belonged to a tiny band of intrepid critics who had been trail-blazing the pop-cultural scene in America for twenty years. Now a new, more media-versed generation was catching up with her almost too rapidly—like an avalanche descending upon someone who cried out too loud in the icebound wilderness. We were approaching that precarious midspan of the sixties, a period whose insurgent style would usher in so many surprises both delightful and appalling. Clare was convinced that movies had played a big part in giving the parental order a well-deserved kick in the pants. "Movies began rubbing the shine off the Social Lie as far back as *film noir* cynicism. Then antiheroes like Brando, Dean, and Newman started dumping all-purpose contempt on Daddy's values. Brando's mumble, Montgomery Clift's slouch, Tony Perkins' sneer—they did more than a thousand political manifestos to rock the pillars of society."

Clare had reservations about much that she saw; she *always* had reservations. Her judgments could be maddeningly convoluted. She claimed to have coined the term "radical chic" (as part of some film notes for *La Dolce Vita*) for the sort of work that glamorizes the corruption it purports to condemn. Of that she saw worrisomely plenty. But she fretted especially whenever the power of a movie outdistanced its intellectual merit.

"What are you *against*, kid?" asks the pretty blonde in *The Wild One*.

"What have you got?" Brando, the brooding delinquent, asks back.

"A lousy movie," Clare thought. "But you put a line like that in the mouth of someone with ten tons of screen charisma and it's dynamite. Though somebody please tell me," she added, picking up on one of her favorite gripes, "why must all our anti-establishment imagery be so exclusively *male?* When do we get the *new* Bette Davis?"

In Clare's view, the French New Wave, the angry young English directors were still way ahead of America in pioneering this new hip populist sensibility that so blithely mingled all levels and tastes with as much irreverence for old line radicalism as for bourgeois propriety. In Paris, street-fighting students would soon be calling themselves "Groucho Marxists." But America was coming on strong. Dr. Spock's first wave of spoiled brats was arriving on the campuses infected with much the same strain of loony left-wing disaffiliation, wanting more fun and freedom than even their ever-indulgent parents would give— above all wanting to make love not war. That choice was coming to seem more and more like a matter of life and death with each news bulletin. America's long-secret maneuvers in Vietnam had boiled up into a major bloodbath that looked to the pampered young not the least bit like the pursuit of happiness.

With alarms like this going off on all sides, I sometimes had honest doubts if the questions that raged among Clare and her friends— heavy, all-night debates about veiled motivations in Cassavetes' *Shadows*, Antonioni's daring use of color in *Red Desert*—really mattered all that much. Did film studies have any defensible place in a world that was going berserk? But whenever I so much as breathed a word of such reservations, Clare was quick to slap me down. "Art civilizes," she insisted. The words were an article of faith for her. "Without aesthetics, no ethics. And vice versa. There isn't a single political issue that couldn't be settled by a heavy dose of good taste. Anyway, Jonny, you've got no call to bad-mouth the movies. You owe them a lot—maybe your life."

She was right about that. By a crazy twist of fate, I had the movies to thank for my civilian status during the war years. When my student deferment lapsed, I fully expected to find myself on the next plane to Saigon. Instead my draft board regretfully notified me that I was judged unfit for service due to "sociopathic tendencies." Namely, I'd once been arrested for conspiring to show an obscene movie. Chipsey Goldenstone's *Venetian Magenta* spared me the horrors of Vietnam. I had, of course, beaten the rap in court; but the military was having nothing to do with shameless pornographers.

What Clare was proposing for my academic future made perfect sense. Looking back now, anybody could see that. Max Castle has long since become a name to conjure with in the art of film; my pioneering studies of his work have become minor classics in their own right. But at the time it took more than a little convincing to overcome my stubborn caution. I was a timid student wanting to stay close to respectability. Under the influence of my thesis adviser (in Clare's opinion an academic drudge; his specialty was publishing pedestrian filmographies on postwar French and Italian directors) I'd been outlining a rather stale project on early Neorealism, a small, secret tribute to those Italian beauties who had lent my youthful lust a touch of artistry. Clare didn't disapprove, but she wouldn't encourage the choice either. "It's just the *usual* thing, Jonny," she kept insisting. "It's so damned *safe.*"

Which, to my unenterprising way of thinking, made it exactly the right choice. But Clare had other, more daring, things in mind for me, and she had her own ways of breaking down the pedagogical barriers.

One night during a memorably steamy bedroom seminar, Clare began to hold forth at some length about the movies of William Keighley. William Keighley? And not his better, later work, but low-grade stuff the likes of *G-Men, Special Agent, Brother Rat.* "*Each Dawn I Die,*" Clare mused. "Probably that's the best of his hack jobs. Stalin once said it was his favorite movie." Oh? And what was I to make of that? "Do you realize what it takes to get through to a Stalin?"

From there, the talk drifted off toward the films of Errol Taggart, William Clemens, Sam Katzman . . . third- and fourth-raters who had once shared quarters with Max Castle along Hollywood's Poverty Row. Clare and I had never discussed such filmmakers before; I assumed because they were outside the boundaries even of her sprawling critical attention. But now she seemed to be saying every good thing in the world about them. About their "raw masculine energy," their "unabashed directness," their "robust narrative line," above all their "sure sense of popular taste."

As she spoke, I discovered she was maneuvering me into a particularly athletic sexual contortion. As always, I went along dutifully and found I was being offered a delicate and highly privileged avenue of access which I'd never have been bold enough to attempt without much urging. By this time, after three years of innovative lovemaking, I assumed our repertoire of postures and pleasures had gone as far as it ever could; for it had indeed achieved an astonishing variety. But I was wrong. With a combination of embarrassment, curiosity, and delight, I followed where Clare guided, though hesitantly.

"What's the matter, lover?" she asked, sensing my uncertainty. "Afraid of entering new territory?" She laughed and coaxed me further along. And, as I toiled away, she began a languid disquisition on the artistic virtues of Val Lewton, the filmmaker she most closely associated with Castle. "Sure, we're getting into the down and dirty side of things," she gasped between rapid and accelerating breaths. "But, believe me, some really interesting things happen in the lower depths. Relax and enjoy."

Very possibly, even in the permissive early morning of the Pop Art sixties, a dissertation on the work of Max Castle, given the reputation he then held, wouldn't have passed muster in the academy. But when I hesitantly mentioned the possibility to my adviser, he was at least curious. "Castle . . . ?" he asked. "You mean *The Martyr* . . . that Castle? Came to a bad end, didn't he? What could you do with him?"

The American career of a once notable German director. That was how I described the project, decking it out with some general remarks about the influence of European talent and techniques during the period. "Sounds more like a historical than an aesthetic effort," he suggested, mulling the idea over. "Maybe, maybe. But how much of his work can you still find?"

"I've got a line on a small private collection of his later films. About a dozen or so, the uncut versions, which are actually a lot better than you might expect."

My adviser perked up at that. I seemed to be suggesting a work of some scholarly value. "I suppose you could come up with some interesting results. A critical commentary on the studio system, something like that. Why not give it a shot and see what you turn up?"

I had the distinct sense that the man was grateful for the chance I was offering to strike out after something new, perhaps even a bit daring. I knew for a fact that he had six students already working on *auteur* theory. (When I reported that to Clare, her comment was: "What a strange hell he must be living through.") As I rose to leave his office, he observed, "You know, there seems to be a growing interest in this sort of thing. Pop culture, all that. I don't think we should be too stuffy about such matters. What the hell, Tom Pittman over in English tells me he's got a student working on Dashiell Hammett. Dashiell Hammett!"

I was launched. And I was never forced to look back. By the time I'd finished my dissertation two years further along, my adviser was guiding (or following) other students through graduate studies of Dick Powell musicals and the comedies of Harold Lloyd—and feeling gleefully liberated. But I was his star pupil. Because my dissertation was submitted with a personal contribution to the UCLA Film Archives of seventeen uncut thirty-five-millimeter Max Castle originals. By then, the films had twice been exhibited in special and exclusive festivals at The Classic, which (I so specified in my bequest) would retain in perpetuity the right to show Castle's works rent-free.

If I spend little time here on the two years of my graduate research, it's because these years did indeed race by like the wind. And that was mainly thanks to Clare. Her help came so generously and abundantly that it was all I could do to keep up with the flow of her thought. At points, I was really little more than her amanuensis taking down lecture notes—in fact, plagiarizing from my mentor. Of course, as long as I was only working at early drafts of the thesis, I could tell myself that everything I took from Clare would finally be reformulated in my own words, filtered through my own thoughts. But swept forward by the pressure Clare placed me under to get the job done, the rough drafts rapidly slid forward into finished chapters that were at best a loose paraphrase of her words. Occasionally, if I dared to introduce a few of my own still embryonic ideas about Castle, Clare would have none of it. She insisted, at times despotically, on recasting all I said and scrapping whatever she couldn't accept.

There was only one point at which I succeeded in making a personal imprint upon my thesis, though it was a minor one. The interviews. Though Clare saw no need for me to do it, I took it upon myself to chase down some of Castle's surviving friends and co-workers. I'd learned a great deal from Zip in our several conversations, points of fact, insights, more than a few mysteries that I was certain belonged in a full account of Castle's work. But I didn't want to base conclusions wholly on Zip's unconfirmed, often wayward, recollection. So I went hunting for others who might supplement what he had told me of Castle's Hollywood years. Though I didn't expect to find many, I made an ambitious start. Using an address supplied by my old pal Geoff Reuben, I sent off a long, flattering, wheedling letter to Louise Brooks. And then a second, and then a third. Rumor had it that she'd retired into hermetical seclusion after jumping off (or being dumped from) the Hollywood roller coaster. When last seen in public during the war years, she was working behind a cosmetics counter in New York. Since then, a small cult had grown up around her early movies. I tried to use that as leverage in approaching her, playing the appreciative scholar to the hilt. Eight letters, no answer.

I had more luck closer to home, beginning with V. V. Valentine, head of Three Vs Studio, an independent filmmaker who had begun producing grade Z movies along the fringes of the troubled and tottering studios during the late forties. Valentine was universally regarded as one of the industry's most carnivorous schlockmeisters. He survived by waylaying greedy young talent as soon as it arrived in town and giving it the chance to make movies at slave wages. The result was a steady, high-earning stream of exploitation films produced at the rate of as many as a dozen a year. My interest in Valentine arose from a few remarks about him Zip had dropped in passing. At some point in the later thirties, the young Valentine, himself an eager greenhorn at the time, had begged his way aboard some of Castle's productions, beginning as a go-for, then as a minor grip. I checked back and, sure enough, there was his name (once as Walter Valentine, once as Virgil Valentine) buried among the lesser credits of Castle's last two films. Zip remembered Valentine as a pushy young pest who was constantly buttonholing Castle, trying to move in close and milk him for filmmaking tips. "Do you think he got much out of Castle?" I had asked.

"Ha!" Zip had scoffed. "All he ever learned was how to make 'em cheap. That guy once made a hot-rod movie in two days. It looked it too. What a louse he was. Tried to cut me out with Max, went around acting like he was number-two man on the set. Max used to string him along just for laughs."

Reportedly, Valentine was a hard man to see, and even harder to like once you saw him. I got to him through a secretary who, as I would soon learn, had screwed up my message in transit. She apparently heard me say I was doing a study of Valentine's films. This, I gather, flattered him sufficiently to gain me an hour's interview in his garish North Hollywood office. Before I met the man his furnishings proclaimed financial success wholly unrelated to taste.

Valentine turned out to be a slovenly, sourpussed little man with a pot belly and a blubbery fish mouth. He was wearing the worst toupee I'd ever seen—and wearing it slightly askew. He bustled in forty minutes late, giving the impression of intense busy-ness.

"A Ph.D. dissertation, huh?" he began, savoring the words like an unfamiliar delicacy as he eased back into a plush chair behind a cluttered desk. His voice was a deep, phlegm-laden growl. "Well, it's about time. I thought they did those just on European types. Rossellini, Bergman. Snob stuff like that."

"Oh no," I assured him. "We're branching out into popular American work."

"*Popular!*" Valentine beamed, punctuating the word with a slap on the desk. "That's the ticket. I mean after all we're talking movies, correct? You know how hard it is to be popular? Plenty hard. Any amateur schnook can make a movie isn't gonna be liked except by a couple hundred stuck-up critics. What's that to do? Ninety-six movies I made here. You know how many tickets I sold? Over five billion worldwide. That's *world*wide, you heard me? In Hong Kong they show my stuff without any subtitles. Don't need 'em. A good story tells itself. Who needs a script, eh?" Swelling with self-satisfaction, he parked one foot on his desk. "Ask away, professor."

I asked—starting with what he had learned from Castle.

"Castle? Max?" Valentine responded, taken by surprise. "Hey, that's going way back. Ancient history. What did I learn from Max? Well, a thing or two, a thing or two." He fixed me with a defensive gaze. "Listen, it wasn't patented. What the hell. In this business everybody steals from everybody. Mostly what Max did for me was he gave me a start. That's important. I'll always be grateful. Just like, right here, I'm giving lots of kids their start. I got some talent working for me you wouldn't believe how talented it is. And what they're willing to work for—shows how grateful they are I'm giving them a break."

"I mean," I continued, pressing the point, "did you learn any technique from Castle. Special, unusual things."

"If you wanna know, you couldn't trust that foxy son of a bitch. These tricks of his he was always using—he'd tell you one thing, it didn't work like that. You could go broke trying to do what he told you. Split lighting. Ha! I musta burned up a million bucks on that one. Buncha baloney."

"What about the flicker? Did you ever talk with him about that?" I tried to put the question as casually as possible, as if I might be asking about common knowledge.

All I got back was a blank stare and a gruff "Huh?"

"Or the underhold?" I hastened to get the word in, hoping it might ring a bell. "Did Castle ever mention something like that?"

Now the stare turned suspicious. "Am I supposed to know what you're talkin' about here, sonny?" he asked back with distinct impatience.

I moved on rapidly. "What was Castle like—as a person, as a friend?"

Valentine gave me a shifty-eyed squint. "A spy. That's what I think he was. Don't quote me."

"A spy?"

"A kraut spy, yeah."

"Why do you say that?"

"All these shady types around the place he worked with, all talking kraut, you know. *Jawohl, jawohl, ach du lieber, gesundheit.* Fifth columnists. Don't quote me."

"You're sure of that?"

He sniffed knowingly. "He told me."

"Castle told you? What?"

He dropped into a husky whisper. "Secret messages. In the movies. Like, you know, code. 'Val,' he said to me (we were very close, very close), 'Val, you could conquer the world with the movies. You just gotta know how to stick the messages in there.' That's Nazi talk, am I right?"

I started to ask further about his conversations with Castle when Valentine cut me off, his face suddenly darkening with distrust. "Hey, what the fuck is this? Are we talking about Castle or are we talking about me?"

"Castle," I answered, admitting, before I could think better of it, that we were at cross-purposes. Three minutes later I was on my way out of Valentine's office, washed along on a stream of abuse.

"You think I got time to waste on crap like this? Castle's a dead doornail, for God's sake. What's to talk about? He never taught shit, if you wanna know. Nobody does nobody any favors in this business. I got eight pictures in production right now. I'm a busy man. Go peddle your papers someplace else, sonny."

My second interview was less abrasive but not much more informative. I was able to run down one Leroy Pusey, who had been a studio executive at Universal in the years Castle worked there. His name appeared as an associate producer on one of the Count Lazarus films. He was now well along into his seventies, surviving on one lung in a Pasadena rest home. He proved to be a pleasant, cooperative man, though he spent a long while catching his breath between sen-

Theodore Roszak

tences. He clearly enjoyed having my company. Unfortunately, his recollection of Castle was dim and unreliable. "Arrogant," he recalled, "very arrogant. They were like that, those German directors. Von Sternberg, Von Stroheim. Max wasn't in that league, but he could be just as arrogant. Never enough money. Complaining, complaining. Let's see, there was some picture we made about airplanes. What was it? *Dive Bomber, Crash Dive* . . . something like that."

"I don't think Castle ever worked on any aviation pictures," I corrected. I knew he hadn't.

"*Test Dive* . . . I think. Something of that sort. With Robert Armstrong. We had a pretty good budget for that. But Max—listen to this—he wanted us to buy him three real airplanes. Just to crash them. No models, you see. Realism. We rented one plane for him finally, but not to crash. He crashed it anyway."

"I don't think that was Castle," I tactfully insisted, absolutely certain there was no such film in Castle's repertory.

"Sure, that was Max. He thought of himself as expensive talent. An MGM budget, that's what he expected. That's when we fired him—after he crashed the airplane. That finished him at Universal. To tell you the truth, I always believed he did it just to get himself fired. Airplanes—that wasn't his kind of movie. We replaced him with . . . I can't remember. Was it Otis Garrett?"

Now I wasn't sure if I should believe him or not. Perhaps Castle had sabotaged his way out of a contract at Universal. I tried to move the conversation toward more familiar ground. "What about *Count Lazarus*? Do you remember that?"

He stared back vaguely, as if through a heavy fog. "Count Lazarus . . . the vampire? Max made that? No, I believe that was Bob Siodmak."

"Count Lazarus was Castle's vampire—definitely," I corrected.

"Was he? Lord, we made so many of those." He laughed. "Vampires! We had them hanging from the rafters. Yes, you're right. Lazarus. That was Max. We had trouble with that too."

"What kind of trouble?"

He wagged his head grimly. "Very unpleasant. What Max gave us . . . well, it was very, very *dirty*. Never could have cleared the censors. Naked women. He wanted to put naked women on the screen. In America."

"There's no nudity in the film," I reminded him.

"We spent hours, days cutting that movie. Jack Wasserman, Neal

205

Davies . . . practically the whole Universal executive staff. Lewd, very lewd. How did he expect to get away with that? Native girls, maybe. But white women . . ."

"I mean, Mr. Pusey, there's no actual, real nudity. Even in the original version. I've seen the original version."

"No, that would have been kept by the studio. Probably long since destroyed."

"Castle's cameraman, Zip Lipsky, saved a lot of Castle's films— the uncut versions. I've seen them. He showed them to me."

"Zip! Excellent man. Whatever became of him?"

I filled him in on what I knew about Zip down to his death. Pusey showed honest sorrow.

"He was one of the best. Too good for Universal, I'll admit that. Just a natural-born shooter."

"Mr. Pusey, I've seen the uncut prints of both *Count Lazarus* and *Feast of the Undead*," I went on, returning to the point in question. "There's nothing you could call obscene in either movie, certainly no nudity."

Pusey seemed to be scouring the dusty corners of his memory. "Well, no, not that you could *see*."

"I beg your pardon."

"It wasn't anything you could see."

"I don't understand. Either you see it or you don't."

He was thinking strenuously now, digging deep. "Well, it wasn't that simple. I remember we argued a lot about that movie—where to cut, how much to cut. We even . . . yes, now I recall, we even brought in some of the secretaries and receptionists. We asked them to look at the movie. They all agreed it was a dirty movie. There was one girl, she walked out. Very angry. Very embarrassed. She thought the whole movie was practically pornography. The trouble was: we couldn't seem to agree on *what* we had seen, the group of us. Isn't that strange? We all had these different ideas about it. Myself, I don't think I saw any nudity, not really. But . . . something else."

"What do you mean?"

"Have you ever walked into someplace . . . a house, a neighborhood? And you just know it's bad. A bad, a nasty place. You don't have to *see* anything. You have a feeling. It can be worse than seeing. Because it's everywhere, soaked in deep." Pusey's voice faltered and went fuzzy. He seemed now at last to be bringing his distant memories of Castle into sharp focus across the years. The reminiscing had ceased being enjoyable. "He was not a nice man. I never liked working with him. It wasn't just the arrogance. Something else. We made lots of morbid movies at Universal. They were our big earners. Dracula, the werewolf, zombies. But really, you know, they were sort of jokes. Who could take them seriously? Bela Lugosi . . . you see what I mean. When we were finished, we walked away from them, left it all behind. But not Max. Max was morbid. Inside, a morbid man. These things were in him, not just in the movie. I think he was very sick, do you know what I mean?"

There was little more I could draw out of Pusey, though he rambled on for another hour or so, mixing clear recollections with obvious mistakes. One thing was abundantly clear: the longer we talked about Castle, the more his distaste for the man returned to mind and deepened, until at last, when I turned to leave, he asked with genuine concern, "Why do you want to study about a man like this? There were so many good and talented people, even at Universal. James Whale, Al Cosland . . . why Castle?"

I tried to answer that I found significant qualities in Castle's work, but Pusey made me feel ashamed to say it.

There was only one more interview of any possible value I went after. Helen Chandler had been immortalized for film fans as Bela Lugosi's victim-in-chief in *Dracula*. From there she drifted through a series of undistinguished films, including three of Castle's. There was no record of her film work, if any, after the late thirties. I was able to trace her to an address in Santa Barbara. She was a soft, refined, and very fragile voice on the phone when I got through to her.

"Max Castle," she repeated when I mentioned the name. And then there was a long pause. "Oh yes, I worked with him. Twice."

"Three times actually," I reminded her. When I requested a visit, her reluctance was obvious.

"I'm not sure it would be worth your trouble. There are many things I wouldn't feel free to talk about."

"There are just a few details I'd be interested in. Nothing personal."

"What sort of details?"

"Oh, some of his directorial techniques, the way he handled his actors."

"I think that would turn out to be quite personal, especially in my case."

"I'm willing to let you be as nonpersonal as you wish," I assured her. "Wouldn't we be able to stick to technical matters?"

"Max was a most unusual man. He made unusual demands. Frankly, I wouldn't be able to explain a great deal of what he expected of us. Some of it might sound . . . quite mad."

"If I could just have what you remembered most vividly, your major impressions."

Another long pause. "You see, there were things we were asked not to talk about."

"By Castle?"

"Yes, by Max. Things he wanted to keep to himself."

"What sort of things?"

"I suppose I shouldn't say. Little tricks of the trade he probably didn't want other directors to know about. There was a great deal about lights . . . I never understood about that. It was all very unusual."

"Well, he is dead now. It's a long while to be keeping secrets."

"Perhaps you're right." But she still hesitated.

"Do you remember some of these things well enough to describe them?"

"Oh yes. One remembers things like that . . . so far out of the ordinary."

"If we could talk, that might make it possible for more people to appreciate his work."

Her tone took on a quizzical chill. "Should I care about that? They were rather frightful pictures . . . perhaps best forgotten."

"But don't you think Castle would want his work to be appreciated?"

"I really have no idea. He seemed to have a very low opinion of the films we worked on. In any case, Max and I . . . we didn't part as great friends. He wasn't a man who made friends. Sometimes I felt . . . the closer he let you come, the less friendly he became. He could be . . . very cruel."

I begged and wheedled a bit longer and finally got an invitation to visit in the following week. Accordingly, I made the drive to Santa Barbara, only to be met at the door by a housekeeper who told me Miss Chandler had been taken ill and was in the hospital. She suggested I leave my name and wait for a call. I waited. Weeks, months. When I finally phoned again, I learned that Miss Chandler was too weak to receive visitors. I wasn't encouraged to call back. Even so, over the next few years I made two or three routine calls. I was never put through to her. When I finally came across her obituary in the papers, it was too late even to send flowers.

There was very little in what Valentine, Pusey, and Helen Chandler told me that could qualify as fact, let alone anything that contributed to an analysis of Castle's work. Nevertheless, the biographical tidbits I collected along the way had their value. They sharpened my mental picture of Castle. I saw him now as an even more formidable, if more distasteful, personality: cool, domineering, manipulative. Above all, I was more convinced than ever that he was the guardian of some highly unorthodox filmmaking techniques that remained unknown nearly thirty years after his death. Clare, on the other hand, refused to take the least interest in anything I gleaned from my interviews with Castle's surviving associates. She regarded my dissertation (she might just as well have called it *our* dissertation) as an exercise in criticism, not history. Stick to the films, she insisted. Everything else is mere back-lot gossip. But even she couldn't help being curious about one item of biographical trivia I turned up. Its source lent it dignity.

"Seems Castle was quite a boozer," I mentioned to her one morning as casually as possible. "At least in his latter days in Hollywood. All-night sessions. Interesting letter I have here from one of his drinking companions." Clare, seated across the breakfast table, her nose buried in the newspaper, refused to be drawn. "Letter came from Ireland," I went on. "From a guy who knew Castle at Warners." No reaction. "Man says he's just finished filming something called *Night of the Iguana*. Tennessee Williams play, isn't that?" She looked up, frowned. "His name is . . . yes, Huston, that's it. John Huston. Ever hear of him?"

The newspaper dropped. "John Huston sent *you* a letter? About Castle?"

He had. A generously long one. It graciously confirmed everything Zip Lipsky had told me about Castle's tenuous and apparently fateful connection with *The Maltese Falcon*. Clare snatched the letter from me.

It began with a lengthy apology for the time I'd been kept waiting for a response. Then:

> I'm so pleased to know that Max Castle is finally receiving the schol-
> arly attention he deserves. He was a very great director. Had he been
> given the largesse the studios have lavished on many lesser talents (I

include myself) he would surely be remembered today as one of the three or four leading filmmakers of the century. As it was, working on a frayed shoestring, he often achieved results that many of us would be proud to claim as our own.

With respect to *The Maltese Falcon*: it is true as Zip Lipsky told you that Max and I had many discussions about the movie. If I say I cannot recall them in any detail, you will understand that memory dims across a span of a quarter century. (Lord! is it so long?) I will also confess that many of these conversations transpired in a haze of inebriation that made it somewhat difficult to remember the night before on the morning after. As befalls so many of us in the turbulent and troubled film world, Max had entered an advanced alcoholic phase of life when I knew him. In addition, I must say that a great deal of what Max told me was both bizarre and obscure. Given the intoxicated state in which I audited his often long and rambling disquisitions, I could hardly be expected to retain more than fragments.

As I recollect, Max had an odd fix on *The Maltese Falcon*. He had the quaint idea that the bird—or rather the statue of the bird—should be the focus of the story. Accordingly, he wanted to surround it with a great deal of fabulous history and iconography that would have made the movie more of a Gothic romance than a hard-boiled detective thriller. For example, I remember that the business of coating the bird with enamel in order to hide its value (a negligible part of the Hammett tale) was very important to Max. He wanted a big scene depicting that. I found all this intriguing but hardly useful. I had already decided quite simply to lift the tale right out of the book chapter by chapter. A cautious approach, but one which seems to have met with critical approval over the years.

Max also had the notion of framing the story within a flashback delivered by Sam Spade on death row the evening before his execution. Max would have deviated from the novel by having Spade kill Gutmann at the prompting of Bridget O'Shaughnessy. He wanted to include this element of the fallen and persecuted hero led to his doom by the wily temptress. All very Arthurian-Wagnerian but hardly what a studio like Warners was likely to buy.

My hunch is that all this had to do with the fact that Max belonged to an unusual religious sect. These of course grow thick on the ground in the permissive cultural climate of southern California; but I was surprised to find that someone of Max's intellect would have been drawn into what I recall as some form of Rosicrucianism. Though I cannot remember the name of the cult, Max did tell me quite a bit about it in a wandering and haphazard way. More than I wished to know, and possibly more than I was supposed to know. He seemed to take a perverse satisfaction in imparting what I gathered were secret doctrines to me. I recall none of these except those that had to do with *outré* sexual practices. These stick with me because on one occasion, Max prevailed upon his lovely friend Olga Tell to demonstrate some of them for me. Since the lady is still alive, modesty forbids me to tell you more.

I do hope you won't find any of this too shocking. You must understand that there was a great deal of this sort of thing happening in the film community in those days. One swami after ananda. My impression is that Max wanted to use his movies as a vehicle for the cult. I'm not certain if he ever succeeded in doing so or how he might have gone about it. I do believe he was trying to persuade me to embed some of the symbols and rites of his sect in *The Maltese Falcon*—for what reason I cannot say. I'm sure it wouldn't have contributed to the quality of the film.

My recollection is that Max was really up against it at the time. The studios wouldn't trust him with anything but low-budget assignments and very few of those. He was understandably bitter and, frankly, desperate. I tried to smuggle him on to the payroll for *Falcon*, but Warners wouldn't hear of it. His only contribution to the film—an indirect one—was to put me on to a peculiar team of editors, two German lads whose name eludes me. (Reinhardt? Reingold?) Twins, as I recall. They assisted Tom Richards somewhat in the editing. I believe all that survives of their work is an interesting twist they gave the closing scene—the parallel descent of Spade on the staircase and the elevator behind, a shot I had not intended to use. They found a few odd shadows to work with which Richards and I had unaccountably overlooked. Brief as it is, I have always found that this shot lends a hauntingly bleak tone to the conclusion, though I'm not sure why. I suppose that might count as contributing a few tail feathers on the bird. Otherwise, the movie as we have it is, alas! mine own from first to last.

But in a larger sense, I will gladly concede that the movie is indebted to Max for its bleak and seedy atmospherics. When it comes to *film noir*, Max was the unsung master. His role in creating the genre is an unwritten chapter in movie history—perhaps now to be supplied by you? (In this regard, I suggest you look closely at his *Man into Monster* if you can find an uncut print. For my money, it is the best B-movie ever made and the *noirest* of all *noir*.)

Best of luck with your study. Do send me a copy upon its completion.
Yours sincerely,
John Huston

P.S. Did Zip Lipsky ever tell you that I asked him to film *Falcon* for me? Unfortunately, he was not available.

P.P.S. Your letter prompted a rapid excavation of my personal archives. Lo! I discovered a memento of my long-ago evenings with Max Castle. The enclosed renderings are by him. Like myself, he was a trained graphic artist and frequently sketched his settings in detail before the shoot. I learned the technique from him and it has served me well over the years. I can no longer identify which scenes these rather lugubrious drawings were meant to be, but I'm sure you can appreciate that mixing the streets of San Francisco with the dungeons of medieval Europe would have been a grievous error. In better days, Max would surely have realized as much. I present the drawings to you for your scholarly use.

I'd hoped a letter from John Huston might mellow Clare's opinion of Castle. Huston was one of her idols; if he was willing to call Castle a great director, that ought to make some difference. Not a chance. Clare had staked out her intellectual ground and was prepared to defend it against all comers. Far from moderating her views on Castle, the letter provided grist for her mill.

"A religious cult," she sneered. "It figures. There's a twisted mind at work here. Gifted, but twisted. Look at these drawings. How did he expect to work this into *The Maltese Falcon*? Looks like old Zip was right. Toward the end, the man was off his rocker."

I had to admit she was right on that point. Two of the three sketches showed what might very well have been dungeons: a vast, lightless interior in which two hirsute artisans were shown toiling by firelight over the statue of a bird, apparently smearing its golden surface with a black coating. In the background, three regally dressed figures looked on. The tunic of one was emblazoned with the emblem Sharkey had first called to my attention: the Maltese cross.

The third sketch had even less obvious relevance to any movie Warner Brothers might have been willing to make. It was a voluptuous female form, naked, suspended in space above three kneeling and prayerful men. There was a large dark bird hovering above her with wings spread. The bird was all that even remotely connected the sketch with *The Maltese Falcon*. I was pleased to have the drawings. They were well-executed by a deft hand. But all they seemed to provide was evidence of Castle's increasing instability. I decided, as an act of scholarly mercy, to make no reference to them in my research until I had some clearer way of interpreting what they had to tell me about Castle's later intellectual development—or degeneration. I wasn't the Sam Spade to do that yet without a lot more clues.

My dissertation, *Max Castle: The Hollywood Years 1925–1941*, was a neatly competent job covering my entire collection of Castle films, except for the *Judas*. I presented a souvenir copy of the bound work to Clare one evening with more ceremonial care than I'd shown my thesis adviser. She brought it to bed that night and, to my surprise, proceeded to read it from cover to cover. I couldn't see why, since she had worked through the whole volume with me chapter by chapter, page by page. I lay beside her, watching for signs of approval, perhaps even praise that I had given her thoughts the prominence and polish they deserved. Her face remained a mask, at times seeming to darken menacingly. When she finished, she lay the thesis on the bedsheets and slowly smoked her cigarette down to a stub, her eyes staring off distantly. It wasn't a look I cared to interrupt with questions.

After a long interval, I saw tears gleam at the corner of her eyes; but her expression remained dead cold. At last she turned to me. She drew down her nightgown revealing her ample left breast. Quite deliberately she offered it to me, extending it toward my lips. It was a familiar invitation. I leaned forward to taste the gift of her nipple, but just as I grazed it with a kiss, she plucked it away leaving me puckered into thin air.

"All right, baby," she snapped, a sneer of dismissal in her voice. "Consider yourself weaned."

At that, she ordered me out of the bedroom onto the living-room couch. Bewildered, I sat alone outside her closed door, trying to make sense of my abrupt banishment. After several minutes, the bedroom door opened and Clare stepped forward to fling my dissertation on the rug. "And take this piece of brain-picking plagiarism with you!" she shouted.

The door slammed. It didn't open for the rest of that night. I knew without being told that I mustn't expect it to admit me again as Clare's lover.

The next morning, as brutally as if I were a hotel guest who had used up his credit, I was ordered to pack and leave.

12 ORSON

I always had my suspicions about the way Clare cut me out of her life. There was no denying the truth of her accusation. My thesis and for that matter almost everything I was to write about Max Castle for the next few years was borrowed from her. I'd even be willing to admit that it was stolen, if it made any sense to say I stole goods that were forced upon me. But I couldn't really believe Clare was wounded by a result she'd collaborated in bringing about. No, there was something more to the matter.

Looking back now, I realize she'd decided to end our affair months before that final wrenching break. At a certain point, she began rushing my research along at a breakneck pace. It was a symptom of impatience; she was racing to get free of the responsibility she'd assumed for my intellectual development. Her sense of fairness wouldn't permit her to dump me until she was sure I'd been well installed in as promising an academic career as her efforts could gain for me. Nor would she let go of my dissertation until, using my voice, she'd said all she cared to commit to print about Max Castle. But once that was accomplished to her satisfaction, she took the nearest excuse at hand to throw me over, and that turned out to be a trumped-up charge of intellectual larceny. It was Clare's style of doing things. No tear-stained apologies, no lingering fond farewells. Just one well-aimed kick in the teeth, an emotional mercy killing quickly and cleanly executed.

Why? Because all the while I was plodding through my graduate studies, great changes were taking place in Clare's life. It began with the local papers. Thanks to the *Venetian Magenta* episode, Clare had become a name. The *Los Angeles Times* took some of her reviews, then requested the occasional article. Her reputation began to grow, at first on the West Coast, then nationally, as her essays on film broke through into major magazines. Opportunities too enticing to ignore were presenting themselves; she had every good reason for wanting all the freedom of maneuver she could get. And of course that meant

214

dropping her rather gauche, still vastly dependent, young lover. Within a year of our parting, Clare was in New York lecturing on film at NYU. For a brief period, she became *The New Yorker's* backup critic, playing a discordant second fiddle to Pauline Kael, with whom she saw eye to eye on practically nothing. A year after that, *The New York Times* hired her as its lead movie reviewer, and a volume of her collected essays and reviews was ready for publication, the first in a succession of best-selling books. Clare had arrived.

I was happy for her success; no one deserved it more. But I was also sadly certain that we'd now be parted permanently not only by the miles between us, but more so by the separate paths we'd chosen. I found myself more and more deeply embedded in the world of the university that she still treated with disdain. I'd been hired into the UCLA Film Studies Department. It was a rock-bottom appointment, but lacking Clare's ambition, I was content to creep slowly up the academic ladder, far removed from the high visibility and lively debate of her new career. From time to time, I sent her little notes of congratulations on an article or a review I'd seen. If she responded at all, it was with a quick postcard. I didn't expect more; in her own hard-as-nails way, Clare had been supremely generous to me, sharing her sophistication and sexual favors with someone too unformed to give her anything in return. I was neither hurt nor surprised that she'd outgrown me and The Classic. I frankly didn't expect to see her again for a long, long time. When we did meet again, it was thanks to Max Castle.

Two years after Clare left Los Angeles, I received a letter from the editor of the Sunday *New York Times Magazine*. He was curious about the rising popularity of Max Castle's movies, which were now playing steadily in the art and repertory houses. The films had become staple items of late-night television, though they usually appeared there in their truncated studio versions, sometimes cut even more drastically. Some of Castle's work—the more lurid horror films—were even acquiring a devoted following as midnight movies. Why Castle, and why now? the editor asked. Would I be willing to try an article that answered these questions? He noted in his closing paragraph that Clarissa Swann had put him on to me as "the country's foremost authority" on the subject. I was overjoyed, as much by Clare's recommendation as by the editor's request. I of course accepted the invitation and at once sent off a gushing note of thanks to Clare. She gave no response.

FLICKER

I realized from the outset that this was a great opportunity for me. Accordingly, I slaved over the piece, packing into it all I could of my years of research. There was, however, one problem at the heart of the project which nearly defeated me. I'd been asked especially to account for Castle's remarkable and growing popularity with young audiences. In my dissertation, I'd handled this question by discussing the timeliness of Castle's films. Or rather I should say that *Clare* had handled it, since the critical judgments on this point were hers not mine. Her interpretation fastened primarily on matters of character and mood, the bleakly *noir* aspects of Castle's movie world. But by the time the dissertation was completed, I no longer felt certain she was right about that. Probably wisely, Clare dissuaded me from mentioning anything about Zip Lipsky's sallyrand. She insisted that such a gimmick, even if I could describe it accurately (which I couldn't), was nothing more than a marginal curiosity that had no place in a serious critical work. Yet even the little I'd learned about Castle's films from that strange device convinced me that the man's power lay in some subterranean dimension of the mind that was still waiting to be unearthed. Did I dare bring that conviction out of the closet now?

I decided not. Instead, I took the easy way out and simply fell back on Clare's interpretation. What was it audiences found in Castle's films? It was, I answered, the characteristic protagonist who appeared in almost every one of his movies: "the outsider," as I called him, using a then-fashionable phrase. A man for our time: isolated, besieged by invincible evil, himself flawed by that evil, fighting against it unsuccessfully in the name of no certain cause. It was an idea my readers would understand. Castle, I suggested (following Clare), had invented an early version of the existentialist hero who had since become so prominent in the films of Bergman, Godard, Antonioni. His central character is invariably an outcast, living in a state of exile or disgrace. In the early silents, he might appear as the traitor Judas or the persecuted heretic. Later, in the B-films, he might be the imprisoned criminal, the hunted spy, or Jack the Ripper hounded through the streets and sewers of the city as much by his own self-loathing as by the fear of punishment. In his fully developed form, he becomes Castle's most popular character, Count Lazarus the vampire. The Count's hunger for blood, always intertwined with a morbid sexuality, is never so much frightening as pathetic, a man driven by his domineering will to survive, even though the price of his survival is a constant horror to him. Invariably, Castle succeeds in enlisting our sympathies on the side of these outcast monsters, even when their crimes are repulsive. We see them as victims of a cruel fate which has blighted their better nature. We feel their struggle, knowing it is futile, knowing that the wrong they oppose is too great, the evil too formidable.

My editor at the *Times* approved the thesis of the piece, though he insisted on paring away its academic refinements. He also pressed me to make a concluding judgment I was reluctant to offer and finally sidestepped. "A sympathetic vampire . . . a Ripper who wins our hearts. Granting it takes some skill to pull that off, isn't there something pretty sick about all this? And dangerous? What sort of 'heroes' are these for a young audience? Bloodsuckers and mass murderers! Any comments?"

What comment could I offer but worried acquiescence? I'd been aware of the morbidity that infected Castle's work since I saw the *Judas.* But my fascination with that work was more and more mixed with admiration. I couldn't bring myself to make the damning judgment.

My article spent some six months being churned through the *Times's* editorial mill, steadily shedding its scholarly tone with each revision. I balked at many of the changes that were demanded, primarily because, as I soon realized, the farther I moved from academic restraint, the more my writing began to echo Clare's direct and pungent style, which was still there embedded in all I had to say about Castle. With some embarrassment, I was forced to recognize that I really hadn't yet added much more to my teacher's critical views than footnotes and bibliography. This led me at one point to suggest to the *Times* that Clare be asked to take over the assignment. She *had* been asked, I was told; she was their first choice for the piece. She'd recommended me instead. So I saw: I was still functioning as Clare's means of distancing herself from Castle.

Finally, the article reached print under the title (rather too sensational for my tastes) "Max Castle, Maker of Likable Monsters: Rediscovering a Forgotten Master of the Fast-Film Trade."

The piece brought me a small flood of enthusiastic mail, the most dramatic indication I'd yet received of Castle's new following. The response wasn't all encouraging. A sizable part of it came from college students, some of the letters so inarticulate I wondered how their authors could possibly have understood what I wrote. Very likely they didn't; they were simply Castle fans whose mindless infatuation glowed on the page. His movies I was told again and again were "incredible" and "fantastic." One freshman from Columbia told me he was now "tripping out" on Count Lazarus regularly every Saturday at the Charles, a run-down old movie house on Avenue B that specialized in midnight movies. He went on to tell me all about his absolutely most favorite flick of all! *Venetian Magenta.* Had I seen it? I really, really should. Because it was very, very groovy.

Mail like this worried me. Its minimal literacy made me fear for the audience I might be cultivating. Fortunately, there were also a number of flattering responses from scholarly peers and critics. But there were two letters that mattered more than all the rest.

The first was from Arlene Fleischer, the film archivist at the Museum of Modern Art. She was toying with the idea of holding a Max Castle retrospective in the coming year. Would I be willing to discuss a brochure and filmography for the event, and perhaps offer some lectures? The invitation was dazzling enough; but more exciting still, she went on to note that the archives were in the process of purchasing all the Castle films they could find, and these now included prints of some of his early German films, which had been located in the Vienna School of Cinema, as well as in several private collections. The search had also turned up a few more B-films to which Castle might have contributed. Would I care to come to New York and look over the material? The archives would pay my travel and accommodations.

It was a windfall. I leapt at the offer.

The second letter was a postcard, a curt one-liner. It said "Congratulations, lover . . . couldn't have done better myself. As ever, Clare." Even MOMA's invitation paled in importance for me beside that single terse compliment.

But if I expected Clare's note to introduce Phase Two of our disjunctive love affair, I was dead wrong. When I got to New York that summer to make plans for the Castle retro, she treated me to a month of carefully contrived elusiveness. Calling her from my hotel the moment I arrived, I received a hasty, last-minute goodbye. Clare was on her way out the door and off to Europe. There followed three weeks during which she toured film festivals and conference-hopped her way from Edinburgh to Athens. When she got back, my calls to her home and office went unanswered. I sent letters; twice they produced phone messages in my box at the Granada telling me please to try again. I got the point. This wasn't the way a prospective lover greets a prospective lover. So I quietly lowered my expectations and soldiered on with my duties at the museum, screening and annotating the films of Max Castle.

My work put me in daily touch with Arlene Fleischer, a hard-edged but always courteous lady who ran the archives with the precision and authority of a ship's captain. One day when she dropped by to check on my progress, I asked, "How did you happen to start collecting Castles?"

"Clarissa Swann," was her answer. "We were discussing acquisitions over lunch some time last summer. Clarissa is the only critic in town whose recommendations I'd spend money on. I was trying at the time to decide between some Renoirs and some Pabsts that were being offered. To my surprise, Clarissa advised that I buy Castle instead of either. To tell you the truth, I thought she meant *William* Castle, you know, the man with all the awful gimmicks. When she said *Max* Castle, I pretty much drew a blank. After all, this was before your excellent article appeared in the *Times*. All I could associate with *that* Castle was vampires. As it turned out Clarissa had compiled a list of available Castle material. Most of what we purchased from private collections are items she'd scouted out, often in very unlikely places. She put me on to one collector, a certain Hermann Von Schachter in Paraguay. I do believe the man was some kind of runaway Nazi. But he did own a couple of Castle's silent films. That's where we found *The Dreaming Eyes*. Clarissa was also the one who clued me into the fact that Castle and Maurice Roche were one and the same. That's how we picked up the five Roche films we have. So you see, I could have bought Renoirs, and instead I bought Castles. I didn't realize Clarissa was such a fan of his."

"I don't think she is," I replied. "In fact, I think she rather despises him."

"Oh? I wouldn't have guessed it to see how she went after the films once they began to arrive."

"She watched these movies?"

"Oh yes, every single one, some of them several times over. With that look of hers, you know—when she really cares about a movie. She watches it as if she might burn a hole through the screen."

"Did she make any comments?"

Arlene thought back. "Now that you ask, nothing really memorable.

Just noncommittal little remarks like 'interesting.' But I assume she found the films worth serious attention. It was her idea to do the retrospective."

"Oh, was it?"

"Yes, but when I invited her to organize it, she put me on to you. So here you are." She smiled rather too condescendingly, as if it should be gratification enough for the likes of me to play second fiddle to Clarissa Swann.

Two days before I was scheduled to return to California, I discovered a letter in my box at the hotel. Clare's handwriting. I opened it at once. It contained the usual brief communiqué.

Jonny My Dear,
    If you can spare the time to drop by this coming Thursday evening, I may be able to offer you the thrill of a lifetime. Say about nine-thirtyish . . . ? (No false promises. All the thrills will happen in the dining room, not the boudoir. Okay?)
Clare

"This coming Thursday" was tomorrow, just twenty-four hours before I had to leave town. Had she planned it that way? Of course I'd go. But from what I knew of Clare's cooking, I couldn't imagine what sort of thrill she might be serving up in the dining room. Nine-thirty sounded like dessert time. Clare was quite lavish about desserts. But I was sure she had more than that in mind.

She did. The evening's entertainment announced itself before I'd knocked at the door of the smallish flat she was renting in the West Sixties. A laugh as vast and almost as menacing as a lion's roar penetrated to the hallway. It was vaguely familiar but I couldn't pin a face to it. Then the door opened and the voice attached to the laugh came at me like a baritone avalanche. And I knew at once.

Clare escorted me into a dining room that displayed the messy ruins of a massive Chinese take-out dinner. There was a couple at the table. Clare introduced them first. The Ferrers, Matthew and Barbara. Their accent identified them as English, their dress and manner as rich. The guest of honor needed no introduction. Seated at the head of the table in a blue-gray cloud of his own cigar smoke, Orson Welles looked like a human volcano flirting with the possibility of eruption. Taking my hand in a tight, meaty grip, he grunted a "hello" that managed to be friendly and at the same time haughty.

He was sporting a black dagger beard and hair down to his jowls. His brow was knotted into a permanent frown that made even his smile seem slightly menacing. Already well advanced toward a Falstaffian corpulence, he took up the place of two at his end of the room. Clare, still earning at a subluxury level in cruelly expensive New York, had no air-conditioning to offer her guests that sultry night other than open windows that admitted the roar of Broadway several floors below. Orson, registering the heat of the evening in a sheen of sweat at the brow, the lip, the cheek, was peeled down to a see-through white caftan and bare feet. The robe clung to his chest, revealing masses of hair and nipples large as eggs. His dishabille suggested he was a houseguest. Was he? Clare, seated next to the great man, was lavishing much attention on him. How interesting. Her love life in the big city seemed to have taken on status.

Orson had been talking when I entered. After our brief introduction, he resumed—and held the floor for pretty much the remainder of the evening, with little more time allotted to the rest of us than he needed to catch his breath, swig some drink, or drag on a Havana the size of a baseball bat. Even then, his labored respiration, blown like a whale's spouting from gaping nostrils, was portentous enough to dominate the brief intervals he left for others to speak. The others didn't mind, certainly not the Ferrers. Quiet and courteous, they contributed almost nothing to the evening's talk except polite laughter or an occasional sedate grunt of approval. They were, I gathered, part of Orson's international entourage, possibly patrons of his art who happened to be passing through. Everything about them said money. Accordingly, they were there to be amused and Orson was more than eager to oblige with a veritable raconteurial cornucopia.

My entrance had interrupted an anecdote about the king of Morocco. Orson had been filming in Morocco. Orson, it seemed, had been filming everywhere. He never got back to his story. Nobody cared. He went on to another and another. Stories about movies, plays, parties, intrigues, famous people, scandalous love affairs. It was a glittering performance; you could have sold tickets to hear it. It lasted through coffee, cognac, two servings of Clare's rum-soaked crepes (three for Orson) before, much to my surprise, the talk circled around to me. I have no idea how we got there; as he downed more cognac, Orson's perorations were growing too baroque to follow. At one point, he was going on about dining on camel steaks in Egypt; the next thing I knew, he was paying me what sounded like a well-rehearsed compliment. (But then, everything Orson said sounded well-rehearsed.)

". . . and what our young friend from California here has done for Max Castle shines like a beacon of hope for all of us who know our work, our poor contribution to civilization depends upon rediscovery in some safe haven of the future when the slings and arrows of outrageous criticism have been laid to rest." He raised his glass to propose the fourth or fifth toast since I'd arrived. "To the scholars, who are the final arbiters of taste." But then, turning to Clare at his side, "Of course there are a few critics—not many, a few—who also qualify as intelligent life in the universe." He rumbled with laughter as he clasped her to him in a bear hug. Clare nearly vanished into his bulk. "To Clare!" He lifted his glass. "Champion of the underdog."

I knew what that fond tribute was all about. A couple of prominent critics had recently taken out after Orson, seeking to prove that he hadn't written the screenplay for *Citizen Kane*. Always itching for a good intellectual dustup, Clare had at once sprung to Orson's defense with her usual scorched-earth savagery.

After favoring Clare with a rough nuzzle, Orson, as I hoped he would, turned back to me. "Max was the first of us, you know. Mendicant filmmakers begging our way round the world hat in hand, trying to salvage a few small grains of art from the commercial slag heap. When I first met Max, I felt heartbroken for him. And not a little guilt-stricken. After all, I was the golden boy. And here he was, old and broken and hard up. Not really that old, come to think of it. What would he have been? Early forties at most. He got an even earlier start than I did. The *Wunderknabe* of German cinema. But he looked old as Methuselah and beaten down. A life booked into the theater of disaster. He was carrying a dozen movies in his head, all in bits and pieces, scattered around the world—and none of them likely to get finished.

"I couldn't imagine ever coming to such a pass. Ha! Ten years farther down the road and I was following in his footsteps—a gypsy artist with a ragbag of scripts and treatments and unedited footage on my back, surviving on the generosity of people like Matthew and Barbara here, the last of the great patrons. If any of the four or five films I'm juggling ever gets made, it will be thanks to their unflagging faith and loyalty. To Matthew!" He drank off what was left in his glass at a swallow. Clare filled it in time for the next toast. "And to Barbara!" When the booze had hit bottom and bounced back with a giant-sized hiccup, he continued. "So you see, I hope one day I'll be lucky enough to have a Jonathan Gates to come to my probably posthumous defense, someone who cares enough to salvage the surviving scraps of my labor and see them for what they might have been." And so there was a toast for me.

While he swallowed, I took advantage of the opening. "Zip Lipsky . . ." I began.

"Zip! Brilliant fellow," Orson intruded to tell me. "I always hoped to work with him. A natural. Tried to get him for two or three of my films. It's a tragedy how he was persecuted by the blacklisters."

I waited to see if there would be a toast for Zip. There was. When it was drunk off, I went on. "Zip told me Castle was the first person you looked up in Hollywood when you arrived."

"Not quite," Orson corrected. "It was Max who looked me up. He had work to offer me. Unpaid work, which was the only kind he was in a position to hand out. Did you know I made my screen debut in a Max Castle movie?" When he saw how puzzled everyone at the table was, he burst into a rumbling great laugh. "It had to be a secret at the time, because of my contract with RKO. But that was a million years ago." He took a deep drag on the Havana and settled into the story. "Max was making one of his vampire flicks at the time. I forget the title. This would've been 1939—early 1939. John Abbott was playing the lead. British actor. Competent, not gifted."

"That must have been *House of Blood*," I suggested.

"Yes, that's it. Max was just finishing the movie when he heard I was in town. I'd already sent a letter saying I hoped to meet him. There was so much in his films I admired. Well, no sooner do I check in at the Roosevelt than Max phones. I remember how he introduced himself. 'This is Max Castle. I wish to speak to the greatest Dracula there ever was.' " He paused to sip his cognac, puff the cigar, wait for the predictable question. Clare asked it.

"When did you ever play Dracula? You hadn't even made a movie yet."

Orson roared with delight. "They ought to give prizes for show-biz trivia. This could sell for thousands. 'When did Orson Welles play Dracula?' Answer: on the radio. The premiere broadcast of the Mercury Theater on the Air. As the bloodsucking Count, I had one line."

Leaning across the table, eyes closed, scowling, he recreated the line: a vulpine snarl, mixed with a whine of enraged frustration. "Well, something like that. You see, Max knew that as an actor I was never

anything but a voice. No, it's true. The body is just a sound chest.
All the talent's in the larynx. But a larynx was what Max needed. Not
a human voice, mind you. The voice of the great beast. A voice from
beyond the grave. A voice out of eternal perdition. In short, your
obedient servant.

"Max was struggling with the death scene to his opus. The vampire
has just been impaled. As he expires, he delivers a dying sigh. Max
wanted to pack the whole movie into that sigh. It was supposed to
accompany some spectacular effect on the screen. I don't know what:
the vampire decaying into jelly, something of that sort. Anyway, Max
wasn't getting what he wanted from John Abbott. So he and I go into
a sound studio at Universal and we spend—can you imagine?—two
hours recording groans, gasps, growls." A great guffaw bubbled out
of him. "Anyone listening in would've thought there was an orgy
going on. Finally Max got what he was after. He wasn't much for
voice work in his movies. Like most directors from the silent era, he
was more comfortable working MOS as they used to say: *mit out
sound*. But this time, since I was there and willing, he decided to
make the most of the occasion. He actually had quite a good ear. He
knew exactly what he wanted and worked me until he had it. As I
said, it was all done *gratis*. But I didn't feel ill-used, because I came
away with something that was worth more than money to me just
then. An idea. You see, that's when Max first mentioned *Heart of
Darkness*."

"So it was his idea?"

"Not entirely. I'd been flirting with a radio adaptation off and on
for about a year. But as soon as Max began telling me the movie, I
saw the possibilities. Of course! A movie! And what a movie. With
the whole so-called civilized world sinking into barbarism around us,
what could be more timely than *Heart of Darkness*? Oh, he had some
wild ideas, did Max. He wanted to do the story in first person. The
whole movie seen through the eyes of Marlow the narrator. Quite a
daring idea back then."

I couldn't resist asking the question. "Did you know that Castle
once planned to make a first person movie out of *Oedipus at Colonus*?
The whole movie seen through a blind man's eyes."

Orson's curiosity was immediate. "You mean a totally blank
screen?"

"Not blank. Dark."

"Max never mentioned that one to me." Clearly impressed, he sat pondering the idea for several seconds, his taut breath signaling his concentration. Finally there was a considered nod of approval. "Well, if there was ever anybody in movies who could pull it off, it would've been Max. I would have loved to be his Oedipus." Then, belching up a laugh, "Of course when Joe Cotten heard we were planning something like that for *Heart of Darkness*—he would've been our Marlow—he went through the roof. The star, and he wouldn't get to show his pretty face on screen.

"No, I take that back. Max's idea was that the jungle should be the star. *Heart of Darkness* starring the jungle. The state of nature. Savage nature. A living, devilish presence—right at the core of the story. How did Max put it? 'It will be a mouth—there on the screen. It will eat them alive.' Now that I think of it, he actually did shoot a scene where a severed head opens up its mouth and devours the camera."

Orson paused to give a little mock shudder. " 'A man-eating movie!' That's what he called it. When he talked like that, Max got this fire in his eye. Very commanding. You didn't want to say no to him. John Houseman said he looked positively Hitlerian, which was probably unfair. I don't think Max had any politics one way or the other. But there *was* something of that Teutonic fervor in him. 'The audience must suffer the evil.' That's what he was after. Sounds almost sadistic, doesn't it?"

I glanced across at Clare, who was still seated at Orson's side. I nearly flinched to discover that her eyes were drilling their way into me, a fierce, questioning gaze. I knew what was in her mind. She was asking: *What do you make of that, Jonny? Is that what movies are all about?*

"I can assure you, all this was pretty strong medicine, even for me, the man from Mars. But I tell you, Max had me so spellbound with his vision of the story, I didn't think to ask basic questions. Others did. People close to the production wanted to know, Who's directing this movie, Orson Welles or Max Castle? Yours truly, I assured them. But at times I don't think I really knew. Can you imagine the naïveté! Well, I was the new boy in town. I went with my enthusiasm. Oh, it made no sense, I can see that now. But any time you hear someone accusing me of being an egomaniac, tell him how I once nearly gave away my first movie—to an even bigger egomaniac.

"For that matter, I have no idea what sort of division of labor Max had in mind. He never raised the question. I suppose he was hoping to arrange some sort of shared direction. It wouldn't have worked, of course. You can't have two captains piloting the same ship. We must've both known that. But we were so intoxicated with the project! Well, I finally gave Max the go-ahead to start filming with a small crew of his own, Zip Lipsky and some others. We had this mad notion that between the two of us we might have most of the film in the can before any of the studio heads knew what we were up to. And we might've gotten away with it, as we did later with *Citizen Kane*. We really had them buffaloed. We'd hung out this sign, you see: 'Geniuses At Work—Do Not Disturb.' I don't believe anybody in films ever enjoyed so much artistic freedom . . . at least for the first two months or so.

"Then, as our English friends might say, the excrement hit the fan. Rumors began to circulate. Max Castle was on the lot. And he was doing some very odd things with Olga Tell on a closed set in studio four. Olga was his sweetheart then. Fabulous beauty. She and I . . . well, that's another story. Next thing, I began to receive worried rush memos from the front office. Explanations were in order. Did I know what Castle was up to? Did I approve? I was quite fearless back then, or simply very green and headstrong. I marched right up to George Schaefer's desk, summoned up my best imitation of Westbrook Van Voorhees announcing 'The March of Time,' and asked 'Do I have *carte blanche* here or not?' To which George replied, 'Of course you do, as long as you clear things with me first.' It was like that in the studios.

"Well, about that time Max decided he had to get away for a while. And I decided that was a very good idea. Where did he want to go? To Yucatán, would you believe it! Said he needed some jungle footage, some *real* jungle footage. I don't think that was true. He just wanted to get off on his own, nobody breathing down his neck. So I told him why not? I had money to burn—or so I thought at the time. The fact was, I took a sort of Tom Sawyer delight in playing cat and mouse with the powers that be. I'll admit another thing. I frankly wanted to get everything I could out of Max before I was forced to drop him from the payroll, as I fully expected I would be.

"Now one thing you have to understand. My life in those days was insanely hectic. I was keeping my radio show going in New York, working on *Heart of Darkness* in Hollywood . . . I think I may have been America's first coast-to-coast commuter. Back and forth, eleven hours of air travel, sometimes twice a week. Talk about jet leg, imagine what prop lag was like. So even when Max and Zip got back, I didn't get around to seeing any of their footage until they had five or six rough cuts in the can. When I did, I was staggered.

"Oh, there was some excellent material. The jungle photography was overwhelming. Done with some kind of filter Max had invented. A classic study in moving chiaroscuro. There were darks in Zip's cinematography that were positively 3-D. You could walk right into them and get lost. I don't know how Max did it, but he made that jungle come alive. It stared at you like a beast of prey ready to pounce. And then there was that section with the severed head I mentioned. There was actually a whole chorus line of disembodied heads. If you know the story, you'll recall the heads are mounted on the fence, that infamous fence, which is meant to be the outer boundary of civilization. I never asked Max where he got all those heads. I was afraid to. They looked too real. The rumor I picked up"—Orson paused for the dramatic effect—"was that Max paid some of the Indians to go out and dig them up in the local graveyards. As you see, there might have been a little bit of Mr. Kurtz in our Herr Castle."

It was time for a new cigar. Orson took his time cutting and lighting it while Clare went for more coffee. While we waited, nobody spoke. Nobody wanted to stall the momentum.

"But then," Orson resumed in his own good time, "we got to the heart of *Heart of Darkness* as Max saw it. You see, he'd sold me on the idea that the grand climax of the story takes place when Mr. Kurtz is discovered in his jungle stronghold on the other side of that fence. The novel speaks of 'midnight dances . . . unspeakable rites.' For Max this was the depth of Kurtz's degeneration. Oh, he gave me dances, he gave me rites. I'm not sure they were unspeakable, but they were damn sure unshowable, certainly in any motion picture theater in the civilized world. Though, of course, that's what the story is about, isn't it? How civilized are we, any of us? Civilized—or just fastidious?

"The dances were bad enough. I have no idea how Max got these semi-insurgent Indians to perform them. But there wasn't the ghost of a chance the studio would let them be used. Nudity? Yes, there was nudity. But that was the least of it. The *most* of it was the footage Max had shot with Olga, the stuff that had set off all the rumors. Now I saw, there was good reason for the rumors. Why Olga agreed to do what Max had her do, I'll never understand. Let's be charitable and assume she did it for the sake of art. But *was* this art? No one at RKO would have agreed that it was.

"We came out of that screening quite simply stunned. Myself, Bob Wise, Mark Robson, John Houseman. The question was too obvious to ask, but I asked it. 'Max,' I said, 'how can we put material like that in a movie?' Max never batted an eye. 'We will *hide* it.' That's what he said. 'Hide it?' None of us had any idea what he was talking about. 'There are ways,' he said. 'We will make a movie *within* the movie.' And that's all he'd say. At that point, my colleagues were convinced we were dealing with a loony-bird. But not me. I had too much respect for Max. And now he really had the hook in me. I was determined to find out what he meant.

"Because, you see, I'd always been convinced that, when it came to Max Castle, the camera was quicker than the eye. You may know I have a fascination with magic, sleight-of-hand, now you see it, now you don't. That's what Max's movies were like. Sleight-of-vision, if you see what I mean. How did he do it?

"Well, I never found out. Max kept promising to let me in on his secrets. He used that as bait to keep me close to him. I felt the way an alchemist's apprentice might feel waiting for his master to reveal the secret of the philosopher's stone. Waiting, waiting—until *Heart of Darkness* fell through. As I knew it would. Fact is: when word came down to kill the production, I was relieved. I could see it coming weeks before it happened. If the front office hadn't done it, I would have. There wasn't a chance Max and I could share the movie. Two directors is one director too many. And besides, by then my interest had gravitated to another project. Something more American, more contemporary, and, everybody thought, more commercial. So . . . we decided to make *Citizen Kane*. Which turned out to be a modest success."

A long pause. Again, no one spoke. Orson had an uncanny talent for holding the floor even when he fell silent. He wasn't finished until he let you know he was finished. "Of course I kept Max around while we shot *Kane*. He was a treasure house of ideas. Lighting, camera angles, effects. I was the only person in years to give him the chance to contribute to a first-class production. I pilfered from him shamelessly. He didn't mind. I think he was grateful. The little crystal ball at the beginning of the movie—Max gave me that. He wanted to do more with it, with the light, the snow. 'We can put the whole movie in that little globe.' I remember him saying that. He could have kept us monkeying around with that broken glass for a month. As it stands, I guess it's the image most people remember from the film." He blew out a grumpy laugh. "That's all I need at this point, for the world to find out that even Rosebud isn't mine. And what I couldn't use in *Kane*, I squirreled away for later. The fun-house scene in *The Lady from Shanghai*, all the splintered mirrors, the contorted images— that was totally Max's. He wanted to slip something like it into *Kane*, but there was no room. So I saved it. Mirrors, windows, fog, haze, light on water . . . that's what movies were all about for Max.

"But what I really wanted to learn was how to 'hide' things. How to make a movie within a movie. Max kept teasing me, talking round and about, telling me precisely nothing. It was a great magic act, all diversion and misdirection. What was the word he used? One of those ten-ton Hegelian abstractions. *Der* or *das* . . . *Unenthüllte*. That's it. By God, I remember."

I flashed a glance at Clare, who had also picked up on the word. "Underhold," I blurted out. I explained to Orson, "That's how Zip Lipsky remembered it. The underhold."

"And it means . . . ?" Clare asked.

"The unrevealed, the hidden . . . ," Orson answered. "Something like that. Spooky stuff, what? But maybe a whole new cinematic world waiting to be discovered on the other side of vision. Well, Max promised and promised, but he never delivered. Maybe he would have later on. But, as it turned out, there was no later on.

"Last time I saw him was at the Hollywood premiere of *Citizen Kane*. That would've been May 1941. I know he was pleased with the movie, even though I cut out two or three of his things. That night he was very distracted. He looked a wreck. Sickly, nervous, old before his time. He'd been drinking heavily, using lots of hashish. I know that he and John Huston had their heads together, working on *The Maltese Falcon*. Boozing the picture into existence, I gather. You might talk with John about those last days. I've always been curious how much Max contributed to the movie.

"Next thing I heard was that he'd been torpedoed in the Mediter-ranean—on his way, I don't know where. Quite a shock. And that was the last of Max."

Orson settled back, snorting out a long, satisfied breath like a stallion that had just completed a long, hard race. I finally felt free to speak.

"Clare and I had the chance to see some of the *Heart of Darkness* footage. Zip Lipsky saved a few reels. It's pretty extreme, even by contemporary standards."

Orson gave a confirming rumble. "You can imagine how it came across thirty years ago. The dance Olga Tell does with that marvelously phallic sword. I wish I'd kept a copy of that—for purely artistic purposes, of course. Very powerful." Turning to Clare, he asked, "Don't you think so?"

Clare refused to show a trace of confirming enthusiasm. "Speak for yourself, my dear. Phallic ladies don't exactly turn me on."

I pressed ahead quickly to find out all I could. "I've only seen some outtakes. Did Castle ever get anything produced?"

"Not really," Orson answered. "He did manage to assemble a rough cut of what he wanted in the way of 'unspeakable rites,' a rather hasty mélange of things he and Zip had shot in Yucatán: some gory Indian rituals, a big drunken powwow—with Olga's sword dance, of course, as the master scene. It was a damned clever job of intercutting from limited footage. Couldn't have run for more than three or four minutes, but it was enough to scare the pants off us. The financial pants, that is. We knew that if the boys in the front office ever laid eyes on what Max was after . . . well, they never did. By that time, the picture was dead." He paused, thinking back across the years. "Odd thing was: Max was really very serious about that sequence. I mean, it wasn't just a bit of movie mumbo jumbo for him. He wanted it to be somehow . . . authentic. A real sacrificial rite."

It was getting on toward three in the morning, but Clare's little hotbox of an apartment was becoming no cooler. Orson's caftan had become a second sweating skin, clinging to him from the shoulders down. He had by now downed enough cognac to glaze his eyes and slur the edges of his eloquence. The evening was winding down rapidly, but I had one more item to ask about and I wasn't going to forfeit the opportunity. "Did Castle ever mention anything about orphans?"

"Orphans?" Orson's brows dipped into a thoughtful frown. "Now that you ask . . . Let's see, what do I remember? Some kind of religious order, wasn't it? Took in abandoned children. Yes, Orphans of the Storm. I remember because there was a Griffith movie of that title. Am I right?"

"It's a church," I answered. "It seems to run a network of orphanages. Max was raised in one of them. That's where he learned how to make movies. There were other children who grew up to work in film, not only in this country."

Orson brightened as he reclaimed the memory. "Two very spooky birds. Twins. What was their name?"

"The Reinkings."

"Yes, that's it. They showed up at Max's parties. Film editors they were. Absolutely mute, never said a word. Max introduced them as Orphans of the Storm. They were supposed to be first-class cutters. But Max told me to stay away from them, I don't know why."

"Did he ever tell you anything about the church?"

Orson wagged his head. "Not until the very last, at the premiere for *Kane*. He cornered me at the reception, said he'd decided to go to the orphans for money. Someplace in Europe. Switzerland?"

"That's right. Zurich."

"He was certain he could get the money to make *Heart of Darkness* from them. I didn't understand about that. I considered the movie dead. Anyway, I wasn't listening very closely that night, but it sounded like a wild goose chase to me. I pitied him, little realizing that one day I'd be chasing all sorts of wild geese myself. Like Matthew here, who will, I hope, turn out to be a very tame goose, one that lays at least a few small golden eggs."

Matthew gave a restrained but encouraging nod, and Orson's flagging attention turned to him. They exchanged some enigmatic words about one of Orson's several in-process productions, something called *The Other Side of the Wind*, reels of which seemed to be scattered through four cities in three countries. A half hour later, things were breaking up. Which meant that Matthew, Barbara, and I were preparing to leave. But not Orson. His caftan was a nightgown after all. And there was only one bed in the apartment.

As I rose from the table, Clare gave me a quick, dry kiss goodbye on the cheek, a disappointing token of minimal affection, no more than she bestowed on Matthew and Barbara. But before any of us could move into the hallway, Orson spoke up: a dramatic pronouncement.

"No, no. It isn't fair," he huffed, his voice now down to a growly whisper. We turned as he laboriously hauled himself to his feet. "We've drunk to everybody under the sun—except Max. And who deserves it more?" Clare smiled, sighed, and dutifully poured out a finger of cognac for each of us. "I know exactly the right toast for Max," Orson said. "Something from old radio days. One or two of you will remember." He summoned up a voice from long ago, an impressive imitation of his youthful self which I'd heard only on recordings. " '*Who knows what evil lurks in the hearts of men? The Shadow knows.*' And so does Max Castle, I'm willing to bet. To the shadow in all of us." Orson raised his glass. We drank. "The shadow . . ." he murmured as he eased back into his chair. "Strange man, strange man. But he was one of us."

We took it that we'd been excused from the august presence.

In the hallway, Clare held me back long enough for the Ferrers to depart on their own in the elevator. While we waited, I asked, "How long has he been in town?"

"About a week, not quite."

That led me to voice a small grievance. "I wish I could have met him sooner. There's a lot more I wanted to ask."

"I didn't want you to meet him sooner."

"Why?"

"I was afraid he might tell you what he did tonight—about Castle and *Citizen Kane*. I didn't want you using anything he might say against him at your retrospective. He's a very generous, very trusting man. But just now he's having a hatchet job done on him by a gang of small-minded pedants who're telling the world he didn't write the screenplay for *Citizen Kane*. The last thing he needs is to have somebody announce he didn't direct it either. You take my point?"

I said I did, and blushed to think how eager I would have been to include everything Orson had told me in one of my lectures at the archives. Clare had wisely spared me the temptation.

"Besides," she went on, "you can't take more than half of what he told you seriously. He loves a good story. If I were you, I wouldn't commit anything he said to print until I'd checked it out."

"Does that include the . . ." I groped for the word, but Clare knew what I was after.

"*Das Unenthüllte.* Well, I guess that's what little Zip meant. Even so, I wouldn't put it past Orson to embellish. Handle with care."

Then, as we waited for the pokey elevator to make its way back to her floor, I asked, "Should I congratulate you?" She gave me a puzzled look. I nodded back toward her apartment. "Something permanent?"

She let a few beats go by, then answered. "Hardly. And that's for the best. It's an adventure to have him here, but otherwise . . . well, you remember your little fling with Nylana the Jungle Girl. Things don't always translate off the silver screen as you might like, do they?"

I agreed she was right about that. She allowed another, weightier, pause to set in. Then: "I don't have to tell you this, but whatever the disenchantments, he's the first man I've liked having around the house since I left L.A."

Since L.A. That could include me among the favored few. I wondered if it did, but I didn't have the nerve to ask. Instead I said, "You keep pretty busy, I imagine. No time for romance."

"That's part of it. The least of it." She released a long, weary breath. "Something's going wrong with the men. Have you noticed?" No, I hadn't. Why should I? "You can pick it up in the movies. All this buddy-buddy crap. Shoot 'em up, gross 'em out, hump 'em and dump 'em. Macho little boys making movies for macho little boys. They're scaring off women. Maybe it's a plot against procreation. It'll get worse." I recognized what she was saying. It was a theme she'd been running through her reviews ever since *Butch Cassidy and the Sundance Kid* came along. "Anyway, it puts a woman in a certain frame of mind. You get sick of waking up to find Huckleberry Finn beside you."

The elevator clunked into position, the door rattled open. Clare held it with one hand, drew me toward her with the other, gave me the kiss I had resigned myself to not having.

But why had she waited until my next-to-last day in town to give it?

13 DEEPER INTO CASTLE

"A triumph! A total, absolute, wall-to-wall triumph!"

Arlene Fleischer knew how to lard on the compliments. It was one way of making up for the meager stipend I'd received for staging the First Max Castle Film Retrospective. Another was the customary closing-night reception in the museum's banquet room. I'd been to three of these while working at the archives, cheery little tributes to other visitors who had contributed to the museum's calendar. They were occasions to gush and bubble and wind down in a warm bath of mutual admiration. Many of the same people showed up each time—staff members and friends of the museum—to consume the same catered spread of economy champagne and microwaved canapés. Now, the evening before I was scheduled to leave for California, it was time for me to be hailed and bade farewell at the end of two glorious weeks of films, lectures, and nonstop movie talk.

There was a surprisingly large turnout. In the course of the evening I learned why. Word had gotten around that I was Clare's protégé; there was a rumor she might attend. In New York film circles, she was now a name that drew a crowd. "Will Clarissa Swann be here?" I was asked a dozen times that evening. "I've invited her," I answered, not adding that I had little hope she would come. She didn't. Small talk with a motley collection of prattling film nuts wasn't her thing. She would have been as miserable at the event as Spinoza at a cocktail party, and caustically outspoken about it. I was relieved not to see her.

About the time people began to register Clare's no-show and drift away, Arlene rushed to propose a timely toast. "And we have Jonathan Gates to thank for this splendid success," she concluded, giving me the well-practiced hug and a kiss I'd seen her bestow on others. There was a small shower of applause; I nodded gratefully, genuinely flattered to the point of blushing. It was, after all, my first experience as anybody's guest of honor. But even before the last of the canapés had vanished, I found Arlene huddling with others, swallowed up in a discussion of next month's program: a surrealist film series whose posters had already replaced Max Castle on the museum bulletin board.

Only a year earlier, it might have come as a traumatic letdown for me to realize that my star turn at the archives was merely a fleeting meteor on the busy New York scene. Now I greeted my approaching obsolescence with a secret sense of relief. By the time the retrospective had come and gone, I'd privately crossed a boundary of the mind that allowed me to see it for the minor academic exercise it was. Some old films discovered, selected for screening, and introduced with pedantic enthusiasm. That was the archives' business as usual. But I knew, as no one else did, that Max Castle was no ordinary filmmaker; not even an "ordinary genius" of a filmmaker. Where his retrospective ended, a greater and darker territory began.

It was as if I'd scaled a previously unclimbed peak and planted my flag for all below to see. The appreciative crowd sends up a cheer, a restrained one, since the achievement seems modest enough. But before the accolade dies away, I turn and discover a new range of heights that reduces the summit I stand on to a foothill. The ascent has only just begun, though no one watching from below can know that. From here forward, if I continued the climb, I would be leaving behind everything I'd relied on to bring me this far, including the well-oiled critical apparatus Clare had taught me to use so expertly. As Sharkey once said, Clare's standards were also her limits; I was at those limits. For the first time since my education began, I would have to go it alone.

The break was bound to come. Looking back, I could see it setting in as long ago as my first viewing of the *Judas*, when I came away knowing that I'd seen—or felt—more in the film than Clare did. Now my sojourn at MOMA's archives had given me the chance to see several more of Castle's long-lost silents, which had opened doors for me—especially the apprentice pieces from his UFA days. From that period Arlene Fleischer had recovered four movies in whole or in part, including a reasonably complete print of *The Dreaming Eyes*, his first work. These early efforts were made for quick and profitable release with minimal supervision from the studio. They went out to a still-naive audience for whom movies were little more than a novelty; there was every expectation that, after a brief run, they would promptly be scrapped like old newspapers. Castle and the *Grab-räuber* were, after all, the cinematic equivalent of pulp magazines, disposable items to be enjoyed and destroyed. For that reason, Castle could afford to experiment with less caution. Techniques he would later polish to perfection showed through more crudely in these works and so gave me clues to later films.

The museum had also acquired one short reel of miscellaneous footage cut by MGM from *The Martyr*. It was in miserable condition, jumpy, blurred and cruelly scarred by cinch marks. That might have been reason enough to leave it out of the retrospective. But I had other grounds for omitting it. For one thing, the material had an unsavory character. The reel had been donated to the museum by the grandson of one of the original MGM executives. He recalled being told that it was stashed away by studio moguls for their private use. Publicly, under pressure of the lawsuit Castle had once threatened to lodge against MGM to recover his disputed film, the studio claimed that all the edited material from *The Martyr* had been destroyed. Poor Castle! To the end of his days, he was left to believe that his one great American movie had been consigned to the flames. He might, however, have found it even more galling to learn what the studio had preserved and why.

The sequestered reel was made up entirely of outtakes from bathing and love scenes that captured more incidental nudity than would ever have survived into the finished film. There was, for example, one sequence of the undraped Louise Brooks getting in and out of a pool-sized bathtub over and over again, often caught from highly revealing angles—not the sort of material any actress would have wanted preserved. Had she known at the time she was being filmed? Did she ever know the footage had become a privileged executive pleasure at MGM?

There was only one aspect of this reel that lent it importance— though probably to no one but me. At several points in this waste footage, Castle himself appeared on camera. I don't believe anyone noticed that but me; certainly nobody at the archives mentioned it, perhaps because Castle was far from a familiar face. Or because nobody looked closely enough. The film was badly fogged; watching it was like staring into a snowstorm. But there he was, caught in candid little directorial episodes: handing Louise Brooks her robe, gesturing to the camera, signaling to someone out of sight. At one point, seeking to shield his nearly nude leading lady from the peeping lens, he walked directly forward, playfully thrusting his own disapproving face into the camera.

For me, these fleeting moments touched the man with a reality my research could have achieved in no other way. They animated Max Castle, giving him a living presence, a personality. Up to that time, I'd seen only a few photographs of him; they made him out to be severe and brooding. It was remarkable how the moving pictures of Castle I now possessed shaded that image without essentially softening it. There were some small hints of humor in the man: Castle caught grinning (large, horsey teeth), making a joke, pretending anger, bawling someone out, then giving a brief laugh. But there were many more moments that revealed somber intensity: Castle staring fixedly at some detail, then frowning, gesturing a "no, no, no" correction. Or squinting into the lights, making a sour face, clamping his teeth together, muttering a curse. There was one glimpse of him in a bedroom scene, barely visible to one side, lying flat on his stomach setting a tricky shot. And another that I studied again and again. In the foreground, a bare-breasted Louise Brooks was being powdered and preened; behind her just at the edge of a shadow sat Castle gazing intently off camera, at what I couldn't say: shoulders hunched, his gaze rock-steady, his hand fisted at his mouth, his posture utterly taut. Seventeen seconds of total concentration, then a gesture of command (one finger raised, a word spoken) and he eases back in his chair, suddenly looking deeply fatigued.

Castle, I now learned, was a small man, quite a bit shorter than I'd imagined. His build was slight, his manner highly strung, birdlike. His fingers seemed always to be twitching at his side, his dark locks needing to be brushed back from his high, frowning brow. And when he walked into the camera to block out Louise Brooks in the background, his hard, steady gaze looked for all the world as if it could melt its way through stone. In these fleeting appearances on film, Castle never lost his commanding authority. No question that he had been a domineering character; I would even have said charismatic, though perhaps I was reading too much into what I saw. He was, after all, no more than twenty-six or twenty-seven when this footage was shot.

By the time I'd sat through this reel of film some two dozen times, I realized the true reason I was keeping it to myself. Each time I viewed it, I was staging a sort of private cinematic audience with Castle, probing a little further into the distant and receding mystery of the man, hoping to wring one more intimate nuance out of these dim, oblique images. I was taking a secret, obsessive pleasure in the fact that just possibly there was no one left in the world who knew Castle as well as I did, that no one deserved to.

With the full sweep of the man's work spread before me from his first film to his last, I found myself steadily drawn deeper into Castle than any conventional critical analysis could take me. I had no choice but to follow where Zip Lipsky and his mysterious sallyrand had first pointed the way: into the *Unenthüllte*, the Unrevealed, as Orson had put it, which made itself known only to the dark side of the mind. I was now certain that whatever his studio assignment might be, Castle had found ways to make a second, secret, movie beneath the surface of the first.

I can still remember my excitement when I discovered the first of these hide-and-seek techniques. It appears in one of his earliest silent pictures, *Queen of Swords*, a homicidal thriller about fortune-telling gypsies. I named the effect the Chinese box; it was, in effect, a double subliminal image. In a key scene in the film, the hero, a deranged youth who has murdered his mother in a particularly ghastly way, bends forward to kiss his fiancée. As he does so, there is a brief image of his murdered mother's terror-stricken face superimposed upon the girl. The effect comes across just above the threshold of awareness, so that we catch it at the fringe of consciousness and quickly register the Freudian motif: girlfriend identified with mother. Seeing this for the first time, I could understand the hero's shock; but not the sense of almost unbearable disgust the shot produces. More than merely startling the viewers, the moment imprints a sickly loathing. Why? With the help of a sallyrand, I might have answered the question in short order. Lacking that magical spyglass, I made do as best I could, viewing Castle's film the way nobody has ever looked at a movie, as if it were a specimen under a microscope.

It was only after I ran the film through the museum's analyzer projector, stopping the action frame by frame, that I realized there was a second image that displaces the mother or, rather, skillfully blends with her in the eye. The effect wasn't easy to catch; it appears on just four frames positioned about a quarter-second apart, each underlit in a way that requires careful use of an enhancing filter to tease the image into visibility—and then just barely.

And what does one then see? It is a quick glimpse of a decomposing but still-living body coated with worms. The body even appears to writhe, struggling to claw at the maggots that are feeding on it. These flash frames make use of an astonishing perceptual device. Each of them in the brief sequence is several times double-exposed, the illusion of movement compressed and blurred on the film. Nevertheless, in just that split second, it *takes*. One's attention, picking up the first barely visible image of the mother, is just sufficiently distracted to miss the second completely; it eludes one's guard and gets through unnoticed, but with undiminished impact.

By all the known rules of perception, it ought not to be possible for such an image within an image to register on the eye or the mind at all; it simply comes and goes too quickly. The effect works, however, because Castle has tied all three images together—the fiancée, the mother, the corpse—by a powerful visual signature that appears in the flash frames: a crossed circle that has already appeared several times in the film, always in connection with the themes of lust and violence. Two bloodstained knives crossed on a round table, a prostitute's crossed legs on a circular carpet, a man spreadeagled against a circular window as he is gunned down . . . Castle has systematically schooled the eye in the course of the movie to receive his secret message. When it comes, it penetrates like an invisible dagger.

Even more exciting was my discovery of the device I called miniaturized coding, a far more potent perceptual trick, which Castle was to use again and again in his later movies. It appears in some of his earliest silents, but is introduced nowhere with more precision than in his vampire films. These were the movies that, as Leroy Pusey told me, worried executives at Universal had agonized over for weeks, searching for obscene material that could never be found. To all appearances, the movies were no more suggestive than other vampire pictures of the period. There were the usual sexual overtones, but nothing explicit: not much violence, no blood at all. Finally, the studio settled for arbitrarily cutting several minutes from each of the two films, sections that everyone, though without knowing why, agreed were the most objectionable parts of the movies. In this crudely abridged form they reached their audience, becoming the only Castle films to survive into the late forties.

Zip Lipsky's uncut version of both films preserved the offending sequences; each time I viewed them, I also came away convinced that the movies were intolerably lewd, though I was no more able than the Universal executives to pinpoint the objectionable material. Even when I searched for the sort of subperceptual maneuvers I now regarded as a standard feature of Castle's films, I could find nothing. I was baffled, until I found, among the Castle materials purchased by the museum from private collections, a brief sixteen-millimeter reel of unidentified film in which I was able to recognize some of the actors from *Feast of the Undead*. The reel had clearly been shot at the same time, using the same costumes. Here the cast appeared in a succession of violent, gory, and lurid snippets that had been spliced together in no recognizable order. This was the only film footage of this kind I'd ever come upon in Castle's work. Even by contemporary standards the material would be X-rated. Why, then, had it been made? I searched the movie closely, and it was only after I'd gone through it many times frame by frame that I spotted a clue.

It was in a scene that had been arbitrarily cut by the studio. Once it was gone, people felt less disturbed, though they had no idea why. To all appearances, this sequence is simply a dinner party; amid the feasting and drinking, the host, Count Lazarus, tempts his unwary guests to stay the night. He raises his wineglass in a toast, and for a split second the glass flashes in the candlelight. The result is a star flare that might survive in a contemporary film but that would have been regarded as a flaw in a 1939 production. Castle, however, kept it in the film—a daring move, though at the time probably dismissed as sloppy editing. I knew I'd seen this flare before—in the sixteen-millimeter reel. It appears in a scene where one of the women guests, seminude and vulnerably supine across a bed, is attacked by a bat. (Though the actress is in deep shadows, I was certain it was Olga Tell, once again providing the erotic juice in a Castle movie.) The bat crawls up her body, from the thighs to the breast, and then fastens itself to her throat. As it does so, its eyes catch fire with the same penetrating flash of light—a momentary shock.

I isolated the frames from the dinner-party scene that carried the flare and examined them in every way I could imagine. I found nothing. Finally I printed off a series of stills from the sequence and blew them up to four times their ordinary size. And there, in the Count's upraised glass, I discovered the naked woman and the bat. They appeared miniaturized and upside down, then, in later frames, turning this way and that, as if they might be bubbles floating in the bright wine. When the Count puts down the glass, their image remains there, unobtrusively present and dominating the table.

At once I set about examining the entire scene in this way, making blowups of details from still after still. Every glass and plate on the table carried these ingeniously hidden double exposures. The dinner table fairly seethed with submerged images of lust and death that anticipate the grisly fate of the guests, all of whom will finally become the Count's victims. Yet, even when I'd located this hidden dimension of the scene, the mystery of Castle's craft was only deepened. I had no way to explain how these images were printed on the film or how they could be taken into perception. In no way that made sense could one say they were "seen"; yet this clearly was the material that lent the movie's questionable scenes their undeniable air of obscenity.

I searched further through the dinner-party sequence, probing the deep shadows at the rear of the chamber. Here I discovered still another piece of hide-and-seek filmmaking at work; negative etching, as I called it. Castle had seeded the cavernous darkness of the room with a wealth of veiled images printed in their film-negative form. Here were the eyes that Zip told me Castle loved to collect, an invisible montage of maniacally goggling eyes filled with malice and perverse desire. There are twisting bodies, orgiastic couplings, acts of sadistic violence. Here was all the gore and sexuality that didn't appear at the surface of the film, more of it than the Hays Office would have ever licensed in its day. There was no question about it; Castle had produced the ultimate vampire movie. No one before or since has captured the sick eroticism, the vile carnality of the Undead more powerfully, or in more graphic detail.

Master of visual legerdemain that he was, Castle had even developed a bright-light version of negative etching. This is what accounted for the peculiarly odious atmospherics Clare and I had experienced upon our initial viewing of *The Ripper Strikes*. There, instead of deep shadows, he uses fog to hide his secret imagery, permeating the faintly glowing haze of the London streets with a ghost dance of imperceptible atrocities. The crimes the historical Ripper is said to have committed—brutal rape, mutilation, disembowelings—have never been more than hinted at in the movies. Castle showed them, but below the level of conscious perception. Apparently he filmed these horrors separately, working his actors after hours or off the set. The shooting was slapdash, far from the professional standard; but the aesthetic quality of this material didn't matter, only its shock value. When it is cleverly etched in behind the surface action, it allows the fog that saturates the movie to take on a life of its own, like some evil, disembodied mind hallucinating the Ripper's guilty secrets. Fog, cloud, smoke, dingy mirrors, shimmering water—Castle used them all to ambush his audience with forbidden messages.

Techniques like these, and others I would later find in Castle's films, were inventions of singular importance. Their discovery was exhilarating but at the same time perplexing. Because invariably, on the subconscious level, Castle's movies were psychopathic through and through. Everywhere, blatant sexuality was mixed with a morbidity that deliberately killed any pleasurable effect. Castle's eroticism was a nightmare straight out of the witch's kitchen: bodies tormented by their lust, made loathsome by desire. Once again, as in the case of the *Judas*, I was left with an almost palpable sense of something unclean clinging to my very flesh. Could Castle's techniques be used for any better purpose? What if I revealed his secrets only to see them exploited by other filmmakers for the same sensational and psychotic effects—just that and nothing more?

The question led me to an important decision. In my brochure for the retrospective, I would say nothing about Castle's cinematic innovations. They would remain personally classified information until I understood how they worked and what harm they might do. By then I might be able to surround what I had to say with safeguards, or at least fair warning. That was what Clare would have wanted; her concern for film ethics was still that deeply lodged in my conscience. I might not have been so cautious if I'd discovered Castle's perceptual devices in some more benign context—even if the objective were simply to shock or titillate as all the best or worst horror movies have always sought to do. Castle's films, I was convinced, were linked to something more darkly intended.

I would have been embarrassed to suggest that intention to anyone in connection with the films I was featuring in the retrospective. I wouldn't, at that point, have known how to give such work the weight it needed to be regarded as anything more than at best extraordinarily well-produced little thrillers. That was the pathos of Castle's career. Nobody was prepared to think of him as an artist. The studios handled his work accordingly. Where they found his films jarring, they chopped or slashed them freely. Often it was the endings that proved most troubling and therefore wound up the most butchered. The studios wanted a quick, conventional finish—a joke, a kiss, a platitude accompanied by a final flourish of upbeat music. As I'd learned from Zip, Castle was again and again forced to tack such final scenes on his movies—or had, in fact, anticipated the demand by shooting an alternative climax in advance. Where this happened, the sudden shift in style was so jarring, it became a signal for the sensitive viewer. "Not my work!" it cried out.

Thanks to the Lipsky collection, I'd been able to restore the original endings to almost all of Castle's films, and these were now at last reaching audiences. The effect was universally experienced as startling, perhaps the one repair that was doing the most to refurbish Castle's reputation. Those who could remember seeing Castle's movies in their studio-approved versions recalled pictures that ended with one tired cliché or another, perhaps something insipid enough to erase the entire film from memory.

For example, the finish to the studio version of *Shadows over Sing Sing* is utterly banal. The escaping convict shoots the sadistic prison guard, then is gunned down on the walls. He dies asking his mother to forgive him. There follows a brief scene at his funeral—lots of syrupy violins in the background—where the tear-stained mother assures the understanding warden that "he was a good boy, but he went wrong." The generic ending for prison pictures of the thirties.

The original film ends very differently, a terrifying visual essay on crime and punishment. In it, the young convict, wounded and broken, hides out in the prison basement. He huddles in a dark corner behind a maze of steampipes and debris, more imprisoned than he had been in his cell. Nothing seems to happen, yet the scene quickly takes on an excruciating power. Why? The answer lies in the shadows that lend the finish of the movie a blackness few *noir* films ever achieved. Playing through the shadows we find a run of Castle's negative etching: a rapid series of double exposures in which the convict himself takes on the texture of the stone that imprisons him; he becomes the prison from which he would escape. Nothing could make his plight more hopeless.

Then, as the oily black shadows close about him, a gigantic figure appears barely sketched in an undulating gray light upon the darkness: the villainous guard who has tormented the boy all through the film, now towering vastly above him. He takes on mountainous proportions; the convict shrinks to the size of a mere insect at his feet. The boy gazes up at the punishing form; just beyond it, there is a high window where the sunlight shines through. With his last gesture, he reaches toward the light, but the window draws farther away until it becomes a dying glimmer which is swallowed up in the eye of the guard, then vanishes. The screen goes black.

For the next several seconds, the blackness holds; the eye remains fixed upon it. Why? An unseen vortex fills the unlighted screen; it begins to swirl dimly through our awareness, sucking the mind down and down. On the surface it looks like nothing more than scratches on the film, flickers of light, but the effect is hypnotic. One feels the experience of descent physically in the deep gut, falling, falling. . . . The audience waits for the familiar words "The End" to appear like an act of mercy. Castle withholds them. The falling is without end, the abyss without a bottom. We sit staring at a seemingly blank, unlighted screen, not knowing why the blackness grips us so forcefully. The vortex effect at last diffuses into the dark of the theater, finally freeing the restless audience.

Scholars would one day refer to this closing sequence as the famous "black hole" at the end of *Shadows over Sing Sing*, assuming its power has something to do with the nature of the story. It lasts only sixteen seconds, but those few seconds proved too strenuous for a conventional B-movie, vintage 1936. So the end was crudely lopped off, surviving only thanks to the loyal Zip Lipsky.

Castle was a man with a bag full of tricks. Many of them remain mysteries to this day, unexplored by any filmmaker who came after him, the trade secrets of genius. But there was something I discovered in my close analysis of his work that was quite as remarkable as any of his unorthodox methods. That was the number of times he got what he wanted using no tricks at all. In several of his films I isolated scenes of extraordinary power, convinced that there must be some hidden gimmick at work. All it finally came down to was the lighting, the camera work, the cutting, basic elements of film craft that every director has available. Castle, working on a starvation budget with a hand-me-down screenplay, could do it all better—though only occasionally, by fits and starts, where the deadline might permit or where a few extra dollars might be wangled. When he reached the limit of his resources and could grind nothing more out of his stars or his script, he knew how to work around the weak spots with clever cuts or to frame them with surprising and distracting effects.

But much of this work suffered the same fate as the films that contained hidden material. Found intolerably disturbing by studio heads, they were chopped and scrapped. At the end of *House of Blood*, for example, the vampire is discovered in his coffin just as the sun is about to rise. His pursuers place the deadly wooden stake above his chest and prepare to strike. So far, it is the Hollywood cliché without modification, the predictable end of every Dracula film. But in Zip Lipsky's camera original, the Count's eyes spring open, his hand reaches up—not to defend against the stake but to caress it and position its point above his heart. Eagerly, he invites the blow that will end his detested existence. And when the stake is driven home, there is a profound and grateful sigh. No, it can't be called a "sigh"; it's the ghost given up in an ecstatic exhalation, a breath that might have been held for centuries finally achieving its freedom. Orson, sight unseen, had done himself proud. That single groan-moan-growl was one of his great performances.

The studio, however, found Castle's ending wholly unacceptable. A conventional struggle was substituted, the Count fighting off his pursuers, then, as he screams and writhes, quickly disintegrating in the light of day. There is a fakey dissolve and lots of the usual optical smoke. As the vampire's remains smolder in the background, the hero and heroine of the film walk into the camera, embrace, and kiss. The scene is obviously a hasty afterthought, rapidly improvised and badly acted.

In the wedding scene from *Kiss of the Vampire* there is an even more striking example of Castle working without benefit of the *Unenthüllte*, yet achieving results that directors would kill for. The hero has begun to suspect that his bride may be one of the Undead. Is she or isn't she? We never know for sure, but there are hints. The first comes in this sequence, which the studio decided to excise on the grounds that it was indecent. This is one of the cruelest cuts inflicted on Castle's work. In the release version, the newlyweds—Helen Chandler and David Bruce—kiss goodnight and turn off the light. Abrupt end of scene. But in Castle's version, the scene continues for another forty-nine seconds, a now famous forty-nine seconds studied in film schools everywhere. The quality of Zip's camerawork—jagged black-and-white contrasts that almost give the film fangs—might have been enough to guarantee the sequence a classic status. But this time Castle's sound track makes a contribution that even Orson would have envied. Nothing more than heavy breathing, first the woman, then the man. And then their breathing picks up pace until she is panting nearly orgasmically. The camera snakes around them, almost fondling them. We see the couple up close, their faces and bare shoulders streaked at a bizarre angle and in high contrast by light striking into the dark room through Venetian blinds. The camera lingers over a series of moist, lingering kisses. The woman's lips catch the light, gleaming. The striped lighting, which turns slowly in a crazy spiral, lends an eerie, peekaboo effect, masking and unmasking the actors as they move from dark to light to dark. Her hand, filling the screen, the fingers spread and flexed, passes slowly over his shoulder, through the hair of his chest in a clawlike caress. We think we see scratches where her nails touch. There is a sensuous curve of flesh: her body, his hand tracing the contour, but with the camera in too close for us to know what part of her anatomy it might be. She bends to press a kiss into the hollow of his throat, her open, questing mouth sinking into a stripe of pitch-black darkness. Her lips fill the screen moving forward; there is one faint gleam of teeth. His eyes register shock, then pass into shadow. Did she bite him just then? Just before fade-out, we hear a small, suppressed giggle of delight.

Simply by restoring cuts like these to Castle's films, I managed to give him a secure new identity as one of Hollywood's more gifted minor talents. There were some critics who were already prepared to go further; they believed comparisons with Hitchcock, Lang, or Carol Reed were in order—or would have been had Castle been given a fair chance to make the grade. Privately, I'd reached the conclusion that Castle was a greater talent than any of these, but I wasn't ready to stake that claim for him openly. Instead, I settled for touting him as a solid second-rater whose best efforts had been thwarted by the studio system. That in itself gave him a new status as one of the artistic martyrs of the movie industry. The way forward from there was clear. I needed more study of the *Unenthüllte* in Castle's work. I would then be in the position to press for a radical reevaluation of the man, one that would place him—so I hoped—among the great names of screen history.

Which would, incidentally, pay a neat dividend for me as his discoverer and chief student. As it was, by virtue of my stint at MOMA I'd become a recognized authority in my special little field, strategically positioned to begin collecting grants and fellowships. Accordingly, I applied for them in all directions. At the same time, my *Times* article and my museum brochure had drawn inquiries from interested publishers whose lists were beginning to carry more and more film studies each year, most of them sentimental exercises in nostalgia. With my research fattening to book length, I had every prospect of pinning down a reasonably lucrative contract with one or another of them. Academic promotion was already in the offing; very likely job offers would soon drift my way.

Sure enough, during the next year I received feelers from three major film departments; these in turn shook loose a nicely competitive offer from UCLA, where I decided to remain. But, by way of increasing my bargaining power, I kept that decision to myself for the time being while I accepted a generous Rockefeller Fellowship. I was working the academic marketplace for all it was worth.

There was just one tantalizing loose end left over from my stay at the museum. Among its acquisitions, the archives had turned up an untitled thirty-five-millimeter reel of film that was credited to Castle, but contained nothing Arlene Fleischer or anybody else could connect with the man. The first time I viewed it I also drew a blank. It seemed to be a crudely spliced miscellany of overexposed film with no sound track. Obvious waste. Why had it been saved at all?

It wasn't until I'd run the reel a second time and very nearly peered a hole through the screen that I spotted something familiar. The image was quite dim: a woman's head turning slowly this way and that, striking various angles as if this might be a makeup check. The camera came in closer, masking out most of her face, leaving only the eyes—but these I recognized. They were the two marvelously melancholy eyes of Sylvia Sidney. Zip Lipsky's words came back to me: "Who's got the best eyes next after Garbo?" I recalled what he'd told me about a session he and Castle had once arranged with the actress as part of one of Castle's abortive independent productions. They'd been after her eyes, just her eyes. And here they were, serving as part of some nearly imperceptible montage that involved a long line of marching people, a hooded figure at their head leading them across a vast, featureless plain. The film went blank for several seconds; when it returned, it seemed that the people (they now looked like children) were being gunned down by the masked figure in some terrible slaughter. All the while, Sylvia Sidney's disembodied eyes floated above the scene, watching in mute angelic sorrow.

I had no idea what to make of this grim scene; I couldn't connect it with any of Castle's films. I was ready to write it off as a dead end until I looked to see where this odd scrap of film came from. The museum's files listed the acquisition as a gift from a private collector. Her name was Olga Tell. And there was an address in Amsterdam.

I got off a letter at once, asking for whatever Olga might have to tell me about the material the museum had purchased, and about Max Castle in general. Several weeks later, after I'd returned to California, I received a warm reply written in a gorgeous flowing script: purple ink on scented beige stationery. Olga began with an apology. She knew that the reel of film she'd donated to the museum was largely worthless. She'd been holding it all these years for its sentimental value. Then, the previous summer, she'd met Clarissa Swann at a film festival in Copenhagen. To her surprise, Miss Swann had commented on her performance in Feast of the Undead—one of her later and lesser roles—and had gone on to quiz her about her relationship with Castle. In the course of the conversation, Olga had mentioned some reels of unfinished film Castle once gave her. It was Clare who suggested that she donate the material to the museum. So she had—but not all of it.

There was another reel she owned; she described it as "an unfinished film." This she'd kept because it included material of personal importance: her last movie work, performed as a favor for Max. She wouldn't let the reel out of her possession, but if I ever came visiting, she'd be pleased to let me view it. I should, however, bear in mind (she warned) that this was one of Max's "serious efforts, nothing at all like the things you may be familiar with."

I checked her story out with Clare, who reluctantly admitted that she'd also sat through the reel of waste footage I'd seen. "Not much of any value there," I remarked. "I can see why Olga was willing to give it away."

Clare agreed. "She's holding back."

"Holding *what* back?"

"*Heart of Darkness.* That's mainly what we talked about when we met. Or, rather, it's what I *tried* to talk about—without much luck. Some kind of block there. It'd be interesting to know what it is. I suspect more nastiness on Herr Castle's part. Anyway, she's got a piece of the movie. That much I found out. You should visit the lady, Jonny. She's quite a looker for her age. Hell, I wish I looked that good now. Turn on that boyish charm. Maybe she'll show you what she's got—cinematically speaking, that is."

Had I the time and money just then, I would have been aboard the next plane to the Netherlands. As it turned out, that visit had to wait for another year. And when at last I made the trip, it was for nothing as inviting as a chance to meet Olga Tell.

14 NEUROSEMIOLOGY

Even after I'd translated the title, I couldn't understand what it meant. But I knew intuitively that the drab little journal I held in my hand was a bombshell.

In French, it read *Les Effets Psychologiques de l'Appareil Ciné-matographique de Base dans les Films de Max Castle: Une Analyse Neurosémiologique.* The closest I could come in English was "The Psychological Effects of Basic Cinematic Apparatus in the Films of

Max Castle: A Neurosemiological Analysis." The article that followed ran to some forty densely packed pages in a French periodical called *Zoetrope*. It had arrived with a card that bore the message: "Looks as if you've been scooped, Jonny. Condolences, Clare."

The card sent a small twinge of anxiety along my backbone; after I dipped into the article, I began to feel sick with panic. I *had* been scooped. Not only had the author preempted all the Max Castle moviemaking secrets I knew about, but he'd found *more*. That much I could tell from a cursory survey of the article. What was more alarming: after two more painstaking readings, I found myself totally unable to make sense of the ornate philosophical framework that surrounded these discoveries. It's one thing to lose your scholarly priority; another to be left feeling like a total boob, especially when the boobishness reveals an intellectual soft spot you've been trying your best to conceal for years.

I should explain that, although I'm fluent in French (thanks to Clare, one of her many intellectual gifts), there are realms of French film theory that speak a language all their own and even seem to delight in practicing a self-imposed ethnic isolationism. Thus far in my career, I'd studiously respected their exclusivity. That was the easy way out. Semiology, Structuralism, Deconstructionism . . . one simply waved at these in passing, observing that they were "all very French." Even one's professors went along with that; it was the easy way out for them too. In my case, I felt licensed to dismiss these schools of thought because Clare dismissed them, insisting as a matter of principle that film criticism should stay in touch with the vocabulary of everyday life. In contrast, the currents of thought that had taken hold of French critics and film students swept them away into murky waters where aesthetics, Freudian psychology, and Marxist politics blended into choking ideological vapors.

The monograph I held in my hand was a prize example of the style. The author was one Victor Saint-Cyr, Professor of Cinematic Theory at L'Institut des Hautes Études Cinématographiques. It contained a great deal of highly technical material on the physiology of the eye, including a mathematical treatment of the visual fusion frequencies of the frog and the cat. There followed pages of abstruse calculations having to do with retinal refraction indices, light intensities, and aspect ratios. The paper abounded with graphs and tables. Whatever "Neurosemiology" was, it had nothing to do with the discussion of film as I'd learned it from Clare. This was more like a chilly laboratory report. That much I could in good conscience have ignored as simply an alien academic exercise. But in presenting his obscure thesis, Saint-Cyr had taken Max Castle's subliminal filmmaking methods (my life's work, mind you!) as his case in point, and then dealt with them in a gallingly offhanded way, as if they were of only secondary interest to him, a minor part of some far larger study. At one point he even called them "cheap tricks" used purely for diversionary purposes to mislead superficial analysts—which meant, of course, *me*. What, then, lay beyond them? Saint-Cyr didn't say. This monograph, he explained, was no more than a preliminary treatise on Castle; his definitive analysis would appear in the near future.

For days afterward I was numb with despair. Finally, I swallowed my pride and put in a call to Clare. What could she tell me about Saint-Cyr? Her reply jolted me. She knew the man personally! "We met years ago at the Cinémathèque when he was a smarty-ass little twerp—which I'm sure he remains." Since then their paths had crossed at a few film festivals, but they really weren't on speaking terms. She regarded him as a distinctly minor figure, not worth prolonged attention. Yes, she'd picked up rumors that he was studying Castle, but she never realized how seriously. Some friends had first mentioned the fact several years back—about the time she and I met.

I remembered! The French couple at Moishe's Deli. That was the first time I'd heard Castle's name. "But why didn't you ever tell me about Saint-Cyr?"

"Why should I?"

"Because he and I . . . we're in the same special field. You might have guessed I'd want to know what he's doing. It could be important."

"Oh, don't be so bloody scholarly. Nothing Victor's doing can be important. Just pretentious. Besides I never expected him to produce anything. He's not the type. He doesn't publish; he holds forth—hour after hour to adoring students who don't understand a word he's saying. *Nobody* understands what Victor's saying. *Victor* doesn't understand what Victor's saying. That's why it would have been a waste of time to bring him up. Believe me, there's more solid intellectual meat in one chapter of your dissertation than in everything Victor will ever write on Castle. Put together."

But of course *my* dissertation was at least seven-eighths Clare's work. When is a compliment not a compliment? "Have you read his monograph?"

"Skimmed it. Which is all the time it's worth. You know I don't read academic bullshit like that."

I envied Clare her easy contempt. I could hardly afford to be so cavalier. I was the one who had to show up at department meetings and sherry parties where colleagues—especially American versions of pushy young "smarty-ass twerps," more and more of whom were spelunking in these dark Gallic caverns lately—might soon corner me to ask, ". . . and what do you think of Saint-Cyr's work on Castle?"

"Victor," Clare went on, "is brilliant the way all French semiotic *poseurs* are brilliant. They're in the nature of *idiots-savants*, nutty little kids who can put funny big words together in more or less grammatical order. So who cares? They're not talking to anybody but themselves. Anyway, why don't you get in touch and find out what he knows? You won't understand him, but at least you can tell your colleagues—that's what you're worried about, isn't it?—that you've met Saint-Cyr and discussed his theories and blah-blah-blah. From there on, just fake it. Because, believe me, nobody you meet over here is going to know what Victor is talking about over there. Even in Paris they don't know. They just know how to fake it better than you." She sensed my reluctance to approach Saint-Cyr. "Come on, Jonny," she chided, "don't let the Frenchies shit you. *Courage, mon ami.*" Then, knowing it would prop up my sagging self-esteem, "Incidentally, he's lousy in bed. Tell him I said so."

Using Clare's name by way of introduction, I fired off a letter and a copy of my retrospective brochure to Saint-Cyr care of his school. No answer. Weeks later, months later, still no answer to a second and a third letter. He might have been traveling, he might have been sick, he might have been dead. But my threatened ego wasn't allowing for any such benign possibilities. The man's unresponsiveness irked me, leaving me torn between embarrassment and anger. I imagined him gloating over my work, wondering "Who the hell is *this* to be bothering me with such an infantile effort?" On the other hand, who the hell was he to be snubbing me?

Very well, my foundation grant included money for travel. I would travel. I was long overdue to take up Castle's obscure European trail. Now was my chance. First to Paris to beard the intimidating Saint-Cyr in his den. Then (more enjoyably, I hoped) to Amsterdam to accept Olga Tell's long-deferred invitation. Finally, if it could be arranged, a visit to Zurich to meet the mysterious Orphans of the Storm face to face. There might even be time to scout out a few collectors along the way who might be holding a Castle film or two.

My summer break arrived and I was off to France. Well warned by Clare, I approached my encounter with Saint-Cyr expecting a rough time. Hoping to make the trip something more than a trial by intellectual ordeal, I budgeted a week of purely frivolous Parisian sights, sounds, and flavors. If I'd allowed myself a year, not all the many beauties of the great city would have been enough to offset what followed. Even when one expects to be treated like dirt, it isn't easy to accept the experience. But I had only myself to blame; I went to a lot of trouble to be humiliated. It took me three pleading phone calls with Saint-Cyr to win the favor of a brief audience at a café where, I gathered, he regularly held court. In the course of each call, he tried to accelerate his French beyond my comprehension, but I stuck with him. Maybe that impressed him, or maybe my constant references to Clare made the difference. He finally relented and agreed to squeeze me into his busy schedule. Even so, he kept me waiting at the café for over an hour and arrived without apology.

Boning up for the meeting, I'd learned that Saint-Cyr was the center of an insurgent intellectual clique in the French film community, the latest hot item. Such currents of opinion come and go in France with a regular rhythm, each more audacious, and frequently more recondite, than the last. Even after as much reading as I could do on short notice, I had only the most miserably minimal idea of what Neurosemiology was: jargon surrounded by numbers was all I could make of it. Saint-Cyr brought an unusual background to his film studies; he'd been trained in medicine, mainly neurology. His scientized language showed that influence, along with the fascination for computer calculations. Three paragraphs into any piece of Neurosemiological literature and you were out of sight of anything that sounded remotely like a discussion of the movies. The stars were gone, the stories were gone. But there might be a lot of stuff on frogs. Or pigeons. Or monkeys. And how they saw things. Sometimes human beings were mentioned.

From the ponderous tone of his writings, I expected Saint-Cyr to be a much older, or at least older-looking man. Instead, he might have passed for being middle thirties. Otherwise he was every inch the intellectual cult figure: aloof, magisterial, undisguisedly contemptuous. Even his diminutive height gave him a certain Napoleonic air. Of course, there were the beard, the rumpled clothes, and the admiring entourage: four students, three boys and a remarkably good-looking girl.

Welcoming him to my table, I proffered a copy of my museum brochure, reminding him of my credentials. Yes, he'd received my book. As if he were brushing crumbs from the table, he passed my gift along to one of the students, sniffing dismissively. "The filmography could be useful," he commented. I supposed that consigned the rest of my work to oblivion, but I'd come determined to play deferential. I smiled and thanked him for the kick.

Then we talked about Clare, in whom he showed a genuine interest.

"She is writing now for the capitalist press?" he asked.

"For *The New York Times*."

"Doubtless for handsome pay. And the proletarian theater in California—she is finished with that?"

"Proletarian theater?"

"Where she showed films."

"You mean The Classic? No, it's still going. Her friend Don Sharkey is running it. It's not actually very proletarian."

"In America," he turned to explain to his students, "this is how it goes. Culture is a supermarket. Intellectuals are purchased like merchandise off the shelves—if they have the right flavor. Chocolate, vanilla, tutti-frutti. But it all tastes the same."

"Oh, I don't think that's true about Clare," I protested, though feebly.

Saint-Cyr returned a weary look that made clear how profitless he found it to discuss such matters with the likes of mere me. But he offered a major concession. "Clarissa is of course a facile mind, within the limits of her feminine viewpoint. Unfortunately for her, the day of the aesthete is at an end in the study of film. The critic, historian, scholar—these have nothing more to offer."

I had no interest in arguing general pontifical dictates, so I moved quickly to ask, "Have you had access to many of Castle's films? Your book mentions only two."

"Two films—that is all."

"Only two?"

"In most cases that is more than is necessary. My method does not require exhaustive viewing. In fact, the fewer films the better. Depth, you see, not extent. Reality is interiority. From a single shot, one can reconstruct the entire work of a director. However, Castle is an exception. In his case, I have been forced to make a more extensive survey. Two films."

"Neurosemiology is, I gather, a form of *auteur* theory," I was guessing, trying to keep the conversation rolling long enough to gauge its direction.

Saint-Cyr gave an incredulous smirk. "Not at all! In fact, the contrary. We proceed from the tenet that all human intervention in cinema is negligible. The medium is autonomous."

"I see." I didn't see, but I was eager to press on. That proved difficult to do, since Saint-Cyr was granting me only marginal attention, tossing off table scraps of answers while keeping up a constant stream of discourse with his three male students, who were paying me no attention at all. They were exchanging papers among themselves that looked like computer printouts; what they had to say about them meant nothing to me. At one point, Saint-Cyr displayed one of these esoteric documents for me to study, commenting, "The future of film theory," but not expecting me to understand. I smiled gratefully. He smiled at my smile, then turned back to his students. I noticed at that point that the girl was also being left out of the conversation. She looked reconciled to that. While the others chatted, she stared vacantly into her coffee, at the smoke from her cigarette, at the passing traffic in the street. Finally, her stare drifted in my direction and with it came a question.

"You are from the Los Angeles University?"

"UCLA, yes. I'm doing research on Max Castle." I pushed my brochure across to her.

"Yes," she said. "I have seen this."

"Only a brochure, really."

"Such studies—historical and aesthetic—they are still done in the United States?"

"Yes. And not here?"

"No, no. We have moved on. Victor has opened the frontier." The statement sounded like a liturgical response learned by rote.

She was pretty and pleasant, a slight, fair girl with sharp features and large, watery blue eyes. I wished I'd scheduled more time to lounge around the cafés with people—with girls—like her. No such luck. Saint-Cyr's heavy presence beside me was like a threatening cloud hanging over the city waiting to rain drowning torrents upon me—just me. There were, after all, things he knew that could erase the significance of all my work. Apparently he kept an ear out for his name at all times. He picked up quickly on the girl's remark, using it as the opportunity to issue an edict.

"Within ten years, film scholarship, film criticism will no longer exist," he announced with an air of bored but absolute authority. "They will wither away like the medieval trivium. Cinema will become an adjunct of neurophysiology. On the one hand, there will be studies of the apparatus; on the other, there will be studies of optical perception and brain anatomy. Between them, there will be nothing. Of all art forms, film is doomed to total objective comprehension. That is its destiny as the ultimate cultural artifact of bourgeois society: to be consumed by its own technology."

I followed none of this, but nodded gravely, assuming an "ah yes" expression of profound appreciation. "But why do you concentrate on Castle's work in particular?" I asked.

"Because Castle alone of all directors grasped the essential phenomenology of film. In the entire history of motion pictures, only he and Lefebvre have understood the technology so profoundly. And of course LePrince."

LePrince I recognized; Lefebvre I didn't. I continued to go along as if I understood. "I have a special interest in the subliminal devices you mention in your study. I discovered some of these myself, but I . . ."

Saint-Cyr gave an impatient wave of the hand, a gesture of annoyance that squelched me. His students smirked knowingly. "Tricks. These are really of no significance. Amusing, yes. Castle has his entertaining side. But all this is still in the realm of content. Quite meaningless."

I dared a challenging remark. "Well, I've found these effects to be quite powerful. Audiences seem . . ."

"These tricks are what you call the 'red herring.' Mere matters of aesthetic titillation that serve only to distract from analysis in depth."

I felt like a high school physics student who had just told Einstein the marvelous discovery he'd made about the pendulum. Still, Saint-Cyr had struck upon a point with which I had to agree. "Yes, I've sensed there's something more in Castle's films, something deeper going on underneath the . . . tricks."

"But of course. Neural dialectics." He slipped the phrase into the conversation like a piece of litmus paper.

"Oh yes," I said, having no idea what he meant. Saint-Cyr could tell I was faking. He smiled wickedly and reverted to being cagey.

I got no further with him that evening. He parried or ignored my questions. Would there be time to talk more, I asked. I had so many questions. His only answer was that he might possibly be at the café the following night. When he rose to leave, the girl decided to stay behind. Saint-Cyr lifted a disapproving eyebrow, then shrugged and left with the boys. The bill remained on the table for me to pay. Among them, Saint-Cyr and his students had consumed nine very expensive cognacs and five coffees in less than two hours.

Nursing my wounds, I sat wondering what I might do next to follow up on this abortive meeting. Nothing occurred to me. But here, on the other hand, was a lovely French girl who had decided to stick around. Why?

"Would you care to order another cognac?" I asked.

"Tell me about 'ollywood," she said.

Her name was Jeanette, and she was, as I learned, younger than I would have guessed from her manner—barely seventeen. A bright child already attending the Sorbonne, studying film and a favored pupil of Saint-Cyr's. She was a charming mix of sophistication and naïveté, wise beyond her years, but still girlish. From the French film crowd, she'd picked up a then-fashionable obsession with American movies of the thirties and forties, a subject she felt she could discuss appropriately only in fractured English, the cinematic vulgate. With the taste came a fantasy image of " 'ollywood," the city of glamour and romance that hadn't existed even in the glory days of the big studios.

At first, unthinkingly, I labored to disabuse her of this quaint illusion. "It's not quite like that anymore," I informed her. "It never really was." At this, she looked cross, almost like a little girl whose lollipop had been swiped. At once I realized this was a dumb move on my part. What the hell was I doing? If she preferred to believe, or pretend, that Tinsel Town was still alive and sparkling, why should I be the one to tell her differently? After all, 'ollywood accounted for her interest in me. So out came all the movie-star anecdotes I could remember or concoct. I was surprised how many there were stashed away in the corners of my memory. Thanks to my youthful friendship with Geoff Reuben the consummate movie-trivia magpie, I seemed to be extraordinarily well equipped for this game. Walt Disney . . . Bogart . . . Garbo . . . the Marx Brothers . . . the evening became movie trivia elevated to the level of sophisticated banter, in the sense that we both pretended to be above such things while we wallowed in them. This delighted Jeanette, even though her fascination, I soon saw, was a sort of crazy, wised-up act. By some strange, convoluted logic, she viewed this make-believe movie world, which it was permissible to enjoy, as a compendium of everything American and capitalistic that a French intellectual was required to despise. It was fraudulent, manipulative, crass, tasteless, trashy, cheap, vulgar, philistine—but all the same a brashly authentic culture of the people. She'd learned from Saint-Cyr a way to treat this maze of contradictions as philosophically coherent. The logic escaped me, but the evening was turning out to be a thoroughly rewarding little flirtation.

Toward midnight she asked if I would like to come back to her place and see her collection of old movie posters. Better and better. Two hours later we were in her bed, sharing a postcoital interlude of movie gossip about Hedy Lamarr and Errol Flynn and Clark Gable. Was Hedy really a lesbian, and was Errol really a Nazi, and did Clark really have false teeth? In the course of this cozy, drifting chat, she dropped the phrase "neural dialectics."

"And what exactly does that mean?" I asked at once, but as casually as possible.

"You know, the . . . how do you call it? The 'flicks.' "

"Flicks?"

"How the light goes. Off-on, off-on. You call it 'flicks,' yes? *Les flicks*. The movies."

I didn't follow this; her imprecise English wasn't helping. I moved the conversation back into French.

"You understand," she said, "about the Zoetrope?"

"You mean Victor's magazine."

"No, no. The Zoetrope." She twirled her fingers. "The little toy that makes pictures. Dickson, Reynaud, LePrince, Lefebvre . . ."

Yes, I recognized the names, or most of them. They were men associated with early experiments in motion pictures and film projection. Reynaud was in on the invention of the Zoetrope, Dickson had worked with Edison, LePrince was the mysterious film pioneer Sharkey had once told me about. So what?

"You understand," she continued, "it is all persistence of vision. Without this, there would be no movies, yes?"

She was of course right. Persistence of vision is the optical illusion that underlies motion pictures. Every film-studies textbook dutifully reviews this peculiar quirk of the human eye that allows moviemakers to mobilize photographs and so breathe life into still pictures. To say *les flicks* couldn't exist without it was true. But that was like saying there could be no music without sound waves, no painting without color pigments. What sense did it make to talk about art at such a primitive perceptual level? Why would anyone take a serious interest in primitive old contraptions like the Zoetrope, which was to modern movies what the oxcart was to a rocket ship? I was missing all the connections.

"Is this what Victor means by neural dialectics?" I asked.

"But of course. It is the light against the dark, the conflict of historic forces. This is the basis of Neurosemiology."

We waded a bit farther into the subject, but the waters grew murkier with each step. At a certain point along the way, I began to feel that Jeanette's grip on the ideas we were discussing was far from secure. She had that marvelous French ability to sound canonically certain of all she said, as if she were expounding pure Cartesian principles. But I could tell that she was repeating phrases she'd memorized from Saint-Cyr's lectures and writings. What was more, she had only the foggiest notion how Castle's work related to Saint-Cyr's theories. Here she left me suspended amid nagging questions, until at last we let cinematic metaphysics drop and spent the remainder of the night in other, less mentally taxing, amusements.

Nevertheless, the few fragmentary ideas I salvaged from my night with Jeanette had a certain teasing resonance. I'd heard these things, or something very like them, before. My mind reached back to the hours I'd spent with Sharkey in the projection booth at The Classic. In those wild, rambling exchanges, I'd also been talking to someone who wanted me to believe that the operation of the projector, the fusion frequency and neuromechanics of the eye might be more important than the content of the movies on the screen below. Of course that was kooky old Sharkey, hardly the one to make logical sense of such things. What he'd told me had all but faded from my mind.

But there was another recollection rising out of a fog of confusion: little Zip Lipsky struggling to explain a system of film craft he'd never fully understood, but whose power had touched him more deeply than anybody else associated with Max Castle. All that about the slide, and the split lighting, and . . . yes, the flicker. Something about the flicker. "The flicker's basic," he'd said. "It's like the heartbeat."

Congratulations, Zip! Maybe Saint-Cyr beat me to the punch, but you knew all about it long before either of us.

Thanks to Jeanette's persuasive good graces, over the next several days I made my way into closer intellectual quarters with Saint-Cyr. Periodically the great man staged a soirée for selected pupils and peers. Jeanette, who had a special, obviously sexual, influence over her mentor, prevailed upon him to schedule an evening on Castle and allow me to attend. Perhaps she'd managed to clear me in Saint-Cyr's eyes as a deserving recipient of his gospel; or perhaps Saint-Cyr simply wanted to display some intellectual pyrotechnics for the visiting yahoo. He had at one point let me know that, if he were properly invited for the right sum, he might be willing to squander a few months of his time casting his pearls at an American university . . . UCLA would do. He may have thought I had some pull in such matters. I let him think so, and perhaps for that reason was summoned to the presence.

Saint-Cyr's flat was up a cul-de-sac on the Left Bank quaintly named La Rue du Chat Qui Pêche. From the street, it looked like a crumbly stone tenement leaning precariously above a busy cobblestone court-yard. Inside, the building had been gutted and modernized in a sleek, high-tech style. Saint-Cyr's spacious apartment on the top story was crammed with cinematic equipment for private screenings—includ-ing a pair of old but serviceable thirty-five-millimeter projectors. That evening there were about a dozen of Saint-Cyr's students and col-leagues on hand; they were, I was given to understand, the command structure of the Neurosemiology movement. There wasn't a single person in the room who didn't have an intimidating knowledge of Max Castle's work. He'd become the centerpiece of their theory, in much the same way that Rossellini had once been the darling and chief exemplar of Neorealism.

Learning this was both encouraging and troubling to me. If word ever got around that Castle enjoyed so erudite a French following, his intellectual stock was bound to soar in value, if only by virtue of snob appeal. But it was a value that left me anxious. Among the Neurosemiologists, I felt like a color-blind student at an exhibition of Impressionist paintings; I had no idea what everybody else was seeing in the works on display.

With a careful eye for my reaction, Saint-Cyr announced that the evening's cinematic text would be an excerpt from (he paused for effect) *Simon the Magician.* One of Castle's long-lost films. I registered the appropriate amazement. At once, Saint-Cyr qualified his remark.

He felt reasonably certain the footage he had to show us was from *Simon;* there was no way to be absolutely sure. He possessed several untitled segments of sixteen-millimeter film amounting to some twenty minutes; the best guess he and his students could make was that the material had been culled from *Simon* and then recut many more times. Rather proudly, he explained, mainly for my benefit, that such butchery would render the film valueless to other critical methodologies; Neurosemiology could, however, work with mere scraps. As in the science of holography (a reference that meant nothing to me) every particle of the picture contains the whole.

Simon was a film that had spent nearly fifty years in oblivion. After the German censors drove it from the screen in the early twenties, there was no record that it had ever again been caressed by the light of a projector. There was good reason to believe it might have been among the movies the Nazis destroyed. Eagerly, I asked Saint-Cyr where he'd found the film. In a private collection right here in Paris, he answered. Might I have the collector's name? Perhaps I could track down more of Castle's work. Saint-Cyr was amused to tell me there was little hope of that. The scraps of film he had came from an otherwise worthless collection of erotica, which he had already searched. Did I know, he wondered, that several excerpts from Castle movies had been circulating for years through the pornographic film trade in Europe? The fragments had been crudely chopped from their original context years ago and then reduced to sixteen-millimeter or eight-millimeter stock. The collectors usually had no idea where these snippets came from or what their historical value might be. The reprinting was generally of poor quality—often done by amateurs for home consumption.

Simon had been especially popular among pornographers of the twenties and thirties who freely cut and retitled the more libidinous portions to suit their specialized tastes. In this form, remnants from Castle movies had been circulating for years as peephole scenes usually set in the ancient world. Saint-Cyr had recovered selections under such titles as "The Queen of Sheba's Private Bath," "Roman Nights," "The Pharaoh's Orgy." The excerpt for this evening—his most recent acquisition—had been known to its collector as "A Night with Helen of Troy."

Saint-Cyr switched on the projector. The film, a scratched and grainy square of watery-dull light, began suddenly with a woman being undressed by two dark-skinned attendants. A title frame cut in; it read (in German) "Simon's Consort, the Beautiful Helen of Troy, Entertains the Guests of the Magus." This, Saint-Cyr explained, was what allowed him to identify the excerpt as one of Castle's films. The original movie had been based on the life of the legendary charlatan and heretic Simon Magus, who was accompanied in his travels by a prostitute whom he advertised as the reincarnation of Helen of Troy. All of the extant fragments dealt with Helen: Helen bathing, Helen dancing, Helen lolling about on animal-skin rugs. Here we had Helen disrobing, removing a number of gauzy garments and lounging semi-naked on a luxurious couch. She is a lush, Rubenesque woman with meaty flanks and great, mushy breasts that roll heavily from side to side like unshelled eggs on a plate. But she moves with a fluid grace, her body gleaming with sweat or oil. The print was so blurred I couldn't identify the actress; Saint-Cyr was convinced it was the silent-screen beauty Hanna Ralph.

All along the line, there were jagged splices that apparently cut away any material not related to Helen. Suddenly, after one of these cuts, she appears on a plush rug cuddling a python-sized snake. She strokes it fondly, kisses it, permits it to slither over her body, between her breasts, down her thighs. (How did Castle persuade the actress to do it?) Surrounding her are a number of leering, pop-eyed men. They watch hungrily. Helen teases them, offering her body, but then thrusting the snake at them to drive them off. Finally, she casts the loathsome beast aside and the men converge upon her. Close up, we see several clutching hands paw at her. Helen's form disappears beneath a crowd of bodies as the camera sways drunkenly.

The excerpt, which ran some seven minutes, broke off abruptly, followed by several seconds of leader. Then, just as abruptly, a second, better, print of the same material began. Saint-Cyr explained that this was part of the same reel he had purchased; this time, we should watch for the ending. This turned out to be a remarkable effect that had been edited from the first film we saw. Here at the conclusion Helen, naked and writhing, is caught up in a halo of shimmering light. Her image rolls in a full circle, around and around, and finally becomes a dizzy vortex melting into darkness. The camera draws away at the climactic moment, and we realize we are seeing Helen reflected in the watery curve of an eye. The camera continues to track back and the eye takes its place in a face that is twisted grotesquely with lust. It is one of Helen's spectators. The face is gross and stupid; the mouth gapes; a drop of saliva sparkles on the lips and falls. Suddenly the superimposed form of Helen floats forward and curls about the face, which recedes until it is consumed into a shadowy cavern formed by her pubic thatch. This, in turn, begins to spin slowly, then more rapidly, filling the screen with a swirling darkness. I recognized this at once as the vertigo effect Castle had used at the close of *Shadows over Sing Sing*, less subtly handled here, but with quite as much impact.

Brief as it was, the excerpt explained why *Simon the Magician* had been banned as obscene. Even by the more relaxed censorship standards of the early twenties, the portions we had watched were blatantly lubricious. And, as Saint-Cyr observed, with the final sequence restored, the film's sexuality was touched with a radically unpleasant flavor. "Distasteful" was the word Saint-Cyr used. Another sprang to my mind: unclean.

The room fell hushed as a church as Saint-Cyr began his analysis of the film. His remarks, delivered with wit and energy, filled the next four hours of the evening, an intellectual tour de force that his followers seemed to expect. He began with a number of throwaway observations about the traces one could find, even in these disjointed excerpts, of sophisticated technique: the fluid mobility of the camera, the smooth montage effects, the precocious use of latensification. "At the most superficial level, one can see in Castle's work a polish far beyond anything achieved at this early period by other directors, not excluding Griffith, Murnau, Lang. And bear in mind, we are dealing with the films of a talent still in its early twenties." But all this was made to seem hardly worth mentioning.

Saint-Cyr showed no greater interest in the film's subliminal effects. But over these he lingered for my benefit. His manner was mockingly apologetic, as if he were wasting his audience's time. "These little tricks seem to be of special interest to our American visitor," he explained.

Offhandedly, Saint-Cyr tracked back through the final few minutes of the last sequence we'd seen: Helen's body turning and turning. He slowed the film and brightened the image, then slipped a nozzlelike attachment over the projector lens. This, he explained, was an invention of his own: a low-intensity enhancement filter. My heart gave a quick skip of excitement. My God! It was a *sallyrand*, or the equivalent thereof. Rather than holding it to the eye, Saint-Cyr connected it to the projector; but it was performing the same function as Zip Lipsky's viewer. With the filter in place, Helen's form immediately dematerialized, lost in an undulating tracery of fine lines. A second superimposed pattern took shape. I could make nothing of it, but I distinctly cringed, as I might at an unsavory odor.

"Look closely now," Saint-Cyr ordered. "Tilt your head like so, to the left." I did as instructed. Vaguely, the lines and shadows assumed a shape. I could make out a face turned nearly upside down. It appeared to be masklike, unreal, yet strangely awful. The face of an exotic totem, African perhaps, or Mayan. A stern and scowling deity. The face moved with a solemn animation, filling the screen until it was positioned so that Helen's ample breasts became its eyes and the V of her groin its mouth. As she wheeled about, the face turned with her, coming right side up. The rolling of Helen's nipples in its deep eye sockets now gave it a goggling, maniacal look that was even more menacing. "Watch closely," Saint-Cyr told us again. There was a blur of motion imploding from the edges of the screen, converging upon Helen's belly. Saint-Cyr stopped the film and adjusted the projector to enlarge the image. Now I could see a ghostly array of tiny drawings, figures of men tumbling directly toward the pubic triangle at the center of the screen. Saint-Cyr clicked the frames forward one by one; mechanically the mouth of the stern face opened, closed, opened, closed behind Helen's shadowy sex organ. The tiny figures jigged and cavorted into the vaginal maw. Teeth showed. A streak of blood leaked from the lips and began to spiral across the screen. In the final few seconds, the sheen of Helen's flesh became a watery film, the superimposed mouth and vagina becoming the core of a dark whirlpool that sucked the failing light into itself. In the enveloping darkness, I could, with the aid of Saint-Cyr's filter, discern a multitude of forms— human bodies—raining down into the deepening swirl, helplessly flailing, falling, consumed. When at last the sequence faded from sight altogether, I found myself in the grip of a depression, no, a despair that very nearly left me devoid of words. Deep inside of me, something continued to fall, taking with it all brightness, all vitality. Did the others in the room feel the same? I sensed a somberness all about me that began to grow claustrophobic. I tried to shake myself free of the malaise, asking, "But how was it done?"

"Gray light," Saint-Cyr answered, as if I should understand the term. Then, condescendingly, he explained. "The face is of course an animation—a crude one. Méliès could have done as well. It is projected on a scrim at a low intensity—gray light, as we call it, light that is just below the threshold of conscious perception. The camera photographs through the scrim, superimposing the face upon the scene."

"But why doesn't it show more clearly throughout?"

"Ah, that is the trick. The effect must be carefully balanced with the studio lighting—just dim enough to wash out in the glare. We have not yet worked out these ratios. Incidentally, it is a use of the medium that is restricted to orthochromatic film. One needs the sharp contrast of blacks and whites to distract from the gray."

It was difficult for me to restrain my amazement. "This filter of yours," I hastened to tell him, "I've seen one before."

"Oh? Where?"

"Castle's old cameraman Zip Lipsky had one. He treated it as a great secret. He called it a stripper, because it strips the film down to its underlying imagery. He said Castle invented it."

"I am not surprised," Saint-Cyr replied. "He must have used something of the kind to help with his effects."

"And what you call gray light," I added, "I'm sure it's what Castle referred to as split lighting."

"So you know about these things." Saint-Cyr seemed a bit deflated.

"No, not really. I had no idea how the effects were produced. I didn't even know what kind of lenses were used in the stripper. These are remarkable discoveries. They could revolutionize filmmaking."

Saint-Cyr shrugged off my admiration. "Admittedly they make for a diverting study. But they are of no ideological consequence. You see, they are used here for nothing more than psychological effect. As you have learned from your own preliminary analysis, Castle employs a repertoire of such images to link sex and violence, sex and death. All perfectly banal. This does not get us beyond the level of Wagnerian opera. Here, for example, he plays with the motif of the cannibal vagina." Saint-Cyr smirked contemptuously. "Shocking? Hardly. The bourgeois psyche has long since adjusted to this once-sensational Freudian symbology. It becomes merely a collection of pranks. The significance of film is that it passes beyond the psychological. It penetrates to the neurological: the material foundations of consciousness. Here, Professor Gates, is the *true* substance of Max Castle."

He switched on the projector again, but this time he blurred the focus so that the image that reached the screen was a smudge of moving shadows. For several moments I stared stupidly at the illegible square of light. What was I supposed to see? Saint-Cyr studied my perplexity with malicious delight. Was he putting me on? I felt certain he wasn't. Mocking as his tone might be, there was an intensity about all he said that was clearly sincere. Moreover, the faces of everyone in the room revealed no trace of ridicule, but rather high seriousness.

"But . . . this is *nothing*," I finally said, opening myself deliberately to whatever he would now say to score off my ignorance.

"*Nothing?*" Saint-Cyr retorted. "It is *light*, Professor. Moving light. Is this not the essence of cinema? Now, if we slow the projection, so . . ." and he did, "what do we have?"

As anyone would expect, the blurred square on the wall began to lose continuity and flicker as the film dipped below its fusion frequency. Finally, when he had slowed the projector to its maximum, the shutter was visibly chopping through the beam of light in steady, staccato intervals, like a flashlight being switched on and off. *It flickered.*

"On-off, on-off," Saint-Cyr said, observing the obvious. "*Les flicks.* The objective message of the medium. Always there, even when the eye does not perceive its presence."

He paused to see if I'd taken the idea in. "But what kind of message is that?" I asked. "It's just flickering light."

"Yes. A pulsation. On-off. Light-dark. On against off. Light against dark. *Dialectical structure*, Professor Gates. A message simple enough to penetrate even the lizard brain we carry from the primordial past. Or rather which carries us. The material basis of the dialectic is the cerebral nervous system. With this, the mechanism of projection interfaces objectively. *Here* the machine, *there* the retinal cortex. Technology, anatomy. The rest is nonessential. We run the film forward, backward. Nonessential." He paused again, this time leaning close to study my face. "The light, it fatigues you, does it not?"

In fact, the constant flashing was getting on my nerves. "Yes," I said. "It's really very annoying."

"That is because you are struggling *not* to be hypnotized. The pulse is too obvious; you guard against it. But now . . ." He speeded the film up, refocused, brought the movie back from its blurred condition. The figures in another of Castle's film episodes reappeared, this time a girl shimmying her way through a slow striptease. This piece of film was in even worse condition, blurred almost to the point of being undecipherable, but I was certain I was watching Louise Brooks do the dance that had helped get the film banned. I could see why. Saint-Cyr, noting my concentration, continued, "Now you do not struggle. You watch *the movie*. This is very easy to do, very pleasant. What do we have? A sexy lady doing a sexy dance. Your guard comes down, you take the bait. But the pulse is *still* there. It enters the consciousness, shall we say through a secret door?"

The reel of film ran out, its loose end whipping noisily until Saint-Cyr switched off the projector. Another moment and the lights came on. I turned to ask him a question, many questions . . . they crowded into my mind.

Clearly delighted with the state of mystification in which he had dumped me, Saint-Cyr waved me to silence. "We will talk more," he said and withdrew into the company of his admiring students. He didn't get back to me for another two hours; even then I still couldn't find a question I dared to ask. Whatever came to mind seemed too naively stupid. But Saint-Cyr was in a mood to hold forth and needed no questions from me. After a long evening of wine and adulation from his camp followers, he seemed willing to unbend with the imbecile American in his midst. Toward 3:00 A.M., two of his prize students were still on hand; Jeanette drew herself up receptively on the floor beside her teacher as he slumped in his leather easy chair.

"Study hypnosis, Professor," he advised me. "This is the next great problem in film, as it is in politics."

"You believe movies are a form of hypnosis?"

"The highest form of hypnosis. But this is obvious, a neurophysiological fact. No one disputes it. Let us ask, however, what is the *sociography* of this hypnosis? This has yet to be specified." He gestured toward one of his students in whose company I'd earlier seen him examining a yards-long computer printout. "Julien has made this his special field." As if he were giving his regal permission to speak, he nodded in Julien's direction. He was a bushy-haired, tautly nerved young man who smoked incessantly while he spoke and never once raised his eyes to look at me.

"For each social class," Julien began, rattling off what he had to say in French at a pace that frequently outdistanced me, "there is an optimum fixation ratio. This is a function of the attention span, which is the product of social conditioning. . . ." Julien generously proceeded to unroll his research over the next hour. It was a remarkable theory. He seemed to be saying that in capitalist society there is an inherent tendency for the attention span of each successive generation

to diminish as the experience of alienation increases, with the proletarian nervous system leading the way toward mental disintegration.
Already this psychic mutilation was having its visible cultural effect.
New film and musical forms were pulverizing all content into tinier,
more purely sensational, fragments. Nothing with greater complexity
than advertising copy could be understood even by privileged bourgeois youth. In movies intended for adolescent audiences, directors
would soon be limiting each shot to a five-second duration at longest
and then cutting back from there. The lyrics of songs were fast becoming inarticulate phrases repeated over and over, none more than
three or four seconds long.

At the current rate of accelerating perceptual shrinkage, Julien
predicted that the adolescent generation of the year 2000 would have
no attention span whatever, hence no capacity to absorb any message
longer than a single cinematic flash frame in duration. Even one-line
gags and slapstick comedy would be incomprehensible to them. If,
for example, they were to be shown a classic pie-throwing scene from
the early silent films, they wouldn't be able to recall, when the pie
hit the face, where it had come from.

At that point, language, including the semiological structure of film,
would have lost the last traces of grammatical coherence, which was
based upon the ability to maintain minimal attentiveness from the
beginning to the end of a simple declarative sentence—approximately
three and a half seconds. When this fateful devolutionary moment
arrived, no command issued even on the highest authority could be
supplemented by ideological rationalization. Hypnosis would no
longer be possible; propaganda of the simplest kind would cease to
have any effect. The mystification of the masses would come to an
end. There would be fewer and fewer who could take orders any
longer; the revolution would be at hand, powered by a worldwide
mass of teenage cretins whose means of communication would be
limited to simian grunts, snorts, crude gestures, with only occasionally
recognizable words. This final capitalist generation would be making
its way in the world largely by means of smell, feel, and raw mam-
malian instinct. At that point, the revolutionary vanguard (which
would apparently consist of movie critics and film students who had
preserved enough brain power to understand the historical dialectic)
would take charge of these humanoid primates and salvage whatever
higher-order neurological material might still be functioning in the
world. It would be touch and go until a new socialist state was built

that could once again stretch the attention span and undertake what the Neurosemiologists called "the positive hypnotic reconstruction of consciousness."

Saint-Cyr, slouching deep in his chair and watching me through wine-blurred eyes, was closely gauging my responses, which must have come across to him as a mixture of authentic fascination and barely contained incredulity. "This, you see, Professor Gates, is where Marx went wrong," he explained when Julien had finished. "He was, after all, an economist, hence a man of abstractions. His great concept—the declining rate of profit—poof! it is a figment, a delusionary artifact. All this must now be reinterpreted. In Neurosemiological terms, it is the *declining span of attention* which is crucial. Materialism must become physicalism. The dialectic will have to be grounded in the nervous apparatus."

"Yes, I see," I answered, though I largely didn't. Above all, I didn't see how any of this connected with Castle. So I asked.

"But obviously, Professor Gates," Saint-Cyr answered with a bored, now more than slightly drunken, air, "he more than all others elevates the dialectical fundament of film to the level of conscious manipulation."

"You mean the flicker?"

"But of course. The opposition of light and darkness. The logic of history. The struggle of social forces. In the technology of film, class conflict becomes objective in the dominant expressive form of the industrial period. Castle knew this. He used this. He surrendered to it. Historically, this was the first step in liberating film from the imprisonment of art."

There was an obvious point that needed to be addressed. "But is there any evidence that Castle was a Marxist?" I asked.

Saint-Cyr threw the question out of court. "This is of no consequence. Technology precedes ideology. We do not speak here of subjective preferences. In our view, Castle was an apolitical aesthetic technician, that is all. The essential point is that he grasped the autonomy of the medium. This we can extract from his work. The rest . . . it is so much historical detritus."

"Do you know anything about Castle's subjective preferences?" I asked. "If he wasn't a Marxist, what was he?"

With a dismissive sneer, Saint-Cyr overrode the query. "Like most entertainers, he was prepared to be a bourgeois lackey. He produced for the market. The man himself is without revolutionary significance."

"But you do believe Castle's techniques can be used for Marxist purposes—if a filmmaker wished to do that?"

"For Marxist purposes and *only* for Marxist purposes. This is what the technology dictates. The more essentially filmic a work becomes, the more it becomes the servant of the historical dialectic. Personally, Castle might not have approved; but this is again of no consequence. We deal here with social forces that transcend personal intentions. Castle was prepared to accept the destiny of film for what it is. That is all that matters; it is our only interest in him."

"Do you have any idea how Castle learned what he knew about film?" I asked.

"This has been a matter of passing curiosity with us. There may be a connection between Castle and Etienne Lefebvre. Lefebvre participated in setting up the German UFA. Possibly there was some contact at that point."

"You don't know anything about his connection with a group of orphans?"

Saint-Cyr stared back blankly. "Orphans? No. Biography has no role to play in Neurosemiology. In fact, the less we know of the technician's personal history, the better."

"You mentioned Lefebvre just now. And I believe you have an interest in LePrince. Have you studied their work?"

Saint-Cyr nodded toward his other student, whom he introduced as Alain. Alain's special field was the prehistory of cinema technology. "There is of course no work to study in the narrow aesthetic sense," he informed me. "Lefebvre and LePrince were not filmmakers; they were inventors—like your Edison. Of interest here are the mechanisms they devised. The 'ardware." He put the word in English.

Alain, I discovered, was in the process of reconstructing the early cameras, projectors, and film stock of these movie pioneers. Like most of Saint-Cyr's students, he too seemed to have no interest in movies, but only in machines and optics and nervous reflexes. Alain went on to explain that some of the early technicians, like LePrince, had if only by accident unearthed the dialectical principles of motion pictures. "The machines were so primitive, the film content so negligible," he observed, "that the inventors could not help but recognize the fundamental properties of the technology."

Saint-Cyr broke in to clarify the point. "This is often the case in the growth of technology. Its true nature is more transparent in the initial stages, before a certain sophistication sets in and begins to rationalize the means of production. To take an obvious case: the exploitative nature of steam technology was more apparent in the early factory system than in later historical stages when, for example, the lunchroom was so generously provided alongside the assembly line. The more primitive the mechanism, the more naked is its social function."

Alain resumed, observing that LePrince especially seemed to be aware of the communicative power of the flicker. For pioneers like him, it made no difference *what* they filmed and projected. Any trifling little vignette would do. A man doing somersaults, a horse performing tricks, the waves of the sea washing in. Such early demonstration pieces were, in Alain's eyes, of far greater value than films like those of Griffith that distracted by telling stories. Fred Ott's famous sneeze, as captured on film by Edison, was Alain's ideal "movie," the true culmination of the art. Beyond something like a sneeze, a pure, meaningless, totally uneventful event, the content of the work begins to obscure the basic action of the technology. If I understood Alain correctly, he seemed to be saying that movies were more truly *movies* before there were any movies!

"But, you see," Saint-Cyr went on, "Castle understood that there must be content in order to arrest the attention of the masses. In Castle's case, however—unlike such ignoramuses as Lumière or Griffith—content is expertly layered. The 'flicker,' as you call it, comes through with singular impact."

"Layered" was one of Saint-Cyr's technical terms. I'd come across it several times in his analysis of Castle. I gathered it meant the way the movie as a story connected with the movie as a ribbon of projected film running through the shutter. The story was the upper "layer"; the flicker was the lower "layer." The trick was to join them into a kind of optical sandwich that let the stimulus of the projector penetrate the mind. Saint-Cyr was convinced that Castle had found some optimum means of doing this. Layering seemed to be as close as Saint-Cyr was willing to come to granting that movies had something to do with art. Castle was good at layering; Saint-Cyr admired him for that and was determined to find out how the trick had been turned. When he got into this phase of his theory, the technicalities soon proved too bewildering for me to follow. Yet I felt certain that Saint-Cyr's layering was what Zip Lipsky had once called "compositing," and had tried in vain to explain.

When Saint-Cyr finally gave me the chance to speak, I brought up the one other item that seemed most closely connected with his approach to Castle. I asked, "Have you ever heard of someone—a priest, I believe—named Rosenzweig?"

If the roof had caved in on us, it couldn't have produced a greater shock. A flash of surprise lit up deep inside Saint-Cyr's eyes, followed at once by an ice-cold stare. "You know this person?" he asked.

"Yes. Well, no. I've heard of him."

"In the United States, you have heard of Rosenzweig?" I could sense the rising temper behind his words. I noticed the faces of the students go tense, including Jeanette's. *Back off*, a voice inside me said.

"Just a passing remark or two. Clare met him in Paris at the Cinémathèque. It was many years ago. By now, he may be dead, for all I know. Really, I know next to nothing about him."

"Yes? And why do you see fit to mention this person?" Saint-Cyr's expression shifted from anger to deep suspicion.

"It's simply that some of your work reminds me of his. Or rather, it reminds me of things I've heard said about his theories."

Saint-Cyr's voice was a cold explosion. "I referred to Rosenzweig just now as a 'person.' This was an error. Rosenzweig is not a person. He is a cartoon. A cartoon does not have theories, Professor Gates. A cartoon has, above its head, a small balloon in which little idiotic words are written. One reads these words and laughs. You believe this has some relationship to me?"

"Oh no, not at all," I rushed to assure him. "Not in the least. I'm sure whatever resemblance there may be is a matter of pure coincidence. As I understand it, Rosenzweig also believes the content of films is unimportant. I don't really understand how he comes to that conclusion. In any case, his orientation seems to be theological."

Saint-Cyr spat out the word in a spasm of contempt. "Theological!" I realized I wasn't doing a very good job of placating him. His fury was now just barely controlled. "You do not know that this maniac has made an attempt on my life?"

That jarred me. "No, I didn't know that. I know he tried to shoot Henri Langlois."

"Yes. *And* myself. This was not reported in the United States?"

"Not that I recall."

271

He turned to his students with an exasperated gesture that said "Didn't I tell you?" Then to me: "Of course the capitalist press would not report such matters. And what instead? The measurements of Miss America? The baseball? The price of hot dogs? In the land of the Robber Barons, who would be interested in knowing that the leader of the Neurosemiological movement came within an inch of losing his life? But apparently Rosenzweig, the assassin, is the talk of the town."

"No, please," I protested, "don't misunderstand. Rosenzweig is completely unknown, I assure you. My God, the man's psychopathic. Why wasn't he put away after he tried to shoot Langlois?"

"Our bourgeois law deals very leniently with the mad. Especially when the maniac in question aims his weapon to the *left.* In this case, after his attack upon Langlois, our Jesuitical cineast was placed in a most comfortable asylum for rehabilitation. From this asylum he wanders away again and again. Where does he go? In search of *me.* And why? Because this medieval anachronism, this reactionary obscurantist, this decadent clerical scum has been encouraged to believe there is some similarity of thought between us." A bitter sneer. "So he begins to dog my steps. Wherever I teach, wherever I speak, always he is in my audience. Even if I cannot see him, I can smell him. The man reeks. I try to have him intercepted at the door and turned away. Nevertheless, he insists he is my ally, my *teacher!* This is intolerable. I notify the authorities, who put him back in the booby hatch. And again he walks away. This time he is convinced I have stolen his so-called theories. And—boom, boom. Fortunately for me, as for Langlois, the cur is cross-eyed."

"Then he's still alive?"

"Let us hope not. You will understand if I have not concerned myself with the fate of *le père* Rosenzweig."

"Yes of course. Do forgive me for bringing the subject up."

I could tell I wasn't forgiven. Instead, I was dismissed. "And now, Professor Gates, I believe our *soirée* is at an end. Perhaps you have learned something of value from our little tutorial."

"A great deal," I assured him. But his expression made it clear he felt he had squandered an evening of his precious time.

"Do you understand all that—about the cameras and projectors?" I asked Jeanette the next afternoon when we met for coffee.

"A little," she said. "The subject is very technical." She was by now willing to unbend with me and be more candid. "Victor does not expect all his students to master these technicalities. I, for example, have much more interest in the aesthetic superstructure of the technology."

"Aesthetic superstructure. You mean what the movie is about . . . the story, for example?"

"Yes. Victor feels this is perhaps more appropriate to the feminine mentality. It is less analytical."

"Oh? Well, let me tell you, I care a great deal for what movies are about. I really can't believe it's of no importance what the characters do and say. I mean—that's what people go to the movies for, isn't it?"

"You are very American," she observed playfully. But I gathered she liked me for being very American.

"About this man Rosenzweig," I went on. Did she know if he was still alive and where he might be? She did. After he'd taken a shot at Saint-Cyr—about six years before—there had been a trial. The magistrate had ordered him removed from Paris to a mental institution in Lyons. Unless he'd wandered off again, he must still be there.

We spent one more night together, a gentle, loving night. Somewhere in the languid middle of it, Jeanette confessed that she would rather be a movie star than anything else in the world. She made the admission under her breath, like a child confessing a naughty deed. "You must never tell Victor I said this."

Her secret was surely safe with me. I wasn't likely to be telling Victor very much of anything in the foreseeable future. "Shall I tell you something?" I asked, trading confidence for confidence. "I'd give anything to be Jean-Paul Belmondo for just one day."

That brought her cuddling closer in my arms. "Not Bogie?" she asked. "You would not prefer to be Bogie?"

"Well, sure. Bogie. But first of all Belmondo."

"And I," she returned. "Simone Signoret. Or Jeanne Moreau."

"And of course there's Marlon Brando."

"And Barbara Stanwyck."

"And . . ."

And so on, long into the night.

15 ROSENZWEIG

Before I scheduled the trip to Lyons, I made inquiries with the French police. In which asylum had Victor Saint-Cyr's assailant been placed? And if I went there, would I be able to see him? I had to maneuver my way through several hours of French bureaucratic congestion before I found out what I wanted to know. The answer to the first question was Saint Hilaire Hospice. Despite the religious name, it was part of the state system of mental institutions, in this case a "home" for the criminally insane. The answer to the second question was: yes, there were visiting hours three times each week. I phoned ahead to reserve an hour with Karl-Heinz Rosenzweig (as I learned his name to be). Sooner or later my pursuit of Max Castle was bound to lead me into the world of the mad. The time had apparently arrived.

I might easily have spent my entire fellowship year with Saint-Cyr, seated at the master's feet absorbing the higher mysteries of Neurosemiology. Even if I'd cared to do that, my gaffe about Rosenzweig had queered my chances. Under the best of circumstances, Saint-Cyr would have had little enough time to spare for the bumpkin from California; now that I'd witlessly associated myself with his insane, would-be assassin, I might have had to spend weeks begging my way back into favor. And what would that finally gain me? There wasn't much more I could learn from him without first following the route his students took, a long detour through physiology, mathematics, computer science . . . a hopeless prospect for me. Every fiber of my being rose up in opposition to Saint-Cyr and his clanking, mechanistic system. My love affair with the movies had begun with sexy women and western heroes, high adventure and great romance. I didn't want to get "beyond" such things; I didn't really believe anyone could. If Saint-Cyr was right about movies, then I might as well believe that poetry was created by pencils, not by poets.

At the same time, I had to grant that the man was on to something where Castle's films were concerned. Saint-Cyr had burrowed farther into their technical depths than I had. And he'd found things in those depths: images and motifs of undeniable power, all there even in the seemingly worthless scraps of film he was working with. I sensed too that Saint-Cyr was right in believing that this repertory of subliminal tricks, fascinating as it might be, really served to mask Castle's darker intentions. But I was just as sure that he was dead wrong in taking those intentions to be political. Saint-Cyr talked a glib case for his interpretations, but I knew with all the conviction in me that what I felt when I opened myself to Castle had nothing to do with politics. On the contrary. If I trusted my intuition, it told me that the darkness that lay at the heart of Castle's work reached out to annihilate all loyalties, the political as well as the personal. If there was a message hidden in Castle's art, I was certain it came echoing up from some historical stratum far older than anything accounted for in Saint-Cyr's philosophy. Since I'd first seen the *Judas*, I was haunted by qualities I sensed there that might be called primitive, tribal, even elemental. The categories in which he worked—sin, guilt, sacrilege—were things our age would have to rediscover in his films. Perhaps that was why I was risking a visit to Rosenzweig. I had reason to believe that, mad as he might be, he had the right fix on Castle.

Whatever Saint Hilaire originally was (a convent I was told, dating back to the eighteenth century) it could never have been a happy place. Its gloom went deeper than the centuries of grime and dilapidation that burdened its stones. The sheer brooding bulk of the place, its few and narrow windows, the rusting spear-topped iron fence that girdled it, all marked it out as a place of cheerless confinement. The interior of this antique pile, though renovated, purchased its cleanliness at the cost of sterility; worse than making do on a stingy ration of sunlight, it relied on a surplus of acidically fluorescent illumination in all its rooms and corridors. No shadows were permitted, but the place was a dungeon nonetheless.

The authorities at Saint Hilaire were puzzled by my visit. I presented myself as neither relative nor friend, but a scholar interested in Rosenzweig's writing. The word "writing" elicited a bewildered stare, then a suspicious closer inspection. Was I perhaps a nut case too? I was asked if I realized that this was a mental institution, that Rosenzweig was an inmate here. Yes, I said. Another baffled look, then a shrug. I signed a book, filled out a form (in triplicate), and initialed a slip of paper that had something to do with the legal consequences of any bodily harm I might be exposed to. Then I was led to an overlit, minimally furnished room whose heavy-duty, double-locked door bore the sign "Guests. One hour limit." All the furniture in this room—four chairs and two tables—was made of metal and bolted to the floor. The windows were barred. There without a magazine to read or a picture to study on the wall, I waited for nearly half an hour. Overhead the lights—a row of glowing, ice-blue bars—buzzed like trapped flies. Beneath them, I felt as if I were being disinfected.

I'd never talked to a homicidal maniac before. I wondered if I was in any danger. Would he be wearing a straightjacket or handcuffs? When Rosenzweig finally arrived, I saw I had nothing to fear. If the will to do murder was in the man, there was no muscle to enact the deed. Rosenzweig, though still just marginally ambulatory, might have passed for a walking corpse. Gaunt to the point of emaciation, he was barely able to keep his feet without help. The help was being grudgingly supplied by a burly, sourpussed attendant at his back who seemed to be keeping him upright by the scruff of the neck. Once inside the room, the old man froze in place, gazing intently at me. The attendant had no great trouble forcibly inching him forward; he might have picked up the fragile little man and pitched him at me. Rosenzweig was bundled tightly into a clerical black jacket and trousers that made him seem all the more cadaverously white. A thin gray nimbus of hair and a few wispy white strands of beard surrounded his head; in the harsh light, they took on an eerie glow.

The old man was carrying a disorderly stack of papers—mainly notebooks—clasped to his chest. His writings no doubt. As he was shuffled forward across the floor toward me, bits and pieces of what he held threatened to slip through his grasp; feebly, he clutched where he felt things escaping. Grumbling with annoyance, the attendant stooped to recover the items that floated to the floor; these he crumpled and roughly stuffed back into the heap. After he got Rosenzweig into a chair, he drew off and took a seat by the door where he buried himself in a newspaper.

Making my tone as gentle as possible, I started talking. I talked a long time, receiving no response except long, awkward silences that betrayed not a glimmer of comprehension. All the while, Rosenzweig's dismal and weary eyes stared fixedly at me, a blank, untrusting look. Speaking in French, I said all I could think of saying by way of a carefully benign introduction: that I was a scholar . . . from the

United States . . . from California . . . studying motion pictures . . . interested in his theories . . . planning to write a book . . . a scholarly book. I alluded to an interest in early methods of animation and projection, dropping a few key names. Nothing. When I was talked out, there was a ponderous pause that must have lasted more than five minutes, long enough to make the attendant glance our way to see if the meeting was over. I supposed it might be. My visit was turning into an exercise in futility. Rosenzweig wouldn't speak. Perhaps he didn't even understand. For all I knew, he was deaf or catatonic. I was growing more than willing to break off this unpleasant encounter; twice while we sat together, I was aware that he was wetting his pants. Each time he did so, he wept soundlessly with shame. The clothes he wore, dirty to the point of being vile, were permeated with the odor.

At last, with only ten minutes left, I decided to fish for whatever I could catch. I asked, "Can you tell me about Oculus Dei?" The name was one of the few things I remembered from what Sharkey told me about Rosenzweig years back. He'd spoken of a group, "the ODs" he called them, identifying Rosenzweig as one of them.

The words were no sooner spoken than the little man stiffened, his brows knit, his mouth gaped. I might just as well have administered a jolt of electrotherapy to him. Expecting an outburst, I flinched. But he hadn't the strength for it; he weakened and fell back. The nearly toothless old mouth emitted only a few bubbles of spit; the eyes brimmed with tears. He cried silently in small feeble convulsions. A dry, whispered stream of German leaked from a throat that might not have spoken for years. I picked up only one word I could understand. *"Bitte, bitte, bitte!"* Please, please, please.

Please what? Spastically, with trembling hands, he deposited the papers he held on the table and pushed them toward me, spilling some on the floor. *Please look at these,* he meant. I reached out and opened one of the notebooks. Even if the writing inside had been English (I supposed it was German), I couldn't have read it. It was a madman's scribble, page after page scrawled in all directions, underscored, writ large, writ small, crossed out, blotted. Here and there were drawings, mechanical sketches mainly. Some vaguely suggested movie projectors. One was clearly a Zoetrope. One notebook, the most orderly, was filled from cover to cover with tiny, painstaking drawings of the Maltese cross, one after another, hundreds of them, each, I noticed, slightly rotated beyond the preceding drawing like the turning gear in a projector. Filling the book with these minute sketches must have taken endless hours, a lunatic's pastime. In one of the other books, I noticed little stick figures drawn into the lower right hand corner of each page; if the pages were thumb-riffled through, the little figure seemed to jump and spread its arms in the shape of a cross. A primitive animation. From the offered heap of materials before me, I dislodged a few crumpled paperback pamphlets, one in French, another in German. I noticed there were two or three other copies of these, so I assumed Rosenzweig could spare one of each. Seeing me take them, the old man grew excited. His dry, raspy mouth worked. *"Ja, ja. Oui. Prenez.* Take, take. *Ne permettez pas qu'ils vous voient!"* Don't let them see you. Once again, he was wetting himself.

I shuffled through the remainder of his papers looking for printed matter. There were a few more items I set aside, old and tattered booklets. One I noticed was composed in Latin. As I picked up the materials, I said, "I'm especially interested in the films of Max Castle. Castle, the German director who worked in the United . . ."

I heard a sudden sucking gasp from Rosenzweig, the sound of someone punched hard in the gut. I looked up. And then there was a moment . . . it passed as swiftly as a flash frame in a movie. Had I really seen it at all? A sudden light deep in the old man's cavernously shadowed eyes, there . . . gone before I could draw it into focus. Afterward, immediately, dumb pain twisting his face, Rosenzweig pitched forward in his chair, nearly slipping to the floor.

I thought he might be collapsing and rose to help. But I saw he was struggling to reach across the table for the writings I had set aside. He got hold of them in one desperate clawing gesture and pulled them back protectively into his heap—all except the one I happened to be holding in my hand. His face, twisting up from the table, was now glaring fiercely at me, the look of a man betrayed. Words, probably curses, gagged in his throat. I moved quickly to stash the one pamphlet I still held in my pocket. Rosenzweig saw the move and reached out toward me, wanting it back. By that time, the attendant, who must also have assumed the old man might be throwing a fit, had got hold of him and was roughly straightening him up, all the while scolding him, telling him to keep quiet.

When he had Rosenzweig manhandled back into docility, the attendant let me know my time was up; he jerked his head toward the door and led me off. Behind us, the still floundering Rosenzweig was mouthing things under his breath, urgent little fragments that died away into whimpers; he was too fatigued by his own anxiety to give the words sound. He finally did slide to the floor; the attendant gave his plight a contemptuous wave of the hand and continued to escort me out. I didn't realize how eagerly I was rushing off until I found myself blocked by the attendant, who began fumbling ineffectually with the door as if it presented some major challenge. I finally got the idea; he expected a tip. I fished out a few francs and the door swung open. I was sent on my way with a churlish grunt.

At the front desk, one of the officials stopped me to ask if my visit had been satisfactory. Before I could answer, he rushed on to ask if I could provide the name of a next of kin for Rosenzweig. I said I couldn't help. Why didn't he try the church? The church? I reminded him that Rosenzweig had once been a Jesuit priest. "Surely not," the official replied, and then asked if I'd be willing to have the old man's possessions sent to me in the event of his death.

"Me? Why me?"

"You are his only visitor since he came here."

"What sort of possessions?"

"Not much. He has a small library. A dozen books, some papers, a few small boxes."

"I really don't know the man personally," I told him.

He shrugged. "Then we will just destroy it all. Perhaps there is something of value."

I didn't believe he really thought so, but, on the other hand, what did I have to lose by saying yes? "All right," I agreed. "If nobody else claims it. But none of his clothes, understand?" I left my school address.

I had a leisurely trip back to Paris on a train that seemed to make a hundred stops along the way. It was the route, I presumed, LePrince had taken on his way home from Lyons in, when was it . . . 1887? I used the time to peruse the little volume I'd managed to swipe from Rosenzweig, a cheap self-published effort whose binding had been shedding pages for years. The pamphlet was trouble from the first page. Even before the first page. The title alone occupied me for nearly half the journey. It covered most of a page and let me know at once that Rosenzweig was in no danger of making the best-seller list. Translated from German into Father Rosenzweig's erratic French and now gropingly into my English, it read:

Anathematic Explication of the Dual Hypostases, Most Ancient of Heresies, and of the Accursed Teachings of the Disciples of Abraxas Chronicled since AnteNicean Times, Together with a Documented History Here for the First Time Revealed of Secret Machinations within the Holy Apostolic See at Rome of the Proselytes of Satan Known as Cathari, Unrelenting Enemies of Christ Jesus Truly Proclaimed Redeemer of Both Flesh and Spirit, Covering Eight Centuries of Lies, Deceptions, and Obfuscations, Including an Impregnable Defense of Trinitarian Doctrine Against All Heinous Mechanisms and Unnatural Practices Derived from or Associated with the Delusory Phenomenon Known as the Persistence of Vision, Offered for the Greater Glory of God by His Long-Suffering Servant, K-H. R., S.J.

Below the title, wedged into the remaining space on the page, was an insanely intricate little emblem. I recalled seeing something like it doodled here and there in the pages of Rosenzweig's notebooks. A circle inside a square inside a triangle inside a hexagon inside a square . . . more than the eye could discriminate without blurring. And at the center of this little geometrical jungle, the drawing of an eye with a circular pupil, within which I could just barely make out a cross. Below the eye, there were what looked like two small marks. These I was only able to read later in a stronger light with the help of a magnifying glass. They were the letters OD in a Gothic font: Oculus Dei.

The geometrical symbolism of the emblem meant nothing to me, the gargantuan title little more. Yet the title page was as lucid as the little book was to be. Worse followed. Seventy some (unnumbered) pages that would have been daunting enough if they had been legible. But the cheap pulp paper had yellowed and flaked away at the margins; the densely packed, often microscopic, print had faded. Whole sections were unreadably mildewed and permeated with what I took to be mold possibly mixed with the odor of urine. One day, I mused, after Father Rosenzweig had passed on, a box might arrive from the authorities at Saint Hilaire that brought me more such treasures.

Having gone numb from the title alone, I settled for skimming the rest of the text. Throughout there were lengthy, cramped quotations from obscure sources—Church Fathers mainly and in Latin. Here and there, I picked up recognizable references. Sharkey's old Knights

Templar were much in evidence; there were snippets on magic lanterns of days gone by. LePrince and the Zoetrope were mentioned and roundly denounced. When I reached the point of terminal boredom, I skipped to the end. Amusingly enough, the final paragraphs of this ponderous theological disquisition dealt with Donald Duck and his animated friends. The book closed in the midst of anathemas pronounced upon poor Walt Disney, archcorrupter of the young, which broke off abruptly at the bottom of the last page. There was a concluding line crammed into the last available quarter inch of space. It read, "We resume our inspired defense of the faith in volume two"—which of course I didn't have and which probably didn't exist.

One thing came through my cursory reading with unmistakable clarity; the steady drumbeat of anger and paranoid hostility that animated every word in this ugly little volume. I'd never read anything so filled with spleen. It was the work of a fanatic and a madman, no question of that.

Why had I made this foolish trip? Face it, I said to myself: there's something intellectually masochistic about what you're doing. For if there was anything that could dim my fascination with the movies, it was the possibility that they could have any connection with the dismal and maniacal diatribe I held in my hand. Why not crank down the window of my compartment and consign it to the rushing wind outside? Cast away and forget.

What kept me from that utterly sensible act? A memory that I knew would stay with me always. Rosenzweig's face. The shock, then helpless anguish that filled his eyes when I mentioned Max Castle's name. In that instant, the man's madness gave way to a pathos that cried from inside him like the voice of some still-sane creature imprisoned in the depths of a deranged mind. What was that last lucid fragment of Rosenzweig struggling to tell me?

16 OLGA

I always thought Marlene Dietrich held the world's record for feminine erotic durability, still playing the cabaret vamp into her sixties. Olga Tell, were she still on the screen when I met her, would have made a worthy challenger. I estimated she must be pushing seventy; but the woman seated across from me that afternoon in Amsterdam, though she showed not a trace of makeup or surgical intervention that I could detect, might have been the daughter of the actress I'd come to see. Her hair, straight and flowing the length of her spine, had been allowed to go natural steel-gray; there were even undisguised webs of wrinkles in the still resilient skin at the corners of her eyes and mouth. But every gesture—the easy sway in her hips when she walked, the girlish movement that swept her hair back at the shoulders, the way she crossed her still shapely legs—had the fluidity of youth.

In her golden days, Hollywood had billed Olga as a great "natural beauty." For once the publicity was matched by the truth. Thirty-some years after her last movie, this was still a superbly handsome woman, and without the aid of special lighting. The sheer, clinging silk robe she wore helped with the impression. All the while we chatted, she kept passing in and out of focus: old, not-old, old, not-old . . . but whichever she might seem at the moment, there was an air of casual sexual magnetism surrounding her that both attracted and unsettled. Unsettled, because I'd never experienced such a thing as grandmotherly sexuality. Yet here it was, not three feet away from me emanating from this tall (nearly six feet), still buxom woman, who was playing torrid love scenes when my mother was a schoolgirl.

I came to Amsterdam expecting it to be the most rewarding part of my brief European tour. After the agony of facing Saint-Cyr the egomaniac and Rosenzweig the crackpot—plus several scattered days running down private collectors here and there that had yielded precisely nothing—Olga Tell was bound to be a refreshing change for the better. At least so I judged from her letters, which had continued to be cordial and forthcoming. She showed every sign of wanting to help with my study of Castle, for whom I gathered she still nursed tender feelings.

I'd allowed myself two days in the city, asking in advance that Olga set up a screening of the Castle film she owned. Enough time, I imagined, to view the film, arrange for a copy to be made, and interview Olga. I never would have guessed that what she had to tell me about Castle would be more than my eyes and ears and a notebook could take away.

Olga was clearly a woman of means. Her name now was Van Cuypers. Marriage into old mercantile wealth had brought with it the Van Cuypers house, famous throughout the city as one of Amsterdam's stately homes. It was a high, slender gingerbread mansion that dominated the "Golden Bend" of the Herengracht, the most elegant of the town's canals. While the house had been many times richly renovated, it preserved much of its original seventeenth century marble and plasterwork. The ceilings sported rather awful but obviously costly baroque paintings of cavorting nymphs and satyrs. Why had she settled in Holland, I asked, making small talk while Olga served me hot chocolate and cookies on our first meeting. "It is where I was born and raised," she answered. "My homeland."

"Oh, I thought . . ."

"You thought I was German, yes? You were supposed to. For the studios in my time, German was sexy. You know—Berlin, the twenties, lowlife, decadence. Also Scandinavian was sexy—like Garbo, you see. Even Polish. Pola Negri. But a Dutch girl? Think of Holland, what do you see? Wooden shoes and windmills, yes? Dutch meant cheese and chocolate and the good little boy putting his finger in the dike. Wholesome. Too wholesome. So when I go to Hollywood, your Mr. Goldwyn decides that Ulrika Van Till should become Olga Tell. And then he makes up a whole silly story about me. How I was discovered in a cabaret in Berlin dancing naked. A real floozy. Like in *The Blue Angel*, you remember? Even after the talkies came, a Dutch accent you could mistake for German.

"But you see . . ." she gestured toward a photograph on the mantelpiece that had already caught my eye: a magnificent young woman, blond and glowing—Olga in her glory days fifty years before, posed somewhere on a beach, tall and proud on tiptoe, hands on hips, and completely nude. ". . . it was my great problem. A big, strapping farm girl I was, good bones, good muscles, raised like a workhorse.

What they wanted was vamps, *femmes fatales*. Maybe a little anemic, a little sunken in the chest—like Garbo. Underfed, pale. A life of sin written all over. Ingrid Bergman—she had the same trouble later on. Too big, too healthy. But for her they found saints and nuns to play. For me, it was always scarlet women. But I just wasn't a scarlet woman. It wasn't in me. I took off more clothes in front of the camera than anyone. Oh, I was so brazen. I wanted to be a big star, you see, so I followed orders. Hedy Lamarr in *Ecstasy*—you saw that maybe? Ha! What a sensation they made of her. That skinny little girl, what did she have to show? I did naked swimming, naked bathtub, naked in the woods. But who noticed? I wasn't ashamed to show my body. It was a pretty body. Did it give me a reputation? Dietrich—she showed two inches above her knee, it was a scandal. Me—nobody could believe I was a shady lady. I couldn't believe it myself.

"That was the trouble. I couldn't take myself seriously. God knows I tried to become a fallen woman. Off the screen, I was what you called hell on wheels. I *vluggert* every leading man I acted with. It's so. Every director. Every producer. It did no good. Max once told me, 'Olga, even with all your clothes off, you're still a milkmaid. Fornication with you is just good clean fun.' He said, 'You're the one Dutchman Calvin didn't get.' He was right. I had no shame. Without shame, how can there be any sin? Maybe Mr. Goldwyn got me all wrong. I wasn't Dietrich. I was Mae West. Just a good-time girl."

Since she seemed so willing to talk about it, I asked her, "Did Max Castle ever want you to do any really *very* sexy scenes? I mean the sort of thing they wouldn't show in a movie? There's a reel of film I have . . . extra material from one of his movies. It's rather . . . well, extreme."

She laughed. "With Max, there was always something extra. Not in the script. A little spook show, sometimes, yes, some blue scenes. What for, I don't know; he wasn't in the business. Sure. We did it for . . . how would you say, 'the kicks.' Sometimes he paid a little extra. But he made it like a big party. Max could put on a great party. Which movie you said this was?"

"*Feast of the Undead*. There's a scene with you. . . ."

"And the bat!" She gave a whoop of recognition. "That damn silly thing! They made it all over fuzzy, this fuzzy little toy. It tickled. I was supposed to be scared to death. And all I could do was giggle. Such a morbid thing. Max could be very morbid."

"You didn't mind doing a scene like that?"

"What did I have to lose? I was supposed to be a 'bad girl,' wasn't I? Anyway, by then, Hollywood was finished with me. It didn't matter what I did. I was just working out my contract."

"And the other actors, they went along too?"

"Not everybody. Most, only if Max promised not to show faces. Some, they did it for the reefers."

"The what?"

"You never heard about reefers?"

"Well, yes. You mean . . ."

"What you call now pot. So when Max asks the actors for kinky things to do, it is no, no, no. Everybody is so goody-good. But after he passes around the reefers, or some of his little happy pills, it is sure, sure, sure."

"He used dope to get those scenes?"

"That was how he got lots of favors. He wasn't the only one, you know. It was all over town."

"Do you know what he did with the extra film he shot?"

"Showed it at parties maybe. At all the parties they had films like that. But not so morbid as with Max."

"You never knew he actually used the material in the movie?"

She frowned in disbelief. "No! How could he? Who would show it, a scene like that?"

"It's in the movie, but it's hidden." I wanted to see if she followed what I had to say. She didn't.

"Hidden? Then if it is hidden, nobody can see, yes?"

"Well, you can see it . . . but you don't really know you see it." She was puzzled. "It's a sort of trick."

"Ah, Max was a great one for tricks. Especially with the lights. The flashing lights, you know."

"Tell me about it."

"So long ago, I can't remember. We shoot the same scene over and over. Something small. Thirty seconds. Less. Once with a fast flash, then a slower flash, then slower. Why? 'A little trick,' Max says. So we do it. Nobody else directed like Max. Sometimes we do everything for a whole day behind a . . . what would you say? A veil."

"A scrim?"

"All gauzy, like lace. We don't know why. Later, in the movie, we don't see nothing like that." She shrugged. "With Max there was something mysterious all the time."

"And what about *Heart of Darkness*?" I asked as casually as possible. "That was on the daring side, wasn't it?"

Up to that point, there had been a sunny air about her, a readiness to banter and laugh. Suddenly that vanished; an expression of quiet alarm flashed across her face, as if she'd felt some vital organ rupture inside. After a moment she said in a low, controlled voice, "Not nice. This I did not like." She wasn't going to say more.

I wondered if an apology and a show of innocence might draw something more from her. I tried it. "I'm sorry. Did I say the wrong thing?"

A guarded smile came back to her lips. "With Max I did lots of not so nice things. But this was different. This was not naughty, not just 'take off your clothes, Olga, and do a dance.' This was . . . different." She paused; I waited. "This was religious." And she would say no more.

Come back to this later, I said to myself and allowed a long silence to settle in. Then we passed on to other, less highly charged matters. She'd put out an excellent fruity cordial. I'd downed a couple of glasses and so had she. Under its pleasant influence, we relaxed nicely into the ensuing conversation. It was midafternoon, and we were seated at the spacious front window of her home overlooking the tree-lined canal. On the sun-spangled water, small fleets of ducks drifted by and now and then the occasional barge. Everything I could see of the house, its furnishings, its *objets d'art* bespoke great wealth. After a less than brilliant film career, Olga had cashed out quite comfortably. She was willing to talk about that too.

"The contract your Mr. Goldwyn gave me—I was practically a slave," she told me. "We young things—so greedy to be stars! We accepted whatever they gave us, the big shots. After all, we had to make good before our looks went, didn't we? How long did we have? Eight years? Ten years? Garbo was smart. She quit when she was ahead. Me too, I was smart. I quit when I was behind—way behind. When you got down to making vampire movies on the back lot, the next step was out. Out or into the gutter. But back here in Europe, I was still a glamour girl. Mr. Van Cuypers was in shipping. A great Dutch family. For him, even after the war when I wasn't no spring chicken, I was the gorgeous Olga Tell, the movie queen. So you see, Hollywood paid off very well for me."

"He *was* in shipping? Has he retired?"

"Oh, completely. He is dead. Twelve years now."

Somewhere in the course of that overcast and drowsy afternoon, I became aware that a flirtatious undertone had crept into our conversation, something as warm and soothing as the cordial we were sipping. For one thing, she was now sitting quite close to me on the couch and wearing one of the most intriguing perfumes I'd ever encountered. For another, the long slit at the side of her robe had fallen open at about midthigh to reveal a remarkably well-rounded leg and dimpled knee. With the exception of *Heart of Darkness*, she seemed willing to talk about anything I wanted to know, not least of all her love life. That she related with a more and more seductive lilt as time passed. I had to make a special effort—but why bother?—to remind myself that the woman was old enough to be my grandmother.

"With Max, it was always surprises. When I became his girlfriend, that was the biggest surprise. I expected exciting things. Mad passion, you know. Max had a reputation with the ladies. Ha, if only people knew what was going on!"

I wondered if she would tell me. She did.

"The first time we went to bed, you know what Max says to me? 'Olga, guess what's more fun than sex.' The way he said it, the look he gives me . . . it was a little scary. You see, I was all undressed, completely ready. Not Max, just me. I always got undressed fast. You know, to get the man interested. Well, Max, he was in no hurry. He just looks and looks. I don't know why, but he makes me feel twice as naked as I ever felt in my life. And he just puts his hand right here. . . ." She took my hand and, being very teacherly, placed it across her lower abdomen. "What's more fun than sex? 'No sex,' he says. I think he's joking. But he isn't. That's when I learn from him about *bhoga*."

I let her know I'd never heard the word.

"You are from California, yes? I thought in California everybody would be knowing *bhoga*. With all the swamis. When I was in Hollywood, it was full of them. At every party, there was a swami."

"The swamis seem to have retired," I said.

"Ah, too bad. Max, he knew all the swamis. I think that's where he learned *bhoga*."

"Tell me about that."

"Well, at first, I was sure Max was playing a mean trick on me. Because he always treated me like the big, dumb farmer's daughter. Only the farmer's daughter, she's supposed to get *gestupped*, yes? Just the opposite with Max. He just about don't touch me at all. 'Your innocence is too beautiful,' he tells me. So I think, oh-oh, I made a big mistake. Max Castle, maybe he got some problem. In Hollywood, there was lots of men with this problem. Eyes bigger than their tookies, you know. You had to do circus tricks or they couldn't get it up. But no, that wasn't Max's trouble. Max didn't have no trouble. When he said *bhoga*, he meant *bhoga*. Dear Max! For me, that was the beginning of a whole new life. I learned from a master. 'Olga,' he says the next time we get together, 'how would you like to live forever—almost? Believe me, no sex is the way.' By then, I'm not so sure he's kidding no more. I don't know about his other girlfriends, what went on with them. But me, I bet I was the best student of *bhoga* he ever had. And look." She stood up, displaying herself, whipping her hair back with a flick of the head, running her hands from breasts to hips along the contours of her body. "Maybe Max was right. We wait and see, eh? How long the old lady holds up."

She, along with the heavy cordial, was doing a perfectly charming job of bewildering me. "I may be from California, Olga, but I've never heard of *bhoga*," I told her, hoping she would provide details. She did better than that. Her face, now somewhat drunkenly blurred in my eyes toward a becomingly soft focus, seemed to melt into an expression that was at once lascivious and maternal.

"Well, time you learned, Jon," she answered, her voice dropping into a seductive half-whisper. She tugged me up by both hands and led me off up two flights of stairs toward the top of the house. I was going along but with a certain tactful hesitation. "Now, Jon," she admonished, taking on a schoolmarmish tone, "you want your research on Max to be complete, don't you? So now you're going to find out what kind of crazy lover he was." That made good scholarly sense to me. So I smiled and went along.

After my years as Clare's utterly cooperative paramour, I would have said I'd exhausted the varieties of bizarre eroticism. I was wrong. The weirdest sexual encounter of my life lay ahead of me at the top of one of the Amsterdam's stateliest mansions.

The room she led me to wasn't a bedroom, but a sort of sanctuary, thickly carpeted and hung with dark, lush drapes that covered the windows. The noise of the streets below didn't penetrate here. What little light there was drifted down through a richly colored skylight, a lazy pink, gold, and purple shaft that fell upon a square upholstered mat at the center of the carpet. Beside the mat was the only piece of furniture I could see—a low wooden table on which there rested a few implements, one of them an antique-looking incense burner. Olga bent to light this immediately, and it quickly filled the room with a spiced and musky odor, a stronger version of her own perfume.

The room had a shrinelike solemnity to it, but when Olga summoned me to her side on the mat, it was in a bright, playful voice. "Come on, Jon. Haven't you never been seduced before?" Then, catching me off guard with a movement that was smoothly practiced and which at once dispelled the somber atmosphere, she bowed forward, buried her face in a small cushion and effortlessly straightened herself without a wobble into a solid shoulder stand. I'm not sure she intended a comic effect, but a startled giggle escaped from me at once. Smiling at me with her face turned upside down, she did a little shimmy and the clinging robe she wore slid obediently down her legs and torso, gathering around her shoulders just above the breasts. She held the position for several seconds, allowing me to study her inverted form. She was naked underneath her robe; but, surprisingly, I found that her nude body turned upside down became an object of curiosity more than of sexual attraction. I noted the smooth and milky texture of her skin, flawed only by a few lumpish, purpled veins in the legs. Also, there was a bulge of flesh circling her hips and buttocks that gave some matronly bulk to her figure. She was otherwise straight and strong and remarkably well shaped, still the sturdy dairy maid. Then, as quickly and expertly as she had gone into the shoulder stand, she dropped out of it, her robe smoothly drawn away in a single movement over her head as she settled into an upright, kneeling posture. It was the neatest and most surprising piece of disrobing I ever expected to see. Viewed right side up, her breasts were large and ponderously mushy, betraying more of her age than her face, which was now flushed and glowing.

"Can you go upside down, Jon?" she asked. No, I told her. "Ah, too bad. It clears the brain, you know. Makes you alert. Like I told you, I always like to get undressed first. Now you, eh? Slow, slow. Don't rush. Make a thing of it."

While I removed my clothes, Olga turned over on her back and proceeded to perform a run of slow, graceful exercises. Her back strongly arched, she raised and lowered and circled her pelvis in a ritualized horizontal bump and grind; then, twisting her legs into odd, impossible angles, she rhythmically spread and closed her thighs. All the while, her hands were gently massaging her body back and forth from throat to knees. There was a yogalike precision to her movements, something fixed and well rehearsed. But I'd never seen yoga postures like these. They seemed designed to focus my attention on her slowly gyrating vulva as it boldly flowered and folded in upon itself just below my eye level. If that was the purpose, it was working very well indeed and having the desired effect.

When I was undressed, Olga had me kneel in front of her, sitting back on my heels, my hands clasped behind me. She brought herself around into a strange squatting posture, one leg drawn up under her, the other extended with the toe sharply pointed. "Now," she said, "I teach you just like Max taught me. Only from the woman to the man. It's the same thing, only just the opposite, okay?" I nodded okay, not really knowing what she meant. "Now you breathe very easy, very slowly. And you watch here." She had taken a small silver chain from a lacquered box on the table and fitted it around her head just above the brows. From it a tiny red jewel depended; it reached to the middle of her eyes, glinting there in the queer, colored light of the room. This was where she wanted me to concentrate my attention.

What didn't happen during the next few hours was more remarkable than what did. At the time, I would have said *nothing* happened— at least not between the two of us. Not a kiss, not an embrace. There was no touching; I mean no *real* touching. Olga moved in close enough for me to feel the warmth of her body, and for a long while that was as much contact as there was. The warmth grew until it was like the sun reflecting off a stone wall. Where was all the heat coming from? The odor that arose with it could no longer be called a fragrance. Olga was taking on a decidedly musky aroma, something I wouldn't have called pleasant. It took several minutes for this physical pungency to tone down and lose its disturbing quality. Oddly enough, I would have described it as too sexy for comfort; I was relieved when I became inured to it.

With eyes closed, Olga placed her fingertips just so, a hairbreadth away from my skin, pointed at this and that carefully selected spot on my anatomy: the forehead, between the eyes, the throat, the left and right shoulders, the left and right nipple, the solar plexus, never touching, but palpably there, tingling like a little point of compacted heat. Meanwhile, as instructed, I kept my gaze fixed on the little twinkling jewel. This, together with the enveloping warmth of Olga's presence and the deep quiet of the room, soon flowed me along into a hypnotic calm. I was becoming so relaxed I concluded that Olga's

methods were obviously self-defeating. This not-quite-touching episode, as it went on and on, began to grow tedious. Charitably, I said
to myself—if I could believe her story—perhaps this was the best
Max Castle could do, all those years ago. Queer duck, Castle. Apparently an impotent Don Juan with his actress-lovers, covering up
with mumbo jumbo. My mind wandered. I imagined Olga as a lovely,
eager young thing enduring this baffling treatment from Castle forty
years back. Maybe it was a mean trick. By now I knew he wasn't
above such pranks. But he had convinced her that great things were
happening. Changed her life. Castle, always the illusionist.

Was it all right for my thoughts to ramble like this, I wondered.
How could I prevent it, bored as I was? Imagine my amazement,
then, when Olga's hovering, searching finger came to rest, now really
touching, on the top of my penis right in the crowning cleft. "The
top," I say, because, incredible as it seemed, I was indeed fully,
powerfully aroused, a first-class erection. But how had this happened
without my knowing? And why? Olga hadn't been stimulating me;
just the opposite. I'd nearly dozed off. Now, quite suddenly, as if I'd
awakened from a fast sleep, my juices began to surge. Or maybe I
was simply becoming aware—upstairs, in my head—of what had been
going on in my body all along. I glanced down to see if what I felt
was really so. Yes, there I was at full attention, the good soldier ready
for action. Just at that moment, Olga began to bring her finger—or
rather her fingernail—lightly and slowly down the length of my eagerly upraised shaft. The sensation was so powerful, it brought a rush
of blood to my head, with it an intoxicated, deep-tickling swoon that
bordered dizzily on the edge of release, but not quite, not quite.
Coming, coming, never arriving.

"Careful," Olga cautioned in a low whisper, "we don't want to lose
anything, do we?" She pointed again at the little jewel, fixing my
eyes there. Somehow she prolonged this dry near-orgasm for what
seemed like minutes. My breath was becoming so shallow, I had to
open my mouth to gulp in air. Soon I was panting wildly, greedy to
lay hold on the climax that was almost there, but always just out of
reach. As tormenting as the experience was, I had to admire the
cunning of it. This was prick-teasing raised to a fine art. How long
could Olga hold me on the edge? The answer was a sexual condition
I didn't know existed: until I became too numb to care. In the moment
itself, I couldn't have said if this was a matter of minutes or hours;
I'd lost all reliable sense of time.

But after some endless while, I realized that my excitement—so intense, so painfully sharp—had subsided and the warm calm was returning. Dazzled and distracted as I was, I hardly noticed when Olga shifted around so that she was kneeling behind me, cradling my fatigued body, her arms encircling me at the waist. What had happened? I looked down to see my now collapsed organ nestled peacefully in her cupped hand. There was no sign of a climax; I couldn't remember reaching that point. But I distinctly recalled some crowning moment of fulfillment from which I'd now fallen back like a tired runner leaving the race, grateful for the chance to rest. Somewhere deep inside my sexual tubing there was a feeling of uncomfortable congestion; but Olga's other hand, buried in my crotch, was stoking that away.

Afterward, when we'd showered and dressed, Olga let me know she was entirely satisfied with our session, though whether with my performance or hers, I was uncertain. "You are a fast learner, Jon. Sometimes at first it is hard to control, the excitement is too much. But you see, there was no waste."

Waste. Such an odd word. How many women thought of it like that? "With brainy boys like you," she went on, "there can be too much up here." She tapped her forehead. "You must get the head out of the way, then the body knows what to do. It knows how to enjoy itself."

I wondered how many brainy boys—for that matter, how many boys brainy or not—Olga was including in her generalization. I later learned it was quite a few. Olga's upstairs room was kept in steady use. This is what Olga did with her life. Instructional sessions like this were something of a mission for her, a lesson she wanted to teach far and wide. She did it out of the goodness of her heart, her gift to the world. Her students included women as well as men, old as well as young. Trouble was: when she set about describing this strange vocation more ambitiously, she sounded disappointingly like a quack doctor promoting a bizarre diet. It was all a matter of health and good physical tone, a sort of erotic vitamin pill. I couldn't associate ideas like these with Castle.

"Did Max tell you all this?" I asked her skeptically.

We were back in her living room, drinking a grassy-flavored tea that supposedly had great restorative power. It would, Olga promised me, help reabsorb my unspent seed throughout my tissues, adding

292

years to my life. "No, no," she answered. "I don't learn all this from Max. But I learned the important thing from him."

"Which was?"

Cutely, she shook a teacherly finger at me. *"No babies."*

"Birth control?" I asked in amazement. "You mean Max had to teach you that?"

She wagged her head, "Not just *how* no babies. Of course, this I knew. But *why* no babies—this is what I learned from Max."

I didn't follow her. "What do you mean?"

"Remember when it was that Max and me, we got together—1938, 1939, was it? Such a troubled time. Soon there was to be the war. I was here, all through the occupation. I saw what Max told me, that it was true."

"What was that?"

"The world is hell." She dropped the remark casually between two sips of tea, never letting the sparkle leave her lively eyes. Hers was not the face which I would have connected with such a pronouncement. "It is so, isn't it? One does not bring children into such a hell. That is why there is shame about sex. It makes babies for Herr Hitler's world. The sex is such a craziness! Like a wild animal inside. It is all right for the body to be an animal. But when it runs away with us, then there is a baby, another baby, another . . . on and on. Such a miserable business. There is no joy in this. We know we do wrong. Max called it 'feeding the devil.' You understand? The sex makes babies to feed the devil. But Max, he showed me there is a way to get hold of the animal. You see what good sex you had today? And no waste, no babies. Soon I show you how this can be done in here." She ran my hand over her belly, placing it between her legs, over her heated organ. "That is *bhoga.* The clean joy."

"Clean?"

"When there is no waste, no seed, then the sex is clean. But to feed the devil, that is what makes it unclean."

I felt a distinct thrill as she dropped the word. It was the first time anyone beside myself had connected it with Castle. "Is that how Castle described it—'unclean'?"

"Yes. Unclean. Not because of the pleasure, but because of the suffering it brings."

Still I was puzzled. "But there are other ways to avoid having babies. There are many devices. There's the pill."

She waved my words aside impatiently. "Yes, yes. And still the babies come. All this is birth delay, not control. Sooner or later, the seed gets through. But this way, with *bhoga,* you know there is greater pleasure when there is no seed. We fool the devil at his own game. We take the joy, but he gets no babies." She gave a small, triumphant giggle. "Someday maybe there could be nobody in hell at all."

There was an unsettling dissonance about everything Olga said. Here she was delivering a dire and terrible indictment, a vision of life on earth she might very well have learned from the greatest of the *film noir* directors. And yet, though I could tell she believed all she said, her manner was so buoyant; the smile never left her lips. It was like hearing the words of the prophet Jeremiah sung to a springy little waltz.

"Nobody?" I asked. "I can't believe that. You mean, no reproduction, none at all?"

"Why not? If everybody knew there is greater pleasure and how to have it—then perhaps."

"And this is what Max told you?"

"What I remember, yes. Oh, I forget a lot. Because at first I never knew how serious he was being. Like I said, he was such a joker. So I didn't always listen carefully. I learn *bhoga* because that is fun. Just some kind of tricky sex, like was all over Hollywood. But other things he tells me, I forget. Until I came back here. Until the war. Then I understood what Max meant. The world is hell."

These few dark and simple themes, the evil of the world, the blessings of *bhoga*—that was about as far as I got with Olga on the philosophical level of things. On the more physical plane, she and I made whirlwind progress over the next several days—a longer stay than I had planned for Amsterdam. But I make no complaint. I was receiving a short course of study from her in the sex that was "no sex." She was jubilantly zealous to teach, and, of course, I never found it difficult to drift along in somebody's strong running current. I turned out to be an apt pupil, though I had no idea where this newfound skill might ever be applied. *Bhoga* would have needed a lot of explanation in any company I was ever likely to keep. True, I'd be leaving Amsterdam with a knowledge of sexual postures and practices I could never have imagined; but as enthusiastic as Olga may have been about converting me to her exotic style of sex, I couldn't imagine anyone but another Olga ever getting away with the sort of seduction she had engineered.

In one of our last sessions, for example, we wound up in a contortionistic form of intercourse whose languid rhythm, Olga assured me, could be prolonged through an entire day and night, until hunger displaced sexual appetite and desire faded. She provided some four hours of proof for that claim and was pleased to find that was enough to satisfy my by now less than urgent needs.

"You know," I told her afterward in the leisurely interlude that always followed, "this kind of lovemaking takes a very long time, Olga. It's enjoyable. The best I've ever had. But I really don't think many people have that much time."

"Why not?" she insisted. "If there is such great pleasure."

"I know it sounds crazy, but frankly, I don't believe people care that much about sex. I mean . . . they care; you could even say they're obsessed. It's always on their mind. But it's as if what they really want is fast food, not gourmet cuisine."

For the first time since we met, a shade of sadness passed across Olga's face. She nodded gravely. "Wham, bam, thank you ma'am. You ever heard that? Max told me that. That's how the waste happens. That's why the babies come. Quick, quick, quick. I know. I was like that. Max told me I was like everybody else—a wham-bammer. But I learned better, you see? Like you said, people got it on their mind. *On their mind.* Not in their cock." She reached over to give me a little anatomy lesson, first touching my dozing penis, then the testicles below. "You see: *this* hooked up with *this.* That's what makes the world go round. Here is *bhoga.*" She stroked the penis. "But here is the world." She hefted the balls. "The wars, the suffering, the stupid misery going on and on from father to son, thousands of years. Here is heaven, here is hell. But the two, they been all mixed up. That's the dirty trick."

"Whose dirty trick?"

"The devil," she said simply as a child. "That's what Max told me."

"You believe that?"

She shrugged. "I am not religious. I never understood what Max was talking about exactly. But he was right—this I know."

For all her bouncy high spirits, I'd learned not to underrate Olga's seriousness when she spoke of these matters. After one of our earlier sessions, she'd casually told me something of her wartime experiences. Soon after the Nazis overran the Netherlands, she left Hollywood for England, trying to get closer to her family back home. In London she became involved in the Dutch resistance; eventually that brought her back to Holland, where she ran more than her share of risks. After less than a year with the underground, she was arrested and spent most of the occupation behind barbed wire, enduring all the worst, just barely escaping with her life. A number of her relatives hadn't been as lucky; they perished in the camps. When she spoke of hell and the devil, it was from firsthand knowledge.

17 SIX MINUTES UNTITLED

In the midst of this erotic and philosophical dalliance, what had become of the "unfinished film" Max Castle had left in Olga's safe-keeping, the movie that was "nothing like the things you might be familiar with"? That was, after all, the mysterious object of my visit to Amsterdam.

I soon realized that Olga was using the films, or whatever there was left of them, as bait to keep me coming around day after day. Each time I asked, she promised me she'd set up a screening the next day . . . or soon after. She had a friend who ran a movie house in town; we could use his projector. I waited patiently for the arrangements to be made.

She needn't have been so cagey with me. I was thoroughly charmed by her and honestly curious about what she wanted to teach, even if it left me wondering what I might ever do with this peculiar brand of sexual expertise. More to the point, I was finally prepared to believe what she'd told me about *bhoga:* that she learned the practice from Castle, that it was important to him, that things he believed were intertwined with the discipline. My strange liaison with Olga was, after all, a kind of research.

I realized that Olga must have embroidered Castle's ideas with notions of her own over the years. But these were quite easy to sort out. Anything jovial and fun-loving that smacked of healthy, happy sex was obviously Olga; she was constitutionally a therapeutic optimist. Even though the logical result of *bhoga* universally practiced would be the slow extinction of human life on earth, she honestly saw this as a cheery prospect. Humanity on its way to oblivion, making whoopee all along the way. On the other hand, the darker background against which Olga's jolly mission was being carried out I took to be Castle's brooding Germanic presence.

There were other things Olga had to tell me that made a prolonged stay worthwhile. She remembered the Reinking twins. Yes, it was true as Zip had told me, they were always somewhere near by on the set wherever Castle worked and were constant visitors at his home. Like Zip, she'd found them disconcertingly odd—cold, withdrawn, secretive. Unlike Zip, she'd been able to understand the German that passed between them and Castle. Bickering exchanges, cuts, slights, knocks. The twins were also quite nasty to her, as they were to all Castle's lady friends, as she remembered. She once heard them hectoring Castle about his interest in *bhoga*, using the occasion to take a few unkind swipes at her. She knew Castle disliked them; he complained to her bitterly about them many times. The worst was that they interfered with his movies. "Then why did he keep them on the payroll," I asked. After all, Castle wasn't the man to suffer the opposition of inferiors.

She gave an odd answer. She was under the impression that Castle collected his salary from the twins; he was on *their* payroll. She knew for certain he often went to them for money. What the studios paid him as a director of B-movies was the usual pittance. Olga assumed he was borrowing from the Reinkings to cover his expenses, which ran high. Castle liked his comforts. That was another bone of contention with the twins, who, Castle used to say, were prepared to live in a box like mummies and expected him to do the same. He frequently alluded, with some bitterness, to the abstemiousness the Reinkings demanded of him. "I have left all that behind me," he would insist.

He also went to the twins for funds to produce his independent films. The twins were tight with him on that score too, sometimes using financial leverage to bully him. But where, I wondered, did the Reinkings get their money? She had no idea. She only knew them as film editors working on studio cheapsters. Not much money in that. In fact, she sometimes thought they worked for nothing, just to help Castle get the effects he wanted and couldn't afford on the shoestring budgets he was assigned. As far as she was aware, their names never appeared in the credits of any Castle film, something I'd already found out.

Olga also knew a thing or two about the *Sturmwaisen*, the Orphans of the Storm. Castle and the Reinkings came from the same orphanage, an institution outside Dessau that had been destroyed during the war. That was where they'd learned filmmaking. I mentioned the orphanage in Zurich; it was the next stop on my list before I returned to California. She was familiar with the place. Did she know how many more orphanages there were?

"The *Sturmwaisen* have orphanages all over the world, in the United States, in China even. In Zurich, that is the headquarters. Also there is a school here in Holland. Every year I give them money at Christmas. After the war, they took in many children. They are good people, I think. Very sober, very dark. But good." Then she added something Zip had never told me, though he must have known. "They have a school near Los Angeles. That's where the twins used to live. They were always after Max that he should stay there too, but he wanted his big house in the city. They didn't like that, but Max wouldn't take orders from them."

"Do you remember where this school was?"

She reflected for a moment. "North, in the mountains, I think. I was never there."

"Do you remember its name?"

She gave it a try, but not a very helpful one. "Saint . . . something, I think. Or maybe Holy something."

"What sort of an organization are they, the *Sturmwaisen?*"

"It's a religious thing."

"Like a church?"

"Yes. With nuns and priests."

"They're Catholic?"

"No, no." She shook the question off firmly.

"You're sure?"

"Oh yes. Max told me. Definitely not Catholic. You see the difference? The pope says sex should only be just to have babies, yes? Have lots of babies." She made a sour, angry face, one of the few times her smile went behind a cloud. "I learned from Max—this is the devil's teaching."

"But you say there are nuns and priests at these orphanages?"

"Yes. The sisters, they wear the dark gowns, you know. The funny hats. I said once to Max how Catholic it looks. Max said, 'No, the

Catholics look like *us*. We are much older than them, but they won't admit it.' "

"Do you know what sort of religion it is, what it teaches . . . anything like that?"

She didn't, not beyond the bizarre sexual doctrines she'd already spelled out for me. That seemed to be all she cared to know about. She couldn't tell me much even about the Dutch branch of the order, which was quartered in The Hague. As a generous contributor, she'd been allowed to visit and meet the children. But her relations with the establishment didn't go much farther than that. There was one thing she was certain about, however. "I think Max was in big trouble with these people."

"How do you mean?"

"A few times, somebody comes from the orphans. Always two together: a man, a woman. Very sober, very dark. They bawl Max out for something, I don't know what. He wasn't doing something like they wanted. After he meets them, he mopes around for days. I think they don't want him making movies on his own."

"But why not? They trained him to be a director, didn't they?"

"Yes, but only to make *their* kind of movies."

"What were *their* kind of movies?"

There she drew a blank. "Not good movies, I don't think."

"How do you mean 'good'?"

"Not . . . nice."

In the second week of my visit, after my last session in the upstairs room, Olga asked me to meet her the next morning at the movie theater. True to her word, she'd arranged a screening. It took place at a comfortable little art house in the downtown area. Claus, the owner, was an old friend who still remembered her as a star. He was a movie connoisseur who had screened the Castle material for Olga a few times before, the last time some eight years before. We talked while we waited for her to arrive with the film. Claus was reasonably knowledgeable about Castle's films; he was old enough to remember seeing some of the early silents, some that had long since been lost. "Often the stories were trash," he told me. "But there was always a power, something extraordinary you remembered long afterward. I cannot say why."

Briefly, I mentioned a little of what I'd discovered about the *Unenthüllte* in Castle's films. "Ah, how very clever," Claus said, at once fascinated. "I wonder if you will not find such things in the film Olga

299

is bringing. There is the same power. And one thing I noticed myself. Very odd, very clever. You will see. But this is also very dangerous, don't you think, such a power to sneak inside the mind?"

"Very."

"You must write about this."

"I intend to."

Claus told me that soon after Olga settled in Amsterdam following the war, she'd brought him her small collection of Castle memorabilia, asking his advice about its care and handling. There were two reels, neither of them well produced. The first had a few salvageable scenes on it, plus a vast amount of waste footage which Claus would have scrapped. But Olga refused to see any of Castle's work destroyed, so Claus edited out the good stuff and spun the rest off onto a reel of its own. This was the material Olga finally donated to the Museum of Modern Art.

The second reel was very brief, but, as Claus put it, "very powerful." He had spliced it together with the other small excerpt to make up a single short spool. "But as you will see," he went on, "they are separate films. It would be best, I think, to watch them that way with an intermission between."

Olga arrived about a half hour later, bringing the reel from the bank vault in which it was kept. I was eager to learn what we were going to see. She explained. Part of the material she had to show— the better part, she thought—dated from 1938. In the summer of that year, she and Castle, along with Zip Lipsky, had filmed a number of scenes in Europe for one of the independent productions Castle was always hoping to make when time and money were available. She had no idea what the movie was; Castle rarely discussed his plans with her. When he did, it was facetiously. For example, she remembered asking that summer what the name of the movie was. His answer: "A Damnation Worth Waiting For. What do you think? The title alone will win us the Academy Award."

Olga gave a little shake of the head. "You see what he was like? Well, I made up my own title. Prince of Exile. You will understand why when you see it."

Castle preferred to film in Europe, she told me, because he could find cheaper production facilities there as well as greater freedom. He had friends at a number of French, German, and Danish studios whom he could often persuade to help with equipment, editing, process work. He spent a lot of time dickering with these people, cutting petty deals that involved loans, favors, barter. Sometimes, if he had to, he would grudgingly shell out minuscule fees, but only when he'd exhausted every chance of freeloading. Olga felt it was all very demeaning.

The second film we'd be seeing was, as I hoped, a fragment of the Welles-Castle *Heart of Darkness*. This was footage shot in Mexico by Castle and Zip Lipsky. Olga had been on location with them but didn't take part in the scenes filmed there. Her part of the movie was done at RKO—on the notorious closed set, as I knew but didn't mention. I noticed that in talking about this project, Olga was more than a little ill at ease. She finished by dropping a curious remark. "We can watch it if you wish, but I don't think I am in it."

"You don't know?"

"I don't think so," she repeated, a strange lame note in her voice.

I wondered if she knew of any other surviving segments of the film. She thought there might be. During the years she had known him, Castle was constantly juggling film canisters, moving them in and out of warehouses, studios, or the homes of friends. He carried a list with him at all times detailing which film was where so he could lay hands on this or that project whenever the chance arose to do a little more shooting, a little more cutting. As far as she knew, not a single one of these chronically stalled productions was ever completed. At the time of his death, he might well have left dozens of reels of unfinished work squirreled away with friends and co-workers around the world.

Castle had given Olga the remaining material from the film she called *Prince of Exile* as a memento when she left for Europe at the beginning of the war. She remembered what he said when he presented her with the reel. "You see how prophetic we were? Now there is no need to finish it. The world will finish it for us." As for the segment of *Heart of Darkness,* that was a reel of film he'd entrusted to her in London in the fall of 1941, when they met for what would be the last time. He was hurriedly passing through on his way to Zurich to raise money (so he hoped) from the *Sturmwaisen.* Olga wasn't eager to have the film dumped on her. In fact, she felt irked with Castle for asking the favor. In England, the blitz was under way; in her homeland people dear to her had been killed or imprisoned. Making movies seemed a distinctly minor matter to her just then. But Castle was insistent and as usual got his way with her. He had said he wanted to make sure that at least some of the work was in safekeeping while he was in Zurich. So she agreed to store the film for him until he got back.

No sooner had Castle deposited the film with her than he was on his way, an abrupt, untender departure. He was having difficulty booking passage by land or air across occupied France. The last Olga heard of him, he was planning to fly to Lisbon and improvise an itinerary from there to Switzerland. He was a driven man, obsessed with the single-minded desire to make his movie. Even the war wasn't going to stand in his way.

Olga, meanwhile, was struggling with her own priorities. She was already deeply involved with the activities of the Dutch Resistance in Holland, work that would soon draw her back to her native land to join the underground. She stored Castle's film with friends, and didn't see it again until the war was over. By that time Castle was dead and these few poor reels of film were her only souvenirs of him. Since she appeared in the footage, however briefly, it assumed an emotional value for her. It commemorated her movie career as well as her love affair with Castle, both now part of a world forever lost. True, she'd made a few more pictures in Hollywood after taking part in Castle's final, abortive efforts, but those were trashy B-movies. She thought of these fragments as her last "serious" · work.

From the outset, Olga had been referring to the films she was going to show me as "little pieces," "just scraps," "almost nothing." Nevertheless, her story raised my expectations to a dizzy height. Perhaps I was finally going to see an example of Castle's film artistry at its best. But when I checked in at the projection booth to watch Claus setting up, my heart sank.

"Is that all?" I asked. The reel on the projector couldn't have held more than a few minutes of film.

Claus held up the box that had contained the movie, showing me the label. It read "Six Minutes Untitled."

"Just an hors d'oeuvre," he observed apologetically. "But it will give some idea what a feast there might have been."

As we had agreed, Claus ran the *Prince of Exile* first. That made up the first four minutes of the program. He showed it once, then was good enough to roll it three times more for me, the last time clicking through frame by frame while I took rapid notes. But it was the first showing that made all the difference. I simply let the film wash over me, opening every pore to its impact—the way I'd once watched the *Judas*.

The first image, grainy and out of focus, was that of a bird caught in slow-motion flight against a blank, bright sky. It held the screen for nearly a minute, a mere blur of dark wings swooping, arcing. It was shot from the rear by an unsteady camera that struggled to follow it, focus-pulling into the distance as the bird diminished to a point, to nothing. There was, vaguely, a background sound through the sequence. A low rumble, maybe just empty sound track. When the bird was gone, there was a moment of blank screen, followed by a jumble of leader.

Then, *whoosh, whoosh, whoosh!* an avalanche of images, double-exposed, overprinted, running at many times normal speed. It took me the better part of a minute to get a grip on this runaway movie carousel. When I did, I saw it was a collage of newsreel footage, some of it old as the Pathé Brothers. Scenes of war, mostly World War I, but here and there, material from the thirties. Horrors of the Spanish Civil War perhaps. The Japanese in China. Over and over, one saw soldiers marching, scrambling out of trenches, racing across fields. The tiny figures quick-stepped forward, backward, waved flags. Shells exploded. Planes fell from the sky. Things blew up, then—in reverse—reconstructed themselves. Refugees tore along roads, then reversed direction. The fast motion made everything comic in the extreme, lending it a silent slapstick quaintness, a visual humor only possible on film where human action can be made utterly, absurdly mechanical.

Overlaying and penetrating the battle sequences were other scenes, flashes of social violence. Riots. A lynch mob. Soldiers and police battering crowds of people. Suddenly everything stopped dead; the picture of a begrimed child alone and crying in a war-torn street held the screen. Then again the torrential rush of newsreel footage. On second viewing, I saw this was hardly as chaotic as it seemed; the images were carefully choreographed with rhythmic repetitions. Most memorably, there was a machine gunner (certainly not a newsreel excerpt but an actor shot in that mode) who sat firing directly into the camera. His image popped into view several times, mowing 'em down on all sides. He was masked from brow to chin; the eyeholes showed no eyes.

The film—or the excerpted footage used within the film—looked to be in terrible condition, grainy and scratched, constantly jumping, going too dark, going too light. But I knew better than to take these seeming flaws at face value in a Castle movie. Every one of them might conceal a wealth of hidden imagery. As it was, Castle was drawing upon one of the unique expressive powers of film; the overall effect of the speed and inferior visual quality of what we were watching was to distance the viewer from the images, making them seem an old, old story that had been going on forever. Human folly so persistent and futile it became comic.

And there was sound, racing to keep pace with the rushing film. A superfast, very tinny tune performed on a frenzied calliope. It took me a while to register the piece. When it slowed down, I caught it. "Bye Bye Blackbird."

The black-and-white contrast of the film began to oscillate wildly, the white becoming blindingly hot, finally filling the screen, becoming a blazing sun in the sky. The tinkling calliope faded. A crackling sound like radio static took its place. Below the sun-bright glare, a vast, empty plain appeared, a desert landscape. Then on it a long, endlessly long winding file of figures. This was a sharper version of the scene I'd just barely been able to make out in Olga's reel of waste footage at the museum. Even so, the process work here was quite poor. The marching line was obviously a superimposed shot; it jittered against the desert background.

The camera came in close, closer. The figures were children, shabby and shoeless, trudging across the Sahara waste. They were trailing behind a hooded leader who carried a heavy load on his back. All along the painful line of march, children were sinking down in the sand, expiring. As they did so, their images dissolved into the desert, devoured by the great pitiless dunes.

Then the hooded leader stopped, threw out its arms, welcoming some sight ahead. There was a rough cut, then a long tracking shot of a high stone wall that trailed off across the desert. Another rough cut. Now the children, on their knees, were lined up against the wall, holding hands. In front of them, their leader dropped his hood; it was the masked machine gunner again. He was unstrapping the heavy load from his back. It was his weapon; he was setting it up for use, an act of mass execution. His masked face filled the screen. The crackling sound grew loud and fierce, rose to a high-pitched animal whine, then faded behind a cello performing "Bye Bye Blackbird," now very slowly, dirgelike.

A woman's voice floated up out of the music, a mere whisper at first, speaking French. Overlapped on the sound track, it became its own counterpointing echo, repeating the words of a poem I could only catch in fragments. The voice, which I now recognized as Olga's, fell into a crooning chant, a single haunting line repeating and repeating until it was swallowed by the desert wind as the film ended. I could catch the phrase *"O Prince de l'exil"* before the voice faded away.

I spotted Olga in just the last few moments of the reel, at most a ninety-second appearance. She had indeed been a great beauty in her youth; but Castle wasn't using her for her looks here. He was after a purely dramatic effect. Heavily draped in a white robe, she sat in a bleak lunar landscape cradling a child. Their pose was that of the *Pietà*. Bleeding through the two of them in a double exposure, the desert landscape showed up as an implacable presence. But behind them, just barely visible against the darkening sky, I could pick out a pair of eyes gazing down on the scene with an expression of infinite pity. They weren't Olga's eyes; they were Sylvia Sidney's, finally placed in their rightful setting.

The expiring child stirred in Olga's arms. Her hand moved across its face, its body. Then up close, we see: she is picking at something. Worms. Maggots. They cover the child, a writhing shroud. The task is futile. The woman's eyes fill with tears. The limp body in her arms is withering away, eaten to the bone, to dust. The last shot shows her hands reaching out. The dust, all that remains of the child, blows through her fingers, swirling away, mixing with the anonymous sands of the wasteland. The scene goes dark. There is a rush of leader. End.

Thirty years after the scene had been filmed, Olga still remembered the text that accompanied it. I jotted the lines down as she repeated them for me before Claus rolled the next part of the reel.

> *J'ai plus de souvenirs que si j'avais mille ans . . .*
> *Je suis un cimetière abhorré de la lune*
> *Où comme des remords se traînent de long vers*
> *Qui s'acharnent toujours sur mes morts les plus chers*

Which, roughly translated, I made out to mean something like:

FLICKER

I have more memories than had I lived a thousand years
I am a cemetery that the moon abhors
Where maggots creep like remorse
And feed upon the corpse of my best beloved.

And the other line chanted by Olga as the scene ends:

O Prince de l'exil, à qui l'on a fait tort
O Prince of exile, who has endured such wrong . . .

Short as it was, Olga's sequence in the film brought one innovation with it. At the first viewing, I was annoyed to see a hair caught on the lens, jittering all the way through the scene, picking up bulk, becoming an ugly matted clot that hovered just above her face. The longer it twitched there, the more irritating it became. Finally, just as the reel ran out, it shook loose and scrabbled down the scene, merging with the closing darkness. I expected that would be the end of it; even so, before the second showing I asked Claus to be sure to wipe the lens.

"The lens was clean," he told me. "The dust is on the film. I know this from last time."

But how could that be? Why would Castle have permitted such an obvious flaw to survive on his finished print?

"It is deliberate," Claus said. "If you look closely at the film you will see: it's an animation. This is the innovation I told you about."

Olga winked at me knowingly. "One of Max's tricks. I complained also to him when I first saw it. He said, 'Did you ever notice how it drives you crazy to see a piece of dirt like that on the lens? Well, maybe I want to drive the audience a little crazy here. Like Miss Muffet on the tuffet.' You know what he meant?"

On second viewing I did. The ugly clot of dirt did have a nervous, spiderlike quality to it. It seemed to be reaching down, struggling to get hold of Olga, to snare her in its tangled web. At last it did. Viewing the film frame by frame, I could see the way the animation developed. The clotted dust spread into a web that thickened over Olga's image, strand after strand, until the light was blocked out. The effect brought a note of unrelieved tension to the scene—like a high, screechy sound that will not go away. There was more to that piece of dust than met the eye, of that I was sure.

Though I realized that the excerpt from *Heart of Darkness* wouldn't run more than two minutes, I found myself awaiting it with high anticipation. If I hadn't already seen the first image that appeared on the screen, I would have been suitably startled. It was the hideous fence of severed heads that Castle and Zip had filmed in Mexico. The sequence developed as I remembered, with the camera being swallowed down the gullet of the last head in the series. But this time the ensuing darkness was striped by the flames of a leaping fire.

In front of the blaze, a mass of gleaming, nearly naked bodies writhed, spun, twisted spasmodically, a drunken orgy of cavorting savages. What there was of a sound track was just barely clinging by a thread to the film, but there was enough left to give the idea: a cacophony of frenzied drumming and wailing voices. It sounded a great deal like the sound track Castle had improvised for *Zombie Doctor* but hadn't been permitted to use. Perhaps he'd salvaged it and plugged it in here. Properly recorded, it would have been spectacular.

At the center of the ritual, surrounding the fire were four people bound to stakes: two men, two women, straining at the ropes that held them. They were black, stripped to loincloths, their faces vibrant with fear: eyes rolling, mouths gaping. If they were amateurs, they were doing a damned good job of projecting absolute panic. A grotesquely costumed figure gyrated around them, a witch doctor, I assumed, threatening the captives, lunging at each in turn with what looked like an elephant's tusk equipped with a vicious prong at the tip. I recalled that the Conrad story had to do with the ivory trade in darkest Africa, part of the book's pervasive black-white symbolism; but I was sure no ritual of this kind was described in the book.

The film was by no means a polished piece of work. It was little better than a rough cut. Still, though I couldn't say why, the power of the conception was getting through. To all outward appearances, the scene was a pretty conventional bit of Hollywood jungle high jinx. The captives may have looked more convincingly frightened, the nudity of the women lent a more risqué edge to the action, but even so, there was nothing all that remarkable about what I was watching. Where the scene ended, the camera cut away just as the witch doctor made ready to drive the menacing tusk into the first of his victims. The cry of the dancers punctuated the unseen act, providing it with a jarring impact. Still, it was the sort of censoring cut one would expect in a film of that vintage.

And then, far too soon, the excerpt was over. But it left behind a singularly unsavory aftertaste that I at once identified as the result of one of Castle's subliminal techniques. It was exactly what I remembered feeling when I first saw the *Judas*, the sense that I'd witnessed some holy terror not meant for my eyes, no part of my world.

Claus ran the segment three more times. At my side in the darkened theater, I could feel Olga's tension mounting. She wasn't enjoying this a bit; in fact, she was fighting it. That made it difficult for me to maintain my concentration. I felt guilty to discomfit her so much. When I suggested we end the session, her relief was immediate, like a drowning swimmer finally breaking the surface of the water to take a breath of air. Jokingly, I said, "I didn't see you in the film, unless you were the witch doctor."

Not at all jokingly, she answered, "No, I wasn't there, was I? But I was so close to Max when he worked on this, sometimes I think maybe I see myself dancing there. . . ."

Claus reassured her. "Come now, my dear. If you were in the movie, wouldn't we see you?"

I knew an answer to that question, but for Olga's sake I decided to keep it to myself.

Before we left the theater, I thanked Claus for his time. "My pleasure," he replied, and then thought again. "No, really, it isn't a pleasure to see these films. Especially the second. I feel each time I see it that I have no right to watch. Like once when I was a child, a Catholic friend told me that at the Mass he eats the body of Jesus. I had never heard such a thing before. It was very frightening but also, I thought, very sacred, something I would have no right to see. Taboo. You understand?"

"I understand."

Later, back at Olga's home, I went over my notes with her, using the opportunity to drain her of everything she remembered about the films, every word Castle had said. "I wish I'd seen more of you up there on the screen," I said.

"Oh, but you did," she answered. "I wasn't the witch doctor, but I was the shooter."

"With the machine gun?"

"Yes. Max wanted that I should do that part, the killing of the children. I hated it. It was a real gun, you see. Not the bullets, of course, but the boom-boom-boom. He puts in front of me pictures of children to shoot at. He says it will help me feel the sorrow. The damned gun, it nearly broke my fingers."

"Do you know where the poetry comes from?" I asked.

She did. "The French poet. The sick one." Max had once marked the passage for her in a book. She searched a few shelves and found it. Baudelaire. Two poems. One called "Spleen," the other—for the line "Prince of exile"—entitled "Litanies of Satan."

"Was Castle fond of Baudelaire?" I asked.

Olga shrugged. "Once he said he wanted for this part of the movie that it should feel like decadence. This was poetry of decadence. 'Why so morbid?' I asked him. I remember he said, 'Decay is a great mercy.' " She gave a shudder of disapproval.

Olga actually had little to tell me about *Prince of Exile*. The filming had been done in several sessions scattered over about three months. Castle had rented space in a Paris studio where he had connections. The desert scene was a process shot filmed in the studio; the children Castle used were from one of the orphanages, loaned out for the shoot. He hadn't been happy with the technical work on that part of the movie and intended to redo it. The crew Olga worked with was minimal. A few men on the lights and sound, somebody for makeup, an assistant or two, and Zip Lipsky on camera. There had been more material filmed, using two other actors, but Olga had no idea what became of that. She remembered an eating scene: she and two men richly costumed, gorging themselves at a lavish banquet, stuffing away like hungry pigs, covering themselves with grease. Max had laid out a hefty sum to have the meal catered with disgustingly heavy food from one of the best charcuteries in town, though by the time they were set up the food was cold and far from palatable.

"When we are finished, Max says he wants another take. And out comes more food. By then, we are stuffed to the ears. But he makes us eat again. Right away I start to get sick. One of the others also. But Max doesn't cut, he just keeps shooting. He don't let us even leave the table. You see, he wants that scene—eating till we get sick. That makes me very mad with him. I don't want anybody filming me throwing up. So I just walk off. He could be very mean, very tricky."

Yet she wished now that even this disagreeable scene, along with others Castle had shot that summer so long ago, had survived on the reel she owned. Such as it was, she treated the little scrap of film as a personal treasure. When I asked her to let me copy it, she agreed but insisted the job be done locally in Amsterdam. She wouldn't trust me to take the film away. "There is so little left of the real Max Castle," she reminded me. She was sure her friend Claus could find somebody for the copy job; she would make sure he supervised the work personally.

I waited until I had only an hour or so left to spend with Olga before I left for the airport; then I asked, "Now will you tell me about *Heart of Darkness?*"

She must have known the question would come up again. She unloaded a deep sigh of reluctant consent, then nodded. "Like all Max's serious movies, it wasn't a movie. Just little pieces of things he was going someday to put together. Things shot in Mexico, things shot in the studio, but nothing ever finished, everything all mixed up. This time Max thought maybe he had a big chance to do something high class—because of Orson Welles, you know. Orson had lots of money. And he liked so much this story about the jungle and the natives. Such a terrible story it is. You know the book?"

I said I did.

"Terrible. When Max first tells me the story, right away I hate it. But he says it will be a movie for our time—about the evil inside people, how everywhere we see civilized people becoming savages. So yes, I say, I will be in this movie because it meant so much to Max. Also because I think it will be my last movie. And it was."

She was clearly laboring as she recounted the experience. I realized that asking her to do that was callous on my part. But it was now or never. I kept my questioning pressure upon her.

"You see," she went on, "I don't remember so clearly. It is very fuzzy in my head. I wanted to help Max, but it was so extreme what he wanted. Nudity, yes. This I don't mind. Max and me, we did movies like that before. But this time, he wants more. He wants me to make love to the actor. The real thing, you understand. He wants to have this on film, like a blue movie."

"Who was the actor?"

"A black man. Dandy Wilson was his name. He wasn't an actor. He was a dancer in one of the clubs. Lovely body. Very strong. Max dresses him up like a bird."

"A bird?"

"Yes. I think he is supposed to be some kind of god like the pagan people got, you know? He has such great wings. And over his face a mask like a hawk or eagle. He is very fierce to see. This is an 'unspeakable rite,' Max tells us, like it says in the book. A sacrifice. We got to be very serious about it. We got to feel it."

310

Theodore Roszak

She halted. I could see she was thinking back to something more than unpleasant, possibly traumatic. I sought to keep her talking. "You had to use a sword at one point, didn't you?"

Her eyes gave a sudden flash of recognition. "Yes, there was a sword." She stalled again.

"Was it dangerous?"

She gave herself a shake and continued. "You see, I couldn't do it—what Max wanted. I couldn't make love to this black fellow. I never did that before in the movies. Only make-believe. I told Max, I can't do this. So he gives me something to make it easy."

"What did he give you?"

"One of his evil little pills. It makes me very tipsy. Everything starts to go crazy in my head. This is why I don't remember so good. But I remember . . . I remember what Max was telling me all the time. That Dandy isn't Dandy. He is God, the *true* God. Things get so mixed up with me. I think I am making love with God. I don't know what we did, Dandy and me. But I think it was very wrong. And then Max tells me, I must take the sword. . . ." She fell into a long, tense pause, gazing at the wall behind me as if she were seeing the memory there.

"And do what?" I asked, coaxing the words from her.

Her voice went frigidly brittle. "Chop off his head." She gazed at me with hurt, questioning eyes as if I might be able to tell her why Castle had asked this of her. "But I can't do it. Because the pill is making everything so *real*. I can't tell I'm in a movie no more." A guilty hush came into her voice. "I think I am really killing God." She let out a nervous little laugh. "I am not a religious person. But then, I don't know . . . the pill was doing funny things to me inside. I start to cry. I was hysterical. I couldn't use the sword. But Max makes me do it. 'Kill him!' he says. 'Do it! Do it!' And I get very scared. Because I think Max is becoming crazy. 'Kill him!' he says. And . . . I . . . do . . . it."

I let her take several long, healing breaths. "Well, it was just a movie. I mean afterward Dandy was there."

"Yes, he was. But in my mind, it was all mixed up. For days and days, all mixed up. You see, for me he wasn't Dandy. He was God. And I made love with him and I killed him. For a long time after that I had bad dreams about this. I couldn't forgive Max." Tears had gathered in her eyes. Embarrassed, she brushed them away. "It isn't

311

worth hurting people like that just to make a movie. And the movie never got made anyway, did it? Because how could they show something like that?"

I was more than a little ashamed to have put her through so great a personal ordeal. I waited until she had calmed herself before I asked, "This ritual Castle had you act out—do you know anything about it? What it meant, where he got it from?"

She wagged her head. "Max didn't tell me anything, just to do it. He didn't say so, but I think it was very religious for him. He wanted it done just so, very particular. Me and Dandy, he wanted us to take it serious. I think maybe it was something you shouldn't put in a movie."

"And the pill," I asked. "Do you have any idea what it was?"

She shook her head. "Max had so many pills. For movies, for *bhoga*, for good times. Some he used to get from the twins, the Reinkings. Those were for religious things, I think."

With my taxi waiting at the canal side outside her house, I took a final glance at my notes. At the bottom of the last page I had scribbled "BBB—?" It provided a pleasant note to end on. "That tune—do you know why Castle chose it?" When she failed to understand, I hummed a few bars of "Bye Bye Blackbird."

She smiled. "Ah! It was a favorite song with Max. He was always whistling it. He said he could sing it in fifteen languages. You know the words?" I said I didn't, at least not well. She tried to recall them for me. "Very sad it is. Something . . . something . . . nobody loves me, nobody understands me. Like so?"

"Something like that," I said.

"Max said it was very old, from ancient times."

"I don't believe so."

"He said so. He said it came from the time of the pharaoh."

"Oh come now. Surely not."

We were on her front stoop now, exchanging a good-bye kiss. "Well, Max was a great kidder. You couldn't believe half what he said. Could be he was kidding with Dandy and me in the movie." She thought that one over and wagged her head. "But I don't think so."

Theodore Roszak

18 DR. BYX

The orphanage was a squat stone bastion in the Old Town sector of Zurich west of the river. Even on a bright summer day and framed against the magnificence of the ice-bright Alps, it darkened its neighborhood like some skulking carrion bird. Its cheerless walls seemed stained with more than the grime of years. The streaks left by centuries of rain along its stones might have been made by tears shed from its windows which looked for all the world like eyes darkened with despair. I thought how effectively Castle might have used the world headquarters of the Orphans of the Storm for one of his patented exercises in Gothic atmospherics.

A plaque in the entrance hall informed me in three modern languages plus Latin that I was in one of the oldest surviving structures in the city, dating back to the dawn of the Reformation, when it was built—originally as a school—by the great Swiss Protestant leader Zwingli. The orphans had taken over the site in 1739, adding a few more wings and dedicating it to the service of "the light that shines in the darkness and is comprehended not." In the French, German, and Italian, the plaque left this final phrase in Latin, a language in which I had little proficiency. But I had plenty of time to work it out. Though I'd phoned ahead for an appointment with one Dr. Byx, the chief administrator of the order, I was left to spend over an hour in the chill and gloom of the foyer.

All the while I sat waiting on a stiff wooden bench, black-robed men and women bustled across the floor, eyeing me inhospitably. Their garb suggested they were clerics, but of no order I could identify. Not that I was an authority on religious vestments. Still, I was convinced the costume was more austere than any Catholic monastic dress I'd ever seen. It featured a tight black bonnet that covered the hair, making the men—all clean-shaven—difficult to distinguish from the women. At the cheeks, a high starched white collar blinkered the eyes so that those who looked toward me seemed to be peering surreptitiously around a corner. I remembered Olga had told me the

313

orphans weren't Catholics. "Older than Catholics." Wasn't that what she had said? But what was older than Catholics? Weren't Catholics as old as Christianity got?

That the orphans were Christians I had no doubt. Their emblem—the Maltese cross—had been worked into all the leaded windows and interior decor. A massive version of the cross hung suspended from the ceiling above the door that opened into the central corridor. But this cross had a variation. Where the arms intersected, there was a circled logo. After some study, I concluded that it was the letter A overlapped at its crossbar by the letter X. AX. Which meant nothing to me. I found myself wishing I knew something more about basic religious history. My Sunday-school education in Modesto had been satisfied with teaching me that everything outside the boundaries of Free Methodism was a wilderness strewn with idolatry and popishness. Where, then, did a Christian church older than the Catholic fit in?

Orphanage though this was, I saw no children in any of the halls or rooms I casually inspected while I waited. Then, glancing down from one of the lobby's narrow, fortresslike windows, I spotted a line of kids, about twenty of them, being led double file across a bare, gravel-covered yard by one of the nuns . . . or was it a priest? The children wore uniforms every bit as somber as the clerics', once again with high collars and bonnets. The boys wore knee pants and the girls skirts; below that, long black stockings ending in black, high-topped shoes. The children, rigidly erect, marched in orderly columns, looking neither left nor right, hands folded prayerfully at their waists. My heart went out to them, poor, cheerless little things. They might have been workhouse urchins from a Dickens novel.

As I watched them trudging away toward a rear building, I heard a voice at my shoulder. "Dr. Byx will see you now." It was the nun who had met me at the door more than an hour before. Sister Leonine she'd called herself. A young woman, perhaps quite pretty, but cheated of her good looks by the expressionless mask she had made of her face. Without another word she led me down one of the gloomy halls to a well-appointed but no less gloomy office.

Dr. Byx, a smallish, round-faced man of about fifty, was almost totally bald. His eyes, heavily lidded, gave the impression of chronic boredom. He was dressed less severely than the others: a simple black business suit and dark turtleneck sweater. He wore a necklace bearing the Maltese cross. When I entered his office, a narrow, high-

Theodore Roszak

ceilinged room lined with books and heavily shadowed even in the
bright early-afternoon light, he greeted me with a curt nod and not
very welcoming gaze. I wondered which of the three Swiss languages
he might expect me to speak, but his English was perfect.

"Professor Gates, won't you have a seat?" The invitation was coolly
formal, leading to a long silence. How much did I need to explain?

"I'm a film scholar . . . motion pictures. History, theory. From
California. The university. At Los Angeles. The University of
Cali—"

"UCLA," he volunteered. "Not to be confused with the University
at Berkeley, or at many other locations around the state." He was
showing off, but I smiled gratefully for his help. "Nor with Harvard,"
he added. The cool look that accompanied the remark suggested a
put-down. My smile tightened but held.

"I'm studying the films of Max Castle," I continued. "Von Kastell . . . who was, I believe, raised in one of your orphanages."

He responded with the faintest of nods. "Yes. And?"

"I'm interested in learning about Castle's early years . . . in the
orphanage. I thought perhaps you might have some records. . . ." I
rummaged nervously through my briefcase, but before I could come
up with my MOMA monograph to offer him, he'd picked a copy of
the publication from his desk and set it out before me.

"We know something of your work, Professor Gates. Good, sub-
stantial scholarship." He must have noticed my surprise at seeing the
volume in his hand. "We have a rather good library of film studies,"
he explained. "But I fail to see why you would find Herr Kastell's
years with us of any relevance to your work. It is a long way from
the orphanage to his career in the United States. What connection
could there be?"

"Well, he did learn something about filmmaking at the orphanage,
didn't he? In any case, early influences are always worth considering
in any artist's work."

"Early influences . . ." He repeated the phrase as if it had been
spoken in a language that required translation.

"Things he learned at your schools—about your religion, for example."

I felt as if I'd succeeded in lowering the temperature of the room
by ten degrees. Dr. Byx's already cool tone turned frosty. "Do you
know much about our faith?"

"No, not really. I was hoping . . ."

"May I ask if you have a religious profession of your own?"

"Well, no, not currently."

"Not currently." He gave the phrase a sardonic twist. "But you were perhaps raised in a religious belief."

"Yes, I was. My parents were Methodists."

"Methodists." He pondered the word like some indigestible tidbit, a gourmet palate sampling McDonald's latest creation. "And would you say your scholarship is therefore under the influence of Methodism?"

"Oh hardly. Not at all." I couldn't even imagine what a Methodist influence might be.

"So you see," he continued, "just as you have grown away from the faith in which you were raised, so Max Kastell grew away from his childhood religion. You would do better to look for the influence of Fritz Lang or Josef Von Sternberg on his films."

"But I understood that members of the church, orphans like himself, were always with him while he worked in Hollywood."

"Oh?"

"Are you familiar with the Reinking brothers?"

"Brothers?"

"I believe they were brothers. Well, they were twins in any case. Film editors. They assisted on all of Castle's . . ."

"Yes, yes, yes. I knew them quite well. They taught at this school for a time after the war. But of course, like the Reinkings, many of our alumni worked in films—and not only with Kastell."

"Well, I know he stayed in touch with one of your orphanages in southern California. I believe it's in the mountains north of the city—isn't it?"

Dr. Byx pointedly offered me no more exact location. "In touch, perhaps. But how cordially? That is another matter."

"He did try to raise money from your church, I know that."

"And did he succeed?"

"Well, that I don't know."

Dr. Byx raised his hands in a gesture that implied he'd proved his point. "After a time, Professor Gates, Herr Kastell had very little interest in our church beyond money. Yes, he approached us many times. I cannot say how often he was given some stipend or loan or on what terms. You understand this would have been before my tenure in this office. Our order seeks to be generous with its alumni. Herr Kastell may indeed have taken our money from time to time.

But that is a very different matter from staying loyal to the faith. Consider all the great Renaissance artists who accepted the patronage of the popes. How many of them were obedient sons of the church?"

All I seemed to be learning from Dr. Byx was that the Orphans of the Storm took little pride in Max Castle and retained no fond memories of the man. Still, I pressed on. "Is there any chance that some of his schoolwork . . . papers, essays, drawings, anything, might have been stored away? I might gain some insight into . . ."

He shook his head emphatically. "Herr Kastell attended our school in Dessau, which was totally destroyed in the war. Its records would have been lost along with everything else, sad to say."

I realized I had one bit of information that might be of interest to Dr. Byx. "Actually, a film of Castle's was salvaged from Dessau after the war . . . by the American army."

For the first time, his eyes brightened with attention. "Oh?"

"*Judas Everyman*. It's mentioned in my monograph."

"Ah yes," he said, idly flipping through my little book. "So that is where you found the film. Strictly speaking, one might say that it is the property of our church."

I hadn't expected that. "Well, I suppose we'd have to regard it as part of the fortunes of war." He answered only with a lifted eyebrow. "I don't believe the film was ever released."

"In fact, it was banned, was it not?"

"Yet it contains many unusual effects. A powerful work. Have you ever seen it?"

"No, no."

An idea was taking shape in my thoughts. "You know, I could have the film copied for you. Maybe it would be of interest to your students."

I could see he was drawn by the suggestion. "That would be very good of you. We would of course be willing to defray the costs."

To my relief, I began to feel as if I were at last something more than a nuisance to Dr. Byx. But how much further could I presume upon his time? There was so much more I felt I wanted to learn about this bizarre institution I was in, yet I couldn't think of what to ask. The things that came most readily to mind—questions about the treatment of the children, their discipline, punishments, rewards—seemed impolitic. Others—about ancient heresies—I found it beyond my capacity to formulate. I had the sense that in dealing with Dr. Byx, I was talking—or struggling to talk—across long, dusty centuries to someone for whom the age of the Crusades or the primitive Christian church was still a lively topic. Finally, for the lack of any better way to prolong my visit, I asked, "Might I see some more of your school?"

He seemed surprised by the request. Glancing ostentatiously at his watch, he agreed. "Why, yes, of course . . . if it would interest you. I believe I can spare a short time."

He led me on the brief tour himself, offering little more than minimal identification of the rooms and facilities along the way. Mainly there were classrooms where small groups of somber students sat at desks while one of the priests or nuns conducted the lesson. There was a good-sized though dismal library, a gymnasium, a few science labs that seemed quite well-equipped.

After perhaps an hour, we arrived at a lower level of the main building. Dr. Byx opened a door and ushered me into a brightly lit, freshly painted room that had been recently renovated. If I didn't know a thing or two about the orphans, I would have been astonished by what I saw: row upon row of worktables, and on each a moviola. Several children were working with maximum concentration at the equipment, many of them with obvious great competence. Suddenly the medieval solemnity of the orphanage had given way to the hubbub of a modern trade school.

Dr. Byx allowed me to wander through the room, stopping here and there to observe students at work. He seemed curious to register my responses to what I saw. The children carried on at their chores almost oblivious to my presence. Each was scrutinizing a film on the moviola, running it fast, slow, stopping at certain frames, taking notes. A few were being shown how to cut and splice. We paused beside a table where a girl of perhaps sixteen was intently studying a film, flicking it along frame by frame. The images were those of a man and woman swimming. She ran some thirty seconds of the movie, then rewound and played the sequence through again and then again. Since she didn't seem to mind, I bent closer to the moviola screen and suddenly recognized a face. It was Joel McCrea, the film star. He was cavorting in the water with . . . I stared at the screen again. What was her name . . . ? Ah yes. Dolores Del Rio.

"I know that movie," I announced to Dr. Byx. "It's . . ." But I couldn't recall the title.

Dr. Byx turned to the girl at the machine, questioning her in German. *"Der Paradiesvögel,"* she answered.

"*Bird of Paradise*," he told me.

"Oh yes." I'd seen the film years ago on late-night television, an old Hollywood romance of the islands. A totally undistinguished film. I wondered why the girl should be studying material like this so attentively.

"Hardly a classic," I commented tactfully.

"You must understand," Dr. Byx answered, "our emphasis here is on the technical aspect of film. Also we draw as often as possible upon the work of our own graduates for instructional purposes."

"One of your students worked on this film?"

"Many years ago. Before my time. In this case, the lighting as well as the editing, I would guess."

"Do you mean that if I looked up the credits on this movie I'd find the names of your alumni there?"

Dr. Byx assumed a dubious expression. "Possibly. But also, perhaps not. Often, in the studios, during this early period—especially in America—it was difficult to say who worked on the technical elements of a film. Many times our students went unrecognized for their efforts. In this case, the underwater swimming sequence is rather highly regarded by our teachers. Technically speaking, it is something of a 'classic.'"

I stared again at the moviola screen. Over and over again the girl at the controls was watching Joel McCrea dive and swim out from under the keel of a boat, finally catching Dolores Del Rio in his arms. Then the two splashed and laughed and swam offscreen. As I looked, the scene did seem to take on a certain mesmeric effect. It was the water. It lit the little screen with stripes and spangles of light that were distinctly reminiscent. I'd seen Max Castle use water like that in more than a few of his movies.

When I looked up, Dr. Byx was wearing a small, wry smile. "It has a certain quality, don't you find?"

I turned back to the girl at the moviola, still hard at work, unmindful of my presence. Now she'd taken out an instrument and was holding it to her eye. With it, she was studying the film as it passed in slow motion. I recognized the instrument at once, though it was somewhat different from the one I'd used in Zip Lipsky's screening room: longer and made of some form of plastic, clearly a new product.

"That's a sallyrand, isn't it?" I asked. I could see Dr. Byx didn't understand the term. "The viewing device . . ."

He gave me a surprised look. "You've seen one of these elsewhere?"

"Max Castle's old cameraman had one. He let me use it."

"He still has it?"

"He's dead now. I don't know what became of the sallyrand. I gather that's not its proper name."

"We call it an anamorphic multifilter. It allows a more complex analysis of the light. It is one of our own inventions."

"May I . . . ?" I asked the girl at the moviola, reaching out to take the sallyrand from her. She looked up at Dr. Byx, seeking permission. He deliberated, then nodded yes, but first leaned forward to work the moviola.

"Let me adjust this for you," he said. Quite expertly, he speeded the film forward several seconds. "There. You may find this of interest."

He had moved the film beyond the encounter of Joel McCrea and Dolores Del Rio that the girl had been studying. That left me to wonder what he had elected to pass over before letting me apply the sallyrand. What I saw when I looked was an image with which I was very familiar: Max Castle's vortex of light, the all-consuming maelstrom that sucked everything on the screen down into darkness. As impressive as the effect was, I felt certain I'd missed something earlier. In the grammar of Castle's subliminal techniques, the whirlpool always punctuated the end of a run of images, finishing with a mood of intense depression or anxiety. In "adjusting" the film for me, Dr. Byx had raced by the material I might most have wanted to see.

"Very clever," I said after observing several seconds of the movie. I returned the sallyrand to the girl. "Have you ever considered making your multifilter available commercially?"

Dr. Byx laughed off the suggestion. "Such a primitive little toy! I'm sure no professional filmmaker would find it of value. It is for us a teaching device, nothing more."

"Would you be willing to sell me one?" I asked.

I could see him groping for an excuse to say no. "Just now . . . they are in short supply. We have too few for our own students. But I will keep your request in mind." He wasn't even trying to do a good job of fibbing.

We stopped at the door for one last look back across the room.

"It's so unusual for an orphanage to teach filmmaking," I commented, hoping to draw out some further explanation of this remarkable scene.

"And yet, why not?" Dr. Byx responded. "In the past, orphanages always sought to teach their children useful trades. Carpentry, shoe-making, tailoring. In the modern world, filmmaking is a trade at which our pupils can expect to find employment in many parts of the world."

"I wasn't criticizing," I hastened to add. "In fact, I think it's ad-mirable that you give your students the chance to do creative work."

"Creative? I'm afraid not really so. As I have said, we limit our training to the technical side of cinema. Lighting, cinematography, editing. Especially editing. And, lately, special effects. We expect there will always be a job market for these skills."

"But Max Castle was a director."

"True. But that was a long while ago. You see, in those early days, one could have no idea that directing would ever become something more than a technical function. At first, the director was no more exalted a figure than the cameraman. Very soon, however, thanks to men like your Mr. Griffith, he took on a larger, more artistic role."

"But what's wrong with artistry?"

He answered with a weary sigh. "With artistry comes temperament. And with temperament comes unpredictability. It is not easy to con-trol temperamental people."

"You want to control your students—even when they're out in the world on their own?"

Dr. Byx gave me a long, blank look. I felt he'd said more than he intended. He corrected himself. "Only in the sense that we wish to remain proud of our students' efforts. We want them to respect the highest standards. A man like Herr Kastell . . . he can become quite erratic."

"So you no longer train directors?"

"Not for some time—mainly due to our experience with Herr Kas-tell. But the question has been under discussion now for many years. Perhaps one day again . . ."

As we left the film-editing lab, we passed a door with a small window in it. Through it, I saw a darkened room; the bright shaft of a projector beam cut through the blackness toward a screen I couldn't see. I asked Dr. Byx if I might go in. He weighed the request. "Do you speak German?" he asked.

"No."

"You may not find it very illuminating then. However . . ."

He led me to another door that opened into a projection booth where one of the priests was working the machines. There was a small auditorium out front where perhaps a few dozen students were sitting.

A lecture was in progress. I could follow none of it, but I recognized the movie that was its subject. Performing in jittery, stop-frame slow motion on the screen before me were little Shirley Temple and Bill "Bojangles" Robinson. The excerpt was from *The Littlest Rebel*, a scene frequently reproduced in film histories and on movie posters, an enduring Hollywood icon. Clare, no Shirley Temple fan, had once shown it at The Classic as part of a tribute to Robinson, accompanying the screening with an essay on what even the best black talent had to put up with at the hands of the studios. Without music, Robinson and Shirley pranced up a short flight of stairs, turned, and tap-danced back down. Then the screen went dark, and the sequence, which had been looped in the projector, began again. As in the moviola room, this seemingly inconsequential scene, perhaps a minute long at regular speed, was being studied in fine-grained detail. The priest who was lecturing was pointing to areas of the screen where I could see nothing of special importance. At his direction, the projectionist would from time to time brighten the image or take it almost to total dark.

I did notice, as these transformations took place, that there was an interplay of light and shadow in the background of the shot that shifted across the figures of Shirley and Bojangles; it seemed to counterpoint the juxtaposition of the fair white child and the old black man. The crucial point in the sequence was apparently the moment when the two performers turned at the top of the stairs and started back down. This few seconds of film was shown over and over, with the priest briskly underscoring its importance. As my eyes grew accustomed to the dark, I could see a few of the students scrutinizing the screen through sallyrands. But even without the aid of the instrument, after four or five frame-by-frame repetitions I became aware of something unusual . . . a descending shadow between the girl and the man. It fell across a bright highlight on Bill Robinson's shiny dark brow and then seemed to curl oddly toward Shirley.

Experienced as I was in Max Castle's subliminal techniques, I flashed on this as the sort of effect he might have engineered in one of his films—or allowed to be placed there by the Reinking twins. Of course, without much closer study, I couldn't tell what might be concealed in the images I was watching, but clearly these students were being taught the same craft that Castle had learned two generations ago in his days at the orphanage. And one more thing. As so often when I viewed Castle's work, I felt a subtle unease coming over me, a distaste that utterly undermined the intended innocence and good humor of the movie I saw before me. It was a queasiness that I would never have associated with the likes of Shirley Temple.

I bent toward Dr. Byx and asked in a low voice, "Was this film also worked on by some of your alumni?"

"Yes."

"Another classic moment, I gather."

He smiled back at me. "If one knows what to look for." I had the distinct sense that he was toying with me, trying to discover how I reacted to the few examples of classroom instruction he had allowed me to observe. Dr. Byx had no idea how much more I knew about Max Castle's subliminal methods than I revealed in the writing he'd seen. Was he attempting to find out?

When we left the screening room, I asked, as casually as possible, "Are you familiar with a French film scholar named Victor Saint-Cyr?"

"Oh yes. He has also been studying Kastell's work lately. I have a paper of his. Very typically French. So arid, so geometrical."

"I had a visit with him in Paris a few weeks ago. It was very instructive."

Dr. Byx nodded. "No doubt. These days, film is studied so closely by so many experts. Who would ever have predicted that? It is really no longer possible to have one's little secrets."

"The *Unenthüllte*. Is that what you mean?" The word didn't register with him, or at least he didn't let it show. "I believe that's what Castle called it. The Unrevealed."

"Ah, I see. Very like Kastell to lay it on so thick. If you have read M. Saint-Cyr's paper, you know that his *Unenthülltin* were nothing more than so many optical illusions. Perhaps M. Saint-Cyr analyzed a few of these for you."

"He did. And there were some others I'd already managed to uncover myself."

"Then you recognized what our students were learning just now. A little exercise with split lighting."

"Oh yes. Castle used it extensively. He learned these techniques at the orphanage, then?"

"Some of them, yes. And some we learned from him after he had left us. As the technology developed, he was able to find new devices. A clever man. Better than many of our editors. He would return from time to time to instruct our faculty—usually expecting to be well paid for his lessons. At that time, such methods were known only to our school. That is why I referred to them as 'secrets.' But now . . ."

"Even now, I don't believe most filmmakers know these techniques."

He shrugged. "If not now, soon. It is only a matter of time. We no longer believe there is any point in trying to keep these tricks to ourselves."

"Is that all they really are in your eyes? Tricks?"

He turned the question back on me. "But what else? Little devices to enhance a shot, spice up the story. All rather childish, don't you think?"

We were making our way back to Dr. Byx's office. Along the way, we passed a bulletin board in one of the corridors. On it, among several other notices, was a mimeographed sheet listing movies scheduled on the weekends for the next few months. There were German, French, Indian, and Japanese films. I could identify none of them, except a few of the French selections. Louis Feuillade's old silent serials—*Fantômas* and *Les Vampires*—caught my eye at once. Hardly great stuff, but rare. I recalled that Clare had once tried to track these items down and had come up empty-handed. As I ran my eye down the page, I was impressed that all the movies I saw there seemed to be of the same grubby quality, titles that suggested thrillers, melodramas, low comedies. The American entries were no exception. Four Ritz Brothers movies. I knew two of them: *One in a Million* and *The Gorilla*. Clare had once run them at The Classic, only to decide they weren't worth unearthing.

"More work by your alumni?" I asked Dr. Byx as I drew his attention to the film series.

"Yes, for the most part," he answered casually.

"Louis Feuillade? That goes back a long way, doesn't it?"

"Not Feuillade himself. Perhaps some of his assistants."

"And the Ritz Brothers?"

"There is some interesting work with the ice in the skating film."

He meant *One in a Million*, a Sonja Henie clunker from the later thirties. "Ice, water, glass," I observed, "Max Castle also made the most of them."

Dr. Byx smiled back. "Vehicles of light."

There was only one piece of distinguished architecture on the grounds: the school chapel. Though it was as brooding as the rest of the school, it had a softer Romanesque texture. Dr. Byx would have passed it by, but I politely insisted on stopping for a quick look. Again glancing at his watch, he agreed, but with a note of undisguised impatience.

From outside, the church had seemed a vast, unlit cavern. But as we passed through its imposing stone portal, I very nearly flinched back, thinking the building might be on fire. The interior was alive with dancing shadows. They swirled and spun over the walls and ceiling. It was a spectacular effect produced by the simplest of means. All along the walls were rows of little votive candles. Balanced above each flame was a delicate black metal carousel, its circumference cut open and peeled back at intervals to form a circle of protruding fins. As the fins caught the rising heat of the candles, they gave the carousel a gentle turn, splashing the interior with a dizzy choreography of dark and light. The effect was so distracting I nearly overlooked the artwork that decorated the chapel. There were stained-glass windows and a series of bas-reliefs along the side aisles. Peering more closely through the pulsing darkness, I saw that the work had a single theme. It portrayed atrocities of the most gruesome kind: burnings, beheadings, crucifixions, impalings. Pausing beneath a window that depicted a jarringly graphic disemboweling, I hazarded to comment, "How very grim for a school."

"The martyrs of our church," Dr. Byx explained, but would say no more. The only work in the chapel that dealt with something besides bloodshed was a large wall mural behind the altar table. I moved in on this as soon as I caught sight of it. Like everything else in the building, the picture took on an eerie animation in the flickering candlelight.

In the center foreground, the mural presented three bearded old men kneeling in prayer, eyes elevated. At the top of the picture hovered a dark, haloed bird spreading its wings protectively above the men. Rays of light arrowed down from the bird's breast, striking each man on the forehead. Between the bird and the men, a woman floated in midair. Her body was covered at all the strategic locations by a gauzy veil, but even so seemed too sensuously explicit for a religious painting. In her right hand raised high and pointed toward the bird was a gleaming sword with a bloody heart impaled upon it.

The painting was darkened with age, and in the dancing light of the chapel many of its details were obscured. But what I could see was enough. Not thinking twice, I blurted out, "I've seen this before."

Dr. Byx lifted a skeptical eyebrow. "I don't think so. We have never permitted it to be reproduced."

"But I have. Max Castle made a sketch of this picture before he died. I have it in my office at school. He wanted to use this scene in *The Maltese Falcon.*"

"Indeed!" Dr. Byx's voice took on an edge. "How could he possibly do that?"

"I'm really not sure. I think he intended to introduce it as part of a flashback. I know for certain that he tried to interest the director, John Huston, in restaging the picture in the movie. Huston didn't like the idea."

"A wise choice on Mr. Huston's part. What relevance could this work of art have to a tawdry detective story?"

"Perhaps it had to do with the bird. It is a falcon, isn't it?"

Dr. Byx gave a tight-lipped reply. "A raven. An emblem of our faith."

He was clearly trying to draw me away and out of the chapel, but I stayed put studying the picture. "Who are the three men?"

"Three saints of our church."

"Would I know their names?"

"I doubt it. They are known as the Survivor Saints. The central figure is St. Arnaud."

I admitted I didn't recognize the name. Examining the mural more closely, I now saw that it was hardly as tranquil a scene as I'd at first thought. Like the rest of the artwork in the chapel, it too contained elements of violence and suffering. The three saints were posed against a turbulent background of storm-lashed mountains and valleys. The landscape had the dark, convulsive quality of an El Greco canvas. Not as well done, but as disturbing. There was lightning overhead and in the distance I could discern what I took to be tiny representations of towns, about a score of them scattered through the jagged mountains, all in flames with people streaming from their gates. Men on horseback pursued them with sword and fire.

I wanted to know more about the scene, but I could feel Dr. Byx's impatience at my back like a physical pressure. It told me my time was limited. I selected the question I most wished to ask. "And the woman? Who is she?"

He sighed wearily. "It would really take too long to explain the iconography of our faith to you, Professor Gates. If I were to tell you she symbolizes Sophia, the divine wisdom, would you find that satisfactory?"

"And the sword?"

"The blade of gnosis, as deadly as it is enlightening."

I failed to catch that one, but, having nothing to lose at this point, I risked an impertinence. "What would it symbolize if the woman and the bird were shown"—I quickly sorted through my inventory of euphemisms—"in sexual congress?" When Dr. Byx seemed not to understand, I added, "Making love."

He sneered with strong distaste. "I have no idea what you are talking about. Did Herr Kastell make such a sketch?"

"No, no. I have the impression I've seen such a picture . . . somewhere."

"If you have, it would be quite sacrilegious." The tone of offense in his voice was meant to be emphatic and final. He turned and walked off; I followed, judging it would be wise not to mention Olga Tell's account of *Heart of Darkness*, in which I was certain Castle had cast her as the figure called Sophia, lacking the veil but with the sword spectacularly employed.

A brisk five-minute walk and we were back in Dr. Byx's office. He had only one matter to settle before he bade me good-bye. He wished to make arrangements for having Castle's *Judas* copied and sent. He made it clear that this was the return he expected for having escorted me through the school. I was quite willing to offer the film, but I lingered over the details as long as I could. Before leaving, I was determined to find out more about the Orphans of the Storm, their history, their teachings—above all their fascination with the art of film. My questions, I knew, would be ham-handed, but at this point, with my departure only minutes away, I was prepared to blunder ahead.

I began gingerly. "I hope you understand that I'm curious about your church. I've been told it isn't Catholic . . . exactly . . ."

Dr. Byx returned an inquisitive stare. "Told by whom?"

"An actress friend of mine. Olga Tell. I believe she contributes rather generously to your orphanage in The Hague."

"Ah yes, Fräulein Tell. We are most grateful to her. She is correct. We are not Catholic."

Since he clearly intended to add nothing more, I put out another soft feeler. "Protestant, then?"

He gave me a mildly chastising look. "Those are not the only possibilities. Our church predates these later and lesser divisions of the faith."

Another pause. Another feeler. "But you *are* Christian?"

That brought a note of marked irritation into his voice. "Most certainly." ·

"I'm sorry," I quickly apologized. "It's just that I know so little about religion."

He fixed me with a firm, intimidating gaze. "That is obvious enough, Professor. It is why I am reluctant to speak with you about our beliefs. The modern intellect has lost its receptivity for religious discourse. Consequently, these matters are easily misunderstood. You see, theology is a subtle science. Its nuances and shadings require a trained mind to be fully appreciated. For example, if I were to tell you that our church preceded the Christian revelation, what would you make of that, I wonder? Could there be a Christian church *before* Christ, a state of grace *before* the Mystery of Golgotha? Ah, but perhaps that is what guarantees the purity of our doctrine. That we— our forebears—were primed to hear the gospel when at last it arrived. We were the ear prepared, the eye made ready. As you see, we have here what is surely a paradox. Truly Christian because *older* than Christian. How can we expect this to be understood?"

"Yes . . . I see. I think I . . ."

He could see that his answer was more than I was able to take in, but he continued without waiting for my response, still holding me with his eyes. "There is another reason for my reticence. You come to us out of your interest in Max Kastell. I assure you we would be quite willing to offer you whatever information we might have about his early years, if such material still existed. As I have told you, it does not. Still, it would be a great mistake to associate Kastell's later aesthetic work with our religious teachings, though I'm sure you are tempted to do this. But believe me, Herr Kastell very rapidly grew away from our faith, especially after he traveled to your Hollywood. He then became part of another, more worldly, cultural milieu. As was perhaps inevitable. We continue to respect his craftsmanship as a filmmaker. This is why I will so value having the copy of *Judas Jedermann* that you offer. But I would not be eager to see the content of Kastell's films connected with our doctrines. That would be most improper."

"Are your doctrines . . . secret? I mean, would you prefer that I not ask . . . ?"

"Secret?" He lingered judiciously over the word. "I would prefer to say . . . veiled. Yes, veiled, as you saw that the person of Sophia was veiled in the blessed mural. As one might veil a precious manuscript to protect it from the deleterious effects of the sunlight. We are not a proselytizing order, Professor. We do not even seek scholarly study. There are subjects which can be as distorted by well-meaning objectivity as by outright prejudice."

I felt myself blushing defensively under his steady gaze. "I assure you, Doctor, I would want to treat your teachings with the utmost respect."

Again he continued as if I hadn't spoken. "Fortunately, because of its very materialism, the age we live in is a latitudinarian one. So it is no longer necessary, as it once was, to keep one's beliefs 'secret.' Indeed, secrecy might only draw more prying eyes. In this democratic age, everything must be in full public view, isn't that so? Even though the public scarcely understands a fraction of what it presumes it has the right to inspect. If I were to tell you that we are Katari, I wonder if you would appreciate what secrecy once meant to us and why, even now, we prefer to remain veiled."

"Katari . . ." I almost went on to ask him to spell the word for me.

He searched my face closely. "I assume the name means little to you."

I felt the blood burning in my cheeks. I'd never felt so stupid in my life. "I believe I remember something . . . well, quite honestly . . . no, I . . ." And then it clicked in my mind. He was using the word in the plural and giving it its Latin pronunciation. Katari. He meant Cathars, the heretics against whom Father Rosenzweig had fulminated so wildly in his frenzied little pamphlet. Like someone begging for an intellectual crutch, I asked "Do you mean Cathars?"

He nodded condescendingly. "Cathars, yes."

Of course I knew nearly nothing about Katari even when they were called Cathars. I was way out of my depth and floundering. But one point stuck in my recollection, something that might explain Dr. Byx's reticence. Trying to angle the question as tactfully as possible, I asked, "Weren't they once regarded as heretics? In the Middle Ages, that is. The Templars got involved with them, I recall."

"Regarded as heretics by *whom*?" he asked back stiffly.

"By the church."

"The Church of *Rome*, you mean." He made the correction as if its enormous significance should come down on me like ten tons of bricks. "And we are so regarded still. Heresy does not simply fade away with time. Once a heretic, always a heretic. The brand endures. In the medieval period, that brand was literal. Here!" He pointed to his forehead so forcefully that I almost saw a flame sear his flesh where his finger pressed at his brow, pressed, held, and twisted. "Those who were not burned—*burned alive*—were marked on the brow for life. Mainly these were children, branded with the mark of Cain. Outcasts condemned to wander the roads of a persecuting world. Most of these would have starved, or been beaten to death by angry folk along the way."

There was a rising intensity in his voice that sent a shiver along my bones. He related the fate of these distant believers as if their suffering might have happened just yesterday. As he spoke, the images we had seen in the chapel—tortured and broken bodies, faces twisted with anguish—rose in my memory. Seeking to assuage his indignation, I feebly offered the thought, "Well, fortunately the church—the Church of Rome—no longer persecutes you."

Dr. Byx snapped back with bitter amusement. "It is in no position to do so. Not in Switzerland. Not in Holland, the United States . . . indeed, nowhere. It has lost the power, that is all that has changed."

"But we do live in a more tolerant time," I added.

"A society that does not take religion seriously does not take heresy seriously. We, of course, in our turn, regard the Church of Rome as no less heretical. In the modern world, these doctrinal disputes go on in other forms and by other means. They do not go away, Professor."

He'd at last managed to make me uncomfortable enough to want to leave. Perhaps that had been the objective of his mild, but unsettling outburst. "I don't want to keep you much longer," I said. "But there is so much more I feel I need to learn. Can you recommend a few books I might read on your sect?" The word was no sooner out of my mouth than I realized my mistake.

"Sect?" Dr. Byx's eyes flashed at me, then went ice cold.

"Church, I mean."

He took a deep breath, clearly attempting forbearance. "There are many merely scholarly works on the Cathars. The subject has a certain sensational appeal, the bloodletting and all." He waved his hand toward the bookshelves around us. "Here you see some. I will be frank with you, Professor Gates. I recommend none of these works, not one. Their superficiality is almost indecent. Every one of them is filled with gross distortions. Of course, you are perfectly free to visit any library and take home an armful of such books, read them and flatter yourself that you have learned something about our faith. You will be wrong. If anything, your ignorance will have been supplemented with numerous misconceptions."

He was about to leave me dangling in an intellectual vacuum. "But what would you suggest I do, then, if I wish to learn about your church?"

He leveled his most piercing stare of the afternoon at me. "Because one can ask a question does not mean one will be capable of understanding the answer. You would do our faith a great courtesy and spare yourself great professional embarrassment if you simply put your curiosity to sleep. Pursue your film studies, Professor. Treat your Mr. Castle as what he was—a maker of sometimes clever, often banal, little movies, momentary entertainments for the ignorant millions. I assure you there is no need to implicate our church in your work."

We exchanged a few more words about *Judas Everyman*, which I promised to send as soon as I could have it copied, and I was soon out the door of the orphanage. And, I assumed, out of Dr. Byx's thoughts. I gave the grim old building one last look as my taxi turned away. More than ever its facade resembled a sorrowful, untrusting face gazing after me with guarded eyes. I was leaving without having learned more than a fraction of what I wanted to know.

On the plane back to California, I pondered where my research stood on the strange case of Max Castle. As I did so, I felt like a man working at a jigsaw puzzle. I'd collected a lot of pieces and fitted them together. But the picture they composed was a Martian landscape; I couldn't make head or tail of it even when it all lay before me assembled. What the picture lacked was something that still lay outside its frame. A motivation. I had no idea why Castle and the orphans were making movies. What were they up to with their secret cinematic techniques? And did Castle and his church share the same agenda? Or were they, as Dr. Byx seemed to imply, working at cross purposes?

There was only one way I could think of finding an answer. I would have to make a date with Shirley Temple.

19 SLEAZE AT THE RITZ

And meanwhile, back on Fairfax Avenue, in the basement of the abandoned Ritz Theater between Moishe's Deli and Best Buy Yard Goods—not very far from Hollywood—strange and fateful things were happening.

Once Clare had taken off for New York, and once I'd begun to feather a comfortable academic nest for myself, I would have thought The Classic was out of her life and mine forever, a relic of humble beginnings. For me, the grubby little hole-in-the-wall picture house would always be a sentimental souvenir of first love and intellectual awakening. But Clare, tough-minded as ever, nursed no such fond memories as she prepared to make her getaway. For her, The Classic represented too many years of privation and undeserved obscurity. She was only too happy to bid it good riddance. Her final gesture said it all; she simply gave the place away, making a free gift to Sharkey of her controlling share in the theater, no strings attached, no thanks expected.

As she was at pains to explain, I shouldn't mistake this for an act of generosity; it was euthanasia, the neatest way she could think of to kill off this basket case of a business, avoiding all legal and financial complications. With the weight of Sharkey's bombed-out ineptitude added to its ever-increasing backlog of unpaid bills, she fully expected to see the theater sink out of sight in a matter of weeks. I was sure she was right. But I couldn't help feeling sorry for poor Sharkey, who accepted her offer with the eagerness of a starved dog that has been cast a moldy table scrap. "You won't regret this," he hastened to assure her the last time they met to sign the few miserable papers the transaction required. She gave a contemptuous chuckle as she scribbled her name here and there, not even bothering to correct his misguided gratitude. For Clare, the regrets were all in the past; they attached to Sharkey and to the debt-ridden dump she was bequeathing him where she'd watched herself going bankrupt in spirit as well as finances. She was signing the theater's death warrant and enjoying it.

After Clare's departure, I continued to drop by The Classic to catch the occasional program, as much out of lingering loyalty as any interest in the films. It never failed to tug at my heart to see the hand-lettered placard Sharkey had proudly displayed in the seldom-washed glass case beside the entrance, where it would remain for years to come growing more dusty and faded: "Under New Management." Each time I came by, I was prepared to find the program canceled, the doors closed—perhaps permanently—by that new management.

But that never happened. Much to my surprise, Sharkey's new role in life as proprietor of a terminally ill business worked like some miraculous tonic on him. He more or less sobered up and more or less buckled down, at least sufficiently so to drag into the theater each day, never missing a show, and to struggle through all his managerial duties with enough application to keep the projectors alight and churning. He even added a popcorn machine to the refreshment stand in the lobby, something he had (unsuccessfully) badgered Clare to do for years.

Somehow, as if by magic, he kept coming up with last-minute cash to pay the more pressing bills. When he screwed up, which was often, he could usually joke his way out of the ensuing mess. On his own, and with his dope ration voluntarily cut back by half, he proved to have a kind of loony charm that won him favors and reprieves when he needed them. Now and then he succeeded in talking me into lending a hand in the projection booth or scouting out a film he wanted. Maybe he seemed too vulnerable for even the meanest creditors and distributors to come down on hard. People who knew the old Sharkey had the sense they were helping to build the new, improved Sharkey. And they were. So they made allowances, granted concessions, and the good old Classic just kept rolling along.

All very heartwarming. But when it came to programming—which was the artistic heart of the matter—Sharkey was making it harder and harder for me to justify my continued patronage. Liberated from Clare's "tyranny of good taste" (as he called it) his own bizarre and vulgar predilections quickly asserted themselves. Within a year, he'd converted The Classic into a grind house that showed anything likely to draw an audience, provided the films were cheap and easy to come by. Sharkey still ran art films and the old Hollywood standbys. Every year there was still a Bogart Festival, maybe a few aging New Wave favorites, but these were being steadily crowded out by movies Clare would have refused to show at gunpoint. There was a new species of teenage atrocity film flooding the drive-in circuit, vile little shockers with titles like *Blood Feast* and *She-Devils on Wheels;* Sharkey ran as many of them as he could rent. And there were skin flicks, whose once pulpy core was rapidly hardening into full-frontal gynecological flagrancy.

We were in the later stages of that long forced march into the slough of permissiveness that we remember as "the sixties." The barriers of censorship were crumbling with astonishing speed, and with them the standards of taste. Sharkey was gleefully in the van-guard of the movement. He challenged the authorities to bust him for staging the Los Angeles premiere of Bill Osco's *Virgin Nymph* and again for daring to show *Mondo Trasho.* His defiance went un-requited. The cops were now turning a blind eye, as he well knew. Emboldened by such malign neglect, Sharkey wasn't above running a program of beaver loops in tandem with some old back-lot titillaters like *Sex Maniac* or *Secrets of a Model,* billing the program as "Amer-ican Erotica," as if the fancy title might lend the trash a touch of class.

In time, when Sharkey had prospered sufficiently to leave such items behind him—but hadn't—we had a not-very-coherent talk about the matter, the only kind of talk you could ever have with Sharkey. Why was he still showing stuff like this, I asked with clear disapproval.

"Hey, man, it's a public service. What we're doing is running a how-to, free-for-all, why-not sex-education crusade."

"Oh come on! You don't believe that."

"Damn tootin' I do. We're blazing trails here. You know why it is you can take a nice middle-class chick to a legit house to see *Deep Throat?* It's 'cause the old Classic showed the way."

"And you really think this is a good thing?"

"Wait and see, pal. Another couple years, the men of this country are finally gonna be gettin' some first-class fellation."

Even when Sharkey wasn't wading in the muck, most of what I found playing at The Classic when I checked the listings was just plain awful. Evidence, so I assumed, of the new owner's essential and surely lethal incompetence. *King Kong, Mighty Joe Young,* and *Godzilla* had become staple items. So too the Three Stooges, their films sometimes running in twelve-hour marathons through an entire weekend, a nonstop banquet of witless gags, pratfalls, and the two-fingers-in-the-eyes. There were Scott-Brown westerns in profusion and Wild Bill Elliott retrospectives. Old Saturday serials—all fifteen episodes of *Flash Gordon*, *The Green Hornet*, and *Batman* spliced together for continuous screening—were also a dependable big draw. Even more so were clunky prewar exploitation flicks like *Wild Weed*, *Cocaine Fiends*, *Reefer Madness*. From somewhere in the clammy depths of his distributor's vault, Sharkey had salvaged this celluloid sludge, offering it up as "Vice Squad Week at The Classic." And, oh God! it was just as bad as the titles told you it would be. On what was for Sharkey the more serious side, The Classic organized America's first Radiation Film Festival, movies featuring such monstrosities of the atomic age as fifty-foot women and cockroaches the size of boxcars. This he considered to be a political gesture.

Now this wasn't the kind of fare a respectable professor of film history like myself would want to be caught dead viewing. Which is not to say that, in my capacity as Sharkey's old projection-booth buddy, I didn't come around to sample what he was offering. I was always welcome to walk in free; Sharkey liked having me around the place. He even invited me to resume doing program notes, a feature that had dropped out of sight soon after Clare left. "Program notes?" I scoffed. "For Larry, Curly, and Moe?"

"You're just the man for the job," said Sharkey. I knew he meant it as a compliment, but I let him see me wince.

At first, I gave Sharkey—and myself—the benefit of the doubt when it came to finding some redeeming value in The Classic's new orientation. If I tried hard enough, I could just barely imagine a certain nostalgic justification for dredging up these sub-zilch items. This was, after all, part, a big part, of what Hollywood had offered as entertainment to the generation of kids I belonged to—the film equivalent of comic books. That was something to ponder, wasn't it, if only to bemoan the way our tender young minds had been brutally warped by the likes of a Samuel Z. Arkoff with his *Dragstrip Girls* and *Teenage Werewolves?* And maybe, just maybe, one could see the "clap operas" that were one of Sharkey's prime fascinations—U.S. Army sex and hygiene movies from World War II—as marginally significant social documents. But when we reached the "World's Worst Actress Olympics"—the films of Maria Montez, Vera Hruba Ralston, Adele Jergens—I had to face the fact that Sharkey was drilling a hole through the bottom of the barrel.

I made all the allowances I could for such nearly sadistic trash-mongering. I tried to see it as a belated, childish slap at Clare, at the smug high standards she had used for so long to beat the poor guy over the head. But the perversity of what he was doing went farther than that. Registering his howls of delight as I sat beside him through as much of a Rosemary LaPlanche triple bill as I could stomach (about twenty minutes of *Devil Bat's Daughter,* the first installment of the terrible trilogy), I realized that the man sincerely, authentically enjoyed the stuff he was showing. More troubling still, he wasn't alone. He had company. Lots of it. That came as a surprise. The Classic was prospering on such slop. Each time I dropped by, there was a capacity crowd, even after Sharkey had knocked out a wall and expanded his moldy subterranean auditorium by another twenty rows. Kids mainly—college age, even high school, a raucous assemblage of barely housebroken adolescents who showed up to hoot their way through the show. The crummier the movie, the more they enjoyed it. They liked bad movies. They *loved* bad movies. They relished the low-down imbecility. They might horse around a lot in the theater and burn enough dope to overload The Classic's feeble ventilating system (everybody in the theater wound up sharing the smoke) but they also paid attention to the movies. Close attention, wringing every smug and nasty giggle they could from the pitiful stuff on the screen, waiting to see it again, loitering over the incompetence and inanity, the way a scholar might linger over the fine points of Chaucer or Milton. They were veritable connoisseurs of crap.

The movies Sharkey showed were bad enough to hurt; but his audience hurt more. It worried me. Its laughter had bitterness in it and often cruelty. Sitting among them was like being in a mob that had gathered in the street to throw stones at cripples. I put off facing up to that fact in any very decisive way until the day Sharkey called me up with big news. He'd found a nearly complete version of one of the old Jungle Girl serials. *Nylana and the Cobra Cult.* "Got everything except episodes ten and thirteen. And get this! There are outtakes! Somebody at Republic saved them. Nylana falling out of her leopard skin. Hey, wow!" He was exuberant. And he had a bright idea. "How's about you get on the blower to old Franny Lipsky and ask her to come out for the big opening? You know where she's holed up, don't you?"

"Sharkey, why would she want to do anything like that?"

"She'd do it for you, sure she would. For old times' sake. Hey, tell you what. How about we help her out with the plane fare?"

"We?"

"Well, you'd like to see the old gal again, wouldn't you?"

"Sharkey, this is a really bum idea. *Nylana* is junk. Even Franny knew that. There's just no good reason to put it back on the screen."

"Come on, Jonny! People'll love it. And with the real Kay Allison right there in person as guest of honor—what a gas! Believe me, she's gonna be right up there with the biggies. Buster Crabbe and Charlie Middleton. A classic."

"A trash classic, you mean."

"What else?"

"So you want her to come flying out to your fleapit of a theater so she can watch her boobs bouncing while the audience gives her the big razz. Don't you see how cruel that is?"

He seemed genuinely shocked by the suggestion, even hurt. "Oh, you got it all wrong, amigo. She's a gem. The audience'll love her. She'd get a kick out of it, betcha anything. It's all in good fun."

He wheedled and pleaded, but I wasn't budging. Nothing doing, I insisted, finally hanging up on him. I wouldn't even tell him that I owned episodes ten and thirteen of *Nylana and the Cobra Cult*, part of Franny's going-away present to me. Sharkey ran the serial anyway without Franny's participation. And sure enough: within the next year, after he circulated the film, the Jungle Girl was making it big on the grind-house circuit.

I decided I had to have a long, searching talk with Sharkey, but it wasn't easy to pin him down. While he'd shaped up enormously since taking over The Classic, he was still a breezy, boozy guy who liked to affect a strung-out style even when he was reasonably lucid. I might have taken him as the clown he made himself out to be and brushed him off, but something Clare had told me shortly before she left stuck in my mind. "Don't let Sharkey fool you," she had said. "He may act like a boob. That's because he is a boob. But *that's* because he *believes* in being a boob. Boobiness is a cause with him. He doesn't talk it, he lives it, he thrives on it. Bad taste, sleaze, tackiness. Sharkey is part of something that's been lurking out there along the fringes, and not just among film freaks. Have you seen the comic books the kids are reading? I don't know what to call it, but it's pathological. If it ever gets out of control, God help us all. Of course, if you could ever get Sharkey to talk about it, he'd say he was just having fun. Fun! Beware of people who come bearing fun. Fun is the virus."

Eventually, I did get a shot at an at least semiserious conversation with Sharkey. It came about a week before I was scheduled to take charge of the Castle retrospective at the Museum of Modern Art. Sharkey insisted on giving me a send-off party. Though I gave him no reason to believe I agreed with him, he insisted on seeing *my* success as *our* success, his and mine, something we shared as workers in a common cause. It wasn't much of a party, just a group of us getting together over pastrami and beer and surreptitious joints at Moishe's after the last show. The guests included the usual small band of old Classic regulars, along with some of the kids who helped Sharkey keep the theater perking along—about as many of us as could squeeze into a few booths at the back of the deli.

We spent an hour or two goofing off and kidding around, but that evening's movie had provided me with just the right talking point, so I wasn't going to let the opportunity slip away. It was an absolute atrocity called *Plan Nine from Outer Space*. The movie happened to be Bela Lugosi's last bow; somewhere in the middle of the filming, he had died. That might have lent the picture some barely minimal historical interest for those who cared about whatever became of Bela. But that wasn't why Sharkey was showing it. He was billing it as "The Worst Movie Ever Made," a claim that wasn't likely to be challenged in our lifetime. The production values were actually below those of home movies, the story a mindless improvisation. It was filmmaking at the imbecile level. But it played regularly at The Classic about a half-dozen times a year, always to uproarious full houses.

"*Seriously* now, Sharkey," I began, using the word gingerly, "why are you showing this horror?"

"Because why not?" Sharkey answered, as I might have expected. He inhabited a world where "why not" had long ago replaced "why" as life's great question.

"Because, for one thing," I went on, "it's so damn painful to watch."

"Only if you fight it, pal. See, you're fighting it. Don't fight it."

"I'm not fighting it, Sharkey. I'm just seeing it for what it is. It's garbage. I'd have to fight *not* to see that."

"Yeah, but it's fun. Come on, Jonny, what's wrong with having a little fun?"

I decided not to quote Clare at that point. Mentioning her name was the fastest way to turn Sharkey off. "But don't you see? Mocking—that's all these dopey kids out there in the audience care about. They come to mock. They come to give everything the horse laugh. Stuff like this makes movies ridiculous."

"So what are movies? Sacred or something? Hey, man, this is *your* audience here. These are Maxie Castle's people. Don't knock 'em."

I was waiting for that, because maybe this was what worried me most about Sharkey and his audience. The Classic was at that point one of about a dozen little art and repertory film houses around the country where Max Castle's movies—the whole, uncut originals as Zip Lipsky had preserved them—were playing regularly, gaining a new, youthful following. That was one reason I'd kept up my friendship with Sharkey. In some measure, he'd helped me revive Castle's work and that was adding feathers to my professional hat. I owed him for the favor. Even so, after their first few screenings at The Classic, I found I couldn't come around again when Castle's films were being shown. I was afraid to find out what these movies might mean to an audience that was every bit as eager to watch Captain Marvel kick the Scorpion in the pants.

"Look, Sharkey, Castle isn't junk. That's the whole point. That's why I care about him. I'm trying to show what he's got to offer. Good stuff. Craft. Imagination. Originality. *Plan Nine, Reefer Madness,* all this crud you're showing—it's really awful. There's nothing there. It's just bad, and you know it. With Castle, I'm working in the other direction. I'm trying to pull him out of the garbage can because he doesn't belong there. *Plan Nine* does. In fact, by now it should be landfill. Buried. Out of sight. Gone forever."

By this hour of the evening, Sharkey was just about ready to melt into the cloud of unknowing. But I could tell he was mulling over my protest. His answer, when it came, was a surprise; it sounded like the product of thought. "Lemme give you the inside word here, pal. *Bad is okay.* That's the theory we're working from. Bad is *better* than okay. *Bad is best.* Because bad opens up a space, you understand? It gives things a chance to grow. Listen, it's like in Charlie Chaplin."

"What d'you mean?"

"See, there's the little tramp, right? And there's the big cop. And the cop keeps all the time knocking on the little tramp's ears. Because what right has the little tramp got even to be alive? He's scum, right? So keep him in the gutter, right? You know who the cop is? *Quality* is the cop. The censor. The worst censor. Worse than the sex censor, the politics censor. Quality is the killer. Know why? Cuz it's got Shakespeare Power, and Einstein Power, and Rembrandt Power. That's heavy, man. I mean, after old Will Shakespeare said it all, who's got the nerve to open up his stupid mouth even? So, see, first thing is—you gotta knock off quality. Otherwise, the little tramp never gets his chance. So which side are you on, brother? Which side are you on? The cop or the tramp?"

For Sharkey, this was an astonishingly well-connected answer. It amounted to an aesthetic theory, a vindication of crap culture. I felt almost ashamed to question what he was saying after he'd gone to the trouble of putting so many words together in a speechlike order. But I didn't like what I was hearing, not one little bit. Damned if I didn't feel called upon to defend Taste, Reason, and Civilization. Right there in the back booth of Moishe's Kosher Deli.

"But where do you draw the line, Sharkey?" I asked. "If bad is okay because bad is fun, what're we saying? Anything goes? That worries me. These kids . . ." And there they were, these kids, maybe a half dozen of them crowding around us in our booth like little savages watching this strange thing that was happening—somebody taking something seriously. "They don't know there's quality in the first place. They just want to wallow in the garbage can. They like it in there, can't you see? You show them the World's Worst Movie, it's a big giggle. But did they ever see the World's Best Movie? If we throw out the quality, what happens to civilization?"

The words were no sooner out of my mouth than it came down on me like the bucket of paint that Olsen might rig up to dump on Johnson: a sense of infinite silliness. Here was old Sharkey sinking rapidly under the waves, gazing at me with eyes that seemed to be peering up through three feet of water. And draped around him on all sides were these half-stoned kids giving me a collective subchimpanzee stare. Why was I talking to these people about civilization? They were the barbarians at the gate. Clare was right. Thump them hard, heap them with scorn, kick them out the door. And no apologies. Because there was no little tramp to feel sorry for; there was Charlie Chaplin *playing* the tramp, a rare piece of artistic make-believe, quality all the way through. But Sharkey was trying to stay in touch, he was really trying. He gave his quarter-inch joint a deep, wheezy suck, passed it over his shoulder to the fifteen-year-old behind him, and nodded gravely. "Heavy, man. That's a heavy question." Then, grinning, "Looks like we're gonna have to call in Charlton Heston to guard the fort. Hey, how about that, boys and girls? A Charlton Heston Festival."

And all the boys and girls shouted, "Yeah!"

That night got a lot of things together for me. I realized I wasn't really arguing with Sharkey; I was arguing with myself. I could see so clearly that I should have signed off on The Classic and its trash-loving audience a long time ago. So why hadn't I?

There was one reason I kept coming back to. It had to do with another kind of attraction that was taking up more and more space at Sharkey's picture show. Ever since the *Venetian Magenta* affair, and in spite of everything Clare could do to fight free of the association, The Classic had become the chief West Coast outlet for underground films. Chipsey Goldenstone was willing to spend lavishly to keep that connection alive and well advertised in the public eye year-round, and not just for the length of a two-week festival once a year. Now that Clare was off the scene, Chipsey was nicely positioned to get his way. All the more easily when he became Sharkey's principal means of support, the one deep pocket where Sharkey could look for help when the bills came due. From that point on, whatever Chipsey put on film, Sharkey was sure to show. Maldoror Productions, as Chipsey was then styling himself, were just as awful as ever—mindless, tasteless, nauseatingly prurient—but no more so than the cinematic solid waste Sharkey was importing from the New York underground. In fact, compared to most of what passed for highly touted avant-garde film in those days, Chipsey's work sometimes looked almost well made. He could at least afford decent equipment and fresh film stock.

I inherited all of Clare's reservations about the New American Cinema, but not her capacity for dogged resistance. I could plainly see how overblown these excruciatingly amateurish efforts were. Still, I came to see them all, and to see them again and again. I came to see the bikers' orgy and the gang-bang rape. I came to see six hours of an obscure New York poet sleeping (though, having gotten the idea, I left less than halfway through, leaving only the potheads to finish the course). I came to see the funny fat transvestite eat the puppy dog's turd. I came for the barely visible eight-millimeter eyesores shot by coked-up necrophiliacs on their fire escapes and by seventeen-year-old sadomasochists in their basements. I came for the items Sharkey frankly and lovingly billed as "an evening of dog vomit and sewer gas."

Why? Just keeping up with the latest, I told myself. Part of my professional responsibility. But that was transparently a lie. Because the "latest" had so rapidly grown tiresomely old and was going precisely nowhere. Always the same repertory of smirking perversions and mind-blown improvisation. So why did I sit there for all those hours at The Classic, letting the banality of *The Chelsea Girls* and the mucky fantasies of *Pink Flamingos* wash over me? Fortunately, it wasn't because I'd lost the will to shake myself free and return to the world of judgment and difficult choice; I was attracted, not addicted. But attracted by what? When I finally forced myself to face that question, I realized I was *savoring* the sleaze, letting it cast its spell over me, the seductive sloth that comes of letting the mind mellow out and just having "fun." In another sense, then, I *was* keeping up with the latest. I was watching all the standards crumble before my eyes, all the limits vanish, flirting with the experience of surrender that belongs to the defining terror of my time, the era when human beings confabulate with their own annihilation. So why not, why not, why not?

After my talk with Sharkey that night, feeling more vulnerable than ever, I took off for my assignment at the Museum of Modern Art like the sick man who flees to the spa in search of healing waters. I buried myself in the Max Castle Retrospective, relishing my chance to play the Quality Cop. Even the worst of Castle's productions was fine art compared to the vile and tacky fare on which I'd been too generously feeding. Not that I couldn't have found the same abominations in New York, even more plentifully available. The cult film and midnight-movie trade had originated there; it was holed up all over the city in scruffy little lofts and derelict theaters. The big guns of the underground were mounted in Greenwich Village and Soho.

Resolutely, I stayed away from the plague zone, spending my spare hours in the museum's film archives, saturating myself with Renoir and Bergman, Kurosawa and Kobayashi, masters of the craft. I stayed close to film buffs and scholars, people who served the same high standards Clare had taught me. My time away from The Classic was a purgation and renewal of the senses. It sustained me until my trip to Europe to see Saint-Cyr and Olga. And that in turn extended my period of abstention, so that, by the time I returned to Los Angeles to complete my research on Castle, I felt certain I'd broken the habit of cinematic slumming. I had. But what I didn't foresee was that the sleaze was about to leave the slums and come looking for me.

Theodore Roszak

For some time Sharkey had been making vague noises about "moving upstairs." He meant renovating and reopening the old Ritz Theater. I never listened too closely: this was a vintage dream that I assumed would forever remain out of his reach. True, The Classic was doing better business than ever before; it was making more money in a week on Jujubes and Pepsi-Cola alone than Clare had ever made on a month of art films. But Sharkey was earning in the little hundreds; rebuilding the Ritz was an idea that would cost in the big thousands. Even when I saw the evidence of workmen on the premises, I shook my head in disbelief. I remained convinced that Sharkey would never be able to afford more than a minor renovation. Otherwise he was biting off more than he could chew. I wouldn't have put that past him; he was capable of major financial folly.

What I failed to take into account was Chipsey.

As his reputation in the underground grew, Chipsey began to feel the need of a more fitting showcase for Maldoror Productions. The Goldstein millions were more than adequate to the task; in fact, Chipsey had money to burn. Once the family fortune—much disputed by envious relations after Old Ira's death—had run the gauntlet of seemingly endless litigation and had passed more or less intact into Chipsey's eager grasp, it was his to do with as he pleased. And it pleased him to get his work out of the grungy dungeon. When I returned from Europe, I found The Classic "Closed for Renovation." The entire building spent most of the next year wrapped in a cocoon of canvas and scaffolding. What emerged from the metamorphosis was a true picture palace of yesteryear, an Art Deco monument. Within its spacious interior, the crummy old Classic sank to the status of a storage basement—and even in that lowly capacity looked more humanly accommodating than the moldy crypt I'd first entered . . . was it fifteen years before?

The Ritz Classic was given an exuberant gala opening and deserved it. The theater turned out to be everything that rumors in the newspapers had been promising, a veritable luxury liner dry-docked on Fairfax Avenue. There was carpeting and upholstery, fiesta-colored linoleum floors, Bakelite furniture, and chrome trim galore. The murals on ceiling and walls were restored, revealing whimsical mock-epic scenes of the Muses presiding over the glories of the Jazz Age. Those who could decipher the images when the light of the magnificent frosted glass and sculptured tin chandelier came up found depictions of Paul Whiteman conducting an orchestra of thousands, a

Roxy chorus line that stretched to the stars, Amos and Andy, Rudy Vallee, and the Cliquot Club Eskimos broadcasting to the world via the new network microphones.

And of course there was, stretched from end to end across the ceiling, a heroic montage of movie iconography. Directors in berets and knickers shouting through megaphones, cameramen with rolled-up sleeves and turned-about caps hand-grinding their machines, the caricatured likenesses of John Barrymore, Rudolph Valentino, Mary Pickford, Al Jolson. Even the mighty Wurlitzer was resurrected, gleaming magnificently with lights of a hundred colors. A sprightly old guy named Bertie McGee, who had played at the Chinese and the Pantages during the Golden Age, came in on the weekends wearing a full tux and spats to warm up the audience with medleys of "Singin' in the Rain," "The Good Ship Lollipop," and "Forty-second Street." For someone whose work was touted to be twenty daring years ahead of its time, Chipsey had subsidized a remarkably respectful exercise in cultural archaeology.

But what got served up at the renovated Ritz was Sharkey's same old bill of fare. In fact, trash classics and undergrounders became more prominent than before, taking over the weekends and midnight shows when the theater drew its largest crowds. Sharkey knew his audience. And he knew his backer. "The Films of Chipsey Goldenstone" began to crop up all through the year as weekend retrospectives or a Thursday-night series. Everything Chipsey had ever photographed since junior high school was now on display—and always for a cheering audience of hangers-on and sycophants. New movies from Maldoror began to appear in assembly-line quantities, vying with the output of Andy Warhol's Film Factory in New York—which was also featured on Sharkey's programs.

Attending the Ritz Classic—and I was fast becoming a regular— was now a strangely disorienting experience. Disorienting because so effortless, so inviting, so *guiltless*. It had always struck me as wholly appropriate for underground cinema to make its home in Sharkey's wretched little basement; it belonged in those lower depths like a fungal growth. For shy types like me, it took some psyching up to buy a ticket and walk through the door. Like reaching into a tub full of scummy water. Once inside, you felt you had crossed a line, had left the normal and the respectable behind. Sitting there in the funky dark, your shoe soles sticking to the floor, your rump trying to find a level spot among the splintered slats you sat on, you knew where you were. At the bottom of the world.

But now the sleaze had, in more than one sense, moved upstairs. It had put on clean socks and combed its hair. It advertised its wares on a bright marquee. Its posters were out on the street for all to see. "*Venetian Magenta*. The *film maudit* of the century. Explicit! Outrageous! Unashamed! Children must be accompanied by an adult." You could watch these forbidden delights from an upholstered seat, eating popcorn glopped over with real butter. There were even ushers.

One day, in a high pitch of crusading defiance, Sharkey showed Andy Warhol's latest. *Fuck*. That was the title. There it was, the ultimate word, in lights on the marquee. In his now well-appointed office, Sharkey hunkered down, waiting for the law to strike, coking up, rehearsing his speech to the jury. The cops never arrived. But somebody else did. Moishe from the Deli came knocking at the door, looking sore. "Hey, Sharkey, where d'you get off stickin' that word up there? I got customers complainin'. Rabbi Weintraub, he calls me up, he wants to know what kind of element you are. What'm I gonna tell him? Gimme a break, huh?"

Cowed by his old pal's outrage, Sharkey retitled his program *Andy Warhol's F****.

"What the hell, Moishe's family," he explained to me later. "I wouldn't've done it for the cops, believe me."

"But the cops *didn't* care," I reminded him. "Nobody cares anymore—except Moishe. And he only cares because it's bad for business."

I remembered Clare's words. "If *it* ever gets out of control, God help us all!" But "it" *was* out of control—the assault on standards, the crusade against quality—not running amok, slashing and bashing like Attila the Hun, but writing best-selling books, making top-ten records, showing movies on Main Street. Blending in. Taking over. Smoothly. Linda Lovelace was making appearances on college campuses. Kenneth Anger had won a Ford Foundation grant. Chipsey Goldenstone was touring the talk shows.

The world was making it so very easy to have *fun*. But still not easy enough for Sharkey.

The Ritz had been in business for nearly a year when he called, asking me to drop by his office next time I was in the theater. He was, as he put it, "knocked up with a big idea."

"Trouble is," he told me when we met, "some of us regulars miss the old place."

"The old Classic? You're kidding."

"No, really, we do. It had a certain, I don't know . . . *feel*."

"It sure did. It's called terminal grubbiness."

"Yeah, but you know it was right for a certain kind of show. More intimate, you know. More culty. Upstairs is too mainstream."

"*The Texas Chainsaw Massacre* is mainstream?"

"I'm thinking maybe we could open a second screen, put the old downstairs back in operation, use it mainly for open screenings. What d'you think?"

Open screenings were Sharkey's special pride, regular weekend events to which aspiring "filmsmiths" (as Sharkey called them) brought their own work to show after the midnight movie for those who still weren't too stoned to watch. Sharkey had no shortage of takers for the opportunity; there was a waiting list weeks long of would-be Warhols and Goldenstones jostling one another to be screened at the Ritz. Most brought a single shabby, homemade eight-millimeter reel. Since none of this projected well in a space as large as the Ritz, people would usually work out of the orchestra pit, setting up their own cheesy equipment, struggling to beam a small, blurry square of light on the big Ritz screen, coordinating with a tape recorder if there was any sound at all. Most of what I'd seen from the open-screeners was a tackier version of the same campy clowning you saw in every underground movie: bad imitations of worthless originals. But Sharkey turned nobody away. He believed in what he was doing. He called it "participative film."

"We need some place different for the really far-out stuff," he went on. "Some place with that underground milieu. It would be exclusively for eight- and sixteen-millimeter shows. Got a great name for it. The Catacombs."

"Sounds exactly right. That's a cross between a morgue and a sewer." I didn't mention that I'd once thought of The Classic as a sort of catacombs. That was part of another adventure.

Sharkey looked hurt. "Hey, don't be so down on the idea. Give it a chance. Catacombs. Remember, that's where the chosen few hid out while the empire crumbled. And, sure enough, where something new got born out of the ruins, see what I mean?"

I saw what he meant, and all too clearly. " 'And what rough beast' . . ."

346

"Huh?"

"It's a poem, Sharkey.

> *And what rough beast, its hour come round at last,*
> *Slouches towards Bethlehem to be born?*

Something to chalk on the walls of your catacombs."

Sharkey gave me a grave, pondering squint. "Heavy, man. That's heavy."

It took Sharkey another two months to open his second front at the Ritz. The new downstairs was rather less dungeony than the old Classic; there was fresh paint and better ventilation; the seats, though a well-worn secondhand, were decent quality and bolted to the floor. It was more comfortable than it needed to be to catch on with the local underground. Soon the Catacombs was showing whole weekend evenings of do-it-yourself movies. Financially, the place was an absolute zero, most of the audience taking advantage of the house policy to admit friends of the filmmakers free. But Sharkey didn't care about that. The new screen was his chance to boost participative film. He was in his element, a slap-happy patron of the avant-garde.

And I turned out to be more of a prophet than I realized. For, with the catacombs supplied, the rough beast soon came knocking at the door. His name was Dunkle.

20 BLACK BIRD

"He's got pink eyes."

That was the second thing Sharkey told me about Simon Dunkle. The first thing was: "He's a genius. I discovered a genius." But that was less striking. Ever since the Catacombs had opened, Sharkey had been discovering geniuses at the rate of one a month, calling me up regularly to report the fact, always bubbling over with pride and

excitement. Discovering film geniuses was by now business as usual
for him. But this was the first one with . . .

"Pink eyes?"

"Yeah. Like a bunny rabbit. The kid's a genuine freak. What d'you
call that when you're pure fucking white, even when you're
black?"

"An albino?"

"Right. You ever meet an albino? Weird."

"And he's a genius besides."

"No question. Absolutely."

"Another eight-millimeter genius."

"Super eight. The kid works in Super eight. So help me. You gotta
see his work. You'll love it."

"I doubt it."

"Come on, Jonny, give it a chance."

"When I get the time."

"Tonight? He's running a couple things tonight."

"Not tonight."

"But you'll come. Promise. Soon."

"Yes, yes. When I get the time . . . no, not this week, maybe
next. . . . Sharkey, I'm busy. I have classes, I'm behind on my manuscript. . . . I'll see. . . . I'll try. . . ."

Sharkey knew I was putting him off, and he knew why. He knew
what I thought of the last several talents he'd discovered. I hadn't
pulled my punches with him. Upon returning from Europe, I'd served
notice; I intended to do my duty as Quality Cop. No more wallowing
in the fleshpots of fun. The Ritz might have installed upholstered
seats, but it was the same old grind house that Sharkey's Classic had
been; I'd vowed to protect myself from its corrupting airs.

But Sharkey refused to be offended or even mildly discouraged by
my resistance. Instead he took my evasiveness as a challenge, probably because I represented the ghost of Clare still haunting him. He'd
been happy enough to get her off his back; but he would have liked
to score a couple points with her. Getting her protégé to visit his
theater, maybe to offer a few approving words was as close as he
could come to that. But I wasn't making it easy. I'd disciplined myself.
One visit a month to the Ritz, maximum. Enough to stay in touch
with Sharkey's bizarre film world without, I hoped, suffering contam-
ination.

Theodore Roszak

Why go at all? Because my fascination for the sleaze and its audience, though strictly rationed, was as strong as ever and not to be denied. These were, as Sharkey never let me forget, Max Castle's people. His films were growing in popularity on the cult film and midnight-movie circuit, where they ran in constant tandem with the trash. In several cities, *Count Lazarus* and *Feast of the Undead* played every Saturday night to full houses of exuberant adolescents who had memorized the screenplay and could recite it back word perfect in chorus, a cinematic ritual that had started with *The Rocky Horror Show*. Around the country, kids were showing up at school costumed like the Count. Popularity like that had to mean something to me. There was a secret about movies waiting to be learned from this audience, but only at a distance. A secret to be learned about myself as well, that too at a distance, standing off from my own vulnerabilities, placing them under glass, studying them as in a clinic.

But even with all the detachment I could summon up, monitoring Sharkey's film scene was an ordeal by disgust. Notch by notch, the Ritz was sinking deeper into the mire. I would have found that hard to imagine a few years before. Watching a cult favorite like Jodorowsky's *El Topo*—it screened regularly once a month—I would have said *this* is the antipodean swamp, the absolute, godforsaken edge of the world. Mayhem, mutilation, rape, surrealistic sadism. Beyond this, nothing.

I was wrong. Beyond that swamp there lay another that was even more fetid, filled with stranger, more menacing, fauna. We were passing through an adolescent punk phase that seemed to have no lower limit. Kids were walking the streets wearing electric-blue Mohawks and swastika tattoos, bones in their noses, nails through their earlobes, hunting for still more outrageous fashions. At the rock clubs, performers dressed like the minions of Satan were biting the heads off live chickens, mice, bats. Only the SPCA seemed to object. When these groups took a name like Human Sacrifice, there was cause for alarm.

This wave of adolescent barbarism could hardly leave the movies untouched. Sharkey even boasted (correctly I think) that movies had led the way. First there were Splatter Films, then Sick Flicks, categories he'd long since come to treat as established genres. "Hell," he once commented after reading a hair-raising account of a balls-off-the-wall rock concert that featured simulations of dismemberment, "we were into that years ago. *Night of the Living Dead, The Wizard of Gore*. We're way ahead, way ahead."

"But what sort of competition is this?" I asked. "To see who's first swimming down the drain?"

"Credit where credit is due," Sharkey answered with a proud sniff. "I got stuff playing on my screens they could never even so much as try on a stage. They don't have the reality factor."

Sharkey was right about that. When it came to close-up, hard-focus revulsion, nothing could beat the movies. The most recent item I'd seen at the Ritz ended with the mother of a graphically raped daughter just as graphically castrating the villain with her teeth. On all sides, hoots of delighted approval from an audience of teenage troglodytes munching Big Macs and pizza.

Where did such fury come from? Such vindictive rage? Almost resentfully, I told myself: they don't have the *right* to go so ugly-nuts. They haven't *earned* it. That should be the privilege of age and much suffering.

Or was there, I wondered, some deeper human sensibility rising to the surface here, a thin-skinned, hair-trigger capacity for hurt that would no longer deny itself expression? If so, hurt by *what*? These weren't the casualties of atrocity and historic horror, of which there were many tending their scars with quiet dignity. These were pampered suburban school kids, for God's sake, seemingly unscathed in their enclaves of affluence. Hurt, then, by life itself. Cheated by the act of birth, striking out, hitting back. Was that possible?

True, these tacky little films were a fringe phenomenon. But new growth, including rot, starts at the fringe, working in, and these days traveling at a dizzy pace. No more than a few years after underground and sexploitation films had pioneered the way, major movies at first-run houses were featuring glossier versions of the same sadistic capers, ghoulishness, kinky sex, diabolical obsession. All of which, once it penetrated the mainstream cinema, was apt to be heralded by leading critics as a bold stroke, a daring innovation, a breakthrough. As if everyone, even the best and the brightest, were just waiting for the barriers to crumble.

And here I was at the poisoned source of it all. In this audience, I sensed I was close to some privileged vision into the troubled soul of the time, a truth with a twisted face. The experience took my thoughts back more than a dozen years to that time when movies still largely belonged to an adult culture and the quaint phrase "art film" still held a bright promise. Clare, who was the product and still the game champion of that era, had offered me one of my most memorable lessons in film criticism. It might have been a review of the movie I'd seen that day.

At the time I was still an impressionable undergraduate; in one of my film courses, we were using the famous shower-murder scene from Hitchcock's *Psycho* to learn some fundamentals of film editing. The movie was then Hitchcock's most recent release, and this shocking sequence had quickly been identified as a stunning technical tour de force. Enthusiastically, I reported to Clare how my instructor was deftly combing through the seventy—count them, seventy!—separate shots that compose the single sensational minute of film in which Janet Leigh is hacked to bloody ribbons in the tub. Clare greeted my report with a cold stare and total silence. The following week, she rented Hitchcock's *Strangers on a Train* and arranged to borrow a freeze-frame projector. Then she led me frame by frame through the tennis-match sequence at the end of the movie. She did this quite expertly, delineating the thematic contrast between the sunlit tennis court and the murderer's hand reaching down into the dark sewer.

I was deeply impressed by the analysis. Even so, I ventured to say that the effect in *Psycho* was better. Clare scoffed. With her typical perversity, she let me know she deplored the much-praised *Psycho* and insisted that *Strangers* was Hitchcock's last good movie before he turned psychotically self-indulgent.

"But more important than which film is better," she went on, "is your judgment, Jonny, about what you saw—or *think* you saw. Sure, *Psycho* is razzle-dazzle editing. But did your teacher also call it to your attention that *Psycho* is sick thrills? Never take your eye off the ball, lover. Otherwise, any clever mechanic with a moviola will sucker you in every time. This is a mighty medium. It lends itself to such abuse. Look, I show you a gorgeous sequence from *Strangers on a Train* that has just as much tension, plus elegance, plus symbolic overtones, plus *no* blood. But you tell me *Psycho* is better. Why? It's a crummy script, a contrived plot, badly paced, miserably constructed. So why do you think it's 'better'—*really* why? Admit it. You're a man, sitting here in the protective dark, watching a naked lady getting knifed in all her private parts. That's cliché porn, no matter how you slice it. Believe me, the guys who applaud such mayhem in the shower would be getting their rocks off if Hitchcock gave them the scene in one long take—in slow motion yet."

Exasperated, she made a dire prediction. "*Psycho* is the beginning of something very bad. Mark my words. In another few years, every sadistic nut in the film industry is going to be grinding out mad-slasher-helpless-female-victim flicks, served up with fancy editing. And the same types who are praising *Psycho* will be saluting what they see as 'film art.' Meanwhile, the women of the world will have to start walking the streets dressed in armor. And after that, it's going to be straight ahead into new frontiers of mayhem. I wouldn't be surprised if there comes a day when they hire disposable extras for guaranteed lethal stunts. Just remember, my dear, the pictures *move*—and that's a good trick. But either they move to tell the human truth or they're *just* a trick. Movement that excites without personal contact—that's a good definition of masturbation. And not caring how you fuck over the person you contact—that's the rape of the mind."

A month later, Sharkey was at me again, pressing me to pay a visit to the Catacombs. His pink-eyed genius would be on display that weekend. A retrospective screening yet.

"How old did you say he is?" I asked.

"Hard to tell with an albino. Sixteen, seventeen maybe."

"A retrospective for a sixteen-year-old?"

"He's been making movies since junior high school. Three, four years."

"That long?"

"Oh yeah. Like I said . . ."

". . . the kid's a genius, I know."

"Right. Like what's-his-name . . . Baudelaire. Just a kid, wasn't he?"

"You mean Rimbaud."

"Whoever. That's Dunky's category. Genius child."

"Sharkey, I'm not going to watch any movies made by someone when he was nine years old."

"Ease up, pal. He's one of your fans."

"Oh? How so?"

"He's read everything you've done on Castle. That's why he wants to meet you."

Well, that did cast a more favorable light on things. Even so, I might have held out indefinitely against Sharkey if it weren't for one respect in which I needed his help. My date with Shirley Temple.

I'd returned from Europe determined to investigate the only movies, other than those of Castle, which I could connect with orphan filmmakers. I had no trouble locating *The Littlest Rebel*. Sharkey had shown it and many another Shirley Temple opus at The Classic numerous times. The films played for laughs; their sticky-sweet cuteness and soppy innocence lapped over into the sort of campiness that Sharkey's audience of young cynics relished.

The Ritz Brothers, also on my list of must-see Orphans of the Storm classics, were another matter. Having become nobody's idea of a classic, not even Sharkey's, their films were harder to come by. As for *Bird of Paradise*, it took me six months to track the film down. It finally turned up in a sixteen-millimeter television print so butchered that I spent hours repairing it before it could be screened.

But there was something that proved more difficult than locating these films; that was explaining to my learned colleagues what my interest might be in such questionable materials. As they arrived at the Film Studies department, the canisters produced raised eyebrows and snide queries. Especially so when the Ritz Brothers' *Gorilla* turned up in the same delivery that brought one of the senior professors a print of *The Sorrow and the Pity*. The contrast elicited comments even from our department secretary. "Quite a double bill we have today," she said with pointed sarcasm. I brazened out the embarrassment with feeble explanations, but my courage failed me when it came to screening the films on campus. What if somebody walked in on me in the viewing room? How could I justify the sort of time-consuming, microscopic scrutiny I'd be giving this drivel?

So I turned to Sharkey, prevailing upon him to let me use the Ritz after hours. He was, as ever, compliant, asking no questions. Matters of taste simply didn't register with him.

What I found when I ran the films was the secret cinematic vocabulary I'd learned to look for in Castle's work. Without the benefit of a sallyrand, I could detect little more than surface indications of what lay beneath, but I now knew where to target my attention, and with the aid of a freeze-frame projector borrowed from my school, I was able to pick out the visual cues that marked the orphans' submerged motifs. It was a strenuous exercise that tired the eye, often producing a clanging headache. But after a time I realized, with some pride in the accomplishment, that the hundreds of hours I'd spent studying Max Castle had endowed me with a special facility, a sort of peripheral vision that allowed me to discern what others never consciously saw.

Sharkey, for example, who sat in on the first few *Bird of Paradise* screenings but whose eye wasn't attuned to traces of the *Unenthüllte*, had no idea what I was seeing even when I tried to guide him. Try as he would, he couldn't do more than catch an occasional blur, a suggestive highlight, a squirm of fleeting movement in the deep shadows.

"Tell me again, what're we lookin' at here, man?" he asked, peering, tilting his head this way and that.

"Secret movies," I answered in a hushed tone, trying to sound as mysterious as possible.

"Far out," Sharkey responded, also dropping his voice and squinting harder at the screen. "Where are these movies?"

I laid a finger to the center of my forehead. "You've got to have the mystic eye to see them."

He loved it. "Far out," he said again and after that asked no further questions.

Applying my mystic eye to *Bird of Paradise*, I found what I expected. The vortex effect that Dr. Byx had let me do no more than glimpse with the sallyrand focused on Dolores Del Rio as she swam from the ship; her lissome torso was subtly transformed by the play of light upon the waves into the funnel of an all-engulfing whirlpool, the cannibalizing vagina sucking her helpless lover into the dark, watery depths.

In *The Littlest Rebel*, the buried dimension of the film was more skillfully handled and with a more jolting result. It yielded ghostly images of a black man and a little blond girl, he a leering savage, she an innocent cherub being aggressively fondled. Where had the orphan filmmaker found his performers for a sequence as patently criminal as this? Once again, the association of sexuality with perversity and violation left a nasty taste—though surprisingly less so than in Castle's films, because here the hidden material had so little connection with the surface story, often none at all. This was especially the case in the Ritz Brothers' movies, zany comedies that lacked the macabre texture of Castle's thrillers. Even when the trick was expertly executed—as in *One in a Million* where Sonja Henie spins madly on glittering ice to create the secret sexual vortex—the effect is diminished. She is too bright and bouncy to match Castle's somberly seductive vampires. And the low-comic shtick that follows immediately shatters the mood.

So there was something to be said after all for Saint-Cyr's ideas about "layering." In Castle's movies, tales of terror, suffering, despair worked in tandem with the morbid imagery that moved beneath them. That was the advantage Castle enjoyed as a director over his fellow orphans, who had to connive their way into any cutting room that might be open to them. The whole work, cheap and cheesy as it usually was, was his to fashion. Yet, while the orphan filmmakers might not always equal Castle's power, there was no question but that their vision was every bit as bleak as his. Disowned or not, he was a loyal son of his strange, dour church.

Having begged so many favors from Sharkey, I finally gave in and agreed to visit the Catacombs toward the end of the next Simon Dunkle program to sample the kid's work.

The fact was, something more than gratitude drew me. Twice or three times within the past few months, students had lingered after the lecture in my Contemporary American Film course to ask what I thought of "this Dunkle guy." Who? At first I didn't connect with the name. Then they mentioned the Catacombs and I did. All I could do was apologize, saying I hadn't gotten around to seeing his stuff yet, but I was meaning to. Oh, I should, they told me, I *really* should. Because, oh wow, he was *really* far out. That did it. As a matter of professional pride, I made a point of never letting my students get too far ahead of me.

On the appointed evening, I spent the early hours upstairs at the Ritz suffering through an Andy Warhol double bill: his camped-up versions of *Dracula* and *Frankenstein*. I'd seen the first, not the second, which came in 3-D. I hated 3-D. I hated wearing the little cardboard-and-plastic goggles that never fit the bridge of my nose. The audience, however, was eating it up, yipping and squealing as it cringed back from the splatter and impaling effects. When we reached the scene in which the mad doctor disembowels his female monster, then uses the surgical orifice to have sex (explaining for the benefit of the philosophically minded that "You cannot understand death until you have fucked life in the gall bladder"), I slipped away, goggles and all. It was just past midnight.

I could hear the beat and amplified twanging of rock music from the Catacombs before I opened the fire door that connected it with the Ritz. I could also hear belly laughs and cheering. It sounded like a good-sized crowd. The hastily hand-lettered poster in the lobby gave a full rundown of "The Films of Simon Dunkle" that were being exhibited that evening, some half-dozen items, all of them, I supposed, single-reel eight-millimeter jobs. I ran through the titles, feeling relieved that I'd spared myself most of what I found listed by coming late. *Attack of the Skullsuckers, Insect Anxiety, Kinder-ghoulies* . . . Sharkey, apparently on the lookout for me, came bustling over. "Glad to see you, Jonny. You're just in time for the piece of resistance. World premiere of Dunky's first sixteen-millimeter production."

He pointed to the last title on the program. *Big Stuffer.* "A whole new genre," Sharkey announced portentously. "Barf *noir*. It's a classic."

The *premiere* of a *classic*. Only Sharkey's mind worked like that.

Sharkey gestured me toward the good old projection booth; we slipped in to watch the film from there. Not the most comfortable way to view a movie, but better than crowding into the theater below, which appeared to be packed to the walls. Kids everywhere, including what I took to be some horizontal pairs gyrating in the aisles.

I gave a nod to Gabe, the Catacombs' dirt-cheap projectionist. Gabe, a burned-out Vietnam vet who was a stiff-faced Buster Keaton lookalike, had become one of the resident attractions for the younger film crowd. Sharkey let him live in at the theater where, after the last show, he would drop some acid and spend most of the night running the same movie over and over: the psychedelic fourth section of *2001*. Gabe claimed it was the best turn-on movie ever made— next to *The Sound of Music*. He'd picked up a small following among the kids, several of whom would stay on after hours to offer him their stoned companionship. Not that anybody had to wait that long to get high at the Catacombs. Even here in the booth, the air was bracingly toasted with the aroma of pot. Gabe took the free smoke as a perk.

I'd come in on the middle of a gritty little film which, if I remembered the listing in the lobby, bore the uninviting title *American Fast Food Massacre*. Glancing at the washed-out, jiggling square of light on the screen, I saw at once that it was the usual amateur effort, the product of a single unsteady camera and lousy lighting. But I also noticed that there were cuts; the film had been edited. That was encouraging. So too the fact that there was camera work: close-ups, pans, a change of setups, all quite primitive yet planned. I could see, too, that the movement that filled the meager little patch of light, while wildly frenzied, was rehearsed and organized. In short, there was evidence of direction, a quality one didn't expect to find in the underground, where witless impulse ruled the scene. Turn the camera on and get your friends to horse around in front of it until the

356

Theodore Roszak

film runs out. A bit of slapstick or grab-ass, most of it sliding off camera or going out of focus, anything that avoided the appearance of the dreaded Hollywood decoupage. Unfortunately, the little film before me sported sound: the blasting rock music I'd heard through all intervening doors and walls, and now loud enough to stun the ears. It was low-grade stuff, poorly performed and miserably recorded—but that seemed to be the going standard of the style. Whether the music had anything to do with the film was impossible to tell; the lyrics were an indecipherable avalanche of animal babbling.

What was I watching? And why was the audience so riotously amused? The scene was a fast-food restaurant, the typical McDonald's. All that seemed to be happening is what usually happens in such places. People ordering, eating. Smiling kids on duty behind the counter serving it up. The close-ups, which came cruelly, distortingly close, producing huge noses and bulging cheeks, featured a run of zany adolescent faces clearly selected as a cast of moronic uglies. Pimply skin, crooked teeth in torturous braces, cockeyes behind heavy lenses. All of them were wearing absurdly big, stiff smiles. Then I saw: their mouths had been Scotch-taped into shape.

The customers were just as grotesque, especially the main group, a family—father, mother, four or five kids—all of whom were wearing pig-snout noses and packing the food away in porcine proportions. The action of the movie was made up rhythmically of fast-motion and normal sequences; the music speeded up to a runaway high pitch, then slowed to keep up with the visuals. I quickly got the joke of the piece; it was hardly subtle. As customers left through the exit still chewing on their last mouthful, they were waylaid by a couple of monstrous brutes in leather aprons and boots. They wore masks— the familiar smiley face—and "Have a Nice Day" buttons. The customers were poleaxed, dragged off, and tossed on tables in the kitchen where, now in fast motion, they—or the too-obvious dummies that had taken their place—were chopped, dissected, ground, and cooked. There was plenty of very real-looking gore spread around the kitchen, leavings that I assumed (or hoped) had been purchased from the butcher. Finally, the remnants were served up at the counter to new customers coming in the door who ordered from an overhead menu on which a kid precariously perched on a ladder was chalking the items shouted out to him from the kitchen. It was the sort of turn-green list that a high school imagination might invent. Handburgers. French-fried fingers. Brainballs.

The kids in the pig-family group kept demanding more and chasing back to the counter, where they jumped up and down until they got what they wanted. Sure enough, they returned with hands on a bun, fingers in a paper boat, other such ghoulish treats. In its up-close details, the film was a stomach-turner, no question. But it moved briskly and with great precision, so that, in spite of myself, I was beginning to find it satirically effective. A great American cannibal feast as Mack Sennett might have handled it if he lacked all inhibition. Nobody in the restaurant cared what they were being served, but wolfed down the recognizably human pieces and parts, eating and running, and getting chopped at the door. Meanwhile, at the cash register, the manager, played by a two-ton teenager wearing a Groucho nose and mustache, occupied himself counting scads of money. There was an accelerating slapstick choreography to the little film that made the blood-and-guts elements seem surrealistic, though still sardonically charged.

The ending was predictable enough and rather limp. The pig-family kids, who are insatiable, finally order a couple of handburgers too many. The kitchen has run short. The obnoxious little punks make a scene, throwing fits and rolling on the floor; the parents come running over to join in. The manager intervenes. He checks with the kids and, on their approval, calls in the two bloody brutes who proceed to chop the pig father and mother. The voracious kids cheer. In a jiffy, they are served a platterful of what goes on the menu as two new items: the Daddy-Mac and the Mommy-Mac. Kids rush in from all sides tugging their parents by the hand, demanding the goodies. The pig kids eat hearty, pat their bellies, grin with satisfaction. The brutes begin rounding up parents and leading them to the slaughter. Amidst mayhem in the kitchen, the film vanishes into an old-fashioned iris-out.

By the end of the movie I'd finally succeeded in deciphering some of the lyrics on the sound track. They were barked out in an aggressive growl by abrasively nasal voices.

> *Fast food, yeh, yeh, yeh*
> *Fast food, yeh, yeh, yeh*
> *Meat, meat, generic meat*
> *Meat, meat, s'all that I eat*
> *Don't care what kind, whatever I find*
> *Just gimme generic meat*

Fast food, yeh, yeh, yeh
Fast food, yeh, yeh, yeh
Can't lose my job, same as the mob
No time to chew, I'm tellin' you
Gotta shit on the run, ain't no fun
Ten-hour day, fuckin' bad pay
So what if I'm eatin' you
Fast food, yeh, yeh, yeh . . .

The little movie exhibited all sorts of cheap and amateurish flaws that would have made easy targets for criticism. For one thing, all the so-called actors playing adults were far too young for their roles, a cast of gawky, giggly teenagers. Also the camera work, though ambitious, was strictly substandard. Still, when the picture was over, I had to admit to Sharkey that it showed all the signs of talent working against the limits of a tight budget. My studies of Castle had taught me to be charitable about that, without necessarily conceding that more money meant better movies.

I could feel Sharkey waiting beside me for a comment. "Well, it's pretty gross," I said finally. "But the satire saves it, not that it isn't pretty heavy-handed."

"Satire?" Sharkey answered.

"Satire. It was meant to be a satire. The American family . . . McDonald's . . . have a nice day. What do you suppose everyone was laughing at?"

"Oh yeah, I see what you mean. It's got satire too. That's a groove. But the effects, what d'you think of the effects?"

"You mean the gore, the mayhem?"

"Yeah, that."

"I don't need it, Sharkey."

"But you see why he's catching on. The kid's really into it. And the music. Hey, what about that? Dunky gets all the primo groups. Crib Death, Virginkillers."

"Mostly I couldn't hear a word."

"No, no, it gets in through the pores. Those were the Stinks. Dunky got them together for his flicks."

"Am I supposed to know who the Stinks are?"

"The Extinction Now Boys Choir. They're hot, really hot. Strictly a class act."

Clearly, Sharkey and I hadn't been watching quite the same film. "This is one of his latest things?" I asked.

"This? No. He made this three, four years ago. When he was about thirteen."

"Well, for thirteen, what can I say? Shows promise. The Mack Sennett touches are clever. Does he always work for humor like this?"

"Mostly he does. But his best stuff is pure visual poetry. You gotta see *Insect Anxiety*. Oh, man. Just nothing but this kid pulling apart a cockroach. No, listen, I know how it sounds, but believe me, the way he handles it, it's a thing of beauty."

A couple of apprentice projectionists who looked none too bright had shambled in to help Gabe set up the next movie. On his own, Gabe was far from speedy; with two klutzy trainees assisting him, things slowed to a near stop. It took close to half an hour to get the film on the screen. Meanwhile, down below, the theater was rapidly becoming another Black Hole of Calcutta as more and more latecomers crushed in. The delay raised no complaint from this audience, which seemed to have settled into Sharkey's basement like its natural vermin, ready to spend the night cutting up. They were punky kids mainly, garbed in what passed that year for shattering bad taste. Fringed leather and clanging metal, burlap, shaggy furs, fluorescent hair, Day-Glo makeup. They looked like no human population. Yapping and whooping below me in the pit-dismal wattage of the Catacombs' one bare bulb of an intermission light, they might have been a scene out of Dante's *Inferno*. I was surveying the gathering hoping to spot our guest of honor. But how could I expect a mere albino to stand out in a crowd like this?

"Is Dunkle out there?" I asked.

"Hell no," Sharkey said. "Never goes out in public. Kid's practically a hermit, what with being a freak and all."

"But you've met him."

"Sure. Private audience." Sharkey gave me a smug wink.

"How do you mean?"

"I got driven up to this place of his. Classy limousine and all."

"What place? Where?"

"In the hills behind Zuma Beach. He's got an estate."

"What kind of an estate?"

"Well, maybe it's not his. Probably belongs to the people he works for or with . . . or whatever. Actually, I don't know the arrangement. Nobody was handing out much information. Place looked like a school or maybe a summer camp, I don't know. There were lots of kids over yonder."

"You went all the way to Zuma Beach to look at some kid's amateur movies? A total stranger?"

"Well, the way it played was like this: I get a call from, I guess, the kid's agent. Guy name of Decker. He tells me how he's interested in this great, important thing I'm doing at the Ritz, the open screenings, you know. In other words, a man of cultural savvy. And blah-blah-blah, he thinks I'd be interested in Mr. Dunkle's work. And blah-blah-blah, Mr. Dunkle would be pleased to defray the expenses of showing some of his flicks. It was like that."

"How much?"

"Couple thou. Worth a ride in a limousine, I figure."

"So Dunkle is paying you to show his films."

"Only the first time. Once I saw how he caught on, listen, I was glad to have him aboard. He's a draw, man."

"And that's the only time you saw him, that first trip?"

"First and last. That's when he asked about you. Did I know you? Could he meet you? Now he just sends his flicks in by limo."

Finally, the projector kicked in and a patch of light hit the screen, struggling in and out of focus. The house settled into the slightly subdued uproar that passed for quiet. We waited for *Big Stuffer* to begin.

But Simon Dunkle captured my amazed attention before his movie started. Because the first image to appear was that of a blurred bird flapping away into the distance. It was the image that I'd seen at the beginning of the reel Olga Tell had given me, the sole surviving remnant of a Max Castle independent production. Not a close facsimile, but exactly the same image, here too accompanied by the sound of whistling wind. But added to that were some musical notes—four of them teased out of a synthesizer and slowed to the point of a warbling, abysmal bass. Just as the last note died and the bird faded from sight, three words appeared across the screen:

BLACK BIRD PRODUCTIONS

The audience sent up a cheer, the way I remember kids used to burst out when Tom and Jerry announced themselves on the screen.

"What's that?" I asked Sharkey at once.

"Dunky's logo."

"But where did he get it—that image?"

Of course Sharkey had no way of understanding why I should ask the question. He shrugged. "Shot it himself, I guess. What's so special? Black Bird Productions. So he uses a black bird."

"But why Black Bird? What does it mean?"

Again Sharkey was at a loss. "How come the lion at MGM? What should he call himself?"

The four notes of the logo echoed in my mind. Distorted as they were, I identified them at once. I'd been humming the tune to myself since I left Amsterdam. The notes were those of the last four words of the song.

"Sharkey," I asked in a whisper as the movie began. "This school of Dunkle's . . . could it be an orphanage?"

"Could be. Like I said there were some kids around."

After that, it made no difference how bad *Big Stuffer* might be. I had to meet Simon Dunkle.

21 MORB

Sharkey made all the arrangements for my visit to Simon Dunkle, assuming an irritating air of self-importance as he went about the task. It would be a two-hour drive into the hills behind Malibu. He insisted we use his car, a battered old DeSoto station wagon that was bound to have trouble on the steep and not very improved roads we'd be traveling.

"Why not my car?" I asked. Mine was a spiffy MG in top condition to which I'd recently treated myself upon being promoted to Associate Professor of Film Studies.

"Not enough room," Sharkey answered.

"Holds two," I reminded him.

"But not three. We got a visitor."

"Oh? Who?"

"Some hot ticket," was all he would tell me. "Wait till you see her."

"Sharkey," I protested, "this is business. I want the people we meet to take me seriously. They're not going to do that if we bring one of your"—the word "bimbo" trembled on the edge of speech—"lady friends along."

"Never fear, pal of mine. This is business for her too. You'll like her. She's your kind of chick. Real brainy. She's not my lady friend anyway. Not yet she isn't. Until after I get her a chance to meet Dunkle. Then maybe ha-cha-cha."

No matter what Sharkey said, the image I had of any woman who would keep company with him was far from encouraging. For as long as I'd known him, his taste in femininity had run to strung-out teeny-boppers or giddy carbon copies of Jayne Mansfield. But this time I was wrong. The woman in question was brainy as well as beautiful. I could tell as soon as I laid eyes on her.

"I was planning to look you up," she said brightly when we met. "And then Don tells me that you are his friend."

It was Jeanette, Victor Saint-Cyr's comely young disciple, suddenly there before my eyes in the front seat of Sharkey's car, wearing a skintight T-shirt that read "Hooray For Hollywood" across her pert bosom.

"So you two know each other," Sharkey chimed in, not altogether approvingly, no doubt for fear I might beat his time. Which I had every intention of doing, if I got the chance.

While Jeanette moved into the backseat, I explained. "We met in France. Jeanette is Victor Saint-Cyr's prize pupil."

"No kidding," Sharkey said. "Who's he?"

Before I could answer, Jeanette entered a quick correction. "No, no, not so. Victor and I, we are no longer friends."

"Oh, I'm so sorry," I sympathized in a tone that clearly meant just the opposite.

Our trip north treated Jeanette to an archetypal California vista. Bright if hazy sunshine, crowded beaches observed too distantly to reveal the tar and oil that blighted them, a wave-furrowed ocean populated by stunting surfers. As we drove, she filled me in on her life since we'd last enjoyed one another's company. Most of the tale had to do with what a stinker Victor had turned out to be. A rat, a louse, a world-class prick. I relished hearing her vilification of the great man. I did all I could to draw out the dirty details, which took up most of our traveling time between Santa Monica and Zuma Beach, finishing with a scorching indictment of Saint-Cyr the lover.

"In bed, he was absolutely a nonentity." (Better and better, said the voice of unabashed spite inside me. Tell us more. She did.) "Do you know that he lectures on film while he makes love? Film theory. Long dissertations on film theory, like at the Sorbonne."

"Hey, I know somebody like that," Sharkey blurted out. I threw him a quick disapproving glance; he didn't catch it. "Maybe there's a whole species of people like that. Sexo-cine-maniacs."

"Victor says he learned this from one of his previous lovers. A brilliant woman. Together, they would argue about movies all the while they were screwing. Can you imagine this?"

"Yeah," Sharkey volunteered. "I can imagine it."

Jeanette drew a deep breath, making ready to unload a heavy sigh. On the intake, "Hooray For Hollywood" stretched tight across her nipples, reminding me of what provocative little breasts she had. What were my chances of getting reacquainted with them, I wondered.

"In any case," she went on in a tone of casual dismissiveness, "he will soon be superseded."

"As a boyfriend?" Sharkey asked eagerly.

"As a leading film theorist," she answered, knitting her brows at him.

"Superseded? By whom? Or what?" I wanted to know.

She donned a face of weary indifference. "Who can say? In France, thinkers exist only to be superseded. So too Victor. You have heard of Vulkolof? From Bulgaria?"

I confessed I hadn't.

"Hideous man. Greasy. Fat. He smells like a goat. But since last summer, he is the rage. In the cafés, everybody is discussing Vulkoloff. Existential Kinematics—this is his system. Something about muscles . . . 'muscular intentionality.' You read a poem, you watch a movie, he puts these wires on you, on the chest, the belly, the genitals . . . like you are a mice. What would you expect from a Bulgarian? They are all wrestlers, n'est-ce pas? But perhaps he will supersede Victor. Or"—with an impatient wave of the hand—"Decontextualism. Or Defamiliarization."

She rattled off a small grocery list of cinematic theories as if I should recognize them. To me they sounded like the names of distant jungle tribes. "I see we have a lot to talk about," I said. "You'll have to fill me in on Vulkolof . . . and all the others."

But she shrugged me off. "No, no, no, please. It was too much for

me to learn another system, after Semiotics, Deconstruction, Neurosemiology. I told Victor, no more theory. Now I want just to enjoy
movies."

"And Victor said?"

" 'How very feminine.' This is for him the ultimate condemnation."

So she'd pulled up her intellectual stakes and left for New York,
where her connection with Saint-Cyr had succeeded in opening doors
into the avant-garde film community. She bounced around there for
a few months, managing by way of contacts made at parties to place
a couple of foreign-film reviews with *The Village Voice*. When she
felt bold enough to ask for more work and more money, she was given
an assignment. Go to the West Coast. Find Simon Dunkle. Interview
him. As she described it, the task sounded a little like Stanley being
sent to find Livingstone—but on the cheap. One-way air fare via the
night plane, but no pay and no expenses until the story was submitted
and accepted. Jeanette had arrived with little enough to survive on,
but the plane ticket was enough of an excuse to bring her to California,
her real destination since leaving Paris. At the *Voice*, her editor had
recommended she start out after Dunkle by looking up Sharkey. So
she had, just in time to discover that he was bringing me to see the
man . . . or rather boy.

"Do you know anything about Dunkle?" I asked her. She answered
that she'd seen several of his films, some in Paris, more in New York,
mainly at private screenings or out-of-the-way cult houses. And what
did she think of them?

She fretted over her answer like the serious film student she was.
"They are saying such good things about him in New York. In Paris
too. How daring he is, how apocalyptic. It is true that he is only a
child?"

"About eighteen," I answered, "by Sharkey's calculation."

"Victor says he is a genius, years ahead of his time. . . ."

"Right on!" Sharkey trumpeted. "What'd I tell you? And, hey, I'm
the dude who discovered him."

". . . but myself," Jeanette went on, ignoring Sharkey, "I find him
frightening, especially if he is so young."

"Well, sure," Sharkey agreed. "But also damn funny. Did you see
Fast Food Massacre?"

She had, but she insisted, "No, he is never funny to me. Only
frightening. Not like Hitchcock. Not like Clouzot. Not like vampires
or monsters. Something else is there. Something very negative."

"You're right," I agreed.

"Well, what's wrong with negative?" Sharkey wanted to know. "Negative's the new frontier. Just ask the kids."

I had a question for Jeanette. "Do you associate that quality with anything or anybody else in film?"

"You mean your Max Castle?" She nodded gravely. "Yes, I can see that. There is a connection between Castle and Dunkle?"

"Castle is Dunkle's favorite director," Sharkey told her.

"But it could go deeper than that," I added. "That's what I hope to find out today."

As we passed through Zuma Beach, Sharkey gave out a "Whoa!" and pulled off at a convenience store. "Gimme a minute," he asked as he left the car. I assumed he was after a six-pack, his usual traveling companion. When he returned he had the six-pack, but there was also a package for me. "A little gift for Simon," he explained.

I glanced into the paper bag. It contained several boxes of Milk Duds. "Come on, Sharkey," I protested, "that's pretty tacky."

"Maybe so," Sharkey answered, "but Simon'll love you for it. Kid eats 'em by the ton. Sort of therapeutic."

"How do you mean?"

"He's got this speech thing. Sometimes he gets stalled. You'll see. If he glitches, just slip him a Milk Dud. Probably it's got something to do with his condition, being an albino."

"Albinos eat Milk Duds?"

Sharkey shrugged. "I don't make these rules."

A few miles out of town, we turned off into the hills on a rough, blacktop road whose surface was liberally littered with debris from the eternally crumbling coastal hills. Golden California, forever sliding into the blue Pacific. As Sharkey started the steep climb, I raised a delicate issue with Jeanette. "You do realize that Dunkle's invitation today is for me? He may not wish to be interviewed by you."

"But perhaps I can just listen . . . ?"

"Even so, I don't think you should attempt to publish anything without permission."

"No, no. Of course not."

I suggested that I introduce her as my lady friend and let Dunkle get to know her in that capacity before requesting the interview. She agreed. But there was one more, even touchier, point I felt I must raise. "Do you have anything else to wear?" I asked. "On the top?" She gave me a puzzled look. " 'Hooray For Hollywood' " I pointed out. "It might seem a bit frivolous. You see, this orphanage we're visiting—it's a religious institution. A church, in fact. A very sober, very puritanical church."

"How do you know that?" Sharkey asked in great surprise.

"You've been there," I reminded him. "Didn't you notice?"

"Well, see, they sort of met me in the parking lot. I didn't get to see too much of the place."

"Believe me. I visited one of their branches in Europe. Their world headquarters as a matter of fact. Grim was the word. So while I think the T-shirt is darling, it might not go over very well with the nuns and priests. You do want to make the right impression."

Jeanette looked worried. "But I have nothing else."

I looked across at Sharkey. "Do you have anything in the car she might wear?"

"Dig around under the seat there," Sharkey told Jeanette. "You might find something."

And so she did. A treasure trove of ratty old clothes, mostly female, mostly underwear, bras, panties, slips, some ominous-looking leather garments . . . perhaps a decade's worth of Sharkey's romantic trophies. Finally, among the lingerie, Jeanette found a small, frilly, but reasonably tasteful blouse. It was none too clean, but she judged she could make do with it. Not bothering to ask me to turn around, she tugged the T-shirt over her head, then paused to ask, "Do you think I will need . . . ?" She had fished up a rumpled brassiere and was dangling it fastidiously before me at arm's length like a small dead animal. She was doing quite nicely without one at the moment.

"I think not," I answered, noting the garment's grubbiness. Relieved, she let it drop and proceeded to pull on the salvaged top.

Sharkey, having to catch what he could of Jeanette's quick change in the rearview mirror while he negotiated the twisting road, reached across the seat to give me a dig in the thigh. "So you two know each other *very* well."

The road east from the coast highway switchbacked up steep ravines taking us farther and farther from the beach. Distantly, between the hills, we still caught peekaboo views of the cool Pacific, but the motionless air around us now crackled in the bone-dry September heat. The sun had crisped the scrub and brush into tawny brown tinder that looked eager to burn at the least excuse. The winding road finally produced a signpost that read "St. James the Martyr School" and pointed the way into a small, eucalyptus-lined arroyo. Some three miles more of snaky road brought us to a sturdy, wire-mesh gate with the school's name above it. Below the name, in small letters, were the words "Founded by the Holy Order of the Orphans of the Storm, 1923." Below that, a small plaque read "Black Bird Productions."

There was an intercom box mounted on the fence. I left the car to press a button, got a clipped response from a male voice, identified myself, and, at the buzzer, pushed open the gate. We followed a gravel road around and down to where it ended in a small parking lot beside a low redwood building. "This is where I met Dunkle last time I was up here," Sharkey said. "Never got any farther in."

A security guard looked out a window and frowned. "I heard there were two people comin'," he observed gruffly.

"I brought my lady friend," I said.

He eyed us disapprovingly, but waved us out of the car. "I'll call ahead and let 'em know in the big house." Then he gestured to two children, a boy and a girl—ten-year-olds, I would guess—who were waiting for us in the lot. Each was leading a horse, one spotted, the other chestnut. As we left the car, Sharkey called my attention to the fact that we were sharing the lot with a rather unlikely vehicle: a dusty black van decorated on sides and back with garishly painted mushroom explosions. Over the paintings lay a barely decipherable psychedelic script that I made out to read ENBC. "Check that!" Sharkey said, clearly very impressed by what he saw. When I signaled ignorance, he explained, as if I should know, "It's the Stinks. That's their buggy."

Jeanette looked to me for clarification but Sharkey answered. "The Extinction Now Boys Choir. Real biggies. What're they doing here?"

The two children motioned us to follow them. Leading their horses, they took us down a dirt bridle path.

"Are you pupils here?" I asked them as they led us off.

"Yes, sir," the little boy answered shyly and then said nothing more.

The two were dressed alike. They wore broad-brimmed straw hats, gray shorts, and white T-shirts. Above the breast pocket their tops bore a small, now familiar, emblem: the Maltese cross. Their light-weight uniforms were a merciful concession to the heat. The costume I'd seen in Zurich would have been oppressive under this sun. But while their dress was different, their demeanor displayed the same disciplined cheerlessness. They trudged beside us in silence, eyes down, their expression almost morose.

After several moments, I asked, "Do you study movies?"

The girl said, "He does," nodding at her companion.

"What about you?" She wagged her head. "No movies? What then?"

After a pause, "Physics," she said.

"Physics? They teach that too at the school?"

"Only basic," she answered. "For advanced, I have to go to Copenhagen."

"And when is that?"

"Two years yet."

The children were leading us toward a shaded cluster of buildings behind a high stake fence. Beyond that in the distance, there was a large, rambling redwood house and a barn. Still farther up the hillside, I could see a few cattle grazing and some children dressed the same as our guides, riding or walking horses. The overall feeling of the place was ranchlike, so very different from Zurich.

"Is this all there is to the school?" I asked.

"The school's over there," the boy said. He gestured toward the hills east of us. "You have to ride to get there."

"And what's this?" I asked, indicating the buildings ahead.

"That's the guest house," the boy said, pointing to the structures behind the stake fence. "And that's the studio." He pointed at the more distant house and barn. "It belongs to Simon."

"All that just for Simon?"

"So he can make his movies."

"That's a lot of space for just one pupil, isn't it?"

They both looked up at me, their faces wearing the same astonished expression. "Simon's not a pupil," the girl said. "He's a prophet."

"A prophet?" I asked. "What do you mean?"

The girl shrugged, as if there was nothing more she could add. "A prophet . . ."

Sharkey gave me a skeptical look. Under his breath, he murmured, "I don't think his flicks make a profit."

Ahead, where the path branched, there was an open stone structure surrounded by flowers. It looked like a wayside chapel. Inside stood a piece of marble sculpture. A sign beside the chapel pointed toward the right to "St. James the Martyr School" and left to "Administration and Guest House." We paused to view the sculpture before taking the left fork. It was a pseudomannerist rendering of a three-man group, the sort of kitschy imitation of Michelangelo one might expect to see at Forest Lawn. If the style was unimpressive, the subject matter was plain repulsive. The central figure was a bearded man on his knees. He was stripped to a loincloth, revealing an excessively muscular torso covered with welts from a terrible scourging. The only other item he wore was a large Maltese cross hung about his neck. The man's hands were bound behind him; there was a chain fastened to a manacle at his throat. Two masked and robed figures huddled near him. One held the chain, the other was forcing a brand down upon the man's forehead: the letter X burned deep into the brow. The kneeling man's face was twisted in pain.

"Wow!" Sharkey said. "Here's a man with real problems. What's it all about?"

The girl answered, "It's St. James. His martyrdom."

"Who are the two mean guys?" Sharkey asked.

"Inquisitors."

"Heavy," Sharkey commented. "Never wanna get in trouble with Inquisitors."

Jeanette remembered enough of her Catholic schooling to ask, "But St. James, he was stoned to death, no? Long before there was the Inquisition."

The girl wagged her head. "Not that St. James."

"Then which?"

"St. James of Molay."

Sharkey picked up on the name at once. "Hey, that's the Templars' main man."

"Grand Master of the order, in fact," I added. I recalled coming across the man years before in a book Sharkey had once lent me. "Condemned for heresy."

"Then he cannot be a saint," Jeanette protested.

"I told you, they aren't Catholics."

At the base of the statue was a phrase Gothic-lettered in medieval French. Jeanette worked out the translation.

> *Living or dead, we belong to the Lord.*
> *Glorious be the victors, happy the martyrs!*

She gave a last wincing glance at the sculpture before we turned away to follow the children. "It is a hideous thing for children to see."

I agreed, but I wasn't surprised to find such a work of art on the premises, not after touring the chapel at Zurich. The orphans' taste ran to atrocity. They were a people whose history was written in their wounds.

Some ten yards farther along toward the guest house, I broke the silence to ask the boy, "Do you help Simon with his movies?"

He said, "Not yet. The senior students get to help him."

"With the editing and lighting, things like that?"

The boy nodded.

"Do you like Simon's movies?"

"Yes. The parts that teach, I do."

"Teach about what?"

His voice dropped. "The true God."

We had reached the fence. Behind it, I heard what sounded like people frolicking in a pool. Laughter and splashing. The boy pushed open the gate, indicating we were to enter, but averting his eyes. Then he and the girl mounted their horses and turned quickly toward the hills. The scene that greeted us behind the fence was hardly what I expected to see at an institution run by the Orphans of the Storm. Attached to a large stone-and-redwood house was a sumptuous cabana that opened out on a huge ice-blue swimming pool. In the water was a gang of boisterous adolescents, three girls and a boy, all of them sporting wild punk hairstyles. They were gushing a stream of obscenities as they splashed and dunked one another. One of the girls was doing without a bathing suit.

"I think I could have worn my T-shirt," Jeanette whispered to me. I gave her a bewildered shrug.

On the far side of the pool sat a small group of people. One was another punky youngster whose head was sprouting tufts of multicolored hair. Beside him sat a neatly groomed man in his thirties. With them were an older man and woman wearing lightweight versions of the clerical garb I'd seen in Zurich, but without the concealing bonnets. The well-groomed man rose to greet us, going first to Sharkey, who in turn introduced him to me as Len Decker, Simon's agent.

"Oh, hardly that," Decker corrected him. "Just the school's business manager."

Decker then introduced us to the older couple he'd been sitting with. The man was Brother Justin, the director of St. James School and chairman of Black Bird Productions. He was stooped and balding with weasely little eyes behind small, square spectacles. Shaking my hand and Jeanette's warmly, he assured us that he was delighted we had come and promptly introduced the woman who had risen to greet us. Sister Helena, we learned, was mother superior of the orphanage. She was small and intense, wearing her gray hair skinned back severely from her pallid face.

Sharkey, all the while, had been preoccupied eyeing the kid across the pool, who hadn't so much as glanced our way. "Isn't that Bobby Pox?" he asked Decker in an awed whisper. Decker said it was. "Far out!" Sharkey gushed. "I thought that was his van in the lot." Offering Brother Justin and Sister Helena a quick nod, he rushed us off toward the bored youth as if he were the object of our visit. "It's Bobby Pox, man," Sharkey announced again, clearly puzzled by my lack of enthusiasm.

I vaguely recognized the name. A rock singer who was doing an effective job of poking his finger in the public eye. Rock was not a world I followed. I couldn't have explained the difference between New Wave, Heavy Metal, Maximum Rock . . . or which of these variations on witless cacophony Bobby Pox represented. But his notoriety had oozed out of the pop music subculture and penetrated the daily news. I associated him with riots, drug busts, and sundry public outrages. He was the sort of professional juvenile delinquent who was growing steadily more prominent on the youth scene— though now that I saw him up close, I could tell he was obviously well out of his teens, perhaps as far along as his mid-twenties. But then, I might have been deceived about his age by the several jagged scars that blemished his brow and cheeks. Some of these I saw were tattoos, but not all. When we were introduced, he offered neither Sharkey nor me a hand to shake, but only a minimal surly nod. His glance loitered, however, on Jeanette, a gaze of undisguised lust that lingered until I could very nearly feel her blushing beside me.

The people in the pool weren't introduced and showed no interest in our arrival. In due course we learned that the females were "Bobby's girls," and the youth who was cavorting with them was Bobby's drummer, an entity with lightning bolts tattooed on his cheeks and a phosphorescent Mohawk hairdo. His name was Humper. Just Humper. I had no idea why these people were here. I wished they weren't. Their presence unnerved me. But not Sharkey, who, as proprietor of the Catacombs, had come to regard himself as an honorary teenager. He proceeded to fawn over Bobby Pox as if he might be the Mozart of our time. While he moved in on Pox, I did my best to draw Brother Justin and Sister Helena off to one side, keeping Jeanette close to me.

Theodore Roszak

"I recently visited your headquarters in Zurich," I told Brother Justin, trying to level my voice just above the racket in the pool.

"Dr. Byx has been in touch with us," Brother Justin replied. His voice was tinged with a Germanic accent. "We invited you here on his recommendation. He was most impressed with your scholarship."

"Oh? I didn't realize."

"Yes. He thought you might be of some help to us. Or rather to Simon."

"What sort of help?"

"We will speak of this later. After the screening."

"We're going to see a movie?"

"Simon's latest, yes. Didn't Mr. Sharkey tell you? We would like to have your opinion."

"And will we have the chance to talk to Simon?"

"Of course. He wants very much to meet you. He is also a great admirer of Max Von Kastell. You will have much to talk about, I'm sure. Simon, unfortunately, must avoid the sunlight. His eyes, you know. We will join him at the studio when he is ready for us."

Nodding toward the pool, I remarked, "Your school in Zurich was somewhat more . . . austere."

Brother Justin gave me a toothy smile. "One makes adaptions to local custom. Zurich is the home of Zwingli. California is the home of Woody Woodpecker. Actually, this is not the school. The campus is about two miles in that direction. This is our guest house and production facility. Simon's stamping ground, so to speak. We try to maintain some distinction between the two. I believe you would find the school itself rather more reserved. Here, we meet the people Simon is involved with in his work. Movie people, performers . . ."

"Simon is involved with Bobby Pox?"

"Indeed," Brother Justin announced with obvious pride. "Mr. Pox has done the music for Simon's films. He and his friends are also here for the screening."

There was an outburst from the pool. One of the girls—the one *sans* bathing suit—hauled herself out of the water, screaming, "Screw you, Humper! You tryin' to drown me? Screw you!" She ran to Bobby Pox, wrapped herself in a towel, and cuddled up under his arm, complaining. "You see him tryin' to eat me under water? Whatta pervert!"

Looking not at all apologetic, Brother Justin offered an indulgent nod and smile. "The young people these days . . . so libertine, so outspoken. They are, however, Simon's main audience. What is one to do?"

I didn't know how to put the question delicately. "Don't you find Simon's films rather . . . extreme, especially for a young audience?"

Brother Justin sighed. "I'm sure I needn't tell you, Professor Gates, it is an extreme age. Young people cannot be shielded from this fact. In truth, they seem better adapted to the prevailing moral condition than many of the rest of us. They are able to tolerate stronger stimulation."

"Even to crave it," Sister Helena added.

"And you see fit to encourage that?"

As if it were a law of nature, Sister Helena stated, "Art must reflect its times."

There was a truckload of aesthetic issues I might have raised at that point, but I reminded myself that I'd come to learn, not to argue. "Would I be right in believing that Simon is the first director your church has trained since Max Castle?"

"The first in many years," Brother Justin answered. "There were a few others of Kastell's generation, less prominent than he. Since then, direction has not been our main focus."

"I gathered from Dr. Byx that the church's experience with Max Castle was unsatisfactory. That's why you stopped training directors."

"There is some truth in that. But it is not the whole story. As you well understand, direction is a matter of artistry. And how difficult it is to teach artistry. So much a matter of fashion. We wish to make certain our pupils will find employment. So we have stayed close to the more marketable skills."

"Is that really your only interest—finding jobs for your pupils?"

"What else?" he asked. He smiled pleasantly, but I could sense an intense curiosity behind the grin.

"You might want to use the motion pictures to teach some of the principles of your faith."

Brother Justin and Sister Helena exchanged a bewildered look. "But what might those be?" Brother Justin asked.

"Well, I don't know that much about your church . . . I couldn't say."

Brother Justin gave an amused shrug. "How could that possibly be done, in any case? Do you believe the producers, the studios would permit us to do such a thing? Can you imagine Elizabeth Taylor,

Marlon Brando delivering a sermon in the midst of one of their movies?" He chuckled. Sister Helena echoed his little laugh.

"No, I didn't mean anything like that."

"But what, then?" He spread his hands before him as if sincerely pleading for an answer.

"You understand, Professor," Sister Helena interjected, "that our pupils—with the exception of Simon, who is uniquely gifted—work on film in a purely technical capacity. This gives them very little influence over the content of the work they do."

"Well, yes, that's true," I admitted, not wanting to press the point in the face of their denial.

"Dr. Byx tells me," Brother Justin continued, "that you were surprised to learn that our pupils had once worked upon the films of the Ritz Brothers and Shirley Temple. Now, frankly, Professor Gates, can you imagine the Ritz Brothers associated with a religious teaching?"

They were beginning to make me feel foolish for raising the matter. I tried to think of a way to change the subject when Sharkey came to my rescue.

"Hey, Jonny, you gotta meet the maestro here," he said, pulling at my elbow. "Wait'll you hear. Bobby's doing the music for Dunkle's new flick." He announced the fact as if it were the cultural event of the century.

"So I've just heard," I told him. I turned and edged my chair in Bobby Pox's direction, trying to look impressed and interested. "I know I've heard your group," I lied. Unable to think of how else to begin, I asked, "Let's see . . . it's called . . ."

Pox gave me no answer, only his standard bored-stiff glare. Sharkey reminded me. "The Stinks. Stinks for Extinction. They're the ultimate."

Bobby Pox frowned at Sharkey. "More than ultimate. *Pen*-ultimate."

I wondered if I should correct the misusage, but decided not to. Pox might consider it hostile.

"That's Heavy Metal, isn't it?" I was trying another feeble feeler, but saw at once I was only revealing my ignorance.

The half-naked girl under Pox's arm made a sour face. "Bobby, he way past that shit." When she spoke, I saw that her front upper teeth had been filed into stilettolike fangs. Like Pox, she also had scars tattooed across her cheeks. And emerging from her left nostril there was a tattoo of something like a worm curling down toward her mouth. With one strip of stringy orange hair, stretched across her stubbly scalp, she was without a doubt the ugliest human specimen I'd ever seen.

Sharkey interpreted the meaning of her response for me. "These things change fast. Heavy Metal's big now, sure. But Bobby's into the next thing coming up. Which is Morb Culture."

"Morb? That's postpunk?" I asked.

Pox finally spoke up, answering impatiently. "Shee-it, man, we're postapocalyptic."

I looked back, puzzled. "But how can you be . . ."

"Because on account we're lookin' back at the world from the other side of it. Which is, to wit, we're startin' from total racial suicide."

The girl creature beside him giggled approval. "See, see?" she said. "Real lethal, yum, hum. Tell him 'bout fanny cycler."

"Yeah, sure," Pox went on. "See, that's the evolutionary psycho-rhythmics of the total cosmos. The sixties, the seventies, you raise hell, you kick ass, you give a shit. But what we're gettin' into is the fanny cycler. When you got that comin' down on you, that's absolute depletion."

"The fanny cycler . . . ?" I asked.

Decker intervened to rectify the phrase. "*Fin de siècle*. You see, Punk, Heavy Metal . . . these are highly energized styles, appropriate to the mid-century. They rejected the past and the present as part of their protest. But Morb is rejecting the future as well."

"Which would seem to leave . . . nothing," I observed.

"Fuckin' right," Pox agreed with an arrogant sniff. Loosening up now that he'd found me reasonably respectful, he lay back in his chair, ready to hold forth, a man of ambitious vision. "See, you take a group like, specifistically, the Crucifugs. You know them?"

I didn't, but I said I did.

"The Crucifugs are into balls-out Satanism. Blasphemy, ritual sacrifice, Antichrist, all like that. Which is okay. Which is where the scene is at as of the on-line moment. But, see, they're still fightin'. Because like they got a cause. You got a cause, you wanna win, you wanna survive. Now the Morb stance is as to wit: Why bother? I mean, fuck it, you live, you die, you eat, you get eaten, what's the difference? Like extinction, why fight it, *comprendo?*"

"Just have big fun," said the girl under his arm. "Eat 'em up, eat 'em up. Yum. We the last generation." And she gave a wicked little snicker.

Was I supposed to be agreeing with this dismal line of thought? I nodded, as if engaged by the subject. And then realized I honestly was! This was, after all, part of Simon Dunkle's world and, in some way I didn't yet grasp, part of Max Castle's as well. "Whose idea was Morb?" I asked Pox. "Yours or Simon's?"

"I'd say it was intermutual. See, the time was ripe, this being the bi-lemillion and all comin' up, it was like *ipso facto*."

Decker corrected. "Bi-millennium. The year 2000."

"Yeah, like that," Pox went on. "Dunk and me, we just kicked into the same vibration simul-ten-atiously. Dunk's been scopin' out the rock scene right along. And where I was at, methodologically, was you couldn't do pure Morb without goin' on film. So that's where we synergized, him and me."

"Explain that," I said. "What does film give you?"

"Well, hell," Pox answered as if it should be obvious, "we already pushed theatrics as far as it can go. There's only so much you can do on a stage without crashin' your ass or gettin' busted. I mean, fuck, you do castration or arson on stage, you're limited. People see you're fakin'. And if you're not, hey, lookit crazy old Iggy Pop. That son of a bitch is takin' self-immolation to the max. You know what happened to that dumb fucker last time he jumped into the audience like he does? Somebody tried to bite his pecker off."

Sharkey, always prompt to put the relevant question, piped up to ask, "Who was it tried? Male or female?"

"You ever seen his audience? Who could tell the difference? Anyway, s'pose somebody did eat his dick. How many times can he do that gig? But with film, you do it once and you do it good. And the whole world gets in on it up close. Rape, dismemberment, whatever, you got the intimacy factor, you got the replay factor, you got the actuality factor."

"Actuality?"

"Yeah. Like *real*. On film, you can make it real."

Confusion was compounding painfully in my mind. "But film isn't 'real,' " I protested. "I mean, well, yes, it's 'real' as a work of art. But it's . . . composed, constructed. The way all art is." People were staring at me blankly on all sides. For God's sake, how basic did I have to make this? "Look, film is . . . *film*. Celluloid."

"Acetate, actually," Sharkey volunteered.

"All right, acetate. You know what I mean. It isn't flesh, blood. . . ."

"Well, what you put *on* film is real," Pox insisted, as if he were making the most self-evident point in the world. "I mean, it *can* be real. Which is to wit the beauty part. Because, if you handle yourself right, the law can't tell whether you're fakin' or what the fuck. How they gonna know? You can get away with anything."

"They did *me* in the flick," the vampire-toothed lady at Pox's side put in.

"*Did* you?"

"Bang-bang. Whole tribe." She tittered. "I was the star."

I didn't even want to imagine what she might mean. "What flick was this?" I asked.

"What we gonna see. Hey, it was the real thing, man. There was even blood." She emitted a proud little smirk.

Pox gave her an affectionate hug, leaning over to bite her ear—hard. "Slutty bleeds real good."

Slutty. That was the she-monster's name. And why not?

I passed Sharkey an urgently inquisitive glance. How seriously was I to take all this? Sharkey grinned back gleefully, a man in his element. "It's no holds barred, kiddo. These dudes are into wraparound reality. You heard of MTV?"

At the time, I hadn't. Rock video was still in its infancy, working its way through small production studios around Los Angeles. Briefly, Sharkey, in his role of ambassador to the world of adolescent inanity, described the genre to me, displaying his usual enthusiasm for its most extreme effects: heavy-duty sex, aggressive obscenity, mindless violence. When he had finished, I hazarded to comment that nothing he told me sounded quite like my idea of film art. "Isn't this just a kind of promotional gimmick for the record industry?"

"To a degree, that's true," Decker joined in to agree. "The record companies are bankrolling MTV. But what actually gets put on film— that they leave up to the producers, who have a pretty accurate idea of what their audience wants."

"Rape, dismemberment, all like that," I added, echoing Bobby Pox.

Only Decker detected the sarcasm, acknowledging it with no more than a slightly embarrassed laugh. "Often enough, yes. In some form. Though not necessarily quite so cinema verité as I gather Slutty's experience may have been."

This left me puzzled. "Do you mean Simon is making films to promote rock music?"

"No, no, no," Decker replied. "Simon's into his own thing. His own themes, his own imagery. Film before music. But he has found Bobby here and others quite compatible with his vision."

"Epic," Pox chimed in. "Dunk is givin' us epic MTV. He's gonna be the Cecil Beedee Mill of rock video."

"Of course all the big names in rock are going into film," Decker explained. "Intensified Chaos, Black Sabbath, Toxic Waste . . . But the Stinks have got Simon, who is out-front state of the art."

"Absolutely," Pox concurred. "Dunky is gettin' us into generic evil. No more crappy kid stuff. We're goin' over the fucking edge here."

The one great question I wanted most to ask was too big to squeeze into any words I might expect the likes of Bobby Pox to answer. But I tried anyway, in words of approximately one syllable, aiming my query somewhere between Pox and Decker, hoping for a semiserious response. "Look . . . what's this all about?"

Decker looked blank. Pox said "Huh?"

"The whole scene," I went on. "What's it all about? You, Iggy Pop, the Crucifugs, Kiss . . . What's the goal, the purpose . . . the satisfaction?"

Decker deferred to Pox, who looked bewildered at the question. I might have been asking an Eskimo why he spent so much time in the snow. Finally, he shrugged and said, "I dunno. Shittin' on the world, I guess." A pause and he attached a thoughtful addendum. "And of course collectin' some loot."

"Is that what Simon's after? Loot?"

"Simon? Nah. With Simon, see, it's like a true religious thing."

"Shitting on the world is a religious thing for Simon?"

"Well, Simon . . . I dunno. I don't think he sees it like that." Looking honestly inquisitive, Pox turned to Decker. "What is it with Simon, d'you think?"

Decker wagged his head. "There's no accounting for genius. I would say, yes, there's a religious dimension going with Simon." He asked over his shoulder, "Wouldn't you say so, Brother Justin?"

Brother Justin, who had been listening to every word, now pretended he hadn't heard a thing. "Hm?" he asked, as if Decker's question had just caught his attention.

Decker repeated, "For Simon, the movies have a religious meaning, isn't that so?"

Brother Justin stretched his mouth into his toothsome smile. "I would hope that for our pupils, all honest labor is a spiritual service."

"There, see?" Pox said. "Like what I said. *Ipso facto.*"

Grinning steadily at me, Brother Justin continued. "Perhaps that is what you had in mind, Professor, when you suggested that Simon's films might teach something of our faith. When a devout Christian offers up his work as an act of devotion to the one true God, in effect as a prayer, a hymn of praise to the All-Highest, one might hope it would have some redeeming influence even on the most hardened souls, if only . . ."

He went on. And on. Within a few moments, he'd succeeded in larding the conversation with enough melting religious rhetoric to stifle further talk. All the while he spoke, Simon Dunkle's acts of devotion—those I had so far witnessed—rippled through my memory. Images of cannibal children, butchered parents, kinky eroticism, bloody murder played for laughs.

What manner of faith heaped honor on such a prophet?

22 SUB SUB

After we'd sat by the pool for the better part of two hours, a boy of about sixteen, wearing the school uniform, looked in shyly at the gate, then approached Brother Justin to deliver a message.

"Simon is ready for us," the priest announced.

By this time, Humper and the girls had left the pool and joined the rest of us waiting for the summons. Slutty, who seemed to be Bobby Pox's favorite among the girls, had finally done us all the favor of dressing, though only minimally: bikini panties under a torn T-shirt that bore the motto "Kiss My Mucus," and below the words a crude drawing of someone doing just that. Once again, this drew a teasing nudge from Jeanette.

"And what is that she is wearing around her neck?" she asked in

Theodore Roszak

a worried whisper. I couldn't tell until we had risen to leave the cabana. Then I saw. It was a necklace of bloodstained teeth with a piece of raw meat as its centerpiece. I asked Sharkey to reassure me that her jewelry was a plastic reproduction.

"Nah, it's real," he answered. "Morbs like that kind of thing. Like the teeth there, probably they come from . . ."

"Don't tell me," I pleaded, moving off.

Outside the fence there was an open motorcart not quite large enough to carry the dozen of us who were to view the film. Humper and Decker had to ride the running boards. The boy drove us slowly to the buildings I'd seen farther up the hill: Simon's studio. The ride was a chance to strike up a conversation with Brother Justin, who sat beside me. I'd already decided to weigh my words carefully in speaking to him. I remembered what Zip Lipsky told me about the orphans: "They can be mean as hell." Brother Justin didn't look mean; but, like Dr. Byx, he was guarded in everything he said to me. I wasn't going to be more candid with him than he was with me. I started by asking if it was true that Max Castle had often visited the school during his Hollywood years.

"Yes, but I met him only once," he told me. "That was 1941, not long before America entered the war. I had just arrived from Zurich to begin teaching. He was in a sad state. Very distressed."

"Do you know why?"

"I understand he had been trying to make a film of his own for some years, mainly in Europe. I gather with no success. Apparently what there was of it had been lost when the European war started. A great blow for him. Castle, it seems, only came visiting when he needed money. Unhappily, the order was not able to spare him much at that point. Many of our assets had also been lost in the war— including the orphanage he was raised in. As a result, Castle was forced to take on some rather tawdry directing assignments. Wartime spy thrillers and such. He was most depressed about that. And quite angry, I'm afraid, with us for being so niggardly. The one time I met him, he was throwing a tantrum with Brother Marcion, who was then the director. It was a painful occasion. Soon after that, we learned he had tried to return to Europe—to Switzerland—to plead his case to higher authorities. As you know, his ship was lost at sea. Torpedoed." He sighed heavily. "Perhaps it was a mercy that it ended as it did. I don't believe our people in Zurich would have given him a more generous hearing."

381

"So, at the end, the order disowned him."

"I would rather say Max Castle disowned us. And not at the end. Many years before that. From the time he came to America. The way he was lionized at the beginning, it was quite corrupting. And his work suffered accordingly."

"And yet Simon Dunkle admires him."

Brother Justin nodded thoughtfully. "Yes, that is true. And of course there is a great deal to admire—on the purely technical level—even in Castle's worst work, as you yourself have pointed out in your writing. Well, Simon is still young. Max Castle is apt to be only a phase in his development, one influence among many. I expect he will go on to much finer work than Castle was able to achieve."

An interesting question struck me. "If you had your way, Brother Justin, whose influence would you like to see prevail in Simon's work? Among directors, I mean."

He rolled the matter around in his thoughts for a while. "Renoir, perhaps. Or Dreyer. Cocteau. These are simply my favorites."

I allowed him to see my surprise. "Do you think Simon's work is anything like theirs? You must be aware of the vast difference. . . ."

"In style, of course," he added quickly. "But I have in mind the integrity of the work. Yes, the integrity."

I saw that he was perfectly serious. He believed there was something Jean Renoir had in common with *Fast Food Massacre* and *Insect Anxiety*. He called it "integrity."

Simon Dunkle's studio was housed inside an old, weathered barn that had been gutted and remodeled. Judging from what I could see as we walked through, the place was remarkably well equipped; small, but superior to anything I'd seen on the university campuses I knew. One thing was clear: a production facility like this could certainly have put out more polished work than I had so far seen in Dunkle's films. Which led me to conclude that the style of his movies—slapdash, hastily improvised—was deliberate, an effect he'd carefully crafted for his youthful audience. Dunkle was seeking what Sharkey called a "garagey" look, a primitive surface that gave him access to adolescent minds that were gleefully trashing all established aesthetic standards.

We were led into a screening room off one of the main studio areas. The room was well appointed: a thick carpet and plush seats. In the middle aisle sat a small group of young people. Simon wasn't difficult to pick out among them. He was a small, slight lad with a head of shaggy, dead-white hair and a face that looked powdered with clown white. The pink eyes, however, were not on display; despite the dimness of the room, he wore dark glasses. Sharkey had guessed his age at eighteen; he could have passed for twelve. When he rose to offer his limp, moist hand in greeting, he stood little above five feet tall. Altogether, he had that shrimpy, subglandular physique of a boy whose balls had failed to drop.

Brother Justin made the introductions. Simon answered my how-do-you-do through a cruel stammer, his muscle-bound jaw cramping his words into near incoherence. "I'm gl-gl-glad you c-c'd c-c-c . . ." Giving up, he plumped down in his seat as if overcome with embarrassment. Rapidly, he drew something from his shirt pocket: a crumpled white and green box. He dug into it and, once, twice, three times, his hand shot to his mouth. I saw his fingers and lips were chocolate-stained. ". . . could come," he finished, a brown froth collecting across his lower teeth. It seemed to be the right moment; smiling apologetically, I offered the paper bag I was carrying. "Don told me you like these."

He looked into the bag and then back at me, his face beaming with honest delight. "Oh gee, th-th-th . . ."

My heart sank with each stuttered syllable. This was going to make conversation with Simon difficult, maybe impossible. I'd hoped to quiz him about every aspect of his work. Now I feared I might not get very far—unless the Milk Duds did the trick.

"You have a remarkably fine studio here," I said.

Simon only nodded in reply, his teeth grinding away at some unspoken word.

"Did you learn all your filmmaking here?" I said.

"N-n-no," he answered. "I w-was at V-V-V . . ."

The last I realized might not be a stutter. "Three Vs?" I asked. He nodded. So Simon, like Max Castle before him, had a connection with V. V. Valentine. Sparing Simon the need to tell me more, Len Decker filled in. "You might say Simon served his apprenticeship at Three Vs. A small taste of the commercial film world. We think that's of value to our students. Let's see, Simon did *Happy Kill* for Valentine. And . . ."

"*I W-W-W-W* . . ." Simon added, or rather tried unsuccessfully to add. He popped another Milk Dud and managed to stitch the stutterese into an answer. "*I Wanna Ghoul.*"

At the mention, Sharkey lit up. *"I Want a Ghoul*—that's Simon's flick? I didn't know that."

"Oh yes," Decker assured him. "Script, production, everything."

"Wow! Sensational," Sharkey bubbled. "That's one of my big shows. Kids love it." Turning to me, he asked, "You see it, Jonny? *I Want a Ghoul Just Like the Ghoul Who Buried Dear Old Dad.*"

Trying to sound as if I deeply regretted it, I admitted I hadn't.

"You'd love it," Sharkey told me. "There's this great bit in it. These werewolves dressed like the Beatles, with these Yiddish accents. It's a howl. But also very gross, very gross." In Sharkey's aesthetic system, this last was a high compliment. Turning back to Simon, he asked, "Say, how come your name isn't on the flick?"

This time Decker intervened to answer for him. "I'm afraid Mr. Valentine isn't always too scrupulous about such matters. Actually, not very much that he puts out under his name was made by him."

"Yeah, so I hear," Sharkey said. "Guy's a regular horse thief. But he's broken in lots of talent."

I asked, "Did you know that Valentine helped out with some of Max Castle's films?"

"H-he did?" Simon was surprised to hear.

"That's how Valentine got his start. I gather he wasn't much more than a gofer at the time." Then, as nonchalantly as possible, I added, "He was one of the first people to mention Castle's secret filmmaking techniques to me. He tried to pry them out of Castle, but not with any success."

In the silence that followed, Brother Justin was the first to speak. "Secret techniques? Do you mean the little tricks you discussed with Dr. Byx in Zurich?"

"Those, among others." I turned to Simon. "Are you still using these . . . little tricks?"

Brother Justin hastened to answer for Simon. "Surely what matters most in any film is the total aesthetic effect, however it might be achieved. After all, every director has his methods, the mysteries of his craft. But are they worth serious consideration apart from the work as a whole?" The question was rhetorical. I saw that Brother Justin had a well-developed talent for sidetracking conversation he found uncomfortable. He hurriedly ordered up the film we'd been invited to view and we all settled back to watch.

What is there to say about a movie that has become as familiar— and notorious—as *Sub Sub?* It was intended to propel Simon Dunkle out of the cult-film ghetto, and that it surely did, as explosively as if the young director had been shot from a cannon. Though hardly mainstream fare, it managed to hold out in a number of first-run houses around the country for several weeks, long enough to attract significant critical attention—and then for many months more in the shopping-mall cineplexes, where its largely adolescent audience took to it like an addictive drug. There were reports that some kids had seen the picture more than a hundred times and threatened to riot at theaters where it stopped showing.

Because the film seemed to sneak into circulation without any promotional hoopla, reviewers everywhere could flatter themselves that it was their "discovery"—always a surefire way to hook the critics. And so *Sub Sub* got talked about and talked about, debated and discussed, often with the sort of tantalizing disapproval that creates a *succès de scandale*. I may have little to add to that talk now; still, my reaction to what was, in effect, the movie's premiere screening before an audience of outsiders is part of my adventure with Simon Dunkle and my quest for Max Castle. So I will recount the experience here, noting that my recollection of the work is of the unexpurgated version, never seen by more than a handful. Critics who were subsequently to pronounce *Sub Sub* the most awesomely ghastly vision of our postnuclear future ever produced still have no idea how much of its ghastliness they missed—a full forty minutes that had to be cut before distributors would offer the film to first-run houses.

I'm sure there are long-suffering ganglia deep within my nervous system that continue to reverberate to my first punishing impression of *Sub Sub*. To begin with, the sound, the malignantly inhuman sound. Having borrowed rock video as his genre, Simon didn't hesitate to launch his film with a full-scale assault upon the eardrums of his audience. I understood at the time that rock music, as performed in concert, had reached astronomical levels of amplification; but I had no idea sound of such volume could be etched into celluloid. *Sub Sub* opened like a mountain of noise collapsing on one's head, never relenting by more than a fraction of a decibel from beginning to end. Jeanette, sitting beside me, started in her seat, then clapped her hands over her ears, where they stayed for the remainder of the film. I manfully exposed myself to the cacophony, determined to take in all I could, only to discover that within ten minutes my hearing had gone numb.

Before it did, I was able to make out voices—the constant and incomprehensible yammer of Bobby Pox and the Stinks screaming to be heard above the film's even louder and expertly engineered sound effects, which were, as far as I could tell, a thundering composite of roaring engines, clanging metal, explosions, collisions, gunfire, tumult.

For some five minutes, while we were being bombarded by this nearly unbearable uproar, the screen remained dark, as if the sound-track were offering us an overture for a movie that was yet to begin. The promotion for the film emphasized that it opened with Bobby Pox's hit bumper-sticker ballad "Bend Over, Baby, and Let Me Drive." That's the way audiences continue to experience the beginning of *Sub Sub:* sound without pictures. But my studies of Max Castle had schooled my senses; I couldn't fail to recognize negative etching when I saw it. Or rather felt it. I knew the unlit screen before me was alive with imagery; and my instinct told me it was every bit as brutal as the sounds I heard. Before the movie rose to visibility, I could feel panic and terror welling up inside me. And I wasn't alone. Jeanette, working her shoulder into my chest, let me know she wanted to be shielded. I slipped my arm about her and could feel the tremors that ran through her body.

Once the movie was on the screen bright and clear, it took no more than a few minutes for me to tell that Simon had turned a corner in his career. The boy had come out of the garage. While clearly low-budget, *Sub Sub* was a remarkably well-crafted thirty-five-millimeter color production, the filmmaker's first attempt—and a successful one—to make full professional use of his studio. Even where the film had to cut financial corners, Simon found ingenious ways to mask his economies, if only by way of sensational violence or some nicely designed spoof of the very genre he was using. His skill in this respect was exactly what managed to charm many critics. Wised-up reviewers could tell they were watching a devilishly clever piece of work.

But while Simon had upgraded the technical skill of his work, his message remained as nihilistic as ever. Filmed in the harshest regions of the Mojave Desert, *Sub Sub* is little more than a pageant of unrelieved violence chronicling the endless war between several tribes of inarticulate mutants, the degenerate survivors of a world holocaust. The cast is given only one line, which it lip-syncs from Bobby Pox and the Stinks on the sound track, the only fragment of their lyrics I could make out. "We be sub sub. We be sub sub." Again and again cretinous faces thrust themselves into the camera lens like inquisitive primates to repeat the words. Sub *what?* They are too far gone to know, devolved to a level from which they can no longer recall the humanity they have left so far behind.

For some two hours, these freakish remnants of our species race about a barren landscape in bizarre vehicles improvised from the remains of trucks, fork lifts, tractors, airplanes, bulldozers. The gasoline needed to fuel these makeshift engines is the only wealth they respect. In pursuit of it, they smash and crash into one another, slaughtering everyone in sight with grotesquely savage weapons: harpoons, blowtorches, crossbows, cattle prods, chainsaws. The variations on human carnage reach a level of diabolical inventiveness. Much of the mayhem is so blatantly realistic, it is difficult to see how it could have been filmed without somebody getting maimed or killed. Again and again, I felt Jeanette turn in my embrace to hide her eyes in the hollow of my neck. I felt guilty that my curiosity kept me from yielding to a similar queasiness. Our fellow viewers, however, clearly had no such qualms. The more graphic the violence became, the more exuberant were the howls of sheer delight that went up from Bobby Pox and his party—and from Sharkey, trumpeting his approval right along with them. And theirs would be the response *Sub Sub* would enjoy from adolescent audiences everywhere, who relished the film as the first of what permissive critics would herald as a new genre: genocidal farce.

Yet as excessively brutal as the movie was, it had the same riveting quality that Simon managed to bring to all his work. Arresting images, sly touches of pathos, macabre humor, above all a driving conviction that made one willing to watch just a little more, a little more. There were, quite simply, elements of undeniable artistry to the boy's work. No desert put on film ever looked more utterly desolate than the world of the Sub Subs, a sterile, glowing hell under a merciless sun whose brilliance is allowed to flare the film and batter the eyes throughout. It is the wasteland to end all wastelands, a setting whose inhumanity is as dumbfounding as the mindless carnage that fills it. As time passes in the movie, we have the impression that the sun is expanding, scorching the earth, drying up every last source of life. The light grows more and more blinding until we can scarcely make out the images that move in the sweltering shimmer.

Still the senseless war goes on, the tribes contending for a trophy that lies hidden in a deep underground chamber. Throughout the tale we wonder what the object is, for we glimpse only portions of its shadowy form. It would seem to be the last relic of a civilized sensibility. At last we see it whole. It is an unexploded missile warhead that has been transformed by its brain-damaged possessors into a barbarous icon. It looms up at the end of the movie mounted on an altar that, if examined closely (something Simon's audience wasn't likely to do) reveals itself to be a junkyard jumble of defunct religious images and artifacts: crucifixes, Islamic crescents, Egyptian ankhs, yin-yang circles, Hindu mandalas. Simon's films often included touches like this, details and elaborations that didn't have to be there but which were, usually slipping by too rapidly to be noticed. Finally, inevitably, the Sub Subs accidentally ignite the warhead. Its fireball rises to merge with the blaze of the sun in a marriage of annihilating light that swallows the scene, the story, and all meaning.

For a half minute at the conclusion, the screen pulsates with a light too bright to watch. The voices of the Stinks wail like the cry of the damned, then suddenly fade. The screen goes dark. The end. An end that seems to vibrate through the theater like a vast, cosmic beat. I was sure this hideous interval was filled with one of Max Castle's swirling motifs, the black hole of despair.

When the movie ended, someone brought up the house lights a bit too rapidly. Simon, who was sitting a few aisles in front of me with his dark glasses off, turned, startled, in my direction. Indeed his eyes were bunny-nose pink. He blinked at me painfully out of a paste-white face like some subterranean creature that had been unearthed into the daylight. Quickly he replaced the glasses and then sat staring down into his lap, his jaw knotting and twisting as he chomped on a cheek-bulging wad of Milk Duds.

But his guests—other than Jeanette and myself—were all abubble. Bobby Pox and his contingent—which had consumed more than a joint or two in the course of the viewing—could hardly contain themselves. Slutty was writhing in her seat. "Oh, barfy!" she squealed over and over. "What a barfy flick!"

"It screams real good," one of the other girls added. Humper, his eyeballs now featuring pupils dilated to the size of black nickels, vaulted awkwardly over two rows of seats to thump Simon savagely on the back. "Wild, man! We got a crotch-buster here for sure. But, hey, y'know, we should boost the amps. It don't pierce enough."

Pox, sitting back and dragging deep, judiciously pronounced the work "Epic. Total butt-fuckin' epic."

And, of course, Sharkey was certain we had witnessed a "classic."

I glanced at Jeanette. She stared back at me, her eyes wide and hollow, the face of someone who had just stepped out of a car crash. "Still want your interview?" I asked. She just kept staring. I repeated the question, then realized she hadn't heard me. She was waiting for her ears to stop jangling.

Brother Justin bustled over at once to move in beside me. "So, Professor, what do you think?" A few rows ahead, Simon craned around in his seat, his eager white face staring back at me, a mute but urgent echo of the same question.

This called for a nicely balanced answer. Nothing too severe. There were things I still had to learn from these people. And yet, with Jeanette there beside me, I didn't want to offer outright lies. But for that matter, I wasn't at all certain what I did think. At one level, disgust. At another, admiration. "Well . . . it was surely an experience. I haven't caught my breath yet."

"You found it powerful . . . moving?" Brother Justin's toothy smile pressed in closer.

"I was definitely moved." Playing for time, I raised a question that had troubled me throughout the movie. "Were any of the stuntmen injured?"

"Stuntmen . . . ?" The question caught Brother Justin off balance. Impatiently, he looked across at Decker.

"Actually, we didn't use any stuntmen," Decker answered.

Simon struggled to amend the remark. "Except for f-f-f . . ."

"Oh yes," Decker interpreted. "Except where fire was involved. Otherwise, we just recruited extras on the site. One of our many economies."

"Extras?" I couldn't imagine rank amateurs agreeing to take on the hazards I'd just seen.

"Bikers, scooter nuts, wheel freaks, and such. They hang out in that part of the desert over the weekends. In and around Barstow. They were happy to be in one of Simon's movies."

"Dope 'em up, they'll drive into a truck for you," Pox explained with a mean laugh. "Dumb fuckers! Remember the turkey who ran through the grinder?" His party sent up a howl. "We told him there was a pound of hash at the other end."

Brother Justin, annoyed by the digression, reverted to his line of questioning. "You think the film will prove successful?"

"Successful . . . in what way?"

"In reaching a larger audience for Simon."

I did all I could to conceal the regret behind my answer. "Yes, I believe it will."

"Ah!" He was pleased. "You see, we have invested a great deal in this production, far more than in Simon's other efforts, which were frankly intended for a limited public. We hope that this film . . ."

"It's a breakthrough," Sharkey assured him. "This'll go first run, no question."

Bobby Pox had a deep thought to add. "It's what the world's been waitin' for. *Quid pro quo.*"

But Brother Justin was clearly more interested in my judgment. I tried to assume a professionally objective air. "Of course, I'm no expert on film marketing, but I'd say you have a good chance of getting into some first-run movie theaters in major cities. It's a polished production and in a currently popular genre. Of course, there'd probably have to be a number of cuts. . . ."

Simon leaped at the word. "C-c-c-c . . ."

Offering him an apologetic look, I said, "There are a few sequences that really go too far for a general audience. Not that they aren't done well . . . I mean, convincingly. But the picture does run long, so it could do with some trimming. And it is rather loud."

"What'd he say?" Humper asked in all directions.

"He says it's too loud," Pox shouted, laughing off the idea.

"Oh shit, man!" Humper protested, tossing me a look of aggressive contempt. "You must got bunny ears. We could crank it up to a hundred twenty dbs easy."

"Just don't cut out my big part, that's all," Slutty insisted. She meant the scene in which she'd been the victim-star who gets "done" by the whole tribe. I'd been watching for that especially. To my surprise, it hadn't been so hard to take, primarily because, in her scene as in the rest of the movie, nobody seemed human enough in action or response to evoke sympathy. Like all the Sub Subs, Slutty had emerged as a sort of imbecile simian. Nevertheless, hers was among the first scenes I would have expected to see cut, if only because the sex organs remained recognizably humanoid.

"But otherwise," Brother Justin went on, "allowing for some tactful editing, you believe the film can find critical approval?"

I took a deep breath. It carried me over miles of comments I might have made—severe reservations, agonizing doubts, moral qualms. I knew I hadn't been invited to the screening to offer thoughts like these. Nor, in all honesty, could I say I'd come to present them.

Rather, I was an anxious and uncertain guest in a world that aroused my curiosity as much as it repelled me. My pursuit of Max Castle had brought me here; in Simon Dunkle, I'd found one of his soulmates and disciples. I could hardly allow something as minor as moral revulsion to turn me around at this point.

"Critical approval . . . ? Yes, frankly, I believe it will. Judging from the state of the cultural scene, I think Bobby could be right. This is what the world may be waiting for."

Brother Justin's face lit up with encouragement. "Then we must talk," he said, reaching out to give my arm a grateful pat.

It wasn't until Brother Justin had gotten me aside in an upstairs office that he put his proposition to me. Jeanette, who was sticking close to me as if I were the great white hunter leading her through the wilds of the Congo, asked to come along, but Brother Justin made it clear that he wanted a few words with me in private. Reluctantly, she trailed off with Sharkey and the others back to the cabana where we learned that a buffet was to be served.

"Professor Gates, we believe it is time to present Simon to the world," Brother Justin began, sounding portentous enough to make me feel distinctly uncomfortable. "A young artist with so great a gift, so much to say to his generation . . . Would you be interested in assisting in this project?"

It wasn't clear to me what he expected. "You're not asking me to become Simon's press agent? That's not my line of work."

"Of course not." Irritably, Brother Justin waved the idea aside. "You are an internationally respected film scholar. It is in that capacity that we approach you. We would like to have you treat Simon's work as the subject of a serious critical study, as you have the work of Max Castle—and we would hope with the same result of introducing his films to a larger public. You see, after *Sub Sub* is released, we expect there will be a great deal of interest in Simon. We would prefer to see him brought into the mainstream by someone whose judgment and taste were mature, well schooled, and, above all, in tune with his work."

"You assume I would have a favorable opinion of that work. I couldn't guarantee that."

Brother Justin passed off my reservations with a wave of the hand. "You would of course be free to deal with Simon's films as critically as you might wish. You see, we have every confidence that the more closely you examine his movies, the more merit you will find there."

"You're sure of that?"

"Indeed, yes. Who would be more likely to bring the right sensibility to the job than someone who has been so deeply immersed in the films of Max Castle? That is precisely why we extend this invitation to you. We feel you are uniquely qualified to be Simon's interpreter."

I still wasn't certain what this invitation might mean. "What is it exactly you would have me do?"

Brother Justin spread his arms in a gesture of welcome. "Be our guest here at the school. Come as often as you wish, stay as long as you care to stay. All of Simon's films are here. Screen them. Study them. Above all, Simon is here and at your disposal."

"I could have an interview with him?"

"As many as you wish. As you can see, he's a shy boy. Not at all the sort who might be able to meet his public or the press. But here, on his own grounds, with someone he can trust, I'm sure you will find him forthcoming."

I wondered if this was the point at which to put in a good word for Jeanette, who had come much farther than I had to interview Simon. But there was something else on my mind. "I'm certainly curious to know why the sort of films Simon is making should be so popular with his audience. But I think I must explain: just now I'm trying to finish a major piece of writing on Max Castle. As it is, I'm way behind on the book. I really don't have the time to begin a new study now."

"But there need be no conflict," Brother Justin insisted. "There must be a great deal about Castle you still want to know, details of his life, insights into his films. We could be of some help with your research in this respect. Studying Simon can be a way of studying Castle, do you see?"

The man was offering me a deal. If I helped with Simon, I would, in turn, be helped with Castle. But how? "That's an attractive offer. But I'm not certain what sort of contribution you might make to my research. Dr. Byx told me all the records that had to do with Castle were lost in the war."

Brother Justin nodded. "Yes, that is doubtless true. But there are other matters. For example, you asked about Castle's visits to our school. As I said, that was largely before my time. Still, I'm sure I could remember a bit more, if I set my mind to it. And then there is Brother Marcion. I'm sure he could fill in many details."

Theodore Roszak

"Your predecessor? But you said he was dead."

"No, no. Simply retired . . . some twelve years ago."

"He must be quite along in years."

"It is characteristic of our church: many of our members live to a ripe old age. Brother Marcion must be . . . oh, nearly one hundred. But his mind is as sharp as ever."

"I see. Well, I would of course value an interview with him. But I don't see that this need involve me with Simon's work."

"As to that . . . there are bound to be certain instructive parallels between Castle and Simon, coming as they do from the same religious background. Such early influences would surely be worth your attention."

I flashed at once on the phrase. "As a matter of fact, I asked Dr. Byx about such influences. He was not at all hospitable to the idea. He assured me there was no connection whatever between Castle's education and his later work. He was absolutely firm on that point."

Brother Justin chuckled. "That is very like Dr. Byx, to be so impatient with such a question. He's a busy man with many responsibilities in all parts of the world. You were most fortunate to have as much time with him as you did. I suspect he simply didn't wish to be troubled. Matters of doctrine and education are rather outside his scope."

I squinted hard at Brother Justin, letting him see my bewilderment. "I find that odd. I should think that, as head of your church, Dr. Byx would be exactly the person . . ."

I was stopped by the expression of surprise that came over Brother Justin's face. "Head of our church? Excuse me, Professor. You have that quite wrong. Dr. Byx is not the head of our church. Oh my, no. He is our chief administrator, but his duties are strictly secular. Matters of finance, personnel, international diplomacy. Strictly speaking, our faith has no 'head' except the Saviour Himself. We do have our spiritual authorities. Our elders. They reside in Albi."

"Albi?"

"Near Toulouse, in southern France. A city that has some historical importance for us."

"Dr. Byx never mentioned that to me. I wish he had. I would have arranged a visit."

Brother Justin wagged his head dismissively. "I doubt that would have been possible. The elders live a cloistered life. They rarely meet with people from the outside. Their role is purely inspirational and

393

doctrinal. To set an example of purity, to defend the teachings of our faith."

A small, sharp ripple of irritation ran through me, the same feeling I'd experienced when Dr. Byx mentioned the "veiled" character of his church. Of course, it was really none of my business if the orphans wanted to keep their religion to themselves. But once again their air of secrecy was interfering with my study of Max Castle.

"I wish I could learn something more about these teachings," I told Brother Justin. "That might be necessary if I'm to understand Simon's work. You see, beyond knowing that you are Cathars . . ." I paused to see what effect the word might produce. Nothing special. Brother Justin simply nodded as if to say, yes, you've got that much right. ". . . I really don't have much to go on when it comes to understanding the influences under which Castle worked, and now Simon."

Brother Justin dismissed the problem. "Fortunately, we have a very full library. You can find all the books you need right here."

"Oh? Dr. Byx told me in no uncertain terms that there were no reliable books I could turn to. He said I'd be better off reading nothing."

Brother Justin assumed an indulgent smile. "There are purists in our order—like Dr. Byx—who take such a position. And of course there is a certain truth to what they say. It is difficult for those who are not of our faith to do full justice to our teachings. But I assure you there are many excellent books I can recommend—some by our own scholars. Works you may not find elsewhere. And we are here, myself and my colleagues, to answer any questions you may have."

Once again, Brother Justin was contradicting Dr. Byx, offering me what the doctor had withheld, and offering it eagerly. In Zurich, I'd felt like a beggar turned away at the door. Now, I had the altogether uneasy feeling that I was being enticed, the way a fish is enticed by the angler. I didn't believe Brother Justin had taken it upon himself to initiate so friendly and open a relationship. Clearly, some consultation with Dr. Byx had taken place, and there had been a change of policy. I had no idea why, but I could see no reason to refuse what was offered. "What would you expect to come of my study of Simon?" I asked. "Not a book, I hope."

"Nothing so ambitious at this point. But perhaps something like your very fine article on Castle in *The New York Times*. A critical analysis, but intended for the general public."

It was a realistic enough goal, except in one important respect.

"You understand that the *Times* commissioned me to write my piece on Castle? Nobody's asked me to write about Simon."

Brother Justin wasn't concerned. "I feel certain anything you write on Simon will find its way into print quite promptly, especially after *Sub Sub* is released."

So I agreed to come visiting again, the next time primarily to talk with Simon. I made a point of insisting that I bring Jeanette with me, characterizing her as a serious film student with a deep interest in Simon's work. Brother Justin raised no objections. He was, in fact, being so ingratiating that I was emboldened to raise a challenging issue. "I think I should let you know, Brother Justin, that I have some serious doubts about Simon's work. Not about its technical side. He's a very clever young man, even—or perhaps especially—when he's affecting a primitive style. But, quite honestly, I find the content of his movies . . . well, let's say in dubious taste."

I checked to see how Brother Justin might react to the remark. He sat listening patiently, waiting for more. So I pushed a little farther. "Even in *very bad* taste. Frankly, that leaves me puzzled. I can't see why a church, any church, should be associated with films that are filled with such violence, obscenity, cynicism. To put it bluntly, *Sub Sub* is a chamber of horrors. Many, many people wouldn't have the stomach to sit through it. It may very well be a popular success. But please tell me why your church should want to pour material like this into the minds of young people."

When I finished, I realized I was holding my breath, waiting for some angry or hurt response from Brother Justin. It didn't come. Instead, he answered quietly, in measured phrases, as if he might have expected the question. As he spoke, his eyes never left my face. "Professor, have you ever read the books of the prophets in the Old Testament? Amos, Isaiah, Jeremiah . . ."

"Well, long ago. In Sunday school . . . I think."

"Then possibly you remember. Most of what the prophets preached had to do with sin, fornication, abominations. Not a very pleasant view of life, but true, all too true. And what were they saying? That we live in hell. That we are damned souls. Is that not true?"

I've never heard the prophets interpreted that way, at least within my limited religious background. But who was I to dispute the point with a priest? "I suppose you could read the books that way," I agreed.

"What a picture of the world they painted with their words! But now those words are *mere* words in an old book. Who reads them today with any care? Something more penetrating is required. A new kind of prophecy, appropriate to our time."

I recalled what the little boy had said as he led us from the parking lot to the cabana. "Is that how you see Simon's work, as prophecy?"

He shrugged. "Who can say? Perhaps one day . . . Remember, Simon is still very young, too young to be numbered among the prophets of our faith. But already he has found a way to speak to his peers. He has such a keen eye—and ear—for the spiritual malaise of our time. It is not unthinkable that some day the images that fill his films will become as memorable as those that fill St. John's Revelation. The great beast, the whore of Babylon. For example, this Bobby Pox and his friends, these unfortunate young people who are with us today, would you not describe them as the perfect example of damned souls?" He pressed the point. "Would you?"

"That seems very harsh to say."

Brother Justin rolled right along. "Damned souls, knowing they are damned. Knowing! Wallowing in their depravity, advertising it. Could there be a more vivid image of our condition than that our young people should confabulate with their own damnation, turn it into their art? You may wonder how Sister Helena and I can sit by while they cavort before us. We see them as spiritual cripples, objects of pathos. We view them with pity. Simon has made the only good use that can be made of such wretched human material. He has given them a place in his vision."

There was a smugness to what Brother Justin was saying that I might have found offensive if the words hadn't been tempered with a genuine sorrow. A greater sorrow than I could muster for Pox and his crew, all of whom seemed to me a batch of degenerate bums. It was actually quite charitable of Brother Justin to see them as spiritual cripples. "But Simon's films . . . they're so filled with negativity, with despair. Is that the role of prophecy?"

Brother Justin's smile was now tinged with a deepening melancholy. "You must read your scriptures more closely. The prophet Seth tells us that even the one true God despairs of our condition. 'For this world which thou dost inhabit is itself become the realm of darkness, and this very flesh that clothes thee is thy perdition.' "

We walked from the studio back to the cabana. The path led downhill about a mile over unlighted ground. Brother Justin, carrying a flashlight, led the way. We didn't say much. But just before we reached the stake fence from behind which I could hear bursts of repellent laughter from Humper and Slutty, a final question occurred to me.

"Did Max Castle ever qualify as one of the prophets of your faith?"

"I understand that there were high hopes for him in the early days," Brother Justin answered as he unlocked the gate. "But later . . . well, it is really the role of our elders to designate the prophets in their own good time. So who can say?"

Sharkey, Jeanette, and I didn't get away from St. James School until after eleven o'clock that evening. This time Sharkey occupied the backseat, too stoned to be trusted at the wheel on the rough, winding road back to the beach. I could tell that our visit had had something like a traumatic effect upon Jeanette. She sat in a troubled silence for most of the trip, her sullenness contrasting starkly with Sharkey's carryings-on behind us. He was passing the time at one of his favorite strung-out entertainments: whistling the soundtrack scores of Maria Montez's greatest hits. Finally, after several miles of quiet, Jeanette turned to me. "Surely this movie we have seen, it will never be shown." She was clearly asking me to say it wouldn't.

"Oh yes it will," I said. "With a few minor cuts here and there. In a couple of years, it'll be on prime-time television. Oh yes. It will be a great success, sorry to say."

Sharkey, picking up our remarks, plunked his chin on the top of the seat between us. "Great flick, great flick! Didn't you think it was a great flick?"

I teased him a little. "Do you think Clare would think it was a great flick?"

Sharkey let out a raspy-watery little smirk. "Oh Christ, Clare! Would she have her ass in an uproar. All night long, I can tell you. Boy oh boy, would I like to tie her to a chair and make her watch the whole thing." He gave a wicked laugh. "But what about it, old pal? Didn't you think it was great? I thought you thought it was great. Didn't you think it was groovy-great?"

"Within a certain, special critical category, it was supreme," I answered.

"What's he sayin'?" Sharkey asked Jeanette. "What kind of categal critigory?"

"Like public executions," I said. "Or lynchings. When the mob comes back, it tells everybody it was a great lynching. Or like the

Aztecs, at the end of one of their ceremonies, maybe they used to say 'That was a great human sacrifice. The skin came off all in one piece.' Groovy!"

"It will never be a success in France," Jeanette insisted.

"Wrong," I said. "Victor will love it. They'll all love it. The Semiologists, the Deconstructionists, what's his name, Vulkoloff . . . Mark my words. Simon Dunkle will be the rage of the *rive gauche* by next year."

"But why?" She really wanted to know.

"Wrong question," I corrected. "These days we ask 'Why not?' Why not mayhem and torture and bondage? Why not bloody murder and genocide and apocalyptic fun and games? That's why. Because Simon Dunkle is the prophet of *why not*. And you and I are going to be the first to introduce him to the world that's waiting to hear from him."

23 THE CONNECTION

"The extermination of the Cathars. Jonny, my lad, that is one helluva story! Blood and guts, sword and fire, torture and mayhem. What more could you ask for?"

Faustus Carstad was UCLA's medieval specialist, one of the school's professorial luminaries. Now approaching his emeritus years, he still ranked as an internationally distinguished scholar—though it was rumored that younger members of his department regarded him as an antiquated drum-and-trumpet historian. Faustus would have been the first to admit to the charge, and without apologies. He fairly embodied the indictment. A vast, Falstaffian hulk of a man with a voice that teetered on the edge of a war whoop, he could easily have passed, with a change of costume, for one of the Viking chieftains to whom he proudly traced his ancestry. Barbarians were his kind of people.

Theodore Roszak

Faustus brought a bracing Hemingway air to the academy, the same gruff masculine bravado, the same keen eye for physical prowess. Literally *an* eye. The right one. The other had been left at Okinawa, where he was credited with acts of genuine heroism. The patch he wore over the hollow socket had gained him the nickname Captain Kidd among his students. The piratical persona was more than a matter of appearance; it carried over into a cut-and-thrust lecture style that never failed to wallow in the gory details of his subject matter. The admonition he issued on the first day of class had become legendary. "History," he would growl, "takes a strong stomach—at least the way you're gonna learn it here. Any of you young ladies who might be inclined to toss your lunch, be warned. Violence, vermin, villainy—and plenty of dirt. That's what medieval Europe was all about, and don't let any of my pantywaist colleagues tell you different. Dark Ages? They were dark as hell. That's what makes 'em worth studying."

Even in that period, when the schools were seething with antiwar agitation, his caveat had the predictable effect; it made him one of the biggest draws on campus. As did the reputation for boozing and womanizing, which (to his obvious satisfaction) was pursuing him into his retirement. When Faustus was at his most ebulliently histrionic—as when he offered his expert demonstration in the proper use of the broadsword for splitting one's opponent from gizzard to crotch—you could have sold tickets for the performance.

Dr. Byx had told me I would find no trustworthy information about his church. Maybe so, but that didn't keep me from trying. No sooner had the fall term begun than I went looking for Faustus to learn all I could about the Cathars. Perhaps what he told me was, by Dr. Byx's standards, unreliable; but it was surely engaging. In fact, bloodcurdling. Which made Faustus all the more eager to hold forth. By the time I approached him I'd managed to fill in the general outlines of the story. Brother Justin's books had helped, though they were only a start; I quickly read beyond them. But nothing I found in the dry, scholarly prose of three languages did more to bring the matter to life for me than a few hours with Faustus. "The western world's first holocaust," was the way he described the fate of the Cathars, at once picking up my query with the sort of gusto that all things bloodthirsty brought out in him. "You have to come all the way down to Herr Hitler to find anything that remotely compares. If Pope Innocent (lovely name for the man!) and his minions had had their way, there wouldn't have been one hank of heretical hair left over. The Cathars were called Albigensians back then—after one of their strongholds. Albi. Spectacular siege. Half the town starved. The rest went in the bloodbath. The Provençals had a gorgeous civilization going down there in the south of France. Effete, but gorgeous. Chivalry, troubadours, all that sort of thing, the first lamentable steps away from a healthy state of savagery. By the time the Holy Father and the Inquisitors got finished defending Christian orthodoxy, the place was a smoldering ruin. Carcassonne, Foix, Montségur. If you travel the area, you can still see the scars all over the landscape. Even Toulouse, the cradle of courtly love. Gutted. But why are you interested in this, my boy? As I recall, you were a lousy history student."

I was hoping he wouldn't remember. As an undergraduate, I had, with maximum reluctance, taken a required course from Faustus. It turned out to be a delightful surprise, taught with wit and Faustus' own patented taste for sensational sanguinity. But at the time I was too absorbed in film studies to give the class more than minimal attention. Confronted with flunking, I pled with him for make-up assignments; that's what he recollected—probably with some suspicion that the paper I submitted had been plagiarized. He was more than half right about that. The work was mainly Clare's, something on Joan of Arc that had more to do with the Dreyer film than real history. But it served to get me through. Charitably, Faustus had given me a C−.

"I'm studying a filmmaker," I explained and then elaborated not very truthfully along lines that I thought might pique his interest. "He was planning a movie about the Albigensian Crusade."

"Was he, now? Anybody I might know?"

"His name was Max Castle."

"Never heard of him. Should I?"

"Not really. German, nineteen-thirties. A minor figure. I'm sort of discovering him."

"Man shows good taste. Somebody should've turned the crusade into a major motion picture years ago. De Mille, John Ford . . . somebody like that. Lots of action, lots of carnage. Sam Fuller, now there's a *man's* director. *Fixed Bayonets*—ever see that?" He gave a grumpy little laugh. "Probably you think that's crap."

No, not just crap. *Sad-little-male-delusions-of-genital-grandeur* crap. Clare's precise words, in which I concurred, but not outspokenly at that particularly sensitive moment. "Actually, Fuller is highly regarded in France."

"That's supposed to mean something to me?"

"Well, I only . . ."

"Last Frenchy that had some balls was Napoleon—and he was half Italian. Since then, it's been all downhill." He gave a bitter little snort. "Dien Bien Phu. Hell, you don't surrender just because you lost. That's just when things get interesting." He touched a match to the soggy cigar he'd been gnawing since I entered his office and paused to suck off a deep drag. On the rebound, his lungs blurted out a harsh, wet cough. "These are gonna be the death of me," he half grumbled, half wheezed as he scrunched the butt in a rusty metal ashtray that looked like part of an antique helmet. The mashed butt, however, went right back between his teeth. "Sonny, did you ever think about damnation?" he asked, fixing me with his one hawkish eye. "I mean *seriously?*"

I realized he'd changed the subject. We were back with the Cathars. "You have to understand," he went on, "in the Middle Ages, theology wasn't just airy-fairy talk. It was the principal weapon of psychological warfare. Especially when it got round to discussions of perdition. The worm that never dies, the fire that's never to be quenched, the devil's poker rammed up your ass from here to eternity. Imagine what kind of clout that gives you in a society of piss-poor, moronic peasants. You've heard the one about power flowing from the muzzle of a gun? Believe me, kiddo, that's nothing compared to the power you can wring out of the muzzle of hell. The moral theology of damnation was the H-bomb in the church's arsenal."

He paused to bring forth a bottle of brandy and two glasses. "Officially against the law on university grounds," he reminded me as he poured. "But we don't care about that, do we, my boy? Hell, forming the minds of the young is thirsty work." I accepted the drink, but before I'd finished, he was two ahead of me.

"As of A.D. 1300," he continued, "the Church of Rome was managing an ecclesiastical monopoly that stretched from Ultima Thule to the Bay of Naples. But there was competition in the field—the Albigenses, who were running a rival firm in the most prosperous religious market in Christendom. Their own liturgy, hierarchy, sacraments, a one-stop, full-service operation. They were signing up the richest lords and ladies of Langue d'Oc. The peons too. Why?

Because the Albigenses took their religion to heart. Whereas, most of what passed for clergy in the Roman Church was a herd of hocus-pocus drunken dimwits who couldn't tell the Apostles' Creed from moldy cheese. Most of them had a couple of concubines on the premises, a raft of kids to feed. God knows what they were getting up to with the female penitents in the confessional. Now on the other hand, the Cathar priests, the Parfaits as they were pleased to call themselves, they were living the true Christian life—if you can call that living. No meat, no wine, no creature comforts. Above all no sex. That's what Cathar means. 'Pure'—as in puritan. Meaning, I suppose, they were a batch of obnoxious, cockless prigs. But they were hitting the old pope where it hurt—square in the bank account."

I'd already learned from my reading that the great Albigensian Crusade held its place as one of the bloodiest chapters in the history of human indecency. D. W. Griffith might have included it as a fifth episode in *Intolerance*. But Faustus was putting an angle on the tale that I hadn't considered. "You believe the whole issue was about money?"

"Damn right it was. Biggest land grab of the Middle Ages. A one-two punch. First you call in the crusaders to rape and pillage and just generally mow down the armed opposition. Then you send in the Inquisitors to barbecue the defenseless survivors. Following which, the victorious forces of the Church Militant lined up at the trough. Mass confiscation. That's what happened in the wake of every persecution. Estates, treasure, livestock, castles. That's how the law worked. A heretic's property escheated to the church. Or in this case to the church and King Philip so-called the Fair. Crafty son of a bitch cut one sweet deal with Pope Innocent. He picked up a prize piece of real estate called the whole of southern France—which had only dubiously belonged to the Capetian crown heretofore. Plus the wealth of the Templars, who got railroaded into oblivion as heretical fellow travelers."

"You don't believe the Templars were Cathars?"

"Maybe yes, maybe no. We've got no hard evidence. Not that King Philip cared about that. Templar gold is what he was after. And there was plenty of that. Templars were the first gentile bankers, you know. Along with the Venetians. Handled the whole cash flow between western Europe and the Holy Land. The trade was worth billions. You can just bet the pope couldn't wait to get his hands on assets like that. But the Templars commanded a lot of respect all across

Christendom. Damn good fighters, and—for the most part—true ascetics. The Poor Knights of Christ, that was their original name. Warrior monks. They had to be discredited before they could be plundered. Holy Father did a damn good job of that. He had the Templars vilified in seven shades of lavender. Witchcraft, pederasty, diabolism, blasphemy . . ." He snorted derisively. "Actually pushed it to the point of diminishing returns. They pinned such a reputation for black magic on old Jacques de Molay that after they burned him on the Île de la Cité—that would've been in 1314—some of the spectators snuck across the river in the dead of night to collect his ashes. Made a fertility potion out of them."

"So you don't think doctrine had anything to do with the persecution."

"Doctrine was a weapon of propaganda. It gave you a cover story. Church always had to have a cover story to knock off its opposition. But what you're essentially dealing with here is a power play of major dimensions."

I asked the question that was at the top of my private agenda. "Do you think any of the Cathars might have survived?"

"Of course it's pretty near impossible to wipe out an idea. But the church came damn close. Went after the Albigenses as if they were the devil's own brood. Which in the eyes of the church they were. Of course, for the Cathars the vice was versa. They regarded the Church of Rome as evil incarnate. In their eyes, the god of the popes was the Great Beast in disguise. Now that's a sure prescription for a battle to the death, isn't it? No room for compromise on either side. The pope's goal was total extermination, a final solution if there ever was one. But how do you kill fond memories and old allegiances? You come across stories about Cathars hiding out among the Moors in Spain. Some of the Templars were said to have taken refuge in other knightly orders, like the Hospitalers. Rumors like that kept the Inquisition in business for the next couple centuries. You can still find a few small congregations practicing Cathars in the south of France. People in that area have an ethnic loyalty to the tradition. Very unlikely any of them represent a direct descent from the original Albigenses. Probably later revivals."

I asked if he'd ever heard of a St. Arnaud. He frowned, reached for an old leather volume in his bookcase—it was a hagiography—and thumbed through. "Nope. No such entry. You got the name right?"

"I came across mention of him as a Cathar saint."

"Anybody can call anybody a saint. But heretic saints have no status in the eyes of the church."

"And here in the United States . . . have you ever come across any Cathar sects?"

That produced a quizzical squint, then a raspy laugh. "Now that you bring it up . . ." He'd been poking around his cluttered office picking out books to loan me, about a half dozen so far. Now he returned to the search, clambering atop a teetering foot ladder to investigate a high corner shelf. He brought back a small, yellowed pamphlet. "Surviving Cathars, that's what you're interested in?"

The document he handed me was a cheap pulp publication with a florid cover. The title read "The Passion of Abraxas: An Account by His Suffering Servants of Their History and Teachings." On the back, there was an address: "The Chapel of the Albigensi Fellowship, Hermosa Beach, California." I looked across to him for clarification.

"When it comes to religion, Jonny, Los Angeles is the elephants' graveyard. These folks asked me to come lecture once. Must be eight years ago. Queer old couple, name of Bird . . . something like that. Well along in years, the both of them. I have no idea if they're still around. Probably are. There's something about religious imbecility, seems to keep the tissues supple."

"And did you?" I asked.

"Did I what?"

"Lecture for them?"

"Christ no! I was, at the time, a respectable scholar. Meaning I was a pompous, tight-assed pedant. But I did pay a visit, just out of curiosity. They turned out to be nice enough. Spooky, but nice. Gave me a lovely vegetarian meal. Gooseberry soup. I still remember."

"Are you recommending I look them up?"

"You asked if there were any surviving Cathars. Here's your chance to find out."

There was a sparkle in his one surviving eye that suggested mischief. "Oh, come on. These are just some local cranks." He continued giving me a playful sort of stare. "Aren't they . . . ?"

"This much I'll tell you. The evening turned out to be a rare and memorable experience."

"How so?"

"You ever hear of oral history?"

"Sure."

"Well, that's what happened. A lesson in oral history. An eyewitness account."

"Of what?"

"The Albigensian Crusade."

The teasing stare continued for another several silent seconds. Then he burst out in a blustery laugh. "Listen here, Jonny. This ain't Oxford, and it ain't Cambridge. Thank God! This is the land of the swamiburger and Aimee Semple McPherson. We've got our own native ways to study history. Be brave. Take a chance. What the hell, you might get a bowl of gooseberry soup out of it."

The name was Feather, not Bird. The Reverend Cecil Feather and wife. That much I found out by calling the number listed for the Chapel of the Albigensi Fellowship. It was still there at the same address in Hermosa Beach. An impressively cultivated English accent answered the phone, a quiet-voiced woman who informed me that there would be a lecture by the Reverend Feather at the Saturday afternoon *consolamentum*. She added, as if I would understand, that she expected a "connection" to take place at that time. Yes, all these events were open to the public. I was welcome to attend.

Not that I hastened to do so. The wicked twinkle in Faustus' eye when he mentioned the group left me believing he might be putting me on. The pamphlet he loaned me made the Albigensi Fellowship sound too much like the items one finds listed in the Religious Directory of *The Los Angeles Times* alongside Applied Mindism and the Temple of Colonic Irrigation. It read like a slightly more accessible version of Father Rosenzweig's turgid disquisition, filled with the same arcane references to aeons and pleromas and voids. Reverend Feather's prose sported a kind of mid-Victorian fruitiness that did wonders at frustrating the most minimal understanding; but for that matter, nothing I'd yet read in the way of Cathar theology was any less impenetrable. Dr. Byx had said the teachings of his church were "veiled." That was putting it mildly. The Cathars specialized in maniacally extrapolating involuted cosmic systems jam-packed with celestial entities. The main purpose of these madly subtle discriminations seemed to be putting as much distance as possible between the physical and the spiritual, a sort of metaphysical apartheid. That left their doctrines all but totally sealed in obscurity, at least to my metaphysically underdeveloped mind. And the obscurity tunneled centuries into the past.

In itself, the story of the Albigensian Crusade took me back seven centuries. But the Albigenses, I soon learned, were only the last in a long line of Cathars, the final phase in a heresy that extended to the earliest days of the Christian church. The shadowy figure of Simon Magus was usually named as the first of the Christian Cathars—or Gnostics as they were more often called in those times. But even he may have been a latecomer. Hadn't Dr. Byx said that his faith was "older than Christ"? It might be so. In some accounts, the Cathars were traced back to the dawn of civilization. I was coming to recognize, with a sense of creepy discomfort, how narrow is the fringe of time on which most of us live out our lives and think our thoughts. There are others—like Brother Justin, Dr. Byx, Max Castle—whose lives belong to an immensely larger dimension, a secret history in which our century is only the last page in an enormous volume unknown to the world at large. I felt like an ant crawling over the hide of an elephant, unaware that the few scant inches of terrain beneath my feet are part of some greater life whose goals and purposes I couldn't imagine. Did I really think a group of religious crackpots in a California beach town was going to illuminate my way in this fog?

I was even less prepared to think so after I made the mistake of mentioning the Albigensi Fellowship to Brother Justin on one of my visits to St. James School. Had he, I wondered, ever heard of the Reverend Feather? He squinted at me inquisitively as if the name sounded familiar. "You don't seem to be the only Cathars in the area," I explained. And I showed him the pamphlet Faustus had lent me.

He took it, turned it over, and then, quite spontaneously, erupted into laughter. Making no comment, he handed the pamphlet back, turned, and left the room choking with hilarity. Later that day, at lunch, I caught a glimpse of Sister Helena looking across at me from another table. She was trying, not very successfully, to hold in an explosive giggle. I turned away, blushing, yet at the same time resentful. Who were these people to bully me in this way? What gave Cathars at Zuma Beach the right to treat Cathars at Hermosa Beach with such dismissive contempt?

Still, I might have been persuaded to forget the Reverend Feather if my relations with Brother Justin had turned out to be as rewarding as I'd hoped. But that was hardly the case. When it came to finding out anything about the Orphans of the Storm, the old fellow was proving to be a slippery customer—but in ways that kept me so intrigued that I often didn't realize until several sessions were behind us that I'd learned nothing I didn't already know from my reading.

Or, more often, I came away knowing less. Brother Justin had a positive gift for obfuscation. He would let me ramble on, then vaguely and somewhat condescendingly agree . . . but not quite. "Yes," he would say, "I suppose one might put it that way, though it rather misses the main point." Or, "That is more or less correct." Or, "That is at best a rough approximation." Sometimes he would give me two or three readings of a metaphor or symbol, but without taking sides. The black bird, for example. It came out as the first, then the second, then the third person of the Holy Trinity. But later Brother Justin seemed to reject the whole idea of the Trinity as "ridiculously crude." God, he assured me, had nothing to do with "persons," but with something called "emanations," of which I eventually tallied up a grand total of more than fifty, each more obscure than the last. Was the black bird then the symbol of an "emanation"? To which the only answer I received was another question. "Ah, but if so, which one, eh?"

On another occasion, the black bird was identified with Abraxas, one of the holy names of the Cathar Godhead, which, I was cautioned, must not be confused with God in any of His persons, emanations, or hypostases.

"Hypostases?" I asked, fishing for clarification.

Brother Justin waved me off. "This we will speak of in its proper time." But we never did.

The notes I took on these discussions brimmed with phrases like "uncertain at this point," "this matter much in dispute," "ambiguous meaning." My confusion mounted as I learned that the Cathars of the crusade descended through many sects that could be traced back and back. On each of these Brother Justin was happy to offer me books and articles from his library. There were nights when I found myself delving into the histories of ancient cults that once flourished in lands I never heard of. The Ophites of Hyrcania, the Phibriotes of Cappadocia, the Shiite Gnostics of Seljuk Iconium. Who the hell were these people? And why should I be sitting here to all hours with the roar of a twentieth-century Los Angeles freeway in my ears, losing sleep, trying to understand their differing interpretations of the sixteenth emanation of the androgynous demiurges? Still I soldiered on, looking for just the right piece of information that would make Max Castle and Simon Dunkle part of the enigmatic religious fabric that Brother Justin was unfurling before me an inch at a time. Trusting as I was by nature, it only gradually dawned upon me as the days turned into weeks and the weeks into months that Brother Justin had no serious intention of clarifying anything for me. The man was giving me the metaphysical runaround. At which point I could see no reason why I shouldn't be willing to fritter away an hour or two with the Cathars across town.

The Chapel of the Albigensi Fellowship proved not at all easy to locate. After a long drive on a warm evening, I spent nearly an hour searching for the address I'd noted down. Hermosa Beach was one of those down-on-its-luck coastal towns that spends most of the year hoping the teenagers will show up during the holidays to stage a few orgies and incidentally buy some beer and hot dogs. I spent the better part of an hour cruising one of its seedier ocean-front neighborhoods where nobody was doing very much to maintain property values. The address I had for the chapel belonged to a thrift store. "Aunt Natalie's Antiques and Collectibles" was trying hard to pass itself off as Ye Olde Curiosity Shoppe, but most of what it displayed behind the sun-bleached chintz curtains of its front window looked like little better than you might find at the Salvation Army.

I walked past the store three or four times before I caught sight of a faded hand-lettered sign propped in a rear corner of the window. It informed me that the chapel I was seeking was at the rear, meaning down a driveway, around the back of the store. There, behind a high wooden gate, I discovered a small, neatly kept garden and at its center a structure one could find no place but in southern California: a small wood-frame bungalow sagging beneath a mock-Gothic facade done in cheesy synthetic stone siding. There was a pathetically stunted turret set slightly askew on the roof; at each corner it sported hand-painted gargoyles that might have been rendered by a Disney Studios reject. A glassed-in notice case beside the gate announced not very encouragingly that the Reverend Cecil Feather was Grand Archon of the Fellowship and Natalie Feather its Mater Suprema.

Almost instinctively I found myself edging back toward the street to make my getaway. Too late. A bell attached to the gate tinkled when I entered and I was spotted. A tall, white-haired woman with an extraordinarily thrusting overbite appeared at the entrance of the chapel. She was wearing an ankle-length, silver-fringed white gown that would have made Ginger Rogers look overdressed when she went flying down to Rio. She greeted me with a broad smile that revealed a mouthful of long, misaligned teeth. "Have you come for the lecture?" she called across the garden. It was the voice I'd heard on the telephone, throaty, well-modulated, and very, very English.

"Yes . . ." I said, because what else could I say at that point? I'd apparently interrupted the proceedings. From inside the darkened chapel, curious faces were turned in my direction.

"Oh, how very nice!" she said. "It's always pleasant to have newcomers. Please join us. Cecil is just finishing."

My hope had been to arrive early enough to make this a brief reconnaissance: chat with whoever might be in charge, find out what I could (which I expected wouldn't be much), then make a quick departure before anything ceremonial got started. No such luck. Having spent so long finding the place, I'd come in on the middle of the lecture. Parading me through the dimly lit interior of the tiny chapel like a living trophy, the woman in white sat me in the front row. The curious faces followed me down the aisle, now looking discomfortingly eager—as if, just possibly, a recruit had come their way. There were fewer than a dozen members in the flock, all but two of them women, all of them old. Very old. I couldn't recall ever feeling more agonizingly out of place.

The woman, who had returned to her place at the lecturer's side and who I now gathered must be Aunt Natalie, the Mater Suprema herself, had said Cecil was "just finishing." Twenty minutes later, Cecil was still finishing. By then I had the distinct feeling that he was doubling back and repeating for the newcomer's benefit, lest I miss any of the gems he had to offer. He needn't have bothered. What he said may have had the sound of coherent speech: grammar, syntax—it was all there. But no meaning, none at all. Not that it didn't sound familiar. I'd absorbed enough Cathar vocabulary to recognize themes and variations; it was simply that nothing I read or heard connected with any reality I knew. Even when the reverend paused for my benefit to restate his topic for the evening, it didn't help. With the gusto of a maître d' announcing that day's special, he explained, "We are examining the third syzygy of the Ogoadad." Cathars went in for racy stuff like that. I smiled with polite interest. A mistake. It only encouraged him to prolong the analysis.

The Grand Archon was a small man with a benignly moon-shaped face and goggling watery eyes behind inch-thick spectacles. He was bald except for a wispy fringe of white hair that flared out from behind his ears lending a certain zany wildness to his aspect. Like his wife he also wore an ankle-length robe, but his was black and satiny, tied at the ample waist with a silver sash. Around his neck he wore a Maltese cross that looked heavy enough to drown a cat; it lay unsteadily balanced on his prominent paunch. He too was English, though his accent was tinged with just enough cockney to make its use for heavy metaphysical discourse sound faintly ludicrous.

As he droned on, my attention wandered to take in the decor of the chapel. Behind the Reverend Feather at his lectern there was a small, tastelessly ornate altar constructed of an obviously fake marble veneer. It was cluttered with what must have been a small sampling of Aunt Natalie's pricier collectibles: tinny-looking candelabra, some shiny metal cups and plates, a few framed pictures of faces caught in various beatific raptures, and at the center a large Maltese cross carved from wood. Above the altar in mock-Gothic lettering a foot high were the words *Duo Sunt*. I knew the phrase from my reading: *There are two*, the basic Cathar doctrine.

I turned to survey the rest of the interior, quickly discovering that I would have to do this with a minimal rotation of the head. Whichever way I shifted in my seat to look around, I found a smiling, questioning face staring into mine. The expressions were friendly, but unnerving, all of them obviously asking ". . . and just what might you be doing in this geriatric assembly, young man?" Wondering the same, I smiled back and looked away, knowing that the inquiring eyes of the tiny congregation remained fixed on me. From what I could catch out of the corner of my eye, it seemed the same hand that had done the awful gargoyles on the turret had cartooned the interior walls and ceiling with a thicket of painted columns, arches, buttresses. The place might have been the stage set for a high school production of *The Vagabond King*. The lighting, such as it was—a string of Christmas-tree bulbs stretched along the moldings, some red, some amber, some purple, and about half of them burned out—managed to be both dismal and lurid. Dim as the chapel was, however, I could make out its main aesthetic embellishment: a series of drab and dreadful oil paintings along each wall that depicted atrocities and martyrdoms. Whatever issues of doctrine may have divided the Orphans of the Storm and the Albigensi Fellowship, the tastes of both sects ran to the macabre.

At last, mercifully, the Reverend Feather brought his exhaustive exegesis to what I'm sure he took to be a rousing conclusion. With arms outspread, he intoned, "Once again, beloved sisters and brothers, we stand at the threshold of the Bridal Chamber. Apolytrosis awaits us beyond. May Lord Abraxas bestow upon us the bliss of the Pneumatic Union." With a single voice, the congregation called out "Amen!" I clocked his lecture at just over an hour since I'd arrived. It was now going on toward five in the afternoon. The service was not, however, over. There followed "the sacramentum." After the reverend had mumbled a brief blessing at the altar, he turned, holding out a silver chalice. Each member of the flock rose and walked solemnly forward to the altar to kneel and take a sip from it. As the rite transpired, Mrs. Feather moved to a small pipe organ at one side of the chapel and proceeded to play a potpourri of lugubriously funereal tunes. The organ was powered by a foot-treadle that creaked louder than the tones that were being pumped out of the wheezing bellows. Her playing was wretchedly amateurish, embellished with piercing organ stings and arpeggios that her arthritically stiff fingers could no longer negotiate. But buried in the syrupy cacophony was a recurrent motif that I would have sworn was a doleful version of "Bye Bye Blackbird."

When the last parishioner had taken her taste of the wine, the reverend offered a brief benediction in cockneyfied Latin, wiped the chalice, and stored it away. Then, turning to the congregation, his eyes on me especially, he asked in a cheery tone, "Shall we adjourn to the garden for tea?" He and his wife at once descended upon me offering hospitality. By now stiff in every joint, I more than eagerly accepted. We repaired to a far corner of the yard where a member of the congregation—a wiry little woman named Althea—was already laying out the promised refreshments: some expertly brewed tea and cute little cookies. The rest of the flock bustled after us, gathering to listen at a respectful distance around the umbrella-shaded table where we sat. As soon as I introduced myself as a professor I could tell that the Feathers regarded me as a valuable catch. "We do so appreciate having people from the university join us," the reverend announced, "because, as you know, we move in deep waters here, deep waters. There are so many questions. . . ."

"So *very* many questions," Mrs. Feather echoed.

". . . and all of them requiring the attention of the keenest minds. Because of course, as you realize, these matters are vital."

"*Absolutely* vital, oh yes," Mrs. Feather echoed again. I gathered that it was her habit to provide the verbal italics for her husband's remarks.

"Your field is religion . . . philosophy?" he asked.

"Actually, it's more historical."

"Yes, of course. Reliable scholarship," the reverend went on. "That's what we need. Because, as you realize, the truth . . . "

"The *whole* truth," Mrs. Feather made clear with a decisive wave of the finger.

"Yes, certainly, the whole truth has yet to be told."

"As only those who know it can do so," the wife added.

"So you are a historian, then?" the reverend asked. "Possibly you know Professor Carstad?" I said I did. "Ah, well, then! Excellent. He visited with us just a while ago. . . ."

"Some years ago actually," Mrs. Feather corrected.

"And you gained your interest in our faith from him?"

I decided to keep things simple. "Yes, I did."

"Extraordinary man. Such a vigorous mind. Though not, I might say, gifted in the area of doctrine." Mrs. Feather was nodding her head in sage agreement. "No, definitely not in the area of doctrine. Historical detail—yes, I would say that was his strong point."

"About the sufferings," the wife added.

"The passion, yes. Very good on the passion."

"And yourself?" Mrs. Feather asked me, a certain exuberant light coming into her eyes. "Does passion interest you?"

"Oh, more than interest." This, I saw, pleased them both and sent a ripple of murmured approval through the rest of the flock, a few of whom now edged their chairs forward. "Of course, I'm really no more than a beginner. A seeker."

The reverend nodded with kindly indulgence. "We are always prepared to make room for another among our numbers."

Numbers? There were all of eleven faces before me, not one of them less than twice my age. A dying congregation, I would have said. "Are there others in your church?" I asked, trying not to sound too challenging.

"We have access to many others."

"Here in Hermosa Beach?"

The reverend wagged his head; behind him, his flock mimicked the gesture. "No, no. Those who have gone before."

I failed to pick that one up. "But there are other Cathars in the area." The reverend cocked his head inquisitively. "I believe I've heard of another group in Malibu. They call themselves Orphans. . . ."

The reverend showed not the least curiosity. "No, no. Ours is the only authentic lineage."

One of his parishioners leaned forward over the cane she was using to prop her up and sought to clarify. She was a scrawny old crone who seemed to be in a constant state of hostilities with her dentures. "We are *connected*," she clattered. Grinning rigidly at me, she raised a bent finger to point upward. *"Con-nec-ted."*

The Feathers' prim little garden might have made a gracious enough setting for this more social portion of the service. It was well shielded from the grubby street beyond the gate; but not, unfortunately, from the roar of the occasional jet overhead making its approach to L.A. International only a few miles to our east. The Feathers had clearly adjusted to the intrusion; even during his lecture, I noticed that whenever the planes came growling over, the reverend's voice automatically stepped up a few fractional decibels and then fell back. Seeking for a question that might place us on common ground, I asked, "The slogan above your altar . . ."

"Slogan?" asked the reverend and his wife in chorus.

"Duo sunt."

"Teaching," the reverend corrected, his wife underscoring, "the teaching of teachings."

"Forgive me, I'm rather new at all this. It means 'there are two,' I believe." The reverend and his entire flock nodded gravely in unison. "Two gods, am I right?"

". . . gods." The reverend weighed the word judiciously. "Such a misleading term. So many distorted associations. Should we not rather say 'principle.'"

"Yes," the wife agreed. "Definitely principle."

I groped my way forward. "Gods or principles . . . whichever you prefer. Quite honestly, here in the twentieth century, what difference does it make, there being two . . . or five, or ten? After all, the Hindus worship dozens of gods . . . or principles."

The reverend arched a knowing eyebrow. "Dozens, hundreds even, it makes no difference. Only these numbers are of significance: the One and the Two. For, indeed, these are not quantities at all, but ontological substrata, two being the principle of polarity. You do see?"

Aware that I didn't see a thing, Mrs. Feather hastened to clarify. "Perhaps if we were to consider music . . ."

"Ah yes," the reverend agreed, encouraging her to take a hand with the untutored newcomer. "Natalie is so much more concrete about these things."

"I sometimes think when I'm at the organ: so many notes, but all in harmony. The result is a pleasure to the ear. But to produce discord only two notes are necessary."

"Necessary and, more to the point, sufficient," the reverend added.

"Yes," his wife agreed. "Isn't that it? Sufficient. You see, the Two—where there is no harmony—are a condition." She was holding up fingers, two on one hand, one on the other. "The Two takes over the One. After that, it doesn't matter. Hundreds, thousands. It's simply that the One isn't there."

"Exactly so," the reverend concurred. "The rending of the unity."

"The *war*," his wife interjected gravely. A ripple of consensus passed through the surrounding congregation.

They seemed open to more questions, even dumb ones. I asked again. "But—forgive me—is all this anything more than a fine theological distinction?"

"It depends, does it not, where the principles are quartered?" the reverend answered patiently. "For example, if *bonum* is the spirit, and *malum* is the flesh. You understand?"

". . . not quite."

"Each soul divided. The war *within*. You do see? If the flesh itself, the flesh . . ."

"And this makes enough of a difference to kill for?" I asked.

"The only difference *worth* killing for. Not on *our* side, of course."

"No, no," Mrs. Feather emphasized.

"We are forbidden to shed blood."

"Until . . ." Mrs. Feather reminded him.

"Until the Last Days, of course."

Whether it would have been of any value to continue the little catechism lesson I'd started, I cannot say. At some point, before I'd clearly registered the transition, we were no longer discussing cosmic principles but hollyhocks. The old crone with the chattering teeth had passed an admiring remark about Mrs. Feather's hollyhocks at the foot of the garden. The reverend picked up on the compliment, reminding one and all of his wife's prizewinning talents as a gardener . . . and from there the conversation began to drift and diffuse. I gathered this meant religious instructions were over for the day; apparently I'd drawn a blank—and after such a long drive.

This left me with a tricky problem in social etiquette. How did I extricate myself from this now irredeemably absurd situation without being too brutal to people who were, for all their inanity, cordial and well-intentioned? I was in the process of concocting the best lie I could fabricate on short notice, when my attention was drawn to Mrs. Feather. At first, I assumed she was watching one of the planes pass overhead. For there was an especially thunderous jet in the sky above us—or so I thought until I too looked up and realized that the sky was clear. Apparently the plane had passed behind the trees in the next yard, though its roar continued to rumble menacingly all around us in the air. My gaze returned to the reverend's wife; she was still staring skyward. No, not staring, not looking at all. Her eyes had rolled back in their sockets, so far back that they were nearly out of sight, leaving two gaping white ovals in her face. The effect was so grotesque, I cringed. Had she, I wondered, taken sick? I was about to ask, when the woman rose, opened her mouth, let out a long, thin wail, then pitched forward onto the lawn. There she lay face down, trembling from head to foot. It was only at this point that the others gave her their attention.

"Ah," said the reverend, "Guillemette has joined us. Shall we make the circle?"

I'd already risen to go to Mrs. Feather's assistance, but felt the reverend's hand on my arm restraining me. The others in the flock were busily shifting their chairs with an obviously well-rehearsed precision until they had formed a circle with the fallen Mrs. Feather at the center. I was the only person not yet part of the ring. I glanced at the reverend, who was indicating a place for my chair alongside his own. His expression was calm, there was even the hint of a polite smile. So far no one was making any effort to come to the aid of poor Mrs. Feather, who had rolled over on her back and was now stretched out rigid on the ground undergoing what I assumed must be an epileptic seizure. At that point, one of the men stepped forward to cover her with a comforter; he laid it over her quite casually and withdrew to take his seat. This was clearly the only help the stricken woman was going to receive.

Utterly bewildered, I searched every face in the circle. All were now looking down in a prayerful posture, hands folded in their laps. Only the reverend, with his hands clasped about the cross on his chest, kept his eyes on his writhing wife. After several agonizing moments of gagging and slobbering, Mrs. Feather began to speak, though not at all coherently. It sounded like Italian, soft, fluid, but the vowels were odd: long, drawn out, slightly nasal. A made-up language, I assumed, yet flowing from her at a remarkable clip in a voice nothing like her own. It was a youthful, even girlish voice with a distinctly musical lilt to it, though strained to the point of frenzy.

"In her previous life," I heard the reverend saying at my side as casually as if he were recounting yesterday's weather, "my wife was Guillemette Testanière. She was executed by the Inquisition in 1242 at Montaillou. She was eighteen years old. Four members of her family were burned with her, along with nearly a hundred residents of the village. Her passion was quite terrible. The faggots, you see, were still very green. The fire was not hot enough to kill quickly. There were some who actually survived the flames. For these the garrote was reserved."

He spoke so calmly against the background of his wife's tormented groaning that I felt myself chill. If this was a charade, it was in very bad taste. For by this time, Mrs. Feather's anguish had become extreme. Or was she faking it? The phrase "self-hypnosis" sprang to mind as a conveniently rational alternative to the reverend's totally unacceptable explanation. Yes, that's what it was: simply a bit of hysterical autosuggestion. I wasn't sure I knew what these words meant, but they were helping me keep my nerve—though just barely. The fact was, I didn't like this, not one little bit. And it was getting worse. Mrs. Feather's skin was becoming distinctly raddled, turning a bright, ruddy hue.

"Aren't you going to do something?" I asked—almost demanded.

"This will pass," the reverend assured me. "The connections never last longer than ten or twelve minutes. When she recovers, Mrs. Feather will remember none of the pain. You see, this is a sign on to us, intended for our instruction. Lest we forget the passion."

"You seriously believe she's been . . . possessed?"

"Not possessed. We would say regressed. By the grace of Abraxas, some have received the gift of reentering their previous identity."

Perhaps I shouldn't have been surprised. I now recalled coming across the doctrine of metempsychosis in my reading. It was an article of faith for some Cathar sects. When I brought it up with Brother Justin, he told me we would return to the subject "in good time." That was the last I heard of the matter, which was fine with me. Reincarnation was one of those subjects I preferred to treat with adamant neglect. And still intended to do so. At the back of my mind a small silent curse was taking shape: *Damn you, Faustus, for involving me with these loonies!*

Though I kept reminding myself that the woman was in some kind of hysterical trance and probably feeling nothing, her simulated suffering was growing more unbearable. Moreover, as the moments wore on, my eyes began to play tricks on me. In the dimming light of evening, a dull glow seemed to gather about her body as if she might be engulfed in flames. At one point, I was certain I could see her skin begin to swell into blisters, crack, and turn ashen. I finally had to glance away. All the while her babbling continued, growing more strained, more mingled with suppressed panic.

"She is invoking the true God," the reverend informed me as if he might be describing a spectator sport. "Soon He will take her troubled spirit into His gracious care and leave her corrupted flesh to perish."

As spectacular as Mrs. Feather's tribulations had become, my attention was drawn off across the circle. One of the other women—it was tiny Althea who had served the tea—was now lolling in her chair, eyes rolled back, mouth gaping. She too was connecting, speaking in a voice very different from her own. I couldn't make out what she was saying—Mrs. Feather was now nearly screaming—but I was sure it wasn't English. A few minutes later and still another member of the flock had slipped into trance, this time one of the men. His voice was loud enough for me to overhear. The words definitely weren't English, but some kind of singsong linguistic hash.

Mrs. Feather's passion continued to build until she seemed about to explode. At that point, her howling took on a different quality. She was singing! Her voice became strong and spirited. Though the words were slurred, I guessed they were meant to be Latin. Even more certainly, I could identify the song. It was a wailing, dragged-out version of the tune she'd played on the organ: "Bye Bye Blackbird" in a minor key. Her singing swelled up, then abruptly stopped with a terrible retching cough. Mrs. Feather's eyes popped open, her tongue protruded. I could watch no more.

"Now they are strangling her," Reverend Feather bent to inform me quietly. As if I might be suffering more than his wife, he patted my hand and assured me, "Soon it will be over."

It was. For several seconds there was silence in the garden. I had never been so glad to hear the L.A. freeway. When I looked back, Mrs. Feather was sitting up. As if she had done no more than sneeze, she picked herself off the ground, rubbed at her still-glowing cheeks, smiled, and returned to her seat, waiting for the others to finish their more subdued connections. There was a brief silent prayer; five minutes after that, the congregation was excusing itself and drifting away. I might have done the same, but the Feathers were eagerly soliciting me to stay and talk, perhaps to have dinner. Oddly enough, I felt obliged to linger. After sitting through so singular a performance, I would have felt churlish departing without some word of . . . I couldn't call it appreciation, but at least acknowledgment.

"How long have you had this . . . capacity?" I asked Mrs. Feather as she fussed to brew another pot of tea after the flock had departed. We'd moved into the house that adjoined the antique shop. It was no more than a few rooms behind a curtained doorway that divided it from the store. The kitchen where we were sitting was neat enough, but depressingly dingy. Its only note of cheer was an assortment of china cups and saucers that filled the better part of one wall, probably the best of Aunt Natalie's wares.

"It came to me as a child," she answered brightly. "Guillemette was my secret companion, a sort of make-believe older sister. We did not connect for the first time until I was a young woman of her age. That was when I realized she and I were one."

"But by that time you'd studied the Albigenses?"

"Oh, not at all. I had no idea who these people were. And if I had, I would have regarded them as heretics. I should have had to. My father, you see, was a curate. Very devout. Very High Church, don't you know. That's what led Cecil and me to emigrate. Once my family found out about Guillemette, they were scandalized. Oh, they wouldn't hear of such a thing! I'm afraid they thought I was quite balmy."

"California," the reverend explained, "has proved to be so much more hospitable. There is a certain . . ."

"Yes, isn't there?" Mrs. Feather agreed.

". . . atmosphere."

"An atmosphere, exactly so. Of course later, after I met Cecil, who knew so very much more about it all, I did some reading, not much. The books seem so lifeless after you have known the true story. Guillemette has taught me what I know. I think of it as a deep, deep memory, far more reliable than any book could be."

"The language you were speaking . . . where did you learn it?"

"I never did. It's Guillemette's language. I don't even know common French."

I turned to the reverend. "And do you also experience connections?"

"Oh yes. But nothing as arduous as Natalie. My life stream reaches back to the age of Marcus Aurelius. I was an Alexandrian scholar converted to the faith at that time. That was before the Church of Rome was in a position to strike at its enemies. In that respect I was more fortunate. But it leaves me with less to offer my little flock."

"You are much too modest, my dear," his wife chided. "Cecil was one of the teachers of the great Origen."

"Ah, but the passion of Guillemette, of all our long-departed confreres," the reverend insisted, "it does so much more to teach the evil of this world. That the Children of Light should be made to suffer so."

I mentioned that I'd noticed a few of the others connecting. "Althea, for example . . ."

"Oh yes. Her life stream goes back to ancient Persia, the days of Zoroaster."

Dr. Byx had said "older than Jesus." Apparently the two Cathar congregations agreed on that much. "Your church goes back that far?"

"Brenda McVey goes back even farther. She is the oldest among us. She was a priestess at the Egyptian court in the earliest days of our faith. At the temple of Thoth. All the members of our little flock have manifested their spiritual core."

"Except for poor Mr. Glassman," his wife reminded him. "He is still in search."

"True," the reverend answered. "But he is making excellent progress. We have the highest hopes for him."

"How exactly do you experience a connection?" I asked Mrs. Feather. I was honestly curious to know. Why not take advantage of the occasion? I never expected to meet a team of eccentrics like this again—not if I could help it. "Do you feel any pain?"

Mrs. Feather proved to be blithely forthcoming. "Not really. You see, I am not in my physical body at the time. It's more as if I am observing from somewhere high above, rather than actually being in the scene. But it's all so very horrifying, I can't keep from crying out. Do you follow me?"

I saw what looked like a small, fortuitous opening and moved to squeeze a key question through it. "You mean it's like watching a movie?"

". . . movie?"

"Haven't you ever thought it might make a good movie? The persecution of the Cathars?" The reverend and his wife exchanged a bewildered glance. "It's my particular interest. Movies. The story of the Cathars has so many . . ."

All at once, it was as if I were staring across the table into the eyes of two dead fish. The Feathers had gone cold on me.

"You are from Hollywood?" Mrs. Feather asked, naming the city as if it might rank just behind Sodom and Gomorrah.

"Oh no. I teach film studies."

"Film? I understood you to say you were an historian," the reverend reminded me in a tone that suggested I might be an imposter.

"I am," I hastened to assure him. "The history of the movies. Just now, for example, I'm studying . . ."

But no example was going to save the situation now. Especially not if I should be forced to identify Max Castle as the man who made movies about ghouls, vampires, and zombies. The look Reverend Feather had fixed on me made me feel like a kid who had farted in church. "We have always regarded the motion pictures," he informed me, "as a particularly worldly form of amusement. Not at all compatible with a serious view of life."

"Have you some intention of filming?" Mrs. Feather asked, a distinct note of distress, even insult in her voice. "Here? Us?"

"No, no. Not at all." Under vigorous cross-examination, I issued the disclaimer two or three more times before I resigned myself to the fact that, like it or not, I'd stumbled upon as efficient a way as any to extricate myself from the Albigensi Fellowship. The movies may have ranked high with the Orphans; but not with the two Cathars I was sharing tea and biscuits with that evening. As far as the Feathers were concerned, movies meant Looney Tunes and skin flicks. Even my status as a scholar was sullied by the association. Our conversation was turning more frigid by the moment.

It wasn't as graceful an exit as I might have wished, but it got me moving toward the door. A quarter of an hour later, after the Feathers and I had exchanged some final awkward words, I was headed home along the coast highway, wondering why I should feel the least unease about cutting myself free of the Grand Archon and his schizophrenic wife, no matter how ragged the tear might be. There was nothing I owed them, and I was hardly likely to visit again. Yet I was taking a nagging sense of ingratitude away with me. As rinky-dink as the Albigensi Fellowship might be, Mrs. Feather—and whatever manner of being Guillemette Testanière might be—had filled an important blank in my research. In the days ahead, I would need to know more about the wrath of the Cathars, where it came from, why it might be so enduring. I now had more than books to help me answer that question. I had the memory of Aunt Natalie writhing in unspeakable torment on the lawn among her prize hollyhocks, crying out for pity to a god whose name the world had forgotten.

24 THE GREAT HERESY

The next time we met, I fully intended to let Faustus know how irked my mission to Hermosa Beach had left me. Involving me with the Feathers had all the earmarks of a mean trick played on both them and me. But he was utterly uncontrite. The man actually expected me to thank him.

"Come on now, Jonny, tell the truth. You have to admit that Mrs. What's-her-name puts on a damn good show."

"Shows like that ended, as I recall, when they closed down Bedlam to spectators."

"Could be you're attacking along the wrong epistemological flank." Faustus was giving me his foxy grandpa squint. "Are you so sure the old girl's batty?"

"What else?"

"You heard her speak in tongues, didn't you?"

"Yes. So? Just some kind of gibberish."

"Suppose I were to tell you what you heard the lady speaking was Old Provençal, vintage 1250 or thereabouts?"

"How could it be?"

"Well, I'm not that much of an authority. But I've used plenty of documents from the period, enough to recognize a good imitation of the dialect when I hear it. That struck me right off the night I heard her. I tried to register as much of what she said as I could. Even asked if I could make some recordings, take some pictures. Bad mistake. The reverend wasn't having any of that. 'This isn't a freak show,' he tells me from atop his high horse, as if I was asking his wife to pose for dirty pictures."

"I ran into a bit of that myself," I said. "Made the mistake of mentioning the movies. Clunk. End of the line."

"I gather the reverend and his little band of prophets are more or less at war with the gadgetry of modern life. You didn't use their so-called bathroom by any chance? That's an adventure. Well, anyway, it happens I've got a pretty sharp ear for languages, so I picked up a good deal of what the lady said. And I did take some notes. When I got back to school, I checked with my froggy friend Émile Giraud over in the French Department. 'Sacrebleu,' the man says, 'where did you get this?' Claimed it was as authentic a transcription of the old language as he'd seen—though of course I didn't have much more than fragments. There was most of a prayer she was saying, and part of a curse—on the heads of the Inquisitors. I can't swear to it, but I'd be willing to take an even money bet she was speaking coherent Old Provençal all the way through—and not in her own voice. That language hasn't been heard in Langue d'Oc in seven centuries."

"Did she sing?"

"Now that you mention it, she did. About the dark savior. 'Vale, Domine Tenebrice'. . . something like that. Very woeful. Odd sort of religious chant. And that was a pretty good imitation of Church Latin, what I could catch of it."

"You aren't suggesting . . ."

"Okay, just file that one for a minute. Now suppose I were to tell you that there really was a Guillemette Testanière—burned to death by the Inquisition in 1242 in Montaillou. Age eighteen. I looked it up."

"Mrs. Feather could have looked it up too."

"Not unless she did a lot of digging in a lot of very old, very obscure medieval French sources, which I don't think she'd be likely to find at the Hermosa Beach public library. I had to order photostat copies of records from three or four European colleagues. Cost me a couple hard months' research. Used some of it in a paper I wrote."

"So you're telling me exactly what, Faustus? That Aunt Natalie is the reincarnation of a Cathar heretic?"

He shrugged his shoulders and reached to light his cigar. "Just telling it *wie es eigentlich gewesen,* buddy. The lady spoke the language, and what she says about her doppelgänger (or etheric double or whatever the hell such like ectoplasmic entities are called) checks out with the documents available."

I let my skepticism show, but wasn't about to press the point farther. I could hardly afford to. The Orphans at Zuma Beach were enough for me to cope with just now. One nutty sect at a time. Besides, I had larger issues on my mind. However I might interpret Mrs. Feather's performance—metempsychosis or plain psychosis—it had raised a question that I knew Faustus wouldn't be able to help me with. Convinced that the story of the Cathars was an exercise in political skulduggery, he was not someone I could expect to take matters of doctrine seriously. And now more than ever, doctrine was what I wanted to know about. I'd witnessed the death of a Cathar—or a reasonable facsimile thereof. I'd heard the cries of agony, seen the flesh turn to ashes. Mrs. Feather's connection might have been some kind of hallucinatory simulation, but it had been laid before me in all sincerity as the living recollection of a great historical crime. Even knowing that her travail was a delusionary reenactment, I'd found it nearly too much to stomach.

That had set me to thinking. Once, seven centuries ago, others had stood in the presence of the indisputably real thing, watching the horror approvingly. What manner of theological hairsplitting could steel people to such a deed, blinding them to the inhumanity of what they did? Even more to the point: What about the victims who had gone into the flames singing the praises of a god whose worship had brought them nothing but derision and destruction? What was the faith that sustained them? I wanted more than academic answers to these questions. I was sure the beliefs that had once lived inside the minds of the martyred Cathars lived again in the films of Max Castle, indeed accounted for their strongest qualities. I would be failing the man if I didn't address the teachings of his church with all the seriousness they deserved.

But that wasn't easy for me. My mind simply refused to function theologically. Not that I didn't understand what I read and heard. But when I was finished, the same question was always waiting to be answered: *So what?* Even when it came to the Cathars' principal doctrine, I kept coming up empty-handed. *Duo sunt.* One God or two, why should it make any difference except to religious zealots of a thankfully bygone age? Why would anyone in the modern world, let alone as sophisticated an artist as Max Castle, care about something like that? The Feathers had, in their halting way, tried to explain. "If *bonum* is the spirit and *malum* is the flesh. The flesh itself . . ." I turned what they'd said over and over in my mind, trying to squeeze a drop of living significance from it. I scouted out several works on mind-body dualism, but always finished with the sense that this was one of those long-defunct issues that belonged under glass in the philosophical museum. And just at the point when my mind was going slack with the effort, the words I needed came to me, the memory of one of Max Castle's most unlikely interpreters . . . a spaced-out nitwit of a kid I'd all but totally forgotten.

But let me get this in its proper sequence.

For weeks, as I labored to grasp the significance of the Great Heresy, I'd been scribbling notes, some of which I had to rephrase over and over before their importance broke through to me. And here's where I was when the moment came:

God of Light and God of Darkness *still* at war . . . where? *Within* us, every one of us. Their struggle = the struggle of flesh against spirit. God of Darkness = God of the body . . . this vile body, messy mortal package of unruly appetites and unholy desires. God of Light = God of the body's imprisoned spirit . . . the spark of divinity buried in the corrupting meat of us. Cathars are allies of the God of Light, are body-haters . . . want to set the spark free never to be sullied by the flesh again. . . .

There, I remember, my notes broke off. Because at that moment my mind flashed back to the film that had first thrust Max Castle into my life like a dagger. *Judas Everyman.* More important, I recalled the remark Sharkey's teenybopper girlfriend (what was her name . . . Shannon?) had dropped so casually as we sat taking in the effect of what we had seen.

It's enough to put you off sex for the rest of your life.

At the time, though none of us—Clare, Sharkey, myself—knew why, the comment seemed exactly right. With the words, I could recall my own experience on that day, the creeping sense of *uncleanness* that had come over me for the first time.

Shannon had put her finger on it. *That* was the purpose of Castle's film, of *all* Castle's films, as it was the purpose of his church down through the ages. To kill sex, deny the body, free the incarcerated spark. Faustus had told me that the elders of the Cathar faith (the Perfect as they were called) lived in absolute celibacy when few priests of the Roman Church felt compelled to do the same. They spurned the marriage and family they might have had. And went much farther. The most chilling practice of the religion came at the end of an elder's life. In a final supreme effort to prove their mastery over the flesh, many would voluntarily starve themselves to death.

So hostile were the Cathars to the physical body that extremists among them refused to believe Jesus ever walked the earth as a living man. Instead they insisted that he, the messenger of the God of Light, had appeared among men as a mere phantom to act out a phoney crucifixion. The purest of the pure, how could he possibly have submitted to the indignity of wearing the corruptible flesh? As some Cathars described this strange, illusory Jesus, he almost seemed to have the quality of a motion-picture projection, an actor transformed into an image of light, moving ghostlike across the screen of history, there but not really there.

It was only now that Brother Justin's pronouncement came home to me, and the deep pathos I'd heard behind it.

". . . we live in hell, we are damned souls."

Why? Because hell begins very close to home. This very body we inhabit belongs to the Dark Lord. We are his playthings, his prisoners . . . like the tragic convict in Castle's film, *Shadows over Sing Sing,* trapped in the stone cellar of the universe, his body transformed into the stone of that cellar. This, along with many another image from Castle's movies, flooded into my mind, emblems of torment and decay: the zombies, vampires, ghouls, hounded criminals. . . .

What was it Brother Justin had quoted from a prophet named Seth—a prophet I'd never heard of, but whose writings, I had since discovered, held an honored place in the Cathar Bible? ". . . this very flesh that clothes thee is thy perdition." Brother Justin believed this! He really did. As had Max Castle.

Could I?

I tried, if only for a moment, to imagine believing it, to feel the body I inhabited as if it were a cage, a vault, Count Lazarus' fetid coffin . . . and at once drove the thought from my mind. It stifled me with a claustrophobic panic, as if the whole universe were a locked

tomb in which I'd awakened buried alive. And with that panic, a
stunning new realization came over me, something that turned my
thinking upside down. Since my research began, I'd been regarding
the Cathars as the heroes of the story, the victims of a bigoted church.
What if that were exactly wrong? What if the Cathars, far from being
martyrs who deserved my sympathy, were the carriers of a terrible
doctrine? Sex-denying, love-denying, enemies not only of the Church
of Rome but of life itself. *Of life itself!*

No wonder, then, that Brother Justin could see Simon Dunkle's
ugly little fantasies as works of high art. They were the perfect expression of a world-despising vision. I winced to hear myself wondering:
perhaps it was for the best that the Cathars were hunted down,
liquidated, every last one of them. Except, that is, some few who
managed to survive the holocaust, then vanished from the world's
sight to return centuries later in the unlikely guise of moviemakers.

Faustus might have had little patience for discussions of religious
doctrine. But doctrine connected with sex was sure to get a rise out
of him. As he once told me, "Making love is almost as satisfying as
making war. That's where your generation went wrong, my boy. A
man doesn't have to choose between the two." I tried to maintain a
scholarly air as I broached the subject, but I suspected he would put
his own more salacious construction on the subject. "There were
rumors," I observed, "that the Albigenses went in for some pretty
bizarre forms of eroticism. Do you think there's any truth to that?"

He growled out a dirty laugh. "I've been wondering when you'd
get around to that, Jonny. Always wanted to try a book on the subject.
Strange Sexual Perversions of the Western World. The Cathars would
be worth a whole couple of chapters. The churches—that's where
you find all the best hanky-panky. Hell, every religion in the world
goes back to fertility cults and love feasts. But the Albigenses had a
different slant on things. Their objective was *infertility.* For them,
nothing was a greater abomination than the church's insistence that
sex has got to lead to reproduction. They saw that as delivering another
pure soul into the bondage of the flesh. Now the most obvious way
to frustrate procreation would be celibacy. Which was fine for the
Parfaits, some of whom may actually have been castrati. But there's
never been much of a market for abstinence beyond the chosen fanatical few. So for the swinish many, the Albigenses came up with a
lesser discipline: some kind of genital gymnastics that allowed the

body to enjoy its impure pleasures, but kept the seed corralled. Possibly the practice was imported from the East. There are yogis who go in for that kind of ejaculatory cliff-hanging. They claim it's the secret of eternal life."

"Are there any records of this?" I asked.

"Don't we both wish? With illustrations. No such luck, my boy. Most of what we know comes from the persecutors' side. You have to use your imagination to fill in the blanks."

For the first time I felt one-up on my intimidating mentor. I couldn't resist the temptation. "Actually, I've had some firsthand knowledge of the subject."

Faustus perked up, looking intensely inquisitive. "Well, hotcha-cha! Tell me more."

"I met someone just this last summer who claimed to know a few Cathar sexual techniques. She offers lecture-demonstrations."

"You must give me the lady's phone number. I may write that book after all. Do you suppose I could scare up a Guggenheim to fund some field work?"

Having hooked Faustus' interest, I took the liberty of boasting. "Her name was Olga Tell. You may remember her."

"Wasn't there a movie star of that name some while back?"

"The very woman. She lives in Amsterdam now."

"She must be old as the hills. Older than even me."

"But still going strong. And very good at what she does."

Faustus wanted more details about my adventures with Olga, which I obligingly offered. As I chatted away, blushing inwardly for the unexpurgated frankness of my account, I could tell he was coming to see me in a new light. Up till now, he'd assumed I was nothing more than a cinematic aesthete, meaning another pantywaist colleague. All it took to dispel that image was a little man talk.

"Well then, young fella," Faustus resumed after our brief erotic detour, "you may know better than I what the Albigenses were up to between the sheets. But as you might expect, when rumors of such practices leaked out, the authorities interpreted what they heard as the sin of concupiscence carried to abominable extremes. The Cathars were even willing to countenance homosexuality as a means of birth control. Better to bugger than to beget. That was one of the principal charges against the Templars. And probably it was true. As far back as Sparta, comrades in arms have frequently wound up *in* each other's arms. The rough love of the barracks hall. Never went in for that sort of thing myself, but it has its place. Some of the best fighters I served with were queer as a Turkish corkscrew."

All our conversations eventually circled around to war. And that finally proved to be the undoing of our relationship, thanks to a bad miscalculation on my part. But then, Faustus was a hard man to calculate. It was often impossible to tell how seriously he expected to be taken. It was obvious enough that the figure he chose to cut on campus—that of a barbaric throwback waging war against such effete products of civilization as professors—was played with tongue-in-cheek. So much so that one easily lost sight of the deep conviction that stood behind the pretense. But it was there: an old soldier's loyalty to men he had risked death beside. Politically speaking, this made him a sort of John Wayne superpatriot and pretty much of a bullheaded reactionary on most issues. At the same time, he had been among the most outspoken critics of the Vietnam War on our faculty. His stance was a peculiar one. He was always at pains to distance himself from his colleagues and even more so from the students he had openly reviled as long-haired, yellow-bellied bums. Faustus took his stand alongside veterans returned from the fighting, associating himself with their anger and indignation. His allegiance was pledged not to the flag, but to the Order of Merit, which he wore proudly on his lapel and whose honor Vietnam had shredded beyond repair. Nevertheless, I would have thought the opposition we shared to the war might strengthen the tenuous bond between us. As I was soon to learn, I couldn't have been more mistaken.

Toward the end of the American evacuation from Vietnam, a group of my film students decided to organize a campus showing of antiwar movies, student productions gathered from around the country, a sort of "lest-we-forget" festival to landmark the end of a sad chapter in American history. I agreed to act as sponsor and host. Faustus learned about my role in the event and rang me up to ask if he might sit in on a preview screening I was scheduled to see. The request took me by surprise, but of course I agreed. The films turned out to be pretty much what one would expect: mainly newsreel and video compilations edited to play off the windy rhetoric of public leaders against endless footage of battlefield and civilian atrocities. When the lights came up after the show, I caught Faustus just as he was blotting his cheek with a handkerchief. His one good eye was blazing with tears. I expected some rough but appreciative comment on what was an im-passioned if amateurish statement on the war. What I got was a personal attack.

"Every draft-dodging son of a bitch responsible for this bad-mouth-ing tripe ought to be court-martialed and hung by his thumbs," were his first words. Followed, before I could catch my breath, by, "And *you* right alongside of them, sonny."

Surely he was joking? He wasn't. He meant it. I didn't have to ask for an explanation; it came blasting at me. "When it comes to war, there're those that have the right to criticize, and those that don't. You don't. Not when it makes all the victimized kids who got suckered into this fiasco look like homicidal maniacs. It was a dirty war, sure. But that isn't on their heads." I was struggling to agree and disagree all at once, but he wasn't giving me the chance to do either. "We never got around to discussing the matter, but exactly what is it *you* were doing during the war, my lad? Suffering out a student defer-ment?"

I decided to let him assume the answer was a simple yes. The truth wouldn't have bridged the gap that was suddenly opening between us. Might as well let him think I was a draft dodger. If he found out it was my role in inflicting Chipsey Goldenstone's flagrant penis upon the public that had kept me out of war, he might reach for his broad-sword.

That was the last I saw of Faustus. Even if we hadn't clashed over the war, it might have been months before I could have consulted with him again. A few weeks later, word reached me that the old fellow had undergone a triple bypass, another in a long series. He was expected to be laid up indefinitely. I sent a card and a note; neither was acknowledged. Too bad. For all our differences, he had a kind of rough, warriorly dignity that commanded respect. If anybody could ever convince me that *Sands of Iwo Jima* was a better war movie than *Grand Illusion* (a point we had argued) it would have been Faustus. But that was as far as he could follow me in the dis-cussion of film. And just now I needed to go a lot farther. I was down to the last missing link in my study of the Cathars, the question that had trailed me home from Zurich. *Why movies?* How was I to account for the peculiar association of the orphans with the art of film?

Brother Justin called the movies "a new form of prophecy . . . appropriate to our time." Was that all there was to it: that movies were a popular art, that they reached so many more people than literature did? And—if it was a Castle film (or maybe one day a Simon Dunkle film)—reached those people with more impact?

For a time, I settled for that simple explanation, though with increasing reservations. Something in me wanted to believe there was a deeper connection between the orphans and the movies. But I might never have guessed what it was without help from the most unexpected of all sources.

One day a package arrived at my office at school. The return address told me it was from Le Bureau National des Successions Nonreclamées in Paris, which meant precisely nothing to me. It was lavishly decorated with all manner of official stamps and labels. The U.S. Customs Service had done me the favor of examining it, leaving the outside wrapping in tatters. The Film Studies department secretary had to sign two French-English forms before it could be delivered.

There was a letter taped to the outside of the parcel. In ponderous French bureaucratese, someone whose signature I couldn't read regretfully informed me that Karl-Heinz Rosenzweig was, as of some three months earlier, deceased. He had died still an inmate of the Lyons asylum where I'd visited him. More cheerily, the letter went on to say that as the mad old man's executor, I was herewith in receipt of all his worldly goods—to wit, this parcel, which held a cardboard box about as large as a medium-sized suitcase.

This was totally ridiculous. How could I possibly be Rosenzweig's executor? An attachment to the letter answered my question. It reminded me that the document I'd hastily signed as I left the asylum included an agreement to serve in that capacity if nobody else turned up. Nobody had. The box was all mine. Lucky me.

With less than no enthusiasm I clipped the tape that held the parcel together. From inside a faint, but distinctly evil smell escaped. Had something died in there? At first, the contents seemed to be wrapped in old rags. Then I realized that the old rags *were* the contents. The dead priest's clothes, too poorly laundered to dilute the pervasive odor of urine. (Hadn't I told them, *no clothes?*) There was a pair of well-worn and equally noisome shoes, a pair of eyeglasses with one lens gone, pens, pencils, a rosary, a lower denture, a few photographs.

All this I deposited in the nearest wastebasket—except for the rosary, which I kept as a macabre souvenir of one of the modern world's least celebrated thinkers. Finally, there were some books and papers. I recognized the papers as the inscrutable materials Rosenzweig had brought with him to our one-sided interview. I set these aside for later examination. As for the books, there were eight of them in four languages, all old and edged with mold. Three of these, the most yellowed, were in Latin and looked like self-published works done in broken type on cheap paper. The titles had the ponderously obscure look of Rosenzweig's own fulminations: long, rambling, and probably incomprehensible.

There was also a Latin Bible, a German prayer book, a copy of St. Ignatius Loyola's *Spiritual Exercises*, a withered Greek text whose title I couldn't decipher. Finally, there was a slender, well-printed volume in French that had the look of respectable scholarship. It dated from 1956 and bore a title that translated as *The Manichaean Communities in Eastern Anatolia 329–415 A.D.* The author was a priest named E. D. Angelotti, O.P. A Dominican. He had inscribed the book to Rosenzweig, referring to him as "my dear friend Karl, an ally in the Great Cause." Beneath his signature, Father Angelotti had drawn the little symbol I now recognized as the emblem of Oculus Dei. This was the only book in the Rosenzweig archives I judged worth reading, or at least skimming. A fortunate decision. It made all the difference.

Not that I could have guessed as much at the outset. The style of the work was dry and plodding. Still I persevered, mainly because I'd so often come across references to the Manichees in other works. Like the Cathars who honored them highly, they too were believers in the two gods, for which reason, they'd also suffered persecution at the hands of the church. The book before me was a pedantic little study of some isolated groups of Manichees who had managed to survive longer than most others and had left some documents behind in a few villages of Asia Minor near the Bactrian frontier. It told me nothing I very much cared to know—until toward the end I came upon a section that had been heavily annotated by Rosenzweig. This I read carefully. It turned out to be a revelation.

I learned that the Manichees had once used a peculiar teaching device, a few of which had been found among the remains of the communities under study. It was a little packet of crudely drawn cartoons that could be flicked with the thumb at one side. As the pages riffled by, the cartoons upon them would seem to move.

A flip-book. The most primitive form of moving picture. The oldest example of persistence of vision. Motionless pictures that appear to move because the eye isn't agile enough to catch the gap between

431

them. Every kid has played with one. They come with Cracker Jack.

Father Angelotti didn't think the Manichees had invented the flip-book; he was certain it had a much older history reaching back as far as the Babylonians. But the Manichees had put this toy to a very serious use. It was the basis of their heretical catechism. They taught that the gap between the pictures symbolizes the abyss which is the dwelling place of evil. Whenever the gap flashes by, in just that fleeting split-second, it is like a crack opening up in the walls of the universe, revealing the great lightless void beyond God's creation. The pictures were said to be "real," therefore good. The gap between them was said to be the absence of the real, therefore evil. So—flip, flip, flip—the little books pitted good against evil, Being against Nothingness. Riffle the pages, ponder their meaning. And what did the cartoons depict? Two figures, one white, one black. They rush at one another; they clash. Lord of the Light, Lord of the Darkness, forever at war. Just that.

The first movie.

In a footnote, the author mentioned the continued use of flip-books among the Cathars in later centuries. By the time the Inquisition was on the scene, the little device had become an expensive entertainment. Those found carrying one were arrested on suspicion of heresy. Father Angelotti traced these ancient picture shows on down to the time of the Templars, who, he believed, were indeed Cathars. They were said to have invented a sort of magic lantern that could project flip-book images on a screen. The device was used in their secret rites, which were of course denounced by the Church as an obscene display.

So it turned out that my zany pal Sharkey hadn't been far off the mark back in those days when we shared the duties of the projection booth at The Classic. There had indeed been a kind of medieval movies. Perhaps it was no coincidence that an emblem of the old knightly orders—the Maltese cross—had lent its name and shape to the little gear that rests at the heart of every motion-picture projector and there feeds the film through the light box frame by frame, each illuminated frame divided between light and darkness by the bladed shutter, and all timed to trick the laggardly eye into seeing movement where there is no movement.

Father Angelotti broke off his brief digression into movie machinery with the Templars, but not before he'd dropped one last tantalizing remark: "After the destruction of the Albigenses, such illicit devices disappear from sight. The story of their subsequent clandestine elaboration for dubious religious purposes remains to be told."

So at last I had the key to Max Castle's movies, the secret of their uncanny fascination. The man drew upon an ancient tradition, an art of light and shadow used to teach the war of the two gods. The flicker *was* that war. Twenty-four times a second, as the frames of film raced by—click, click, click—it pounded its way insidiously through the bedazzled eye into the unguarded depths of the mind. Light against Dark. Flesh against Spirit. The Good God, the Evil God locked in combat. Watching movies was a way of being surreptitiously catechized.

Expecting little more than his usual evasive action, I nevertheless brought up what I'd learned with Brother Justin. Had he ever heard about the use of flip-books among the ancient Manichaeans?

"Do you mean those little picture books they put in cereal boxes? Children's toys, are they not?" One of his usual tactics: trying to make my questions seem foolish. "Of what use could they possibly be except for amusement?"

What did he know about the Templars' magic-lantern shows? Why, nothing at all . . . what were they?

How far back did his church's interest in motion-picture machinery go? Why, no farther back than the invention of movies by Thomas Edison . . . or whoever deserved the credit.

Had he ever considered the flicker of the projector to be a sort of a symbolic combat of light and darkness? He pretended total astonishment. What a charming idea! Where had I come across it? I handed him Father Angelotti's monograph, watching closely as he opened it. His glance paused long enough on the inscription to tell me he registered its significance.

"Ah yes. Angelotti. I've come across his work. Not very reliable, actually. The man knows nothing about our tradition. A Dominican, I believe. The inquisitional order."

No thanks to Brother Justin, I'd arrived at an important new level in my understanding of Max Castle. A score of scattered pieces had fallen into place. Now I could see that everybody, each in his or her own way, had been right about some piece of the man and his movies. Saint-Cyr was right about the flicker. But he vastly underestimated the depth of its penetration. Castle was hardly concerned with something as ephemeral as class struggle; his theme was cosmic warfare.

And Clare was right. Castle was out to subvert the conscious art

433

of cinema by his use of sensational subliminal tricks. But she didn't realize how serious was the intention behind those tricks.

And Olga was right. Both in his films and in his strange bedroom antics, Castle, like every good Cathar, was out to "fool the devil at his own game." As prurient as the subliminal imagery of his movies might be, the technology that delivered them to the screen secretly tainted their titillation with persistent shame. At one level, delight, at another disgust. ". . . enough to put you off sex for the rest of your life."

And Rosenzweig had been right about the diabolical agenda of Castle and the orphans. But he, like all the Cathars' persecutors, would never admit that his devil was their god, his god their devil. Every Cathar in history had gone to his grave believing that the God of *this* world, the God of the Church of Rome and of every church except their own, was the God of Darkness, Lord of the hell in which we live out our days as slaves of disease, desire, death. Where the rest of the world saw darkness, they saw light; where they saw darkness, the rest saw light. Because the God of Darkness had turned our mind inside out, upside down. We mistook the negative for the positive photograph of reality. Knowing the true meaning of the words, the Cathars proudly worshiped "the dark God," the light that shines in the darkness and is comprehended not. The black bird was his emblem, the unlit theater his temple. Only at the end of time, when the war of the two gods reached its climax, would these eyes of flesh melt away and our vision become clear enough to see the light as light and the darkness as darkness.

And little Zip Lipsky had been right. Castle was indeed one hell of a filmmaker—though Zip would have been the last to know why. It was because Castle's art served a purpose beyond art. It was the handmaiden of a mighty and ancient teaching.

For my own part, I couldn't endorse that teaching in any religious sense. I surely didn't want to believe that this world, the only one I knew for sure existed, was the Dark Lord's playground. And despite all the antierotic propaganda I'd absorbed from Castle's films, something in my libidinal energy still fought stubbornly to assert its dignity. Maybe I simply hadn't suffered enough to give up on life. Or maybe I'd known the love of too many good women to go the Cathar way.

And yet . . . and yet . . .

The memory of Mrs. Feather acting out a long-dead girl's deadly ordeal by fire would never leave me. Nor would the things Olga had once told me so simply, so earnestly about "making babies for Herr Hitler's world." Her words filled my mind with pictures of the waste and wretchedness that took place all around me, more than I could or cared to take in. The starving children, the butchered thousands, the commonplace terror of the sick, the mad, the poor. News of the day every day. Olga, who had lived through the death camps and had seen the massacre of the innocents, had no doubt that the world was indeed hell. At that brute level of historical fact, I had to admit there was something to be said for the Great Heresy.

25 THE ORACLE OF ZUMA BEACH

"It is like talking to the oracle at Delphi."

Jeanette made the remark with some consternation after our first interview with Simon Dunkle.

"How do you mean?" I asked.

"He babbles, he stutters. You cannot understand a word. Somebody has to translate what he says. And then"—she gave a nice, emphatic French shrug of the shoulders—"it means I don't know what."

It was an apt comparison. Simon's stammer turned out to be so severe that very little managed to fight its way up his spastic larynx and get past his teeth as coherent English. On our first weekend visit to St. James School, we spent three long meetings with the boy. I came away with no more than four sentences from his own lips. The rest had to be mediated by Sister Helena, who never failed to leave the impression that she was doing me a great favor by providing her services. But as time went by, I came to feel she was on hand to function more as censor than translator, intercepting Simon's halting remarks and recasting their meaning entirely. She had little trouble getting away with that. Simon was so shy he never protested, even when I could tell that Sister Helena was rerouting his words in very different directions than he intended. Three times when he struggled to cough up a word I knew to be "flicker," but couldn't get past a spluttery "f," she intervened to construe what he meant to say as "film" or "fun" or "photograph." When he bogged down once more on the word, I mischievously asked if he might not be trying to say "fuck." Sister Helena never missed a beat. Without the sign of a blush, the good lady smiled and said, "Why, yes." By that time, we'd arrived at a tacit understanding. She was misleading me, and I knew she was misleading me, and she knew that I knew she was misleading me. What choice did I have but to go along, hoping to pick up tiny glimmers of the truth here and there?

Caught between the stammering Simon and the devious nun, my frustration grew with each visit. I could never tell if I was learning anything reliable; I certainly didn't feel I was getting any closer to Simon. In that respect, I began to fear my trips to St. James School were going to finish as a total waste of time, except for the chance they offered to view Simon's movies. As it turned out, I was to see his films several times over, because the screenings offered an unexpected benefit. Timid and tongue-tied as he was, Simon was able to relax enormously whenever his films were on the screen. The boy clearly lived for his art—and through his art. It spoke for him, saying all he had to say. In its presence—with the aid of enough Milk Duds— he found the confidence to articulate a great deal more clearly. And sitting by his side in the darkened theater, I could easily lean close to lend him an ear to whisper in without giving Sister Helena the chance to intrude herself between us. Not that she didn't try. While we screened Simon's films, she would sit directly behind him, bent forward to catch whatever remarks we might be passing back and forth. That was awkward for her and besides gave her no excuse to butt in and speak for Simon.

If my attempt to get through to the oracle of Zuma Beach proved frustrating, Jeanette's situation was much worse. I hadn't yet told Brother Justin that she was on hand to conduct a magazine interview with Simon; nevertheless, I encouraged her to take notes along the way for later use. "I'll let Brother Justin know what you want when the time is right," I told her. But it took no more than the first few sessions with Simon for her to realize that her task might be impossible. She was getting nothing from the boy himself; and what Sister Helena was passing along made no sense whatever to her.

Worst of all, poor Jeanette had no idea what most of my questions were all about, since they often related to film techniques or religious doctrines that were a complete mystery to her. I confess it was selfish of me, but I'd decided to tell her nothing about the orphans or the Cathars. All this was mine to reveal when I felt ready to do so. I hardly wanted to see my long years of research scooped by Jeanette in some quick and flashy item published by *Rolling Stone*. So whenever she asked me to clarify one of my mysterious lines of questioning, I obfuscated shamelessly. As a result, after weeks of commuting between L.A. and Zuma Beach, Jeanette was getting nowhere with the project that had brought her to California—though of course she'd gained the opportunity to be saturated with Simon's films, including some juvenilia that had never been released. Unfortunately, that only made her more certain that she detested his work—all of it. Which made her less and less eager to pursue the interview.

The Simon Dunkle assignment may have turned into an ordeal for her, but her pilgrimage to filmland was paying off rather nicely in other ways. Jeanette, whom Sharkey had hastened to offer bed and board the day she showed up in his office, had decided to accept my hospitality instead. Sharkey was magnanimous about it, as if he had ever stood a chance with her. "She's the academic type," he explained to me. "I've sworn off the academic type."

She moved in with me and quickly made herself at home, only to discover that the allure of " 'ollywood" circa the mid-seventies was swiftly exhausted. In fact, it wasn't there at all. But we'd gracefully renewed our affectionate friendship, and that made her prolonged stay a promising possibility for both of us—or at least, so I allowed myself to believe for the next several months. She was a bright, high-spirited, adventure-seeking young woman whose company I found both comfortable and stimulating. Her visit, however, coincided with my full-time research into the Cathars. And this I preferred to do in my office on campus, the better to elude her predictable curiosity. There were also a number of books, among them the most valuable, that Brother Justin wouldn't allow me to remove from the school grounds. These were private publications of the church nowhere else available. I was permitted to see them only in his office. That kept me away from the apartment for whole days at a stretch, leaving Jeanette to amuse herself.

This she managed to do very nicely, finally drifting into marginal jobs around the edges of the movie industry. She had little trouble bringing herself to the attention of company executives who were always happy to have another pretty young thing hanging around, especially one who was willing to work for peanuts and show up unattached at parties. The job offers that came her way were mostly thinly veiled sexual advances, but she soon learned to fend off the savages. She ended up with a job reading for Disney Studios. She complained that the scripts she was given were silly stuff—especially those that went on to earn big bucks—but the work paid well enough and that took the pressure off her to deliver on the Dunkle interview. She soon felt free to skip more and more of our visits to St. James School.

Clearly her heart was no longer in the assignment. On the contrary, Jeanette had become Simon Dunkle's severest critic, always on hand to needle me with questions about his work. Why, she wanted to know, was I spending so much time with this "poor, sad, little boy"? Yes, she agreed, he was very clever. His films showed remarkable low-budget production values. "But they are *sick*. They are decadent." And finally, in a whisper she declared, "they are *evil*." Her words echoed those I'd heard from Clare years back when she'd been exposed to more of Max Castle's films than she could stomach.

"Well," I answered, "Simon is becoming a phenomenon. He deserves critical atttention. That's what I'm giving him. There'll be time to say all these things when I write my piece on him."

Jeanette could appreciate that. She was as astonished as I was to see how Simon's reputation was growing from month to month. *Sub Sub* had all the success Brother Justin expected for it. In its wake, distributors around the country ordered up thirty-five-millimeter versions of some earlier productions he had in reserve. And these too proved themselves at the box office. *Attack of the Skull Suckers* was as gross an example of a splatter flick as anyone would ever dare to put on the screen; but it was also a skillful spoof of the genre that succeeded in charming those reviewers who could pick up its underlying sophistication. As for *Annihilation Derby*, what more need one say than that it was the first Dunkle film that Clarissa Swann saw fit to review. That in itself was enough to give any movie status.

Clare claimed to hate it, calling it "our deepest descent to date into the cesspool of adolescent morbidity." But her critic's conscience obliged her to pay the film a dozen compliments for its wit, skill, daring, and originality before she got around to bum-rapping it. To my surprise, she even praised Simon's distinctly macabre way of handling bullet wounds, each one erupting in slow motion like a small crimson geyser. She called it "a surrealistic embellishment that actually makes the mayhem less offensively graphic."

As for Simon's panoramic treatment of American violence—the film is really nothing more than a fast-paced run of bloody holdups and shoot-outs staged by a gang of teenage ghouls on mom-and-pop grocery stores not for money but for cannibal fare—Clare rather blithely described that as something "Samuel Beckett and the Marquis de Sade might have scripted for Mack Sennett." Of course, for Clare such artistic miscegenation between styles and genres was wholly unacceptable. But she was clearly pitching her rejection at a flatteringly high level.

> Rumor has it [she wrote] that writer-director Dunkle is barely eighteen years old. That might lead one to expect that, in time, his underdeveloped moral and aesthetic intelligence will catch up with his technical talent. But in this case that may be a false hope. His films already reveal the sophistication of premature genius when it comes to dealing with the vile and the violent. In that respect, he has prematurely set aside childish things in favor of a malignant virtuosity. He and the rest of us may be stuck with what he so brilliantly is: a terminally deranged sensibility.

The review prompted me to write to Clare about my new connection with Simon. I didn't tell her much, nothing at all about the orphans. Beyond that, I still assumed there was very little I had to say about movies—even about Simon—she didn't already know. I could tell from the review that she'd seen a number of his other films. But I did ask if she recognized the relationship between Simon and Castle. Two months later I got the usual hasty reply. "Of course. Beware! All my love. Really." And then there was a postscript. "She's cute and she's smart and she's young . . . and I hate her. But give her a kiss for me anyway. What the hell!"

That had to do with Jeanette who, as I'd already learned, had met Clare briefly at a party in New York soon after she arrived from Paris. They had at once struck up a brisk, friendly conversation that grew still chummier when Jeanette hinted at and then revealed her embittered relations with Saint-Cyr. That led to a long spell of hot gossip. But when Jeanette went on to mention knowing me and said she meant to look me up, everything chilled to subzero. That puzzled Jeanette until she learned from me that Clare and I had been lovers.

"But she is three thousand miles away," Jeanette protested. "And she does not even answer your letters. Why should she be so jealous? And besides," she added as if she were scolding me, "she is so old for you. Or perhaps . . . am I too young?"

No, I said. Everybody was just the right age for everything. And of course Clare had no right to be jealous. But I was secretly gratified that she was.

When Clare's review of *Annihilation Derby* came out, I showed it to Jeanette, who believed it was too permissive. "I would not say anything good about his films, not even about how he makes the bullet holes go *plish.*"

I also showed the review to Simon, only to discover that he couldn't read it. The boy was severely dyslexic and struggled as much with the printed as with the spoken word. So I read it to him. He fairly blazed with delight.

"Sh-she l-liked the bul-bul-bul . . ."

"The bullet holes. Yes, I guess she did," I sighed.

Then he asked me to read that part again, "about the cess-cess-cesspool." I did. He took that as a compliment too.

Finally, I laid the review before Brother Justin, who pondered it carefully. I told him a Clarissa Swann review was a breakthrough. He understood that and was pleased. "Though I gather some of Simon's imagery is too robust for her taste."

"Well, I suppose you might put it that way."

"Perhaps after she reads what you have to say about Simon, she will have a more positive opinion."

"I doubt that. Clare's first opinion is always her final opinion."

By this time, some six months since my first visit to St. James School, I had to admit that my relationship with Brother Justin, never more than lukewarm at best, was turning frigid. I'd long since discovered he had nothing more to tell me about Max Castle. And when I asked to talk to Brother Marcion, his predecessor, I was treated to a rude surprise.

"*Talk* to him? Oh no, that would not be possible."

"But I thought you said he could answer some of my questions."

"We may *write* to him."

"You mean he isn't here . . . isn't nearby?"

"I never said so. No, he is in Albi. In seclusion. You see, he has become one of our elders. But he may be willing to correspond with you. I cannot guarantee that. However, if you give me a letter, I will

440

be pleased to forward it and second your request for information."

I let Brother Justin know that I found this highly disappointing. Nevertheless, I doped out a letter asking Brother Marcion for everything he could remember about Castle. I was given no reason to believe there would be a prompt response. There wasn't. Two months later I was asking Brother Justin to write again for me.

Even more frustrating were our discussions of the Cathars and their connection with the orphans. I almost came to admire how artfully evasive Brother Justin could be at every point. He insisted that there was a long dark period following the crusade during which the Cathar church, or what survived of it, dropped out of sight. This subterranean interval lasted for some four centuries, until the church reemerged in Zurich as an orphanage in the late seventeenth century. After that, orphanages sprang up wherever religious tolerance flourished: Holland, England, some of the enlightened German principalities. Two of the oldest establishments were built in the New World—in Pennsylvania and Rhode Island in the early eighteenth century. Within a century after that, the order had reached the Orient, the Near East, Latin America, India.

"But why orphanages?" I asked, a question that had long been on my mind and for which I thought I'd come up with a plausible answer.

"It is the most obvious charitable endeavor, is it not?" he replied. "To save the children."

What could I say to that? But I didn't trust his answer. I tried another question. "Are there any second- or third-generation members of your church?"

He played dumb. "Hm?"

"Kids born into the church. You know, their parents were members and their grandparents."

"Oh yes, yes. All our children are adopted by members of the church."

"*All* of them?"

"Yes. It is our policy to place them in a sympathetic household."

"And do any of them have brothers and sisters who were born Cathars?"

"Often the families have other children, yes."

"Children of their own?"

"Of course."

"I mean *born* to them?"

"Ah well, that is not the only way to have one's own child."

"But that's what I mean."

He stared at me blankly as if he simply couldn't understand. I had to go on tactfully angling the question this way and that several times before I got the picture clear. All the orphans became adopted children of church members around the world. But none of the sons and daughters were the natural offspring of any of the fathers and mothers. Everybody in the church had once been an orphan because nobody in the church ever produced children. Brother Justin wouldn't say as much, but that turned out to be the only possible conclusion. Having elected to become "eunuchs for the sake of the Lord," the Cathars would have nothing to do with baby-making.

As close-mouthed as Brother Justin might have been, I'm sure Jeanette would have found him a fountain of information in comparison with me. There was so little I felt free to tell her. So I swung back and forth between evasion and lying, lying and evasion. But I was doing neither very effectively. Little wonder her patience was evaporating, and she was letting it show. How much more time did I plan to spend with "that ugly child"? "What can you find to talk so much about?" she wanted to know. "You have seen all of his films three times."

"Four," I corrected. "Some of them five."

"So?"

"I'm learning some interesting new techniques from him," I lied.

She shrugged helplessly, then uttered a dark warning. "It is not good for you to let so much of his movies inside you."

Whatever did she mean, I wondered. All she could say was, once again, "It is not good for you." But she said it with intense conviction. More to the point, she let me know she was beginning to resent the weekends I spent away from her—and the evenings I put in at school with my books. In truth, I was neglecting her shamefully. I could hardly blame her for her discontent. And she was giving me fair notice that there was competition in the field for her idle hours. She made no secret of the fact that her job was putting her on the receiving end of lots of aggressive male interest. From time to time she would give me provocative little bulletins across the breakfast table. "Warren Beatty wanted to drive me home last night." "Richard Gere asked me to go with him to a preview."

I believed her. Her stay in California had turned her into a sharp and sexy dresser, enhancing her natural attractiveness. And I knew she could be superbly flirtatious when she cared to be. No doubt she was turning lots of heads. "But that's not why you came to Hollywood, is it?" I asked, only semifacetiously. "To sleep around with madly handsome movie stars?" She returned a look that told me how dumb that question was. Did I think she'd come to wait up nights for the sort of monkish and obsessive bookworm I was becoming?

If my time at St. James School had been limited to fruitless verbal sparring with Brother Justin, I might have shared Jeanette's frustration and simply given up the project. But something else developed over the months that justified my continued visits. Simon Dunkle found his voice—or at least enough of it to carry on reasonably satisfactory conversations. These matured out of the little whispered exchanges between us while watching his films. Gradually he came to feel more at ease with me and, so I noticed, more relaxed still with me alone than when Sister Helena was standing guard. I came to realize that Simon had a rather exaggerated notion of my stature in the film world. He seemed to feel that the research I was doing would lead to an article of decisive importance for his career. I played along with that, using the opportunity it gave to ask prying questions. So we began to take evening walks around the grounds of the school. I'd call for Simon at his studio after Sister Helena had retired and we'd have an hour or two together during the only time of day he could expose his light-sensitive hide to the out-of-doors.

We must have talked a couple of dozen times over the several months I came visiting. Even though his stutter moderated, Simon wasn't the most communicative of people. He remained shy with me, seldom volunteering more than brief answers to questions. Often he sank into pensive moods, and then I couldn't draw more than a grudging yes or no out of him. Even at his most talkative, Simon had a naïveté and awkwardness about him that belied the intricacy of mind he displayed in his films. I had to remind myself that, as childlike as his conversation might seem, this was the director whose knowledge of "the vile and the violent" revealed a menacing depth. In the most threatening sense of the term, I was dealing with an *enfant terrible*.

At first, I wondered if I should keep my conversations with Simon secret from Brother Justin and Sister Helena. But I soon learned that he—and she—knew all about them. That was puzzling, because Simon, though haltingly, was telling me a lot I wanted to know about things that Brother Justin had been withholding for months. Perhaps the priest misjudged how much I was finding out from Simon. Or, more likely, he felt confident that he could subsequently muddle whatever Simon passed along. And so he did on any number of occasions when I came to him seeking elaboration of some point Simon had raised. What Simon left shadowy Brother Justin could quickly submerge in midnight darkness. For that reason, I soon stopped looking to him for any further illumination of Simon's remarks and settled for what the boy told me, as obscure as that often was.

Here then, in composite form—and with the stutter mercifully deleted—is the gist of those extraordinary conversations as I can recall them now.

ABOUT HELL

I ask, "Do you really believe the world we live in is hell?"
He answers, "Yes."
"Why?"
"That's what we're taught."
"But really, actually, literally *hell?*"
"Uh-huh."
"And that God is really the devil?"
"The *true* God isn't the devil. He's God. Ahriman is the devil."
"You call him . . . it . . . Ahriman?"
"Or sometimes Satan. Or sometimes Yahweh."
"Yahweh?"
"Like in the Old Testament. The angry God. He made the world like it is."
"And what is it like?"
"What you see everywhere. All the badness."
"But there are good things too, good people, happiness."
"That doesn't last. It's just to tease us. Yahweh crushes it all. Yahweh hates us."
"Why does he hate us?"
"Because inside, where he can't get, there's a piece of the true God. That makes him wrathful. He's jealous of us."
"But can't he also be merciful . . . loving?"
"Jesus is. Not Yahweh. He just pretends sometimes. And then, wham! He smashes it all."
"Is Jesus the true God?"

444

"Well, not exactly. He's the Messenger."

"But he really existed, really walked the earth, right?"

"Well, not exactly."

"Was he an illusion?"

". . . not exactly." Simon began to become restless with this line of questioning. I tried one more query.

"Maybe he was sort of like a motion-picture projection . . . without a screen?"

Simon perked up at that. "Who said?" he asked eagerly.

"Just an idea," I answered casually and picked up where we'd left off with Yahweh. "So you really believe the God who runs the world is a sadistic monster?"

"Uh-huh."

"Doesn't that make you feel frightened?"

"Uh-huh. I get these nightmares."

"Nightmares?"

"Yeah. That's how I think up my movies."

ABOUT THE BLACK BIRD

"What does the black bird stand for?"

"For the true God."

"And who is that?"

"Well, he's got lots of names."

"Abraxas?"

"Yeah, that's one."

"And Abraxas is fighting with Satan, or Lucifer, or Ahriman, right?"

"Uh-huh."

"Do you think Abraxas will win in the end?"

"Nobody knows that."

"Could he lose?"

"Yeah, he could."

"And then what?"

There was a long pause. He was bringing the answer up from deep inside. "Just dark. Cold. Dead. Forever. Everything would be like . . . black ice. The whole universe just burnt out."

"That sounds peaceful at least."

"No. We'd know it."

"Know it?"

"Know the true God is dead. Know we're lost. Forever. We'll never stop knowing it, and knowing that it was our fault."

"How could it be our fault?"

"Because we kept it all going."

"Kept what going?"

"Life."

"I don't understand. If we stopped life, wouldn't that be death?"

He struggled to explain. "That'd be *one* death. But not the *other* death. It's okay if just the body dies. It's the *other* death that means being damned."

"You mean something like with the vampires? Dead but undead?"

"Yeah. Like that. But like that everywhere. Forever."

ABOUT DEATH

"You believe the body is a bad thing?"

"Uh-huh."

"Why?"

"Because it's . . . the body. It's made of icky stuff. Skin, blood, terrible rotten stuff."

"Some people think the body is a marvelous thing, the way it works and all."

"No. No, it isn't. The Evil God made it. He made it to torment us. He locked us up inside of it to make us suffer."

"Then why don't all the members of your church just kill themselves?"

Simon's eyes widened in authentic horror. "Then we'd be damned."

"Why?"

"Because it isn't allowed to kill. Not yourself, not anybody."

"But why?"

"Because we have to fight against the Evil God as long as we can. We have to redeem all the others, everybody."

"But don't some of the elders starve themselves to death?"

"Yes."

"Why is that all right?"

"Because they're ready to withdraw."

"Withdraw?"

"You'd call it dying. When they're old and ready. So it shows how strong they are. When you're too old to redeem others, then it's okay to withdraw, see?"

446

Theodore Roszak

ABOUT THE FLICKER

"Who discovered it?"

"It wasn't discovered. It was made."

"How do you mean?"

He shrugged as if observing the obvious. "S'how the projector works. It's made to teach the flicker."

"Teach?"

"Uh-huh. The flicker's what movies are, what they teach. It's what you're really seeing, but don't know it."

"And the flicker is . . . "

Very solemnly. "The war."

"Between the two gods?"

"Uh-huh."

"But movies aren't just projected light. There's all the rest. What about the story? The pictures, the music, all that?"

"That's on top of the flicker. If you do it right, the story makes the flicker stronger. You should try to tell a story that helps the flicker get through."

"What kind of story does that?"

"Scary stories, spooky stories. Stories about rottenness and killing people and all very gross things."

"Like your movies."

"Yeah."

"Did the orphans invent the projector?"

"No. Well, sort of. Actually, yes. We helped the inventors. We gave them the idea."

"You mean persistence of vision?"

He nodded.

"But Roget discovered that."

"Yeah, but it's our idea."

"Roget was an orphan?"

"Uh-uh. We gave him the idea."

"Do you know who it was who did that?"

"No. We don't remember the names. Somebody . . ."

Peter Mark Roget—the Roget of the famous thesaurus—was the Victorian Englishman who is usually credited with having written the first scientific paper on the queer phenomenon of persisting vision, the basis of all perceived movement in the motion picture. That was fifty years before a real projector was invented. But soon after his paper appeared, little optical novelties based on his discovery began to catch the public's fancy. Nobody has ever clearly understood where Roget came up with the concept. Now Simon was telling me there were orphans who had passed the idea along to Roget, and who had inspired all the machines that followed.

"Did the orphans help Thomas Edison?"

"Oh yeah."

"And Lumière?"

"Uh-huh."

"And . . ." I ran through the usual textbook list of early movie pioneers. The answer was yes, yes, yes. All of them had somehow been assisted by anonymous orphans somewhere in the shadowy background of history. At least, that's what Simon had been taught.

"What about this man LePrince? Do you know what happened to him?"

Now there was a long pause. After which, very furtively, "He was captured."

"By whom?"

No answer.

"By Oculus Dei?"

No answer, but a sudden amazed stare.

"Was he captured because he was promoting movies?"

No answer. But then a very slight nod.

"You have enemies, don't you?"

No answer.

ABOUT MAX CASTLE

"Why do you admire his work so much?"

"Because he got it just right. The flicker and the story and the lighting . . . everything all together."

"Which movie of his do you like the best?"

He thought the question over carefully. "*House of Blood*, I guess. And *Count Lazarus*. And, ôh yeah, *Zombie Doctor*. I want to remake those. I want to remake lots of his movies."

"Your movies use many of his techniques, don't they? I mean all the things people can't see, or don't know they're seeing."

Simon gave me a quizzical look, as if he wasn't certain I should know about such things. "Yeah, I use all that," he answered hesitantly.

"I think you use them better than Castle did."

His little pink eyes brightened at that. "You do?"

"You have more of a chance to use them. Castle didn't have as much artistic control as you have."

He pondered that. "I guess not."

"Lots of people in the church don't approve of Castle. Why is that?"

"I dunno. I think because he was disobedient."

"About what?"

"He wanted to show things he wasn't supposed to."

"Like what?" He gave no answer. "But you like his work anyway?"

In a solemn tone, "He was a prophet."

"Was he? Even though he was disobedient?"

"Yes. Because his movies spoke the truth."

ABOUT THE SALLYRAND

"Did you ever hear of a sallyrand?"

"Uh-uh. What's that?"

"It's what Castle used to call a multifilter."

"Oh. How come?"

"Just a pet name he had for it. Do you have one?"

"Uh-uh."

"You don't?"

"I don't use one. The editors do, not me."

"You *never* use it?"

"I used to. I don't have to anymore."

"Why?"

"Don't have to hide things. All the sex stuff and blood, you can just show it. People don't care. They like it."

"There was hidden stuff in *Sub Sub*, wasn't there? At the beginning, where the screen was all dark?"

"Yeah. The editors stuck that in. I didn't want it. The worst stuff came later. And I just showed it."

"Do you think I could borrow a multifilter? It would help me with my study of Castle's films."

He gave me a suspicious stare. "You should ask Brother Justin."

"You couldn't get one for me?"

"I'm not allowed."

449

FLICKER

On occasion I met Simon in the little room where he lived in the studio. It was a dim and cluttered cubbyhole; the shades were never raised to admit the light of day. A couple of the windows along with all the walls were covered over with a chaotic collage of posters, clippings, photos . . . the images that animated his genius. Most of the posters were from movies or rock concerts, especially those of the Stinks. There were some reproductions of works of art, a few of which I could identify. Figures from Michelangelo's *Last Judgment,* some Blake prints, some Bosch and Breughel. There was a lot of pop art, plus some rather unlovely cartoony stuff that I discovered were Simon's own sketches and doodles: strange, usually obscene, anatomical variations, monstrous beings, bizarre sexual couplings, tortured faces.

Other than a few catechism pamphlets, the room was heaped with gore and porn comic books. These go by the name "adult comix," but their main audience is kids, most likely unbalanced little boys. There were also several cartons filled with triple-X-rated girly magazines, the vilest kind.

"Do you have any favorite books?" I asked.

With some embarrassment, Simon told me what I already knew. "I have trouble reading." Whenever he wished, however, he could get students from the school to read to him. So what did he like them to read? He seemed reluctant to let me know, even irritated.

"You can tell me, Simon," I coaxed.

He went to a bureau and from deep inside one of the drawers fished out a book. He handed it to me like a precious possession. For the first and only time Simon succeeded in warming my heart. The book was a cheap paperbound edition of *The Wizard of Oz.* It had been leafed through so often the pages had to be held together by a rubber band.

"One of my favorites too," I confided to him.

He lit up at that, then sadly added, "She doesn't like to have the students read it to me."

"Who?"

"Sister Helena. The other teachers too."

"Why not?"

"She says it's a big lie."

"Oh?"

"She says it teaches children wrong things."

"Well, it *is* a fantasy."

"Yeah, that's okay. But it's when everything comes out happy."

"Sister Helena doesn't like that?"

"Uh-uh. Well, I guess she's right."

"You think so?"

"Yeah. But . . ." He fell into a guilty whisper. "Sometimes I like how it comes out in the book."

"Do you know the movie?"

He sneered. "Don't like that."

"No? Why not?"

"It's silly. It isn't really scary at all. Just for little kids. I could make it lots better."

"Have you ever thought of remaking the movie?"

"Oh yeah. I've got it all in my head."

"Have you?" And we talked about that for a while. It was soon clear that what Simon had in mind would be lugubrious in the extreme and as graphically frightening as possible. All the little excitements of the tale came out as ghoulish horrors, while the Tin Woodman, the Scarecrow, and the Cowardly Lion took on the proportions of Wagnerian heroes. Thank God, I thought, that nobody was ever likely to bankroll this production. Worst of all—and it really hit me like a rabbit punch—in the end Simon would have Dorothy die! And not very nicely. Her role was to function as the Cathar symbol of a tragic humanity persecuted by an angry God. An image formed in my mind: Judy Garland nailed like Christ to the cross. It was too much.

"Oh come on, Simon! You can't be serious. You're going to kill off Dorothy—the heroine?"

"Sure. Like Janet Leigh in *Psycho*. And Toto too. Anyway, that's how Sister Helena says it should end. And the Wicked Witch and the Wizard go on struggling . . . and we don't know who's ever going to win."

The next week I made a special trip to a little bookshop I knew in Westwood where I'd seen an illustrated first edition of *The Wizard of Oz*. It was still there. I bought it and gave it to Simon. He was delighted. Quickly he thumbed through. "Pictures aren't very scary," he commented. But he was overjoyed to have the gift.

FLICKER

ABOUT MILK DUDS

"Do you realize how bad that candy is for your teeth?" I asked on one occasion when, counting the Milk Duds as he crammed them in rapid succession into his bulging cheeks, I reached the number fourteen. The candy seemed to make it easier for him to talk, but when he was that loaded up, he drooled chocolate with every word.

"Yeah," he answered with a giggle. "It makes them all fulla holes. I get terrible toothaches."

"Maybe you should try to control that."

"I was gonna make a movie about it that maybe would scare me into cuttin' it out. This kid, see, he keeps eatin' these Milk Duds— like me—until one night his teeth get so mad they all give him a toothache at once." He burst out in a big, chocolate-spluttering laugh. "Only there's nothing scary about toothaches. It's just funny, y'know, this guy rollin' around in bed moanin'." More laughter, more chocolate.

"Well, it's a bad habit, Simon."

"Maybe what could happen is the guy's teeth decide to have like a mutiny against him . . . and eat his head."

He salted the idea away for later consideration.

ABOUT HIS PLANS

Simon seemed to have movies lined up in his mind for years into the future. I asked him to tell me about them. It was the one question that got him talking a blue streak—though in such a state of excitement that his stutter accelerated. I had to slow him down if I was going to learn anything from him.

His next film at the time was going to be called *The Birth Defectors*. This would be "sort of science fiction, about all the poisons and everything that're everywhere, and how that made all the babies become birth defectors."

"Birth defectors?"

"Yeah. Because they don't wanna be born. So they try to hide."

"Hide? Where?"

"Inside of the mothers."

"I don't get it."

"See, they have to be hunted around for and forced to be born.

452

And anyway, when the mothers see them they wanna kill them because of how they look."

"The babies hide inside their mothers? Babies can't do that."

"If they're different they can—because of how the poisons made them."

"Different?"

"Sort of wormylike. Or all oozy."

Again, I could discern the Cathar angle behind all this; the allegorized rejection of birth, the degradation of sex and the body. But Simon saw I found it pretty gross. He hastened to assure me, "It'll be funny. Like how they make it a crime not to want to be born. So all the birth defectors get arrested and sentenced to death by the big, bad judge." That brought on a wheezy sort of laugh, which I didn't share with him. "But first, the cops have to chase them all around inside, and the mothers get all twitchy and twisted up. . . ."

I decided I didn't want to hear any more about that one. So we went on to something called *American Mouth*. This, Simon told me, would be about shopping.

"Shopping?"

He explained. "First time somebody told me about this mall in Santa Monica, I thought he said 'maw.' Shopping maw. I had this dream about it. A big maw—where you go to shop. And it would chop you. A chopping maw. So we're gonna rent this mall in Ventura. We got that just about worked out. And see, this mall is really the mouth of hell. Like this." Simon pointed to a half wall of illustrations he had collected. A couple of them were from Bosch: people being gobbled down a vast demonic muzzle. The rest were mainly medieval sketches of the proverbial mouth of hell with devils at work pitchforking the damned to their fate.

"Most of the picture," Simon went on, "is just of people buying and buying and buying. Real greedy. We speed that up like the Old Keystone Cops. And then the whole inside of the maw becomes alive and opens up and they get swallowed, and they can't get away because they're loaded down with everything they bought, all this crazy stuff."

"Will this be funny too?"

"Oh yeah."

More distant projects included the working titles *They Came from Toxic Seepage, Cannibal Salad, Interviews with Assassins*. Somewhere three or four years down the line he had plans for an especially

dreadful item called *The President's Other Head.* This was so nauseatingly extreme that I cut him off abruptly after a couple minutes
of description. "God, Simon," I blurted out, "just stop, will you?" A
mistake, I realized. I'd wounded his feelings.

After a few moments of hurt silence, he turned to me with a malicious gleam in his eye. This was a Simon I hadn't seen before, a
vicious little imp whose voice suddenly took on an unexpected
strength and steadiness. "You think that's bad?" he asked. "Maybe
you'd like to see something."

"What?"

"Something. Tomorrow. I'll show you." It was almost a menacing
promise.

And that was how I came to know about the sad sewer babies.

26 THE SAD SEWER BABIES

Even in the darkness, I knew she was in tears as she spoke the
words. I could hear them in her voice, the deep pity that lay beneath
the anger. "It is worse when you are here than when you stay away."

"But you're always telling me I spend too much time away," I
protested, knowing there was nothing I could say that would placate
her.

"Yes. But when you are here, you still are not with me. Not really.
You don't want to be with me. Not like this. Tell the truth!"

Jeanette could mount an effective attack when she had to, a combination of little-girl poutiness and legalistic pugnacity. It always got
to me. "Oh no," I insisted, reaching across the bed to draw her close.
But even as I did so, I could feel the fibers of my body turning liquid,
going limp, rejecting the scent and moisture of her. She was right,
I couldn't stand having her flesh against my own. But I wouldn't
admit it, refused to admit it.

"Do you know how long it has been like this?" she asked, freeing

herself from my insultingly feeble embrace and moving farther off.
"Since the beginning. Since the first night I was here. Always there
is nothing. You think that is satisfactory?"

"Oh come on, we've made good love many times." My heart sank
to hear the words. When you have to say things like that, the cause
is already lost.

"Oh, is that how you remember?" She was sitting up now against
the back of the bed, her knees drawn up defensively against her
breasts. "You are wrong. Do you know how many times we have
made love in all the months I am here? Two times, three times. That
is all."

"That can't be right." Or could it be? I found myself struggling to
remember, like a man fighting off amnesia.

"Yes. It is right. And almost never complete. Like in Paris. There
is no finish."

"Paris?"

"Yes. You don't remember also that? Then too, there was nothing.
But I do not know you so well. So I think perhaps you are very shy
or very tired. I think perhaps that is how people make love from
California, because that is how they learn from the swamis." Even
though she was berating me, that brought a laugh. "Well, I do not
know. That is what Victor tells me."

And that choked the laugh in my throat. "You told Victor about
us?"

"Why not? I did not expect to see you again. But now, here, it is
again the same. And not because of the swamis. Always you tell me
you are not in the mood. Not in the mood! But now it is worse. Now
instead of nothing, there is something. Something *bad*. Disgust. I
disgust you."

"No, no, no."

"No? Then tell me how you feel. Tell the truth!" She rolled toward
me, searched to find my hand and forced it tight between her legs,
against her damp, fleshy cleft. I let her do it, but there was no denying
the fact that I wanted to flinch and draw back. At the touch, my mind
teemed with sensations of loathing. But I stubbornly kept my hand
where she'd placed it, hoping to prove her wrong. It was useless.
She could tell what my true response was.

"There, see?" I said. But my hand was making no effort to caress
her, to offer pleasure or take it.

"You lie to yourself, Jon," she said, thrusting my hand away. "You pretend we are lovers. No, we are not. There has been no love in this bed. You are not . . . capable."

By this time, there was no turning back. I realized that Jeanette and I were in the stormy middle of a decisive conversation. I could already see where it would end. For a while longer I argued back as best I could, offering excuses, telling her how fatigued I often was, how distracted, or perhaps how jealous of the other men in her life. But I knew these were lies. She was right. I'd been deceiving myself. And not only with her, but for some time, through several transient relationships that had left the recent women I'd been seeing bewildered, hurt, even outraged. One—a student of mine whom I briefly dated before Jeanette came visiting—had finally asked me, with infinite pity, if I was gay, so tenuous and inconclusive were our intimacies. I'd laughed the question off and quickly broken with her. Before that, there had been another fleeting episode with a woman in the English Department from which I'd begged off on grounds of illness after a second disastrous night. I could tell she would have been pleased to learn that it was a terminal condition.

Amazingly, I'd managed to sweep these embarrassments out of mind as if my sexual false starts didn't really matter. And they didn't. That was the worst of it. I had to admit that the end of each relationship, no matter how wrenching, had come as a relief. I was chilled to realize that the same would be true even now of Jeanette, with whom I'd been waking each morning in a cold and loveless bed, pretending there had been many nights of passion sometime in the past. But that wasn't so. Night after night—but less often in recent months when I'd been sleeping away—I'd lain beside this lovely, utterly compliant young woman and done nothing more than stroke her shoulder and kiss her once goodnight. Sleep always seemed more urgent than desire. I could recall the many times she'd teased me about it in little, hesitant ways. I'd offered excuses; she'd been patient. But this time she was having none of it.

"Don't you know why this is, Jon? It is the boy."

"The boy . . . ?"

"Don't be stupid with me. Simon. His films. They are poisoning you. I can see it happening. So much morbidity, ugliness. It is too much for you. You cannot tell?"

Her words were echoing what Clare had told me years before when she called Castle's movies "evil." I hadn't taken that warning. I was so certain I could ward off the effects, especially since I knew what they were intended to be. But if Jeanette was right about Paris—and I knew she was—I hadn't succeeded in defending myself. The movies I'd exposed myself to for so long—Castle's dark thrillers, Simon Dunkle's nihilistic nightmares—had taken their toll.

As far as I could clearly remember through layer upon layer of stubborn denial, the only real sexual arousal I'd experienced in years had been Olga Tell's kinky exercises in Amsterdam. I might have continued denying that fact now. I might have been ready to turn Jeanette out and shore up my sagging psychological defenses once again. But the conversation we were having came three days after Simon had introduced me to the sewer babies. The impact of that was too vivid to be waved aside.

The full title of the movie was *The Lonesome Lovesong of the Sad Sewer Babies*. Simon had never shown me an unfinished work before. This one might not be completed for years to come, due, he said, to certain technical problems—a mysterious remark that was made to sound like a military secret. Nevertheless, he seemed eager to screen the film for me. In part, his motivation was prankish. He brought the film to me the way teasing little boys exchange disgusting stories when they're playing "turn green," trying to gross one another out to see who has the strongest stomach. But there was something more to it than that. Simon seemed to have something to prove as a matter of professional pride. He wanted to demonstrate how "good" a "bad" film could be, meaning how serious a message could be wrapped in one of his cheap little shockers. Accordingly, I prepared myself for another onslaught of gore and horror, only to find I'd been outflanked. *Sewer Babies* aimed at a different, more disturbing effect. No violence, no mad slashers or cannibal gangs. And no earsplitting soundtrack. Instead, only a quiet descent into absolute despair.

As I write these words, I realize that the *Sad Sewer Babies* offers me my one chance to describe a Simon Dunkle film the world hasn't seen—and may never see. But I take no satisfaction in this cinematic scoop. If I could, I would prefer to erase the film from my memory, hoping that it survived nowhere else. Or perhaps that Simon Dunkle himself won't find the stamina to complete it. If he does, I suppose it might be his masterpiece—given the purpose his films are meant to serve. Other than its producers, I may be the film's only audience. Or rather victim. Because the *Sewer Babies* isn't a movie—not really. It's a kind of optical acid that burns through from the eye straight down into the vital organs.

As in a number of Max Castle's films, the movie begins before the eye has ingested a single image. There is—for some ninety seconds—nothing but the broiling dark screen, writhing with invisible or barely perceptible movement. Sound predominates. Heavy, labored breathing, counterpointed with whines and low groans, cleverly composed, but prolonged to intolerability. Stifled cries, clearly female, struggle to be heard but are held back. At last, a murky, slow-motion montage emerges from the darkness. Flesh, flesh, flesh in gaudy, flared colors. Body parts. Women's bodies. Legs, stomachs, knotted muscles, blood streaming over bare skin in small, turgid rivulets. The camera jostles maddeningly, refusing to yield a whole and solid image.

Then, deep in the background, seeming to rise from beneath the floor, there is a rhythmic pulse, a water sound, surging and fading, familiar but elusive. It takes many minutes to become identifiable. A toilet flushing. Then more toilets. Gradually, against ever more contorted glimpses of female anatomy, the sound builds to a crescendo loud as a waterfall. Finally, voices emerge. The Stinks, but this time their raw, amateurish caterwauling has been disciplined into a somber, elegiac, and highly sophisticated fugue constructed out of just a few phrases.

> *Wasted . . .*
> *Ripped and torn,*
> *Unwanted . . .*
> *Never born.*

We see great gloved hands wielding menacing and bizarre instruments: prongs, pincers, tubes, clamps. Behind them, sweating and straining faces, all women. At last, the suggestive fragments take on meaning. These are the sounds and images of abortion. There is nothing clear or graphic, yet we are seeing the essence of the act captured at its most grueling extreme. It was more than I cared to watch. I looked away until the sound told me the scene had changed. Now the screen was filled with a dizzy swirl of stained water, the embryos being flushed away by the hundreds. The camera goes into a drunken spin following them down and down into darkness. The scene descends into a yawning void. The only light is a damp glimmer here and there reflected off water. All around there are high, whining voices chattering in a vastly echoing abyss.

Where are we? In the dank sewers of the city, a subaqueous labyrinth, the perfect Cathar symbol of our earthly condition. Here the embryos survive to become the sewer babies. They huddle together in clusters and grow into gelatinous creatures with sad human eyes. They feed and fight among themselves; swim, wallow, and creep along the walls looking for light. The film as a work-in-progress became somewhat jumbled at this point, a collection of shots upon shots of the babies in their noisome habitat. Though I assumed much of this would be mercifully edited from the finished version, the camera carefully investigates every fetid inch of this infernal landscape. At last the film breaks off in the inconclusive middle of a struggle between the embryos and the indigenous rat population for control of the sewers. There is every indication that the predatory vermin will prevail over the defenseless babies who seem able to do little more than wail and retreat.

Vile as the mewling, grublike embryos were to watch, they were a remarkable screen effect. Though they riveted my attention, for the life of me, I couldn't make out what they really were. Obviously not costumed actors; their diminutive size ruled that out. Nor were they animations; they were far too organically mobile. They looked like actual living things. But if they were, I was glad to say I'd never come upon their like. I asked Simon what they were while we waited for the reels to be changed.

"G-guess," he challenged me.

"Some sort of puppet . . . ?"

He gave a dismissive smirk. "You c-can't guess?"

"No, I can't."

"N-n-nobody will," he answered smugly. "It t-took a long time to grow them," he added, but would say no more.

In the second section of the film—also still in rough cut—the embryos have made their way back into the world. But what a world! Simon managed to suffuse the scene with an oppressive yellowish-gray atmosphere, an acidic twilight that might be the last glimmer of a dying sun. It left ominous gulfs and pits of shadow everywhere. What little color remained in the streets was a mix of diseased greens and purples. People moved in this sickly half-light like zombies in the making, the life being slowly drained from them. The effect was a variation on the split-lighting I'd seen in so many of Max Castle's films, but much more expertly achieved. Simon later referred to the result as "granulated light," a term I hoped he would get around to explaining.

FLICKER

In this darkling environment, the desperate embryos emerge timidly from the sewers and storm drains to slither along the gutters and lurk in unlit corners. They don't mean to menace or attack; they do worse. Pathetically, they beg for a love they are too hideous to reclaim. Still, when the chance comes their way, they approach, stroke, cling—especially to sleeping women. We have scene after scene of the babies squeezing under doors, creeping over the bedclothes, fastening themselves to the mothers who have rejected them. In the background, The Stinks take up their wailing chant, sounding now like bats in the night sky.

> *Love you so much,*
> *Ooh wanna touch,*
> *Love you a lot,*
> *You all I got,*
> *Luba, luba, luba,*
> *Gluba, gluba, gluba.*

Where the film breaks off, the lovelorn embryos have become unintentionally menacing in their futile pursuit of acceptance. In their numbers, they too often choke the life out of those they would caress. Simon had no idea as yet how he would end the story, but my sense was that he had in mind a sort of lethal worldwide pestilence, the human race smothered with love by its aborted progeny.

Putting it that way might make the film seem like an exercise in antiabortion propaganda. But that it surely isn't. The movie isn't "pro-life." Like all Simon's work, but this time more crushingly than ever, it is *anti*. Anti everything. Antisex, antimotherhood, antilove . . . antilife. In Simon's hands abortion becomes a visual metaphor of contempt and loathing. The babies are the quintessential Cathar vision of physical existence: the blind animal rage to survive at all costs, the maniacal appetite of the flesh that devours the spirit within. They don't enlist our sympathy, they aren't victims but persecuting little monstrosities. Their hunger for love is wholly repulsive. One longs to see them flushed away, expunged.

But that hardly puts Simon on the side of the hounded mothers in his film. Without exception, they are bovine, stupid-faced women, the female type Simon so often features, especially in the role of mothers. Gross physical specimens, they would seem to have no function in life but to make babies. Yet that role is made to seem thoroughly disgusting. One simply wants to see the entire cycle of begetting, birthing, dying, come to a merciful end.

This, then, was the stew of life-denying imagery I carried home in my head to Jeanette. I sat through only that one screening of the film, but it was enough to cripple my vitality. Max Castle, with the benefit of all the subliminal motifs at his command, couldn't have done a better job of that.

Simon, of course, was eager to know my opinion of his work, but I wouldn't give him a quick answer. Instead, I resorted to peripheral questions.

"How long did you say you've been working on this?"

"F-four years."

"Why so long?" I asked. As far as I could estimate, Simon rarely spent more than three or four months on a movie. Many were true quickies, done in a few days.

He screwed his face up in annoyance. "L-lots of dumb tech-technical things."

That puzzled me. Simon had never referred to "technical things" before. Though there was a great deal in the way of special effects and tricky editing in all his work, these matters seemed almost routine for him, never the sort of difficulty that held up production. "Seemed quite effective to me," I commented, hoping to draw him out. "Some very powerful images. The lighting, the sound . . ."

"Oh yeah. The f-film's okay."

"Well then?"

"It's the tr-tr-transfer."

I'd never heard this term before. "Transfer. To what?"

"T-T-TV."

"TV? You mean this is supposed to be a *television* movie?"

"Yeah. That's why we g-got to get it tr-transferred just right."

"Transfer," he went on to explain, meant preparing the movie so that it could be shown on a television screen with no loss of power. Simon had never talked technicalities with me before, and he wasn't the easiest person to follow when he did. But I got the main point. Television, although still an art of light and shadow, significantly altered the characteristics of a film, especially the flicker. The flicker was still there, but it required a different treatment. Simon went into the engineering fine points of the matter, running off lots of numbers that meant next to nothing to me. I couldn't help but be impressed, however, by how much he knew about the medium.

I'd always smugly regarded television, especially its technical side, as unworthy of serious artistic attention. Not so Simon. He was intensely concerned about the problem of transfer. As I understood it from his hasty and stammering exposition, the little video screen was very unlike the big movie screen. On the big screen, the dark and light alternated in time as the film flipped through the projector. On the little screen, the dark and light—which still embodied "the war"—were simultaneously present at every moment as a result of the rapid scanning action that went on inside the picture tube. The flicker was thus laced across the entire screen.

From Simon's viewpoint as an orphan filmmaker, this made a big difference. It meant that whole scenarios had to be handled in ways for which the movies provided no guide. The deep darks and sharp lights of the film screen had to yield to more intricate blendings, muted grays, fuzzy contours. Images and sound had to be scaled down and made more sensuously intimate. More had to be done with close-ups and interiors. The edges of the picture tube, being beveled, could be exploited for a new range of effects.

Above all, there was the phenomenon Simon called "beaming." In film, light is projected from behind the viewer upon the screen and there perceived by reflection. In video, the light is invasive, almost like an assault; it is beamed directly at the viewer from the front. The human retina is the screen. The pictures are shot straight through the optic nerve into the brain—"like millions and millions of little needles," as Simon put it. Potentially, that drives every cinematic effect more deeply and surely into the mind. From Simon's viewpoint, this made television a far more potent medium—if it was properly used. "Movies're gonna be dead," Simon predicted confidently and without a tinge of regret. "Everybody's gonna s-stay home w-w-watching the TV all day. Hours and hours. You g-got 'em sitting there like t-t-targets. You c-can just keep zapping it at 'em, wham, wham, wham!"

How much progress, I asked, had Simon made so far in transferring any of his films to the TV format?

"Oh, lots. C-course I'm n-not working on it all b-by myself. But there's still problems, so I c-can't f-finish anything yet." He went on to explain something about the trouble he was having with "blacks." The black part of a TV movie—shadows, depths—were still not "negative" enough. Television color (which Simon hated) was part of the difficulty. But even if the harsh video color spectrum could be softened, the beaming made the blacks too luminous. That was where the granulated light came in. It was an experiment seeking to create an eerie gray that might suffice for the time being whenever ghastliness was needed, the effect in which Simon was most interested. But eventually Simon wanted a video-dark that would be as "pitlike" as the darks in a good *film noir*.

"Real h-hellish, you know?" That would "strengthen the evil." As it was, "you r-really can't scare anybody, especially with all the lights on in the room." What Simon was working toward was a "vampire black" that would "suck all the light right out of the people's heads" and produce an "inside darkness" deeper than any movie theater. "It'll be like the gr-grave," Simon predicted eagerly. "Then you'll really get the f-f-flicker in there."

"And you think," I asked, "that when you get it all worked out, with the vampire black and the beaming and all, that the television networks are going to broadcast movies like the *Sad Sewer Babies*?" I was trying tactfully to remind Simon that he was after all a marginal, avant-garde filmmaker who couldn't be certain of placing his work in first-run theaters or outside the video ghetto of MTV. My skepticism hardly fazed him.

"Oh yeah. They'll be showing everything on the TV, another t-t-t-ten years. All k-kinds of j-junk. There's gonna be so m-many ch-channels. H-h-hundreds of 'em."

"Hundreds?"

"Oh sure. It's being invented. So my stuff will be th-there. The kids'll want it. But th-that's not what matters anyway. That's just broadcasting. Th-that's how the TV is now, but it's gonna be all d-different. Wh-what'll happen is the kids'll b-buy the f-flicks and stick 'em on at home. Par-parents won't even know what they're w-watching."

"*Buy* them? Kids are going to *buy* movies?"

"Sure," he answered in a wised-up tone.

"Simon, I think you're being unrealistic. Do you know what it costs to buy movies for home projection—even *if* the producers are willing to sell them?"

He gave a knowing little smirk. "That's *now*, you're talking about. But p-pretty soon . . ." He fished into his pants pocket and drew out a small circular object about the size of a poker chip. Casually, he flipped it toward me. I caught it and turned it over a few times. It was made of plastic with a square hole at the center. Along the edges there were tiny slots. Otherwise there were no distinguishing features. ". . . movies'll look like that," Simon went on. "Even smaller. And re-real cheap. I could stick all my stuff on just that one."

Simon called the little trinket a "flick pack." He was convinced that in the near future people would have some means of playing these devices in their own homes on television—as inexpensively as playing phonograph records. All the movies in the world would wind up being fed into television sets and shown at the push of a button. For years I'd been hearing rumors of such a technology; recently, a kind of "cassette" had been put on the market which might one day hold an entire movie. What Simon was describing still lay in the realm of science fiction, but he had no doubt about the matter.

"People'll be b-buying movies like"—he popped a Milk Dud into his chocolate-ringed mouth—"candy. N-nothing special. Th-they'll just be playing in the background all the t-time, every room of the h-house. That's when we'll really *g-g-get* 'em. And my fl-flicks'll be the most popular of all."

I drove home from St. James School that weekend in a condition of emotional and intellectual overload. The images of Simon's film were swimming through my memory, reminding me that I'd seen a true masterpiece of morbidity. But what I carried away of the movie jostled for attention with what Simon had told me about his plans. I understood very little of what he'd said about the possibilities of video technology, but I'd learned better than to dismiss anything the orphans had to say about the cinematic arts. Their skill at manipulating the medium was formidable.

Yet, if I could believe Simon, everything the church had thus far accomplished with the movies was as nothing compared to the latest phase of their work. Within the next several years, the orphans planned to invade new territory, the world of the video screen, and with an even more fearful arsenal of psychic weaponry. For most of the drive back to L.A., I tried to hold that one thought in mind, concentrating on its significance. I now realized that Simon's career was meant to reach far beyond that of a promising underground filmmaker. His destiny lay in a new medium, which he predicted would soon be open to the most extreme forms of artistic license.

I couldn't dispute what he said. Clearly the Reign of Excess was upon us. On all sides, the walls of taste and intelligence were tumbling down. Why should I doubt that if a means could be found to bring porn and gore into the living rooms of the world, it would be done?

There were probably orphan inventors already at work on the project. And when the dust settled at the advent of that new Dark Age, there would stand a little, snow-white and bunny-pink-eyed Antichrist, Simon the Dark, holding out a handful of tiny flick chips that contained the nightmares of his diseased imagination. So far, only I in all the infidel world outside the circle of the chosen Cathar few could see it coming. And what are you going to do about that, Professor Gates, you who alone can chronicle the history of the movies from Lumière to Dunkle, from light onto darkness? Or do you even care?

All this was on my mind the night Jeanette opened her barrage upon my sexual failure. I might have tried to explain that the future of civilization was weighing upon my poor, unresponsive organ. But that would have been a dodge. Because she was right, as only the woman who shares your bed can be right about such things. It was Simon's sewer babies that had emasculated me, they and all the horror and despair with which his movies had been flooding my senses. His nihilism had saturated me and claimed me for the Great Heresy. As a result, Jeanette's elegant young flesh had turned rank for me. I couldn't bear to touch her, smell her, share my space with her. Of course we would have to part.

That happened three days later. It was neat and friendly. A sharply dressed older man named Barry dropped by to help Jeanette move her few modest possessions to his condo in Century City. I vaguely remembered him from studio parties in the past. He was a low-level Disney executive whom I could recall she'd mentioned meeting several weeks ago. Sizing him up with a frankly jaundiced eye, I concluded Jeanette was better than he deserved. But then, every guy I'd ever met in the film industry was accompanied by a woman who was better than he deserved. In any case, Barry seemed suave and polished smooth around the edges, so I judged he would be kind to her for a while and, so I hoped, pass her along in better shape than I was leaving her.

Jeanette was relieved to be going but not happy. She showed true concern when I gave her a goodbye kiss—probably the warmest kiss I'd bestowed on her in months.

"Remember what I have warned you," she said.

"You were right," I answered. "I intend to stop with Simon."

That brought a sudden light into her teary eyes. "Ah, then maybe . . ."

"Then . . . I'll be leaving town for a while."

"To go where?"
"New York. I need help."
She knew at once what I meant. "To see . . . ?"
"Yes. To see . . ."
She offered a final kiss. "I think it is the right thing."

27 ANGELOTTI

Success had done good things for Clare. Under its influence, she'd flowered astonishingly like some tough desert cactus one wouldn't have thought kept the promise of a blossom hidden among its thorns. When I'd first known her during her long years of obscurity, she was a bitter woman torn by hurt and envy. It showed in her sullen moods, her belligerent swagger, her aggressive arrogance with one and all. Rebelling against the intellectual establishment and, more immediately, against the glitz of a Los Angeles she regarded as a philistine slum, she'd affected a Parisian Left Bank slovenliness, her hair a riot of tangles, her clothing the same drab sweater and skirt each day. I'd fallen madly in love with that surly, unkempt woman, though I knew at the time that much of what I found exciting about her were the wounds left by years of heartache. Still, at a certain stage in my life, she'd been the living image of daring and defiance, holding out the promise of hot new ideas and forbidden sex.

That Clare was now gone forever. Her years in New York had transformed her radically—and, I had to admit, all for the better. With the exception of that one glowing evening she'd arranged with Orson, she never spared me more of her time when I came visiting than a quick luncheon or a drink during the happy hour. But on each occasion she looked brighter, more chic, more contented than before. That made me happy for her. It was hard to imagine Clare mellowing, but so she had, even in her reviews. She no longer indulged in the vitriolic contempt and studied aesthetic dissection that were once the trademark of her criticism. She'd learned that such intellectual acrobatics strain the pages of any publication paying enough to cover the cost of lunch in New York. Instead, she'd perfected a style that managed to both chafe and charm her public. While the mordant wit was still there, she now tempered its use to champion struggling talent: the little film, the marginal effort, the one redeeming performance that deserved praise in an otherwise dreary production. She made her readers feel they were partners in discovering these few bright grains of gold in the growing mountain of cinematic slag. At least with me, she stopped pretending she felt compromised by the rewards her popularity brought her: a string of successful books, top-dollar lecture stints, invitations to festivals and conferences across the country and abroad. These days she was as apt to be traveling as to be at home in the small but luxurious condo she now owned in the East Eighties. She'd spent years resentfully convinced that the world owed her its recognition. Now that the world had come across, she relaxed into its applause gratefully.

Though I admitted it with reluctance, the new Clare had acquired sexiness with success. It was nothing like the steamy bohemian appeal that had once stirred my boyish lust. Her features took on a confident glow, a relaxed grace of manner. Her figure had grown trimmer and she dressed to show it off to the best advantage. There was always a lover or two in the background—not penniless students, but men of substance. I felt like such a prehistoric relic in her life that I approached her with apologies even as I wrote her the long, urgent tale of Simon, the orphans, and the Cathars. I didn't mention Jeanette, but I hinted at the strange enfeebling effect the films were having on me. I knew I ran the risk of sounding loony, but I was beyond caring about that. This was no academic query; it was a cry for help. I wanted her to know it was.

To my amazement, I got a phone call the very day my letter reached her. It was a brief but pressing invitation couched in unmistakably affectionate terms.

"Darling, you may be in a lot deeper than you realize. I want to see you right away. Can you come soon?"

"How soon?"

"Now. Tomorrow. Possible?"

"Well . . . I'm teaching. I'd have to make . . ."

"Sweetheart, I'm worried for you."

Worried for me! The tone in her voice made *me* even more worried. "Next week. I'll be there first thing."

"Don't bother to book a hotel. Stay here. But hurry. It's important."

Clare was telling me it was "important" for us to meet. I couldn't believe my ears. The last thing I expected from her was therapeutic consolation. But her voice on the phone raised my hopes. Maybe I was going to have the chance to pour my heart out.

I did. But not to Clare. To a stranger who, as it turned out, already knew my story better than she did.

When I arrived in New York, I headed straight for Clare's, where I'd been promised a modest meal and a long evening's talk. To my intense disappointment, I discovered our dinner was not to be *à deux*. There was someone else on hand, a dark, excessively lean but strikingly good-looking man in his late forties, dressed in a baggy black suit and high-necked sweater. His hair, lightly streaked with gray, was a curly, minimally combed mane that straggled down his cheeks into a rough, short beard and mustache. His English was good enough to make his accent nearly imperceptible. Clare called him "Eddy." I wouldn't have guessed he was Italian until she mentioned his last name: Angelotti. "Eddy is the new film archivist at NYU," she told me.

"Thanks to Clare," Eddy acknowledged. "She rather smuggled me into the job."

I assumed, with a small, well-disguised twinge of jealousy, that he was the new love in her life. And why not? Though on the ascetic side, he was a gorgeous sort of man, and clearly gifted at exactly the sort of verbal fencing Clare enjoyed. The two of them traded film talk across the table like champion Ping-Pong players—fast, tricky volleys of likes and dislikes, with plenty of spin on each judgment. The well-chewed bone of contention that evening was Pasolini's posthumous shocker *Salo*, which they had seen the night before, the grand climax of a Sadistic Cinema Festival that was the hot topic of the film crowd. I gathered they'd been arguing over it ever since. Eddy considered it "the definitive anti-fascist statement." Clare disagreed passionately. "But it *isn't*. Fascists would love it; it's an outright surrender to their aesthetic. The beauty of atrocity. With the Carl Orff music yet. *Salo* would have had an extended run in the officers' quarters at Buchenwald."

"But surely," Eddy protested, "the film is done with a certain formalistic rigor that objectively distances . . ."

Clare was having none of that. "Eddy, please! You don't defeat brutes by showing them what they are—least of all 'objectively.' They're proud of what they are. They *like* it. That's what sadism means: beyond shame. Films like *Salo* just appeal to the same in the rest of us. The only way to deal with fascism is to show people what it *isn't* over and over again. Joy, love, innocence. *Singin' in the Rain—that's* the ultimate anti-fascist movie."

Backing off the argument, Eddy turned to tell me that Clare had insisted they leave after the first half hour. "Perhaps it was too strong at points," he conceded but with rather too much condescension.

"Too strong, yes, but not for the eye," Clare countered. "For the nose. You didn't notice that the theater reeked of vomit? Which was actually very encouraging. There are still people going to movies who can have their stomachs turned. The visceral index of civilization. I'd given up hope. Or does the Trans-Lux East always smell like that? In any case, I left before I made my contribution."

Good old Clare, still the same bright spirit fighting for the Good, the True, and the Beautiful. And here I was, back in her life again to bring word that worse than *Salo* lay in store for us. Simon Dunkle, impresario of the Bad, the False, and the Hideous.

We were halfway through dinner before I concluded that I was wrong about the relationship between Clare and Eddy. The talk between them had the ring of recent acquaintance and purely academic interest. Clare was doing nothing along the way to clue me in about the man except to say they'd met at a screenwriters' symposium in Milan the year before. I had the feeling Clare was making every effort to build up Angelotti's expertise for me. By the time we got to her usual epic dessert—a *tarte tatin* with heaps of crème Chantilly, one of my old favorites—I was suitably impressed, but also puzzled. After all, Clare knew I hadn't rushed across the country for an evening of movie chatter, no matter how scintillating. At last, a bit impatiently, I decided to move the conversation to new ground. The question was a clumsy one, but I simply dropped it on the table. "I once read a book by an Angelotti. Any relation of yours?" I'd flashed on the name when Clare introduced us. Since the man didn't look, dress, or talk like a priest, I hardly expected the answer he gave.

"My little monograph on the Manichaeans? How remarkable you should have come across it."

Clare shot me a mock-angry glance. "There now, you've spoiled my surprise. Father Angelotti is a member of Oculus Dei."

My pulse gave a heavy twitch, but I tried to keep the tone relaxed. "Oh? Any connection with Father Rosenzweig?"

"One of our more militant members," Angelotti answered, picking up smoothly on the reference. "A gifted man, though I am afraid he became an embarrassment. He recently passed away, did you know?"

"Yes, a sad death. I visited him in Lyons, at the asylum just shortly before he died."

"Did you? For what reason?"

"An interview. About Max Castle's work. It was quite hopeless. He was beyond communication."

"Still, I'm sure he appreciated the visit. None of us dared put in an appearance, as I'm sure you can understand."

" 'Us'? How many of you are there?"

Angelotti unloaded a sad sigh. "Barely a handful. I'm not sure you would any longer call us a group at all. I keep in touch with four or five others. We rarely meet, and never in gatherings of more than three. We keep a low profile. Except, that is, for Rosenzweig. But he paid dearly for his outspokenness. Poor man."

"As a matter of fact," I said, "I can tell you just *how* poor. Crazy as it may seem, I'm the old boy's heir. They sent me all his worldly goods after he passed on."

I could see that drew Angelotti's interest. "Anything of importance?"

"Oh, some real treasures. A heap of very smelly old clothes and very moldy books. That's where I came across your book."

"Was there also perhaps a Greek text among them?"

"Yes, there was. I have it with me. That and the rest of his stuff. Not the clothes. The books, pamphlets, notebooks."

Clare lifted a curious eyebrow. "For me?" she asked.

"I thought I'd bring what I had for show and tell."

"If you have no use for them," Angelotti suggested, "I'd be willing to take them. I've been trying to collect a small archive of materials. Our members' writing, their personal libraries, that sort of thing."

"And the Greek book is of some value, you think?"

He shrugged. "Only to a specialist in the field. A Gnostic catechism, I believe. I know Rosenzweig had such a work."

"You're a Dominican, I gather."

"Formerly, I should say. In my own eyes, still. But officially defrocked—like all our members. As you have learned, our views are not welcome in the church."

We'd finished dessert. Oddly enough, Clare, who was never the most efficient of hostesses, went to work quickly clearing dishes. Minutes later, she reappeared wearing her jacket. "There's a flick I have to catch tonight. Plus a party after, where they'll try to get me drunk enough to write a favorable review. I'm sure you and Eddy will find plenty to talk about."

I was startled to see her leaving. "I thought . . ."

She came close and put a hand gently on my cheek. "I think you should talk to Eddy first. I've heard it all. We'll be sure to chat before you leave. I'll try to be back by midnight. Wait for me." She rose on tiptoe to brush a kiss across my cheek. She was wearing perfume, my Clare! Then, in my ear, she whispered, "Trust him."

So I found myself alone with an Italian monk who seemed perfectly at home in Clare's apartment. He knew where the liquor was kept, fetched a few bottles, and poured us each a cognac. "She is quite odd, Clare," he said. "She listens to me, but I think she only half believes—or less than that. Sometimes she simply laughs. But then she asks to hear more."

I settled across from him in a deep leather love seat, a coffee table between us. "She loves film," I explained. "I suspect you and I know something about that love she'd rather not hear. Like the betrayed wife who wants and doesn't want to know what her husband's been up to."

He nodded. "So I gather. A pity. She could help us."

"The only member of Oculus Dei I ever met was a madman," I said. "Are you a madman?"

"Would I be Clare's friend if I were?"

"Are you going to tell me about medieval movies?"

He laughed. "But this I think you already know about. The Templars' magic lantern, Manichaean flip-books . . ."

"All leading up to Max Castle."

"The master of the art. Now, thanks to your diligent labors, restored to posthumous prominence and once again ready to smuggle his heresies into the public consciousness."

"And Simon Dunkle?"

"Ah, there *you* may have something to tell *me*." He reached for an inside pocket and drew out an envelope. My letter to Clare. Laying it on the coffee table, he said, "Clare took the liberty of letting me

471

read it. She thought it would help." Angelotti was astute enough to notice my resentment. "I did try to skip over the more personal matters. In any case, do bear in mind that I am a priest. I have some respect for people's confidences."

I reminded him that I hadn't asked him to hear my confession, but let the issue slide. He was a courteous man with a compassionate air. And Clare had told me to trust him. "You didn't know about Simon?" I asked.

"Only a little. That he was the great new hope of the orphans, their first attempt to train a major director since Castle, this I have heard. But his work—what I know of it—seems still very marginal, very underground. How seriously to take it, I have no idea."

Before I told him what I knew, I decided to go back to the beginning. The remote, original, primordial, once-upon-a-time beginning, if he could escort me that far. "Where does it all start—the orphans, the heresy? Seventeenth century? Thirteenth century?"

Angelotti settled into his chair and took a long sip of cognac, then cast his eyes to the ceiling. "How far back . . . ? For our purposes, or at least *my* purposes, we would need to reach back to Simon's namesake. You have come across him, Simon Magus, Simon the Magician?"

I had. I gave Angelotti a quick read-out. "The original Christian heretic, a rival of Jesus himself, taken by some to be the Antichrist." Angelotti nodded. "That's quite a way to go, isn't it? Two thousand years?"

He gave a soft chuckle. "Well, if we were to believe the dualists . . ."

I knew the term but asked him to explain it as he understood it.

"That is what we call our heretical friends, making no distinction among their many sects and cults and schools. There have been many religious dualists, but all share one central doctrine. *Duo sunt.* There are Two. Two gods, not one. All the rest follows from this. And for them, this leads back to the beginning of time. A cosmic condition. As a human teaching, it can be found in the oldest superstitions— and in the latest news of the day."

"The latest news?"

"The belief in the ultimate enemy. It is all around us. The communists. The Mafia. The blacks. The Jews. The street gangs. These are all variations on the ancient theme. Good Us versus Wicked Them.

Theodore Roszak

That, of course, is what the dualists play upon, that fear, perhaps as old as the shadows in the ancestral cave. What lies hidden there, eh? What lurks in every dark corner, waiting to pounce and kill? Every child is born with that same dread of the wholly other. And from it grows the great hatred and the great despair: the conviction that evil is invincible, that we have no power against it. It is the devil's trump card."

He sighed and sipped his drink again, then asked whether I cared if he smoked. He took out a crooked cheroot, dipped it in his cognac, lit up, and relaxed into a deep drag. "These excellent little luxuries . . . I have a weakness for them."

"All right, then," I said, "starting with Simon the Magician. Are you saying the orphans date back that far?"

"Not as orphans, no. But some of their predecessors do. And as far back as that, we can find the little flip-books used as a teaching device, a catechism. The world as the struggle of the Dark God against the God of Light. The early church did all it could to root out the heresy wherever it appeared."

"But it failed."

"Alas, yes. There was always a corner of the world where some small infestation of dualists could take shelter, especially by moving east or into the deserts. Later, the Moslem world proved more hospitable to their teachings, and from there they could make continued forays into Europe, Southern Italy, the Balkans, the south of France."

All this was the background to the great Albigensian crusade. We could skip that; it was a history with which I'd made myself familiar. "And after the crusade, then what becomes of them?"

"The struggle against the Albigenses—that was the most determined effort the church undertook. And still, we know that certain Cathar elements survived."

"By 'elements' you mean people."

"Yes, people."

"Whom the church would have slaughtered, burned . . ."

A sadness came into his eyes, but his voice was firm with no note of apology in it. "They were brutal times."

"Would you have preferred to see the crusade succeed in wiping out every last Cathar?"

His eyes held me with their candor, the look of a man who was entrusting me with a terrible admission. "The persecution came

473

within inches of its goal. If it had succeeded, that might have been for the best. This way, the church has the blood on its hands, but without the benefit."

"The benefit? Of what? Massacring women, children . . ."

Angelotti didn't waver, but the sorrow in his voice was unmistakable. "You know what the dualists teach. That the physical world is evil, the earth we live upon is hell. It is an obscene teaching. Suppose all this could have been blotted out seven centuries ago by that one act of unspeakable cruelty, a single righteous blow. Would you now look back and regret that it had happened?"

There was a cunning inflection to the question, almost as if Angelotti knew where his thrust would lodge. I thought at once of Simon's *Sad Sewer Babies*. True enough, if the crusade had succeeded, the world might have been spared this ugly descent into nihilism. Was that what I was defending here, Simon's right to make life look vile beyond description? The best answer I could come up with was, "I don't believe you can ever wipe out an idea by killing the people who hold it. Surely the idea would have survived somehow, somewhere, no matter how much blood was spilled."

Angelotti nodded gravely. "A good answer. So let us agree that old Pope Innocent was profoundly misguided when he launched the crusade. So too the members of my own order, who, as you know, organized the Inquisition. Please understand I am not here to speak in behalf of this ancient atrocity. At the time, St. Francis hoped to convert the heretics by kindness and preaching. I would like to believe that would have been my choice as well."

I backed off, realizing there was nothing to be gained by reviling Angelotti, who had, after all, been cast out by the church. "So then," I went on, "the orphans trace back to the surviving Cathars."

"We can be more specific. They descend from three elders who fled before the sack of Montségur, March 16, 1244. . . ."

"St. Arnaud the Survivor . . . and two others," I added. Angelotti gave me an impressed and quizzical stare. I answered the implied question. "There's a painting over the altar in the chapel in Zurich."

"You have seen it?"

"Yes. It was explained to me by a Dr. Byx."

"Byx, yes. An important man. And he told you . . . ?"

"Nothing much. He was pretty close-mouthed."

"The story is quite dramatic. A hairbreadth escape in the dead of night before the crusaders strike, and then the three old men flee to three widely scattered cities. Toledo, Aix-la-Chapelle, possibly Prague. Some say they took with them a great Cathar treasure. Others say they fled with nothing but the clothes they wore to live in poverty, begging along the roads. Gradually, small troops of refugees, hungry, ragged, frightened, find their way to the elders. The largest congregation may be no more than a dozen. This is the saving remnant. By agreement the elders meet again secretly three years later in a village near Barcelona—safe territory. They meet on the anniversary of the razing of Montségur. A fateful occasion. From that meeting—the Council of Gerona, as the dualists remember it—the risen Cathar Church takes its origin. There all the ground plans are laid. Or rather, I should say, *under*ground plans. A crucial decision is made. The church of the Albigenses will become clandestine, a church in exile, never again revealing its existence, never again openly recruiting or teaching. Yet it will continue its mission, which is to man the front line against the Evil God.

"But how to do this with the Inquisition still so doggedly at work? Here the elders came up with a daring stratagem. They would train a small elite corps of young Cathars to infiltrate one of the knightly orders. The Templars were chosen because of their wealth and power. But, as you know, the papacy soon detected the scheme. It does not hesitate. It strikes the Templars a death blow. Even so, some of the survivors flee to other orders, the Hospitalers, the Knights of Malta. Here again they are hunted down. Eventually this strategy is given up. The military orders were too prominent, too close to the Roman Curia.

"So there follows a period, some two centuries, when we know little of how or where the heretics survived. We assume in small, scattered bands, often passing themselves off as orthodox Catholics. Finally, in the seventeenth century, in the chaos of the Thirty Years' War, they emerge into the light once more, this time in the guise of a charitable institution. The Orphans of the Storm. This becomes their new public identity—and their mission. To save the children. And in the wake of the wars, there were all too many orphans throughout Europe waiting to be saved. How commendable that these good Christian souls should come forward to care for the innocent. In the confusion of the times, nobody could any longer be certain of anyone's religious orientation. There were so many sects, so many wild-eyed prophets in the streets, so many millennial cults. Quite often the orphans were mistaken for a Catholic religious order—a confusion that continues today and which they encourage for protective coloring.

"In any case they are doing so much good, who bothers to examine their credentials? So they slip back into history. As it turns out, the orphanages were a solution to more than one problem for the dualists. They allowed our friends to recruit new members at a tender young age, when the mind is ripe to be formed. For you realize, all the orphans are schooled to become Cathars. Think of it. A church that has had total control over the education and upbringing of its every member for four centuries. And then, there was the question of concupiscence. You're familiar with the Cathar teaching?"

"Yes. They seek to become 'eunuchs for the kingdom of God.' Meaning, no sex."

Angelotti corrected me. "Not quite. Oh yes, there are Cathars— the so-called Perfect of the faith—who deny themselves all recourse to sex, as do our own celibate clergy in the church. But the remainder of the flock are permitted to indulge. A necessary concession to the frailties of the flesh. Indeed, I am told that Cathar sexuality can achieve the most baroque extremes. A sort of western Tantric yoga. You understand that the Cathars are not prudish about the pleasures of the flesh. No, it is procreation they reject. That is where their church and ours part company most decisively. Indeed, if you have ever wondered why our church is so fiercely opposed to contraception, it is because we regard it as a Cathar ploy. It is not a victory we intend to allow them. So you see their position is, sex yes, but babies no. This creates an obvious problem. How do our friends replenish their numbers generation after generation?"

"By taking in orphans."

"Exactly. Or, where the opportunity presents itself, by creating orphans."

"You don't mean by killing the parents?"

"No, no. They will not shed blood—not even the blood of animals. They are strict vegetarians, you know. They will not even taste milk and eggs. But they have been known to kidnap children. Or to buy them."

"Buy them?"

"There are parts of the third world where that is possible. You see how nicely it all fits together? The ranks of the faithful are amply restocked from the orphanages with minds that have been shaped from infancy by the Great Heresy."

Angelotti spoke in a smooth, rolling baritone that modulated all he said with a tone of absolute authority. I realized I was being carried along on the current of his conviction as he narrated this astonishing tale of survival and conspiracy. But there were questions that had to be asked. "Look here, there's something that's bothered me all along. In the eyes of the church, the orphans are heretics. No doubt about that, am I right?"

"Correct."

"All right, then. Here are these particularly malignant heretics who are still with us today making mischief. And you tell me the church knows all about them—because you, I mean Oculus Dei, have been sounding the alarm loud and clear inside the Vatican for a century or more. But the church does *nothing*. Or rather, it turns against *you*. Denounces you, defrocks you. Why?"

Angelotti squinted at me, a twinkle of curious amusement in his eyes. "What would you expect?"

"That the church would listen to you, believe you, go after the culprits. After all, once upon a time, it was willing to slaughter the Albigenses down to the last man, woman, and child."

"But that option is thankfully no longer open, is it?"

"There are other ways to strike at them. The pope could speak out, condemn the heresy . . ."

"And if he did, what would that accomplish but to make the church look like an intolerant bully all over again? Besides, do you really think anybody in the modern world cares about heresy? If the church once began anathematizing heretics, where would it stop? From the church's point of view, the Lutherans are heretics, the Baptists are heretics, the Holy Rollers are heretics. So what? Who cares? Even loyal Catholics have no interest in resurrecting these old disputes."

"But surely people would be alarmed to learn that the movies— the movies they grew up on, that their kids are watching—are being used as a proselytizing device by a small, conspiratorial movement."

Angelotti gave a bitter little chuckle. "Have you ever noticed what happens when the charge of conspiracy is introduced into any discussion? Automatically, everything one says is discredited. Why? Because no right-thinking person believes in such a thing. Only charlatans or cranks like poor Rosenzweig invoke conspiratorial rumors. The word alone is enough to mark you as suspect. Can you imagine the pope lecturing the world about a seven-hundred-year-old conspiracy and expecting to be taken seriously? He would become a laughingstock." Angelotti took a long sip of cognac. "And even if the church had the nerve, it would not be free to speak out."

"Why not?"

Now Angelotti's face turned several shades more somber. "You cannot guess how it grieves me to tell you. Of course we know that all human institutions are doomed to be imperfect. In the hands of fallible men, nothing remains infallible. And yet did not our Lord proclaim that 'the gates of hell shall not prevail' against this church, *his* church?"

He seemed now to be looking into the distance beyond me. There was a glitter in his eyes that might have been tears. "It is like this, my friend. Listen closely. Somewhere in the world there is a box. Not very large. The size of a small suitcase. Possibly it lies in the vaults of a Swiss bank deep beneath the Alps where it would survive even the atomic apocalypse. Or so I have always imagined. Where exactly this box is hidden is the deepest secret of our age. There is only one secret that approaches it in importance: Who holds the keys to this box? I say 'keys,' but there may be only *one* key. Perhaps there is only one person who can find that key and open that box. And that person's identity is guarded by the massed ranks of the orphans with such dedication that they would surely die to the last man to defend his name.

"What does this box contain?" Here Angelotti swallowed hard as if his throat had locked down on the words. "Shame. Filth. Corruption. Moral horror. What form does this horror take? Numbers for the most part. Mere numbers. Amounts of money. Bank accounts. Deposits. Withdrawals. Payments rendered. Investments. Stocks. Bonds. Loans. Debts. To these numbers are attached names, dates, small annotated reports of meetings, agreements, bargains. Also court records, affidavits, deathbed confessions, the accounts of various investigators. Some of the materials are very old, yellow with age. But I would assume that by now, the box also contains more contemporary forms of evidence. Photographs, Xerox copies, tape recordings."

He paused to study my reaction. It was one of blank bewilderment. I had no idea what he was talking about. He poured more cognac and went on. "The Roman Catholic Church is a rich institution. This all the world knows. But *how* rich, and what the sources of that wealth might be, and to what uses it has been put—this the world does not know. These are matters the church has sought to guard more closely than anything ever spoken in the confessional. But that effort has not been a success. *The orphans know.* Yes, they have done their work cleverly and completely, working from within over centuries, documenting the invisible finances of the Vatican. In this box one might find records reaching back to the papacy's dealings with the House of Fugger, before Columbus sailed for the New World. Arrangements with the Doge of Venice in the time of the scandalous Fourth Crusade. Transactions with Saracen moneylenders and Moslem potentates. And, yes, the disposition of the Templars' treasures, that too would be there.

"Disgraceful beyond description. Nothing short of the betrayal of the faith. Ah, but all so long ago. Such quaint matters would be of little more than antiquarian interest today. There are, however, more contemporary documents in the box, and these no less disgraceful. Indeed, more so. Worse than merely illegal. Deeds so heinous that no laws have been framed to cope with them. Things that one kills to keep hidden. Profitable investments made in the most unspeakable trades. Moneys paid to thugs, cutthroats, assassins. Contributions made to clandestine agencies, to unscrupulous despots, to movements dedicated to violence and terror. Treasures taken as security from the bloodiest regimes on the planet. Loans to the sorts of governments that pledge the gold collected from human teeth as their collateral. Do you follow me?"

"I'm not a Catholic," I reminded him, "so probably this should make no difference to me. But, well . . . I'm frankly shocked. Are you telling me these things are true?"

"Of course Vatican authorities would dispute much of it. But I assure you, Jon, if only *one* accusation in ten is true, it is enough. Enough to blacken the name of the Catholic Church for the rest of time. And there is every reason to believe that far more than a tenth is true, more than half. Perhaps *all*. Consider the centuries over which the church has accumulated its riches and power. Where does the control of this wealth and power reside? In the iron-clad secrecy of the Holy Curia, a clique of faceless men who are a law unto themselves. Do you know what kind of men flourish in such an environment? I have met them, shared their private moments, their gossip, their sometimes drunken ruminations. Bring just these two things together—vast power, absolute secrecy—and you have built the gates of Hell *inside* Christ's church!

"Ah, but, as it turns out, the secrecy was not absolute after all.

There were those who were more cunning, more ruthless than the Machiavellian princes of the church. The masters of another church, an ancient rival driven by infinite hatred, willing to work with infinite patience. Yes, the orphans penetrated the *sanctum sanctorum*, laboring with the cold, meticulous fury of ants, boring deep, collecting every scrap of the Vatican's dung, storing up every dropping. For this, they knew, would finally be their only defense against annihilation on that day when Rome once again identified them for what they were.

"Why does the church not strike at its detested enemy? Because, my friend, to put it crudely, that enemy has the goods on us. One threatening word from the Holy See, and the orphans would drown St. Peter's in an avalanche of muck, muck of its own making."

For the next few hours, Angelotti dilated upon the crimes of the Vatican, describing to me what he knew of the devices the orphans had used to discover and document them. There were moles the orphans had sequestered in the ranks of the most highly placed prelates for thirty and forty years, there to filch one document, to record a single conversation. It was a story of ecclesiastical espionage that dwarfed anything I knew in the world of modern politics.

Somewhere after 1:00 A.M. I heard Clare's key in the door. I hadn't glanced at the clock since I sat down with Angelotti hours before. Clare looked in on us as she passed along the corridor.

"Don't let me interrupt," she said, standing in the doorway to the living room. She was swaying slightly and her eyes were glassy. I realized I hadn't seen Clare drunk since the old days, though I knew she was still a heavy drinker. "I'm just going to collapse. Lousy film, great party. Feel free to use the facilities for the night." She studied me, bleary-eyed, for a moment, then tottered across to where I sat to bend over me. "We can talk tomorrow . . . some time, yes?" And she leaned to give me a long, clinging kiss. As if she were confessing a crime, she whispered to me, "Supposed to get the review in tonight. You know, I can't remember the bloody film." She giggled, then kissed me again, this time holding her lips on mine an ambiguous few seconds too long.

Feebly, I mentioned that I'd brought a paper with me for her to read. "About Simon Dunkle . . . and everything." I pulled a copy of the article from my briefcase and held it out to her, but her attention had drifted. She laid it on the coffee table, and turned to move unsteadily toward the door, murmuring, "Tomorrow, tomorrow," then stopped in the hall to look back and add histrionically, "After all, tomorrow is another day." Shoes off, she padded down the corridor, humming off-key the theme that went with the line. After I heard her bedroom door close, I tried to pick up the thread of my conversation with Angelotti.

"All this you're telling me—top-secret stuff, right? How do you know about it?"

He gave a sad little smile. "For my sins, I once moved within these inner precincts. Oh yes, for the greater part of my life in the church, I was I suppose what you might call an up-and-comer in the Vatican elite. You have heard of Cardinal Mazzarini? No? Very important, very powerful. Also quite vicious. The old Medici prelates would have paled beside him. I was his personal secretary for eight years. Even so, it took years longer before I could put the pieces together. 'We have enemies,' the cardinal tells me one day. I am given a new position, to take over one of Mazzarini's most sensitive responsibilities. Monitoring the orphans. I learn their story. It is well documented in the Vatican archives, a file in which your FBI would take pride, but going back before the American Revolution. In the course of my duties, I come upon mention of Oculus Dei. I seek out one of its members. We. We meet several times. I am astonished by what I am told. And even more astonished to find that the cardinal is *not* astonished. Yes, he knows all about Oculus Dei. 'Stay away from these people,' he warns me. But why? Isn't that like ignoring a fire alarm?

"The cardinal grows stern with me. I seem to have disappointed him. Next I am removed from my assignment. I learn that I will be sent to some distant new position. At this point, I find myself asking my superiors the very question you have raised this evening. And slowly, slowly I unearth the truth, a scrap here, a fragment there. The church is paralyzed by its dirty secrets, blackmailed into silence. Unwisely, I now realize, I make a nuisance of myself. Mazzarini disciplines me, but it does no good. And soon I find myself cast out like others before me. Like Rosenzweig. He too was a Vatican insider."

He went on to tell me the strange, twisted history of Oculus Dei. It was more than I cared to know, but he told the tale with a certain relish, as if he had been waiting to find a friendly audience for a long while. The organization, I discovered, had been hatched within the Vatican at the time of the Napoleonic Wars. It was the original intelligence unit assigned to report on the orphans. Angelotti seemed to know the names of its every member for the past century. At some point, the small circle of orphan-watchers became alarmed at what it saw happening. That was about the time the first Zoetrope motion-picture instruments came on the scene. This was no mere toy, Oculus Dei realized. It was an orphan invention meant to inculcate the Great Heresy. Angelotti was convinced the ODs had a clear idea even then of what would follow from these early cinematic experiments. They clamored for the Holy See to take action. But it refused. Instead, it clamped down on Oculus Dei, at least as an official operation of the church. But several members of the agency wouldn't play dumb. They bolted the church and became an independent, unsanctioned crusade against the orphans.

"But you can imagine," Angelotti continued, "how much success they had trying to convince anybody that there was some great danger attached to amusements like the Zoetrope, the phenakistoscope, Edison's peep-show. 'Wheel of the Devil'—that is what Oculus Dei named Horner's Daedalum, the first mechanical animation. But who would listen? What harm could there be in such toys, eh? Besides, in most parts of the so enlightened western world, my predecessors found themselves confronted by anticlerical prejudice, especially where Catholics or, worst of all, Jesuits, were concerned. This was the great age of science and reason. And now along come these renegade priests ranting about some ancient heresy. Even their own benighted church rejects them. You see why, after a certain point, our members might be tempted to turn to other methods."

"You mean like abduction . . . murder?"

"Never murder," Angelotti was quick to insist. "Not as far as I am aware."

"But they did kidnap LePrince, is that so?"

He nodded. "I fear so. A futile gesture. LePrince was the most active promoter of the cinema in his day, but abducting him was quite useless. By then there were too many inventors, entrepreneurs, film-makers at work. And the public was already too fascinated to be denied. It was only a matter of time before the movies would be born."

"And is it true that all the most important inventions were the work of the orphans, feeding their ideas to Edison, Dickson, Lumière, all the others?"

Again he nodded. "If not all the inventions, enough of them to inspire the rest."

It was going on toward three in the morning when we finally got around to Simon Dunkle. I explained that "my agreement with Brother Justin is to let him and his superiors approve my article before I publish."

"I would be surprised," Angelotti interjected, "if they really wished to see you publish anything."

"Possibly that's so," I agreed. "God knows, they've given me enough of a runaround. But I think they want to pump up Simon's reputation a bit. Anyway, I don't intend to honor that agreement." I fetched my briefcase, took my article on Simon from it, a manuscript of seventy-some pages, and laid it on the coffee table. "I've finished the piece. Last week. After Clare asked me to come, I decided to get it all down for her to read. I worked around the clock. It's only a rough draft but it covers the ground. You'll find yourself generously credited in the footnotes. I'll see what Clare says, polish it up, and put it in print wherever I find the chance."

Angelotti flipped through the manuscript. "Of course I can understand that you should want to see your article published. But am I right in detecting a note of urgency in your voice? Why is that?"

"The reason is there in the paper. There are developments afoot that I think justify some haste."

"And these are . . . ?"

"Simon's going into television." For the first time that evening Angelotti's eyes lit up with surprise. I didn't have to spell out the significance of my announcement to him.

"How soon?"

"Not for a while. A few years yet. There are technical problems. I gather orphan inventors somewhere are working on them at top speed."

Angelotti released a tense sigh. "The flicker on television. Well, well . . ."

"You agree I should go public with this as soon as possible?"

He took his time answering. "Yes . . . and yet, I would like to see the article first. I hope you appreciate that one must go about this in exactly the right way. Recall that poor Rosenzweig made an effort to go public. You see what came of that."

The comparison jarred me. "But Rosenzweig was a nut."

Angelotti smiled indulgently. "At the end, yes. But not always. He went crazy. But why? Because he was driven crazy—by contempt, ridicule, scorn. Believe me, once he was as sane, as lucid—and as concerned as ourselves. But when he took his message to the world . . ."

"I hope you'll agree that my style, my approach, my credentials lend me a bit more credibility."

"Without question. But remember, please, what I have told you about raising the cry of conspiracy. There are secrets that guard themselves, because even when they are revealed, they will not be believed."

I agreed he had a point. "That's all the more reason to try this out on Clare. I'll be guided by her reaction. And by yours."

At this late hour, Angelotti decided to take Clare up on her offer to spend the night, or what was left of it. Reaching to flip through my article on the table, he asked, "Would it be possible for me to glance over this tomorrow? I may be able to make a few suggestions." I had a copy; I fished it out of my briefcase and handed it to him. He started to shuffle off toward the small guest room where Clare kept a daybed, then stopped in the doorway and looked back. "Am I presuming? You will be staying with . . . ?" He gestured down the hall toward Clare's room.

"Actually, I'll just use the couch in here," I answered, wondering what he might think my relationship with Clare was.

"Ah, I see. Then perhaps you will want the guest room?"

"No, no, it's all right," I assured him as I pulled off my shoes and loosened my clothes. When he was gone, I stretched out for several minutes trying to review all we had talked about. Most of what he said really boiled down to little more than rumor and conjecture—though he had certainly made it sound spellbindingly convincing. But like so much else about the orphans and Oculus Dei, it was a history that defied documentation. Despairingly, I realized that everything I'd written about these subjects was simply a pedantic version of what zany old Sharkey had once told me years ago in the projection booth at The Classic. And how had that sounded to me at the time?

After a while, still too restless to sleep, I made my way quietly down the corridor to Clare's room. I stood outside the door for several long moments wondering if I dared knock. From behind the door I could hear Clare's heavy, boozy breathing. She would be in no mood to be awakened. Still, just that muffled sound of her light snoring nudged my memory; I was comforted to be that close to the woman whose onetime love had started me out on this improbable adventure which now left me shaken, fearful, and plain helpless. My forehead pressed against her door, I whispered a small appeal. *Clare, tell me how to live with this evil.*

28 2014

I used a few good-sized belts of Clare's whiskey to put me down for the night. The drinks were more effective than I intended. When I woke, cramped, rumpled, and headachy on the couch the next day, it was nearly ten-thirty and the apartment was empty. Clare had left a scribbled note.

> Busy day. Home late. Wait up, love, do. Took the article. (Weighs a ton! Who's going to print this?) I'll give it a read today. Promise. Eddy says will ring you. Ask him about 2014. That's the zinger.

2014?

As I sat over a cold meal salvaged from Clare's none too ample larder, Angelotti called. Was I free to meet him later that day? Of course I was. "Excellent," he said. I should expect him in the late afternoon. I spent the day reorganizing my notes from the previous evening, wondering how much of this I should try to squeeze into my already overlong article. About four o'clock, Clare's doorman phoned to tell me there was a delivery. I told him to send it up. A few minutes later a Puerto Rican kid was at the door with two smallish bags of groceries from one of the town's upscale delicatessens. Pinned to the bags was a hefty bill. Since there was no one else to pay the tab but me, I paid, adding the usual exorbitant New York tip, and stored the supplies in the refrigerator.

I assumed the provisions were for Clare; but when Angelotti arrived an hour later, his first words were to ask if "our food" had come. "I took the liberty of ordering for us," he explained. "It is so difficult to find a decent cheap restaurant in New York."

Judging from what I'd shelled out for "our food," it was no less difficult to find decent cheap take-out. I wondered if I should mention how much the delivery had set me back. But here was a man of God, providing me with a ton of valuable information. So I kept it to myself. I noticed that Angelotti never asked.

We gravitated into the same seats as the night before, but with a fresh bottle of cognac from Clare's liquor cabinet between us on the table. Angelotti drew out his copy of my manuscript; I could see a wealth of pencil notes up and down the margins.

His first words were high praise, but I could hear the hint of serious reservations that lay behind them. "What you have to say about Dunkle is illuminating. I had no idea he was making such inroads among the young. That is very worrisome. These movies he makes, they are the Cathar gospel in its very essence. The message comes closer and closer to the surface. My God! we have come so far. I found your critical commentary excellent, very persuasive. I see so much of Clare's influence there, the precision, the ethical clarity. . . ." His voice trailed off, his brow taking on a deep frown.

"But I gather you have some doubts."

He hesitated, then felt his way forward gingerly. "There are certain details that need correction."

"Oh?"

"I have made some marginal notes. Fine points, for the most part. Theological matters, a few historical references . . ."

And for the next hour or so, Angelotti ran through my paper fastidiously offering revisions. A few were important, most were nitpicking. When he finished, I thanked him, but knew we were skirting the edge of larger issues. "There's something more, isn't there?"

He sighed deeply and shook his head, a gesture of honest regret. "Yes, something more. How to say it? Even with corrections, everything you say about the Cathars, the orphans . . . I am bound to tell you, Jon, I believe it will make you look foolish."

"But it's what we both know to be true."

"You and I, yes. That makes two. And all the rest of Oculus Dei, which is perhaps a dozen more. Also there are those in the Vatican— ten or twenty, let us say—who will believe you, since they already know the truth. Beyond these, and of course the orphans themselves,

I think you will find not one sympathetic reader who is not a psychotic." He saw the disappointment in my face. "Please understand, I want to be helpful. Let me assure you, what you have done here is what I have sat down to do a hundred times. To tell the whole story from beginning to end. Now I see why I have never done so. Because this is how it would read. Like a paranoid fantasy. I'm sorry. . . ."

He meant the apology sincerely, but his words stung nonetheless. "What else can I do but tell what I've learned? Are you saying there's no way to do that and sound sane?"

He pondered what I said. "Hitler spoke of the big lie—so big that people had to believe it. I begin to think there is also the big truth—so big nobody can believe it. You realize what you are up against, Jon? We suffer from the reflex of trivialization so ingrained in the modern world. People live off the surface. Even our so-called deep thinkers only wade the shallows. And in the shallows the mind can find no true clarity, no satisfactory answers for its questions. It is like trying to comprehend the cube by means of the square: the depth dimension is missing.

"What are the big issues of our day? Justice for the oppressed, peace in the Middle East, prosperity or depression, communism versus capitalism. For many there is nothing more urgent than the baseball, the football. Such transient matters, but enough to distract one's attention for a lifetime. How many live and die never once touching the greater questions which are the source of all the rest? *One God or two?* There you have the question that lies at the root of all conflict between nations, cultures, races. It is quite simply the second most important question in the world."

"What's first?" I asked.

"Is there a God at all? Until one answers that, there is no point in thinking, or living, is there?"

In consternation, I slugged down my cognac, at once reaching to pour another. "Then I have no idea what to do."

He was thumbing through my paper. "Frankly, I think there is simply too much here. Too much to tell all at once. It becomes a jumble. Perhaps . . ."

"Yes?"

"Perhaps you should consider limiting yourself to Simon, to his films, and perhaps to Castle. A good, solid piece of film criticism. That might be enough to warn the film community to raise its guard."

"You mean I shouldn't mention the orphans at all?"

He thought carefully. "Not yet. That is another, more delicate, project. On that I could be of assistance. We might work together. Of course, I would not want any credit. In fact, I would prefer to go unnamed."

"How long do you think such a collaboration might take?"

He wagged his head uncertainly. "That is hard to say."

"Weeks? Months?"

". . . hard to say."

"Years? Are you talking about years? A major piece of scholarship? Is that what you have in mind?"

"Possibly."

Did he know how exasperating he was being? "Eduardo, how long have you been part of Oculus Dei?"

"Some twenty years. Why do you ask?"

"In all that time, you haven't published a thing on this subject, have you?"

He assumed a defensive tone. "I have a wealth of notes, years of research. You would be welcome to it all."

"I'm not prepared to spend twenty years of my life getting ready to write. Frankly, I'd rather take my chances on public ridicule."

He nodded judiciously. "I understand your impatience. I admit my own approach has been laggardly. But you see, I have felt the need to be thorough, to prove every point solidly. I haven't wanted to become another Rosenzweig."

I rose and paced the room, letting my frustration show. "I don't know, I don't know. I can't keep something like this bottled up inside me indefinitely."

"I understand," he said, trying to soothe me. "But there is good reason to plan what we do carefully for the maximum effect. You may, for example, have a unique opportunity that should not be overlooked."

"What do you mean?"

"To get closer to the orphans, to enter their world."

"How?"

"They want your help with Simon. In return, they let you talk to the boy, they tell you things."

"Mostly they just run me around in circles."

"Ah, but each time you go around the circle, you learn a little bit more, yes? They may believe they are misleading you . . . but nevertheless you find here a fact, there an insight. And with my help to sort through the gleanings . . ." He grew suddenly more intense, leaning forward in his seat. "Jon, I believe you could be admitted to Albi itself, if you played your cards right."

"Albi?"

"You would be working behind enemy lines. Certainly you could return to Zurich, to Dr. Byx. You could find out more than any outsider has yet known. Your tour of the Zurich orphanage with Byx, do you realize how remarkable that was? I doubt such a thing has happened before. And some of the volumes Brother Justin has loaned you from his private library, these are unknown outside the orphans' own circle. With time, who knows how much more you might learn?"

"Look, Eduardo, I'm a scholar, not a spy. And anyway, what would I be after? What else is there to know? It's all there in my article, isn't it?"

Angelotti settled back, reining himself in with great deliberation. "What if I were to tell you, my friend, that everything you have learned so far, the entire amazing tale of the orphans, their survival, their connection with the cinema—all this is but a fraction of what there is to know? The tip of the iceberg, no more. Have you not sometimes suspected as much?"

He caught me off guard, but he was on the button. "Yes, I have."

"You see, Jon, that is why Oculus Dei has moved so slowly, more slowly than poor Rosenzweig could tolerate. It is because there is so much more that must be brought to light."

"Yes, but what? What exactly?"

He smiled enigmatically and suddenly said, "Eggplant parmigiana. The best in New York." He bounced up and gestured me toward the kitchen. I glanced at my watch. Dinner time so soon? "I hope you don't mind if we go vegetarian."

"No, not at all."

"Good. I guarantee you will be delighted." Once he'd unpacked the makings and spread them on the table, Angelotti was a whirlwind of activity: a hungry man preparing a feast. He'd assembled an impressive spread at my expense. Lots of pricey antipasti in little cartons and a main course that he popped into the oven.

"Salad?" he asked. "The Italian dressing is excellent."

"Yes, yes."

"Then perhaps you will not mind?" He was putting me to work on a head of lettuce, some endive, tomatoes, red peppers. While I started in at my chore, he bustled about setting the table, humming all the while. From one of the bags, he drew out some small brown bottles and clinked them at me. "German beer. My favorite. Will you join me?"

I said yes. I would have said yes to anything. My mind wasn't on eating; I wondered how his could be. "You have rather extravagant tastes," I commented as he arranged some giant-sized olives and an artichoke on a plate.

He folded his hands prayerfully as if pleading for forgiveness. "It is an indulgence I permit myself when I am on special assignment."

"What's the special assignment?"

For just a moment, he fixed me with an odd, blank stare. "Why, *you* are, my friend. I expect great things to come of our meeting."

"Do those things have to do with 2014?"

That brought an end to his bustling and humming. "Indeed so— 2014 is the answer to the one question you have not asked. The most obvious question of all. I'm not surprised you have not raised it. No doubt you believe there is no answer to be had. But there is. I know the answer. Or at least a part of it. And until you have that, your research is incomplete. You know what I mean? The great hole at the center of the story."

I knew. I asked. "*Why?* Why are the orphans doing it? What are they after?"

"Exactly."

"At first, I assumed it was to convert the world to their religion. They were using the movies to peddle their heresy."

Angelotti smiled knowingly. "But clearly that is *not* what they are doing."

"Because it's all too subliminal. What sort of victory would it be for people to become Cathars and not know it? It doesn't make sense."

"They have no intention of converting the world, Jon. They may be fanatics, but not fools. In any event, they have no time for that. How many converts could they expect to make by 2014?"

". . . it's a date?"

"You didn't know?"

"Clare left a note. She said, 'Ask Eddy about 2014. That's the zinger.' "

We took our places at the table and began working our way through the breadsticks and antipasto. Or rather Angelotti did. He ate; I nibbled and watched. "Ah well, then we must return to basics. True: 2014 is a date. And it is indeed a zinger. The end of the world." He dropped the words so casually I wondered if I'd heard him correctly. I simply stared back at him, waiting. "Our dualist friends work from a different calendar. Our 2014 is their 2000. Two thousand years after the Supplantation." He saw that I didn't understand. "The most important earthly event in history, as the orphans see it. The moment at which the physical Jesus was supplanted by his ghostly double. It is their equivalent of Easter."

"That's what they're waiting for? The end of the world . . . in 2014?"

"Not waiting. Working. Remember, it is their belief that the true God must be assisted by his followers. Christmas morning 2014, they will put an end to history."

He wasn't joking; he wasn't mocking the idea. But I thought he should be. "So ultimately they're a bunch of cranks after all."

"Hardly. They intend to do it, Jon. And there is every chance they will."

"But how?"

"Consider what you have learned about the orphans and the motion pictures, how they have worked in the shadows to midwife this technology step by step, so skillfully, so secretly. A remarkable achievement, is it not?"

"Yes, I agree."

"People gifted with such patience, such cunning . . . they might be capable of accomplishing anything, given enough time, enough secrecy."

"I suppose."

"Very well, then. Apply the same pattern elsewhere."

"Elsewhere?"

"At Zurich, at Zuma Beach, at several other orphanages, the students study film. But in Edinburgh, in Frankfort, in Tokyo, in Copenhagen . . ."

Copenhagen clicked. I remembered the little girl I'd met at St. James School on my first visit. "Physics. In Copenhagen, they study physics."

"Correct. And so too in Tokyo. In Edinburgh, it is microbiology. So too in Frankfort." He continued talking while he fetched the eggplant from the oven and placed it carefully on the table. It was a magnificent-looking dish, but I didn't have the appetite to do more than pick at it. "From these schools come not film editors, but high-energy physicists, neurobiologists, genetic engineers. A small, steady stream of scientists and technicians—gifted pupils, all excellently trained. An intellectual elite corps that finds its way into the best research facilities, the finest laboratories. Incidentally, they earn quite well at what they do. Top-dollar men and women. A major source of the orphans' wealth."

"And what's this all about? What are they up to?"

"It can be easily summed up. Bombs and germs."

"Weapons?"

"The deadliest. The means of universal destruction. Understand, Jon, they are soldiers in a great war. For them that war is not a mere metaphor. The combat is invisible but real. They have every intention of winning that war—right here on this earth, a palpable victory. Come, you know their teachings. The body is the stronghold of evil, the prison of the spirit. How else can the God of Darkness be defeated but by the destruction of that body—all bodies, every single one, gone in the flames."

"War? They mean to start a war?"

"*The* war, my friend. The final event in history. The great cleansing. It was all laid down by the three elders at Gerona, the grand strategy of Armageddon. The church in exile would struggle on two fronts. In their parlance, these were called *voluntas et potestas*. Will and power. What you have learned so far has all to do with one front, the struggle to propagate *voluntas*, the will to self-destruction. For this, the movies have been their chosen medium. No better way to infiltrate the mind of the masses, to fill it with nihilistic imagery, to loosen the grip on life.

"But how actually to *do* the deed? How to annihilate the physical basis of life which is the Dark Lord's citadel? Of course, the elders at Gerona had no clear idea. They knew it would take centuries. Still, the orphans never wavered in their commitment. Somewhere, they knew there must lie the secret of a power great enough to overthrow their cosmic enemy. One hundred years ago, this would have seemed like madness. But as we now see, it is all within the realm of possibility. You and I, we would regard the bomb, the toxic gas, the lethal virus as tools of the devil. But that is not how the orphans see things. For them, these are the means of salvation."

"But you said they don't believe in killing."

"And it is so. They will not shed blood. There is one exception. At the final hour, on the field of battle, it will be the true God's will that all flesh be expunged, if possible every last living cell."

"In other words, murder no, but universal genocide, okay."

"You call it universal genocide, they would call it universal deliverance. In their theology, it makes perfect sense. It is blasphemy, I grant you, but there is an undeniable grandeur to the project, no? One can almost admire the dedication, the dogged persistence, the unflinching discipline."

He was speaking now with an exuberant intensity that touched me with a small, secret shudder. If I'd found the least trace of admiration in myself for the orphans' grand design, I would have smothered it immediately.

"You do not care for the food?" he asked, noticing I'd hardly done more than rearrange what was on my plate. My stomach was knotted in a combination of excitement, alarm, horror. I apologized and offered to let him finish my serving. He didn't have to be coaxed, but dug in with gusto, talking all the while. The story he proceeded to unfold was far more than I could take in. The sudden shift in our conversation left me groping. It was as if, in the middle of the movie I'd come to see, a reel from some other film had been slipped on the projector; without warning the screen was filled with scenes from some far grander production.

Angelotti was drawing in a vast array of new historical allusions and a whole new cast of characters. He must have spent the better part of an hour picking his way through a thicket of late medieval alchemists whose relations with the orphans seemed of supreme importance. He spent nearly as much time on the Rosicrucians (the *original* Rosicrucians, Angelotti was at pains to specify, as if that would make some difference to me). Their connection with Galileo and Newton (a few names I could finally recognize) was also highly significant, though for no reason I could grasp. As if he were delivering a prepared lecture, Angelotti skipped rapidly through the early history of modern chemistry, biology, atomic physics. Behind all the great figures, he was convinced the dim outlines of orphan scientists could be discerned filtering their research into the mainstream, steadily moving the world toward newer, greater forms of energy. And damned if it didn't make a weird, seductive kind of sense. It was surely a dazzling display of erudition; beside it, my slender research in the secret history of the movies began to shrink to nothing. What was a Max Castle compared to a Pasteur, a Curie, an Einstein?

But how much of this could I believe? Was this anything more than another, grander paranoid rhapsody? If so, Angelotti was quite swept up in its drama. His eyes had taken on an eager shine, and his words flowed from him with flawless eloquence. By the time he'd brought his narrative down to the development of the intercontinental ballistic missile, I decided to rein him in if I could.

"Eduardo," I interrupted, struggling to introduce a note of healthy skepticism, "you're saying that the whole course of modern history has been practically dictated by a very small number of people, who . . ."

"Small? Minute. Not more than several hundred over four, five hundred years."

"You honestly believe so few can be credited with so much power?"

"Not power. Influence. The orphans rarely wield power. Power is too visible. But they are masters of the art of influence. They position themselves next to people of power. They move those people; those people move the world. Leverage, Jon. That is the secret. As Archimedes taught: one man standing in the right place can move the earth. The orphans have a gift for finding the right place. That is where they station their members. And of course there is the factor of time. They have not been in a hurry. Can you imagine the infinite patience? There must have been periods when generations of Cathars came and went, their entire lives devoted to achieving just a few small steps forward along their path, never knowing for certain that they had chosen the right way, never expecting to see the final result of their efforts, but believing steadfastly that there must be a means to accomplish their great end. Can there be such a thing as diabolical faith? Surely this is it. If you are leaving this . . ."

What? I looked down to see him pointing at a breadstick I'd left uneaten on my side of the table. I suddenly realized that the food was gone; Angelotti had consumed it all, the eggplant, the antipasto, the salad, the beer. I pushed the breadstick toward him. How could I eat even crumbs at a time like this? My head was spinning. In the course of the last hour alone, he'd been telling me the inside story of the first atomic bomb, marking out the obscure figures, presumably orphans, who had guided J. Robert Oppenheimer along the road to Hiroshima. He'd made it sound utterly convincing. But the tale left me in a state of cruel perplexity.

"Yes, I know how you feel," he said at last in a pitying tone. "I have lived with these facts for so long they have ceased to amaze me.

494

But I can remember when I was first told, I also found it hard to accept."

I needed to know if there was any proof for what he had told me. He laughed softly. "Such as? Documents? Authoritative records? Of course not. Nothing that matters in the history of the world is ever set down in writing. Word-of-mouth, private conversations, gentlemen's agreements, a nod, a whisper, a wink. This is how fortunes are built, great crimes planned, atrocities and holocausts perpetrated. Among the powerful, there is almost a form of ESP. Very little needs to be said, let alone committed to paper. But what could documents tell us that is not already staring us in the face? I mean the whole shape of modern times. Is that not the real evidence, all that a reasonable man requires?"

"What do you mean?"

Angelotti took a deep breath, then fell silent, his eyes closed. He seemed to have sunk into a small meditation. His eyes were still shut when he spoke. "You are a student of film, Jon. Very well, imagine the last five centuries running by as if they were a movie compressed into an hour's time. Doesn't the story tell itself? What do we see? A love affair with power, more and more power. Our infamous but ever so exhilarating Faustian bargain. And all the power becomes weapons, every great discovery, all the great theories. Guns, bombs, rockets, poison gas, tanks, planes, missiles. The nations grow bigger, the wars grow bigger . . . until at last the wars become bigger than the world itself.

"The next war will be the last war. We all know this. We are only left to wonder if anything—the termites, the roaches, the bacteria—will survive. Put the bomb together with the germs, perhaps finally nothing will outlive the catastrophe. There will be the hellfire of the bomb, the scourge of the plague, a final worldwide winter blotting out the light for a thousand years, and then nothing, a sterile rock in place of the fruitful earth.

"We agree, don't we, this is no fantasy? This is the news of the day. The movie we are watching is one mad rush toward annihilation. Yet think of the genius that has gone into this production! The machines, the medicines, the instruments that explore the great world and the small. Think how much has been perverted, twisted, poisoned. How are we to account for this, for the amazing coherence of this terrifying scenario? Can it be purely fortuitous? Or is there not obviously a design here before us, the design of a story? If a person knew nothing whatever of the orphans, might he not in a moment of frightening insight say to himself, 'It is *as if* someone has planned it'? But you and I know better, don't we? We can say, 'It is *because* someone has planned it.' "

He left me dazzled and depressed while he exited to the kitchen to brew the coffee and lay out dessert. Listening to his fine, strong baritone voice—he was crooning what sounded like a Gregorian chant—I realized what it meant to be a man of faith connected with a tradition that taught one to think across centuries. Angelotti had clearly learned how to keep his morale flying high while he pursued his small, secret, probably futile war against the orphans. I envied him his resiliency. Myself, I was feeling just flattened. When he returned with two steaming cups and a plate of biscotti—more food he'd have to finish for me—I let him know how hopeless the prospect seemed to me.

"But if all you say is true, Eduardo, I don't see what you expect me to achieve by continuing my study of the orphans. What can I do between now and 2014 that others haven't been able to do?"

"I cannot say exactly. Possibly if you could get hold of this device you describe in your article . . . the sallyrand, as you call it. Think what that would prove about the orphans' film technique."

"They'd never let me have one."

"Are you certain? Perhaps you might, shall we say, 'liberate' one?"

"Steal it, you mean?"

Angelotti smiled slyly. "If I were a Jesuit, I might be able to offer an acceptable justification. Dominican casuistry is rather primitive. Shall we say 'all's fair in war'?"

A bit shamefacedly I admitted, "I've tried to do it already."

"Oh?"

"With Simon. I asked him to loan me one, but he wouldn't. If he had, I would've swiped it."

"But possibly if you could return to Zurich, to their film laboratory . . . who knows? The opportunity might present itself. As it is, your description of this device sounds not at all convincing."

"Frankly, Eduardo, I don't think I have much talent as a thief, if that's what it comes down to."

"I'm sure we can think of other things," he hastened to assure me. "We must talk more. Now I only ask that you consider what I suggest. Of this much I am certain—that in the whole history of the grand conspiracy, you are uniquely placed. I know of no one who has been given such privileged access. And at a time when the orphans are more exposed to risk than ever before."

"Why is that?"

"Because they must reveal more and more of their work to more and more people. Dunkle's films will go out to hundreds of millions around the world. Dunkle himself will become a celebrity. There would seem to be no way to avoid this. Perhaps—one hesitates to raise the hope—perhaps this is a mistake, the one mistake our friends have made. I assure you, Jon, I do not overestimate our chances. But my faith teaches that we are not permitted to despair."

As I walked Angelotti to the elevator, I asked a last question, something I'd stowed away earlier that evening. "That tune you were humming during dinner . . . do you know what it is?"

"I'm sorry. Was I humming?"

I whistled a bit of what I remembered. "Ah yes," he said, picking up on the fragment of melody and adding several notes more. "A French folk song. Still quite popular. Truffaut uses it in *Les Mistons*. I was working with the film today." He held the door of the elevator long enough to hum a few bars more. "Catchy, is it not?"

Back in the apartment, I turned off the lights and lay back on the couch, waiting for Clare to come home. It was now almost beside the point what she might have to say about the article I'd written. Angelotti had succeeded in making the piece seem hopelessly inadequate. Not because it tried to say too much, but because I now had some idea of how much more needed to be said, things which led into fields where my ignorance was total. It might indeed be the work of years to study up, dig through, muster the facts, make the case. The prospect exhausted me. All the more so when I realized how uncertain was my loyalty to Angelotti's cause. There was no question but that he had painted a monstrous picture of the orphans for me that evening. If I believed all he said, no doubt I would share his fanatical dedication. But I simply couldn't take seriously the apocalyptic intention he had described. Not yet, not without more thought, more evidence. And short of that, I was bound to be an unreliable ally.

How it would have surprised Angelotti to know that my doubts arose from the little tune I'd asked about. I couldn't have explained my curiosity about it, so I hadn't tried. But I was certain the melody I overheard him humming as he prepared our dinner was the same that Natalie Feather had sung that Saturday afternoon in Hermosa

Beach when she experienced her passion. Since that extraordinary occasion, I'd frequently caught myself humming it. So it was nothing more after all than a folk song that Mrs. Feather had unconsciously picked up along the way. Whatever its true source, Guillemette's song (as I'd come to call it) still had a special significance for me. It brought with it the memory of an ancient atrocity that had taken the lives of thousands. Were the orphans victims or villains? Was it my role to be their enemy, their advocate—or simply a neutral observer on hand to chronicle a long-lost chapter in the history of human intolerance? Without a clear decision on that point, I would never find the will to do what Angelotti was proposing.

"These days I go to more parties than movies. The parties are better than the movies. That is, until some asshole starts talking about movies, which some asshole always does. That's when you know it's time to leave—or get drunk. Tonight I left. No drinking. I didn't want to flake out on you again, sweetheart."

Clare staying sober just for me. I was flattered.

It was just short of ten o'clock when she came bustling in, eager to talk. But it took another hour for the talk to begin. First there was taking phone messages, and showering, and slipping-into-something-comfortable. It was worth the wait. To my barely concealed delight, Clare decided to make this a special audience held in her bedroom. On her bed. Only then, when the two of us were nested across from one another on her lush comforter, was she prepared to trust herself with a drink, something bitter and bubbly for the two of us. She was in a simple but elegant black robe, settled back against a small mountain of pillows, surrounded by an odor of spiced bath splash. She looked and smelled and sounded simply great—though not at all like the Clare with whom I'd once shared a bed for more than conversation. Still, it brought back sweet memories.

"Do you remember the last time we were on a bed together?" I asked.

Clare pointed the finger of doom in my face. "Absolutely no reminiscing. I'm too vulnerable at this age. And no seducing."

"*Me* seduce *you?*"

"Well, it won't happen any other way."

"What won't happen?"

"What's not going to happen. Down to business." She took her copy of my article from the bedstand and dropped it in front of me.

"If you publish this—and believe me, nobody's going to publish it—I'll disown you."

She wasn't kidding. "Why?" I asked.

"It makes you sound like a crackpot. You aren't a crackpot, are you?"

"I believe it's all true."

"Exactly what a crackpot would say. Anyway, I don't care if it's true. The point is, there's no wit to it, no polish, no style. It's so damned, relentlessly journalistic."

"Does that make any difference?"

"All the difference, love. Especially when you're serving up such dismally serious stuff. It's just too breathless, and earnest, and . . . unrelieved. Christ, you come on like Stanley discovering Livingstone. Extra, extra, scoop of the century! At least people could believe in Livingstone. Nobody except other crackpots would believe this. The trick would be to write it as if you weren't sure you believed it yourself. Hook them with a good story, make them wonder. Probably you should do the whole thing as fiction. As it is . . ."

My insides began to go watery. Because I knew she was right. I just didn't have the touch for this assignment. Gloomily, I told her, "That's what Eduardo said too. Nobody's going to believe me."

"Did he? Well, well. Shows that even a Jesuit can be right sometimes."

"He's a Dominican."

"Whichever."

"What about the stuff on Dunkle?"

"Oh, that's first-rate. My advice is to fillet this thing. Throw away the bone and gristle and messy innards, leave the meat, and you've got something. A good, sound critical thrashing for this depraved adolescent. Go for it."

"But the critique of Simon connects with Castle. And that connects with subliminal techniques. And that connects with the orphans, their religious teachings, their history. . . . Where do I apply the knife?"

"Simple. Save all the stuff on Castle for your definitive study, which I gather you're still planning to finish before you go on Social Security, am I right?"

"Well, it's gotten a little bogged down lately. . . ."

She sighed wearily. "Typical. Scholarly constipation. I expected better of you, Jonny." I started to explain, but she waved me to silence. "Save it for your promotion-and-tenure committee. Otherwise, I suggest you go through this and wherever the word 'orphan' appears, *cut*. Keep cutting. Make it a piece of film criticism, not conspiratorial reportage."

"Also what Eduardo advised."

Clare was surprised. "He shows better judgment than I expected." With honest bewilderment, she added, "He's an odd bird. I can't really figure him."

"You met him at a conference . . . in Milan?"

"I was at the conference, not him. We met at a party after some marathon panel discussion. I can't recall what we said. I was pretty well smashed. Then we met again through mutual friends."

"Did he tell you he was part of Oculus Dei right away?"

"If he had, I'd have run for cover. Usually fruitcakes like that come at you wild-eyed and raving. But Eddy was smart enough to keep his affiliation sub rosa until we were three or four meetings along. By that time I was semicaptivated. You may have noticed the resemblance to Marcello Mastroianni. A sort of starved-down version. How can a poor girl resist? Of course, I didn't know he was a priest—and a seriously celibate one—until later. But he makes up for that with conversation. Very sharp, very engaging. And he knows a lot of people in Italian film. He kept arranging introductions for me, which I appreciated. Then, at one meeting, he got into a heavy exchange with somebody about movie projectors. I flashed on his train of thought immediately. I was the one to bring up Oculus Dei. 'Are you one of *them?*' I asked. He admitted he was. Next thing, we were having long conversations about the Albigensian origins of Mickey Mouse. And I was listening closely, much to my amazement."

"Eduardo wants me to hold off on writing about the orphans for now. . . ."

"Good idea."

". . . and to work with him on a bigger, more definitive piece of scholarship."

"Oh, oh, bad idea. Give it up, Jonny. Eduardo is a fanatic. A cultivated fanatic, I grant you, but a fanatic nonetheless."

"Then why did you introduce us?"

"*Not* to get you involved with him. It'll be the end of your career if you do. You'll spend the rest of your life scratching around for crumbs of arcane lore, sniffing out rumors, chasing shadows. You're too good to be wasted on that. Besides, Eddy is a sponger. Amiable, engaging, but totally penniless. Collaborate with him and I assure you, he'll have you paying all the expenses. If he hangs around much longer, I'm putting a lock on my liquor cabinet."

"So how do you want me to handle the man?"

"Be warned, that's all. I wanted Eddy to give you some idea of what you might be up against so that you'd steer clear."

"Steer clear? How can I do that? Hasn't he told you what's at stake? Everything's at stake."

"That's fanatical talk. Everything is *never* at stake."

"How can you say that? Is it because you don't believe him?" Clare didn't answer. Instead, she returned a smoldering, fixed stare, her eyes loaded with anger. Had I said the wrong thing? But this was the inevitable question. I couldn't let her sidestep. "Clare, you asked me to come here. You said it was important. You put me in touch with Angelotti. You vouched for him. *Why*, if you don't believe him?" She kept staring, but now I could see a rim of tears collecting under her eyes. One tear welled over and started down her cheek. "Clare, you must've known I'd ask you. Why else would I have come? Is it true about the orphans, the medieval movies, all that? Do you *think* it's true?"

She put her drink down carefully, turned and crawled awkwardly toward me across the bedclothes. Very tenderly, she buried her face in my shoulder, embracing me tightly. "I got you tangled up in all this. Believe me, I didn't see it coming. I really didn't. I just wanted to share . . . I wanted to . . ." Her voice was washing away into little sobs.

"Clare," I said, "please tell me, do you think . . ."

"*Yes*," she answered, hissing it out. "I think it's true. There. Happy?"

"My God," I said and hugged her to me. "So Angelotti convinced you."

"Oh shit, no. I didn't need him. In here . . ." She pulled back and rubbed her hand over her breast. "I knew it was true years ago—when I heard it from Rosenzweig in Paris."

"Rosenzweig? But you always said he was a nut."

"Yes, an obnoxious, smelly, little old nut. But I listened to what he was saying. I read his miserable little pamphlet. And I knew."

"But how could you be sure? I mean there's still no good evidence. . . ."

She slumped back, but stayed in my arms, letting me cradle her. "Evidence! What does that mean? In *here*, that's where I knew. Pure instinct. Because they're so beautiful and so exciting . . . movies. They have a life, more real than our so-called real lives. They have a power. I knew that power went deep. It wasn't just the stories or the stars or camera angles or anything like that. Something underneath all that, something that *connects*. I always knew it was there, but I didn't know what it was, how to talk about it. Then I read this thing of Rosenzweig's. It was half gibberish, but only half. The rest got through. Or let's say I heard it in my own way. I didn't care if Rosenzweig had all the details right. I was ready to believe there was something uncanny about movies, a charm, a magic, something demonic. They capture the attention so fiercely, they eat you alive. Movies aren't *just* movies.

"Then along comes this ranting old crackpot . . . maybe it takes a crackpot to recognize the demonic, or maybe that's how he got to be a crackpot, from staring the awful truth in the eye. Anyway, he was saying . . . what? That there was an echo of some cosmic encounter in this art. Between *what* and *what*, who knows? It didn't matter to me what names you used—Good and Evil, Being and Nothingness, Abbott and Costello. The main idea clicked, it just . . . clicked. Not that I wanted to believe it. But I knew I'd felt it, in between the frames, getting through to me. I never tried to put it in words, never wanted to talk about it. But I knew." She had been wiping away the tears with the heel of her hand. Now she gave a defiant toss of her head. "I decided to rise above it."

"How can you do that?"

"Art, Jonny. Believe in the art. Art conquers all. It does. Homer turned war into art, Dante turned all the terrors of hell into art, Kafka turned nightmares into art. Same with the orphans' demon machine. Fuck it, I said, fuck the flicker and all the optical illusions. In the hands of Charlie Chaplin, Orson Welles, Jean Renoir, it's all redeemed. Because these are beautiful souls. I don't give a damn who invented the film sprocket and the Maltese cross gear and the arclight, or for what nefarious purpose. What we've got is forty or fifty great works. I decided to go on loving those works and enjoying them. That's the only way to deal with the orphans. Just live right through them. That's what I intend to keep on doing. And so should you. Don't burn yourself out raking this muck."

"But what about 2014? What about the rest of the story?"

"You mean all that about the wars and the weapons?"

"Of course."

She nodded gravely, reached to pour out more liquor, straight this time, and swallowed it down fast. "That is a kick in the ass, isn't it? That was new to me. I don't know, I don't know . . . Eddy made it sound convincing. Oh, probably he's right. Frankly, I didn't really try to follow him. I found it all rather grubby. Part of some other world, not mine."

"You can just ignore what they're planning?"

"What they're planning is forty years off. Not likely I'll be around to see how things turn out."

"But they're going to destroy the world . . . Eduardo says."

"Well, *somebody* sure as hell is. I've known that since Hiroshima. There was the power to do it. And the human perversity. If the orphans don't do it, somebody else will."

"But that's the point. There isn't any 'somebody else.' The orphans are *everybody* else, the Russians, the Americans, the Nazis, the Jews, the Arabs. They're all the enemies, both sides, all sides. *They're* the perversity. *They're* the power too. They've been inching us along toward their final solution for seven hundred years. All our little wars have been rehearsals for their one big war. If Eduardo's right about that, I don't think I'm going to be able to let go of this thing. Can't you see that, Clare?"

She pulled away from me petulantly and curled up against her mound of pillows, her knees tucked under her chin. "I think I'll disown you anyway, even if you don't publish your miserable article."

"Why?"

"Because you came to me for advice and now you won't take it."

"I will about the article. I'll trim it down to a commentary on Simon, hold back on the rest. But about Eduardo's proposition . . . it's tempting."

Clare's eyes were getting colder, more remote. And the liquor was beginning to affect her, lending a meaner edge to her words. "Save the world, that's what you have in mind?"

"Well, maybe."

"That's grubby too. People who set out to save the world always do more harm than good. Remember, Pope Innocent's crusade was supposed to make the world safe for Catholicism. Look what came of that. Oh, Jonny, can't you understand? Everything about politics, even apocalyptic politics, is just shit. It's dealing dirty, and plotting plots, and telling lies, and kicking ass . . . and none of it makes anybody one bit nobler or wiser."

I felt myself getting angry with Clare, though I couldn't bring myself to show it. I simply couldn't tell if her withdrawal was honorable or just cowardly. "So what's worth doing, then?" I asked with a visible sulk.

At that she lit up and leaned toward me, as if she might pounce. "Jesus, you haven't learned a thing from me, have you? Let your heart answer that question. Do you remember how, at the end of *Les Enfants*, Garance gives up Baptiste? The whole scene from where Nathalie enters the room. Oh God, the architecture of that scene! Every word, every gesture. And then, how Garance melts into the crowd, that long, slow track back and back, until the crowd becomes the river. And Baptiste tries to find her, tries to make the crowd give her back, but it won't. It tears your heart out. Yet you know it must be that way. The camera is telling you it *must*, because it won't stop tracking back. And you say, yes, yes . . . because the crowd is the river, and the river rolls on. Nothing lasts longer than a moment. Oh, but there are some moments, like that shot . . ." Her tears had returned now, not the tears of sorrow, but of some stronger, more savage emotion. "If saving the world means anything, it means creating a moment like that before the lights go out. Because the lights will go out, if not in 2014, then in 20,014. Those moments are the real stars in the darkness. They're all we've got. And if that's not enough to teach people what's what, to make them a little kinder, a little more human . . ." She wanted to stop there, I could tell. But the words kept coming, spat out in anger. ". . . then maybe the orphans deserve to win. After all, just because Pope Innocent called them heretics doesn't mean they can't be right . . . in some sense."

In some sense . . . Clare and I would hardly be the ones to say in *what* sense. Neither of us could have formulated the metaphysics. But we knew that ever since we'd seen Castle's *Judas Everyman*, there was something compelling about the Great Heresy. A teaching so grim—and yet it had survived for centuries in the teeth of fierce persecution. Why, unless it had spoken the truth to thousands of people?

"I've wondered about that," I said. "Sometimes it's pretty easy to believe we're living in hell. Just read the front pages. The cruelty, the bloodshed, the endless, senseless violence . . ."

Clare nodded, but then was quick to add, "Of course, that's only half the story." She didn't want to wander too far along this path.

I reminded her, "Half is all the orphans need in order to be right. Half light, half dark, the constant struggle."

She shrugged me off, impatient now. "It's such a damned childish explanation. There's evil because an evil god is out to get us."

"Except if you try to explain things any other way, it gets nearly absurd. Why do the innocent suffer? Why do any of us suffer? Or doesn't life make any moral sense at all?"

Clare interrupted with a throaty laugh. "Jesus! I do believe this is the absolute first time I've talked theology in bed. And with you— the best lover I ever had."

That stopped me dead in my tracks. "Do you mean that?"

"Why else would I say it? Of course, I taught you everything you know. Admit it."

"I admit it. But, oh, Clare, it might not be true anymore. I told you in the letter, Dunkle's films . . . I think they've done me some damage, where it hurts most."

Clare came a little closer across the bed, stretching her hand out to stroke my arm and draw me to her. "That's what worried me," she said. "I didn't want to see you hurt that way. How bad is it?"

"Very—according to someone who was in a position to know."

"The little French girl."

"Yes." And haltingly I told her about my amorous misadventures with Jeanette. As I did, Clare gathered me still nearer. She was more caring than I could remember at any time in the past. "Maybe that's why I'm so anxious to have it all out with the orphans. I want to hit back."

"Yes, yes, yes," she was saying as she nuzzled me. "I warned you about this, remember? When we saw Castle's films at Zip Lipsky's?"

"I know."

"Poor baby. But it's nothing that can't be fixed."

"You think so?"

She leaned to brush a kiss across my lips. "I got you into this. I owe you something."

"Don't think of it that way."

"But I do. I don't know why I've been so cold toward you for so long. Trying to put my much-regretted past behind me, I guess. But not you. You were the good part. Did you know, when we met, I was about ready to chuck it all away?"

"How do you mean?"

Quite casually she answered, "Knock myself off, dear friend."
"No!"

"It was on my mind." That shocked me. I remembered how often
Clare had been morose; but there had always been an underlying
vitality about her, a cantankerous sense of high purpose. I couldn't
imagine she'd ever contemplated anything so extreme. "I was sick of
Sharkey and The Classic. I didn't see any future ahead of me. The
quicksand was up to my chin. But then having you as a student—
that's what kept me going. You were just so beautifully naive and
impressionable. You still are, do you know? Oh, I used you for all I
was worth. Every time you lit up with a new idea, you added a year
to my life. I rediscovered a lot while we were together. And it kept
my head above the mire just long enough for better things to come
my way. You saved my life, lover."

My heart glowed to hear her say it. And meanwhile, Clare's old
erotic magic was beginning to take effect, stirring the cold ashes,
finding an ember that was still barely alive. I felt myself slipping into
the boyish passivity that I always assumed with her. I could tell she
found that arousing. Would she have called this "seduction"? If so,
it was the way a fly seduces a spider, for Clare came at me with an
appetite that seemed to have been stored up for years. Yet, as insistent
as she was, she was patient and gentle. It took a long time, but it
was exactly what I needed.

Afterward, as the night glided into dawn, Clare lit a cigarette, and
settled back into the pillows. "Christ! I'll have to reschedule the whole
day. We're going to sleep till noon, aren't we?"

Judging by our mutual exhaustion, I would have guessed longer.
"Hope you don't mind," I said.

But she ignored the remark, her eyes staring off across the now
dimly lit city beyond the windows. "I'm getting married. Later this
year. In the summer probably."

She delivered the news in so melancholy a voice, I wondered if I
should offer condolences. "Anyone I know?" I asked lamely.

"Not unless you're into world-class money. He's a broker. One of
the ten biggest, five biggest, three biggest, depending on which financial journal you take from."

"You don't sound overjoyed."

She sighed pensively. "Right now, with you here, it seems like a
defeat. Harold—imagine marrying somebody named Harold!—Harold isn't going to light any fires in my boudoir, I can tell you that."

"Then why?"

"It's the easy way out. I don't see why I shouldn't take it. I'm going stale at the *Times*, turning in fewer reviews, enjoying each one less. Movies really are getting shitty, you know. Ten years from now, there isn't going to be a filmgoer older than thirteen, but they'll be making more money than ever. As it is, all the talk about movies is becoming talk about deals, big bucks, careers, who's going up, who's going down. Our whole bloody culture's just an extension of high finance. Harold can save me from the grind. We've come close to marriage twice before, but I scared off. Why, I can't say. I have no idea what I'm defending. We're comfortable together. Frictionless, nonpossessive, both of a certain battle-scarred age. He's a nice man. Very cultivated in that utterly dutiful, Ivy League seminar way that comes with fourth-generation wealth." She laughed. "Such are the circles I move in now, Jonny. The sons of the sons of the Robber Barons, trying to make amends for their forebears' philistine ways. Harold spends more time these days sitting on museum boards than on the stock exchange. Philanthropy and yachting—would you believe it?— his grand passions. I suspect I would come third on the list. But who knows, maybe I can help put his ill-gotten gains to some good use. I come across young filmmakers all the time who tell me all they need is a grubstake to produce the next *Birth of a Nation*. Probably most of them can't get a movie past the talking stage. But what the hell!"

"Well . . . congratulations." I put as much sincerity into the remark as I could, but it still came out as more of a question than a statement.

My head was cushioned in Clare's still humid lap. Hovering over me, she looked down into my eyes. "This doesn't have to be a final fling, Jonny. Harold's very liberal, very understanding. Also very busy. He travels a lot. So do I. We can still be affectionate friends— provided you don't run off to the crusades with Father Angelotti."

Good old Clare! She was giving it all she had. "Is that a bribe?" I asked.

"An inducement. I mean everything I said tonight. You've got better ways to spend your life than hunting heretics. I could be one of those ways . . . at least until another Jeanette comes along."

Clare was bargaining cutely with me, but I could hear the worry and concern that lay behind her words. "Will you let me think about it?" I asked. "This has been quite a mind-numbing few days, especially the last three hours."

"I would've hoped the last three hours had blotted out everything else. They were meant to. If not, we can give it another try—and sleep until tea time."

"Thanks, but I don't have it in me. Honestly."

She ran her hand softly down my body. "That's what you always used to say. But I managed to surprise you, didn't I?"

And she did again.

29 INNER SANCTUM

"I have the distinct feeling," Clare said over late brunch the next morning, "that I have labored in vain." Her look was both challenging and hurt, meant to make me feel supremely guilty.

"Not in the least," I hastened to assure her. "My God, I was beginning to feel like a zombie." And I thanked her and thanked her until she had to tell me I was becoming soppy and would I please cut it out. Even so, she wasn't mollified.

"I had something more than your gonads in mind. Not that the poor neglected little things aren't important. But there's also a minor matter called your life's work. If you get tangled up with Eddy, mark my words, you'll go down the tube professionally. Don't let it happen, please."

As far as I could remember, Clare had never said "please" to me. Her advice had always come as a quasi-parental command.

"I promise," I answered.

"Promise what?"

"Not to get tangled up with him."

"I'd rather have you promise not to talk with him again."

But on that point, I equivocated until Clare must have sensed my mind was made up and tending away from her wishes. Angelotti's proposition was too enticing to pass up, exactly the sort of once-in-a-lifetime adventure every timid, desk-bound scholar hopes will some day come his way.

"At least promise to call me before you decide to do anything rash," Clare asked when she was dressed and ready to leave for the day. I said I would, and we kissed at the door. It was a long, loving kiss. It couldn't have been better even if we had known at the time it would be our last.

I met Angelotti one more time before returning to California. Lunch at a restaurant of his choosing, but at my expense. He wanted all the details I could give him about my relations with Brother Justin and Simon. As I went over the ground, he hit upon an idea. "So you were promised an interview with this Brother Marcion."

"That's what I thought at first. Later Brother Justin said that wasn't possible."

"But you must insist. Tell him you will not continue with your article on Simon unless he secures a meeting for you with Brother Marcion face to face."

"That'll never work. Brother Marcion is at Albi. He's one of the Perfect. He lives a cloistered life."

"Insist!" Angelotti said again. "What have you to lose? If you succeed, you will be inside the inner sanctum."

I shook my head. "It's not even worth trying."

"Let us be cunning like the serpents we must deal with," Angelotti said with a sly wink. "Suppose you revise your article on Simon. Make it highly laudatory. Exactly what Brother Justin would like to see. But say it is not quite finished. This will be the bait, yes? Tell him unless you can have your interview with Brother Marcion, the article will never reach print. Perhaps then . . ."

This seemed to me a pretty feeble ploy, though it was the best Angelotti could come up with. I took the idea back to Los Angeles with me, feeling certain I'd never have the courage to try what he proposed. But over the next two weeks, he phoned me no fewer than seven times—always collect—to urge me on. At last, if for no other reason than to be able to tell him I'd tried and failed, I made up my mind to approach Brother Justin.

He had no idea I'd been away. And if he did, so what? But with my usual total lack of self-assurance, I quickly gave away the fact that I was hiding something. Some secret agent I was going to make! "You seem nervous," Brother Justin observed with concern when we met, and he fixed me with a stare that made me even more unsettled. "Is there something you would care to talk about?"

Taking a deep breath, I put Angelotti's plan of attack into operation.

"In fact, there is," I answered. "This." And I deposited on his desk a not-quite-finished article on the films of Simon Dunkle. It was an almost absurdly glowing tribute to the boy's work, expressing none of my doubts or reservations, exactly the sort of puff piece Angelotti had suggested I dangle before Brother Justin as an inducement. After he'd rapidly scanned the manuscript, he looked up, an expression of surprised delight on his face.

"But this is excellent," he said. "I had no idea your view of Simon's work was so unexceptionably positive."

"As you see," I said, "the article lacks a conclusion. It will remain that way until you fulfill your end of the bargain."

He seemed frankly puzzled. "Which is?"

"You do remember that I requested some information from Brother Marcion."

"Oh yes."

"About Max Castle."

"Yes."

"I gather there still hasn't been a response."

Brother Justin began combing abstractly through the papers on his desk. "Let me see now . . ." he mused, as if I should expect him to discover a letter there from Brother Marcion.

Impatiently, I pressed my advantage. "You realize that my main interest all along has been Castle. That's what brought me here in the first place. I've delayed finishing my book because you led me to believe that Brother Marcion might be able to provide me with some valuable material about his relations with Castle. Well, I've been waiting now for . . ."

Brother Justin plucked an envelope from his desk and held it up. "A letter arrived just a few weeks ago. It slipped my mind. I tried to call you when it came, but you were apparently away."

"A letter from whom?"

"Brother Marcion. Actually Father Marcion now; that is how we refer to our elders." He drew out the letter and skimmed it. "Yes . . . he apologizes for taking so long to reply. He has been on a hermetical retreat. He says he would be pleased to pass along what he knows about Max Castle. Only . . ."

"Yes?" I waited to hear his excuse for telling me precisely nothing, as usual.

Brother Justin's eyes were still on the letter. "He says there is so very much to tell, more than he will have time to set down in writing just now."

As I expected, another evasion. But it was also the perfect opening for Angelotti's stratagem. Why not suggest that I visit Father Marcion at Albi to spare him the trouble of writing? Not that it would work. But Angelotti was right: What did I have to lose? I began to speak just as Brother Justin looked up from the letter. "He wonders if you would care to visit him at Albi."

Brother Justin gazed at me. I gazed at Brother Justin. A questioning pause on both sides. "He wants me to come to Albi?"

"At your convenience."

"But I thought visitors weren't welcome."

"Why did you think so?"

"Isn't it cloistered? Doesn't that mean . . . ?"

"Yes, but there are accommodations for meetings. It isn't a prison, after all." He studied me for a moment. "You seem surprised."

"Well, I assumed . . . I mean, would Father Marcion actually be free to see me, free to talk?"

"If he chooses, yes." His face was taking on a progressively more puzzled expression as I stared back at him incredulously. Finally he said, "Of course, if you have no interest in meeting him, he may find time to write at some point in the future. I realize it would be a long trip for you."

That brought me up short. One more question and I might talk myself out of what I most wanted. Of course I would go. But when? How? Brother Justin agreed to consult with Dr. Byx about all that.

"Dr. Byx would be willing to have me visit Albi?" I asked.

Brother Justin cocked his head at me inquisitively. "Byx? What has it to do with him? If Father Marcion wishes to see you, the matter is settled. But it would be convenient to coordinate through Zurich."

A few days later Brother Justin phoned to confirm my travel arrangements. We decided on a date at the beginning of my summer vacation. I was to book my flight to Zurich. From there, Dr. Byx would provide my transport to Albi. The orphanage, I learned, kept its own plane at the airport.

Two weeks before I was to leave, I phoned Clare. I'd been rehearsing what I would tell her during every free hour for days. I got no answer, not even her machine. I tried several times more before somebody at last picked up the phone. The voice at the other end wasn't Clare. It was Angelotti. He explained that he was staying in Clare's apartment while she was away. Away where? Hadn't I heard? She'd gotten married the previous week. "All very quick and private," Angelotti explained. "A stockbroker. I forget his name. She did not inform you?"

"She mentioned the possibility. . . . I didn't expect it to happen so soon. Where is she now?"

"On the high seas, would you believe it? He is an avid yachtsman, this husband of hers. The honeymoon is a world cruise."

When I was off the phone, I turned to a weeks-old stack of correspondence on my kitchen table. Junk mail I assumed. I dug through and found a formal-looking envelope which looked like better than junk. It had a printed return address I didn't recognize. Inside was a very tasteful little notice embossed on plush lavender paper.

Clarissa Swann and Harold C. Dumbarton Jr. announce their marriage, June 12, 1976

On the back I found Clare's scribble.

As I warned you . . . Off to see the world. Back in the fall maybe. Hope the crusade can wait till then. Must talk more.
As ever . . . no, make that, as of our last meeting.
C.

I believe I can honestly say I felt glad for Clare. Good old Harold might finally give her the opportunity she deserved in life to do the sort of writing she wanted to do, even get in on producing a daring little film or two. And liberal as the man was (if Clare could be believed) there was every good chance I'd be seeing her again for intimate advice.

But meanwhile, I felt odd undertaking the trip ahead of me without anyone knowing what I was up to. Yet whom could I tell, besides Angelotti, who, for all the phone calls we'd exchanged, was still a stranger in my life? No one in the Film Studies department would understand why I should be on my way to a monastery in southern France. My colleagues still hadn't come to grips with what little they knew of my research on Castle. I realized with some regret how cloistered my work had become over the last few years. I'd systematically isolated myself, waiting to amaze the scholarly world with my magnum opus. Now didn't seem to be the time to start making lengthy explanations. There was, of course, Faustus Carstad, who knew at least half of the story. But the last I'd heard, the poor man was on indefinite sick leave following his recent surgery. Not the best time to begin mending fences in that quarter.

I considered letting Jeanette know my plans, but she was bound to ask more questions than I cared to answer at this point. Well, as a last resort, there was Sharkey. He'd have to do. It took three days of playing telephone tag to get through to him, and when I did, it was hardly encouraging. He was so strung out I had to tell him twice who I was. As for explaining about my trip, that proved to be a Herculean effort.

"You're goin' to South America? Far out!"

"No, Sharkey. The south of France. First Zurich, then Albi. Near Toulouse."

"Right. Yeah. Where that little crippled painter came from."

"That's got nothing to do with it. I'm visiting the orphans there. They have a monastery. In Albi."

"Right. What orphans are these, pal?"

"Simon's people, remember?"

"Oh, hey, you seen Dunky's latest flick? *They Came from Toxage Seepy*. Wild, man!"

"*Toxic Seepage*, Sharkey. Yes, I've seen it."

"Wild."

"We're not talking about that."

"We're not?"

"No. We're talking about my trip to southern France, remember?"

"Yeah, right. To Albuquerque."

"Albi."

"Albi. Right. Hey, when'm I gonna get to see little old little Jeanette again? Huh?"

"Forget about that now. Listen, while I'm away, I'd like to leave my manuscript with you. Okay?"

"Sure. But, hey, where're you goin'?"

Poor Sharkey. His short-term memory had shrunk to the last three words he managed to hear. I decided to give up on everything beyond saying goodbye, but even that was a struggle. "I'll be in touch with you when I get back," I told him. "In about four or five weeks. I'll have quite a story to tell you, old man. It looks as if you were right about everything."

"No kidding? Well, congratulations to me."

Hopeless.

I was relieved when, in the week before I left, Angelotti asked if he might see my Max Castle manuscript while I was away. "Of course," I told him. "Fact is, I'd appreciate leaving it in sympathetic hands . . . just in case."

"In case of what?"

"Oh, in case I get lost at sea," I laughed.

Angelotti didn't understand. Why should he? "At sea? But you are flying, yes?"

"Of course. Castle was lost at sea."

"Oh?"

"On his way to Zurich in 1941."

"Oh. I didn't know."

And then I wondered why I'd brought the point up at all.

Somewhere in the course of the last several days before my departure, I became aware of a curious change. Something was displacing the many reservations, even the real fear I'd been nursing about my mission to Zurich. Instead, I was experiencing a rising sense of giddiness, rather like the feeling that sets in on the steep uphill approach to the first dip of a roller coaster. Perhaps some of Angelotti's eagerness was rubbing off on me. In any case, I was actually enjoying the anticipation of risk. And there was something more. A sense of power. Just to be privy to the orphans' great project seemed to confer an importance upon my every thought and move. Never in all my life could I have imagined an enterprise as vast as theirs, a dedication as fierce. I found myself deliberately suppressing my incredulity about Angelotti's story. I *wanted* him to be right. Because then *I* would be the man who knew! And soon, like one of Hitchcock's lovably bumbling innocents—Jimmy Stewart, Cary Grant—I might be moving inside the conspiratorial depths, sharing some part of the terrible adventure. This was a side of myself I hadn't known was there. Once I did, I issued a stern warning: *Careful, Jonathan! That way lies madness.*

Los Angeles to New York. New York to Rome. Rome to Zurich. Then, by way of a waiting limousine, to the orphanage where I was scheduled to spend the night before continuing to Albi.

The old, weather-stained building was as cheerless as I remembered it, but Dr. Byx had changed markedly. While as stiffly formal as he'd been the previous summer, he was clearly making a supreme effort to be affable. I could almost believe he was pleased to have me back. I had to remind myself that this couldn't be so, since I was an interloper here to ask more unwelcome questions. I'd been in his office making small talk for nearly an hour before I began to get a fix on my situation. A priest named Brother Basil happened by and Dr. Byx hastened to introduce me as "a guest of Father Marcion" on my way to the abbey. There was a buoyant note in his voice as he spoke that led Brother Basil to respond with a more than polite handshake and a "Congratulations." I gathered that receiving an invitation from one of the Perfect conferred a certain distinction. Dr. Byx went on to let me know it was a rare privilege.

"I believe it is some three years since we last arranged a formal audience at the abbey. Let me see, that was for an official of the Red Cross with whom we were cooperating in a venture. But a scholar . . . I can't recall it has ever happened."

I wanted to know how long I'd be permitted to stay. "That will be up to Father Marcion. There are accommodations at the monastery. You may find the food on the frugal side. Vegetarian, you know. Modest portions. But you may send out for things of your own."

"Father Marcion must be very old," I observed. "Will I be tiring him?"

"The elders are all very old. Many in their nineties. The oldest— Father Valentinius—is one hundred and nine. Living to a ripe old age is a characteristic of our faith. Our diet perhaps. I expect you will find Father Marcion lively and alert."

I'd arrived at the orphanage in the late afternoon with no clear plans for dinner. I discovered that Dr. Byx expected me to dine with him at his residence. In fact, he insisted. As far as I could tell, the only reason for the invitation was to let me know how "very, very grateful" the church was for my "brilliant article" on Simon Dunkle. Dr. Byx had received a copy of the piece from Brother Justin and had taken the liberty of showing it to some of the elders, especially Father Marcion, who was delighted with my analysis. As Angelotti had surmised, my opinion of the boy wonder was of great importance to the orphans. It made me uncomfortable to do it, but I persevered in my deception, agreeing to everything Dr. Byx said about Simon's skill and promise, holding back my severe reservations.

At last, when I saw my opening, I reminded him that the article was still subject to revision.

"But your opinion of Simon will finish in the same positive vein, will it not?" Dr. Byx asked with marked concern.

"I hope so. To be frank, just now I'm not certain that the article will get finished at all. Because, you see, that depends . . ."

"On?"

"On whether I make some progress with my research on Max Castle."

"I'm sure you will find Father Marcion very helpful in that respect."

"So I hope. And what about you, Doctor? You could also be of great help to me."

"Please, in what respect?" he asked eagerly.

I took a deep breath and made my play. "I've brought a film with me. Actually, it's only a clip, a few minutes long. Max Castle's last serious piece of work. It's been stored away for years in a private collection. I'd like to look at it tonight."

The eagerness melted from his voice. "You haven't seen this film yet?"

"Yes, I've seen it. But not all of it. I think you know what I mean."

He did. Offering me the steady, searching look of a man weighing a difficult bargain, he pushed back from the table and strode across the room to a cabinet. He unlocked a drawer and took out a flashlight-sized box. "What was the amusing name you had for it?" he asked.

"A sallyrand. She was a famous striptease dancer."

"Striptease . . . yes. A dance that hides more than it reveals."

We left his quarters and walked across the courtyard outside. In his office, where I'd deposited my luggage, I unpacked the reel of film Olga Tell had sent me and followed him to the lower floors of the school. I remembered this part of the orphanage; it was where the film labs were. We entered one of the rooms containing a dozen or so moviolas. Dr. Byx chose one, took the reel of film from its canister, inspected it with undisguised displeasure, and began to thread it into the machine.

"Perhaps we should have a fanfare. Max Von Kastell's last serious piece of work. Is that what you called it? As usual, it would seem to be incomplete." He switched on the moviola. A familiar but still startling scene from *Heart of Darkness* sprang into view on the small screen: the fence of severed heads. It was followed by the raucous native dance and gory ritual. Dr. Byx and I watched the short clip all the way through. Or, rather, he watched it; I watched him from the corner of my eye, eager to gauge his reaction. I expected it to be unfavorable, but it was more than that. His face was that of a man struggling to hold back a convulsive repugnance. Still, when the film ran out, he managed a controlled response. "Quite shoddy, don't you find?" he asked coolly. "The man was finished, at the end of his rope."

"But we haven't seen it all, have we?" I replied.

Without being asked, Dr. Byx rewound the reel and handed me the sallyrand. I aimed the device at the moviola and watched the film for a second time. I had a strong hunch what I might see, and I was right.

There they were, Olga Tell and the man she had called Dandy Wilson, their wraithlike images emerging in a run of negative etching that coiled through the interlaced smoke and shadow of the scene. He was wearing his ritual costume, the great black wings and beaked headpiece. She, while as completely naked as I'd seen her in the footage Zip Lipsky managed to salvage, was now ingeniously if minimally clothed in the flashing light of the sword she wielded. This was cleverly done, lending her marvelously contoured body an angelic luster. At the same time, in the close-ups Zip had filmed, Olga's face showed unmistakable signs that she was indeed doped up and not at all in control of what she was doing. That was painful to watch. Her eyes were spacey and blurred, filled with an unfocused fear, her movements somnambulistic as she and her partner performed the graphic, totally joyless sexual maneuver Zip had been so eager to deny was porn. The outtakes he'd saved made that denial a great deal less than convincing. But in this version, using the shot Castle must have been hunting for all along, the act had taken on a more ritualized and at the same time more tortured quality. This was partly because the scene had been filmed in super-slow motion. The black man and the white woman seemed to be making both love and war simultaneously, embracing and tearing at one another, caressing and clawing with an achingly labored underwater heaviness.

But there was something else happening. The subliminal footage of Olga and her partner was shifting back and forth between its positive and negative images: black man, white woman; black woman, white man. As their sexual encounter mounted in intensity, these reversals accelerated, producing a dizzying effect. Finally, at the moment of climax, the camera went into a slow spin that swirled the wildly flickering forms of the man and woman into a yin-yang configuration, an animated union of the opposites. But this came to a sudden, jolting halt as Olga took up the sword she'd laid to one side, and struck at her lover with one swift blow, a graphic act of decapitation.

At just that moment, the surface film that overlay Olga's ritual murder brightened and pressed forward. The first of the victims in the "unspeakable rite"—it was one of the women—was swiftly immolated by the witch doctor. That moment had been edited from the visible footage; but Castle had preserved it subliminally. It was a terrifying image: the black native woman impaled upon the fierce white tusk. I couldn't have put the symbolism of all this into words. I didn't have to. I was left knowing that I had witnessed a sacrificial act that was at once sacred and obscene. When the film finished, I felt as if I'd been punched in the gut. I took a moment to compose myself, then offered Dr. Byx the sallyrand so that he might watch the sequence in its entirety.

"No need," he sniffed as he rewound the reel. "I have seen this little piece of work."

"Oh? When?"

"When I first took up my duties here in Zurich. This excerpt was in our film library."

"But how did it get there?"

"I was told that some of our people in Hollywood helped with the editing and effects—such as they are. When the studio—RKO, was it?—wisely elected to abandon the movie, our editors took whatever footage they could find into safekeeping. How it eventually found its way here, I cannot say. It is an even greater mystery to me why it was preserved. I'm sure my predecessors found it as distasteful as I do."

His reply raised more questions than it answered. "My understanding was that Castle took this excerpt with him when he left on his final trip to come here."

"Indeed? I wonder why he should have done so?"

"He thought it might persuade your church to help finance a production of *Heart of Darkness*."

Dr. Byx stared at me, confounded. "I can't believe he would make such a misjudgment. In any case, if he did take the film with him, it would have perished when he did, not so?"

"Yes, that's true." Dr. Byx was giving me an owlish stare, as if he were trying to read my thoughts. I decided to let him know what was on my mind. "Is there any chance that the film was delivered here by Castle?"

He frowned at me. It was a smiling, inquisitive frown. "How could that be?"

"I mean, is there any chance Castle actually got to Zurich in 1941?"

Dr. Byx pursed his lips, furrowed his brow, and made a great show of pondering my question. "I can't recall that this was ever reported to me."

"Do you still have the film here?"

A quick, bitter laugh burst from him. "Hardly! It was one of my first acts as director to dispose of this little horror."

"Do you really find it so disagreeable?" I asked, hoping he would open up for me. "I grant you the scene isn't up to the best technical standards, but Castle was quite handicapped at the time he shot this. He was working fast, trying to avoid the supervision of the studio. . . ."

Dr. Byx broke in impatiently. "This has nothing to do with artistic values." He hissed the last two words at me as if it burned his lips to pronounce them. "There are things you have seen here in this wretched little scrap of film that are precious to our faith. Kastell was given no permission to make use of them, let alone to desecrate them. We place a very high value on obedience in our church. Perhaps this is difficult for you to appreciate with your rather exaggerated modern concern for artistic freedom."

"I don't understand what you mean by 'desecrate.' "

He answered as if he were doing me a great favor to be responding at all, though hardly expecting me to appreciate what he said. "I wonder what the concept of *sacrifice* means to you, Professor Gates. Does it convey any spiritual import at all? Suppose I were to tell you that what you have seen in the multifilter is a gross parody of a sacrificial rite that has been honored in our church since ancient days. Would that clarify anything at all for you? I suspect not. You would have to understand a great deal more about our theology to know how offensive we find this crude piece of burlesque. Suffice it to say, that even if this effort were not blasphemous, it would be intolerable that the emblems of our faith should be placed on public display in such a film, in *any* film."

Now I was getting what I wanted, teasing the spleen out of the man and with it a few anguished truths about the last days of Max Castle. "But why? You teach your pupils to make movies."

Dr. Byx's tone became crushingly sententious. "Motion pictures are a profane art. They have their function. It is not to dabble in sacred doctrine, especially when one has no higher goal than aesthetic sensation."

"Do you really believe that's all Castle was after here? I happen to know that he took this movie very seriously. He wanted it to be a commentary upon the barbarism of our time, the revolt against civilization. I believe he was looking for the most powerful images he could find to make that statement."

There was a frozen sneer on Dr. Byx's face that showed me I wasn't getting through. "And in order to make this very important statement, Herr Kastell sees fit to associate the holiest symbols of our faith with drunken savages and striptease dancing."

I decided it was best to back off. We were skirting matters of doctrine and religious discipline that were well beyond my grasp. Besides, it wasn't my job to defend Castle to his spiritual superiors. But I ventured one final remark. "There are some members of your church who regard Castle as a prophet." I angled the observation to sound inquisitive: a question, not a statement. Dr. Byx threw me an expression of challenging incredulity. Feeling intimidated, I qualified my remark. "Well, at least one member said so."

"I'd be interested to know who."

Not wanting to rat on Simon, I retreated rapidly. "I may have misunderstood."

Dr. Byx gave a small, dismissive shrug. "I can assure you that is *not* how Max Kastell will be remembered in the annals of our church."

By the time we returned to the doctor's residence, he'd managed to cool down enough to recapture his sense of hospitality. He offered me a final brandy for the night and, much to my surprise, an apology. "You will excuse me if at times this evening I seemed in bad temper. I find this film so very offensive. It marks the failure of someone in whom we invested high hopes. Perhaps now you have some better idea why our church came to be so displeased with Max Kastell."

Before I lost touch with the more ingratiating mood that had come over him, I hastened to thank him for letting me view the film and then decided to press my luck. "I'm sure you realize how greatly my research would be helped if I had the use of a multifilter. That might allow me to finish my article on Simon all the sooner."

Dr. Byx lifted an eyebrow, weighing the request. "No doubt, no doubt. I will see if that can be arranged."

Theodore Roszak

I thanked him in advance for a favor I hardly expected to receive and finished my brandy. Dr. Byx showed me to my quarters for the night, a room on the same floor of the main building as his office. It was impeccably clean and quite comfortable, though monastically spare in its furnishings; the only decoration on view was a Maltese cross above the bed. Although I felt beaten flat by jet lag and an evening of strained conversation, I at once set to work recording all I'd learned that evening in my notebook. I didn't want to forget a word. Unless I was mistaken, I'd found the last missing fragment of Max Castle's story.

He'd set out for Zurich in the fall of 1941 hoping to raise the money he needed to finance his own production of *Heart of Darkness*. It was a long shot, actually a fool's errand, but the best hope he had at that dismal stage of his career. Possibly the orphans, trying to bring him home for disciplining, deliberately created the impression they might strike a bargain with him. There was never a chance of that, even though I felt certain Castle didn't intend the blasphemy his superiors saw in his version of *Heart of Darkness*. If he had, he wouldn't have planned to show them the excerpts he took with him. It was more likely he'd grown so estranged from his church and so immersed in his art that he could no longer tell where aesthetics left off and religion began. Or he'd ceased caring.

At least tentatively I was able to identify more of the symbolism contained in the little film clip than Dr. Byx realized; my studies in Cathar history had taught me a thing or two along the way. Castle had wanted to imbue his key scene with as much in the way of holy terror as possible. So he pulled out all stops and gave it the works. He drew upon the most vivid image of sacrifice and expiation he knew: the eternal love affair between the black bird and the lady Sophia. From what Dr. Byx told me, I gathered the Cathars still celebrated a sacramental rite which depicted that ambiguously erotic encounter between the true God and the fickle human mind that would embrace divine knowledge at the risk of profaning it. Was that rite as blatantly sexual as Castle made it in his film? Was it—I shuddered to think so—as murderously gory? I supposed not, though I'd given up guessing what might or might not be too extreme for the orphans.

What was clear was that Castle had, for his own artistic purposes, played fast and loose with images and ideas his church regarded as taboo in the deepest primordial sense of that word. For him, the mysteries of the faith were the legitimate stuff of art. He saw nothing sacrilegious in using the love dance of the black bird and the white lady to imbue the primitive ritual of Conrad's savages with as much juice and power as he could bring to the scene. I remembered Faustus Carstad's remark. "Every religion in the world goes back to fertility rites and love feasts." A rigid fanatic like Dr. Byx was hardly likely to admit that, let alone permit that fact to be exploited for its cinematic effect on an audience of unbelievers.

I could imagine how desperate Castle must have felt traveling so far to lay his proposition before the scorning authorities of his church. Even if he had succeeded in reaching Zurich with his meager bit of film, it was a doomed mission. The powers that dominated his church had lost all patience with him. "Movies have their function," Dr. Byx had said. He meant they were an instrument for mental manipulation, a means of twisting the psyche of the infidel masses. Just that, nothing more. For Dr. Byx, artists like Max Castle and Simon Dunkle were mere technicians whose task it was to work in absolute obedience to their superiors. Castle was bound to be sent away empty-handed.

And then what? Zip Lipsky had said he was ready to resort to extortion if the orphans failed to come across with the cash he needed. He'd already been shooting his mouth off around the studios, telling outsiders—like John Huston—more about the church than the orphans cared to have known. Was he still in that rebellious frame of mind when he set out for Zurich? Would he have been willing to spill the beans if he'd made it back to the States? Zip Lipsky had hinted darkly that the orphans might be quite ruthless about muzzling their enemies. But how, if they refused to shed blood?

It was nearly midnight by the time the fatigue of the day overcame me. I was just opening the window of my room to bring in the fresh night air when I heard a distant singing. It came from the direction of the chapel, the priests and nuns, no doubt, performing a late service of some kind. The music was soft and crooning, rather like a Gregorian chant. At that moment, within sight of the moon-blanched Alps, I would have said it was the most touching music I'd ever heard: sweet, dark, and infinitely plaintive. A deep melancholy washed over me. Though I couldn't make out the words of the song (they were probably Latin anyway), I felt certain they hymned some ancient memory of hardship and persecution. Somber praise offered to long-suffering ancestors whose only crime was that they honored an austere faith in the face of brutal opposition. Despite all I knew about them now—

their maniacal vengefulness, their secret machinations devoted to an act of universal extermination—still, in that moment, caught in the spell of those mournful voices, my heart went out to the unhappy orphans for all they had endured. It was the last generous thought I was ever to spare them.

That night I didn't sleep well. Early on I had a dream that left me too jumpy to settle down. I saw myself in the limousine from the orphanage. I was on my way to the airport. Dr. Byx sat on one side of me; on the other sat a second man whose presence made me afraid, so afraid that I could not bring myself to look in his direction. Rather I averted my eyes, trying not to see him. When we arrived, there was no plane in sight. "Don't worry," Dr. Byx said cheerily. "We can provide an alternate carrier. But first we must mark the spot."

"Of course," I agreed.

At once, he and the second man took large pieces of chalk from their pockets, knelt down, and began to draw a series of long, straight lines on the tarmac. Once again, I turned my eyes away, not wanting to see the second man's face. The lines that he and Dr. Byx were drawing came together in the shape of a large Maltese cross and I was at the center of it. I stood admiring the precision of their work. "No wonder your church has lasted so long," I commented. "You take such great care with every detail."

"Exactly so," said Dr. Byx. He scanned the sky, then pointed. "You see?"

I looked up and saw a dark speck circling slowly overhead. It turned and swooped, coming lower. It was the black bird. But now it was very large. Very, very large. Larger than an airplane. Suddenly it dived—straight at me. I tried to run, but the chalk cross was holding me in like an invisible fence; I couldn't step across any of its lines. The bird, sweeping overhead like a windstorm, snatched me by the shoulders and lifted off. We were soaring away, climbing steeply. I tried to cry out, but the rushing air stifled me. Looking down in terror, I saw the rapidly receding figures of Dr. Byx and the second man smiling after me, waving.

I wanted desperately to wake up but couldn't. The dream had a fierce grip on my mind; it wouldn't be shaken off. The great bird was carrying me over the Alps, over forests and farms. It seemed to be holding me by the threads of my jacket. Fearful that I might fall, I strained to reach around and grab hold of its talons, but each time I tried, I seemed to slip. Then we were over open ocean, traveling at a fierce speed. I could hear the gigantic wings beating above me. In a panic, I wrenched myself around—and the bird let go. My blood froze as I felt myself falling, falling. Now I'll wake up, I said to myself. But I didn't. As if in slow motion, I splashed into the water. It closed about me, cold and thick and damp. I sank and sank. All around me the darkness deepened. I should have been drowning, but I wasn't. And this frightened me more than I would have feared dying, for I realized I was passing into some hideously unnatural condition: hopelessly trapped in a kind of living death.

I became aware of music . . . voices singing, reaching me with a deep, wavery distortion there below the water. A familiar song. The words of "Bye, Bye, Blackbird," that old vaudeville dirge about hard luck, lovelessness, and everybody's long dark way home.

And then, far below me, I saw blurred yellow lights. It was a city under the sea, at the bottom of the world. *No*, I said, *I don't want to live here!* And with a convulsive effort, I woke. But just before I did, I made out a sign in the sickly lights below me. It said "Hollywood."

As I pulled myself up from the bed, I could still hear the singing voices from my dream. They were there in the room with me. No, outside . . . coming from the chapel. I listened intently. Silence. Yet I was certain I'd awakened in time to catch just the final strains of their singing. I waited for several minutes to see if they would sing again. There was nothing.

I spent the rest of the night afraid to sleep again. Toward dawn, I managed to doze for about an hour.

That morning I was served breakfast in my room. Soon after, a priest came to tell me my car was at the front door. I'd been told that someone from the orphanage would escort me to Albi to make introductions. This turned out to be a young nun named Sister Angeline. She had a pleasant, fresh face, too pretty, I thought, to be encased in the close black bonnet of her order. As we sat together in the back of the car waiting for the driver to return from a last minute errand, I wondered what color her hair might be beneath her censoring habit and how she might look if it were free to frame her face. All the while we waited, she wore a small, strained smile, trying hard to please, it seemed. Instead, the tension in her face unsettled me, as did her silence. She said nothing except to answer questions, and then only briefly. She didn't, for example, tell me we would have a traveling companion. It was Dr. Byx, who came bustling out of the orphanage with the driver. He hurried to the car holding out a small box. It was a gift. "By all means, open it," he said, smiling benevolently.

I did. It was a sallyrand. It was shiny new. "Well, thank you," I managed to say. My surprise was evident. I asked if he expected me to return it.

"Not at all," he said. "It is yours. After so many severe criticisms of Max Kastell last evening, it seemed appropriate, as, shall we say, a goodwill offering? I want you to start your long journey in the right frame of mind, so to speak."

I thanked him again. "It will be put to good use."

"I'm sure." And he waved me on my way.

At the airport, a sleek little twin-engine commuter plane was waiting for us. Sister Angeline quickly climbed in and took her seat; I followed. The pilot, a personable young priest named Brother Jerome, welcomed me aboard and began to taxi us toward a distant runway as soon as I was buckled in.

I settled down for the trip with a distinct sense of triumph. I had a sallyrand! Dr. Byx had simply given it to me. Everything was falling into place, just as Angelotti had said it would. I began to make a mental list of the people to whom I would show the multifilter, starting with Clare. I might even schedule an invitational screening of the works of Max Castle and Simon Dunkle at the Museum of Modern Art and let the films be viewed with this remarkable instrument. It would provide all the proof I needed of the orphans' cinematic techniques. My God, it would make history!

It wasn't until we were floating west over the Alps that I became aware of something buzzing away at the back of my mind like a persistent alarm one wakes and hears distantly in the darkness. I was remembering another flight I'd taken above the landscape I now saw below me. In my dream the night before, the great bird had flown with me across these mountains, had dropped me in the cold sea. But there was something about that dream that was more frightening than those experiences. That fear was still there, refusing to leave my memory. The second man, whose face I refused to see. I knew now as I had known in the dream who he was. Angelotti.

An uneventful flight, a smooth landing at Toulouse, a quick passage through French customs, and Sister Angeline and I were at the curb outside the arrivals lobby, where another limousine awaited us, this one larger and more luxurious than the one in Zurich. A driver, also a priest, greeted me cheerily and rushed to take charge of my luggage. In short order, Sister Angeline and I were sharing the spacious backseat nested in a cloud bank of velour and gliding noiselessly away into the mountain country north of the city. The limo seemed to float over the roads. I soon found myself nodding off, a sleepless night and a backlog of jet lag catching up with me. I shook myself awake and glanced across at Sister Angeline. Poor girl, I thought as I studied her. Young, pretty, bright . . . probably she knew nothing of life beyond the narrow precinct of her church. Taken in as an orphan, she'd been raised since infancy on the cheerless teachings of the Cathars. Did her own experience give her any reason to believe that the world she lived in was hell, that she was born to be an innocent, lifelong victim of the persecuting Dark Lord? And then before I realized it, she'd turned; her eyes met mine. The look was neither shy nor innocent. Her stiff little smile was gone, replaced by a cool, clinical stare.

Reaching into my overnight case, I took out the sallyrand Dr. Byx had given me. "Have you ever used one of these?" I asked, just to make conversation.

"Yes, when I was at school," she said.

"Did you study filmmaking?" I asked.

"No. I prepared for the religious faculty."

After we'd driven a few minutes more, I said, "Last night at the orphanage there was some singing in the chapel. What was it?"

"Compline," she answered. "The midnight service."

"I'm not sure . . . I thought I heard a song. It went something like . . ." and I whistled a fragment of the melody I remembered.

"Oh yes. One of our hymns."

"Does it have a name?"

"Vale Avis Tenebrica."

"And that means . . . ?"

She hesitated, frowning over her answer. " 'Farewell, Bird of the Night,' I suppose. It is symbolic."

It was the tune I'd heard Angelotti humming that night at Clare's.

Something like carsickness began to uncoil inside me. But it wasn't carsickness. It wasn't fear either. It was disgust arising from a realization of my total, lethal stupidity. I was the man who, after seeing *Psycho*, checks in at the Bates Motel . . . and rings for room service.

"How long a trip is it?" I asked.

"Less than two hours," she answered. "Would you care for some coffee?" I said I would. She tapped the driver on the shoulder and he passed back a large silver thermos and two mugs. Sister Angeline unfolded a small table from the armrest between us and poured out the coffee. It was a strong, bitter brew and very hot. I nursed it along, taking small sips.

"Is there a telephone at the abbey?" I asked.

"Oh yes," Sister Angeline replied.

"Good," I said. And I put my mind to work trying to think of someone to call when I had the chance. But with Clare out of reach, who else was there? Someone in my department at UCLA. At least to tell them that there was a copy of my Max Castle manuscript and of my complete, fully critical article on Simon Dunkle locked away in my desk. Someone besides Angelotti should know about my writing just in case.

In case of what? I turned to Sister Angeline and coughed up a little giggle. "I guess there's no chance of being lost at sea around here."

She looked back at me pleasantly, though of course she had no idea what I meant. "No, you need have no fear of that." Her eyes had grown more penetrating still.

"Good," I said. "That's very good."

"As you see, you are a long way from the ocean." She gestured out the window toward a magnificent vista of jagged and precipitous cliffs on all sides.

"Good," I said again, feeling strangely comforted by her reassurance. I realized that there was a great silly smile on my face. It shouldn't be there. But it would be such an effort to remove it. So I let it stay. My mouth was talking again. I wondered what it would say this time. It said, "No chance of being carried off by the big bird either." I thought that deserved a good laugh, so I laughed, spluttering some of my coffee on the cushions.

"No chance of that," Sister Angeline agreed.

"Good," I said. "Soon I'll be in the inner sanctum, won't I?"

"Oh yes," she answered. "You will be very safe, very well taken care of."

"Good," I said still again. Because it was good to be safe and well taken care of. And it was very good coffee. It was making me feel warm and tingly. But very sleepy. Nicely sleepy. Well, there was nothing wrong with that. I needed the rest.

Sister Angeline must have known that. She was taking the mug out of my hand so it wouldn't spill. That was good too, because my hand was so tired, it could hardly move.

"Here," she said, "you can lean on me if you wish."

I wished. But I asked, "Is it all right?" Because she was a nun, and that meant she was a virgin. A beautiful, friendly, comforting virgin.

"Perfectly all right," she said as she propped me against her shoulder just to make sure I wouldn't fall.

I really should thank her, I thought. But that would take so much work to do. I managed to glance up and move my lips, saying something, I didn't know what. But Sister Angeline understood. She smiled down and drew me closer.

"Will you sing . . . that song?" I asked, not at all sure she understood me. I seemed to be mumbling under my breath. But she knew what I wanted. Above me, she began to croon the sad little song about lovelessness and hard luck and the dark, dark night. I decided that Angeline was exactly the right name for her. She looked like an angel, hovering over me, protecting me. Her eyes were bright and pretty, pretty and bright. And, yes, right behind them, just as everything grew dark and then darker, I could see it. Opening its doors to take me in.

The inner sanctum.

I was there.

Now I could rest

for a long, long time. . . .

30 THE CONQUEROR WORM

Again and again—over the weeks that seem like months, the months that seem like years—I run it past my mind's eye like a movie. Something I watch on an imagined screen still in rough cut, happening to somebody else, not me. Seeing it that way keeps the truth at a merciful distance.

How do I cast myself, the astonished protagonist in this farce *noir*? I try to imagine a nice guy. A really nice guy. Personable, well-intentioned, trusting. Too trusting. All right—dumb. But charmingly so. Like that affable boob Joseph Cotten plays in *The Third Man*. A total innocent fallen among rascals. It's the best face I can put on things.

(The casting makes me reflect . . . in the mental motion picture I've been producing for the last thirty-seven years—*The Jonathan Gates Story*—I seem to have gone from naive youth to naive middle age with remarkably little character development along the way. I begin to think this film needs a script doctor.)

So then . . .

Our hero awakes to find himself alone in a strange bed, in a strange room, in a strange land. He is still weak and dazzled, head pounding, cramps in every joint. How long has he been unconscious? Hours? Days?

What's the last thing he remembers?

Ah yes. The beautiful eyes of a woman gazing down at him, sending him gently on his way to oblivion. Sweet Sister Angeline. The treacherous bitch! Slipped him a Mickey on the road to Albi.

But why?

And where is he now?

Could *this* be the abbey?

He lifts his thundering head and looks around. A room made of rough timbers and bamboo, a low thatched roof overhead, a single window covered with mesh, a few sticks of furniture. Through an open door he sees bright sunlight streaming in. He rises unsteadily to find his clothing drenched with sweat. An oppressive warmth fills the room. He stumbles to the door. Outside it is no better. Sweltering humidity, blinding sun. And nothing in sight but palm trees, fern groves. Beyond that, unbroken ocean, smooth and blue as far as the eye can see. The little cabin where he woke is the only habitation in view.

One thing for sure. This is no abbey, and this isn't Albi.

He walks this way, that way, around the cabin, which perches atop a hill. There is open sea on all sides. He is on an island in a tropic climate. Alone.

Back inside the cabin, exploring, he finds a tiny alcove meant to serve as a kitchen. There is a small sink with a primitive pump attached. He tries the pump; it has been kept lubricated. After several thrusts, water flows, rusty at first, then clear. Beside the sink he finds a grimy hot plate resting atop a miniature refrigerator. Electricity? Yes. Both appliances work. Where does the juice come from, he wonders. He puts the question on hold. Just now, he is more interested in the food he finds. Fruit, chocolate, nuts, some tinned fish. Suddenly thirst and hunger report their presence. Famished, he wolfs down enough to blunt his appetite, but stops when his belly starts to gripe. Against one wall, he finds a water cooler with extra bottles. He drinks. Drinks lots. And then becomes aware of more urgent needs.

Behind a narrow door off the kitchen he finds a closet-sized lavatory. Here too there is a pump—a formidable contraption rising out of the floor, connecting to a high cistern that services a sink, shower, toilet. He rushes to use the toilet. It flushes. Running water. He uses the sink to splash his blazing face and chest. Cold! But there is a propane water heater that can be lit with a match. There are matches. In the mirror above the sink he sees his face for the first time since waking. His eyes are red and glazed, the pupils as small as pinholes. He estimates the growth of beard on his cheeks is at least two days' worth. He looks a sight. He sinks down at the toilet. His belly convulses. He cries like a baby.

So he has been shanghaied. Duped, doped, and shanghaied. The road to Albi has led him to a tropic Alcatraz. At this point, our make-believe movie might use a brief flashback to explain the protagonist's outrageous predicament. But how far back would we need to go? To his first meeting with Dr. Byx? His first visit to St. James School? When did the orphans begin to take a secret hand in his life? At the very least, we would have to go back to Angelotti, that weasel! Devilishly clever, getting at our hero through Clare. Or is it possible the orphans had Clare staked out all along, wondering if she would ever open up on them? Was there always an Angelotti somewhere, tracking her, watching for any threatening move? He feels sick. Not with hunger or fatigue, but with pure disgust, ashamed of his own wraparound gullibility. Walked right into it, eyes wide open.

And now what?

For the next few hours our hero sits depressed and bedraggled on his small stone veranda, drinking an exotic juice, surveying his imprisoning domain. He estimates the island is a few miles wide by

Theodore Roszak

more than a few miles long, trailing off toward a high promontory in the long direction. But for the overgrowth, he might be able to circle the place in a few hours at a moderate jog. The only work of man he can see besides his cabin is a rugged stone breakwater at one end of the island and something that could be a jetty running out from a yellow sandbar several yards into the ocean. He notices that the wires feeding electricity to his cabin run off in that direction. When his strength returns, he decides to explore his territory, beginning with where the wires go.

The hill he is on proves to be higher than he realized—and steeper. There is a dirt path that cuts through the dense foliage, but it is precarious, studded with loose rocks. He stumbles often, slides, must leap and skip. The descent exhausts him, leaving his clothing again sopping with sweat. At last he is again in sight of the jetty. Under the trees at the water's edge, he sees another cabin much like his own—and in front of it a person! A swarthy, youngish woman with bushy black hair, bare to the waist, wearing a ragged skirt. Her dark, narrow eyes are already on him, impassive, not friendly.

Assuming his most winning Joseph Cotten persona, he approaches his female Friday, offers his most winsome "hello," begins to ask all the obvious questions. The woman stares back, unspeaking, then shuffles into the house. Inside, he hears her voice, a language he does not know. He hears another sound from inside. A low mechanical chugging and rasping. The sound of a generator? He notices the wires run to a small shed at the rear; near it, there is a coal pile. The source of the electricity. He notices something more. Above the house, there is a tall metal rod that widens into a kitelike shape. An antenna. There must be a radio inside, a link to the world beyond.

The woman returns, behind her a man who is nearly a foot taller than our hero and easily twice as wide. He is wearing a sort of abbreviated diaper, nothing more. Like the woman, he is dark-skinned, with a shaggy mane of black hair. He looks no friendlier than she does.

"Do you understand English?" our hero asks. *"Français? Deutsch?"* No answer, no answer. Instead, the man steps forward, takes him by the hand and leads him away, not forcibly but firmly, as if he were a naughty child.

"Where are you taking me?" our worried hero cries. But that is already apparent. He is being led back up the path to his cabin. Should he resist? The man towers over him. For that matter, the woman looks robust enough to be intimidating. Our hero follows where he is taken, continuing to jabber questions that elicit no answer.

Is it really possible that these people speak no English? Everybody in the world speaks English. He shouts, demanding an answer, still receives none. The man pulls him over the steep parts of the path and at last deposits him on his veranda with a commanding grunt. No translation needed. *Stay put!*

"You can't do this!" our hero calls after the man until he vanishes away down the hill. "Who's in charge here?" he shouts. By this time, his voice is quavering with enraged humiliation. He is once again weeping.

Later that day, it rains furiously for perhaps an hour. The island steams until evening. As the sun fades into the sea, the woman comes striding up the path, taking long powerful paces, carrying a well-laden wooden tray. Food. A covered bowl containing a fish stew. Bread, hard, but tasty. Unidentifiable fruits. Nuts and figs. She answers no questions, leaves the tray, goes. Our hero eats, sullenly but with good appetite. The food is really excellent, nicely spiced, well balanced. He reflects: a restaurant featuring such cuisine would do very well in Los Angeles.

Los Angeles!

When darkness falls, he spies a point of light by the jetty where the man and woman stay. And he is sure he sees another winking through the trees at the opposite end of the island. His head pounding with weariness and confusion, he sleeps undisturbed by the echoing rush of the waves, the chatter of birds in the trees.

End of day one.

Day two, day three, day four . . . no different. Same heat, same rain. Each day there is a crashing downpour in the afternoon. It starts and stops as if a faucet were being turned on and off in heaven. If our hero did not, like the dungeoned prisoners of fiction, scratch marks in the wall of his cabin, the identical days would begin to blur into an unmeasurable stream. He uses his time to explore his new home, the grounds around it, to venture along the path far enough to spy on the man and woman. This proves to be a boring project. The woman washes clothes in a big tub; the man carries coal to the generator. The man goes fishing in a tiny, primitive boat that he keeps inside the house, never paddling farther out than the break- water. The woman cooks. In the evening, they sit together on their porch. They rarely talk. When they do, it is in the same strange language.

In his cabin, our hero has found his luggage—most of it—stowed beneath his bed. Olga Tell's film is missing, so too his wallet and passport. And of course the sallyrand. It was not an honest gift, only a ploy to win his confidence and send him merrily on his way into captivity. He has hung up his clothes and set out his bathroom supplies as if for a long stay. In the drawer of his single table, he finds pencils (replete with the prints of the previous user's teeth) and paper—a couple of notepads with yellowing pages. He begins a diary (the notes on which this scenario will be based) but with no clear idea of the date. The days simply become day one, day two, day three. And soon, because after all he has no choice, he settles into the simple routine of his Napoleonic exile.

His condition is benign enough. The native couple are his servants, though not obedient to his orders. The woman brings food, launders his clothes, cleans his cabin. Apparently she has been instructed to meet other needs. One afternoon, after a perfunctory sweeping, she removes her skirt, stretches out across the bed, spreads her legs, fixes him with a balefully submissive stare. She needs no language to make the offer. Though none too clean, she is otherwise a reasonably attractive female; but our hero finds nothing arousing in her stolid dutifulness. She understands his refusal, accepts it impassively, leaves with skirt and broom in hand. With the exception of the woman's casual erotic invitation, one day is so much like the next that his diary often remains blank for long intervals. What is there to write after he has filled pages with his anger, fear, self-pity, unanswered questions?

One morning our hero wakes to see a ship anchored inside the breakwater. Well, hardly a ship. An ancient packet boat belching wreaths of sooty smoke. Without a second thought, he rushes off down the path. As he approaches the jetty, he spots two seamen at work unloading barrels, boxes, crates. Supplies from the outside world. The sailors are also of the swarthy native type, shouting to one another in the same lingo the servants use. Our hero makes a dash for the boat, covers several yards of open ground, sets foot on the jetty . . . and goes sprawling, a sharp bar of pain across his shin. He turns over to see the frowning male servant beside him holding a shovel. The man was there, guarding the way, reached out to trip his fleeing charge and bring him down. Now he gestures, pointing sternly back up the hill; our hero retreats, limping, his hands and knees badly scraped by his fall. This is, thus far, his first experience of serious physical coercion. A warning.

The next day a different woman brings breakfast. She is of the same race, speaks the same language, but is a little older, half of the new couple that has taken the place of the other. This rotation scheme will be repeated several times in the weeks ahead. Always a dark-skinned man and woman, the man large, gruff, and intimidatingly strong. None are friendly, none will admit to understanding English. They all do their jobs with the same sullen punctiliousness. At some point, governed for all our hero knows by the phases of the moon, each of the women offers her body and indifferently registers his rejection. Whatever else they may be better or worse at, all guard the harbor steadfastly whenever the supply boat comes—which seems to be every month. But by the time of its fourth arrival, our hero's attention has drifted to the opposite end of the island, where, he has become convinced, there is another inhabitant. He has seen a light there and smoke rising above the trees. And on several occasions, he has seen one or another of the men travel to the promontory by boat, paddling close to shore with a load of parcels and a heap of coal bags. Making a delivery. To whom?

He has tried for some weeks now to explore this region of his domain but made halting progress. Beneath the tropic canopy, the island in that direction is sliced across by two rugged ravines. Through these he has had to pick his way carefully, fighting against abrasive under-growth, stubborn vines. But then, having laboriously cleared a path, he discovers that the promontory which commands that end of the island, is, in effect, a second, smaller, island, a sharp rise in the terrain that is cut off for most of each day by the sea. For a few hours the water recedes, leaving behind a soggy sandbar. The sand is a problem. It is fluid enough to suck the shoes off his feet and then his feet up to the ankle. Our hero hesitates to cross it for fear of getting caught by the tide, trapped by the sand.

He wonders if the unknown inhabitant is another prisoner like himself. If so, he must make contact at all costs. And so, one day, casting away all caution, he races across the sandbar at low tide, sliding and tripping in the viscous muck. The distance is greater than he guessed—perhaps a hundred yards. He calculates he has at most an hour to reconnoiter before the sea cuts him off.

The promontory lifts sharply, then drops away toward the sea. Just over the rise, there is a building, a ramshackle bungalow fashioned from irregular stones. Cautiously peeping inside as he makes his way forward, he notes a table, chairs, a bed, some lamps—furnishings no finer than in his own cramped cabin. Behind the building, from a rough-hewn log shed against the hillside, he hears the chug-chug-chug of a generator. Sacks of coal lean against one outer wall. The shed, he notices, is padlocked. Why? No need to fear burglars in this neighborhood. There are two windows of glass-bottle bottoms cemented in at either side of the door. He looks in, but can see nothing in the dark interior.

Sloping away from the bungalow is a stand of trees neatly spaced and pruned, each tree different, many bearing fruit. An orchard. He steps into the luxuriant grove, looking this way and that. He passes a row of trees, another, another . . . and suddenly, it is as if he has stepped into an Hieronymus Bosch painting. For there, to his left, stands a resplendent tropical tree loaded with great, succulent red blossoms that might be the disembodied sex organs of some unearthly species. And beneath the tree, seen straight on, is a pair of skinny human buttocks wearing a wide-brimmed straw hat. Our hero halts, stares, shifts his position and sees that, of course, the buttocks are attached to a man who is bent over, facing away, scratching at the base of the tree with a rake. The man is naked except for the hat on his lowered head. His skin, stretched taut over his protruding bones, is nut-brown and gleaming under the noonday sun.

Our hero calls out—a good, cheery "Hello there!" The man gives no response. Our hero inches in closer, calls again. No answer. Closer. At last the bending man catches sight of him from the corner of one eye. He cranes his head around effortfully, not the least startled, gazes coolly, then straightens up on creaking limbs. He is old, very old, scrawny and wrinkled from top to bottom. His leathery flesh hangs loose at the breast and loins, but hugs his bones tightly at every joint. Our hero calls out again. The old man cocks his head and squints, gestures earward with one hand and shakes his head. *Can't hear. Deaf.* Then pointing to a small basket of berries at his feet, he mimes the question "Something to eat?"

So this is where all the exotic fruits come from. And this is the gardener, a deaf old man, now grinning somewhat stupidly, revealing a nearly toothless mouth. Our hero steps forward, tries a question or two. No luck. The old guy shrugs and points at his ears, smiling apologetically. It occurs to our hero that by now the tide may be closing in behind him. He waves goodbye, turns, and makes his way rapidly back across the sandbar, which is now ankle deep in swirling brine.

Having found another resident of his island, Robinson Crusoe feels lonelier than ever.

These words were written eight days ago, ten days ago . . . I can't be sure. But here my mock scenario ends. Reality begins—with a jolt. What has happened is too serious a development to allow me to go on playing games. I return to my diary in earnest.

I've been forming habits in my captivity, little routines that help me get through the long, vacuous days. One of these has been to sleep until I hear the sound of my breakfast tray being deposited on the veranda. One or another of the silent native women—there have been four so far in the series, with one repeat—leaves my food there in the early morning, with usually enough to get me through lunch and keep me until dinner is delivered. For prison fare, it is surprisingly good. In truth, I've been eating better and more regularly than in my days of freedom. I can tell that the diet is intended to be wholesome and well balanced. Frequently there are little treats that come as appetizers or desserts. And invariably a generous serving of strange fruits, nuts, berries. Even those I can half recognize are unusual variants of the pears or citrus or bananas I knew in the outside world. These, as my recent explorations have taught me, come from the orchard at the far end of the island, lovingly raised by the decrepit old geezer I encountered there.

Then one morning several days after I had visited the promontory, there was a change. My morning tray arrived as usual, but this time accompanied by a basket piled high with a choice selection of produce. Amid the produce there was a clamshell containing a heap of perfect dates. And among the dates a note. I spotted it at once and snatched it up. It was in English, scratched in a light, unsteady hand. It read: "With my compliments. Please do me the honor to be my guest for dinner any evening soon."

I shook off my drowsiness at once and took off at full tilt after the woman, who was already several yards down the path. As I raced along, I couldn't help but reflect on what an absolute savage this professor of film studies had become in some five months' time. My hair a haystack of uncombed locks, my face wearing the tatters of a

536

badly scissored beard (my electric shaver had proved unpluggable in the only outlet my cabin provided), my sunburned hide half browned and half peeling, my unsheathed penis flapping like an animated sausage against my churning thighs. For I was stark naked. I slept that way now and spent most of each lonely, torrid day not bothering to put on a stitch. Anything I wore would only be sweated through within a quarter hour. What was the point? The women who served me were used to the sight and totally unfazed. They frequently went about their chores unclothed themselves. Oh yes, we were a regular little tropical paradise.

When I caught up with the woman, I waved the note in her face and breathlessly asked her to confirm what I believed. "What? Who? Where?" At last, understanding, she pointed toward the far end of the island. The invitation was from the old man who worked there. Who else? More to the point, I mimed the problem of crossing the waterlogged sandbar. Was there any other way to get to him? This she had, or pretended to have a difficult time grasping. Finally she gestured toward one side of the island and mimed back the action of stepping on stones. I gathered she meant there was more secure ground to that side, though I'd never noticed. When I mimed the possibility of using her man's boat to make my way to the promontory by water, she frowned and gave an emphatic negative wag of the head—as I expected. That way might lie escape.

The note said "any day soon." Why not that very day?

I was on my way to my unexpected soiree well before the dinner hour. By now I'd worked out a reasonably accessible route through the ravines and marked it well. As for the sandbar, I found it already under a half foot of water with the level rising. Following the woman's instructions, I explored the side she'd pointed out and discovered that, after one waist-deep section several paces long, there was indeed a series of boulders and clumps of coral that were only slightly submerged. They hardly provided the most secure footing; I took a few dips negotiating them, but the crossing did prove shorter than others I'd tried. About forty yards out there was an underwater walkway of lichen-covered sandstone that was only knee-deep. I was soon across into the old man's territory.

I found him once again at work, this time betrousered in a pair of shredded dungarees. Seeing me, he smiled his fey, picket-fence grin and doffed his straw hat to reveal a totally bald pate. Before I could approach to offer my hand, he turned and hobbled away into his house. Was I being dismissed? No. In a moment he was back outside, puffing with the strain of his exertion. And now he was wearing a new item of apparel: a necklace whose centerpiece was the tiny black box of a hearing aid wired along the side of his neck and behind his head.

"You see," he said in a dry, wispy voice, "this time my ears are working. Our friends have been good enough to bring me batteries from civilization. I ordered them when you arrived. They came just a few days ago. Ordinarily, there is no need, you see."

It was British English, not American. And too perfect. The sort of English a foreigner learns, though there wasn't the trace of an accent.

Too eagerly I rushed forward to shake his hand. "My name is Jonathan Gates. . . ."

"Yes," he said, as if he knew as much. He gripped my hand limply with fragile fingers. Though my eyes were asking "And you . . . ?" he gave no answer. I pressed for his name. "You're . . . ?"

". . . gard . . ." he mumbled. Something like that.

"Gardener?" I asked. "Mr. Gardener?"

". . . gardener." He gestured to the trees and shrubs.

"You're . . . the gardener?"

"Yes. The gardener," he answered. And nothing more. The small, vague smile he wore began to take on a faintly idiotic contour. Was I perhaps dealing with a senile loony? He turned and led me into the shade of his front porch.

"Are you a prisoner too?" I hastened to ask.

He squinted straight ahead as if the answer might be written on the wall of his bungalow. "Prisoner?" He shook his head. "After all these years . . ."

"You want to be here?"

He gave a why-not? sort of shrug. "It is quite lovely . . . if you don't mind the heat. The heat is good for these old bones." He walked beside me with a gimpy shuffle, still pondering my question. "No, not a prisoner. I wouldn't say so." He spoke with a distracted air, slowly, unfocused. When we reached his veranda, he was breathing hard, ready to rest, but he insisted on offering me his one roughly made cane chair. There was a bowl of fruit on the table; beside it an earthenware jug. From the jug, with unsteady hands, he poured a pinkish juice into a small tin cup and nudged it toward me. "One chair, one cup. One of everything, you see. A solitary life." He eased himself down into a crumpled sitting posture on the board floor, leaned against the railing, and removed his hat from his sweat-beaded brow. "My children . . . I can't take care of them any longer. Poor things."

Oh God, I thought, he *is* a loonybird. "Children?" I asked. He gestured widely out toward the orchard. He was talking about the trees. "My children. Soon they will all go wild. I have not the strength."

"You planted all this? By yourself?"

His eyes narrowed, pondering. "Once there was someone. . . ." Then he fell sadly silent.

If he wasn't a prisoner, then my next question was, "Are you an orphan?" The words burst out, sounding too angry. An accusation.

He stared back at me a long while, then murmured distractedly, "Orphans. Yes. We are all orphans. *Born* orphans."

"I mean Orphans of the Storm. *Sturmwaisen.* Are you one of them? Are you here to guard me?"

"No need of guards. Only those out there who never sleep." He waved toward the sea. "You should be warned. Were you not?"

"Of what?"

He hinged his two hands at the wrist making a jaw-snapping movement.

"Sharks?" I asked. Walking the beaches, I'd several times seen what I thought to be fins moving out to sea. "Nobody told me. Nobody told me anything. I was abducted. Drugged, kidnapped." I could hear the rising note of rage in my voice. I tried to throttle back. "I don't know where I am. Do you? Do you know where this is?"

He stretched out his emaciated arm and plucked a brownish-orange fruit from the bowl on the table. "This is . . . ?" he asked, turning the fruit in his hand. Again, I began to fear he might be a crazy man.

"A fruit," I answered. "A mango, isn't it?"

He held up an instructive finger. "*Mangifera ameranta.* A rare species. It thrives only within a narrow band of islands in the western Indian Ocean."

He replaced the mango and gazed toward the horizon. "At night, the Southern Cross appears just there, very low. I believe we are somewhere near the Seychelles. That way . . . or that way. My teeth tell me about five hundred miles distant."

"Your teeth?"

He opened his mouth wide to show me two higgledy-piggledy rows of decaying dentition. "Three times when I had a toothache, a doctor

came by seaplane. Also a nurse. I judge from the time involved—
once it took them only a few hours to make the trip—that they are
stationed somewhere nearby. Two hours by plane . . . five hundred
miles? This is a sensible estimate, you believe? They don't always
come so promptly. My advice: don't get sick."

"But how did this doctor know you needed him?"

"There is a radio down by the jetty. The caretakers use it." When
he saw an eager look flash across my face, he cautioned me. "The
radio is kept under lock and key. Always guarded. I did my best to
get at it years ago. No success."

"But the doctor—wouldn't he help you?"

"He was a priest from the church. The nurse was a sister. They
were under orders to say nothing, except to ask where it hurts. Of
course, each time they came, I appealed to them to let me go free.
It does no good. But they have sent me books and other small favors."

"Then you *are* a prisoner."

"I have stopped thinking of it that way. A compulsory guest, I
would say. Well cared for. I have no complaints."

"How long have you been here?"

He shrugged. "No way to tell." He smoothed the air between us
with his hand. "Here the time, it is so flat. Like a desert. Endless
sand. No landmarks. No way to tell the distance. We have no seasons.
Nothing to count. Only day and night. Soon one loses track."

I noticed that he didn't ask me for any better date than he may
have had in mind. I volunteered the information. "It's 1976. July
when I arrived." But then I wondered: hadn't that been months and
months ago? "Possibly 1977 now."

He nodded, taking the information carefully into account. "I
thought later than that."

I asked, "What's the last thing you remember from the outside?"

"A war. There was a war."

"Which war?"

"Have there been more since then?"

"Since when? Who was fighting?"

He smiled bitterly. "All the civilized nations. But not your people
yet. The Americans. They had not gone to war yet."

"Against whom?"

He knitted his face into a mock scowl, held three fingers slanted
down over one eye like a lock of hair, held a finger of the other hand
under his nose like a mustache. "Him."

"Hitler? You're talking about the Second World War?"

"There have been more?"

"That was over thirty years ago! You've been here since then? My God! Have you ever tried to get away?"

He gestured to the sea, then again made jaws of his hands. "No way to escape. Believe me. It has been tried."

"By whom?"

He pondered the memory deeply before he answered. "You aren't my first companion. There was a young German—younger than you. A student. Albrecht. Lovely fellow. We became great friends. He built a raft." His voice trailed off as he remembered.

"What happened?"

He held out his hand and turned it in a slow flip-flop: the raft being capsized, I gathered. "There," he said, pointing at the sea just off the nearest bit of shore. "The water turned red. The last of Albrecht." Then, brightening, he added, "He was a great help with the garden . . . and other things."

"Don't ships ever come?" I asked.

"We aren't on the sea lanes here. A few times small boats have come inside the breakwater. It's difficult to land anyplace else. Only passersby. The caretakers shooshed them away before I could cross the island."

"Have there been others here—besides Albrecht?"

He nodded. "A Frenchwoman. She was my first companion. She was sent soon after the war. But she was quite ill. She didn't last long, poor thing."

"The orphans let her die?"

"I think it was the caretakers' fault. They didn't send for the doctor in time. Perhaps they thought she was faking."

I waited for his eyes to come back to me, tried to fix him, drill the question in. "Why are you a prisoner?"

"For the same reason as yourself," he answered calmly.

I stared hard into his old, vague face. Almost afraid to ask, I asked nonetheless. "What do you know about me?"

He rose on unsteady legs and shambled into his bungalow, beckoning me to follow. I did. The building was smaller than I'd estimated, but extraordinarily cool inside. There were thick walls coated with a syrupy white plaster coating that held out the heat. As I'd seen from the outside, there was little more in the way of furniture than an easy chair, a table, a desk, a bed. But something I hadn't sighted through the window took my eye at once: a bookcase, packed full, against one wall. I stared across at it hungrily. Books! Dozens of them. Little of what I could see looked new; many of the volumes bore antique bindings and had the appearance of non-English editions. Even so, I offered up a silent prayer of thanks. I'd have something to read.

The old man sank down at his desk wearily and pushed a mound of disorderly papers toward me. A few pages fluttered to the floor joining others there. It was a typescript, though I could see no type-writer in the room. The uppermost pages were filled with penciled notes along the margins and between the lines, a weak, crabbed hand too small to make out, though I could tell the words weren't English. The notes caught my eye before the text did. Then, looking across the pages, I realized. It was *my* work, a copy of *my* manuscript. There was the title page: "The Hollywood Years." *My book. Here.* On this old codger's desk. Passages circled, scratched out, words underlined. His comments everywhere. In (now I saw) German.

I looked up. His eyes were on me. *"Auch ich wusste zu viel."*

And the truth collapsed on me with the force of a mountain. What should have been self-evident. The last thing I could have imagined. The unthinkable obvious.

When my head cleared, I found myself bent above the table, strug-gling to hold my knees solid under me. The daze couldn't have lasted more than a few moments, but it was time enough for him to cross and take me by the shoulders. Not that he had the strength to steady me. He walked me to his bed and sat me down. "I will make some tea," he said soothingly and moved into a small adjoining room. Wait-ing, I found my mind subsiding into a comalike blankness. A hundred questions to ask but none I cared to voice. Instead, I felt only de-spairingly sick. For him. For myself. What I most wanted to do was to scream with sheer fury like a caged animal in useless protest. Thirty-five years he'd been here. Is that what they had in mind for me? *They.* Of whom I'd met no more than some half dozen face to face, the rest a shadowy throng I would never know. Who were *they* to do this to me?

When he returned, I asked, "Since 1941? Has it been all that time?" He nodded, handing me some lukewarm tea in the same tin cup. "How did you . . . can you stand it?" Asking the question, I felt the tears coming. Rage. Self-pity.

He reached out to stroke my shoulder, an authentically caring gesture. "The first five years are the worst. After that . . . it becomes unreal. Of course, for me everything was at an end. Nowhere to turn. Why not here? I came to think of it as . . . retirement. Yes, a comfortable retirement. There was a great deal to keep me busy. The garden. It was already planted, but in need of much care. And the house—it was a wreck when I came. Albrecht helped me make repairs. And I found other ways to pass the time."

His tired old voice had grown thick with a muzzy resignation that was starting to suffocate me. Perhaps he was prepared to accept his lifelong incarceration, but not me. It was absurd! "They wouldn't dare keep me here that long!" I blurted out. "Not for the rest of my . . ." And then choking on the words, I fell silent. At once my mind began to dart this way and that, contemplating escape. Not now, but someday. A plan would emerge as new opportunities presented themselves. The packet boat. I would find some way to swim out to it, hang from the anchor chain. Isn't that what people did in novels I'd read, films I'd seen? Hang from the . . . But what about the sharks? No. Fight my way on board. Steal the ship. Take off at full speed. Which way? Oh God, I had no idea about directions. For that matter, I had no idea how to pilot a ship. Hopeless.

Watching me, he must have read my thoughts. Again he patted my shoulder. "Perhaps one day you will find a way." There wasn't much conviction in his words. "You have more reason than I."

A pause set in, a silence of prisoners that might last forever. Finally, having nothing better to say, I asked, "Where did you get my manuscript?"

"It was sent. Soon after you arrived. By the next boat. I believe it was meant for you. The caretakers delivered it to me. I took the liberty. . . . Forgive me. I found it diverting. The first reading I've done in years. I've made some corrections, as you see. Things you couldn't know. It may amuse you."

"Sent from where?"

"From New York."

"By whom?"

"One of the brothers. He sends things from time to time."

"Angelotti? Is that his name?"

"Brother Eduardo, yes. We've never met. You know him?"

"I know him. I'm here because of him."

"Ah! And, I fear, because of me."

"It's hardly your fault."

"But you liked my movies so much. If you hadn't . . ."

543

"Yes, if I hadn't . . ."

He sighed. "Pity. They weren't very good movies, you know." It wasn't false modesty. He meant what he said. I didn't feel like arguing the point. He mused on. "I never thought a day would come, these little amusements of mine would be studied so closely. Griffith, Eisenstein, I could understand. Dreyer . . ."

"Everything gets studied now," I told him. "All the classics."

"But my things, such nonsense they were. People like them?"

"You're what is called a cult phenomenon. First you're a cult, then you're a classic."

He chuckled dryly. "Cult!"

"Along with Buster Keaton, the Marx Brothers, Fred Astaire."

"Hoot Gibson," he added, his soundless laughter deepening.

"You didn't know about all this? Film culture?"

"A little, a little. They send me books, our friends. Sometimes magazines. After a while, one loses interest. What is the point, after all? There was something a long time ago . . . Nouvelle Vague. By now, no doubt, Vieille Vague."

"Yes. Late fifties."

"About that time I stopped keeping track. *Mise en scène*, montage . . . it seemed such nonsense, especially from this distance. Brother Eduardo sent me your brochure from the Museum of Modern Art. My retrospective. I remember that."

"It was your rediscovery."

"You found so many of my things! I thought they would be scrapped."

"Many were."

He cocked his head inquisitively. "There was something in the brochure. At the back. An announcement. Another series. Hitchcock. They study Hitchcock?"

"He's very highly regarded."

He rasped out his dry little laugh. "Amazing. Hitchcock."

"A definite classic."

"Amazing. Such a boor he was, that man. Quite deranged. The thing about the blond women. Very sad. If I had been given just half the money he . . ." Then, catching himself, he fell silent. "That's the first time in years I've thought such a thing. I had hoped all that was behind me." He wagged his finger at me in a half-serious reprimand. "You are a bad influence on me."

Theodore Roszak

That night we talked late, rambling on and on in the tropic darkness, following wherever his curiosity and ragged attention took us. He was fascinated to know how I'd reconstructed so much of his career, the shreds and fragments I'd collected here and there over the years. The story of his *Judas Everyman,* its hairbreadth escape from obliteration, amazed him, though he remembered the film only dimly as a flawed and abandoned effort. As for his later B-movies, he showed some embarrassment at their mention. He regarded them all as gravely compromised works done only to keep him financially afloat. I told him how Zip Lipsky had tried to burn them on his funeral pyre; he told me he wished the little man had succeeded. "So much better for you if he had done it. I would have gone up in a puff of smoke. And you could now be safely at the university studying . . . Hitchcock." We talked at length about Zip. "A great natural talent. A perfect eye." Sadly, he confessed, "I didn't always treat him well. Still, I gave him his chance, didn't I?" He lit up to hear about Olga Tell, pleased to know she remembered him fondly. "And she kept the film I gave her! For so many years. She was the most beautiful girl."

In the course of the early evening, he managed to assemble a modest repast for us. Cheese, fruit, berries, nuts, a creamy coconut pudding, a highly spiced vegetable broth. I gathered it was the diet he lived on. Meager fare. Still he was, for his age, agile enough to meet his own needs and tend his garden: all in all, a wiry vital old guy. We ate from a single plate, sharing the tin cup, a fork, a spoon, a knife. One of everything, including a single wineglass from which we sipped our brandy, he quite a bit more than I. He seemed well supplied with drink. I caught sight of a couple of still unopened bottles in a cabinet. There was but one dope pipe as well. That came out toward midnight, with a small canister of hashish. I wasn't yet in the market for the habit; I let him puff away alone.

I did most of the talking that evening, though with less and less certainty that I was getting through to him as the liquor and hash began to take effect. His attention would come and go like clouds blowing across the sky. At times, I had the disturbing sense that I was in the presence of incipient senility, a growing mental vacuum where my words sank into uncomprehending blackness. But then, he would brighten, smile gently, make some remarkably sharp observation. I could only conclude that much of what I had to say bored him, things he'd lived beyond caring about. Finally, sometime well past midnight as I judged, he slipped into a deep, snoring snooze. Outside, in the silence, the strange night birds I never managed to see took over the conversation, chattering and warbling into the wee hours.

Still wakeful myself, I crossed the room to check his bookcase. There were three shelves of books on horticulture, natural history, geography. These seemed the most used of his books, the bindings cracked, the pages dog-eared. Beyond that, there was a collection of German literary classics, Grimm's fairy tales, E. T. A. Hoffmann. Old editions, dust-covered. There was exactly one book on film: Kracauer's *From Caligari to Hitler*. But then what did one of the century's greatest directors need with film studies? There were some Gnostic gospels and Cathar tracts. Like his German literature, these volumes were well along the way to acquiring a patina of dust and mold. The only English works I could see were anthologies of Verne and Conrad, W. H. Hudson's *A Crystal Age*, Bulwer-Lytton's *Zanoni*, a few Raymond Chandler paperbacks . . . and mercifully, a collection of S. J. Perelman which I decided at once to borrow. The only comic relief in sight from here to eternity.

On the pillow of his bed lay an open book face down. The works of Poe, copiously annotated. The volume was stuffed with scribbled sheets of paper. I couldn't make out the German chicken scratching, but I could tell what I was looking at. A collection of pencil-drawn movie-screen squares, each filled with an exquisitely delicate little sketch. A storyboard in the making. Mental movies. The best the old boy could manage with pencil and paper in his solitary confinement. Sad, sad.

I dropped down on the bed and, having nothing better to do, began to read where he'd left off. The last stanza of a poem.

> *Out—out are the lights—out all!*
> *And over each quivering form,*
> *The curtain, a funeral pall,*
> *Comes down with the rush of a storm,*
> *And the angels, all pallid and wan,*
> *Uprising, unveiling, affirm*
> *That the play is the tragedy "Man,"*
> *And the hero the Conqueror Worm.*

I'd never been able to take Poe seriously; as horror fiction, time had brought his work to the borders of campiness. But that night, lost as I was up some blind alley of the universe never to be found, his Gothic elegy turned the tropic night cold about me. The shadows of the room closed in like a fist of bone. I listened, chilled, to my host's labored snore, an old, old man struggling to suck the thick air into his frail and failing lungs. So this was how he read himself to sleep, doting on images of death and decay. He was an Orphan of the Storm all right, even in his exile and disgrace.

Suddenly feeling claustrophobic, I wandered onto the porch, snatching up the bottle of brandy that stood open on the table as I passed. The air, though warm and heavy, was fragrant with the flowering of the old man's garden. The pungent odors of fertility momentarily chased away the morbid images of the poem. I plumped down on the steps and took a few swigs from the bottle. Studying the stars at the horizon, I picked out the Southern Cross where he said it would be. So that was south. I'd learned that much today. Not the way to go, if I ever got the chance to sail away. Next stop in that direction was—my God!—Antarctica. My heart gave a tremor. I was staring out over the edge of the earth. I took another mouthful of brandy and stretched out on the floorboards, my thoughts filled with the contemplation of cold stars, glacial landscapes. Dante believed that the core of hell is ice. As far as you can get from the fire of divine love.

When I woke, the dawn was a thin veil of light across the sky. A familiar chatter—hungry and pugnacious birds—cluttered the morning with song here as it did at my end of the island. A bit stiff but sufficiently rested, I rose and looked back into the bungalow. My host was still snoring away where I'd left him, slumped in his chair. I decided to let him enjoy his lingering dope dreams. But before departing, I gathered up the scattered remnants of my manuscript to take away. It was *my* work, after all. Probably there were dozens of pages missing, but what difference did that make? I used my belt to package the manuscript and set off for home.

I decided to let several days pass before I visited again. There was no rush. The company of my aged cellmate was hardly exhilarating. In fact, it was spooky—to be accepting the hospitality of a dead man. Something to be taken in small doses, especially if I had another ten, twenty, thirty years to spend with him. ("Them orphans," I remembered Zip Lipsky saying, "they live forever.") What a thought! Besides, I had something to busy myself with: my manuscript. I reassembled it, discovering there were only fifteen pages missing—probably lying around his bungalow—and began to comb through his notes. His handwriting was almost a code—and in German yet. Even if it had been English, I doubt I could have deciphered more than half of what he'd written. But I could understand enough to learn how much I'd overlooked or gotten wrong.

There was a ton of commentary on the inside politics of the early German movie studios and their many hidden connections with the orphans. What he had to say on that topic alone would have been a revelation of the highest order—if the tale could ever be told to the outside world. Most of it had to do with *Judas Everyman;* there was more behind the film than I'd realized. It was begun by all concerned with high hopes. Even after the failure of *Simon the Magician,* UFA gamely went ahead with *Judas,* fully intending to make it the great expressionist epic of the era. Quite a vote of confidence in its young director. The film was to be the orphans' supreme bid for mass influence. The poet Rilke was to write the titles—in verse; Alban Berg was commissioned to produce a special orchestral score for the premiere. As for the sets and lighting—I'd always wondered who was responsible for designing this grisly little masterpiece; now I found out. It was the celebrated sick-Gothic fantasist Alfred Kubin. Offhand, I couldn't recall when a comparable collection of talent had been put to work on a movie. And to think the project was entrusted to a youth not yet twenty-five years old. But then the orphans, at that early stage of film history, expected their director to do little more than play traffic cop on the set. And take orders from his elders in the church. That wasn't what happened.

Instead, their star pupil turned out to be a spoiled-brat-genius who wanted to make his own movie in his own way. The result was two years of aesthetic warfare over every detail of the film. He remembered the episode now as his first serious clash with the orphans, who found the movie too purely "artistic" for their tastes, too short on doctrinal teachings. They demanded changes he wouldn't make. Finally, they quashed the project and served notice that he was expected to return to the cheap sensationalism of his Grave Robber period, formula films that could be more easily freighted with approved themes and imagery. It was a prophetic encounter, his earliest realization that the orphans, who had trained him and who dominated so much of the film industry around him, had no essential interest in art, much less in autocratic directors who wanted to set their own priorities. More than anything else, this falling out over the *Judas* made him decide to leave for America, where he hoped to find more latitude for his talents.

The same grievance ran through his comments on *The Martyr,* which filled the backs of eight pages of my manuscript. I couldn't make out more than every third word of what he'd written, but the slash and thrust of his handwriting on the page would have been enough to make his feelings clear. Anger, outrage, insult. The old wound still bled beneath the scab. He claimed any number of innovations for the film, remembering it as the only movie spectacle that could be said to possess artistic merit. Of course he was free to attribute all the excellence he could imagine to footage that had been destroyed a half century before.

It was interesting to me to learn that the orphans had done more to scuttle the movie than MGM; their influence in the American studios could be that great. The issue was the same: a demand for changes he wouldn't agree to make even when the orphans threatened to disown him. Which they soon did, providing less and less support as he slid into the shadow zone of Hollywood. The relationship remained cruelly ambiguous for the next several years, the orphans offering minor stipends, marginal connections, always seeming to promise that, in return for good behavior and submissive cooperation, they might rehabilitate his dwindling reputation.

Meanwhile, he carried on as best he could, smuggling small measures of quality into the shoestringers he found himself directing. He admitted to taking some pride in a few of these efforts. There were lengthy comments attached to my analysis of the *Count Lazarus* films; they detailed all that I'd missed, in some cases referring to scenes or shots I couldn't remember seeing. Perhaps he was making it up or his memory had, over the years, embroidered this distant work with fantasies that never found their way into film. Most intriguing of all, I came across mention of several films he claimed to have directed under other names: not his own, not Maurice Roche. And others still on which he assisted without credit. A few of these—Karl Freund's *Mummy*, Paul Leni's *The Cat and the Canary*, Edgar Ulmer's *Black Cat*—I already knew about. They were minor classics of their genre— "trash classics," as Sharkey would have called them. Others—*Casino*

549

Lady, Swamp Creature, Murder Thumbs a Ride—couldn't claim that much distinction. What hell it must have been for him to sink his talents in such wretched stuff.

One point that jarred. I kept coming upon references to movies that had appeared *since* his captivity; usually these arose in connection with innovations he claimed to have anticipated in his films. The French director Georges Franju seemed to be his special hangup. He was convinced Franju had learned all his more macabre touches from him—and that was a distinct possibility. Only how did he know about Franju's films of the late forties and fifties? Moreover, he was convinced that by way of Franju he'd influenced two or three of the New Wave directors of the sixties—and he knew their work in remarkable detail down to specific scenes and shots. It was more than he could have learned from the occasional newspaper or journal Angelotti sent his way. This was something we'd have to discuss.

So now at last I had my definitive study of the great director, supplemented by his own posthumous commentary. Never to see print, unless I should be given a reprieve by my captors. Or escape. Or be rescued. Would any of the above ever happen? I spent nights turning the question over in my mind, wondering if anyone was looking for me. *Anyone.* I confess that more than once I collapsed into tears of self-pity, bawling like an abandoned child. Could I have simply burst and vanished into thin air like a soap bubble? And nobody cared? My parents, my colleagues, my students, above all Clare . . . weren't any of them trying to find me?

Of course that depended on how well the orphans had covered up my abduction. I now knew they had some experience at this sort of thing. I wasn't the first or even the second prisoner to roam this island.

One evening I brought the matter up with my partner in captivity. Was my case hopeless, I asked. To my surprise, he brightened up at once and began to rehearse my plight far too zealously. He wanted to hear every detail of my trip to Europe right up to the point of my disappearance. When I'd gone back over the ground for him a second and third time, he clapped hands and said, "Ah, you see. Your trail goes cold as soon as you arrive at the airport in Zurich."

"It does?"

"Did you tell anyone where you would go when you left the airport?"

"No."

Theodore Roszak

"Then, you see, from the moment you arrive in the city, you are entirely in the hands of your abductors, yes? A private limousine, a private plane. You are a very trusting person."

He meant it kindly, but I felt like such a fool. "Wouldn't somebody have a record? The authorities . . . at the airport in Toulouse?"

"Did they check your papers?"

I reached back into my memory. "No. They waved everybody through."

"So? What record would there be? Who could tell where you landed? Who knows you took off?"

"But people don't just vanish. I have parents, friends who would demand an investigation."

"From whom? The Swiss? The French? Who would be responsible?"

"Well . . . *somebody.*"

A sly look came over his face. "Of course, they might have provided for a body. Do you still have your papers with you?"

"No. My passport, my wallet . . . when I woke, they were gone. You don't mean they'd murder somebody to have a body."

"Nothing so crude. Besides, it is against our religion. If not, they might just as well have killed you. Or me. With enough money, there are ways to procure a body. And then, let us see . . . a car is found, crashed and burned, the body mutilated, even the teeth, eh? But your papers manage to survive intact." He stopped short, frowning with thought. "I have often wondered—was 'my' body ever found?"

"No body," I told him.

"No body." He seemed mildly miffed by the information. "And no one ever came looking?"

"Well, it was wartime, so much confusion. You were reported missing at sea. Torpedoed off the coast of Spain. Were you?"

"Was I what?"

"Torpedoed."

"Only by a glass of schnapps. I never boarded the ship. I was met in Algiers by a delegation of two of my fellow religionists sent to escort me to Zurich by private plane. Such a generous offer. We downed a few snifters. The next thing, I find myself on this island paradise."

"Coffee," I said. "With me it was a cup of coffee on the road to Albi."

"Ah yes." After a moment of frowning reflection, he resumed his line of speculation. "And then perhaps they arrange to have someone

551

impersonate you. One of the brothers, someone of your age and build. He checks into a hotel in Toulouse, carefully calling attention to himself so he will be remembered. The next day he announces that he plans to take a hike. He asks directions, he hires a car, he leaves for the day . . . and never returns. The car is found parked in rough terrain outside of town. The country in those parts can be quite rugged. One could easily get lost. There is a search; they find nothing." He thought that one over for a while, then shook his head. "But why draw attention to Toulouse, so close to Albi? Perhaps the imposter, with your papers, heads in another direction entirely. Germany, Italy . . . he sends a few postcards in a forged hand to dear friends. A false trail. And then he does his disappearing act."

This was more than he'd said on any subject since my arrival, and all of it with such relish. I finally realized why. He was making up scenarios, one, two, three, four of them, turning my sad plight into a cheap thriller. The experience, so diverting for him, left me depressed for days afterward. It served to show me: there were a dozen ways I could have been erased from the face of the earth. I had only one hope to cling to. Clare. When she learned I'd vanished on a trip to Zurich, surely *she* would suspect the worst. Good old Clare! She'd come through for me. She'd find a way to track me down. She'd be relentless.

And then there came the day when that last slender hope died, suddenly, totally, almost too cruelly to be remembered.

From time to time—unpredictably and with no particular logic—I receive missives from the outside world. Newspapers, magazines, always months out of date, arrive—usually the day after the supply ship makes its call. One of the women drops the material on my veranda when she brings my breakfast. Somebody's idea of a kindness, I gather. Perhaps Angelotti—though there's never a note attached. The publication might be American or French, English or German. Whatever it is, why ever it was sent, I read it avidly, every page, every word, lingering over it as long as possible, drawing out the pleasure, and then reading it again from first to last.

On the day in question—two weeks into the eleventh month of my captivity (I was at the time still marking the days)—I woke to discover a book beside my breakfast tray, a much-handled paperback with a broken binding. The title: *This Is Where I Came In.* The subtitle: *Infantile Obsessions and Premature Senility in Contempo-*

rary Film Culture. The author: Clarissa Swann. Still another collection of her reviews and essays; there had been three before this.

I felt myself flush with gratitude and anticipation. I turned the precious little volume over and there, as I hoped, was a photo of Clare staring out at me, looking sharp and smart and sexy. It brought on the tears, blurring my vision so that I couldn't read the cover copy for several seconds. As my eyes cleared, they fell haphazardly upon the text before them, as if I were reading through a blowing cloud.

> . . . last book . . . sorely missed . . . prepared for publication before the author's still unexplained disappearance . . . stands as a fitting tribute to the memory of America's most acclaimed film critic . . . her many fans will not soon forget . . .

I was leaping and racing over the words, trying to devour them all at once, rereading before I'd read once through. Finally I got the meaning. They were saying this was Clare's *last book.* "Last" in the sense of final, in the sense of never another. And why? Because Clare had "disappeared," was gone, was no more.

My hands, tightening on the book, were twisting it out of shape, trying to wring more out of what I'd read there. Quickly, I turned to the preface. It was a brief piece by Arlene Fleischer of the Museum of Modern Art that did little more than lavish praise on Clare. There were only two phrases that half answered the questions raging in my head. One referred to Clare's "tragic disappearance in a boating accident last summer." The other located the accident as having taken place "just after she had attended a film festival in Sydney, Australia." That was all. Boating accident. What kind of boat? What kind of accident? And why "disappearance," not death? Presumably because no body had been found.

In pure frustration I wanted to scream. I did scream, a long, miserable howl of hurt and fury. I had no doubt, none whatever, that Clare had suffered the same fate I had. Lost at sea, but not drowned. Imprisoned. Somewhere in a place like this. How could it have happened? Why was she sailing to Sydney? My God! The world cruise! Her husband the yachtsman. Had it happened on her honeymoon? Was her new husband, like Angelotti, an orphan in disguise, lying in ambush? I knew what film festival this was. It would have taken place the previous August, three months after Clare set to sea. That made the time about right. She could have stopped over in Australia, attended the festival, boarded her yacht, sailed away . . . and vanished.

One question hammered insistently inside my skull. *Had it happened because of me?* Because Clare was an inconvenient loose end in my story? Because the orphans feared she'd come looking for me, make trouble, spill the beans? Oh God, oh God! I had (effectively) killed the woman I loved.

After that morning, my wretchedness lasted for days. It never went away, but simply settled in, a permanent condition of guilt and grief that hurt less only when I became numb with pain. Often I fell asleep exhausted from weeping, Clare's name on my lips repeated again and again. But the weeping wasn't just for her. Whatever her fate might be, I knew her disappearance made my captivity a life sentence. Nothing ahead of me but one day as lost and hopeless as the last.

And finally . . . the Conqueror Worm.

31 PALEOLITHIC PRODUCTIONS PRESENTS . . .

It was over a month before I paid another visit to the far end of the island. Since I could hardly go there seeking consolation for the sad news about Clare, what was the point of going at all? Nothing awaited me there but the senile shell of a once possibly great film director, who, when he was in his prime, Clare had warned me to avoid as a force of pure evil. Perhaps I wouldn't have gone back for months more, had I not stepped out on my veranda one morning to see a column of jet-black smoke rising from what I took to be the site of his bungalow. Had the old fool set his house on fire?

I made my way across the island as rapidly as I could, struggling through the thicket of undergrowth that was forever renewing itself in the ravines. Just as I cleared the semisubmerged sandbar, the wind shifted enough to blow a few whiffs of smoke toward me. I stopped in my tracks as if I'd run into a wall of glass. The acrid chemical odor was unmistakable. Burning film. But, my God! it would take a truckload of the stuff to make that much smoke. What was happening?

I clambered over the rise and came within sight of the bungalow. No sign of damage there. The smoke was issuing from another source: a rock-lined pit off to one side of the house. I'd noticed it before but never bothered to investigate. I assumed it was for burning garbage. There was no fire in sight above the rim now, only a few wisps of gray vapor gusting up. And there he was, his back to me, squatting down beside the pit, rocking on his heels. He was wearing no more than his straw hat and a tattered loincloth. At his side was a wheelbarrow; like all the rest of his gardening equipment, it was rusted and broken down. Without looking, he reached back into it and drew out what looked like a tangled handful of shiny black snakes. It was film stock cut into strands and coils. He casually cast it into the smoldering hole. There was a brief flash of flame, then a puff of black smoke ascending. A moment later, he threw in another fistful.

Even with his back toward me, I saw he wasn't wearing his hearing aid, so he couldn't hear me approach. When I got closer, I heard him whistling to himself, a dry breathy little tune. "Bye Bye Blackbird." Not wanting to startle him, I slowly circled around to come into his view. When he caught sight of me, he gave an unexpectedly cheery greeting. Then, at once pointing to his ears, he indicated that his hearing aid was in the bungalow. I signaled him to stay put and went to fetch it. I found it lying atop several rumpled pages of my manuscript that he must have found about the house since my last visit. These I folded and stuck into my shirt pocket.

As he worked to plug the hearing aid into his head, I asked, "What the devil's going on here?"

"I hope the batteries still work," was his answer as he fiddled with the little device.

I asked again, "What are you doing? Where did this film come from?"

This time I was sure he heard me, but, still adjusting his earplug, he pretended he hadn't. Instead he gazed at me with his gap-toothed semismile and asked where I'd been for so long.

"New York, Paris, Rome, the Riviera," I answered. "I returned when I got homesick. What have you been doing here?"

He noticed the typed pages in my shirt. "You took the book with you last time."

"It *is* mine."

"Yes, of course."

"There are still some pages missing," I informed him, as if it really mattered.

He nodded apologetically. "So sorry. Did you find my comments helpful?"

I said I had. "I'll be sure to include them before the book goes to press."

He couldn't mistake the bitterness in my voice. He reached up to pat my arm. "One day, you will leave here."

He meant to be comforting, but his grandfatherly tone made the words sound condescending. I wagged my head disconsolately. "No, I won't. I lost my one best chance." And then, though I'd decided not to, I told him about Clare. The story spilled out in a stream of anger.

He listened patiently until I was finished. "Clarissa Swann. I know this name. I've seen reviews by her in the American papers they send me sometimes."

"I'm sure they've kidnapped her."

He nodded gravely. "Very likely. The others that were here, they knew less than she did. Yet even that was too much. The French-woman had only interviewed me once. Before the war. Perhaps I was somewhat indiscreet with her; I was quite angry at the time. But there was no need to send her here."

His words sparked an old memory. "What was her name, the Frenchwoman?"

He wagged his head, unable to remember. "Geneviève . . . ?"

"Geneviève Joubert?"

"Ah yes."

"I looked for her in Paris a few years ago. People said she was dead. You mean they kidnapped her because of that one interview?"

"Afterward, when the war ended, she went digging a little deeper. She met a crazy old Jesuit. You know about Oculus Dei?"

"Rosenzweig?"

"Yes. He used to write me letters threatening to kill me. Imagine! She got too interested in what he told her. Still, she could have done no harm. It was cruel to bring her here. Cruel." He must have known how madly curious I was about the film he'd been burning, but when I asked again, he continued to ignore the question. "I'm sorry about your friend Clare." It was a touching remark sincerely intended. "She

556

was a very fine writer. Too good to be a critic really. Such a parasitic trade! Film critics . . . who reads them?"

That irked. I couldn't keep myself from putting in a good word for Clare and her "trade." "She believed criticism has a high moral purpose." He emitted a superior little smirk that irritated me still more. "For example, she regarded you as an unhealthy influence on film."

He raised a curious eyebrow. "Unhealthy?"

"Evil, in fact." *Take that! Score one for Clare.*

He clucked under his breath indulgently. "There are so few who understand evil. It is bound to be shocking when we tell what we know. Most people would prefer to think of evil as a small, superficial blemish. Nothing permanent, nothing that *has* to be. An occasional cloud that passes across the sun. But no. It is the equal of the sun. It is the whole black night, in fact. You know the phrase—'an act of God.' Ah, but *which* god? It is very odd. In the church, they didn't believe I took evil seriously enough. They said I *played* with it for the aesthetic effect. But how else to teach its power to nonbelievers?" He mused upon the thought to himself for several moments. "But perhaps Miss Swann was right. My treatment of evil was very narrow, very sober. I never saw the humor there—like Browning, you know, with his freaks."

Humor? In Todd Browning's *Freaks*? I'd seen the movie only once, and left partway through, fighting down nausea. I let the remark slip by unqueried, allowing a punctuating silence to settle in. As he well knew, there was another matter on my mind. Namely, the smoldering fire pit at our feet. I kicked a few pebbles into it and then asked more emphatically, "Now will you tell me what you're doing here?"

He smiled slyly. "Smoke signals. I hoped they would bring you— if you were still here to see them. I missed your company. I wondered if they had taken you away. So I decided to incinerate some excess stock."

"Don't you know how dangerous it is to burn film?"

"Yes, yes, yes. But what can I damage here that matters? I wouldn't care if the whole island went up in flames. For me, worse than the danger, I hate the stink. I used to wait until I could see a ship or a plane. I hoped the smoke would attract attention. It never did."

"But where did you get all this?"

"Where else? From our friendly jailers. Every supply ship brings me at least a few films. Once there were sixty-five in one delivery. Nazi propaganda, all of it. So many scenes of *der Führer* receiving flowers from children. What do you suppose he did with all those flowers?"

"You mean to say you have some way to show these films?"

"If there is electricity, all one needs is a projector and a blank wall."

Without another word, he shuffled away toward the bungalow, more sprightly in his step than he'd ever been before. I followed. But we didn't enter the house; we went around it to the generator shed that stood against the hillside. Inside I could hear the machine chugging away. The door was still padlocked as it had been when I paid my first visit.

"Why bother?" I asked as he took hold of the lock. "Afraid of burglars?"

He chuckled. "Afraid of *you*—when you first arrived. After all, what did I know about you? I was simply told that I had a companion. I didn't want you snooping."

"Told? By whom?"

"Our faithful native retainers. Oh yes, they speak our language. French, English. It took me years to find this out." He gave the rusty old lock a couple of tugs and it opened with a creak. "Anyway, it was only a dummy." He threw the lock into the nearby shrubs, pushed open the door, and felt in the air for the string that turned on the one bare bulb hanging from the ceiling. Waving me inside, he said, "Welcome to Paleolithic Productions. I will guide your tour personally."

What I'd mistaken for a mere shed turned out to be the facade of a longish tunnel that had been dug into a shallow cave in the hillside. All the walls, including the rough natural rock and dirt at the rear, had been heavily coated with the same gummy whitewash used to brighten and cool the bungalow. The only light came from the bulb and the two bottle-glass windows, one on either side of the doorway. What I saw before me at once brought the phrase "medieval movies" to mind. It was the sort of motion-picture theater our Gothic ancestors might have built if the Dark Ages had been illuminated by electrical power. Indeed, it was more primitive than that. As my guide had said, it was a Stone Age cinema. *Sharkey would love this place*, I thought as I gazed around. It was a true catacombs, as busted-down minimal as a movie house could get, perfectly designed for an audience of vermin and grubs: Sharkey's kind of people. How I wished he were there to see it with me.

There at the far end, about twenty feet into the cave, was a small soiled movie screen suspended crookedly from the stone ceiling. And at the center of the space just inside the door stood an archaic sixteen-millimeter projector mounted on an olive-oil barrel. The projector had been mended at several points with friction tape, wire, string; I couldn't believe it worked. Along the walls on both sides and at the rear were scores of film cans and cartons stacked on the dirt floor or precariously positioned in various crates and boxes that looked like the jetsam of the sea. Were there actually movies in all those canisters and boxes? If so, the man had an archive of a few hundred films.

"So this is how you amuse yourself, watching movies."

He made a sour face. "Watching? Hardly. Most of what they send is *dreck*. The worst. I don't watch. There is nothing I care to watch anymore. I *make*. This isn't a theater. It's a studio." He moved across to some lumpy, blanket-covered objects standing beside the metal casing that housed the generator. He slipped the cloth away from one of the objects, revealing a moviola—or rather, the skeletal remains of a dismantled moviola that had been stripped of about half of its parts. "For the first few years, I was lucky enough to have this. I cobbled it together from three machines. Then it wore out, more than I could repair. They wouldn't replace it. But some of the parts proved useful. Now I have only this, but it suffices."

He drew back the blanket from another object. Under it was a bewildering Rube Goldberg mélange of machinery. I had to study it before I recognized it as a makeshift editing bench. Nearly lost among empty or half-filled film reels were two rewinds, and bolted to the table between them a battered Moviescope viewer that was even more taped and wired than the projector. "This actually works?" I asked.

He reached across the bench and gingerly connected two bare wires that were pinned against the wall. At once the little viewer lit up inside. In it, I could see a frame of film displayed in the machine. A woman's face upside down. He cranked the handle on one of the rewinds and, sure enough, the still film became a moving picture racing past the lens. Beneath a panning camera, the woman's torso emerged naked and gleaming with sweat; it was at once submerged in a tangle of bodies male and female. A riot of genitalia filled the screen. A skin flick. The dirty old man!

Conceivably one *could* cut film on a contraption like this. I noticed there was an antique Griswold splicer beside the viewer, some splice blocks, razor blades, bottles of cement, rolls of Mylar tape, something that looked like a surgeon's scalpel. There was also a collection of paint jars, some brushes, and colored pencils.

"The cement and the tape are the most precious," he explained. "I send letters begging for more with every supply boat. Sometimes I have to wait months. Then, a small mercy, I receive a few bottles, a few rolls . . . never enough. I've tried making synthetic mixtures. Beeswax, resin, bird dung, various juices. My best results have been with lime and tree sap, if one lets it harden sufficiently. Sometimes it sticks in the projector and the film burns. But often it holds until more cement arrives."

I didn't believe a word he was saying. I knew at some point I'd have to recognize that I was living with a madman. This was the point. But even if none of this equipment was working, why was it here at all? "The orphans let you have this? They send it to you?"

"Most was here when I arrived. More than you see now. There were cameras, moviolas, projectors. It was all heaped up in the bungalow, which was a wreck when I first came. And movies. Cans and cans of them. A small mountain of movies. I was elated to find them, because, of course, there was a generator, electricity, all I needed to run the machines. This elation lasted, I would say for one minute. For then I saw. It was all rubbish, all of it. Useless, worn out, scrap. It came from the film schools. Whatever was used up or broken was sent here, a movie graveyard. I understood. It was somebody's sadistic idea of a fit punishment. I too was scrap. And this was my torment. Condemned to live out my days among decaying equipment, torn film. As a concept of damnation, it was worthy of Dante.

"But having nothing better to do with my time, I set to work tinkering. In the depths of the junkpile I found what I most needed: a box of Mylar. Twenty-four rolls. With this I could repair the film, I could even patch some of the machines. Then, with pieces from here and there, I succeeded in getting one of the projectors to run. Not for long. Nothing ever works for long. Bulbs burn out, belts snap, film breaks. I remember that first movie of my exile. It brought tears to my eyes. Josephine Baker. *Zou Zou.* Projected on a bedsheet without sound. Such a delight. I knew her in Paris. Alas, she was with me here for only ten minutes. Then the film caught fire—perhaps from her performance. *Le jazz hot*, eh?

"Still, I persisted. More equipment arrived, more film. Practice film, outtakes from editing classes, the most worthless kind of refuse, an insult to the taste. But even in this trash I found pieces of other movies I could use—stock footage, newsreels, little snippets from the classics, even a few snatches from my own work as improved upon by some adolescent film butcher.

"It was not until three or four years later that things changed. One day, I received a good projector—used, but good—and some film that was in decent condition. Perhaps it was felt I had suffered sufficiently. Perhaps somewhere in the higher echelons of the church I have a secret benefactor—a fan, a former student of mine, someone who has decided to take mercy on me. In any case, I at once sent letters back by the supply ship pleading for forgiveness and requesting things. More and more often, my requests were granted. What they send is still secondhand, but usable. And then Albrecht came. Like yourself, he was a film scholar interested in my work. Poor boy! he had been contaminated with curiosity about Oculus Dei. So he was sent here to finish out his days. He was younger than you. Together, we built what you see, our 'studio.' That solved my worst problem. The climate. Too hot. The film decays so rapidly in such heat, especially the splices. We dug out this cave and painted the walls. You see how cool it is. Too damp, yes. But the film lasts a little longer."

Machines held together by string, film spliced with lime and sap . . . even if this was something more than a batty old man's wishful make-believe, an editing bench does not a movie make—not unless there is a movie to edit. If he was producing movies of any kind, how did he shoot them? And what was he shooting? There was no sign of a camera on the premises. "How do you do your filming?" I asked.

"No camera," he said dismissively.

"Then where does your movie come from?"

He gestured imperiously to the canisters at the rear of the cave. "I have become the world's first cannibal moviemaker. My movie eats their movies. It is the survival of the fittest."

"You're just sticking things together, that's all?"

"I think of it as pruning. As in the orchard. I prune away the excess until only the essence remains. Even in the best movie, there is excess; even in the worst, there is an essence—something humorous, something mysterious, something uncanny. Perhaps it is only a single shot: an eye, a smile, an actor's instinctive gesture, light reflected from a jewel. In my own films, there was often no more than a few seconds that really mattered. This would have been true, even if I had been blessed with all the money I wanted, all the resources. You see, I am God here in my little celluloid universe. I decide what survives and what perishes. I have become the director of directors."

I walked into the depths of the cave to examine the shelves of what was indisputably the most complete film library in the entire Indian Ocean. Scanning the labels I could manage to read in the thick shadows, I had to agree that most of what he had on hand was *dreck*. Monogram Studios horse operas, Saturday serials, coming attractions, stag movies. There was an entire shelf of what appeared to be industrial training films all having to do with the proper handling of machines and chemicals. Another shelf was taken up with something called "Collision Derby Highlights." But my eye, traveling fast, also picked out titles by Renoir, Truffaut, Buñuel, Kurosawa, Hitchcock, Bergman, Rossellini. There were Disney cartoons, John Ford westerns, Bette Davis tearjerkers, Pete Smith Specialties, Preston Sturges comedies sandwiched between old newsreels, travelogues, *The March of Time*. On the lowest shelf of the last rack I came upon some half-dozen cartons whose labels simply read "Student Projects—Outtakes." And next to these, the last films in the collection, were two titles that caught my attention at once. *Big Stuffer* and *Sub Sub*. So he'd seen the work of his most important disciple. What did he think of it? I filed the question away for the moment and returned from my brief survey. "A pretty mixed bag you have here."

"Without rhyme or reason it comes. Mostly scrap quality, whatever they no longer need. Some of it I cannot even run through the viewer. It is quite challenging. I never know what each delivery might bring. The Pathé news, the Dead End Kids. . . . You know perhaps the Roadrunner, this moronic little bird? I have, I think, the entire corpus. Also blue movies—many of these. The pupils study them to learn certain effects. Lately for some reason I am receiving the work of one Run Run Shaw. From Hong Kong, I believe. You know this person?"

"I'm afraid so."

"Simply amazing. The man seems to make a movie every fifteen minutes. You cannot tell one from the other. People kicking, people punching, people screaming . . . From forty miles of his creations, I have been able to salvage exactly sixteen decent frames. Would you believe, once I was sent eight defunct prints of *Citizen Kane*, each in worse condition than the last. From all eight, I could not glue together one complete version. At the schools, they study the film so intensely, it is torn to pieces by the time they are done." He paused, a small, smug grin on his lips. "I take that to be a great compliment, though my captors wouldn't know. It is my film, you realize. All the best parts. Orson would tell you so."

"I know. He told me. I intended to include that in my book." I could see that pleased him.

"Well now, as you see, I've become the garbage can of the film world. The waste, the trash, the crap, it all comes finally to me. But whatever comes, I work with it."

"But exactly *how?*" I asked. I'd seen compilation movies that stitched together excerpts from many sources. They were a staple of film schools, an amateur exercise in cheap production. I couldn't believe he'd find enough artistic sustenance in that to satisfy his creative hunger. "What can you do with this stuff except splice your cuts together end to end?"

"Ah, but there are such possibilities in this splicing. You would never guess, as I didn't myself until I found that my whole art had at last come down to this one skill. With nothing to do with one's days and nights for—how long has it been? thirty-some years—one finds ways to work wonders with the razor blade, the X-acto knife, a dab of cement, a sliver of tape. Of course, we work here without sound. As it was in the beginning. Pure cinema. The image and nothing but the image. It is the pristine art."

"But what about the *Unenthüllte?* No chance for much of that, is there?"

He returned an amused stare. "You know this word?"

"I picked it up from Orson."

"Ah yes. He would remember. He had a weakness for the spook stuff. Well, as you will see, I have not had to leave the *Unenthüllte* behind."

"You mean you have something to show me?"

"You have studied my minor efforts, why not my *magnum opus?*" Proudly he drew back a curtain that covered the bottom half of his makeshift editing bench. There on a shelf stood a number of film cartons piled on their sides. I bent down in the dim light to study them. They bore no title, only numbers.

"This is your work?" I asked.

"Awaiting its world premiere."

I looked for the highest number I could find among the cartons. "This is all one movie? Forty-two reels?"

"Forty-three, actually. But not all the reels are full. On some there is only five minutes, ten minutes. Whatever the overall structure of the work required at that point."

"And it's finished?"

"Let's say it's ready to be seen at any time. Today in fact." Almost tenderly he added, "You see why I was fearful you had been taken away? I've waited half my lifetime for an audience. For *you*."

I had to admire the brave front he was putting on his sad plight, playing the cinematic Prospero in his island exile. I was certain that behind the ironic facade there lay the pieces of a heart long since shattered. He wasn't an easy man to like, especially in this cut-down, quasi-senile version, but I felt sorry for him nonetheless. "You deserve so much better than this," I said.

He smiled gratefully, but waved off my solicitude. "At first, it seemed to me a great pity to find myself in such reduced circumstances. But then I came to see, as more and more of my raw materials arrived, that in fact I had at my disposal all that the motion picture has to offer. The work of the very best, as well as the very worst. All of it mine. Through the films, I can treat myself to a kind of animated museum of modern times: the great ideals, the great lies, the unholy loves, the follies. What more could I ask for?"

His graceful resignation became grating. "*What more?* At the very least, if they insist on keeping you here—which is a crime and a shame—some decent equipment. You're working here like a savage, for God's sake."

"Exactly so!" he chirped with a clap of his hands. "The way our barbaric forebears salvaged the ruins of Rome to make their barns, pigsties, churches. And yet, I have come to see my work as the film of the future. I imagine the French would call it *cinéma brutal*, the way movies will have to be made if there is any future at all for us."

He'd finally struck on the one great subject we'd left undiscussed. I was saving it up. "You mean after 2014." To my surprise, he didn't flash on the date; I had to explain it. "Armageddon," I said. "It's the date of Armageddon—at least as your church sees it." He returned an inquisitive stare. All I saw in his face was total incomprehension. "Your church *does* subscribe to an apocalyptic teaching, doesn't it? The end of the world. The day of wrath."

"Oh yes, yes. But as to *when* this will be, frankly it strikes me as pedantic to ask—2014, 2114, 2214 . . . the date is immaterial. *That* this thing will happen—this is all that matters. In fact, some might say it has already happened." He looked at me with an owlish expression, waiting to see if I followed him. I didn't. "The religious wars, the witch hunts, the death camps. Surely these represent the end of the only world that matters, wouldn't you agree? The Great Whore rules over us long since."

Confounded by his apparently sincere ignorance, I hastened to brief him on everything I'd learned from Angelotti about the bomb, the germs, the seven-hundred-year conspiracy. I was moving over the ground so rapidly, trying to elicit some sign of recognition from him, that I feared I must be making a hash of the story. Nevertheless, he listened with great concentration and just a touch of irritating amusement.

"Amazing," was all he said when I finished. Wagging his head, he led me out of Paleolithic Productions, which had by now become intolerably clammy with the moisture of our breath and bodies. The cave might have solved his heat problem, but I guessed the humidity was still dense enough to be a film killer in its own right. Outside, he slumped down on a fallen tree that lay against one wall of the bungalow. He was showing signs of the fatigue that usually preceded a long snooze. "And you believe all this?" he asked as I settled in beside him.

"I hardly want to. But our mutual friend Angelotti assured me it was true." He emitted a dry soundless cackle, a laugh that implied, boy, had I been taken in.

"Now I see. This is what impelled you to go to Zurich and to Albi. You thought you were saving the world."

The way he put it made me fairly blush with embarrassment for my own presumption. But worse, he was raising the possibility that my gullibility had cost me my freedom and had led to Clare's captivity. If that were true, I didn't want it rubbed in. In fact, I now wanted desperately to believe that the great Cathar plot was real. It was all that made sense of my otherwise idiotic adventure. "You mean to say you've never heard about any of this? How the orphans are planning World War III?"

"There was always talk of this kind around the church. Big apocalyptic fantasies. When the Great War came—in 1914, I mean—I recall my schoolmates in the orphanage cheering. Most disturbing. But you see, they believed 'we' had made the war happen. Soon we would see the end of the world. For them, this was a thing devoutly to be wished. Myself, I had bad dreams for months. Perhaps because in my mind, the end became so graphically vivid. I could see it before my eyes like a movie, an Eisenstein epic. Terrible, terrible. Of course, as it turned out, 1914 was not the end of the world, only of European civilization. My schoolmates found this most disappointing. Accordingly, when the second war came in 1939, they once again rushed to claim credit for initiating *Götterdämmerung*. It didn't trouble them that this meant accepting Herr Hitler as the unwitting instrument of the true God. For my own part, I was not prepared to regard Auschwitz as the gateway to salvation. I would just as soon see us remain indefinitely in our normal human state of semidamnation."

"You're saying that Angelotti duped me? There's no truth to his story?"

He reached back a long way in his memory. "I do remember hearing of schoolmates who went into the sciences—biology, physics. No doubt they have made their significant contribution to the patriotic carnage on all sides. But as you see, the world goes limping on. Abraxas is not omnipotent, nor are his followers."

"But you have to admit," I insisted, "that we get closer to the brink all the time."

"True. And still the brink remains a long way off."

"Does it? You *have* heard of the bomb—the H-bomb?"

"H? I thought A. The atom bomb. Like in *Hiroshima Mon Amour*. Did it really wipe out the whole city?"

"You *are* behind the times. H for hydrogen. Millions of times more powerful."

"Millions?" He was struck by that. "Ah well . . ."

"And the chemicals, the germs. You don't believe there are malignant little orphan geniuses at work in germ labs all over the world cooking up better poisons by the day?"

"Ah yes, the germs." His eyes narrowed thoughtfully. "I remember . . ." He brought the fingers of his hands together to form an arrow point and placed it against his upper lip as he thought back across the years. "I remember some talk of a project many years ago. Brother Marcion told me about it one day at St. James School. A disease that would someday make sexual relations—fucking, you understand—absolutely lethal. The ultimate *Liebestod*. The man was quite exhilarated by this prospect. As you know, our faith takes a rather dim view of human concupiscence. There have always been militants among us who advocate the example of Origen." When he saw that I didn't understand, he clarified. "Castration for all male

members. Literally so. No pun intended. Fortunately, these extremists have been outnumbered by those who recognize that a congregation of obese countertenors might have some difficulty keeping itself
unnoticed. Still, these fanatics persist in their efforts. This fellow Byx
that you've told me about, he would seem to be one of the zealots.
For them to concoct a little antilove germ and send it out into the
world . . . it's all too possible. It would be their kind of choice: celibacy or certain death."

In the midst of the tropic afternoon, I chilled at his words. I found
this notion more nauseatingly hideous than nuclear annihilation. I
could more easily contemplate the world going up in flames than the
thought of our universal extermination insinuating itself so silently
into the act of love. "They'd never do such a thing," I protested.

"I wouldn't put it past them. Still, if you find that so hard to swallow,
why believe the rest?"

"But you do believe there will be an apocalypse. Inside just now,
you spoke of a dark age to come, a future when there might be no
survivors."

"Who can doubt it? We are surely a doomed species. Look with
what ingenuity we destroy all we create. But this requires no grand
conspiracy. Only our own twisted will. Perhaps it doesn't even matter
if the end happens as a physical event." He leaned toward me to
whisper. "Don't tell the orphans I said so, but these great religious
teachings really shouldn't be taken so literally. You see what a heretic
I am? All artists are. We turn all things into metaphors—the better
to play with them. What matters is that in some sense we are at war
with all that is best in ourselves, that the forces of darkness and light
here inside us can never be at peace until we have been shattered
in the struggle. This is what makes us dramatically interesting. The
end of man. To ponder this is all that art requires." After a long pause,
he added, "And to laugh at the idiocy of it all. *Vanitas vanitatum.*"
Another pause. And then a silent, wheezy chuckle welled up inside
him, finally growing to a choking guffaw. "Do you remember Stan
Laurel's little film, where they tear the cars to pieces? And then"—
he was fighting against his laughter to get the words out—"and then
the suits . . . they tear the suits." He doubled over laughing. When
he caught his breath again, he leaned back against the wall of the
bungalow, gasping. "That says it all."

When he'd recovered, I raised a subject that I knew would interest him despite the weariness I could see taking hold of him. "I noticed you had a few Simon Dunkle films in your collection." He squinted at me, not understanding. *"Big Stuffer. Sub Sub."*

He recognized the titles. "Yes, yes. Student projects. Very rough, very primitive. Also quite clever, though still immature. Rather too strong for my taste."

This from the man who found Todd Browning's *Freaks* redeemingly humorous. How Simon would have appreciated the compliment. I explained, "He's primitive because he *wants* to be, not because he has to be. Also he's immature because he *wants* to be. His films are meant for a young audience. For kids."

He was genuinely startled. "These films are being shown? Children see them? With the nakedness, the exploding bodies?"

"These films are a great success. Children love them. You see how it is? Less and less has to be hidden. Everything's coming to the surface. All your old subliminal techniques—not necessary. Nothing's forbidden. You should send back a request for more of Dunkle's movies. I'm sure the orphans can supply you with all his work."

"He's an important man, you believe?"

"Not a man. A boy. Hardly twenty. As young as yourself when you started." When he had taken that in, I let him know the rest, the one item of news I had left to tell him. "He's your disciple and successor." He cocked his head inquisitively. "The first director the church has trained since its misadventure with you."

"He is one of the orphans?"

"Like yourself. Only they've given him his own private studio at St. James School. Everything he needs—except, of course, his freedom."

He reflected a long while on what I had told him. "After me I didn't think they would ever try again."

"They have him well under control—at least for now. They plan to use him to invade television."

"Television?"

"Movies at home. It's an invention that became popular after the war. Everybody in the world watches television now—even the Eskimos in their igloos."

"Yes, the little box. I've come across it in many movies. Tell me, where do the pictures come from?"

"Out of thin air. They're broadcast like radio waves."

"But then it isn't a projection. Where is the flicker?"

"I can't explain the technicalities. But television is still an art of light and shadow. There is a flicker. It's sort of braided into the picture. Dunkle uses it very effectively."

"Movies in the home. How remarkable. What will happen to all the picture palaces?"

"Going out of business."

He gave a bemoaning sigh for an era that had long since passed from the scene. "When they watch in the home, do they turn out the lights?"

"No, they leave them on. They eat supper, do homework, have arguments, carry on."

"But that changes everything. There can be no feeling of isolation. For the flicker, you need darkness, like in a temple, a cave. Every person alone with his fantasies."

"It works differently with television. The image projects itself directly on the viewer. The picture tube is like an eye that looks into its audience, a sort of hypnotic stare. Even together in the same room, people can be isolated, vulnerable."

"Ah! Interesting."

"Dunkle claims the video flicker drives every effect in deeper. The real screen is the retina of the eye—inside the skull. The skull is the cave. Imagine the psyche sitting inside there in its own dark, private theater."

I could see he was impressed. Nodding thoughtfully, he said, "There are possibilities here."

"I think you'd appreciate Dunkle's work. I know he admires yours. He plans to remake some of your films. *Count Lazarus, House of Blood.*"

"My films? Remarkable."

"He regards you as a prophet of the church." He let out an incredulous little gasp, then waved his hand dismissively; but I could see he was moved by Simon's judgment. "Dunkle asked me not to let anyone know that. But I guess it's safe to tell you."

"Well, well. A pity he won't be able to see my finest effort. That privilege seems to have fallen to you, my friend. Are you ready for the prophet's last prophecy?" He gestured back toward the shed. "The studio is yours for as long as you need. There is plenty of coal for the generator." He rose and trudged off toward the bungalow. "I look forward to hearing your opinion. If you care to nominate me for an Oscar, I will be highly honored."

Astonished, I called after him. "Aren't you going to run the film for me?"

"No, no. Too tired. Time for my siesta."

"Don't you want to watch with me?"

"No need to. I have it all up here." He tapped his forehead. "The pure original. To tell the truth, I'm afraid what you find on the film may not live up to what I intended."

"Haven't you ever looked at it?"

"I never looked at any of my work after it was finished. For that matter, I never really had to shoot the film. Once it was in my mind, it was complete, perfect. Of course, the studios insisted on having a product to sell."

"You trust me to run the film myself? What if I damage it? It must be very delicate."

He laughed. "Damage it? I expect you to *destroy* it. The splices could never go through the projector more than once. Maybe not even once. For all I know, some of the film may already have decayed. Thirty years in the can. Pity. It would be best if you could see the whole thing, take in the total structure. But it will be enough if you see reel thirty-seven—about ten minutes in, the parody on Dov-zhenko. And the end of reel sixteen. Also the material from Lubitsch in reel twenty-one, toward the end. Notice how I have managed to touch up his lighting; the man never knew how to use shadows properly. And, ah yes, there is a sequence in reel twenty-nine—the best use of the flicker I ever put on film. Watch for Busby Berkeley at the Crucifixion. You can't miss it. Very irreverent—but only on the surface."

He turned and started away again. I stared after him in disbelief. "You mean this is going to be the *only* screening?"

He stopped to look back, giving me his gap-toothed grin. "Did you think I was waiting to have an opening at Grauman's Chinese? In this case, my premiere is my dernière."

Almost imploringly, I stammered, "Please, it's too much of a responsibility. I don't want to be the one to destroy your work."

"What responsibility? Please. Be my guest. Enjoy yourself. There is an old American folk saying: 'It's only a movie,' right? Let it fall to pieces, burn to a crisp. I told you, the only film that matters is in here." Again he tapped his forehead. He turned the corner of the bungalow and was out of sight—but only for a moment. Then he stepped back into view, looking deeply thoughtful, something on his mind. "Is it still there?" he asked. "Grauman's Chinese?"

32 THE END OF THE WORLD AND SELECTED SHORT SUBJECTS

I waited a long while before I approached the little shed against the hillside. Despite the curiosity that bubbled inside me, I wasn't eager to enter. In my bones, I knew what I'd find there. More for his sake than mine, I wanted to put off the moment of dread discovery. Meanwhile, I let my thoughts drift back in time, remembering . . . I'd first encountered the great man's work in one sort of cave—a funky cinematic crypt called The Classic. Now, so many years later, somewhere at the crumbling edge of the world, I was entering another cave—a real one—to see what he regarded as his masterpiece. My quest would seem to have brought me full circle. But not really. The circle had turned into a descending spiral and I was riding it down and down toward unfathomed depths.

When I finally returned to the shelf of cartons that held his last movie, I looked for one of the numbers he'd recommended. Reel twenty-one came to hand; I quickly pried open the dusty, mold-enshrouded box. It was like opening a coffin expecting to find a corpse . . . and finding a corpse. Not shocking, just sickening. As I feared, reel twenty-one, exposed to the light perhaps for the first time in years, turned out to be a wild tangle of curled, split, and corkscrewed film stock. It stuck out of its spool at all points like a dead porcupine flattened in the road. At the touch, shreds and coils of film came away in my fingers.

What else could I expect? He'd started with decayed film, had cut and pared it with crude instruments, smeared it with cement, and stuck it away to molder in a musty dungeon. Hopeless.

I opened another carton. Reel thirty-seven, which he told me improved on Dovzhenko. At first the half spool of film I found in the box looked to be in better shape—until I touched it and found it annealed into a solid disk of nitrate, never to be peeled apart and threaded through a projector. After that, I despaired of finding as much as a few yards of viewable footage; still, I continued opening cartons. Each revealed a new plastic pathology. Film reduced to crumbs, to jelly, to dust. Film melting into goo, cracked into splinters, shredded into black spaghetti. I was learning all over again how fragile this greatest of all art forms is, a dream drawn by light on an evanescent polymer ribbon. As I explored the ruins, I was treated to a nasal montage of odors, the smell of old chemicals yielding to rancid organic vapors where he'd used one of his experimental cements— bird droppings perhaps, or resin. One carton, at my touch, set my skin to crawling—literally. My hand came back covered with ants. The carton, once opened, proved to be filled with them, busily devouring some sticky juice or tree sap he had spread over his splices.

I'd gone through some two dozen cartons before I stopped, heartsick. What was the point of searching further? The lower the numbers of the reels went, the more deteriorated their contents. For curiosity's sake, I hunted out box number one, presumably his earliest work. It was filled with a yellowish grit. Nothing recognizable as film survived; only scores, hundreds of pieces of the Mylar tape that had sealed his splices. Sifting through the rubble, I paused, my attention fixed upon what I found lying in my hand. How intricately, how fastidiously the tape had been cut; evidence of a maniacal precision. I'd never seen splices like these. They were sliced at bizarre angles, notched, pierced with holes, shaped into strange geometries. What had he been trying to do?

I searched back through the other cartons, looking for whatever remnants I could find of his editing craftsmanship. In one box I discovered a longish strip of newer film stock that still held together; it stretched out from the reel to some twelve feet in length before it cracked. Along the strip I found several oddly shaped splices both cement and tape. They made up a weird jigsaw of patterns. With infinite care, I lifted the strip to the editing bench and fitted one end into the viewer. I lit up the lens and delicately drew the film through, studying it frame by frame, especially at the splices, which in this case were at two or three points holding overlapping lengths of film in place—something no film editor would ever attempt to do. Staring into the viewer, I was able to make out a familiar figure, though not at all what I might have expected to see.

Betty Boop.

The little mock-sexy vamp was doing her rubbery strut back and forth over a grainy background that, on closer inspection, turned out to be newsreel footage from one of the Nazi death camps. The scene was one of those hideous, slow panning shots of bodies, bodies, bodies laid out like broken dolls. I suppose that image holds a permanent place in the iconography of our time; but I've never been able to view the pictures without wincing and turning away—except this time. The juxtaposition of Betty Boop with this nauseating atrocity took stubborn hold of my attention. It was bizarre, even obscene. But it was so well done! Betty Boop, reaching down, skipping along, was gathering a bouquet of cartoon posies from the piled-up corpses, blithely gliding over horrors beneath her dainty, high-heeled feet. What I held in my hand couldn't have been more than a few minutes of a movie, yet it was enough to show me a prodigious skill at work fashioning virtuoso splices that produced a jarring marriage of images.

But what was the intention? Mockery? Sick humor? Or perhaps to capture in an offbeat way the sense of life renewing itself out of genocidal carnage? Without seeing more than this fragment, there was no way to know. For that matter, I would never have the chance to see this fragment again. As I cranked the film strip through the viewer, it was already disintegrating.

I went back to the cartons, searching for more samples. In reel twenty-nine I was able to salvage as much as three or four minutes of a sequence that featured Fred Astaire. I could recognize the scene. It was his famous "Puttin' on the Ritz" number from *Top Hat*. But here the high-spirited dance had been radically transformed. Tiny human figures had been etched along the bottom of the film. Under Fred's wildly tapping feet, they had been animated to flee for cover. When he pounded his cane on the floor, he seemed to be beating them flat. Sudden close-ups that had been spliced into his choreography showed anguished faces, broken bodies. Fred's face had been painted a lurid scarlet; he had become a cruel, punishing giant, laughing as he smashed and swatted in all directions. I guessed he was meant to represent the Cathar's unpitying Other God who lorded it over a suffering mankind. His lighthearted performance had become the bloody dance of Shiva.

FLICKER

In reel forty-two I found another several feet of film even more precariously patched together. In this case, he had achieved a longitudinal splice, two half films joined down the middle. The splice came apart in my hands even as I studied it, but I was able to feed the two halves into the viewer one by one. The left side of the film was an animal form—a panther on the prowl in a shadowy jungle. The right side was difficult to make out. Finally, after investing several minutes of eyestrain and using a magnifying glass I found in a drawer of the bench, I saw that it was a woman—or at least the lower torso of a woman—giving birth. I supposed this unsparingly clinical scene came from a medical documentary. The baby seemed to be struggling out of the womb directly into the claws of the hunting cat. Another familiar Cathar theme: we are born into death.

Searching further, I now began to pay attention to segments of film no more than a few frames long. Even these revealed the man's skill and daring. Here and there, I noted traces of color added to the film, things drawn or painted on the emulsion, overlapping the photographed picture. To see these I had to use the same magnifying glass he must have employed to make the additions. My God! the labor that had gone into these primitive animations, frame by frame, twenty-four frames for every running second of movement. It was plain crazy. He had toiled for days to paint, pencil, scratch words, figures, shapes upon film stock he knew was doomed to rot away unseen. The task must have required a ferocious concentration, like that of a bee or termite single-mindedly driven by its tyrannical instinct to achieve some minute insect project.

I soon discovered that my scholarly habits of mind hadn't deserted me. Sorting through the debris, I automatically began to categorize the images and motifs I was finding, heaping them up in little mounds on the bench. In one there was the recurrent image of a polyp or tentaclelike shape; it usually crept out of holes, tunnels, dark corners to slither over scenes of love, sex, romance. This nasty little cartoon exuded weblike tendrils that spread and tangled across the frame, finally knitting the lovers up like a spider's victims. Then there were any number of examples of the black bird flying over scenes of atrocity and devastation. This I recognized as the Cathar emblem of divine but powerless mercy. And pitted against the bird, there was the stalking panther, tiger, jaguar, usually spliced into idyllic scenes where it became the shadow that fell across all earthly delight. And finally there was the most intriguing footage of all, frame after frame that seemed to be nothing more than the play of light and darkness: infernal blacks alternating with blazing whites, pinpoints of light against night skies, starbursts, lightning streaks. Where I could recover as much as several feet of such film intact, I could tell he'd been experimenting with wild rhythms and counterpoints of light and dark that were meant to enhance the effect of the flicker.

There was no way to tell if these artfully edited and altered fragments added up to some overall story, or if the various reels might simply be so many variations of Cathar themes of good and evil, suffering and salvation, heaven and hell. I was studying nothing more than pitiful scraps of the man's work. But even that little brought me a welcome sense of relief. I'd listened to his description of his work suspecting he was totally nuts. If there was film in the cans, it might be imbecilic hash revealing nothing but its maker's madness. Now at least I had the proof of a surviving talent at work—though it had been expended on a project that many, myself included, might be inclined to regard as psychotic. On the other hand, what are the standards of sanity for a one-man society existing in such isolated exile? Was there anything he might better have spent his time doing?

But having satisfied myself to that extent, what did I do next? I could, I suppose, amuse myself for the rest of my life combing through the ruins of his work, seeking out surviving images here and there, admiring the ingenuity of his utterly impractical editing techniques. For all that task might teach me, it would be a heartbreaking pastime.

Even more urgently, what did I say to him later today when he woke from his nap? He told me the movie would fall apart; but that was supposed to happen *after* I had screened it. Could I bring myself to tell him that he wasn't to have even the most minimal audience after all these years? Or did he know that? No one who handled film with such dexterity could really believe his work would survive the self-destructive chemistry of celluloid, the inherent instability of these zany splices. But if that was so, did he expect me to play along with the fantasy and humor him the next time we met by pretending I'd seen the film?

After this brief intermission, I glumly set about closing up the cartons and stacking them under the editing bench. As I did so, I came upon a half-opened carton that bore no number. It was less dusty than the others, possibly a recent piece of work. I looked inside and found a reel that was about half full. The film looked to be in decidedly better condition than anything I'd seen so far. Along the coiled edge of the reel I could make out an extraordinary number of splices; the film must be a kaleidoscope of imagery. I unrolled a few feet of it; the stock was supple, the sprockets in good shape. Unrolling more, I came upon a segment that looked like a long stretch of eight-millimeter film cemented along one edge to a strip of blank film meant to lend it enough width to pass through the projector. The splice seemed to go on and on well into the reel. This was a very tricky piece of work, unlikely to stay together under the pull of the machine. Looking more closely, I saw that this part of the movie had been elaborately worked on. A sort of muddy glaze had been painted over it, then pocked and pitted. I was madly curious to know what effect these awesome labors had produced. Dared I try running it through the projector? Well, what did I have to lose?

I fastened the reel to the battered little Bell & Howell and carefully threaded the film through its creaky innards. Like the viewer on the bench, the projector also had to be hot-wired to pull its juice. As soon as the connection was made, it came to life with a grumpy little growl like an animal waking from hibernation. I switched the lamp on; it stabbed its blank shaft of light across the room to brighten the lopsided screen. I turned off the overhead bulb, took a deep breath, and pressed the FORWARD button. There was a lurch and a slap as the leader began to click through the film gate. By God, the thing worked! I brought the beam to a sharp focus. Two big words occupied the screen. . . .

"The End."

Then, just as they faded away, a Castle trademark appeared. Eyes. Just eyes, the face around them blacked out. But even masked off, there was no mistaking these eyes. Large, mascara-ringed, shining with tears, they were the eyes of Charlie Chaplin, the closing shot from *City Lights*. They held the screen for only a few seconds and then were replaced by another image, blending in rapidly . . . and then another, another, another. Split-second cuts flashing by, too quick to register. Still I was certain I caught the faces of familiar stars. Bogart, Gérard Philipe, Garbo, Marlon Brando. Then something I couldn't miss, a favorite film: a snatch from the cremation scene at the end of Truffaut's *Jules et Jim*.

About then, I got the point. These were memorable endings, the sort of invasive final images that stake out a lifelong claim in the mind. A death, a closing door, a farewell wave. The ending of a movie—so I'd long believed—was a moment out of time, a spectral transition from the illusion of the film to the illusion that passes for real life. In its own small way, it's an aesthetic apocalypse, the end of one world, the resumption of that other which begins on the streets beyond the theater. Where it's done well, it packs the whole picture into a single, persisting memory. Flashing before my eyes now was a prize collection of just those moments clipped from scores of movies, each one precisely cut to capture that experience of completion. But they were all sorrowful completions. None of the shots I could identify was a happy ending; all were moments of grief, loss, resignation. The last in the series was the terrible immolation from Dreyer's *Joan of Arc,* just that instant when the body slumps against the ropes and the flames take it.

And then the flames were fading, replaced by the segment of eight-millimeter film I'd inspected before I rolled the movie. This was at first so grainy and dismally lit that I couldn't get a fix on it. It did, however, manage to produce an immediate mood. Absolute, total despair. I couldn't tell why; I had no idea what I was looking at. It had the appearance of yellowed newspaper photos blown up ten or twenty times, so gritty I could feel it like sand rubbed into my eyes. It hurt to stare at the screen, as I struggled in vain to piece the picture together.

Again, the words "The End" took shape on the screen, this time followed in an accelerating succession by "Fin," "Das Ende," "Fine," a graceful cascade of final frames artfully arranged into a mobile collage from scores of movies in all languages. The grainy image returned. This time I succeeded in getting a visual grip on it. I was looking at a super-slow-motion overhead shot of people on a city street all moving toward one point, a dark square at the center where they vanished. What was it? A pit, a tunnel? Squinting hard, I felt sure it was a subway entrance. New York? No, more likely the London Underground. The crowd, slowed to a crawl, flowed like a dirty, turgid river along the sidewalk, turned, headed down the stairs. That was all. Just that, endlessly *that.* At a few points, I thought I spotted helmeted or uniformed figures. That, and the style of the clothing, gave a wartime atmosphere to the scene. London during the blitz? Possibly. Somebody had planted a camera above a London sidewalk and let it run, relentlessly recording this commonplace street scene. Why would anyone do that? No telling. Yet as utterly uneventful as the film was, after several moments its very ordinariness began to assume an eerie quality. The ceaseless funereal tread of the crowd became a death march, thousands trudging with robotic deliberation toward the concrete underworld. There was nothing to watch, yet I was watching, certain that something was about to happen. It was that experience only movies can capture: impending action off-camera about to intrude from the edges of the screen—the mummy's hand, the blow to the head, the pie in the face. One feels it coming, waits for its arrival with strained expectation.

What was it that held me so tenaciously? I decided it had to do with the texture of the picture. The grain had been made so coarse that I felt I was observing a world reduced to its very atoms. Below the visible surface, every constituent particle of the scene was on the verge of flying apart. And I was waiting to see that happen, wanting to see what lay underneath.

I might not have realized how gripped I was by this strange excerpt if my attention hadn't been diverted from the screen. I heard a snapping sound and, looking down, saw the first break in the film, the loose end coming through and falling short of the take-up reel. Only when I looked away did I experience how unwilling my eyes were to stop watching. I felt angry, even slightly panicked, to be distracted. I reached out to catch the end of the film and tried to provide enough tension to keep the movie flowing. That wasn't easy to do; twice the projector jammed, leaving no choice but to stop and rethread. The film continued to break, and twice more, when splices caught in the gate, the picture on the screen turned slowly brown, then red, as the film sizzled under the lens. Each time I lost several feet of the movie. Still I persevered, finally getting the feel of the tension right in my hands as I took over from the take-up reel. I was simply letting the film fall away on the floor with no thought of how I'd ever reassemble this mess on the spool.

But as these problems drew my eye from the screen, I realized that the room about me had changed. It was suffused with a pulsing, subaqueous light. The movie reflecting off the screen was producing the same uncanny fascination I had found long ago when I first saw the *Judas* and fell under the hypnotic spell of the flicker. What a pity I'd never have the chance to study the effect, or even to witness it a second time. The movie was dying in my hands while I watched, breaking, spilling away in pieces after the only viewing it would ever have—just as its maker had said it would.

Back on the screen, the unending parade of the doomed millions continued. If my attention hadn't been jerked away by the projector,

Theodore Roszak

how deeply I might by now be immersed in the scene, still waiting for its disintegrating surface to crumble—as at last it did. I'm sure it was well before my eye registered their appearance, subtle hairline fissures began to form across the crowd. They grew deeper, opened wider. Something behind was emerging, something I both wanted and feared to see. A thought leapt to mind as vividly as if it had been recorded on the sound track: we live on film, on *a* film, the skin of a bubble, what is real lies behind, waiting to push through, swallow us up, reclaim us. It may not be nice.

What was emerging? A light whose brightness punished my sight. The atoms of the picture were spinning off into that light. How had he managed to achieve such a brilliant intensity? Finally the light began to fold and crinkle, taking on shadows, a shape. It assumed a familiar outline, a nuclear cloud mushrooming up and up, ever so slowly, I was certain I saw something inside that cloud. An eye, was it? A single, terrible, unblinking eye fixed upon me, driving its cruel gaze into me. A sudden irrational impulse came over me. I wanted to hide. I didn't want that eye to see me. Because I knew it was there to judge me. I blushed to realize how childish the response was. It was exactly the way I had once felt as a kid when the monster appeared on the screen and I tried to hide under the seat. But this monster was nothing but that eye . . . if indeed there really was an eye there.

Before I could decide for sure, it was gone. Or at least I sensed it was gone, replaced by a mercifully blank white screen. Nothing. Just white leader running through, running and running. But not so. Like the blackness that filled the screen at the end of *Shadows over Sing Sing*, this white also riveted the attention. There was some absorbing tempo to what I watched; it stroked like a finger in the dark of the room, a sensuous tickling at the rear of the retina, deep in, reaching deeper. I became aware of a small gyrating spot on the screen. Yes, that's what I was watching for. Or was it a trick of the eye? At first I couldn't tell. In the pulsing white void, the spot writhed and grew larger. Yes, it was really there. It had wings. It was the black bird, or rather an animation of the bird etched on the film. Not even a smooth animation, but a crude, jumpy little cartoon.

Nothing special. But I felt it held out the promise of comforting darkness. My eyes invited it nearer. It spread larger on the screen, then fell away teasingly, returned, swelled. I waited for it eagerly; it would be an end to watching, to the strain of alertness. It would be shelter—from the light, from the mushroom cloud, from the vin-

579

dictive eye. The dark shape closed on my field of vision, filling the screen with its black breast, sponging away the light, putting everything to rest.

And then the film was over. "The End" had come to its end.

I never saw Busby Berkeley at the Crucifixion. Reel twenty-nine, where I was told I would find this supreme moment enshrined, turned out to be dust and fragments like all the rest. But how much more powerful an example of the flicker could it have offered? "The End" was as strong a dose as I could have handled—and accomplished with the most primitive means, with nothing more than a razor blade and some strands of tape. Whether he believed in the orphans' version of the teaching or not, he'd cobbled together the apocalypse to end all apocalypses. At least my exile had brought the satisfaction of proving me right. He was without doubt as great a moviemaker as I'd told the world he was.

Later that day when he woke from his nap, we talked it over.

"Some of the films were damaged," I told him hesitantly.

"A lot of them, I should think."

"Quite a lot."

"Most of them?"

"I'm afraid so."

"*All* of them?"

"Not all."

"You were able to see something?"

"A little. Mainly 'The End.' "

"Good. I finished that not so long ago."

"Is it really 'the end'? Of the whole movie, I mean?"

"It more or less rounds things off. If more of the rest had survived, I might go back and make changes. Reel five, for example. Very rough. And twelve, I would have blushed to have you see that. However, as things stand . . ."

"It was very effective, what I could see of it."

"You liked it?"

"I wouldn't say 'like.' I can't honestly say I ever liked any of your movies. But I appreciated it."

"Good."

"I'm afraid it came apart in the machine."

"Only to be expected."

"I mean *all* apart. It's . . . ruined."

"You expect me to be heartbroken?"

"I saved the pieces."

"No need. As I said, the real movie is in here."

I breathed a sigh of deep relief and went on to ask about some fine points. Among them: "The street scene . . . what was it?"

"I really have no idea. I assumed it was some kind of drill. From the war. In London. People taking shelter during an air raid perhaps. Maybe to see how smoothly things went. Would you believe, there were reels and reels of it, some fast, some slow. I took out the slow parts and worked on them a little."

"Ingenious."

"You think so?"

"Who else would have seen the possibilities?"

He gave a modest shrug that wasn't really meant to disguise the pride behind it. "I work with what I have." After a moment, a question occurred to him. "At the conclusion, the big explosion I put in . . . I came across it in a science fiction film. This was the J-bomb?"

"H-bomb, yes."

"One bomb?"

"Just one."

"Very powerful."

"Very."

"It's quite magnificent to see—the great cloud, the burst of light."

"It covers the world with radiation." He was unfamiliar with the word. "A sort of electrical poison. It kills everything it touches. They say a few hundred of them could wipe out all life on earth . . . except possibly for the cockroaches."

"And how many of these bombs are there?"

"The last I remember, thousands. Tens of thousands."

"Ah!"

"So you see."

"Yes, I see. Well, we must get down to work."

"Work?"

"You and I. We have a lot of films to use up before 2014."

"You want me to work on films with you?"

"You have other plans?"

When he put it that way, I had no choice but to accept his proposition. How else was I going to pass the time? All I had to do was move myself across the island and furnish a corner of his bungalow, which was quite a bit more livable than my cramped little hotbox of a cabin. I informed the caretakers of my change of address, letting them know that I expected my food and supplies to be forwarded. They pretended not to understand, but I didn't bother repeating myself. The next morning after I'd relocated myself, my breakfast arrived on schedule, brought in the little boat. Since then I talk to the man and woman, whichever pair is on the job, assuming they know what I'm saying. They do, but they never answer.

My new roommate isn't difficult to live with. Between his work in the garden, his long naps, his frequent evenings with the dope pipe— which I now share in moderation—I'm left with a good deal of time on my hands. One of my ongoing projects: compiling the great man's filmography, which needs to be revised every month or so as his memory dims or brightens. Otherwise, I read, very slowly, making the books last. My German is becoming much better, thanks to his collection of classics and his tutoring. I memorize poems. I begin pieces of writing and then throw them away.

"Don't waste the paper," he once warned me.

"Why not? What am I saving it for?"

"You may want to write your memoirs."

"Are you kidding?"

"You never can tell. Boredom is a great stimulus. See what it has done for my art."

Our sessions at Paleolithic Productions happen unpredictably as the spirit moves him. Sometimes we work for several days in succession; sometimes the studio stands empty for a month or two at a time. I let him set the pace. A great deal has to do with the supplies on hand. When the cement runs out or the tape is used up, he keeps the film in his head for weeks. But when we finally get down to work, it can be with a mind-splitting intensity, hour after hour. He's shown me lots of his tricks, but I leave the difficult work to him, preferring less demanding assignments. As for example: clipping the logo off all the Universal Studios movies made before 1946. He tells me the old Universal globe was worked over by orphan editors who smuggled a peculiarly potent subliminal glimmer into three of the twinkling highlights. I cut these out and save them up.

Another task I've been assigned: assembling yards and yards of blank leader, white or black, on which he spreads his glazes and then makes cryptic scribbles—usually his weirdly disturbing polyp-and-tentacle animations. He uses these grotesque little doodles for certain grisly montage effects. He tells me they represent carnal appetite running wild. Since the carnal appetite gets no more exercise on this godforsaken island than the native ladies are willing to provide once a lunar month or so, I say the more of that the better. I've managed to teach them the rudiments of *bhoga*, which seems the ideal diversion for one in my circumstances.

As for anything beyond low-level jobs, I'm far too clumsy to achieve the precision my boss at Paleolithic Productions requires. Even with his dimming eyesight, he can dissect the figures in a frame of film with surgical skill, or finesse a splice within a hairbreadth—all with instruments that remain stubbornly blunt no matter how many times I sharpen them for him on a tiny fragment of whetstone. The other month he devoted three days to excising tiny, tiny cutouts of Brigitte Helm from a tattered print of Fritz Lang's *Metropolis*. He wanted "just that movement, that gesture . . . the shoulders this way, the head cocked just so"—some seventy seconds of action to be grafted over jungle footage salvaged from a Tarzan film. "You see," he explained. "The Lady of the Beasts. Perfect casting."

Early on, I asked him the obvious question: Why does he take the trouble, since he never watches the results of his efforts? Why not keep the movie wholly mental? He tells me he needs the discipline. The task implants the image in his memory. It has another function: it allows him to decide when a film is "done" so he can forget it and pass on. "Otherwise," he says, "I would keep monkeying and monkeying."

So it goes. We work in our cave like a brace of witches concocting the most unlikely cinematic hybrids. William S. Hart shoots it out with Benito Mussolini, King Kong sails aboard Battleship *Potemkin*, Mae West makes love with Woody Allen beneath a downpour of Olympic diving champions. *Eye of newt, toe of frog.* However he wishes to spend our time, I raise no questions. I'm content to be his gofer. Not that I have far to go for what he needs. No farther than the back of the cave to search the shelves for stock on hand and bring back what hasn't rotted away in the box. His memory for film imagery is phenomenal. He tells me, "The khalif in *The Thief of Baghdad*—Conrad Veidt, isn't it?—he wears a green jewel here on his chest. It catches the light just so . . . about twenty minutes into the movie. Please to look for it." Or "In *Umberto D.*, at the end, the wall in the corridor, it has a certain texture, very diseased, very morbid. Find that." I look, and sure enough I find what he wants in the viewer.

When the supply boat brings us movies he hasn't seen, we run them on the little projector. He watches once and remembers every frame for future reference.

Sometimes he does go wrong, though not often. Once he instructed me: "In *Lady from Shanghai*, look for the shot where Rita Hayworth shows her garter when she steps from the boat. About twelve minutes in. So very provocative how she does it. We need about twenty frames of the thigh, especially the shadow under the skirt."

I looked. I couldn't find what he wanted. "No such shot," I reported.

"You're certain?" He frowned. "There should have been. Orson slipped up."

Like him, I never watch the films we make. It would hurt too much to see them come apart in the machine, as they surely would. My gratification lies in trying to watch the movie that's running through the camera of his mind. That isn't easy. From his description, he's working for effects never achieved before, and possibly not by him either. He calls what we make "short subjects," some of them only a few minutes long, but each seemingly drawn out of a vast backlog of planned films he has stored up over a lifetime.

Another job I've mastered: composing the titles for these brief novelties. I cut words from the films on hand, lay them out at random on the editing bench for him to ponder. He hovers over the scrambled language like an ancient sibyl searching to find the will of the gods in leafmeal or marrow shards. Then—"Aha!"—he hits upon something he likes and I go to work with magnifying glass and tweezers cementing the verbal confetti on a piece of selected film. I've become very quick and neat at this kindergarten task, though I have no idea what to make of the names he assigns to his productions. *My Favorite Executioner, Half a God Is Better Than One, The Punisher Who Loved Too Much, Beauty and the Beast Discover the Pleasures of Prohibition, The Devil Among the Daffodils*. Do the titles have any relationship to the films? I doubt it. I think he invented the job to keep me occupied.

From time to time, he draws a rusted oil can from under the editing bench; it contains a collection of bottles, boxes, pouches made from knotted rags. He calls it his "Special Effects Department"—a motley assortment of items he saves from our supplies or finds along the beaches. These he sets aside to stick, smear, or tape on film stock with the hope of producing strange visual results. He was overjoyed

584

to discover that I had a small tin of talcum powder in my shaving kit. Might he borrow some for his Special Effects Department, he asked eagerly. Take the whole tin, I told him. Talcum, it turns out, is among his favorite materials; under Scotch tape, he says, it will create the same ghostly atmosphere Carl Dreyer once achieved by blowing flour across his sets in *Vampyr*.

Just the other day, I came upon him rummaging through the can; he brought out a rag packet containing a glittery dust. This he began sprinkling over a strip of film; then he cemented it down. He had a pile of the stuff on the bench; it looked like nearly microscopic, translucent sequins. "What's this?" I asked.

"Fly's wings," he answered. "I've been catching them in the orchard. They get trapped in the fruit when it rots, thousands of them. The wings have a prismatic surface. Very ethereal. They will fill the screen with rainbows."

Would they? He could only be guessing. I took his word for it, trying to imagine the effect as he must see it in his imagination. The movie he was adorning with his magic dust had the working title *High Marx for the Greatest Jesus Ever Sold*. He calls it "An antimonophysite political exposé farce." He makes up genres like that, leaving me to wonder what the hell he's talking about. The film uses some of the most boring footage we've ever received: a Catholic instructional documentary on the making of communion wafers. Lots of nuns rolling dough. But cut into it is one of his most precious possessions: excerpts from *The Maltese Falcon*. Over the years he's acquired four or five scrappy prints of the movie, none of them complete. Now and then he hauls it out to retouch a scene here, a shot there. We've talked about the film several times.

"Huston never saw the possibilities of the story," he complains. "He was so very pure, so reportorial. I gave him such good ideas. What a movie that could have been!"

So he's been making up for that ever since. Holding a piece of the film to the light, I saw it was a shot of the bird itself. He was flocking it with an iridescent gossamer coating. "It does catch the light," I said, noticing the evanescent colors that shimmered against the emulsion.

"So much could be hidden in that light," he sighed. "Movies within movies within movies." Pointing to the cartons beneath the bench, he assured me, "If I could shoot my own scenes, I could bury all this—forty reels—in just three minutes of that light. The entire history of human obsolescence packed into less time than it takes Abbott to tell Costello who's on first."

"It's a pity you had to spend your career hiding things. Don't you wish you might've simply said what you had to say, shown what you had to show?"

He was jarred by the words. "Never! The art of it all is in the hiding. Don't you know by now? One works always under the surface. That's the only way you get inside their minds: when they don't see you coming."

That's his main criticism of Simon Dunkle's work. The *Sad Sewer Babies* arrived about a month back. He watched it through three times—the only film to be so honored by him since I've been here. He found it clever, but his conclusion was negative. "The sport has gone out of it," he commented. "There's less and less to conceal."

Apropos of Simon, it seems that somebody sees fit to keep me abreast of his ever-prospering career. Probably it's Brother Eduardo. About once a year I receive a packet of reviews and clippings that detail the boy's steady, meteoric rise in the world. (Ah, but he's not a boy anymore, is he?) He moves farther into the mainstream all the time. At last report, Fox Studios had signed him to do a cablevision series described as "serio-comic Grand Guignol."

Accompanying this bulletin was an item that could only have been sent to rub salt in the wound. It was a feature from *The New York Times Magazine* dating all the way back to the summer of my unexplained disappearance, in fact to before my disappearance had been officially noted and announced. I have no idea how long ago that was. My organic clock—graying hair, dimming eyesight—tells me several years. The subject of the piece was the then boy genius Simon Dunkle, described as "the most daringly original and controversial film talent to appear since Orson Welles."

So described by whom? Why, of course, Jonathan Gates, Professor of Film Studies at UCLA. And Professor Gates goes on to praise the courage and candor with which this superbly gifted youth is throwing open new frontiers of once-forbidden subject matter . . . and clichés to that effect. It was the article Angelotti once persuaded me to use as leverage with Brother Justin. The orphans had given it a neat ending and submitted it for publication. They probably even pocketed my fee.

I complained about the matter to the only audience I had available to hear my grievances. "I wouldn't be caught dead saying things like this about that little monster. I don't want to be implicated in his success."

He listened sympathetically, assuring me I had no reason to concern myself. "Nobody pays attention to scholars and critics."

Maybe we'll go on like this for years and years—until he drops dead of old age or I fall victim to tropical fever. In time, I'm sure I won't even remember that once I used to think of our experiments in Stone Age cinema as shared insanity. It will simply become my way of life, the normal routine for the population of an island where time has ceased. That's become my principal means of survival. Killing time. Killing it dead. Nothing can be crazy or wicked or worth worrying over when there is no "before" or "after" to distinguish cause from effect, means from end, hope from disappointment. I'm at the point now that the only trace of time's arrow I can still detect is the almost nonexistent seasonal variation that passes over us. Sometimes it rains a lot; sometimes it rains a lot more. One of these means spring, one means winter. I'm no longer sure which is which, nor can I remember how many springs or winters have passed since I last tried to recall how many springs or winters had passed. There's only one landmark I'm watching for on the event-horizon of the black hole I inhabit. If one day I wake to find the sky on fire, I'll know it's 2014 and that the orphans' death wish has been granted.

On the other hand, the fateful day may pass so unobtrusively I won't know it has come and gone until some old newspaper arrives bearing a later date. Of course that's how I should hope things will turn out. But over the years, I've soaked up too much of the Great Heresy. I've come to see that all wisdom lies in what may have been the first muffled lines of dialogue to reach my fetal sensibilities before I too was born into death.

"Frankly, my dear, I don't give a damn."

He turned out to be right about the memoirs. They started happening just the other day, while he was on the dope pipe. Doodling on the flyleaf of a book (it was the S. J. Perelman anthology, reread for the dozenth time), I discovered I'd written a sentence.

"I saw my first Max Castle movie in a stuffy basement in west Los Angeles. . . ."

Stuffy? Or grubby? Or grungy? Or all of the above?

Whichever . . . it makes as good a beginning as any. I scrounged around for some paper, found a few scrap sheets, and pressed on. By the time he came back from never-never land, I was describing my first encounter with Clare. Now I am sorry I wasted so much paper. I've begun scrubbing old newspapers and letting them bleach in the sun. If I slow myself down to about five pages a week, I may be able to stretch the job out over the next ten years. And then what? Perhaps I'll stuff the pages in bottles and float them out to sea.

With my luck, they'll wind up heading south. Entertainment for the penguins.

THE FILMOGRAPHY OF MAX CASTLE

At UFA Studios, Germany

As Art Director

1919   *The Cabinet of Dr. Caligari* (assisted)
1920   *The Golem* (assisted)

As Director

1919   *The Other Side* (abandoned)
1920   *The Dreaming Eyes*
         Masque of the Red Death (lost)
1921   *Phantom of the Wax Museum* (lost)
         Mark of Cain (lost)
1922   *Ghoul of Limehouse*
         Queen of Swords
         Lilith the Temptress (collaboration with Fritz Lang, lost)
1923   *Wozzeck* (collaboration with Alban Berg, abandoned)
         Simon the Magician (withdrawn, lost)
1924   *The Hands of Orlac* (uncredited collaboration with Robert Wiene)
1925   *Judas Everyman* (withdrawn; rediscovered in unfinished form 1960)

In the United States

1927   *The Martyr* (released in studio-edited version by MGM, withdrawn
         and destroyed)

FLICKER

1931   *The Ripper Strikes* (Paramount)

1932   *The Ripper Returns* (Paramount)

1933   *Hands of the Strangler* (Monogram, under the name of Maurice Roche)

       Track of the Strangler (Monogram, under the name of Maurice Roche)

1934   *Isle of Terror* (Paramount, partially destroyed)

       Woman of the Shadows (Paramount, under the name of M. M. Valdemar, partially destroyed)

       Zombie Doctor (Universal, with Edgar Ulmer, under the name of Maurice Roche)

1935   *Man into Monster* (Universal)

       Revenge of the Ghoul (Universal)

1936   *Blood Vengeance* (Republic, under the name of Marcus I. Cain, lost)

       Bum Rap (Republic, rereleased 1937 under the name of Maurice Roche as *Phantom of Murderers' Row*)

1937   *Revenge of the Zombie* (Universal, under the name of Maurice Roche)

       Hour of the Hangman (Monogram)

1938   *Blackjacked* (Prestige International, under the name of M. M. Valdemar)

       Count Lazarus (Universal)

       Voodoo Mistress (Allied Eagle, under the name of Mark Cain, lost)

       Feast of the Undead (Universal)

1939   *Shadows over Sing Sing* (Monogram)

       House of Blood (Universal)

1940   *Kiss of the Vampire* (Universal)

1941   *Axis Agent* (Monogram)

Uncredited collaboration as director, production adviser, screenwriter

1927   *The Cat and the Canary* (Universal, with Paul Leni)

1930   *Nosferatu the Vampire* (Fox, American remake of original, with F. W. Murnau)

1931   *Fangs of Fu Manchu* (Universal, with Ford Beebe, serial)

1932   *White Zombie* (United Artists, with Victor Halperin)

       The Mummy (Universal, with Karl Freund)

1934   *The Black Cat* (Universal, with Edgar Ulmer)

       Murder Thumbs a Ride (Warners, with William Keighley)

       Mad Love (MGM, with Karl Freund)

1935   *The Brute of Broadway* (Columbia, with Robert Florey)

       Casino Lady (Monogram, with Sam Katzman, lost)

1937   *Swamp Creature* (Prestige International, with William B. Clemens)

       Casino Lady Takes a Chance (Monogram, with Sam Katzman)

Theodore Roszak

1938   *Revenge of the Swamp Creature* (Prestige International, with William B. Clemens, lost)

         King of Alcatraz (Monogram, with Robert Florey)

1939   *Heart of Darkness* (RKO, with Orson Welles, abandoned)

         Citizen Kane (RKO, with Orson Welles, assisted in production)

1940   *The Devil Bat* (PRC, with Jean Yarbrough)

1941   *The Maltese Falcon* (Warners, with John Huston, assisted in production)

1946– *The End* (Paleolithic Productions, work in progress)

APPENDIX
The Secret History of the Movies:
Miscellaneous Documents

Novels, like movies, have their outtakes—passages and chapters that never make it into the final cut. The following are outtakes from *Flicker*, items Jonathan Gates elected to delete from his study of Max Castle. Fortunately this lost literary footage survived among his notes. It serves to remind us that some highly intriguing material often winds up on the cutting-room floor.

THE DEVIL'S PLAYTHING

[The following document recounting the inquisition of Raymond Lizier was passed to Jonathan by Eduardo Angelotti, Dominican friar, film buff, and militant member of Oculus Dei. Copied by Angelotti from faded originals in the archives of the Dominican Court at Comte de Foix, the report describes a case that took place in 1324 at the height of the Albigensian Crusade. Angelotti came across Lizier's case while he was preparing his study of heretical Manichaean communities in Eastern Anatolia. His interest at the time was in tracing the heresy into western Europe. As he explained to Jonathan, "Here you will see how cleverly, indeed how subliminally the Great Heresy put down roots in the western world. What do we have here? A mere plaything, as innocent as the flip books of ancient times. Gradually, over the centuries, cunning moving-picture machines of this kind spread throughout the south of France into the Moorish Kingdom of Grenada and from there further east. They ranked among the most popular courtly amusements of the High Middle Ages. As for the lower orders, there were more primitive versions of such mechanisms like that described in this account. Except for the ever-watchful inquisitors—members of my own order—who would have raised the least objection to such harmless pleasures? We can imagine the unsuspecting peasants gathering for the show, completely enthralled by this remarkable device, never realizing the spiritual poison that was being introduced through their eyes and into their minds. After all, what do they see? A fox chasing a hare, the dance of Salome. A bit naughty perhaps, but all in good fun. For what does any of this have to do with religion? Of course, they knew nothing of persistence of vision, the optical trick that the heretics were exploiting below the level of awareness. Stupid clods, we might say. Ah, but what do the moviegoers of our own sophisticated age know of the diabolical corruption that is insinuating itself into their very souls as they sit watching a love scene, a shoot-out, a car chase on the screen? Are they any less mesmerized by Humphrey Bogart, Groucho Marx, Mickey Mouse? They laugh, they thrill, they gaze with amazement at the delightful dance of light and shadow. Have they any inkling that they are taking the bait? That they are descending to their damnation?" The translation is by Father Angelotti.]

Here follows the sworn deposition of Raymond Lizier, millwright of the village of Junac in the principality of Comte de Foix, taken down at the diocesan court held at the château of Allemans, Thursday, the feast of St. Lawrence in the year of Our Lord 1324. The said Raymond, being vehemently suspected of the heresy of the Cathari, was brought before the Reverend Father in Christ Monseigneur Jacques Fournier, by the grace of God Bishop of Pamiers, to be questioned with the assistance of the venerable and religious person Brother Arnaud de Beaune, chief inquisitor of heretical depravity in the kingdom of France as commissioned by the Apostolic See. Also present were diverse other worships of the court wishing to make inquiry of a certain diabolical device said to be of Raymond Lizier's invention and purported to have a pernicious effect upon the mind and soul with respect to assailing the faith and unity of the Roman church.

The accused, having been brought to this audience after several weeks of strict confinement, was closely examined to confirm that he should be capable of speaking and understanding. The court having unanimously affirmed his competency, he was sworn with his hand upon the Holy Gospels to tell the truth pure, simple, and entire, as much concerning himself as principal as concerning others both alive and dead as witness.

The question put by Monseigneur Fournier: What was the origin of the device by which your offense came to be broadly known in this region?
To which, Lizier of his own volition made answer as follows:

It was in the year of Esclarmonde my youngest daughter's birth, she now being seven years of age, that Guillaume Panissoles, bayle of the most honorable Seigneur Berenger de Rocquefort, châtelaine of Foix, summoned me to make certain repairs to the windmill which stands among three others atop the ridge overlooking the village of Aix-les-Thermes. The wind upon this height is famously potent and drives the mills most vigorously by day and night through all seasons, for which reason the valley below has long since been known as the Vale of Aeolus. The mill that was in disrepair was the oldest on the demesne, having been many times mended to my knowledge as far back as my grandfather some sixty and ten years before. A sturdy mill it is, but having been crafted of elm (as was common in earlier time) its sails were heavy and slow and prone to grind to a halt. After examining the structure, I proposed to replace the old sails as well as their inner workings with eight sails of birch, a wood of lesser weight. This being agreeable to the bayle and a price being settled, I began my work hoping to finish before the winter rains began.

According to the custom of my family as I learned it from my father, I first constructed a model of the mill as I intended to build it in full scale so that I might make sure of the balance. This I did, finishing with a fine, small prototype that measured perhaps two cubits in height. When I had completed the full repair of the Seigneur's mill to the satisfaction of the bayle, I did as I have done in the past and gave this model to the children to be a sort of toy. But before doing this, in a moment of idleness, I undertook to paint pictures on the sails, placing on each a horse and rider depicted at the gallop, in each image carefully showing the legs of the horse in a different position as if the beast and its rider were progressing along a road. This was no more, my lords, than an act of whimsy intended to entertain the children. I then placed the model, so decorated with its pictures, out of doors where the wind could take hold of it. And to my amazement I noticed this remarkable thing that followed. As the sails turned in the wind, the pictures flashing before my eyes at a great speed, the horse and rider painted on the spinning sails did seem to move, as if they were indeed traversing an open road. And the objects I had placed behind them, which were a tree and a rock and a post and such like, did seem to glide by as if I were myself riding this beast. This was how my device was born, sires, as no more than such a trivial plaything and with no malicious intent.

The question put by Monseigneur Fournier: And what ensued from this?
Only that I was inspired to paint a similar succession of images on the sails of the other models I had at hand from previous work. One of these was a twelve-sail mill, which is as many sails as ever I have tried to attach at the hub, for there is a limit to the weight and the twist that a mill can bear if one intends to use it for grinding the grain. But since my intention now was mere amusement, I dared to place still more sails on the hub, each light and narrow but large enough to carry a picture. I then amused myself by choosing some several kinds of pictures, as for instance two tumbling clowns, a fox in pursuit of chickens, two swordsmen locked in combat. With each new effort of this kind I studied the illusion I had created and soon learned what was the best speed for the sails to travel roundabout.

The question put by Monseigneur Ladurie: What speed was that?
If the sails are turned so that two dozen pictures pass in the time required for a drop of water to fall six handbreadths, the eye sees, as it were, a single passage of motion.

Appendix

The question put by Monseigneur Ladurie: You were able to perform so cunning a calculation?
With much patience, my lord.

The question put by Monseigneur Ladurie: You did not feel it was unnatural to divide God's time so minutely that the very eye is misled?
I did not stop to think this, so absorbed was I in finding ways to improve the appearance of motion.

The question put by Monseigneur Ladurie: What were these ways?
Since the wind cannot be summoned or controlled as one might wish, I attached a pedal and treadle like those used on the weaver's hand loom to my models and so determined the speed of turning with the pressure of my foot. I also discovered that I could more closely direct the eye as to what it should see by placing before the sails a leather sheet in which I had cut a hole. In this way, one might fix one's eye on the hole and see nothing but the pictures as they wheeled by. This vastly improved the illusion I sought. And indeed I now recognized that there was no need to mount the sails on the model of a mill, but simply to design a wheel of sails that could turn as on a central pivot.

The question put by Monseigneur Fournier: At what point then did you employ candles in this work?
Quite by accident on one occasion, while I labored by candlelight indoors, I noticed that the material from which I had fashioned the sails, which was cloth that had been soaked in oil to protect from rain, transmitted light through itself, though not so clearly that the candle itself could be seen, but only the shine thereof.

—It was translucent, you mean.
I have learned that word, my lord, and that is what I mean.

—Continue.
Having observed the effect of the translucent cloth, namely that it made the spinning pictures brighter and so enhanced the illusion of motion, I tried other materials and soon discovered that silk cloth achieved the most satisfactory result. So I acquired several pieces of clear, unpainted silk to use.

The question put by Monseigneur Fournier: Where did you acquire this silk?
At the market fair at Prades d'Aillon, which is yearly held at the time of the grape harvest until the Feast of St. Bartholomew.

The question put by Monseigneur Fournier: And from whom did you buy the silk at the fair?
From a Moorish merchant who comes there occasionally.

Appendix

The question put by Brother Bernard of the Dominican court at Carcassonne: A Moorish merchant you say. A resident of your district?
No, my lord, he travels from the lands beyond the mountains, I know not where.

The question put by Brother Bernard: He is an infidel, then?
I did not inquire, but very like. But I have never been told it is forbidden in Comte de Foix to do commerce with infidels, my lord.

The question put by Monseigneur Ladurie: What use did you make of the infidel's silk?
(At this point the accused swooned, and upon being restored to his senses asked if he might have water and a modicum of food, as he had eaten but meagerly in many days during his confinement. The water, as prescribed in the amount of four drams, was given. At the bidding of Monseigneur Fournier, the audience continued. The accused resumed.)
As I have mentioned, my lord, I replaced the cloth I had used for the sails with silk, which was the more translucent and also smoother of surface, which allowed me to execute more detailed pictures.

The question put by Brother Antoine of the Dominican court at Carcassonne: This work, did it not take you away from your livelihood?
It did, and concerning that my good wife complained most resolutely.

The question put by Brother Antoine: In what terms did your wife complain?
Indeed, she said, but only jokingly, that the devil was leading me stray, so wholly sunk in this strange work had I become, often spending whole days and nights at it while I neglected my proper trade.

The question put by Brother Antoine: She said the devil was misleading you?
But only jokingly, my lord, as she has sometimes said such playful things when I am lost in gaming or some other irregular thing.

—Let it be noted that the wife spoke of this as a trick of the devil. Continue.
The question put by Brother Bernard: After you had perfected this strange device, what then?
In time I came to see that this amusement might prove to be of some profit.

The question put by Monseigneur Fournier: In what way?
People from the village, hearing of this strange device, asked to witness its wonders. And so I showed them what I had created. Those who came soon told others and in time there were great numbers who came to our door, indeed too many to crowd into my small workshop. So I set up the device in the ostel at the rear of our domus.

I then discovered that because the ostel was so poorly lit, the building having no windows, the illusion created by my device, as lit by candles, showed up all the more brightly. And here I could accommodate more observers if the kine and sheep were removed.

The question put by Monseigneur Fournier: How many observers?
As many as two score at one time. It then occurred to me that I might ask for a small payment for my efforts which were now costing me a great deal of time. Indeed, I was no longer regarded as a millwright in Junac but as a sort of wonder worker and conjuror, though not so of my own choosing.

The question put by Brother Bernard: What manner of pictures were you displaying to these observers?
At first I showed the few things I have mentioned, the running horse, the tumbling clowns, the swordsmen. But these made for such brief amusements that I soon wished to attempt something more. At which point it struck me that if I were to use several of my devices one after another, I might move from the one to the next and so present a greater show, indeed one that told a story.

The question put by Brother Bernard: How so a story?
Like the mysteries that the jongleurs enact at the fair on feast days in which they progress from scene to scene, as in the story of the three Marys at Our Lord's tomb.

The question put by Brother Bernard: And how would you accomplish this?
By dividing the story, as it were in portions, and reserving for each device a single portion. Thus, I would paint on the first device how the devil might tempt a good Christian man and on the next paint how he succumbs to that temptation and on the next how he begs forgiveness of the Virgin Mother as he lies a-dying and in the last how he ascends to Heaven.

The question put by Monseigneur Fournier: You assume the right to make such a judgment of a man's sins?
Nay, my lord, but it is how the jongleurs present their work, nothing more.

The question put by Monseigneur Fournier: And do not the jongleurs first solicit the approval of the bishop?
I do not know of this.

The question put by Monseigneur Fournier: But you, a millwright, assume the right to teach such lessons?
My purpose is not to teach, my lord, but only to amuse.

The question put by Brother Bernard: And in what way did this lead you to include Our Blessed Lord in your amusement?

Only because I have seen at the fair at Eastertide an interlude in which Our Lord's resurrection was enacted.

The question put by Brother Bernard: And so you presumed that you might also enact this greatest of mysteries in your ostel where the kine and sheep make their home?

Only to amuse and perhaps to uplift the spirit.

The question put by Monseigneur Ladurie: Tell us what your performance depicted.

Only what the Fathers of the Church have taught us, that Our Lord was crucified, died and was buried, and on the third day rose again.

The question put by Monseigneur Ladurie: All this you show with your devices?

A humble facsimile, though one which onlookers found powerfully instructive.

The question put by Brother Bernard: In what way powerful?

In that many said that they felt they could see the contention of the Good and the Evil most vividly in the flickering light.

Brother Arnaud de Beaune, inquisitor of heretical depravity, being present, he intervened to note well the informant's particular words, namely that he voiced the foul and odious teachings of the Cathari, to wit that the Good and the Evil rank as equals in their contention, which is gross heresy.

The question put by Brother Bernard: Who has taught you this doctrine that the Good and Evil are equal in power?

My lords, I am a simple man. I present only what I have learned since childhood, namely that the world is torn between the darkness and the light and that this struggle has endured since time out of mind and shall not be resolved until the end of days, no man knowing which party to the struggle will emerge triumphant, for indeed the power of the dark god is great.

The question put by Brother Bernard: And are you not aware that this is a false teaching contrary to scripture and tradition?

I am not a learned man, my lord. I know nothing more than I have been taught.

The question put by Brother Antoine: Taught by whom?

By the good Father Joseph of our village and by others besides who preach in the churches of our Comte de Foix.

(At which Brother Arnaud de Beaune intervened to remind the court that Father Joseph curate of the parish of St. Catharine's in Junac is among those under confinement at Carcassonne, having been denounced by several informants as a priest of the Cathari.)

The question put by Monseigneur Fournier: What payment did you exact for these entertainments?
Only a few sous, my lord, no more. Less than the mimes take for their performance.

The question put by Monseigneur Fournier: But do not the mimes also solicit the permission of the bishop? And do they not share their earnings with Mother Church?
I do not know this.

At this point in the proceedings, Brother Arnaud de Beaune requested that he be permitted to speak at length so that he might report what he had learned in his capacity as a covert informant after secretly attending several performances of Lizier's device and in this manner observing with his own eyes the harm inflicted upon the vulgar folk. For, said Brother Arnaud de Beaune, the untutored people who came to watch what transpired in Lizier's ostel spoke of the spectacle they witnessed there as being more pleasing and more instructive than lessons read from Holy Scripture, and that they found it difficult to remove their eyes from the performance, this being the case because the delightful play of light and shadow upon their eyes brought with it a sort of excitement, as if they were seeing into another world through the peephole. Pray tell, Brother Arnaud de Beaune asked, what man has not the sense to see this as tantamount to witchcraft? And the attraction of these moving pictures was all the more enthralling when salacious images and carnal acts were shown, such as depictions of our parents Adam and Eve disporting themselves lasciviously in the garden of Eden, and of the temptress Salome dancing before King Herod, and of Queen Bathsheba making her toilet, and of the harlot Mary Magdalene offering her favors to Our Lord and His apostles.

The question put by Monseigneur Ladurie: Is this true? Does Lizier show such unseemly matters?
To which Brother Arnaud de Beaune replied: He does, and with women as well as men in attendance.
(At the bidding of Monseigneur Fournier and the other worships, it was ordered that these lewd depictions be placed in evidence so that they might better be examined by the court. Brother Arnaud resumed.)
In addition, does it not smack of a kind of idolatry that Holy Persons should be delineated in so lurid and deceiving a way that an image crafted by human hands should appear more real than that which it represents? Indeed, by my own ear I heard Lizier boast that animating these painted images made him like God the creator.

The question put by Monseigneur Ladurie: And did you, sirrah, compare yourself to God?

Only as if far off, my lord. I spoke of myself being, as it were, a creator in small, for there is something in this art that gives a taste of bringing the dead dust to life.

To all this Brother Arnaud de Beaune added the following admonition:
My lords, these are troubled days for Mother Church. False doctrines have been spread throughout Langue d'Oc and especially the perverted teachings of the Cathari which threaten the very survival of our faith. Wherefore it is my opinion that the moving picture mechanism created by Raymond Lizier is a fiendish invention capable of seducing all who come to watch its deceitful figments, even as the serpent seduced our Mother Eve. Accordingly I appeal to you as my fellow inquisitors to seek out and destroy all such engines of delusion and punish their makers as corrupters of souls. Further, a warning should be issued throughout the district of Comte de Foix that those who have witnessed such presentations are infected with poisonous heresy and stand in danger of damnation, for which reason they must report to their confessor to be shriven at the earliest moment.

Following Brother Arnaud de Beaune's denunciation and upon due deliberation, the above-named Raymond was admonished, begged, and ordered by our said lords bishop and inquisitor once, twice, and three times for charity to leave and abandon the said errors and heresies of the Cathari and to denounce all his companions, accomplices, and fellow believers, imploring them to return to the faith and unity of the Roman Church.

To this the accused replied that he knew not what his heresy was, and that he was a poor, unlettered man who believed only that in which he had been instructed from his childhood, which teachings he could not truly foreswear for he did indeed believe that the world is torn between the light and the darkness and no man can tell which of the two gods shall prove victorious.

It was accordingly decided by the lords bishop and inquisitor that Raymond Lizier should be returned to the château of Allemans and there racked until he gave the names of any who aided him in devising his infernal engine, which is, in truth, the devil's plaything. Following which he and all those who participated in the making of the said devices should, in penalty and for penance for their offense, remain in strict confinement of the highest degree until the sentence of the court be determined. And further that Lizier's property should be forthwith confiscated to Mother Church, and that all other persons discovered to be in possession of moving picture machinery should be summoned for close examination.

Submitted to the diocesan court at Pamiers this twenty-second day of September in the year of Our Lord 1324 by master Guillaume Peyre-Barthe, notary of the diocesan court, who wrote and received all of the above by order of my lords bishop and inquisitor.

Addendum: On Wednesday, the 30th of November 1324, I, master Guillaume Peyre-Barthe, notary of my lord the bishop of Pamiers, came in person to the château of Allemans and presented myself by the order of my lords the bishop and the inquisitor to the said Raymond Lizier to ask that he appear in person the following day to hear the sentence passed on his above confessions. The said Raymond accepted this summons purely and simply.

The sentence having been given, it is inscribed in the Book of Sentences of the Inquisition. Upon being transferred to the hands of the secular authority, Raymond and his sons were burned and his wife placed in strict confinement for the remainder of her life. His youngest child Esclarmonde was spared and placed in the convent of the Poor Clares at Limoux.

THE GREAT ART OF LIGHT AND SHADOW

[The following document is perhaps the most puzzling to be found in Jonathan Gates's possession. It was among Father Rosenzweig's tattered papers and urine-soaked clothing as they were sent to him by the French authorities after the priest's death in the asylum at Lyons. Jonathan preserved the papers, even though they seemed to be sheer gibberish, page after page of Roman numerals in no sensible order. What could it possibly mean? Some years later he found out from a surprising source. "It's a cipher," Professor Faustus Carstad said at once when Jonathan showed him the papers. "The most secure cipher ever invented—used to record the top secret proceedings of the Holy Curia, the real inside dope. Absolutely impenetrable. The Mafia was once willing to pay millions to learn the code, but no deal. There are no more than a dozen men in the world who can read what you have here. Perhaps your Father Rosenzweig was one of them." Turning to Jonathan with a wink, he added, "And I'm one of the others." Carstad had learned the cipher while he was working in the Vatican archives on issues related to late medieval heresies. His teacher was a Polish Jesuit who was in charge of classified documents. "I pretended learning the cipher was just a lark, a sort of game. I taught him a few medieval military codes in return. Even so, it cost me over four hundred dollars' worth of pornographic books to get him to play ball. As unbreakable as the code may be, notice what you see scribbled here at the bottom probably by the Holy Father himself. *Hoc delenda est.* 'This must be destroyed.' That's ordinarily what happens to documents like this. They shouldn't even exist. Father Rosenzweig was either an insider or a thief." Was Carstad willing to decode the papers, Jonathan asked. "Willing? You couldn't keep me from it at gunpoint. Drop by my house this evening—and bring some decent Scotch. No, make that gourmet coffee. This is going to be an all-nighter, my boy." That night, as Carstad worked his way through page after page of the cipher, Jonathan took rapid notes. Of all the documents, the following struck both men as the most important.]

Minutes of the Synod for the Preservation of the Faith summoned at the order of His Holiness Innocent XI, March 23, 1679, for the purpose of granting audience to Father

Appendix

Athanasius Kircher S.J. at his request.

Father A. brought to the attention of the Holy Curia certain facts in connection with his recent examination of the device known as the magic lantern. He explained how he was drawn to the study of this mechanism by his interest in optical phenomena, and especially the behavior of lenses. The which study had revealed to him ways in which this cunning device might be employed for the corrupting of souls. The results of his research have since been published in his treatise *Magna Ars de Lucis et Umbris,* with the exception of the material presented to the Holy Father at this synod.

Father A. recounted the principles of his research, namely the capacity of a well-crafted, illuminated lens to cast an image upon a surface and in what way a lens might be used to enhance this image, whether making it larger or more impressive to the eye. He reminded the synod that he had demonstrated the fruits of his research on several previous occasions, including public audiences. And while his use of the magic lantern, it seemed to him, was harmless and diverting, he discovered that there lay a more pernicious purpose to which this phenomenon might be put. Namely, it was possible to animate a succession of images and so to give them a kind of fabulous life. And this accomplished, the image then becomes a kind of sorcery, capturing the observer's attention with so ruthless a tenacity that observers subjected to these enlivened images fall under an irresistible attraction as if their very soul had been ensnared.

And further, in answer to an inquiry from His Holiness, Father A. recounted how he had learned of this practice from a visitor from Toledo, one Don Pedro Molina y Perez who had served for eight years as Spanish ambassador at the court of the Sultan Al-Rashid of Morocco. During this period of service, Don Pedro was on two occasions invited to attend the sultan's court where certain entertainers styling themselves the Theatre of Miracles performed. These entertainers, who claimed to make their home in Turkish Anatolia, had invented a means of projecting images of inordinate size upon an illuminated screen, and then of tricking the eye in such a way that these images might simulate movement, as for example a match between wrestlers, the slaying of a lion, or the dance of a woman, the latter a shamefully indecent display. In this fashion the Theatre of Miracles was able to present something in the nature of a drama made up of animated images. Upon inquiring further into this remarkable phenomenon, Don Pedro was troubled to learn that some in the visiting troupe regarded this amusement more seriously, taking it to be a device for spiritual instruction. In this way Don Pedro learned that the perfecters of this mechanism spoke of themselves as Manichees, that is, believers in the two gods, though in what way the faith of the Manichees was contained in this entertainment, he was not able to discover.

Recognizing this to be heresy, Don Pedro reported what he had learned to certain officers of the Sultan's court, for he believed that those who believe so adamantly in the oneness of God as do the Musselmen would perceive the danger lurking in this seemingly innocent contrivance. But so slack was the sultan's spiritual authority that little was done to censor or impede the Theatre.

Don Pedro then offered the same warning to Father A., who, upon making further researches, was able to reproduce the illusion of movement and accordingly submitted

Appendix

his designs for an animated magic lantern to the Holy Curia, with the further admonition that a body be formed to monitor and guard against such machines and keep careful watch for any group attempting to present entertainments based upon the illusion of movement. Upon further deliberation, the Holy Curia, with the firm endorsement of His Holiness, commissioned such a body under Father A.'s direction and designated that its name should be Oculus Dei . . .

THE ZOOPRAXISCOPE

[The following packet was also found among Father Rosenzweig's papers. The engraved invitation was addressed to Dr. Augustus LePlongeon, the French physician, photographer, and Mayan archaeologist who was then residing in San Francisco.]

October 5, 1885

Governor Leland Stanford requests the honor of your presence at a significant scientific event to be hosted at his home on the evening of October 18 at 7 P.M. Eadweard Muybridge, the distinguished photographer and the world's leading authority on animal locomotion, will demonstrate his Zoopraxiscope. This remarkable device captures and then projects photographic images on an illuminated screen in a manner that faithfully reproduces the perception of motion. This will be Mr. Muybridge's first presentation of his invention in the western United States since returning from his lecture tour to the capitals of Europe.

RSVP

[Attached to the invitation was the following clipping from the *San Francisco Call-Bulletin* for June 15, 1878.]

Amazing Photographic Feat

At the Palo Alto racetrack near the campus of Stanford University on June 15, 1878, the noted English photographer Eadweard Muybridge, currently resident in San Francisco, succeeded in photographing the movement of a horse running at full speed. The glass-plate negatives on which the successive images of the horse had been captured were developed immediately after the event and made available to the press for inspection. The event was sponsored by Governor Leland Stanford, who invited Mr. Muybridge to undertake this experiment and financed the equipment required. This consisted of twelve box cameras which were carefully located at fixed intervals along the track. The cameras were outfitted with electrical-operated shutters timed to open and close faster than in any previous photographic device. Scientists in

603

attendance predicted that a similar mechanism might one day be able to reproduce the illusion of movement as perfectly as the human eye itself.

Adding to the excitement of the day's events was the report that, on the evening before, a would-be assassin had made an attempt on Mr. Muybridge's life. Armed with a Colt Army pistol, the man found his way on to Governor Stanford's estate, where Mr. Muybridge was staying. He attacked his victim in the garden just before nightfall. After getting off three shots in Mr. Muybridge's direction, the intruder was wrestled to the ground by several servants and a groundskeeper who succeeded in disarming him and turning him over to the local police. Though he spoke no English, the culprit was branded on his chest with a symbol that might be that of a religious order. Why he should bear Mr. Muybridge a grudge remains a mystery. The man, whose name remains unknown, is being held for trial.

THE BLACK CAT

[As Jonathan learned from Zip Lipsky, Max Castle worked with the legendary poverty-row director Edgar Ulmer on two films: *Zombie Doctor* and *The Black Cat*, both produced at Universal Studios in 1934. Shortly before his death in 1972, Ulmer agreed to critique the page proofs of Jonathan's study of Castle. As this letter from Ulmer reveals, his friendship with Castle ended abruptly while *The Black Cat* was in production. In the years that followed, Castle's career continued to decline, but Ulmer went on the become "the king of B's," as Peter Bogdanovich has called him. Among film scholars, the best of his low-budget productions, especially *Detour, Ruthless,* and *The Black Cat,* now hold a classic status. Jonathan may have felt he could not trust Ulmer's embittered and derogatory evaluation of Castle and so decided not to introduce the information in this letter into his interpretation of Castle's films.]

February 11, 1972

Dear Mr Gates:

I have received your manuscript and read it carefully. I hope you will understand my reluctance to take up many of the questions you raise about my relationship with Max Castle. This is a particularly painful subject for me which I prefer to avoid.

It is true that Max and I were friends for many years, dating back to our days at UFA studios. You might say we served our apprenticeship there. But you have greatly exaggerated how much Max, as a young man, contributed to the design of *Caligari* and other UFA productions. He can hardly be credited with being the genius behind the camera. In fact, if anybody can be credited with inventing expressionist design in *Caligari*, it would be myself—a technique I went on the develop throughout my career, though without fair recognition. I won't go so far as to say that I taught Max everything he knew, but it came close to that.

Later, in Hollywood, after Max's projected extravaganza *The Martyr* came to a disastrous end, he might not have survived at all if it were not for friends like Lang, Freund, and me. Though I was struggling myself, I pushed work in Max's direction whenever possible. Bear in mind, the studios of that period had come to regard Max as a jinx and were unwilling to have his name associated with their films. I was taking a great risk when I decided to bring him in to assist on *Zombie Doctor*; it was also more than I could afford to do at the time, since I had to pay him out of my own pocket. But a few months after he joined me on that film, I was lucky enough to land a better contract. Universal decided to produce *The Black Cat*. That allowed me to be more generous with an old friend. In effect, I let Max have *Zombie Doctor* and the salary. I believe he directed the film under one of his assumed names; as "Max Castle," he was still anathema in the industry. You are correct in giving him full credit for the result—a brilliant low-budget job. He was working on an even thinner shoestring than I was.

But you are outrageously wrong about *The Black Cat*, and I must ask you to revise your chapter dealing with that film. Don't believe a word you hear from Zip Lipsky, that vindictive dwarf. The man was Max's stooge, his toady. Contrary to what he has told you, *The Black Cat* was mine, all mine—one of my few big-budget productions. Max's role was strictly subordinate, little more than a gofer. I am willing to give him credit for only one aspect of the film. After I had designed it in a traditional horror-film mode—clammy stone walls, a shadowy crypt, winding staircases—Max came up with the intriguing notion of revamping all the sets as art deco. Imagine! Gothic art deco! A marvelous blending of the modern and the medieval, lending exactly the contemporary note I wanted. I saw the possibilities at once.

I knew better, however, than to leave the actual design up to Max. If I had, the film would have been a calamity. For one thing, Max actually proposed letting the design of the movie dominate everything else—script, acting, music. He imagined whole sequences in which the characters appeared simply as a huddled crowd or as hooded and faceless figures in the shadows with very nearly no dialogue. Only the design and lighting were to stand out. He insisted that the *mise-en-scène* in and of itself would be enough to tell the story—"the essential story," as I recall him saying. Since I had no idea what this "essential story" was, I ignored the suggestion. Even so, I remember Boris Karloff complaining that he felt severely crowded by the scenic effects, as if they were doing more acting than he was.

I have tried never to speak ill of the dead, but now, for the sake of the historical record, I will be frank with you. My relationship with Max reached a nasty climax during the making of *The Black Cat*. This was destined to be the end of our friendship. Things happened between us, words were spoken that left me unwilling to associate with him again on any level. As I'm sure other sources will confirm, there were aspects of Max's personality that I was not alone in finding obnoxious in the extreme. Why did I not notice these disturbing traits before? I believe Max underwent a significant change of character after coming to the United States. Hollywood warped him. He became another man, one for whom film seemed at times to be of secondary importance.

I do not refer to the crass commercialism or the general immorality of the culture. It was something more purely personal. How shall I put it? Max got religion. What kind of religion? I cannot say. Nothing I could recognize or put a name to. He was now in the constant company of people who seemed to have a hold over him. There was an arrogant young priest of some sort named Justin who claimed to be Max's business manager and was never far from his side, as if he were keeping Max under close observation. And, of course, there were the twins you write about at some length, the Reinking Brothers who worked with him as editors. There were others whose names I forget, strange, dark figures who were clearly controlling Max's career, though to what end I cannot say. They were certainly not making a financial success out of him. Quite the opposite. And there was an orphanage involved in this, a place in Zuma Beach. I cannot connect all these things for you. I can only say the entire arrangement had an unsavory odor.

As we worked on *The Black Cat*, I became more and more aware that Max was no longer his own man. He was laboring under an iron discipline. I have seen this kind of regimentation only once before. Friends of mine who belonged to the German communist party during the Weimar period. I do not know if you are old enough to remember the ethos of that time. Total, unquestioning subordination to the cause. That was the order of the day. Men—rational, well-educated men—became robots of their ideological masters. Absolute obedience, complete subservience. Only in Max's case, the cause was not political, but religious. Max was using movies for some purpose that went beyond art or entertainment. Whatever he and the Reinkings touched took on a quality that I can only call metaphysical. Exactly how they managed to infuse their productions with such an uncanny air, I cannot say. But I shudder to think of what *The Black Cat* would have become if it had been Max's film.

Perhaps you know something of my own political views. Notoriously, I was a radical lefty, very close to the New Deal. I was deeply committed to racial justice. I fought against anti-Semitism. I hope you appreciate that *The Black Cat* was one of the first movies to dramatize the dangers of fascism. If this was not appreciated at the time, that was only because the world did not yet know how crazy and how cruel fascism was. The cult in the movie is a Nazi cult. The protagonist, Hjalmar Poelzig—so brilliantly portrayed by Karloff—was the first totalitarian leader to appear on film. Some thought he was patterned on Svengali. But no. Hitler. That was the pattern. A charismatic sadist. That was the very core of Hitler's appeal. Long before anyone in Hollywood got round to taking Nazism seriously, I created this image of totalitarian madness, how sick, how superstitious it was.

Max and I had long discussions of these matters. He was a great one for all-night drinking sessions. To my amazement, he kept insisting that Poelzig must be the hero of the film. "The priest of the unknown god." That was what he saw in Poelzig. He believed that Poelzig's death—he is flayed alive by Bela Lugosi—should be a sacrificial act, a martyrdom. We spent night after night making such crazy talk. The more he rambled on, the more incoherent and hostile he became. Finally, things became very heated. I refused to consider making Poelzig a heroic figure. I asked him, "Can you imagine making Adolf Hitler the hero of a film?"

To my utter amazement, Max waved the question aside with a shrug. Hitler? What did Hitler matter? What did fascism matter? Not that Max doubted the harm that would come of Nazism. His view of the future was very dark. "So? There will be another war. Worse than the last. There will be terror, the slaughter of the innocents. The Jews will get the worst of it. They may not survive. But this will not be the first holocaust in the sad history of Europe, nor the most consequential."

Can you imagine him saying this to me—a Jew? It was the first time I heard the word "holocaust" in connection with anti-Semitism.

"And this does not matter to you?" I asked.

"Edgar, there will be worse to come, a greater horror."

You may know something of my work in Yiddish film, a little-known aspect of my career. For love, not money, I produced several movies based on Yiddish literature and Jewish history. This work was close to my heart. Then to hear Max dismissing the plight of the Jews in Nazi Germany—it was too much. Our collaboration and our friendship was at an end. I had to ask him to leave the set and not return.

But that was not the end of my connection with Max Castle. You may be interested to know that afterward I conceived of a film based on Max himself, a Gothic tale about movies. I imagined a power-mad film director, a Svengali of the silver screen who finds a way to hypnotize his audience and then bring his movies to life. Monsters, werewolves, vampires, the whole Universal Studios menagerie, he releases them into the world to do his bidding. An army of phantoms. They kill, they pillage, they rape. Whole societies fall under the director's spell. The title was to be *Hypnogogia*. Universal was interested. They signed Peter Lorre to play the lead. He had just arrived in Hollywood. He would have made the perfect Max Castle. In fact, he worked with Max on *Mad Love*. But then my luck turned. As you may know, I made an unwise marriage with the daughter of the studio head. People still say that was why I was blackballed. I never believed my marriage was the issue. I think it was the film. *Hypnogogia*. Somebody wanted to make sure it was never made. Maybe it was Max or his mysterious friends.

I once said I would go on making movies if I had to direct from a wheelchair. But that has not proven to be possible. I can only hope that scholars like yourself will find the artistic value in my work. Look at *Detour*. Then think what I could have done with a *Gone With the Wind* budget!

Sincerely Yours,
Edgar Ulmer

ABOUT THE AUTHOR

Theodore Roszak is professor emeritus of history at California State University–Hayward. He holds a B.A. from the University of California–Los Angeles and a Ph.D. in history from Princeton University. He has taught at Stanford University, the University of British Columbia, San Francisco State University, California State University–Hayward, and Schumacher College in the United Kingdom.

His books include *Longevity Revolution: As Boomers Become Elders,* a comprehensive study of the cultural and political implications of our society's lengthening life expectancy, and the widely acclaimed *The Making of a Counter Culture,* a much-discussed, bestselling interpretation of the turbulent 1960s. He has also written *The Cult of Information,* a study of the use and abuse of computers in all walks of life, and *The Gendered Atom: Reflections on the Sexual Psychology of Science,* a study of gender bias in scientific theory and practice, which includes a preface by Jane Goodall. His books *The Voice of the Earth* and *Ecopsychology: Healing the Mind, Restoring the Earth* are the founding texts of the ecopsychology movement. With his wife, Betty, he is coeditor of the anthology *Masculine/Feminine: Essays on Sexual Mythology and the Liberation of Women.*

His fiction includes *Flicker* and the award-winning *Memoirs of Elizabeth Frankenstein,* both of which are under option for major feature films. His most recent novel, published in 2003, is *The Devil and Daniel Silverman.*

Theodore Roszak has been a Guggenheim Fellow and was twice nominated for the National Book Award. He lives in Berkeley, California.